GOOD COMPANY

Cully nodded. "We are not alone, and I don't think I care for the company."

The Khan was whispering to Gray; Gray let his hand rest upon the cold steel of the sword.

Danger. Release me.

No.

Release me. Death and destruction is what I am all about.

"Darklings," Bear said, saying it as the curse he would confess and do penance for later, if there was a later.

Gray finally saw them as they started to move out of the shadows.

They were mostly shadow themselves. Their dark robes, flapping in the light breeze, were every bit as real and substantial as the sharp blades that they carried, but the bodies beneath the robes gained and lost substance as they glided across the plaza, the tips of their boots touching only every few feet. Gray had the sensation that if he only looked more closely, he could see the faces hidden in the folds of the robes, but he didn't know that they had faces, or took any more substantial form than necessary to defile and kill whatever they touched.

Now, the sword insisted. *These are unclean. Even more so than you and me, and we're both damned.*

"No," Gray said. "I'll handle this."

You're a fool, Gray. What have you to lose? Your soul? That was lost the first time you pulled me from my sheath. You need me.

The three knights moved forward, spreading out. Bear to his left; Cully to his right.

If a Knight of the order was to die, this was the proper sort of company with which to do it. . . .

BAEN BOOKS
By Joel Rosenberg

Paladins
Knight Moves: Paladins II

Guardians of the Flame: Legacy
Guardians of the Flame: To Home and Ehvenor

PALADINS

Joel Rosenberg

PALADINS

Copyright © 2004 by Joel Rosenberg

A Baen Book

Baen Publishing Enterprises
P.O. Box 1403
Riverdale, NY 10471
www.baen.com

ISBN 10: 1-4165-2094-5
ISBN 13: 978-1-4165-2094-8

Cover art by Kurt Miller

First Baen paperback printing, November 2006

Distributed by Simon & Schuster
1230 Avenue of the Americas
New York, NY 10020

Library of Congress Cataloging-in-Publication Data:
2004011689

Printed in the United States of America

10 9 8 7 6 5 4 3 2 1

DEDICATION

This one's for Lydy. Which is only fair.

Boys throw stones at frogs in sport, but the frogs do not die in sport.

They die in earnest.

—Plutarch

Chapter 1: Into the Fire

I'll begin at the beginning, because with Cully, the beginning is always the same: a man standing between the sharp and the soft.

"Not while I breathe," he's saying.

I've always thought that's a better oath than "service, honor, faith, and obedience," and not just because I've been the soft more often than the sharp.

That's the beginning.

Knowing Cully, it'll likely be the end.

        —Gray

"Leave the child alone," Cully said quietly, barely above a whisper.

Cully didn't sound like he had been looking for a fight. He never did—although he had certainly found more than enough.

Gray hadn't been looking for a fight, either. Gray was looking for Cully; he had been doing just that for weeks, all up and down the Pironesian coast, and far enough up into the hills to come down on the other side of more than one of the bigger islands.

Given that they were looking for Cully in the city of Pironesia itself, and particularly given Cully's background, there was no need to try any of the estates nestled high in the hills, so they had made the obvious split: Bear wandered through the markets and the warehouses, while Gray took the taverns. There were advantages to rank, and, besides, Bear didn't seem to mind.

Gray had quickly made his way through the various dockside sections that catered to Shqiperese, Boyaliri, Italians, and the local trade, on the grounds that Cully would likely prefer to hear English spoken while he was drinking, but also that likelihood was not a certainty, and diligence a virtue.

Still, eventually, Gray had found himself on English Row, where the readable letters on hanging placards, the drunken sea chanties that would have been comprehensible if they hadn't been quite *so* drunken, and above all the ever-pervasive smell of roast mutton felt almost homey. With the narrow, twisty streets and the tall, three-story buildings concealing the hills that rose beyond the city, he could have squinted and almost have fooled himself that he was back in Londinium, if it wasn't for the pleasant smell of fish oil emanating from the too-dim lanterns, rather than the bitter reek of black whale oil that would have filled the air at home. But this wasn't Londinium, and he didn't try to fool himself. Gray prided himself on very few things, but a lack of self-deception was one of them.

The Dangling Sacerdote was the fifth of those dockside taverns that Gray had checked out as afternoon was already giving way to evening.

Gray had been on his way in through the mudroom when he had heard the quiet sound of the blow and the loud cry of pain, and quickened his pace, making his way through the men streaming for the exit without more pushing than necessary. More than a few pairs of eyes widened at the sight of his two swords, but none of the men stopped to ask about that, not knowing—or, more likely more interested in getting away than finding out— if the two swords and his distinctive clothing meant what they should have meant.

It hadn't quite started yet, not quite.

Cully stood between the three sailors and boy; a fourth sailor lay on the floor in a disgusting puddle of something that was probably his own vomit, trying to breathe.

Cully himself was dressed in a loose woven sailor's tunic over calf-length breeches and sandals, the tunic belted with a length of rope, but other than that, he was about the same as he had been the last time Gray had seen him.

Oh, there were a few more lines in his face, but the collection was already large enough that a few additions didn't much matter. His dull gray hair might have been a little thinner, although what with it being tied back in a sailor's ponytail, it was hard to tell. His hooked nose hadn't any new breaks, and the deep-set eyes still seemed to see everything without moving. When Gray had been in first form, the novices used to say that Father Cully could see more out of the corner of an eye than most priests could during a focused meditation.

It figured that Gray would find Cully standing between the wolves and their prey. He should be used to it by now. Jenn certainly would have been, but Jenn wasn't at Cully's waist—where she belonged, no matter what the Council said.

The boy-child was about what you would expect in a waterfront tavern: barefoot, bare-chested, and skinny; bruised and scabbed; clad only in a kirtle that had once been a burlap sack, and almost certainly was his only clothing.

One hand was clamped to where blood dripped from the right side of his face, and the blocky man looming over him told the rest of the story. The wars and the Occupation had left a plentiful harvest of orphans behind them, and many of them gravitated to the waterfront, eking out what miserable existence they could while trying to avoid the impressment gangs—and worse.

Some lucky ones would manage to get themselves jobs as cabin boys on merchantmen and avoid the Press that way, and a few would find work in the olive groves and vineyards outside the city, but most just got by as best they could.

Gray knew something of that himself, although not from recent experience.

"I told him to leave the boy alone," Cully said, again, quietly, to the sailors. Cully prided himself on his patience; he never seemed to mind repeating himself. And: "I've told you three, as well."

They were now alone in the common room; Gray assumed that the innkeeper had already made his way up on the roof, and was at this moment signaling manically for the Watch. From the way the smell of scorched fish was starting to fill the air, the pot of some oily fish stew burbling on its hook in the fireplace badly needed stirring, but apparently not as much as whoever had the responsibility for the stirring of it needed to be elsewhere.

Understandably so. Fights weren't uncommon along the waterfront, although the separation of nationalities seemed to keep them to a minimum, but drunken sailors would fight, and fighting would upon more than rare occasion turn to killing, and as far as the Crown could reach, murder would be punished. Many satrapal governors preferred to open their monthly reports to Londinium with dry statistics of hangings—and Halloran, the Pironesian governor, was famous for it, even going to far as to, upon occasion, send ropes as mementos home to England. Government wasn't for the squeamish.

Neither was what Gray did, for that matter.

One of the sailors looked over at Gray, then nudged the nearest of the others.

"This isn't any of your concern, Sir . . . ?"

"My name is Grayling," Gray said. "Joshua Grayling. Grayling, like the fish."

"He meant to say that this doesn't need to be any of your concern, Sir Joshua," another put in. He ducked his head quickly, then straightened it—he didn't like taking his eyes off of Cully.

Cully still didn't look at Gray; he just smiled at the sailor, in a way that reminded Gray, not for the first time, that what looks like a smile is the way a wolf bares his teeth to rip and rend and tear.

"Don't look to Sir Joshua to interfere," Cully said, quietly. "He's unlikely to. 'Sides, I gave up taking orders from priests some years ago."

Gray smiled. That was pure Cully. To most people, a Knight of the Order was first, foremost, and always, a knight; to Cully, an Order Knight was first and always a priest. Granted, both were dedicated to service, and if the service Cully chose hadn't always made sense to the Council, to the Abbot General, or to Gray, that probably didn't bother Cully any more than it would bother—*had* bothered—Jenn.

Cully knelt over the man he had downed, and snatched the purse from his belt—snapping the thong with no apparent effort—and tossed the purse to the boy. The sailor made some vague batting movements with his hands, but Cully just brushed his arms aside, more gently than Gray would have expected. Gray would have hurt the sailor. A lot.

"You should leave," Cully said gently, turning to the boy, one sandaled foot pinning the sailor's nearest hand to the floor, the other resting lightly on the sailor's throat. "Just walk. There is no need to run from the likes of these."

The boy had snatched the purse out of the air, and dashed past Gray, ducking to one side, as though to avoid a blow, and was through the beaded curtain and gone in a heartbeat, leaving nothing behind but the clicking of the beads.

"Sir . . . Joshua?" one of the sailors asked, turning to Gray. "You haven't said anything." His singsong accent spoke of a Brigstow origin—there had been that telltale el-sound at end of his vowels.

Gray nodded. "True enough. There's little point in me saying much of anything, since I'm not here, after all," he said, throwing a hip over the edge of a table.

He crossed his arms over his chest. Let them work it

out themselves. There were arguments that it was his duty to intervene, but Gray had once been enough like that barefoot, bruised boy to be his twin, and he would save arguing with Cully over matters that he cared about; the fate of a bunch of bullies wasn't among those.

But perhaps it was his duty to say something. It was possible that they'd listen, after all.

"If I *was* here, mind you," he said, "I'd suggest running away—I've known Father Cully for some years—but since I'm not here, I'm not saying anything, and, besides, I don't think he'd let you leave now, anyway." The boy was probably long-gone by now, and the sailors would be unlikely to find him quickly, if at all—but that was the sort of risk on the boy's part that Cully would be unlikely to permit.

"True enough." Cully had finally turned to him, and a thin smile creased his face. "Gray," he said, "it's been a long—"

That was when the nearest sailor made his move. The fool. Laying hands on a knight of the Order?

You could take away the robes, the sword, and the honors, but taking away the training was another matter entirely, and Cully had been in training since around the time that Gray was born. It was possible, of course, despite the legends, to take a knight of the Order by stealth, surprise, or overwhelming force.

But Cully had—also of course—been watching carefully for just this sort of foolishness.

And there were only three of them, after all, and he was, after all, still Cully.

He blurred into motion, and when he stopped, just moments later, there were now four sailors groaning on the floor amid the wreckage.

Gray counted three broken arms, and from the gasping sounds that the biggest of them was making, one possibly broken trachea. All of them had broken noses, of course; Cully was one of those who had taught Gray how a painful, distracting blow set the opponent up for the real attack.

If they'd actually laid a hand on Cully, Gray would have drawn his own sword and been on them, but—but, no.

The sailors had had no chance at all. They were tough and brutal, of course, but they hadn't spent decades studying and practicing how to damage and kill at close range the way that knights of the Order did. A knight would use his sword if he could—his mundane sword by preference, even if he was Red or White—but there were only some times that you could walk about with a sword, live or mundane, naked in your hands, and as fast as you could get the sword into your hands, there was no guarantee that that would be fast enough.

And Cully had no sword at all—he had, for some reason, left it at his table.

Cully, despite his age, wasn't even breathing heavily as he walked over to the table where he had been sitting, and retrieved his sheathed sword, a mundane weapon—of course—made up to look like a simple, straight walking stick. Gray had a sheath like that for the Khan, for those rare occasions that he both wanted to and was able to appear in public in something other than the robes of the Order. There were few places that a commoner not in uniform but carrying a sword would not draw unwanted attention. He had left that scabbard, along with the rest of his gear, aboard the *Wellesley*; he didn't mind drawing attention in the city.

At Gray's knowing nod, Cully shook his head and rapped the sword against the table. "No, it's just a stick, Father," he said, without a trace of hesitation or mockery in his use of the title. "I've long since given up the sword. *All* kinds of swords."

Gray made a face. "That's unfortunate. Swords are what I was sent to find you about."

"Swords?" Cully didn't like that. Neither did Gray, for that matter. Life was like that. What you liked or didn't like rarely mattered.

Gray nodded. "Yes."

"She sent you?"

"Of course. The Abbot General, as well." Well, he hadn't been sent to find Cully, not specifically—but She, at least, had known that was likely, if this had turned out to be anything, and it had.

No, it was more than that. She knew that Gray would turn to Cully if there was any possible way to justify it, just as Bear knew that, and just as Gray himself did. Cully would know that, too.

Still, Cully made a face. There was little love lost between Cully and the Abbot General, for good reason and ill. She was a different matter, although all of the Order knights always fell in love with Her, at least for a time. Gray had, in his own way, but there was little of love in Gray, after all, and it had long since ceased being an obsession or a burden. Gray and Cully were, of course, very different.

"For what purpose?" Cully finally asked.

"For purpose enough. More than that, you'll have to accompany me to the Governor's palace to discover," he said, as he had planned to.

Cully grinned. "Ah. Curiosity has always been my downfall, and you think that it shall trap me again, eh?"

It was not curiosity that had been Cully's downfall, but Gray didn't rise to the bait. Cully was just trying to distract him.

"It's not an invitation, but a command," Gray said. "I'm not trying to tease your curiosity." That was almost true; he wasn't *just* trying to do that.

"Not with more powerful means at your disposal."

"Yes. If I have to use the words, Father Cully—"

" '*Cully*.' Not 'Sir Cully,' not 'Brother Cully,' and most certainly not 'Father Cully.' Just 'Cully,' if you please."

It would have been easier to concede the point, if only for the moment, but with Cully, the easy way had rarely been the best way.

So Gray shook his head, slowly. "No. You were released from active service in the Order, true; and you surrendered your sword and rank—but you were not relieved of your vows, Sir Cully of Cully's Woode," he said, as though daring Cully to contradict him.

"Vows." Cully didn't respond to the dare, not directly. " 'Service, honor, faith, obedience. Justice tempered only by mercy; mercy tempered only by justice.' " He shrugged. "My honor is a sad joke, and I long ago lost my faith— and, well, obedience was never one of my virtues; and neither was I ever much for mercy."

Gray could have argued with that latter, but Cully went on: "Justice? You might have me there, but then you'd have to persuade me that *She* has much of anything to do with justice, and that would be . . . difficult, although not as difficult as persuading me that the Abbot has anything to do with it, except by coincidence."

Gray could have argued with him about that, too, but . . .

There was no point in wasting his time trying, even absent Cully's stubbornness—not when Gray had a simpler alternative. He raised his hand in the Sign: thumb folded in tightly against the palm; all four fingers spread widely, symbolizing service, honor, faith, and obedience.

"In the name of the Order of Crown, Shield, and Dragon," Gray said, "by the power vested in me by the Abbot General of that Order, I do call you into service, Sir, Brother, and Father Cully of Cully's Woode, upon your oath, Sir Cully; upon peril of your soul."

Cully's face went blank. "You—*you* speak of souls, Joshua?"

Gray would have liked to have taken offense at that, but there was no offense to be found in the truth, no matter how brutal that truth was.

"Yes, I do—just as a thirsty man speaks of water: hoarsely."

Cully laughed. "You've not persuaded me, Father." He carefully toed a knife away from the outstretched hand of one of the sailors before turning toward Gray. "But I'll walk with you to the Governor's palace, I'll wish you a good evening, and then I'll let my soul take care of itself."

Well, that would do for the moment—as long as Gray didn't commit himself to leaving it at that. "The governor's palace it is."

"Let's be off, then, shall we?" Cully raised his stick as though to slide it under his belt, but caught himself, smiled, and set it down on the table next to him. He folded his hands over his waist, bowing deeply—like a peasant, not a knight!—then picked up his stick and followed Gray out into the street, leaving the sailors behind.

The first time Gray had seen Pironesia, it had been as a second-form novice, aboard the old *Resurgent*, and the smells and tastes and colors were still fresh in his mind, even decades later.

It had been different then, on his maiden voyage. The sails of the *Resurgent* and her sister ships making their way into the harbor had seemed to be of an impossibly pure white, ballooning out to catch the last breath of the wind, while the dark sea whooshed beneath the hull. The same wind had brought hints of the garlic-laden lamb cooking on the fires atop the lighthouses guarding the harbor entrance, as the golden light of the setting sun had caught the marble spires and high bridges, making them glow with an inner fire.

It wasn't the same now.

Under what was left of the fading, fiery glow of the setting sun that had all but vanished behind the hills, the dockside reeked of rotting fish and ancient sin, and the sails of the one fat-bellied sloop wheezing its way into the harbor were patched and stained, and seemed to hang limp from the masts, even when filled.

Was it Pironesia that had changed, or was it Gray? It could have been both, of course, and that was the most likely explanation.

Some things had definitely changed—back when he had been a shaved-headed novice, eyes hadn't widened when he walked down these same streets, nor had people avoided meeting his gaze.

They did now; that didn't bother him at all.

Before they had walked for more than a few minutes, the sun had completely set behind the hills to the west, and night was edging in across the harbor, chased by the faint glow remaining along the horizon.

They walked in silence for some time as darkness crept in on the port, step by stealthy step.

Gray wanted to say something, anything, but he feared that if he spoke too soon, or too loudly, Cully would simply disappear into the shadows, as though he were some sort of ghost that could only be compelled to take substance briefly and reluctantly, to vanish at the slightest sound.

It was silly to worry about that, but . . . it felt absurdly good to be walking beside Cully once again, even though the old man had long since stopped towering over the nameless, bruised little boy that had been called Grayling—and much worse—on the Southampton docks. It wasn't terribly unusual for nameless orphans to be given a tryout at Alton, although few made it through the first form. It was, in fact, much more common that a commoner rather than a noble would end up kneeling before His Majesty. The Order was loyal to His Majesty, and only to him, and even a whiff of suspicion that family loyalties might ever take precedence over that was enough to get a novice called into the Abbot's office to be persuaded to leave Alton, one way or the other.

Gray had had no such extraneous loyalties, then or later, of course; when he had served with His Own, he would have struck down the Duchess of Cumberland had she approached the King with a weapon, just as he would—and had—struck down anybody, of any rank, who he thought might endanger His Majesty.

There were always people with grievances against the King, and ofttimes Gray could see some validity in those grievances—not that they had ever stayed his hand, or his sword. You were allowed objectivity in this life, as long as you didn't let it rule you.

"How have you been?" Cully finally asked.

"As well as can be expected," Gray said. "Under the circumstances."

"Could you, perhaps, be a little more detailed?" Cully almost smiled. "Brevity is a virtue, true enough, but it is a minor virtue."

Gray shrugged. "Life goes on," he said, "until it stops. I'm trying to go on."

"Oh." Cully made a face. "You are going to make me come out and ask, aren't you?"

"No, not really," Gray said. "Only if you really want to know."

Cully nodded, as though to himself. "Very well: you win, Joshua. How is She?"

There it was. "She's as well as can be expected, She says. She misses you, and wishes you'd return to Her service." That was the way She had put it. Not the King's service, or the Order's—Hers. She said that Cully would understand.

He nodded. "As do I, Sir Joshua. Miss Her, that is." No pain showed on his face; he said it far too matter-of-factly.

Gray believed the true words, not the lying tone and manner. "You don't have to call me 'sir.' "

"Ah, but I must, of course. It's either 'Sir' or 'Father,' in recognition of your rank; I can hardly call you 'Brother,' after all. You're a priest, Gray; a sworn and sealed Knight of Order of Crown, Shield, and Dragon—a knight of the Red Sword, in fact, honored and deservedly raised in estate. Me? I'm just an old man with a walking stick." He furrowed his brow, and gestured at the two swords under Gray's sash. "You are still carrying the Khan, aren't you?"

"Of course." His hand started to move toward the Khan's hilt, but he stopped it. The last thing he needed right now was the Khan telling him how to handle Cully.

"That's a pity. I had hoped that Ralph would have, eventually, thought better of that." Cully shook his head. "I always thought and often said you should have been given something less dark, but . . ."

"It suits me," Gray said. "It's a perfect weapon, in its way."

"In its way." He gave Gray a look that could have meant anything, or nothing. Then: "Alexander once said just those words to me: 'it's a perfect weapon, in its way.' "

It was Gray's turn to shrug. "I'm not Alexander, the Khan isn't the Sandoval—I was *given* the Khan by the Council."

He should have been angry at the comparison, but he wasn't. He would have to sit by himself and try to figure out why some other time. Focus on the moment, he reminded himself. The moment usually held enough peril as it was.

"No, you're not Alexander," Cully said, a duck of his head making it a concession, rather than an accusation. He let out a long breath. "I've wondered, from time to time, just how many innocents I murdered by letting him live."

Gray didn't have an answer for that, so he changed the subject. "Would you have preferred that I had been given the Sandoval?"

A silly question, but Cully seemed to consider it seriously for a moment, then: "No; of course not."

"He wouldn't have been able to take it from me." Sister Mary had been too trusting of Alexander. They all had been too trusting of Alexander.

"I'm none too certain of that; you would have turned your back on him for a moment, just as Sister Mary did, just as I would have. As I did, time and time again, and never thought it a risk. No, I wasn't thinking about that." Cully shook his head. "I was thinking that the Khan's more than enough of a burden on you, Joshua. It's something I've thought about much, over the past years."

Gray shrugged again, and let his hand rest against the Khan's hilt, the familiar exposed band of steel cold against his palm, as it always was, no matter how long Gray's hand rested there.

Burden, am I?

Well, yes. The Khan was certainly that, and more.

Silly of him; sillier of you.

The Khan was more amused than offended. The notion that being able to kill one's enemies could ever be a burden wasn't exactly beyond the Khan's comprehension. He understood it, but he understood it as an effete bit of Western stupidity, something to be tolerated under the circumstances, but hardly anything to be taken seriously.

The Great Khan had been bloody-handed, true, and he and his horde had left a trail of bodies across from what was now Nova Monglia to the Caspian Sea, never regretting it—relishing every moment, in fact. But the Khan hadn't taken any joy in the carnage itself, as Gray knew better than any man living. To the Great Khan, killing was only and always the way of conquest, and conquest was only and always what made a man great, and it was the conquest, the victory, the triumph that he loved so dearly, an insatiable hunger that grew sharper with each victory, and which could never be satisfied, any more than a fire could be doused by pouring lamp oil on it.

Damned, the Great Khan was, of that Gray was certain, but he was honestly so.

Emil Sandoval, on the other hand—at least so it was said—had actively enjoyed the family business of waylaying, robbing, and murdering travelers. Why as gentle a soul as Sister Mary had ever been selected to bear the Sandoval was another of the mysteries that Gray had never been able to puzzle out for himself, any more than why he himself had been chosen for the Khan.

Service; honor; faith; obedience—the only one he was sure he was capable of was the latter, and he had carried the Khan willingly, and as well as he could, although Gray wondered, as he always did, how it would have been if he'd been given a White Sword instead of Red.

The Goatboy, say; or the Hermit. Or Jenn.

"I see envy on your face, young Father," Cully said, softly.

"Yes. My sins are legion. Envy is hardly the worst of them."

"You're thinking of Jenn?"

"As you are."

"Of course." Cully nodded. "I always thought you should have gone White. I pressed for it in the Council— I even offered to surrender Jenn, in your favor—but among my many flaws is that I've never been a very persuasive fellow."

"It's too late for that, Father," Gray said. "Since Vlaovic—if not before." A city in revolt; a single knight of the Red Sword sent to handle it, who handled it in the only way that he could, and the screams of the dying would have haunted Gray's dreams ever after, if he ever allowed himself the luxury of dreaming. "A White Sword would turn in my hands, if it didn't burn me alive—"

"Now it would, perhaps. That wasn't always so. And don't be overly sure that Jenn is as White as you believe."

Gray would have thought that he was beyond surprise, at least when it came to Cully. He had been wrong, yet again. "You're claiming—"

"I'm claiming nothing. I'm suggesting that the difference between White and Red is a matter of individual observation, theological doctrine, and historical interpretation, and not one of hard, cold fact."

"But—"

"But nothing. I know what you see when you take the Khan in hand, but if you believed things were always as they seem, you'd not have dragged an old shepherd away from his bread and beer—and where are you leading me? We should have turned right down the Street of Sails to get to the governor's palace."

"I told Bear to meet me at the Plaza of the Order when he finished his rounds, with you in tow if he had better luck than I'd expected either of us would. He'll be happy to see you."

As was Gray, for that matter. He was happier about being with Cully again than he thought he could be happy about anything.

"The Plaza, eh?" Cully chuckled. "That seems fitting— there may be statues of the two of you around the Fountain of Heroes some day. So sure you were that you'd find me?"

"No, I thought it unlikely. I originally thought you'd

be most likely found up in the hills, tending to your sheep. We've been looking for you for long enough that I was starting to think we might not find you and have to consider . . . other options. Still, I thought that if you *were* in town, you'd more likely be nearer the beer than farther from it."

Cully laughed. "Ah. You do know me well. A shepherd's life is not the easiest or most pleasant. A man can use a few beers when he takes a break from it, and while it's not going to make me rich, I can afford enough beer for a good drunk. Can't stomach enough of the local wine to get drunk on it—tastes like chewing a pine tree."

"Who's tending your flock?"

"Do you mean that as the usual metaphor, Father, or are you talking about actual sheep?" Cully grinned and went on without waiting for an answer: "Nobody, thankfully—the hills are filled with thieves. What was my flock is probably hanging from hooks in the slaughterhouse by now." He patted the pouch at his waist. "Safer to just buy more ewes and rams and start over again. It's an honest life, as long as you don't tempt your neighbors."

"Yes, I suppose it is."

"Which, you should say, since that's what you're thinking, makes it very unlike me—and here we are." Before Gray could interrupt to say that he had been thinking nothing of the sort, Cully raised a hand, and his voice: "Sir David—over here."

Bear had been at the fountain in the center of the square, refreshing himself in the way that the light breeze caught and shattered the spray, mindless of the way that it was soaking his robes.

Was it a coincidence that of the seven statues placed

around the circumference of the fountain he had positioned himself beneath that of Woltan the Smith? Perhaps not; Sir Woltan, after all, had been the first to carry the Nameless, the same, now-scabbarded sword that was stuck through the sash around Bear's thick waist, above his mundane weapon.

Bear was a big man, more than a head taller than Cully or Gray, and built along thick, peasant lines that belied his putative parentage. Gray had always wondered if it was that that had caused Baron Shanley to pledge his son to the Order by way of ridding himself of the boy, or if the Baron had simply intended that Bear add a year or two at Alton to his curriculum vitae as preparation for an Army or Navy or Administration career, as was common for second sons. Not likely that he had expected young David to end up kneeling before the King, to arise as a knight of the Order, after all.

There was no way of knowing, not really. Gray, having spent awkward hours-that-felt-like-days and days-that-felt-like-weeks with both of Bear's parents several times while on leave, found it hard to imagine Bear's slight, delicate mother engaged in a sweaty coupling with some unbathed peasant—but, then again, Gray had found it difficult to imagine the baroness coupling with her always elegantly attired, aristocratic husband.

Bear's five brothers and sisters, all of whom physically resembled the Baron, were ample evidence that Gray's imagination, once again, had fallen short.

Bear walked quickly toward them, then stopped and dropped to one knee before Cully, his left hand properly pushing down on the hilts of his swords, sweeping them up and behind him so that their scabbards didn't touch the ground as he knelt—not bothering to arrange his robes to cushion his knee against the hard stones, as Gray certainly would have, if he'd chosen to kneel, which he *most* certainly would not have.

"Bless me, Father, if you think me worthy," Bear said, his head bowed.

"Up, up, up, foolish boy," Cully said. "Even a shaved-headed first-form novice, much less a sealed knight of the Order, doesn't drop to a knee before a mere shepherd. It's . . . unbecoming, boy, most undignified."

Gray had been about to say the same thing—although not nearly so gently, nor with even a trace of a catch in his voice. Not that it would have done any good. Bear defered to Gray on much, but not all, and he certainly would not on this.

Bear didn't look up. If anything, he lowered his head further.

"Holiness is not resident in estate, Father Cully," he said, quietly. "Saint Peter was a fisherman, Saint Albert of Leeds a beggar, and Our Lord Himself a humble carpenter. I'll rise in gratitude when I have your blessing, Father, or in shame when you tell me that I'm unworthy of it. Not before. Not otherwise."

"And if I just walk away and leave you kneeling in the square? You'll look foolish here."

Bear didn't answer, and he didn't move. Bear wasn't the brightest of men, but he was famous in the Order for his stubbornness. Back when Gray had been in the fourth form and Bear in the first, Gray had once set Bear to saying the rosary before dinner for some minor or imagined failing, and had uncharacteristically forgotten about it, only to find Bear still on his knees, his naked head still bowed in prayer, beads still clicking between his fingers, when Gray had led the rest of his cohort into the chapel for morning mass.

"I should leave you here on your knees, Bear, and hope that the pain helps you come to your senses by morning," Cully said, with a quick glance at Gray that told him that Cully fully remembered the rosary incident, "by which time I intend to be well on my way home."

"If that is your will, Father and Brother Cully, then so be it," Bear said, his head still bowed.

Cully sighed, and surrendered, laying a hand atop Bear's head. "You were always a stubborn pupil, Bear, and it's far too late to break you of that now, so I'll not try. You do have my blessing, for what it's worth, which I suspect isn't much. You always have that, Bear; you always have, and you always shall." He removed his hand and turned to Gray. "As do you, Joshua, whether it's asked for or not."

Gray started to speak, but Cully held up a peremptory hand. "I did say 'for what it's worth.' "

Bear started to rise, a broad smile across his thick face. "Thank you, Father," he said, his voice thick and husky. He got to his feet and reflexively adjusted his swords in his sash. "It's—*Gray*." His eyes widened.

Gray felt it too. Something cold, and dark, at the edges of his perception. He didn't have to drop his hand to the cold metal to feel the Khan stir with excitement.

"Shh." He held up a hand.

Cully nodded. "We are not alone, and I don't think I care for the company." His nostrils flared, as though smelling something horridly rank.

But he had said *we*, after all, and at that realization, Gray found himself on the verge of tears, and was furious with himself for that. It was silly for a grown man to be so moved by one word, even if that word had come from Cully.

We.

The Khan was whispering to Gray; Gray let his hand rest upon the cold steel.

Danger. Release me.

No.

"Over there. Can you see them?" Cully had caught it first, and Bear was only a heartbeat behind him. "I can't. Not yet—but they're there. I can feel them."

Them, not it.

There was something, but Gray couldn't see it, couldn't feel it, not specifically.

Release me. Death and destruction is what I am all about.

No. Not now. Not if it wasn't necessary, despite the temptation—or perhaps because of it.

"Darklings," Bear said, saying it as the curse he would confess and do penance for later, if there was a later. Bear never shirked a penance; there were disadvantages to carrying White, and holiness was a burden in more ways than that.

Bear took a step to one side and drew his mundane sword, tossing the scabbard aside; it clattered loudly, painfully so, on the hard cobblestones. With his left hand freed, he pulled the Nameless from his belt, but held it by the center of the scabbard, making no motion to draw it.

Gray finally saw them as they started to move out of the shadows.

They were mostly shadow themselves. Their dark robes, flapping in the light breeze, were every bit as real and substantial as the sharp blades that they carried, but the bodies beneath the robes gained and lost substance as they glided across the plaza, the tips of their boots touching only every few feet. Gray had the sensation that if he only looked more closely, he could see the faces hidden in the folds of the robes, but he didn't know that they had faces, or took any more substantial form than necessary to defile and kill whatever they touched.

Now. These are unclean. Even more so than you and me, and we're both damned.

"No," Gray said. "I'll handle this." He didn't need to look or whistle a command to know that Bear would move out to his left and Cully to his right as Gray walked forward, his mundane sword in his hand, although he hadn't remembered drawing it, or tossing aside the scabbard so that his free hand could rest on the Khan's steel.

That won't be enough. I shall live again, eh?

Not yet. Maybe not ever. He hoped it would be never, at least never as long as he lived, but . . .

You're a fool, Gray. What have you to lose? Your soul? That was lost the first time you pulled me from my sheath. You need me.

He set himself for their approach. The Khan was probably right, as he usually was in such circumstances. Any mundane sword could cut through the flesh and clothing, and a good dwarven sword—knights of the Order were never equipped with less—would not shatter on lesser steel.

But it wasn't the steel. Gray's mundane sword was of this world, not the next, and carried no trace of curse or blessing; darklings were only enough of this world to make it possible for them to manipulate cold objects. Theologians argued whether they were really demons from Hell, or something less, but there was no argument that they were foul as foul could be, that their touch burned, that wounds received from their hands wounded the soul as much as the body, and that neither body nor soul ever completely healed.

It could still be that he would have to release the Khan, again. And even that, horrible as it was, might not be enough.

Oh, it will be enough. More than enough. If you don't mind taking another few souls, or whatever a darkling has in its place. I certainly don't.

The three knights moved forward, spreading out. You often had to retreat before you could advance in a fight, and the best way to be sure that you had stable ground behind you was to walk forward over it.

This was the sort of thing that he had practiced, over three decades, from novice through sealed brother and sworn knight, and after, on more practice floors than Gray could count: he would take the lead, and the other two would drop back, one to each side, close enough to protect him, but not so close that he would have to worry about cutting them with even the broadest slash.

Bear to his left; Cully to his right. If a Knight of the Order was to die, this was the proper sort of company with which to do it. It would be a good death, better than such as Joshua Grayling deserved.

You don't have to die. Release me.

Concentrate on the weapon, not on the one who carried it. In the Zone, at the juncture of nightmare and substance, the darklings had other, far greater threats at their disposal, but here, without the ability to draw strength and substance from cursed soil, they were limited by the same lack of substance that made them almost invulnerable to ordinary weapons.

Attack the weapon, not the wielder. That might work; in their weakened state, they might draw sustenance from the metal. And if it didn't, if it took unleashing the Khan to do so, well, then, that's what a live sword did better than anything else, after all, and that's why he carried it.

"No," Cully said. "I count six. And—"

Cully launched himself at them, his stick held high, and batted one darkling sword hard, sending it spinning off into the night, then spun about to strike at another that was moving, more swiftly than a darkling should have been able to, toward his side.

Gray had already followed Cully. He struck up at one sword, then across at another, frustrated when both of the darklings spun away into the dark, not losing their weapons, circling around back.

You can watch him die, or you can release me.

If I have to release you, I will. Otherwise, you can stay locked in your prison of steel, Khan.

If you wait too long, you can release me to protect his corpse, Gray.

Stop bothering me . . .

He would let Bear go first. Releasing holiness was not to be done casually, but it fell more lightly on the world than did unleashing evil.

Bear might as well have read his mind. "Move back, the two of you," he said. "They're not hurt by the metal, but if God does not will otherwise, it shall end now." It sounded more like a threat than a prayer.

As Gray moved to the side, the white, pure light flared from behind him, dazzling his mind even more than its reflection from the stones did his eyes.

The darkling in front of him seemed to waver, and when Cully slapped his stick down on the darkling's sword, the sword clanged on the stones, as though the old man had met no resistance.

The light flared brighter and brighter, until Gray couldn't see at all, and even through eyelids jammed closed over hot tears, it still dazzled him; even with his free arm held up over his eyes, he could still feel its icy brightness that shone through flesh.

And then, as suddenly as a soap bubble disappears on the tip of a needle, it was gone, and they were alone in the plaza, surrounded by half a dozen swords, and an equal number of empty robes lying limp on the cobblestones.

Bear's face was pale and sweat-slickened, and as he took a step toward Gray and Cully, his knees began to tremble. Gray knew better than to approach him—not with the Nameless naked in his hands—but Cully dove for the Nameless's scabbard, retrieved it, then rose and, moving slowly, too slowly, proffered it to Bear, who accepted it.

Bear sheathed the Nameless, and sat down, hard, on the cold cobblestones.

It was only then that he fainted.

Now it was safe for even Gray to approach him. He put to fingers to Bear's neck: his pulse was fast, but strong.

I guess you don't need me this time.

Not this time.

I'm patient. You'll need me before this is all over.

The Khan sounded happy.

Then again, the Khan usually seemed happy, and was always so when there was the possibility of blood and death—and the more imminent the possibility and the greater the number of possible dead bodies, the better.

"I think," Cully said slowly, carefully, "that I shall accompany you to see the Governor, after all. Take his shoulders; I'll take the feet." He grunted. "He hasn't gotten any lighter over the years, has he?"

Interlude 1: Knight Moves

━━━◆━━━

Creating the Order wasn't a mistake, I think.

Turning a gang of Arroy Forest brigands into his personal bodyguard was an obvious sort of thing for Mordred the Great to do, what with most noble families firmly aligned with the Tyrant since the Battle of Bedegraine, and all the rest save the Orkneys studiously neutral, as though if they didn't involve themselves, it would all resolve without bloodshed—their bloodshed.

They were, of course, wrong. Wars are like that, and civil wars are anything but civil.

Mordred the Great wouldn't have survived the first years without us—the remaining Knights of the Table Round were hardly the only ones out to kill him, after all, even before he broke with Rome. And if the truth be told—as it often isn't, but I've spent some time with the Archivist, and he's certain—the stories you read about the people greeting the new Pendragon as a savior from both the Tyrant and the Roman Empire and Church are, at best, greatly exaggerated. We were needed.

Then.

But perhaps by the sixth or seventh Pendragon—certainly by the conquest of Rome under Harold II—the Crown and Dragon were as safe as a dynasty can ever be. Avalon, at least supposedly, waited, yes, but it had been waiting for centuries then, and it's waited longer now; possibly it will wait until the Final Trump.

Perhaps it would have been better to retire the Order entirely.

Or perhaps I'm just trying to excuse my own damnation.

—Gray

Halloran didn't quite hate knights.

For one thing, he *was* one—a Knight of the Guard, although Lord Sir Albert Halloran, OKG, OPE, and KHMG, had never stood a guard watch in his life, and was vanishingly unlikely ever to do so.

The Guard was a military order, yes, and not a priestly one, but that didn't make him a soldier; it just made it possible for His Majesty's troops to take orders from a man to whom they were not fealty-bound. The Administration was not a bad career for the second son of a minor land-baron, and Halloran's promotion to Governor almost guaranteed that the use-peerage that came along with the promotion would be confirmed and become a court-peerage upon his retirement, but that didn't mean that he had to like this assignment.

And the sooner this was over, the better. He had been up for a governorship in one of the New England colonies, and had some supporters in Parliament on that, despite the stiff competition—but the Pironesian governorship had come up at the same time that his name had topped the list, and while one could, in theory, pass up an assignment, that was only theory; he had taken it, of course, when it was offered.

Pironesia was too hot, too dry, and much too far from the Court for his taste. Not just the court in Londinium, although it certainly was that—Pironesia was too far from *any* court, in fact. His wife spent most of the year in Milan or Napoli, for just that reason, and if their marriage had been a warmer one, he would have resented that, as he thought her notion of his ending up with a land-peerage in Italy was even more a fantasy than his own dreams of one in New England had become.

He was sure that he would have resented her absence if there had been issue, as he sometimes wished there had been. It would have been pleasant to raise some sons, or even daughters; and any man who could govern His Majesty's Possession of Pironesia would have no difficulty with a bunch of children, after all.

The locals were like wilfull children in their own irritating way. In almost six years as governor, he still hadn't managed to get the majordomo—a local, of course—to teach the cook staff—also locals, of course—that spices were to be used with a light and judicious hand, and not put on and in everything, leaving a normal man sweating in his clothes by the end of a meal.

Perhaps it would have been better if the Crown had never conquered Inja, as the Injans and their thrice-damned peppers had infected all of the south, certainly, and much of the rest of the Crown. He had heard that there were even curry shops in Londinium itself of late, as strange an idea as that seemed. Why an Englishman would choke down spoonfuls of burning mush when there was good English food to be had, well, it just didn't stand to reason.

He put his fork down with a muttered curse, and turned back to the ever-growing stack of paperwork on his desk. The joke, back when he had been in school, was that the answer to any question about Pironesia was either "olives," "dried fish," or "resined wine," but it hadn't been very funny then, and it was less so now, when the answer was usually "more paperwork."

An empire floated on a sea of paper, yes, and the Crown was that, certainly, but why did all of it seem to flow across Halloran's desk? Taxation reports from all over the central islands, and supplements for the surrounding islands that were administratively bunched with Pironesia—and never mind that the inhabitants of the islands didn't think of themselves as Pironesian, and resented being thought so.

And then there were the proctors' reports, each one of which had to be read, responded to, and both the report and the response passed up the administrative chain through Malta and Gibraltar, to eventually arrive in Londinium.

About twice a year, that idiot McLowery out on Keliphnia would decide that some lateen sails that he spotted from his watchtower were the first signs of an approaching Caliphate invasion fleet, and each time a messenger arrived, Halloran would have to notify Londinium that he was investigating, and then, once again, report that no, it was nothing of the sort; just another Guild felucca that had gone south of the usual central Mediterranean trading routes.

And then there were the intelligence reports. Several

dozen beached Navy officers had taken up homes in the outer Pironesian islands. Understandably so; there, they could live remarkably well on the half pay that would leave them barely able to feed and clothe themselves at home. But each one of them seemed to have some relationship with Crown Intelligence, and as every ship that called in the port arrived, it fed the constant stream of coded messages flowing in both directions, each one of which had to be copied—there were clerks for that, of course—and logged.

And since any coded message that passed through the office might, at least in theory, be for Halloran's attention, and since he couldn't share his own private codes with his clerks, he had to examine each and every one at least briefly, looking for any of the six prefatory headers that indicated it was addressed to him.

Occasionally—rarely—one of them was, and he would have to go to the safe to break out his code books, and not only decode it so that he would read it, but then search through yet another stack of code books to make sure that the signatures on it were valid.

And this latest, well, that was about as annoying as it could be, and if he hadn't been a man who prided himself on self-control, he would have slammed the signature book shut, or thrown it across the room.

Sir Joshua travels under my orders and with my full authority, the letter said, *and I humbly beseech your full cooperation with any requests he might make.*

The Archbishop had signed it with his tight, cribbed hand, although that wasn't necessary; his coded signatures—as Archbishop of Canterbury, as well, and not just as Abbot General!—proved its origin. The lack of any counter-signature showed that it had not gone through the usual channels, but had been, as Halloran had been told, handed directly by the Archbishop to Joshua Grayling—and proper protocols be damned.

Given that, Halloran would have been well within his rights to send it back through channels for verification and endorsement, although he hadn't. That would only anger the Archbishop, who considered himself above the Administration, on matters political as well as canonical, an opinion Halloran neither shared nor wished to dispute, even implicitly. Best just to go along.

Halloran shook his head. That was not his problem; he had already referred that matter—through the proper channels, of course—to the minister. Let him argue it out with the Archbishop.

Besides, the way that this message was sent was a message itself, and it was utterly clear. Halloran would just have to trust that His Grace knew what he was doing, even though he doubted it.

He wouldn't even give a hint in private, not even to his wife, that he thought making an archbishop of the Abbot General of the Order of the Sword had been foolish of His Majesty, and making him the Archbishop of Canterbury even more so, but Halloran didn't believe in practicing dishonesty within the confines of his own mind. It was a bad idea.

Yes, the Order of the Crown, Shield, and Dragon— what those insufferably pompous knights almost invariably insisted on referring to as *the* Order, as though there were no other orders of knighthood worth mentioning—was utterly loyal to the Crown and Dragon shield, and had been, ever since the old days, when they had originally been Mordred the Great's bodyguards, the origin of both their longstanding feud with the Order of the Table Round and their special relationship with the royal family.

But that was then, and this was now, and as prized a commodity as loyalty was, it had no longer been the special provenance of the Order of the Crown, Shield, and Dragon for centuries.

What was needed in politics was, by and large, more flexibility—a much rarer commodity, and one that Halloran prided himself on having. The destiny of Pironesia had yet to be settled, and wouldn't be, by royal edict, for another thirty-odd years. In the meantime, the Shqiperese and Macedoni intrigued in ducal courts from Taranto to Normandie for support for their possession of it in return for incorporation as federated states into the Crown, and Boyaliristan continued its ancient balancing act between Crown, Empire, and Dar as it sat astride the exit of the Black Sea, while Halloran simply tried to keep his head down and not involve himself in matters beyond the Administration.

It could have been worse, he supposed. The Prime Minister could have prevailed on His Majesty to send a Knight of the Table Round again, and Halloran would have had to—again—spend his days and nights entertaining one of those pompous twits, instead of attending to his real duties. He had been through that before, and his head still ached in memory of the morning after. Nobody could put away wine the way a Knight of the Table could, and even pretending to try to keep up was punishing.

At least these two had simply left the . . . item in his safekeeping—as though he were some sort of clerk!—

and then gone about their business, leaving him to his own, of which there was always more than enough.

He didn't complain, though. It would have been unseemly, and, while it was less important, in fact he liked his work; it suited him, and—

There was a knock on his door, and it immediately opened, before he had a chance to ask who it was.

He looked up in annoyance.

"I'm sorry to bother you, Lord Albert," that damned Grayling said.

A handsome enough man, Halloran would have said at first glance, but there was something about his eyes that was dark and ugly, although Halloran couldn't have quite said what that something was.

"Not at all." Halloran forced a smile to his face. "And I'm even more sorry that one of the carls didn't announce you, Sir Joshua. I'll have to have a word with Miconou; he's been much more reliable."

Grayling blinked. "May we come in?"

You are already *in*, he didn't say. "Of course, and be welcome," he said, pulling at the bell rope as he rose to greet the knight.

Grayling and his peasant-looking companion had some sort of unwashed, raggedy peasant in tow. The old man carried himself with a self-confidence than Halloran thought quite improper.

The other knight, the big man who was—supposedly, although he didn't look it—the third son of Baron Shanley, seemed to have trouble keeping his legs underneath him. Without so much as a by-your-leave, Grayling settled the big man into Halloran's own chair by the fire, laid Shanley's swords across his lap, then turned back to

Halloran, and drew himself up straight.

"Lord Sir Albert Halloran," Grayling said, "I have the honor to present Sir Cully of Cully's Woode, of the Order."

So the ragged peasant was supposedly a knight? And of the Order, at that?

"The Order of the Crown, Shield, and Dragon, I take it?" Halloran asked, trying to keep the sarcasm out of his voice.

"Of course."

This Sir Cully—if indeed he was a knight at all, much less the famous Cully of Cully's Woode, and not some peasant that Grayling was passing off as a strange sort of joke—smiled, and touched the end of his rough-hewn walking stick to his forehead in a mockery of a salute. "Your servant, Lord Albert. I beg the governor's pardon for my appearance," he said. "I'm . . . largely retired, these days."

"Nothing to apologize for, of course, but accepted nonetheless." He forced himself not to sniff. "Please," Halloran said, waving to the chairs in front of the unlit fireplace, "make yourselves comfortable." He did his best to make it sound as though he had nothing better to do with the evening than entertain the three of them, and, as critical as he tended to be of his own performance, thought that it came off as sincere.

Halloran's valet, Miconou, was nowhere to be seen, but Papilodos, the majordomo, appeared in the doorway, a heavily laden silver tray balanced easily on one palm, and Halloran excused himself for a quick moment to cap his inkwell and tidy his desk before joining the others, while Papilodos set out a small repast of bread, cheese, and wine. Good man, Papilodos, despite his affection for spices; he anticipated most of Halloran's needs without much prompting, and from the looks of it, had had the tray under preparation from the moment the knights had passed through the gates.

It was nothing terribly fancy, thankfully; in Pironesia, "fancy" meant "unbearably hot," and it would be bad manners indeed to inflict on his guests a so-called mild local sausage that would be doing the dance of a thousand knives in their colons before the next morning, as amusing as the mental image of Sir Joshua Grayling squatting over a chamberpot in agony might be.

"I've taken the liberty of sending for the bishop," Grayling said, from around a huge mouthful of bread and cheese, without the decency of engaging in any small talk first.

"How interesting."

"Not nearly as interesting as the half dozen darklings we chased away in the Plaza of Heroes," Grayling said. "Well, Bear—Sir David and the Nameless did that; Sir Cully and I just kept them off him while he did so." He washed the food down with half his wine. Apparently, Grayling thought that wine was for drinking, not for tasting.

Are you certain? Halloran didn't ask. He tried to avoid stupid questions—Grayling wouldn't make such an absurd claim if he wasn't sure.

Halloran was reaching for the bell rope when Grayling spoke up again—"And I've also had words with Father Czerny. He's blessing the grounds right now."

It was typical of a Knight of the Order to impinge on a local governor's prerogatives, but Halloran tried not to bristle. It was, after all, more important that it be done, and quickly, than that Halloran himself order it done.

Halloran nodded. "I see."

"Then Your Lordship is doing far better than am I," Grayling said. "I haven't heard any reports of darklings south of Aba-Paluoja in a generation."

"Nor have I," he said. "But it should be a simple matter. The right blessings, and we shouldn't be bothered."

North of the southernmost border of the Zone, of course, darklings were just this side of unkillable, but the ground of every square mile of both Crown and Empire had long since been hallowed, and cursed ones were unable to draw sustenance from it—even if the blessings to keep darklings in particular away had apparently evaporated.

Understandable. Pironesia was not connected by land to the north, and running water was supposed to be a barrier to darklings, and to all the unholy.

Still, the bishop probably should have renewed the blessings as a matter of course. Halloran would have to have words with him, which would be a pleasure, of sorts—Anastadiadis was a native, and his natural hot-bloodedness had not been cooled a whit by his years in the seminary in Norwich; handling him with the right delicacy was a matter of some art, and Halloran took pleasure in doing his job properly. But with this Grayling having sent for him, it would be best to get his business done and him out of here before Anastadiadis arrived—native or not, the bishop was an Anglian, and jealous of his prerogatives. It would probably take a full hour to unruffle his feathers at the thought of having been sent for by an Order knight.

"And we still don't know why they were here," Grayling

said. "They're not like termites, you know, Your Excellency."

"You think it has something to do with that . . . item you came for?"

"It would seem likely." Grayling shrugged. "I'd ask Brother William of Occam, but I don't think it's worth raising his spirit for this."

Cully smiled. "You have indeed risen in estate, Joshua, to speak of such things so casually, even if only to dismiss them. As for me, I've never lost the common fear of wizards, and would rather avoid the whole matter—"

"Shh." Grayling turned back to Halloran. "You still have the sword?"

"Of course," he said. "I'd hardly throw it away, after all."

Grayling nodded. "We need to examine it more closely, and while I think we'll have things under control, it might become more . . . interesting than it ought to be. You might wish to take the evening air while we look at it?"

The nerve of the man! Halloran didn't know whether he found the notion of Grayling trying to commandeer his office more irritating than Grayling's imputation of cowardice, but he didn't much like either.

"I'd just as soon observe," he said, pleased with how calm his voice sounded. "If, of course, that meets with your approval, Sir Joshua."

"As you wish." Grayling looked over at Sir David. "Bear? Do you need a few moments?"

"There's no need to wait on me," Sir David said. "I can manage, if need be, with little difficulty."

"It can wait until you're ready."

"I *am* ready, Gray."

Shanley rose to his feet, the wobbliness of his knees giving the lie to his claim; he had to catch himself against the chair as he bent and retrieved one of his scabbarded swords. It was the White one, no doubt, although there was no way that Halloran could tell from the scabbard or grips; they were plain wood, wound with brass wire for a better grip. Halloran had been presented with a fine-looking sword when he had ascended to the Guard, but knights of the Order of Crown, Shield, and Dragon were boastful in the affected simplicity that extended even to their weapons. Halloran had no doubt that even with the ornate surplice and miter of his office, the Archbishop of Canterbury still kept an ostentatiously plain sword belted around his ample waist—two ostentatiously plain swords, in fact.

"If Your Excellency wouldn't mind having the sword fetched?" Gray more ordered than asked.

"That's not necessary." Halloran allowed himself to show some slight irritation. "I'd hardly put such a thing in another's hands," he said, rising from his seat.

The safe was set into the wall behind a tapestry of lambs frolicking in a meadow, as it had been when Halloran had assumed his duties here, and—unlike when Halloran had assumed his duties—the heavy iron door was now well maintained, and swung silently open upon its regularly whale-oiled hinges when Halloran put his hand into the recess and grabbed the handle. His wrist always tingled when he did that—from fear, not from the magic—even though he knew full well that the safe door had been attuned to his own vibrations. This was an old safe door, from the time of the first Pironesian governor, and in those days, the trap was set to cut off the hand, whether from the influence of what was done to thieves in the Dar al-Islam, Halloran didn't know. He would have preferred the more modern type, where the mechanism would simply clamp down, holding a would-be thief in place, unless he was willing and able to cut his hand free.

He stepped inside, and walked past the the carefully labeled bags of coins and jewels on the racks, as well as the ever-growing pile of account books that were a history of his tenancy in the governor's palace. At the very back of the safe was the shelf where the sword lay, carefully wrapped in layers of burlap. He picked it up then backed out of the safe, reflexively if somewhat awkwardly closed the safe door with his boot before turning to set the package on the table before the knights.

Grayling had pulled a pair of lambskin gloves from his belt pouch, and already had them on as he untied the twine and unrolled the burlap, deftly working the knots and cloth with his gloved fingers.

The sword lay there, what there was of it; it was just a bare sword, with no hilt or pommel covering the naked tang.

Without being asked—and without deigning to ask permission—Sir Cully took the lamp from Halloran's desk and brought it over, peering closely at the bright steel.

It was a good-enough-looking blade, the swirls of the Damascus pattern fine and close. The blade was thicker and wider than was common these days, although it was a typical length for a modern sword. The blade was bright and unmarked, save for a spot, about the width of a palm, halfway down the blade, which was caked with some tarry substance that Halloran presumed was dried blood.

Save for that, there were no markings on the sword at

all, none that Halloran could see. The only swords he had ever heard of without makers' marks were Army- or Navy-issue weapons, and each of those was always stamped with acceptance marks. While Halloran knew little and cared less about such ordinary occupations as smithing, he knew that Crown, Empire, Dar al-Islam, or elsewhere, the making of a sword was an affair of some great effort, and any smith that Halloran had ever heard of would surely wish to sign the product of his art.

"Mmph," Sir Cully said. "An awfully plain blade. I couldn't place it to country, much less to century. Pattern-welded steel, yes, but that doesn't help much."

"Easier to say what it's not," Grayling said. "About the only thing I can say for sure is that it doesn't look Byzantine or Damask. Tien-shin weapons tend toward the plain, when they aren't overly fancy."

Sir Cully shook his head. "A Tien-shin straight-sword? Possible, I suppose, but not likely."

"Look at the hammer marks, though," Sir David said. "It's either reasonably new, or it's been preserved well without being much polished."

Grayling nodded. "That was my thinking, as well. It was, so I understand, in seawater for some time. Even if rust had been polished away, there would be some pitting."

"Red? White?" Cully asked. "Is it live at all, or just devilishly cursed?"

Grayling shrugged. "I haven't . . . tested it. The only thing I know is that the fisherman who picked it up is dead." He gestured at the mottled markings. "Which doesn't necessarily mean that it is live; a cursed sword can certainly kill, true enough, but—

Sir Cully nodded in approval, then nodded some more, as Grayling went on: "But it is definitely enchanted, if that's what you're asking, and it's likely something beyond what would be needed to protect it from rust."

"Indeed." Sir Cully's fingers trembled as he brought them near the blade, and he yanked his hand away sharply. "Shit," he said, in a decidedly unknightly exclamation. "It moved."

"Easy, Father—"

"Cully. Just Cully." He gestured at the blade, then seated himself heavily in the chair. "Take it off the burlap and set it on the table. You hold it down, and I'll slide my hand along the table toward. Safer, I think, to have it solidly under control." His smile seemed forced. "As it would be for me, too, I suspect, but there's little that can be done about that, eh?"

Grayling nodded, and did just that, then gestured to Sir David to take his place to one side of Sir Cully, while he took a position on the other side.

"Be careful, Just-Cully," Grayling said, with a thin smile. "Brother Bear and the Nameless One have had enough exercise for one night—"

"And if they are to have more, we'd all rather it not be them hacking through this ancient neck, eh? I know I would, and that's a fact." He gave a glance down at Grayling's hands, as though to reassure himself that Grayling was still wearing gloves. "Hold it down, please."

Grayling set his own, still-scabbarded blade on the table, and held down the naked sword with both gloved hands, leaning heavily on his palms, his fingers spread widely, as though to keep his fingers, even though gloved, away from the sword's sharpened edges. "Anytime you're ready."

Sir Cully took a deep breath, closed his eyes tightly for a moment, then laid his hand on the table and inched his long fingers forward with excruciating slowness—and were those fingers trembling? It was probably just Halloran's eyes, but perhaps not.

Halloran had never seen a knight of the Order actually make contact with a live blade—their mundane swords were invariably used for ceremony, and for all but the direst of other occasions—but he had certainly heard enough about it.

Before, the blade had seemed to want to move toward Cully's fingers, but now the very air around it seemed to jell in opposition to his movement, and Sir Cully's forehead beaded with sweat as he forced his fingers ever closer to its surface, never quite touching it.

His head sagged forward on his neck, and his eyes closed. Ancient, cracked lips parted slightly, but his breathing became slower, much slower—not faster, as Halloran had thought it would, as his lined face drained of color.

"Pull him away, Gray," Sir David said. "I don't like the looks of this."

Gray took a step toward the old man, but stopped himself; Halloran couldn't tell whether because he would have to remove one of his hands from the hilt or scabbard of his sword, or because Grayling immediately made a patting motion with the fingers of his hands, telling Sir David to move back, although not releasing the pressure of his gloved palms that kept the sword anchored to the table as tightly as though it had been welded there.

"No," Grayling said. "Leave him be, Bear."

"That wasn't my suggestion, Father," Sir David said, gesturing with his scabbard.

"The Nameless One is much holier than I have a hope of ever being, but it doesn't know Father Cully as well as I do. We leave him be, Sir David."

"But—"

"There's no buts about it, Bear—just stand by."

Sir Cully stopped the argument by leaning back in his chair, his head coming erect. His eyes opened slowly, and his breath left him in a quiet whoosh.

"Shush, the both of you," he said. His face was pale, and sweat stained his tunic dark as blood under his arms and across his chest. He shook his head. "Well, you were right to use an expendable old man for this."

Sir Joshua Grayling smiled. "Not a White blade, I take it?" he asked, casually, his question more rhetorical than anything else. The only way a White blade could be created would be with the consent of one who was dying anyway—suicide was incompatible with a blade of virtue—and while saints tended to have short lives, they had always been in short supply.

Even during the Age of Crisis, when Mordred III had ordered the making of as many White Swords as could be created, it had been more a matter of luck for the Order to bring a willing volunteer, a talented smith, and an accomplished wizard together at the right moment, and then even more luck if the volunteer turned out to have the requisite purity of soul—something you could only know after the fact.

Most often, the attempt had failed, and a Red Sword had been the result. A Red Sword, after all, didn't require that the volunteer already be dying, or even that the subject be a volunteer, and legends to the contrary, most Red Swords now in existence had come from failed attempts to create a White, rather than by the execution of the guilty; the Khan and Sandoval were two of a half dozen exceptions.

Turning murderers and would-be conquerors into weapons of justice and defenses against the ungodly was, in the long run, one of those sensible-sounding ideas that had far too many unintended consequences, most of them negative. Halloran had visited Linfield, once, which was at least one time more than enough.

"Hardly." Cully shook his head. "But it's not like, say, the Khan or Sandoval, or even Jude." His brow furrowed. "No sense of cruelty; no thirst for revenge, nor a hunger for blood. Anguish without anger; fear without thought of retribution; innocence, rather than virtue. A blank slate, I think, not one set in sin or sanctity." He shrugged. "But it's Red, sure enough. And worse."

"What could be worse than a Red Sword that nobody's ever heard of?" Halloran asked.

Sir Cully closed his eyes.

"It's no more than a year or two old," he said, softly, as though by making the words soft it would soften the truth. He opened them again. "And it remembers lying quietly, in a wooden rack, aboard a ship, with a dozen others."

Chapter 2: Red Rain

———◆———

The world does not revolve around the live swords, although there's always the temptation for those in the Order to think that way, when we're not thinking that it revolves around the Crown, Shield, and Dragon.

No: the three pillars of the world are faith, wisdom, and justice. They're shaky supports, at their best; and there are times when I think we have damnall to do with any of them.

—Gray

A storm was coming.

While the morning sun was hidden behind the bulk of the island, it had risen only a little later than Niko had; beyond the cove, the horizon was clear as far as he could see, and the sea was calm, with only the wide deep swells that gently raised and lowered the skiff at the cove's mouth, and barely a trace of chop beyond.

Still, the east wind was far too strong for the smoke from Kela's island, just now a smudge at the very limit of visibility, to carry any messages—save for the fact that the paucity of the smoke suggested that her family's smokehouse wasn't nearly as busy as Niko's was. He found himself somewhat smug about that, and felt even more guilty at his smugness.

But the storm was coming. Niko could feel it in his bones, just like Grandfather could, although with Grandfather it was always his knees and knuckles that hurt. At least, that's what Grandfather always said. Niko thought it was worse than that, not that Grandfather ever complained.

For Niko it was just, well, his bones, in a general sort of way, without any pain. What pain he had was inside, and could be kept there. He had even stopped crying himself to sleep weeks ago. Father was dead, that was all, just as Mother and his dimly remembered Grandmother died before him—although, granted, not in front of his eyes.

But he could save those thoughts for late at night, when he couldn't push them away.

Now, he ran easily along the almost invisible path across the rocks, his feet landing on the usual almost-flat spots on the stones without much thinking about it, ignoring the way that the occasional tide-scattered sharp stone cut into the long-hardened soles of his feet. He would soak his feet in brine again, tonight, as usual, while working on the nets, and they would grow even tougher. His one pair of sandals was for visiting neighbors—Kela, more often than not—or the rare trip to Pironesia.

He didn't want to look like a barefoot fisherman, not

in front of her father or on the streets of Pironesia.

Though that's what he was, after all. Just that, and nothing more. A fisherman, who would spend his life hauling bounty from the sea to be exchanged with traders for those necessities that the sea itself couldn't provide.

He would live with that, and, were it not for the traders bringing stories of distant lands, it probably wouldn't have occurred to him that there even might be anything else to live with.

In the meantime, ignoring the way that the salt on the stones increased the pain from the cuts in his feet was something he was used to, and might as well stay used to—today he was working the net alone, and the longer he left one end open while the other was staked down, the more fish would escape, and this looked to be a large haul. They would spend the rest of the day salting down the sardines and smoking the rest, and have a larger-than-usual load for Captain Andros when the *Kalends* arrived on its latest trip, which meant a larger than usual payment.

He smiled at the thought of a new bolt of sailcloth and one of woven cotton, a roll of good netting-string and another one of brass wire, a few sacks of flour and turnips, a bag of nails, even a few carefully wrapped injan candies for the girls, and a small leather pouch filled with bright coppers—and perhaps even a new knife for Niko, as repeated sharpenings had worn Father's old knife down to less than a finger's width.

And perhaps they would buy some hickory, if the *Kalends* had some, and had a good price on it— hickory-smoked fish brought a higher price than seaweed-smoked, although both Niko and Grandfather thought that it didn't taste nearly as good, not that they ever mentioned that to Captain O'Reilly of the *O'Reilly*; he either had a taste for it himself, or more likely had a better market for smoked tunnyfish than Andros did.

Niko made the sign of the trident, and touched it to his lips in hope. The gods were cruel, although you weren't supposed to talk about the gods.

It had always been that way. In Grandfather's youth, they had been supposed to worship the three-in-one Triune God; by Father's boyhood, that had changed to the One God, although Grandfather said that the only difference he could tell was that the language the new priests in Pironesia insisted that they pray in was trader-talk, rather than Latin; the priests even dressed the same, after all, and the only difference between a One True Church priest's cross and a Triune's crucifix was, Grandfather explained, that a crucifix was usually heavier, generally fancier, and always hung around a Triune priest's neck.

But, of course, Niko's family did worship the old gods—just not in Pironesia. High on the ragged peak that topped the island, the midday sun still shone brightly over the ancient stone altar for its seasonal joint sacrifice to Zeus and Demeter, and every full moon saw the monthly sacrifice to Poseidon, and while the altar was scrubbed fresh of blood immediately after, that was just from habitual caution that had long ago become part of the ritual, not because there had been any danger of a ship of the Inquisition anchoring offshore since Grandfather had been a boy—the Inquisition was an office of the Triunes, not the One True Church.

Regardless of which church claimed hegemony over

the islands, the gods would have their blood, and it was best that it be a sacrificial goat for Zeus and Demeter and a fat tunnyfish for Poseidon; the red blood was the same, and the same as that which flowed through Niko's veins, and it was safest to offer the red blood willingly and freely, lest the gods decide to choose their own sacrifices.

And, besides, Zeus and Demeter only wanted the liver and heart consumed by fire for them, and Poseidon only the blood and viscera of the tunnyfish dumped into the sea; Niko's family was free to eat the rest, as long as they properly thanked the gods for their generosity with every bite, lest the food turn to ashes—or worse—in their mouths.

Yes, the gods were cruel, but their cruelty was every bit as unreliable as their kindness; Father's death had been followed by a dramatic improvement in fishing off the island, as though Poseidon himself was sending them fish in apology for the awful, fiery death that had been brought to shore in the nets; and, of course, they had always offered the odd sacrifice to Him, even though they weren't supposed to worship the God of the Sea anymore, the priests said.

Grandfather said that it was more important to show appropriate gratitude than it was to keep the priests theoretically happy over things that wouldn't bother them because they'd never know about if you just keep your mouth shut when outlanders are around, like a good boy, Niko, eh?

And while there was much to resent, there was much to be grateful for.

The cave that they used as a storehouse was filled with baskets of salted and smoked fish, so much so that Niko and the girls were spending almost as much time gathering salt at the salt pans and stretching out seaweed to dry on the sand as they did in anything else. Very strange to be in a situation where they had more of a shortage of salt and seaweed than of fish, but that was easily enough remedied. There was no luck involved in that—all it took was work.

There had always been more than enough work to go around, and it was more so now that Father was dead. Even with a lighter catch, handling the net was really a job for at least two, but the morning wind had carried Grandfather and the boat out past the mouth of the cove and into the heavier seas beyond, leaving him barely enough time to set the net—the combination of handling the skiff and setting the net was really another two-man job in any kind of wind—and Niko wasn't about to wait until Grandfather could manage to make his way back around the point before hauling in the catch.

He pulled harder on the net, feeling it struggle back against him.

He smiled. It never failed—the fish could feel the storm coming, too, and that drove them in closer to shore for reasons that even Grandfather couldn't explain. With Father dead, and Lina and Mara up on the ridge salting down what remained of the morning's disappointing previous catch, that left Niko to handle the net by himself. Neither of the girls had enough strength to handle the lines, and would be more of a hindrance than a help— although he envied the way that their smaller fingers could gut a fish far faster than his thick, clumsy ones could.

Each to his own, he decided, and set his feet firmly against the rocks and pulled.

He had to be the man of the family, Grandfather said, although at fourteen summers he didn't know that he felt like a man.

A fisherman, well, yes. Niko couldn't remember the first time he had held nets in his hands, and balancing his pull on the two lines to keep the edges of the nets together was almost second nature to him. He had to set his feet into familiar indentations in the rocks and pull hard, but balance was the way of it. Too much pull on the float line, and the ends would open; too much pull on the weight line, and it would tilt the flat wooden float, making it impossible for even someone with much more than Niko's weight and strength to move the net ashore.

But pull it ashore he did, and the nets were heavy with wriggling silver flashes of sardines, leavened with the occasional bulk of a blue-and-gold tunnyfish or silvery mackerel, the odd dragonet and ermine, and even a few crabs.

The crabs had to be dealt with first. He took the short wooden club from his belt and quickly cracked their shells, even before he opened the net. A panicky crab would damage valuable fish with its sharp pincers—and worse, the net. As it was, his evenings were too often spent with thread and awl, patching the nets.

They did crab, of course—a shorebound fisherman couldn't neglect any of the bounty of the sea—but Grandfather and Niko had set the brass-wire basket crab traps the day before, and wouldn't return to them until tomorrow, at the earliest. Let the sea hold them until the *Kalends* arrived again, and let Captain Andros's crew pack them in seaweed to keep them alive for the relatively short trip into Pironesia.

He smiled, remembering the unusual oaths that the sailors swore when a crab managed to move its nimble pincers faster than the sailors could move their clumsy fingers. Listening to sailors was one of the best ways to learn parts of the trader-language that weren't in the Bible.

That was much more fun than this, he decided, not for the first time, as he sorted through the fish, pitching the sardines into a broad, shallow indentation in the rock that served, at low tide, as a holding-pool. The tunnyfish he quickly gutted with his sharp knife, spilling their guts into the chum bucket—a fisherman wastes nothing of the fish—then stooped to rinse off the bright red blood from fish, knife, and hands in the water, digging his fingers into the cuts on his feet to make sure that it cleared out the sand. Sand and dirt, left alone, would fester, and cleaning it out was a constant irritation; he would rather have been on the boat, where he could merely have dipped each foot in the water in turn, and expected the wounds to have closed themselves up before he had to return to shore.

But Niko was stuck on the shore for the day, and despite the necessity he resented it, and missed the water.

There was something pleasant about diving down, into the dark sea, the heavy basket-hook in his hands pulling him down, down, down, all the while searching through the haze for a glint of brass that showed where the trap was, his feet kicking him over as he fell through the cool blue, then quickly examining the trap to see if it was full, or simply needed to be rebaited. Rebaiting could be done quickly—it was just a matter of taking a handful of chum from the bag at his waist and thrusting it into the cage. If the trap was full, it was even easier; that was just a matter of fastening the hook to the lip of the cage, and then kicking himself up toward the surface, pulling himself up along the line, assisted by his fast-kicking feet.

There he had to move fast, while the fire burned hotter and hotter in his lungs, as the roof of sky grew ever closer, until he finally broke into the air that always, always tasted sweeter than honeyed wine.

Here, the only thrill came from carefully avoiding the spines of the two dragonets that had apparently been injudiciously away from their usual hiding places in the rocky bottom. Pretty fish—while their backs were the dull gray colors and mottled patterns of the rocks on which they hid, these two had lovely bellies the colors of a summer sunset—and tasty, but the flesh didn't keep well, even when salted down, and tended to fall apart in the smokehouse. Eating-fish, not selling-fish. Well, the family had to eat, as well as sell, after all.

He carefully gripped first one then the other by their tails, and threw them back up the beach along with the cracked crabs, smiling as Lina squealed in delight from the ridge above. Lina was more than passingly fond of dragonet, and while all of the flesh would go into the stewpot, Niko was more than certain that most of it would, eventually, find its way into Lina's bowl.

Which was fine with Niko.

The skiff appeared from around the point, tacking back and forth. Niko beckoned to the girls on the ridge above, although they were already making their way down the path. He walked back above the high waterline and took off first his belt, and then his kirtle, and then carefully set belt down on top of the kirtle to keep it from blowing away.

Yes, it was soaked, but he once had had a kirtle blown away by an offshore wind very much like this one, and Father had explained to him, in great detail, just how many sardines they had to salt down to pay for that small scrap of cloth that he had carelessly offered to the sea.

He waded into the water waist-deep, then set out for it with quick, sure strokes that kept his eyes above the water. Connecting with the moving skiff was tricky, and Grandfather, who had little patience for Niko's occasional clumsiness, would be as likely to come about one final time as he would be to drop the sail.

But this time he not only dropped the sail at Niko's approach, but actually knelt in the skiff and reached out his hand.

Niko gripped it; it was rough and calloused as his own; the gunwale tipped dangerously close to the water as Grandfather pulled him aboard, but righted itself with the aid of a gust of wind.

"Ah, Niko," Grandfather said, "I see you've left the girls to do the work while you went for a swim, eh?" His smile took the sting out of his words.

"Well, Grandfather," Niko said, putting one hand on the gunwale, as though he were about to vault back into the water, "if you want to beach the skiff all by yourself, I'll be more than happy to let you."

"No need to go that far." Grandfather laughed. "I'm happy of the help, at that," he said, as he finished lashing the sail in place. He gave a glance at the beach. "The nets look good and fat."

"That they do." Niko followed Grandfather's gaze. The girls were already busy at work; there was certainly plenty of it to do.

Grandfather unshipped the long oar, and set it in the oarlock at the rear of the skiff behind the tiller; Niko took up the long gaff, and took up his usual position at the bow, ready to shove the skiff away from the rocks that seemed ready to bite it. Beaching the skiff was easy at high tide, as the rock formations were buried far enough beneath the surface that they couldn't endanger the hull, even with the centerboard down. It it was tricky at low tide—there was a narrow passage that had to be carefully navigated, with the waiting rocks always eager to reach out and stave in the hull, and Grandfather would be busy with sail and tiller and centerboard.

Niko had a scary moment when a gust of wind combined with a swell almost made the butt of the gaff slip off the tall rock that Father had named Acharis—Father had been much for naming things—but he recovered at the last second and swung the bow away, into the safety of the final approach to the slip. Grandfather's grandfather had, so the family legend had it, carved it from the stones all by himself, with long-worn-out tools, and generations of sliding boats up and down from the water had left it almost glassy smooth, polished enough that two men could slide the boat up and far enough beyond high tide to be safe even from a storm.

A quick plunge into the water, and several minutes of grunting and pulling, and the skiff was safe ashore.

And then the day's work really began.

It was midafternoon before he finally had to take a break. It wasn't the work as much as the smoke—there were only so many times that he could unload slabs of smoked fish and replace them with raw slabs on the racks before the combination of the smoke and the heat made it impossible. Years of practice had given him the timing of it; his last stoking of each smoldering fire pit with just the right amount of dried seaweed left just enough so that it would have almost died out when it was time to unload it, but the difference between "almost died out" and "really died out" had his eyes tearing, his lungs on fire, and his body sweating so much that even guzzling water in between trips into the smoke-tents had left him ready to pass out.

Mara set the long wooden spoon down on the flat rock next to the kettle and ran over to him, the waterskin held in her skinny arms. She was every bit as nut brown from the sun as he was—at least as he was under his present coating of smoky dirt and streaked sweat.

"It's going well," she said, with a sage little nod that she had inherited from Father, accompanied by the usual broad smile, revealing the gap where her new front tooth hadn't quite grown in.

"Oh, and you say this from your long experience?" he asked, returning the smile to take any sting out of his words. He gave her head an affectionate shake as he accepted the waterskin, then used both hands to tilt it back, careful not to waste any—the pool refilled itself just fine from the rainstorm runoffs, but every cup had to be carried uphill.

She frowned. "You don't think so?"

"No, I think it's going very well," he said. He lowered himself to a squat to rest, while she laced up the smokehouse door, her small fingers working the lacing more quickly than his thick ones could have.

He looked around for the next basket, and was rewarded by a smile.

"That was the last one. And Lina's got all the sardines salted down," Mara said.

Grandfather walked up the path that led to the cave, stacked empty baskets dangling from each end of the yoke that he easily balanced across one broad shoulder. His long beard, a few black strands still visible among the white, was caked with smoke and salt, but there was a decided bounce in his step that couldn't be accounted for merely by his light burden.

"Not a bad day's work, eh?" he asked, snatching the waterskin out of the air when Niko threw it to him. He drank deeply, and wiped his mouth on the back of one sun-browned arm. "I think we can take the rest of the day off," he said, frowning judiciously. "It's possible that I might even be prevailed upon to read some."

Mara squealed. "In the *daytime*?"

Reading lessons were for nighttime, when the family gathered around the fish oil lamp with one of the few, precious scrolls and printed books. Niko and Lina knew all the books by heart—they had learned most of the trading-language from the thick Bible scroll—but Mara had yet to memorize most of them.

He shrugged. "Why not? We're very low on seaweed, and I've just finished cleaning out the salt pans and putting away the nets. There's a nice patch of kelp beyond Nicarus, but even if we filled the skiff with it, it would be a week before it was dry enough, and I think that sailing toward the storm would be a bad idea, all in all." He gave a quick glance at the darkening sky to the west. "I'd be tempted to send Niko over to Ari's to see if they've got any extra seaweed for trade."

Ari's island was closer, yes, but Kela's family generally

had more seaweed—they had a good patch just south of their island. "Perhaps Stavros's, instead?" he asked.

Grandfather smiled knowingly, and shook his head. "Or Stavros's, instead, but with the storm coming, he'd likely have to stay overnight, and I'm not sure that Kela will tolerate his presence for that long," he said. "Too windy to smoke a message, asking," he said, rubbing his knuckles. His mouth twisted. "Think you'd be welcome?"

That, of course, was a deliberately silly question. Neighbors, of course, were always welcome, and too little seen in the islands.

"It's a possibility," Niko said.

"I could help you get the skiff into the water, if you'd like to go."

He didn't need to be asked twice.

There isn't much in the world that's easier and lazier than sailing with a full wind at your back, Niko decided, not for the first time. The wind blew from the west more often than not, and the trip out to Kela's was almost always much quicker than the trip back, when he would have to tack back and forth. It didn't feel quicker, of course— sailing close-hauled to the wind made you think you were going faster than you really were, just as running before it deceived you the other way.

It was faster, easier—the only tradeoff was that it was hotter; the aft wind pushed the skiff along quickly, but it left little breeze to cool Niko as he sat at the tiller, sweating under the sun.

He cast a look over his shoulder. The dark, oily clouds were growing closer and closer as they chased the skiff ahead of them, and he thought, when he squinted, that he could even see an occasional flash of lightning, although he couldn't be quite sure.

The skiff rode high in the water, which made it jounce across the chop even more than usual. What cargo there was—a doll for Kela's little sister that Niko had carved out of a piece of driftwood; a small sack of wild onions; a bag of salt; and a half dozen pots of Grandfather's famous pickled octopus—wasn't much ballast at all.

But there wasn't much to do except to tie the tiller down, and then bathe himself with the bailing bucket while the skiff jounced around so hard that the loose cake of soap slipped out of his fingers more than once, and if he hadn't been careful to be lying on the soap as he bathed himself, it would have easily gone over the side, and along with it all the work that soapmaking was.

As it was, he banged his head hard against the mast, and cursed the waves almost as much as he cursed himself for having been in too much of a rush to add some rocks for ballast. The two things that they were never short of were seawater and rocks.

But, still, by the time he was ready to come about so that he could round the island and approach the leeside cove, he was clean and dry, and his kirtle—which was the first thing he had washed, and which had spent the trip hanging from the mast, not drying much in the absence of a felt breeze—was only annoyingly damp around his waist. His sandals, along with his gifts, were safely—he hoped—sealed in the oilskin bag, shortly to be joined by his kirtle. If none of the Antillides family saw his arrival, he would have to anchor the skiff until he could get some help beaching it, and he would no more think of arriving at a neighbor's empty-handed than he would of spitting in their shadow or failing to belch loudly at the end of a meal. Niko was a simple fisherman, but Father and Grandfather had raised him to understand simple courtesy, even though it had taken a clout or two.

He was so busy coming about to swing wide of the rock spit that spiked out of the north side of the island—jibing would have been quicker and easier, yes, but a jibe in a heavy wind could capsize the skiff, and was harder on the boom rigging—that the ship seemed to appear in front of him.

His jaw dropped.

He had always thought of the *Kalends* as large—and certainly it was not only larger than any of the other regular trading ships that called on them, and larger than most of the ships he had seen in his rare trips to Pironesia—but this ship could almost have carried it as a launch, and the launch being raised by a dozen seamen was itself easily twice the size of Niko's skiff.

The ship was a long and sleek monster, two-masted, with rigging for probably a full dozen sails, although none were flying as it lay at anchor, of course. Niko could count easily a dozen men on the deck, besides those working the pulleys and ropes to raise the launch.

The black flag of the Crown, Shield, and Dragon fluttered atop the foremast; and below it, the red-and-gold pennant of the Royal Navy, and below that a golden cross on a white field, representing the One True Church, and, finally, a blue and white one that Niko couldn't identify.

The deck was crowded with half a dozen ballistae, and large traps in the side of the hull more promised than suggested that there were catapults below; Niko didn't need to see the flags to know that it was a ship of war, not of trade.

"Ahoy the skiff! Drop your sails!" the watchman shouted in trading-language from the raised rear deck. "This is the *Wellesley*—what ship are you?"

I'm not a ship—I'm just a fisherman on a skiff didn't seem to be a good answer. The Navy wasn't known for having a sense of humor or brooking disobedience, so he let the boom swing free, and quickly dropped the sail.

"Niko Christofolous," he called back, using the family name that the Triune Church had given the family, and the One God Church had left alone. "The skiff doesn't have a name—it's bad luck to name a skiff." He was surprised that the outlander didn't know that, although he shouldn't have been; outlanders were notoriously ignorant. "I'm a fisherman."

The wind and the current kept carrying him closer to the man-of-war, and he started to reach for the gaff before he decided that that might be seen as a challenge, and you *didn't* challenge the Crown, so he made his way forward, slowly, empty-handed. He could always hang on to the bow and stop the skiff from bumping into the ship with his feet.

"More like a fisher*boy*, I'd say," the man said, with a chuckle. His comment was directed at somebody just out of sight behind one of the wooden boxes stacked on the rear deck, but the wind carried it to Niko's ears, and he felt the tips of his ears reddening. "And your business here, fisherboy?"

"Visiting," Niko answered, "and seeing if I can get some dried seaweed—we use it to smoke fish, and—"

"Enough." The seaman cut him off with an upraised

hand. "I don't have all watch to stand and listen to you chatter. On your way, then. You'll need a call-and-challenge from ashore before you leave." He looked up at the sky. "Not that anybody's going to be going anywhere for a while," he said, turning away in dismissal. "Hey, you—yes, you, Blodgett, you clove-footed son of a Byzantine whore and her priest-pimp—get that rack lashed down, and smartly now. There's a storm coming, and while I don't care if a wave shoved a rack up your back passage, it probably wouldn't be good for the rack and I suspect the captain wouldn't like the spectacle of you jumping around and capering about while squealing like a stuck pig, and yes it *will* end up up your back passage if it's not smartly lashed down, as I'd shove it up there myself, so move your lazy ass . . ."

Niko didn't have any intention of leaving until the storm passed, and he didn't envy the sailors who would be aboard the ship when the storm hit, but it wasn't his problem, and he was still being carried toward the ship.

He raised sail, pulled hard on the tiller, and tacked into the cove.

A party was waiting for him on the beach.

Niko had always envied Kela her beach: broad and sandy and with only a few boulders, and a deep cove, instead of rocky outcroppings, which made landing a lot easier.

A small launch was beached just above the waterline. The family skiff had been beached, as well, although the skiff had been pulled far up the beach, dismasted and flipped over, in anticipation of the storm.

Kela was nowhere to be seen but her father, Stavros,

and brother Andrea were waiting, along with three out-landers, the two younger ones in the overly heavy outlander clothes that Niko didn't envy, while the old one was dressed more sensibly, at least for an outlander. All three of the outlanders stood silently watching Niko without comment, while both Stavros and Andrea waved a greeting.

The two younger outlanders were obviously nobility, of some sort—each man carried two sheathed swords, stuck through the black sash around his waist.

Niko dropped his sail, raised the centerboard, and let the skiff coast in to where he knew it was shallow enough to beach himself, since Stavros and Andrea weren't dropping their kirtles to the sand and swimming out to help him. He was about to toss off his own kirtle and lever himself over the side when Stavros and Andrea dropped their clothing and waded into the light surf, Stavros making a be-still patting with both hands, and Andrea beckoning for the line, which Niko obediently tossed him.

"No need to get wet," he said, in a friendly enough way, although without the usual smile. "The outlanders want to talk to you," he said, quietly, as he gripped the gunwale, and leaned over.

"Me?"

"I don't think they know of another Niko Christofolous, son of Niko Christofolous; I certainly don't. It's about your father, and that sword. Just as well you came here—they were talking about heading over to see you, even with a storm coming."

"They're not sailors." Niko didn't know the ins and outs of it, but some Crown sailors were nobles—you could tell by the fancy clothing, and the swords. A sailor would know enough of storms to stay anchored on the lee side of the island.

"No. They're priests, among other things," Andrea said, with a frown that flashed into a smile. "The big one insisted on confessing all of us."

"Priests, with swords?"

"Either that, or they were just playing with us. Me, I confessed the usual sins, and muttered the right phrases, and suggest you do the same, when it's your turn."

Niko went through the rituals at the church in Pironesia, of course, whenever they went there, but those priests wore simple caftans, with the strange high collars and the silly cloth caps that barely covered the top of the head, and couldn't possibly have been of any real use in the sun, and the priests were, well, *priests*, not nobles.

The islands had, in their time, been ruled by adherents of other religions than the Triunes and the One True Church, and the islanders had always simply gone along with whatever the foreign rulers insisted on; fisherfolk were, of necessity, practical folk. But compared to tales of the days of the Triunes and their Inquisition, or even to the Musselmen that the Triunes had replaced, the One True Church that was bound to the Crown and Dragon was an easy master.

Keeping their priests as happy as priests could be was just a matter of learning their rituals in the trading language, paying an occasional visit and contribution to the church in Pironesia, and confessing the appropriate sins— and never, ever mentioning offerings to the gods—and there was no trouble that Niko had ever heard of.

Perhaps their One God could read the mind and soul

of a man, but of a certainty the priests couldn't, and largely left the islanders alone.

Maybe that was changing—priests coming out to the islands? It would hardly be worth their trouble to collect the scant offerings that were all fisherfolk could afford—a ship that large would easily cost a dozen coppers a day, just for the hire of the sailors!—but perhaps they had religious reasons? To take confessions? That sounded too much like the tales of the Triune Inquisition—did they think that Father had been worshipping that sword?

That would be very bad. The tolerance of the One True Church didn't extend to what it called idolatry, any more than to heresy, and though Niko wasn't exactly sure of the difference between the two, he was very sure that he had no wish to be hanged for either.

Niko wanted nothing more than to turn the boat around and make for the open sea, but there was no point in that, even if these strange priests would let him, even if he could slip by the anchored ship. The storm was coming, and even without that, the *Wellesley's* sleek two-masted launch could easily have caught up with his skiff, in light air or heavy.

And, besides, if this was to be the One True Church's version of the Inquisition, it wasn't just Niko who was at risk, but the rest of the family.

Flee? That was a fine idea, but how? Where? There was nowhere to go. He squared his shoulders and walked over to where the three men stood.

They were a strange-looking group, even for a trio of outlanders. Their skin was outlander pale, even paler than city folk, although the old one, who was wearing only a blousy white shirt and trousers, rather than the robes of the others, had darkened some; Niko could tell by the fish-belly white where the shirt was open to mid-chest.

The old one had a full white beard, but the other two had theirs close-cropped, and had shaped their beards in that strange outlander way, leaving the skin on their upper cheeks naked, save for some stubble. None of them had their hair bound back in a proper queue, or even hanging loose around their shoulders, but had the hairs trimmed, to perhaps a finger's length.

Priests? Nobles? Or some combination?

Niko stopped before the old one, and dropped to one knee. "I am Niko Christofolous, Your Excellency," he said in the trading language, not sure if "Excellency" was the right honorific. British noblemen were addressed that way, but priests were to be addressed as "Father."

"You don't need to kneel," the old one said—in unaccented language, not in trader-talk. "And we're not 'Excellencies.' Come on, boy—on your feet, on your feet. That's better. Sir Joshua Grayling, sometimes known as Gray," he said, indicating the tall, gloomy-looking one with the long face and deep-set eyes. "Sir David Shanley"— the big one, with the wide nose and the gentle smile—"sometimes called Bear. You call them 'Sir Joshua' and 'Sir David.' They're knights—addressed as 'sir.' And I'm 'Cully.' Just 'Cully.' "

"Sir Cully," Grayling put in. "At the very least, Father." His voice was lower in pitch and volume than Niko had expected, although he wasn't sure why.

Cully ignored him. "We're looking into the matter of the sword that we're told your father found."

Yes, Father had found the sword in their nets, and picking it up had killed him, right in front of Niko's eyes.

"Yes," Niko said. "It came ashore in our nets, and when he picked it up—"

"It killed him." Grayling nodded. "In fact, it ate—"

"It was very sad, I'm sure," Cully said, interrupting. "And from there?"

Niko explained that Grandfather had prodded it with a stick, at first gingerly, then more vigorously, and finally worked it onto a net and dragged it away, offering it over to Andros of the *Kalends*. He had heard of cursed swords, and passing the curse along to someone else only made sense, even though Andros insisted on halving what he would have paid for their catch in payment for taking it and its curse away.

"He did, did he?" Grayling tilted his head to one side. "That's interesting, and—yes? What is it?"

"I mean no offense to the Sirs," Stavros said, "but we do have a storm coming."

Grayling, who seemed to be the leader, nodded, as he looked at the darkening sky. "Well, then, we probably should return to the ship and continue this discussion there," he said without any visible sign of relishing the prospect of riding out a storm on even so large a ship.

"Will you honor my home?" Stavros asked, as custom required. "And you, too, Niko, of course."

There was no particular enthusiasm in either request. Visitors were one thing, but outlanders—outlanders with swords, no less—were another thing entirely.

Grayling didn't seem to notice. "We'd be delighted," he said, smiling, patting at his stomach. "I was hoping you'd invite us; I really hate the rolling aboard a ship even in clear weather."

While Niko was trying to sort that out—how could

somebody possibly be bothered by something so ordinary?—Grayling raised a hand, and a man that Niko hadn't seen before appeared from behind the trees, tucking his pipe into his belt as he approached. Thickset, fiftyish, and with the same sort of outlander beard that the others had, although the only weapon he carried was a knife at his belt.

Niko would have guessed him to be a sailor, except for the fact of his wearing a pair of fine boots—what would a sailor need with boots? How could he afford such?

"Bosun," Grayling said, "unload the launch, please; the three of us will be staying the night. Tell Michael that he is not to come ashore; we can see to our own needs for one night, without being waited upon."

Bosun—was he one of the outlanders with only one name?—had leaped into a curious position when he was first addressed by name: his arms held straight down at his sides, his legs and feet close together, his eyes staring straight ahead. It wasn't just that he didn't meet the Sir's eyes—he stared off into the distance, his face blank and expressionless.

Outlanders were very strange.

"Aye, aye, *sir*," he said, far too loudly. "Will there be anything else, sir?"

"Yes. My compliments to the captain, and tell him that he's free to ride out the storm where and as he sees fit— we'll expect to see the *Wellesley* offshore in the morning, if it's clear; otherwise, the day after."

"Yes, sir. Compliments to the captain, and he's to ride out the storm as he wishes; return in the morning if it's clear, return the day after if not. By your leave?"

"On your way, Bosun." Grayling smiled. "And good luck to you."

"Aye, aye, sir." He stuck two fingers in his mouth and whistled, and half a dozen more men, dressed similarly, even to the boots, ran out of the woods and to the small launch and quickly removed a half a dozen canvas bags, then removed their boots and launched the boat with Bosun climbing aboard at the last moment that he could without wetting his boots.

Bosun kept up a stream of invective at how slowly and clumsily they were moving, although Niko couldn't find any fault with it, and it was in just a matter of moments that the six men, three on a side, were quickly pulling at their oars, all in perfect unison, while Bosun glared at and insulted them, his words and his glances not seeming to have any effect, one way or another, on their precision.

Grayling beckoned the others over to the canvas bags. "Your hospitality, Stavros, is most generous—I wasn't looking forward to a night riding out the storm. You'll find that we're good guests, I trust," he said, "and where I was raised, a guest always brings gifts."

"That is our custom, as well," Stavros said, with a smile. "Although I wouldn't take offense if it wasn't yours, Excellency."

"Would a full bolt of good Londinium denim be insultingly small?"

"Small? Not at all, Excellency—you are far too generous. Guest-gifts are usually some trifle; I couldn't think of—"

"Then a bolt of denim it shall be." Grayling handed one of the bags to Niko. "You'll favor me by carrying this?"

"Of course, your—I mean, of course, *sir*." Niko tried to draw himself up straight, like Bosun had.

Grayling smiled, and Cully laughed.

The storm hit.

Outside the cave, rain sheeted down, and below, waves shattered themselves upon the rocks, as though trying to claw their way up and to the cave mouth. Lightning lanced from cloud to cloud, occasionally painfully bright, crooked fingers dazzling his eyes while the thunder rang in his ears as they reached down to claw at the sea itself, in Zeus's ancient reminder to Poseidon that while Poseidon ruled the sea, Zeus ruled all.

Niko thought that he envied the Antillides their cave even more than their beach—it was much larger than his own, and bent back into a fishhook shape, leaving the sleeping chamber completely protected from the elements.

The only thing about it that he didn't envy was the crack along the roof of the outer chamber, which quickly started dripping water in even the lightest storm. While rain barrels had been carefully placed to catch the stream, they now had all been filled to overflowing, and the leak had become a constant stream that ran down and exited the cave mouth, only part of it obediently adhering to the too-shallow channel that had, ages before, been carved into the stone.

Even so, there were advantages; one could relieve oneself into the stream without getting battered by the storm, as strange as it felt to piss into fresh water.

He could hear Kela splash up from behind him, and adjusted his kirtle before he turned.

"Kela."

"Niko."

There was only a little light leaking out from the oil

lanterns farther back, and what little there was illuminated her outline, though not her face. That didn't matter. He knew it almost as well as he knew his sisters'. And while Grandfather said that his sister Lina and Kela looked enough alike to be able to pass as twins, Niko didn't think so. Certainly being alone with Lina didn't give him that strange feeling in the pit of his stomach, much less farther down.

It was strange to be left alone with her without a proper escort—Niko was no more left alone with Kela than that gangly Arno that found every opportunity to visit Niko's family would be left alone with Lina; it was indecent for a girl who had reached her bleeding-time to be alone with a boy—but he guessed that it wasn't a problem. With a dozen people gathered around the fire in the sleeping chamber, they weren't really alone, were they?

Still, it seemed almost indecent, and it made him nervous.

"I'm very sorry about your father," she said, just as she had said when she, Andrea, and Stavros had come visiting to pay their call. She glanced behind before she made the sign of the Trident and touched it to her lips. "The outlander priests talk about the sea giving up their dead someday, and they could be right."

He shrugged. There was no point in talking about it, after all. That just made it worse. Better to think about other things.

"How have you been?" he asked.

Has that Milos Abdullah been visiting you again? he didn't ask. He didn't like Milos, and it wasn't just because Milos insisted on being called by both first name and surname, as though he was some sort of outlander nobility.

The Abdullah family had not been assigned a surname by the One True Church. While proclaiming their loyalty to the One True Church, and still making it a point to visit Pironesia more often than anybody else Niko knew of, the Abdullahs had given up the hated surname that the Triunes had laid upon them and resumed their Musselman name, although—so it was said; Niko didn't know nor care—they had not resumed their Musselman rituals, whatever those rites might be.

Niko didn't know why he disliked Milos so, unless it was simple jealousy. He didn't much care about whether or not they were performing whatever Musselman rituals were, although he had never seen any sign of such; everybody knew that only sacrifices to the old gods mattered, after all, and the rest was just superstition or going-along.

The Abdullah family's island was actually a trio of close-set islands, and the smallest one was larger than Niko and Kela's families' islands put together. A preposterously huge number of people lived on the Abdullah island; Stavros said it might be as many as three, perhaps even four hundred, although surely that was an exaggeration. Their great numbers let them be traders, as well as fishermen, and their fleet of three ships seemed to be in constant motion, whether fishing in deeper waters and for more days than the shorebound could, or carrying their catch and what they traded for not just to Pironesia, but sometimes as far away as Gazipasa, or—rarely—even to Konya, braving the dangerous waters around the pirate havens on Seeproosh to trade for gemstones from the Dar al-Islam.

They even managed to keep livestock. Not just the chickens that Niko's family kept, or the wild goats that roamed about the high ground of their island, the goats that Father or Grandfather would, once or twice a year, take with bow and arrow for meat and leather. Kela's family did the same, as did most of the families on the islands, although a few supplemented that with the occasional pigs.

The Abdullahs, on the other hand, had chickens, and *tamed* goats, *and* a huge flock of dozens of sheep and even a few cows; when the wind blew the wrong way on a Sunday, distant hints of the tantalizing smell of roasting meat were often carried across the water.

"Yes," Kela said. He could more hear than feel her smile. "Milos Abdullah has found quite a *few* occasions to guest here, of late."

"Oh."

"Then again, Father wonders aloud, every now and then, how I'd feel being a junior wife in the Abdullah family, and he seems to worry about that."

Niko smiled.

"Then again, he also wonders out loud, even more often, as to what sort of bride-price an Abdullah might be able to offer, as compared to some other people I might name."

His smile went away.

She laughed at him, which only made him angry. Niko didn't like being laughed at.

"Don't be so silly," she said. She reached out a hand and touched his arm. "I've told you that I'll ask Father to set my bride-price at something you can afford, although I don't know what he'll say."

"I hope you manage to find a moment to bring it up before he marries you off to Milos."

"I'll talk to him soon, I promise," she said. "I'd rather . . . be a big sister to your sisters than be a scullery maid for Milos and his mother."

"I—"

"Kela," the harsh voice sounded from behind him. "This is *not* proper."

Stavros' face was stern in the flickering light of the lantern that he held high above and in front of him, probably more for the benefit of the three Sirs, who picked their way carefully across the unfamiliar cave floor.

Her mother, Nikea, waddled around from behind, and fastened her thick hand on Kela's arm. Kela ducked her head as her mother pulled her away.

"I'm *sorry*, Father," she said. "But we weren't—we were just—"

"You were just alone and unaccompanied with a man not of our family," Stavros said, shaking his head. "And with honored guests present, as though you were some shorebound whore, and—" He stopped himself when Sir Cully cleared his throat.

"There's no problem on our account, good Stavros," Cully said, gently. "And, as a guest, I'd take any insult to your daughter's virtue as a personal slight," he went on, less gently, "were there someone here who would be so crude as to utter such—as of course, I believe that there isn't."

As if in answer, lightning flashed and thunder roared so loudly that Cully had to wait a moment before going on. A smile flickered across his thin lips. "And, truth to tell, where I grew up it was not unknown for a couple of young people to find some private time by themselves, when they could—just to talk. Speaking of talk, we need to talk to young Niko; embarrassing you or your family is not our intent."

Stavros didn't like it, but they were both guests and nobility, and he ducked his head briefly. He hung the lantern in a wall niche, and ushered Kela and Nikea back toward the residence chamber.

"So, young Niko . . ." Cully said. He tilted his head to one side. "You don't like being called that?"

"I've no complaint, sir."

"Then why did you look like you'd bitten into a piece of meat and found half a maggot?" Sir Joshua asked.

"I've no complaint, sir," he repeated. But he wasn't 'young' Niko, not anymore. With Father dead, that made him the man of the family, Grandfather said, and entitled to his name without the diminutive. But he could hardly say that to these outlanders; they might take offense.

"Niko, then? Is that better?"

Niko nodded. "I don't mind if you call me Niko, sir," he said, choosing his words carefully.

"Well, then, Niko-sir," Cully said, smiling, "we—"

"Stand *easy*, boy," Sir David said, his growl somehow more reassuring than frightening, although Niko couldn't have said why it was so. "We don't mean you any harm, but you look like you're about to bolt." He gestured toward the storm outside. "Which doesn't seem to me like a good idea, even if we did mean you any harm—"

"Which we don't." Cully raised both hands, fingers spread, the thumbs tight against the palms. "Truly, we don't. We just need your help."

Niko was having a hard time figuring out which one of them was in charge. At first, he had thought it was Grayling, despite Cully being the elder. And then it seemed that Grayling was taking his lead from Cully, but they kept interrupting each other—even Sir David, who he had thought was the junior of the three of them.

Niko didn't know which one he was supposed to be addressing, so he just stared off into the distance, not meeting any of their eyes. "Anything you want, sirs, I'll tell you. It's all about that cursed sword?"

"Cursed sword, indeed," Grayling said. "More than you know." He patted at the hilt of the uppermost of the swords supported by the sash around his waist. "Like this one. That one is locked in a strongbox on the *Wellesley* at the moment, and the only key is around my neck, even though there's not a jack aboard who would be foolish enough to touch his flesh to its steel."

"Yes, sir."

"Do you have any idea where it came from?"

"It came from the sea, sir," Niko said. "Father and Grandfather just hauled it up in our nets, just a short ways beyond Silver Point, off Marcosia; there's good bottom there." He started to shrug, then stopped himself. They might think he meant he didn't care about answering their questions. "You get an odd thing in the nets every now and then, particularly when you're deep-dragging on a sandy bottom."

"Silver Point? Marcosia?" Grayling asked. "I don't recall those names on any of the charts."

"I don't know anything about chartages, sir—"

"Charts."

"Marcosia is probably a local name," Sir David, the one they called Bear, said. "This region hasn't been properly surveyed—we're still using the Byzantines' charts."

"There were probably better ones in the Vatican—if

they hadn't been carried off to Byzantium," Cully said. "Not that it would make much of a difference. Idiotic to put it to the torch, I always said."

Sir Joshua snorted. "Well, take that up with His late Majesty, when next you see him, Cully. He had his reasons, I'm sure."

Cully snorted. "Always the obedient servant, eh?"

"Always." Grayling answered Cully's smile with a stern expression.

"I've never thought that loyalty ought to be blinding; it's supposed to be enlightening."

"Some other time, Cully." Grayling made a patting, be-still motion. "This still leaves us without a proper chart." He turned to Niko, a raised eyebrow asking the question.

"Yes," Niko said. "I could show you where Silver Point is. Or Stavros could—anybody could."

"It's a big sea. Do you think you could find that exact spot again?"

"Of course, sir."

It was a silly question. When you found a good spot for bottom-dragging, one where your nets wouldn't catch on rocks, you always memorized it. This one wasn't difficult. Niko could see in his mind's eye how, at that spot, Scolia's Rock, the big boulder that stood like a watchman at the shore of Silver Point, was just left of the big, jagged crack in the rock face of the island itself.

"The Crown will pay for your time, Niko," Cully said.

"I wasn't trying to cadge money, sir," he said, although it was nice to hear. An extra copper or two would always be more than welcome. "I was thinking that my family will expect me back by dark tomorrow, at the latest, or they'll start to worry about the skiff."

"Easily enough handled—Stavros or one of his sons can be dispatched there in the morning, along with some guesting-gifts, and perhaps an advance payment on your account. This could take a few days—not that you're likely to need the few coppers. Easy, boy—there's no threat meant in that."

"The reward." Grayling nodded. "Live swords belong to the Crown—and there's always a reward for their return."

Do you lose them a lot? he didn't ask. "But we paid Captain Andros to take the cursed thing away!"

"The Crown will settle with Captain Andros as to that. By rights, your family should split the reward with him— you for the finding of it, him for the surrendering of it," Grayling said. "It was substantial—"

"I should say so," Sir David, the one they called Bear, said. "And it's cheap, at two hundred golden crowns, to have that in hand."

Two hundred crowns? That was a preposterous amount of money. Niko couldn't imagine what one could buy with five or ten crowns of gold—and hundreds?

He had to ask: "My family is entitled to some of that? Sir?"

"Oh, I think your family is entitled to all of it," Grayling said. "I'm not pleased at all by this Captain Andros cheating you; I'll have a word or two with the Governor about that."

Niko's hopes had been raised only to be dashed. The Governor? Who would such an important man side with? A well-to-do ship's captain, or a barefoot fisherman? It wasn't difficult to guess.

Well, it had been a nice fantasy, even better than visions of a huge net filled with struggling fat tunnyfish, but that was all it had been.

Cully chuckled. "Sometimes, Gray, you can be such a fool—Niko, *Gray* will pay you the reward, out of his own funds, and get the Governor to reimburse him. Halloran can squeeze the money out of Andros—and it's a thing he should do personally, and a thing he'll probably enjoy."

"Of course." Grayling appeared puzzled. "I'd give you the money right now, but our traveling funds are in the strongbox aboard the ship, and I've barely got a couple of crowns in my purse."

A preposterous claim—why would even a noble need to travel with such wealth?

"So give him that now," Cully said.

"Excuse me?" Grayling drew himself up straight. "Is there some reason that my word is not good enough?"

Bear laid a hand on his arm. "Your word, Brother and Father Gray, is better than gold for me, and, I trust, for Father Cully, as well—"

" 'Cully.' Just 'Cully,' Bear. I don't wish to have occasion to tell you that again."

"—but for an island boy? One who only knows the Crown, Shield, and Dragon from the Occupation?"

Bear reached down to his waist and produced a small leather pouch, dipping his fingers into it momentarily to remove a ring and small glass vial, which he tucked into the sleeve of his robes before he handed the pouch to Niko. "I believe there's three or four crowns in there, Niko. Does that make you feel better?"

Well, of course it did, he thought, as he let the half-dozen-or-so coins fall into his hand, and made a fist around the hard, cold weight after a quick glance downward.

Niko had never held a gold coin before, although he knew that you were supposed to bite into a gold coin, to make sure that it was gold, but the knights would surely take offense at that, and he did believe that these were indeed gold. Niko didn't believe in this nonsense about almost two hundred more to come, but what of that?

This money alone could purchase enough hickory to smoke a lifetime's-worth of fish, a pile of hard candy that was taller than his sisters, and still leave more than enough left for a calf and a bull and enough oats to feed them forever.

New nets, bronze wire for more crab traps—he was suddenly a rich man, one more than able to meet any bride-price that Stavros could think of asking. If Father had known that his death would bring such wealth to his family, he would surely have thrown himself on that cursed sword with a smile on his worry-lined face.

And for the promise, a believable promise, of almost two hundred more?

Bear was still waiting for him to respond, and Gray's face had clouded over.

"I would have taken your word, sir," Niko said, choosing his words carefully.

"But gold in the hand is even better, eh?" Bear smiled.

Gray glowered.

Cully laughed out loud.

The lightning flashed, and the thunder roared.

The storm had passed, leaving behind good fortune in its wake.

For the third day in a row, the *Wellesley* lay at anchor

just off Silver Point, rolling slowly in the gentle, post-storm swells. Off in the distance, the ship's launch was moving quickly, close-hauled, toward where the twin masts of the Abdullahs' fishing sloop was just barely visible, while the *Wellesley*'s longboat was beached on Marcosia next to Scolia's Rock so that a hunting party could try for some more goats to supplement the ship's stores with fresh meat.

That last vaguely bothered Niko, although he didn't know why; Marcosia hadn't been inhabited in living memory, and there was nobody to care if the Navy swept it clear of life, and nobody who would object, even if they did care.

Niko took a secret pleasure in the Abdullahs being shooed away like they were bunch of chickens, and he surreptitiously patted at the pouch concealed beneath his kirtle, trying to ignore the discomfort of the doubled thong he had tied too tightly around his waist.

It was a fair enough trade. Most of the coins, of course, were still in the knights' strongbox, although Sir David had ceremoniously counted them out for him, and separated them into a separate leather bag, not commenting at all when Niko had taken out a handful, and put them in the pouch that Sir David had given him.

He needed to keep that with him. He didn't really believe that he'd be allowed to keep the entire fortune, but a dozen crowns was a sum so large he could barely wrap his mind around it, and if the thong bit into his flesh, what of that?

Much better to put up with that discomfort than have to worry about losing all his family's newfound fortune, which he did, day and night, sleeping only a little, and waking at the lightest sound. He had been billeted with what were called the mid-ship-men, although they seemed to have little to do with the middle of the ship, and were not men at all, any more than Niko was—less, if anything; not one of them had a proper beard.

Their quarters were well toward the bow of the ship, on the second deck, and the "men" were boys of about his age who, strangely, seemed to be given deference by the sailors, although he couldn't see why. It wasn't that the sailors treated boys that way—the "runners" got their share of muttered curses and occasional clouts.

Maybe it was the clothing. The mid-ship-men wore officers' clothes, while the runners had merely sailors' trousers and jerkins.

Still, it was interesting to listen to the mid-ship-men talk at table, with the oldest one presiding, and enough of that strangely potent wine regularly served to have him reeling off to bed to lie down on his pouch and fall asleep immediately thereafter.

The main result of him being billeted with these men-who-were-boys was that sailors and soldiers treated him with the same deference they treated the mid-ship-men, and, unless engaged in some work, all but the officers would stand and assume that curious stiff posture when he walked by, although they didn't bring their hands to their foreheads for him.

Outlanders were strange, but he could get used to that part of it, as funny as it looked.

It was strange not having any real work to do since the skiff had been taken aboard, and in fact he was going to leave the ship with it in better shape than it was taken aboard in, as a bunch of particularly scruffy-looking sailors—mid-ship-man Reifer had called them "prisoners at large," whatever that meant—had been set to working on its hull with bricks, sand, and tar in the middle hold, while the boy who seemed to be the sailmaker's servant busied himself with reinforcing seams and patches on the skiff's sails. Mid-ship-man Reifer had explained that Niko was not to speak to the men working on the hull—and certainly not pay them—but that a few coppers to the sailmaker's boy were traditional, and had shown disdain when Niko had inquired precisely how many were "a few."

Niko could live with the scorn. They were all outlanders, after all.

The only thing that was uncomfortable was being required to help supervise things from the raised rear deck, along with another man named Bosun, while the captain and Sir Bear looked on, saying little.

This bosun was strange-looking in a different way than the other one; where the other one was squat and muscular, this one was tall and lean—with hair the color of straw!—and a peg where of his right foot and part of his leg should have been. That lack didn't inhibit either his movement or his mouth—he kept moving about the raised deck, the brass ferule capping his peg maintaining the beat of his incessant stream of abuse to the sailors walking round and round, pushing the wooden arms of the strange device that, so Sir Bear had said, constantly delivered fresh air to the divers below, and that surely kept the calm sea churning with bubbles.

Shipboard life was apparently not terribly busy, as easily a dozen sailors were lolling against the rail below, just standing and watching what was going on, apparently not having any real work to do, other than staying out of the way of the soldiers—Sir Bear said they were called "marines"—engaged in some bizarre outlander rituals that involved all performing the same motions on space that had been cleared on the main deck.

Other groups of sailors took turns seeing how quickly they could load and fire the foremost mangonels and catapults, the mangonels apparently for distance—rocks were cheap, and could easily be resupplied from shore—and the catapults for accuracy, using one of the several targets that had been towed some distance away, then anchored in place.

There was, unsurprisingly, some cursing from the bosun's friend supervising it when the catapulters missed, but only silence when, about one time in five, the bolts actually hit the floating target.

Still, there was constant talking, and that took some getting used to, and he still wasn't quite used to it.

The man standing on the platform at the top of the main mast was constantly shouting out reports to nobody in particular, and one of the young boys called "runners" were always coming up to the captain, taking that strange stiff position, and rattling off something that always began with somebody's compliments and ended with the captain gravely nodding, taking a puff on his pipe, and giving a set of instructions that always ended with "on your way, and smartly."

How anybody was able to think with all this chatter was beyond Niko's comprehension. A fisherman's life was much simpler.

Grayling and Cully were nowhere to be seen. For the past days they had mainly stayed below, which left Niko thinking that Bear was the junior of the three, minding to

their affairs while his seniors got away from the noise and
clatter. As far as Niko had seen, the only time that the
two other knights were regularly on deck was for their
late-afternoon sparring sessions, where all three knights
would don padded clothing and go at each other—
sometimes one-on-one; other times two-on-one, or each
on all—with various wooden implements as well as bare
hands, only quitting when all were breathing heavily and
bathed in sweat, and would unselfconsciously strip down
to their bare skins and go over the side for a quick swim,
leaving behind their gear to be gathered up and washed
by some of the same "prisoners-at-large" who were working on Niko's skiff.

A couple of times Bear and Gray had even put on that
strange metal clothing over their padding, and that had
been even stranger to see.

Bear looked over the side at the diver on the raft below,
and shook his head. "Nothing, he says." He opened his
mouth, closed it, and opened it again. "I've got something to ask you, Niko, but I don't want you to think it a
threat. I mean you no ill, I swear."

He kept saying things like that, as though the words
would reassure Niko, and, well, maybe they did, at least a
little. Anything was better than the piercing stares that
Sir Joshua gave him.

"Yes, sir," Niko said.

"Oh, don't stand at attention. It looks silly on you—
you're not in His Majesty's service, or in Hers, either. Are
you sure that we're at the right spot? The same spot where
you brought it up?"

"Yes, sir." The question had been hanging in the air for
the past three days, and he had checked, time and time

again, but he went through the motions of looking at Scolia's Rock again, but the jagged rock face was just to the left of it, as he remembered.

"I could take a turn below, if you'd like," he said, hopefully.

Niko was more than a little curious about the diving bell. The notion of being able to get the benefit of returning to the surface without returning to the surface was enticing, although it seemed like cheating.

But, as Grandfather always said, anything that filled the nets with fish was the right thing to do, and it might be possible to use even a hoop-net to gather fish, if you could simply loiter around on the bottom and wait.

"I've thought on that," Sir Bear said, then shook his head. "But there's some tricks to using a diving bell—it's not quite as easy as it looks, and there's a sickness you can get if you stay down too long or come up too quickly—and I'd not want to lose you, even if I didn't find you pleasant company. As I do." He smiled and gave Niko a friendly pat on the arm, then beckoned to the captain, who dispatched the latest runner with the usual "on your way, and smartly now," and stalked over to join them.

"I'm thinking," Sir Bear said, "of moving the ship again—of asking you to move the ship again, that is. Perhaps a hundred yards out?"

Captain Johansen puffed a few times on his pipe before answering. "Hmm. Begging your pardon and all, Sir David, but perhaps you could tend to your knitting and permit me to tend to mine?"

Niko half expected the sky to split open and vomit lightning and thunder, but the big knight just smiled. "I could. Perhaps you could explain to me why?"

"Of course." Johansen nodded. "Of course. It's a big sea, Sir David. Very big," he said slowly, as though he wasn't sure that the knight had noticed that the sea was large. Perhaps he hadn't been told that it was wet, either? Outlanders were strange. "And the currents hereabouts are damnably tricky," the captain went on, "and change with every tide; something on the bottom could easily tend to be pushed this way and that, and *this* way might be a much longer distance than *that*." He pointed the stem of his pipe at the windward shore of the island. "Anything driven to a stable position would be likely driven there, which is why I've had the longboat over there most of the past two days, in water shallow enough that the divers don't need the bell, and they've found nothing there, either, save for some old pottery shards, which suggests to me that the currents sweep things clean hereabouts."

"Which is why—"

"If you'll excuse me, sir, that's why, if we're going to find anything that was on the bottom here, we're going to find it near here, or we're not going to find it at all." He took a few puffs from his pipe, thinking it over, or at least affecting to.

"You give me half the Fleet and half a century, and I could search this stretch of sea, perhaps. But steel is heavy, and metal, when it's thrown in the water, it *sinks*—steel rarely floats, sir; not even small pieces—and if something or some things, if you take my meaning, were thrown over the side here, even some long time ago, they're likely on the bottom here, even now, unless they're too far away to find. I'm assuming that if there is another sword here—and I say *if*—it was covered and uncovered by sand, not blown about like a bit of fluff, or driftwood." He puffed some more. "The bottom sand is deep here, deeper than any of the sounding poles can reach. I've got my divers searching the bottom, of course, but poling the entire bottom, even for just a few leagues, would take months, or longer."

"And if we can't find it?"

"Then either it's not here, or nobody else could find it here, any more than we could, without a fleet and a century, and some bloody good luck. Sir."

Sir Bear nodded. "Which will have to do."

"There is the other alternative, sir. A master wizard, sir, of the Royal Academy—"

"Would be no more capable finding a live sword than a diver would, and much less so, unless he were a skilled diver himself. It's not like the swords announce themselves, Captain, although I wouldn't doubt that most would want to, some exceptions aside." He patted at the hilt of the sword at his hip. "Red Swords tend toward the thirsty," he said, with a quick glance at Niko, "and they call out as loudly as they can, so I'm told, but you have to be in contact with them, metal to flesh, to hear it—at least, very close to that contact." He shook his head. "Perhaps one of the Great Wizards could hear the call a short ways away, but even She wouldn't be of much use in this—we're talking about a few feet, at the most."

The captain started to say something, but then stopped himself.

"No," Sir Bear said. "I didn't ask Her myself; I wouldn't disturb her. But Gray—Sir Joshua did. Well, She summoned him—that's why we're here. Word of what sounded like it might have been an unknown live sword worried Her, Captain. As it should." He shook his head. "No; the only way we could locate it by unearthly means is if God Himself takes a hand."

"He answers prayers upon occasion, I'm told," the captain said.

"He always answers prayers, Captain. And that's what Father Cully and Sir Joshua have spent every spare moment doing, over the past three days. I've spent a moment in prayer on the matter myself, as well."

"A moment?"

"Yes; just a moment." Bear nodded. "It's one of the things I disagree with many of my fathers and brothers on. It seems to me that since He notes the sparrow's fall, a quiet word or two is sufficient; He does not need to be shouted at. I pray thrice a day, but I do so for the sake of my own soul, not to nag Him." Once again, he touched his hand to the hilt of one of his swords; once again, he sighed. "So be it. We're done here. Please be so kind as to recall the divers, the cutter, and the longboat; prepare to raise anchor."

"Aye, sir." The captain casually touched the stem of his pipe to his forehead and walked away, already beckoning to the waiting runner.

Bear turned to Niko. "We'll get you home, and then return to Pironesia. Perhaps there have been some developments there, or perhaps Cully or Gray will have some other idea." He smiled. "I'll see that you're paid your full reward before you're off-loaded; there's no need to worry on that score."

Niko nodded. "Thank you."

"Then why the concern?"

"I—I don't know." He still couldn't understand these knights.

"Really, Niko—it's safe to ask me any question; I'm not easily offended."

"Well, sir, meaning no offense, honestly, sir, but I've been trying to figure things out, and if I understand it correctly, you're the junior of the three knights—but you didn't ask permission from the other two before ordering the captain about, and, well, this is a big ship and . . ."

He let his voice trail off; Bear was smiling, and Niko was just rambling.

"Well," Bear said, "when it comes to Father Cully, it's much more complicated than that, although, yes, Gray's my senior in the Order, not just in years, but in rank. But I am a Knight of the Crown, Shield, and Dragon, Niko, and a knight is expected to be able to make decisions by himself—and I don't need to beg Gray's permission when it comes to matters so obvious." His grin widened. "Although when we were boys at Alton, matters were somewhat different. But we were both just novices then, not knights.

"But enough of that. Mmmm . . . and I should hear your confession, and that of the rest of your family, as well, unless you'd prefer that Gray hears it? I know that you don't travel to the port very often, and the local bishop seems rather lax in dispatching priests," he said, frowning in disapproval.

"Whichever, sir. You'd be fine. So would either of the other two." He tried to seem eager; you were supposed to be eager about that sort of thing.

Bear smiled. "Good. Not that it should make any difference to you, but I'm a lighter penance than Gray is, and Father Cully . . ." He let his voice trail off, then shook his head. "Well, Father Cully is of the opinion that he's not a priest anymore, so he probably wouldn't hear your confession in any case. Let's find ourselves some privacy and get to it, shall we?"

"Yes, sir."

It had been an interesting few days, but not as interesting as the thoughts of what two hundred crowns of gold could buy. This business with the swords was the knights' affair, not his, and while they had treated him well, he'd be more than happy to see the *Wellesley* vanish over the horizon, leaving the gold—two hundred crowns!—behind.

"You say that your—that the One True God often answers prayers, Sir Bear?"

"Always." Bear nodded. "He always answers prayers, Niko. But often, so often, the answer is no."

Home.

Even a shallow-water fisherman could find rounding the lee side of his island a warming time, and this time Niko had more to be warmed about than the usual. The gold had been loaded into a small strongbox—they had just given it to him!—and locked with a key that even now hung from the thong around Niko's waist beneath his kirtle, along with the small pouch that he couldn't quite bear to let go of.

Unsurprisingly, the family was still working hard—the wisps of smoke blowing across the water spoke of active smokehouses and that spoke of some remarkably good shore fishing.

There was much to think about. His first thought was that they should keep the fortune a secret—let Grandfather negotiate a decent bride-price, before Stavros found out about it. But would Stavros feel that he had been taken advantage of?

And what would they do with it? Father Cully had spent an evening talking to Niko about what he called investment, as though a fisherman could just walk into Pironesia, lay down gold to purchase, say, a dockside warehouse, and expect to keep it.

Probably the best thing to do would be to let out word that the outlanders had given him some relatively small amount of money. Word of this sort of fortune would spread fast and far, and might even reach as far away as Seeproosh and draw pirates. That kind of money might make the risk of entering Navy-patrolled waters appeal to a pirate, although perhaps not.

Another thing to think about.

But it was probably worth spending at least some of the money on an appropriate sacrifice. The very idea of buying a bull to offer up to Poseidon would have seemed preposterous a week ago, but now it seemed like it could be a useful investment. What did a bull cost, anyway? Two silver crowns, perhaps four? It would have to be handled carefully, making it clear that the bull was being bought for breeding, lest the One True Church think that they were sacrificing it.

As, indeed, they would.

It could be that the sea would disgorge itself of another of these cursed swords, and the reward would turn that into a blessing—this time, he would know better than Father had, not to touch hand to metal, and would know better than Grandfather had that there was not only a curse on the sword, but a reward, as well.

It was a—

Wait. There wasn't too much smoke, but it was too broadly spread.

And there was something strange on the shoreline. The remnants of a fire? But why would Grandfather make a fire on the shore?

"Three bodies, sir, lying on the shore," the lookout called from atop the mast. He raised the glass to his eye again. "Hard to say for sure, but I don't think they're moving."

No.

Niko's gorge rose. He dropped to his knees, his bowels heaving.

Chapter 3: Dark Star

> Revenge is Mine, saith the Lord.
> Bear used to remind me of that, every now and then.
> I used to remind him that the Bible does not add, "and
> it's never, ever for the likes of you, Joshua Grayling."
> —Gray

Gray sat, quietly, cross-legged, on the cold stones, the Khan, still sheathed, across his lap. Prayer hadn't helped; meditation wasn't of any more use.

The Khan spoke to him, begging, pleading, promising.

Kill them, kill them all, he said.

Kill who? How?

Everybody. Anybody. You believe your God will sort

out the righteous. Let Him do his job, let you and me do ours. It's one thing that you're very good at, Gray. Better than anybody who has carried me before. It's what you and I do, Gray—and we're better than Alexander, even, no matter what they say about him and the Sandoval.

No.

He became aware that Cully had been standing in front of him, silently watching him.

Moonlight shattered on the waters below, and the wind had changed, now carrying the smell of smoke away. Off in the distance, a gull screeched in triumph or frustration, or perhaps both. Gray was beyond frustration now, and perhaps beyond anger. He just felt cold and empty.

"Feeling better, now?" Cully asked, leaning on his staff. "Or has the Khan persuaded you that killing everybody at hand is still and always the best and only solution to any problem?" His face was pale and ashen in the moonlight, but his voice was calm and level, as always.

"How is the boy?" Gray asked, not because he particularly cared, but to change the subject. Gray had to live with the Khan; he didn't have to talk about him.

"Asleep. Bear not quite forced half a bottle of wine down his throat; the surgeon had it spiked with some concoction or other—probably laudanum, although he didn't say. It seems to have worked." He smiled. "It worked on Bear, too; I had him drink the rest of it. He's going to need his sleep. As will you."

"Yes." Gray nodded. "Much to do, come morning. Too much to do."

"First things first, Gray," Cully said. "We still don't know near enough—"

"We know that somebody murdered those three

people. And for all we know, they died unconfessed, in sin, sent straight to hell without having had the wit about them to make a final act of contrition." He shook his head. Horrible.

"As could be." Cully nodded. "And if you believe that sitting here on the cold stones, letting the Khan stoke your anger, would cool those fires, then sit here and commune with him. Failing that, get to your feet and come with me." He rapped his staff on the stones. "Now, if you please."

"Give me a few moments."

"I've given you several hours, and I've come to the conclusion that you're just letting yourself go because I'm here. If it was just you and Bear, you'd have attended to necessary matters yourself, and not left them to an old man."

"Could you please—"

Cully slapped him across the face, hard enough to make the lights dance in Gray's head.

"Enough," he said. "If you don't care to be treated like a wilfull boy, then act like a man, Joshua."

Kill him, the Khan said.

No.

Cully struck down at him again, but Gray caught his wrist easily, and fastened his fingers around it.

The wrist felt bonier than it should have, and when Cully tried to pull away, Gray was more than strong enough to hold him in place, and Cully just stopped pulling. When had he gotten so feeble?

Gray could have snapped the old man like a twig, but he just let the wrist drop, and stood.

"Very well, Father Cully—"

"Just—"

"—and if you're going to treat me like a stripling, shaved-headed novice boy, by *God* you'll stop your endless complaining about me calling you Father, or we'll have that out, right here, right now, you and me, *Cully*."

Yes.

Oh, shut up.

He untied his sash and set his swords down on the cold stone, then turned to face Cully.

Cully's smile was ghostly and ghastly in the moonlight. "As you wish. It seems strange that you'll tolerate me slapping you about, but not correcting your misstatements—but leave it be, leave it be. Call me whatever you wish," he said, raising his hands in surrender.

"And that goes for Bear, too. Enough of this playing at being a shepherd."

"Very, very well—have it your way. Just understand, if you please, that I'm surrendering to the intensity of your feeling, and not for any other reason. I won't say I'm not afraid of you, Joshua, but I will say that I don't let fear rule me. As you well know."

For a moment, the smile dropped, and Gray remembered that this was still Cully, after all, with all the relentlessness of a saint, if little of the equanimity that supposedly came with a saintly personality.

Cully dropped his hands and squatted to pick up his stick. "Now, if you're quite done with your tantrum, would you pick up your swords and come with me . . . ?"

Gray nodded.

Cully led him down the stone path, toward the shore.

The bodies were still there, but now they lay wrapped in shrouds. Two of the marines, each with a lantern set nearby on the stone, stood watch over the bodies, from a respectful distance away.

Cully gave him a look. "Somebody had to attend to the necessary."

"Thank you, Father," he said, accepting the reproof.

"You there—Sterling is it?—I'll need your lantern, again." The marine, a compact sort of man with a bristle of a mustache, stalked over and handed Cully the lantern, then returned to his post.

"Look here," Cully said, unwrapping one of the bundles.

Gray put his hand on the Khan's hilt to calm himself. Death and mutilation didn't bother the Khan at all, and the emotion, or lack of it, was infectious. Carrying the Khan was, all in all, more of a burden than a blessing, but that didn't mean that there weren't some benefits.

It was the body of a girl, of perhaps twelve, thirteen or so. She had probably been pretty in life, in the olive-skinned Mediterranean sort of way, although it was hard to tell. There were dark, gaping holes where her eyes should have been, and all of the left breast and most of the right had been cut entirely away. Cully started to pull the blanket past her waist, but stopped himself.

"Torture," Cully said, his voice low and even, too low and even. "Same with the younger one. Bodies stiffened up, but haven't started to loosen yet—figure they're dead at least a day, but not much more."

So while the *Wellesley* had been bobbing around at anchor, somebody had been hacking little girls' breasts off in front of their grandfather.

Gray knelt and covered her face up. Even with his right hand on the Khan, it was difficult; the fingers of his left hand couldn't stop trembling, even when he fastened them on his belt for support.

We will avenge them, the Khan said.

Yes.

There were many times that Gray had wished he had been picked to carry a sword less dark than the Khan, but this wasn't one of them.

I've never wanted affection. Respect, yes; blood, more often. Affection is for women.

"And the grandfather?" Gray asked. "Should I look at his body, as well?"

"I see no need. He had some scratches and bruises, and then a slit throat." Cully shook his head. "Very unsystematic, the lot of it. Not the Inquisition or the Caliphate's style at all."

Which didn't mean much of anything. The Congregation of the Defense of the Faith was not what it once had been, what with the power and reach of Byzantium a remnant of what it had been at the height of the Church's power; although the Ministry for Promotion of Virtue was, if anything, more of a force in the Caliphate than it had ever been.

But centuries of virtual stalemate among the Crown, Empire, and the Caliphate had taught the agents of the Caliphate even more of the subtlety that seemed to come naturally in the Levant, and those of the Empire had always been so, both in history and in legend, from before the time of Mordred the First, Arthur the Tyrant, and the beginning of the Age.

"It looks piratical," Cully said. "Not exactly unusual for Seeproosh pirates to torture his children in front of a man to extract his secret cache, and they're a remarkably clumsy lot." He shrugged. "But I doubt that we'd have pirates in these waters without them having struck somewhere nearby first."

Gray nodded. Pironesia didn't produce much. Fish, some wine—particularly on the larger islands—and the mutton and wool, as well as the olives. Neither fish nor mutton traveled particularly well, and better wine, although not cheaper, was available just across the Channel from England, although certainly both fish and sheep helped to feed the Malta fleet. And while olives were tasty, certainly, and traveled well after being pickled, they were, after all, only olives.

Pironesia had nothing like the wealth that poured out of Inja or New England. Which made them a relatively unattractive target, what with Antalya, Kizmir, and Koosh closer to hand, and if not much richer, at least much more vulnerable. With the Caliphate controlling the south, the Crown the north and east, and the Byzantines the north and west, there were still ample uncivilized regions along the ragged ex-Turkish boundaries for those pirates who didn't want to sneak past Gibby and go out to sea, traveling for months to get into the rich pickings of the Kareeb, some never to return.

Besides, while the old man wouldn't be of much value to pirates, it would take some serious motivation for a pirate to kill a couple of young girls who could easily be sold for good money on any beach in Suryah, or more likely auctioned off in the markets of Aladikyah.

Of course, a live sword would have been more than sufficient motivation for a raid into Pironesia, and more— if they believed that the old man was hiding one.

Alexander was living like a king in Qabilyah, at last

report, at least whenever he and the Sandoval weren't off running bloody errands for the Caliph. The docents of the Royal College didn't have a high opinion of their equivalents in the Caliphate, but there was no reason at all to believe that a Caliphate wizard was no more incapable of joining a live sword to live man than a Royal Wizard was; of a certainty they were every bit as capable of producing cursed weapons, although nothing as powerful as the live swords.

Fastening a curse or a blessing on a sword was difficult, yes; and while Gray didn't know much about the details, and wished he knew less, he knew creating a live sword was another order of difficulty entirely, and that the doing of it entailed serious risks for all involved. Since the end of the Age, it was supposed to have grown more difficult, year by year, to create such a focus of power, and even She couldn't do so, not anymore.

He would have said that it was impossible, until just a few days before.

"What are you thinking?" Cully asked.

"I'm thinking that we'd have heard of pirates, or Caliphate raiders, or anybody else out of place in these waters," Gray said.

"Probably. Almost certainly. All those half-pay officers in the islands?"

Gray nodded. "Which means that whoever did this is somebody who belongs here."

"A local?"

"Possibly. Or a trader, more likely." Guild traders, whose only homes were their boats, plied the Mediterranean from end to end, just as they did the European coast, protected here more by the fear that local authorities would lose trade if they were interfered with than with the Navy or the Caliphate's protection—although that was scant protection from the Seeproosh pirates, or the Barbaries.

The richer clans of the remnants of the ancient Hanseatics had taken up the newer routes to New England and Darmosh Kowayes, some for pure trade, and some others for whaling, competing with the New England industry, although avoiding sailing too close to any of the colonies; it was best, for a trader, to avoid the obvious conflict.

The Atlantic was much harder on ships than the Mediterranean, and more than a few ships simply disappeared—there was more profit to be had, but more risk in the taking of it. Much safer to trade in the Med, where there were dozens of established routes, bringing spices or gold or cedar from here to trade for fish or wool or wine from there, those to be traded for something else somewhere else, the route established by custom and need as well as opportunity. Gray had always thought that direct trade, from point to point, made more sense, all in all, but the world seemed to work in ways that Gray found sensible only by accident, if at all.

"Somebody who heard about the sword in Pironesia," he said, idly, "or somebody who heard something from somebody who heard something. Or one of Niko's neighbors?"

Neighborliness was of high value in the islands, as it was in many places, but the thought of what a live sword would go for, from the Caliphate or the Empire, if one were to ignore the law, would be a huge temptation, no matter how neighborly one was.

But that was the sort of secret that couldn't be kept, not long. Somebody would talk to somebody, no matter how insular the island families were.

If, of course, they'd gotten a live sword.

If there had been another.

If—

Cully shook his head. "If there was, the boy doesn't know about it, and his story made sense to me," he said, answering Gray's thoughts, instead of his words. "It's possible, I suppose, that what they found was a cache of these, instead of the single one that they said had been swept up in the nets, but I think not. Not everybody betrays everybody else, Gray, and the boy seemed genuinely surprised at the amount of the reward—wouldn't he have said something if there were more here?"

"If he knew. If his grandfather wasn't hiding something from him. If he isn't being duplicitous. Hard to tell." He was fairly sure that Niko was as ignorant as he seemed to be, but Gray would very much have liked to take the measure of his grandfather for himself.

"So you'll want to keep him nearby?" Cully asked.

"That seems sensible, no matter what I believe." Gray shrugged. "But if it was a Guild ship, that speaks of some foreknowledge—risky thing, isn't it?"

Cully nodded. "Yes, it would be, at that. Be interesting to take a look at the records and reports in Pironesia, and see what ship hasn't shown up that should have."

Gray nodded. Pity that it was just him and Bear and Cully—pouring over records was the sort of thing that Brother Linsen doted on. While the loss of his left arm had barely slowed him down, the age and feebleness that went with it had made Linsen give up the Goatboy five years before, accompanied by the traditional and suitably hypocritical protestations that it was more in relief than regret, despite it being a White Sword.

But Linsen had been and still was a Knight of the Order, by the grace of God; and a Knight of the Order of Crown, Shield, and Dragon could still practice service, honor, faith, and obedience from a chair in a library as much as from the back of a horse or the deck of a ship, as long as his mind was clear.

"We might make a guess as to where they'd head," Gray said. "*Wellesley*'s a fast ship. Make at least twice a fat-bellied merchantman's speed, better in a stiff wind—"

"Which is just fine when you know where you're going. Useless if you're just picking a direction. Doubly useless if you don't even know what you're chasing."

"Maybe not." The fastest way to get away from anywhere on the open sea was to put the wind at your back. "East, with the wind at our back—"

"—and if whoever it was took flight that way, but headed just a point or two off the wind? With a day's head start?" Cully shrugged. "If you had three or four fast sloops to spare, maybe. But *Wellesley* and the cutter? How quickly do you give up?"

Well, if they were both wrong—Gray agreed with Cully—there would soon be somebody missing from the islands, or some ship that had been plying the trade routes having disappeared. That part of it could be left to the Administration in Pironesia. Halloran seemed to be a capable enough man, and the capable surrounded themselves with the equally capable.

Gray was about to say something to that effect when Cully beckoned to the nearer marine, who more marched than walked over. "What do you think?" Cully asked.

"Sir. It's not my place to listen in, nor to say, sir."

"Yes, but you *have* been listening," Gray said, "while trying to look like you haven't. Just stand easy and talk—" he beckoned to the other "—the both of you."

"Sir, I'm supposed to be on station."

"I'll square things with your corporal, if he comes by," Cully said. "Go ahead and smoke, if you'd like to. Flaherty, is it?"

He nodded. "Sir. Private Seamus Flaherty—" he dropped the brace at a gesture from the other marine. "I dunno, sir. I seen places that have been raided by pirates, and this just doesn't smell right for that." He reached for his belt pouch, presumably for his pipe, but desisted at a head-shake from the other.

Sterling nodded. "Yeah—Shim's got the right of it. Never knew a pirate to waste flesh, or leave anything that isn't nailed down, not even when there's more valuable stuff to be had. It's like . . ."

"Well, go ahead."

"It feels like somebody's trying to make me mad. I got kids myself, back home—a boy and a girl. Haven't seen them in better than a year, but the boy should be just about ready to make his mark and join the Fleet, and the girl's just about the age of the older one of those, by now." His face barely held a trace of any expression, but his voice had some heat in it. "What I want to do is find the bastards, no matter where the hunt'd take me. Me, I'd start with every fucking one of these little islands around here, and see who jumped when I said boo, and since everybody'd jump, I'd be chasing things down for a good time to come—which is why if it wasn't one of the natives what done it, whoever it was'd have plenty of time to put enough sea between himself and here to drown a fish, and be off to wherever the hell he thinks he's off to, if you get my meaning.

"Shit—me, I'd say that it smells of the Dar, say to hell with them all, and Shim 'nd me send the cutter to Pironesia, and have the Gov send one fast sloop to Malta and another to Gibby, telling the *Pelican* and the *Refuge* and the *Ark* to load up the King's Own, the Red Watch, and what they've got of the Scots Guard, and set sail with the rest of the Fleet around them, stop off on Seeproosh to put it to the torch from end to end, then put in at Aldikyah, burn that, and carve our way east all the way to M'dina." He smiled. "Which'd be a damn fool thing to try to do, I know, given the size of the Fleet and the size of the Dar and all, but I'm just a marine private, sir, and not no Admiral or General or Duke or the King—God save him, sir—which is why it's just as well that decisions about such things aren't made by the likes of Shim and me, but by you folks with the titles and the swords and the responsibilities, eh, Father? Begging your pardon, and all."

Gray nodded. "Somebody who didn't know better might think that a Knight of the Order would feel the same way."

Someone who didn't know any better, for that matter, might think that a Knight of the Order would have that kind of authority, which Gray certainly didn't, and no Knight of the Order had, during living memory. Gareth and Gaharis had been their half-brother's commanders in chief; Dinadan of the Isles had been first sea lord and Sir Alex the MacPhee field marshal to Good King John, true, but that was just history. Giving military commands to Knights of the Order had long become uncommon, and both military and nobility resented the Order Knights' authority and royal access enough as it was.

You heard mutterings around Court about how they were fine as bodyguards, but that they shouldn't make such a habit of overreaching themselves.

Gray thought that the mutterers had a point.

Getting the *Wellesley* seconded into their service had not been a battle only because Admiral Dougherty knew full well that Gray was utterly capable of doing as he threatened. Had Dougherty continued to delay, he knew that could have looked out his window to see Gray hopping into a jitney to ride across the city, and coming back with a letter from the King, or perhaps even the King himself.

At that, even after winning the concession on the *Wellesley*, Gray had had to threaten the direst consequences at Dougherty's attempt to strip off both the senior officers and the marine contingent and send the *Wellesley* out with a green crew of mainly landsmen and a training company of marine recruits, rather than its present master and seasoned sailing crew, along with the marine company from the Blue Watch that Gray had firmly insisted on.

"All that service, honor, and justice stuff, sir," Sterling said, "going for justice the way we marines go after blood. Instead of whatever you should be doing. Sir."

Cully nodded, and smiled approvingly. "One can always trust a marine to obey orders, even if the order's to be insolent, eh?"

"Yes, sir." Sterling drew himself up straight. "And you can count on this marine to take the consequences of overreaching himself, *sir*."

"Oh, be still." Cully snorted. "The only consequence you've got to worry about is me asking you some other time what you think; I told you to speak your mind, so drop the brace and relax, man."

There was another player in this game—at least one. Gray didn't believe in coincidences—somebody had gone to some trouble to turn darklings loose in Pironesia.

And now this? Coincidence? No.

"Yes," Cully said, "Private Sterling has a point. Let the governor and the Navy handle whatever happened here. If there was another sword here, let him try to find out where it's gone. It's our job to find out where it came from."

Gray nodded. Our job, eh?

He smells blood, he does. The Khan was amused, and, for a change, Gray shared his amusement.

"And how exactly do you propose we do that?" he asked.

Cully shrugged. "Well, we know it's a live sword, and we know it's new—finding anything else out from it requires more magic than holiness. Nearest place to find that, in more supply than I like to think about, is you-know-where."

Gray nodded. "Pantelleria?" He wasn't afraid to speak its name; in the old days, Cully wouldn't have been, either. Too much time among superstitious Pironesians, Gray supposed. Not that there wasn't reason enough to be nervous about Pantelleria.

"Yes. Likely a wizard or two on Malta, but nothing like what we'd find you-know-where."

"More reliability, though."

"Gray, you're thoroughly reliable, and I trust your considered opinion completely—what do *you* make of the sword?"

"Nothing. I don't know enough."

"My point precisely."

There was that. "Very well."

Sterling made a face, then resumed his blank expression. "By your leave, sir?"

"Carry on, Private."

Niko went along without protest. He didn't have a choice, and it was hard to care, and impossible to try.

He just went along, whether it was having the ship's tailor fit him out with more of these strange-looking outlander clothes—which, bizarrely, included clothes that he was expected to wear *under* his clothes—and the cobbler and his assistant busy at work on not just one but two pairs of boots, each of which would have done justice to a wealthy trader.

He just went along. He had donned the under-clothes, and the blouse, and then the heavy but elegant jacket and trousers that he had been given—just like the officers' and mid-ship-men's clothes, save for the lack of decoration on the sleeves—and he padded barefoot up the ladder to the quarterdeck behind Bear and Cully, as he had been told to do. If he was to be outfitted with strange clothes, he would have preferred the looser and more clearly comfortable tunic, trousers, and robes of the knights, but nobody was asking him, and walking about the deck in these garments, as though he had any business wearing them, was more than enough pretentiousness, at that.

"The matter that we need to decide," Cully said, "is precisely what to do with you."

Niko shrugged. "I should just take the skiff and go home."

"That would not be possible, I'm afraid," Cully said, shaking his head. "At least, at the moment. But, after we're done with you, if you want to return to the islands, it can be arranged. You'd have your choice of families to marry into, what with the gold, and all. I'm sure that Stavros could use another hand, and, if not, arrangements can be made."

"I can help with that," Bear said. "A word or two—"

"I just want to go home."

Bear's eyes widened at the interruption, which had surprised Niko probably even more than it had surprised the big knight.

But instead of cuffing him for the impertinence, as Niko no doubt deserved, Bear just nodded. "Understandable, at that."

"Whether it's understandable or not," Cully went on, "as I said, it's not possible, not at the moment. In due course, perhaps. Or you might want to try life in Pironesia, at least for a while."

"He's more than old enough to interest the Press, Father," Bear said. "No, Niko, I'm not threatening you— it's just a matter that has to be handled. A letter from Gray or me can give him immunity—with a note that a copy has been filed with the Governor to remove any temptation from the press gangs to lose the letter." He turned to Niko. "If you're accosted, you'd just need to be sure that they see the letter. Not that the Navy's a bad life, mind."

"Not when seen from guest quarters," Cully said. "It's somewhat a different thing when seen from the aft hold. Well, as the Founder said, 'when you don't know what to do, do what you know how to do.' "

"Train him? I don't see much point, Father."

Train him to do what? Niko's brow hurt from all the furrowing.

"I don't see any harm, and for a fact I'm finding his constant cringing around everybody a little irritating." Cully's smile took some of the sting out of the words. "Bruises heal, and giving one good hit on a breastplate can have a boy walking about as though he thinks he's ten feet tall, as you might remember. It's been some years since I faced a novice on a training square, but I think I can remember how, eh?"

Both of the knights smiled at that.

"You and Gray might as well do the formal part," Cully went on. "Start him on first position in the morning—the Wellington sequence, not the Cumberland, I think. See if Lieutenant Haversham has any objection to him drilling with the marines in the afternoon."

"Well, there's enough practice swords aboard, and leather enough, but he'll need both sword and dagger for the Wellington."

"The armorer will have ample spares—make sure he's given good steel, not some Bombay pot metal."

"One advantage to seconding a taut ship like the *Wellesley*, Father, is that one doesn't have to worry about such things. Nor about some lazy armorer not properly fitting grips to the hand." Cully started to say something, and Bear raised his palms in surrender. "But I'll see to it, Father."

Niko's fingers clenched on the rail, and the pouch beneath his kirtle was cold and leaden. He had been staring off into the distance so long that it took him a while to realize that both Father Cully and Sir Bear had stopped talking to each other, and were just looking at him.

"Lust is a sin, Niko," Bear said, gently, "whether it's lusting after flesh or anything else—gold, or vengeance. It's also pointless, as Saint Paul says."

"It's also incomplete, Bear," Cully said. "You know the previous verse, as well?"

"Previous verse?"

"You were about to quote from Romans 22— 'Vengeance is mine,' no? You do know what comes before and after it, don't you?"

"Of course. 'If possible, so far as it depends on you, live peaceably with all.' Then: 'My loved ones, never seek for vengeance for yourselves, but leave it to the wrath of God; for it is written, vengeance is mine, I will repay, says the Lord.' "

"I never much cared for that letter to the Romans," Cully said. "Saint Paul was too flexible."

"That's not a common criticism of him."

"No, it's not." Cully shrugged. "But it's mine—too much of the if-it's-possible, and if-you-can, and such. You do remember the next verse?"

"Yes. 'But if you do wrong, be afraid, for he does not bear the sword in vain; he is the servant of God to execute his wrath on the wrongdoer.' " Sir Bear patted at the sword at his waist. "But one has to find the wrongdoer, first, and be sure that he is a wrongdoer, and be sure that one is serving God."

Cully nodded. "Standard, sound doctrine, that. The devil is, of course, in the details." He jerked his chin toward the shoreline. "But if it is sound doctrine, would you explain Gray to me?"

Bear shrugged. "There's logical reasons for it—there's always reasons for what he does. If there is another sword hidden somewhere on the island, it's best that it not be left for easy discovery, and important enough that he draw the Khan to make that so."

"But he could have left a dozen marines to search for it, along with one of the bigger launches to bring them back to Pironesia, in success or failure."

Bear smiled. "I'm not saying that he's being reasonable, just logical."

"I'm thinking that the Khan wants to destroy something, anything, and that Gray's letting him."

"There is that, too, I expect." He turned to face the shore, although Niko couldn't say what he was looking at, what signal he'd seen.

But there must have been one.

Without warning, without lightning or thunder to presage it, the island burst into flame, drawing incoherent gasps from Niko's throat.

The night flashed into an awful red brightness. Fire roared, and the wind brought more than a trace of sulfur with it. Even from this distance, Niko could feel the heat on his face. Sparks flew up into the air.

The sailors had apparently been warned of that— buckets of water were already being hauled up on ropes to wet the sails, accompanied by imprecations from the bosuns.

The launch was cast off, and rowed swiftly toward the cloud of smoke and steam that covered where the island was. Had been. Rocks still remained, but they were just rocks, and no longer the home to any living thing.

"I would hope he gave them a proper, Christian burial

first," Sir Bear said, making the One True Church gesture over his massive chest.

"Shh. Of course he did."

The island seemed to collapse in on itself, in a fountain of fire—and steam, as the melted rock hit the water.

"The Injans used to talk about Shiva, God of Destruction," Cully said. "Probably still do. Probably talking about somebody a lot like Gray."

"Blasphemous, too many of the Injans," Bear said. "They worship Christ out of one side of their mouths, and then turn around and pray to the rest of their absurd pantheon out of the rest, with their filthy fakirs encouraging them the moment that the Church turns its back."

"And what would you do to stop that, Bear? Turn the Order into the Inquisition? Turn the whole *Church* into the Inquisition?"

"*No*." Niko had never seen Bear angry before. "No, Father, I would do no such thing, as you should know. For my part, I would preach to them. With the Gospels under one arm, and the Analects of the Order under the other, with no sword at my waist, and with no shoes on my feet."

"You would preach peace, and love, and turning the other cheek, as He did?"

"Yes; although He preached that and more, as I would. And if you wish to remind me how He died—"

"No. I'll not tempt you to martyrdom, David. You already are far too tempted in that direction." Cully gestured to where the launch had emerged from the cloud of smoke and steam. Gray stood at the bow, as though attached there, not wavering for a moment as the bow rose and fell in the swells, not even as he sheathed his sword, and replaced the sheath in his belt. "No. I'd say this: preach to Gray first."

Bear nodded. "As you wish, Father Cully."

Chapter 4: Pantelleria

> Wizards. I don't much like wizards. I'd rather deal with
> with a company of saracens than with one such. At least
> I know what to *do* to a company of saracens.
>
> —Gray

Dark clouds gathered over the sea behind them.

Niko couldn't help turning in his saddle to look nervously over his shoulder, and he tried to act reassured when Bear would smile and nod at him, although he didn't feel in any way reassured. It felt like the clouds were herding them, like a pair of netters funneling a school of tunnies into a small cove for the slaughter. And the wind kept blowing—more so the farther inland they rode, as though the netters were getting more and more excited.

Cully seemed to catch his nervousness. "Interesting

island, even if you don't include you-know-who," he said, his voice raised just enough to easily carry over the wind. "You notice the groves down by the port?"

"You mean with the walls?" It had seemed strange, at that. "Thieves?"

"No, wind—orange trees and lemon trees, well, don't like a lot of wind, for some reason. Neither do vines— they're planted in sconches. And you might want to look at those olive groves outside of Porto Pantelleria—they've been trimmed to grow out, rather than up. Arabs used to call it Bent el-Rhia—the island of the wind." His horse was starting to edge ahead; Niko envied the quick and easy tug on the reins and click of the tongue that brought it back beside his own animal, every bit as easily as Niko could have pulled a skiff into a slip on a perfect day.

Niko had always thought that it would be pleasant to ride on a horse. Sort of like a skiff, except that a horse would know enough to keep its feet on the right course, and not have to be constantly watched to prevent it from capsizing.

So much for dreams; even when they turned out to be true, they turned out to be unsatisfactory. For one thing, a horse walked so much more slowly than a skiff moved; he could probably have kept up with it by walking, not that he had been offered the choice.

And yes, the horse didn't tip over, or threaten to, and it certainly kept its feet on the trail without any urging, but what he hadn't dreamed was that every step that the animal took would bounce his tailbone against the hard leather saddle, any more than he had that getting off the animal was largely a matter of tumbling to the ground in a controlled way.

And getting on the horse was far more difficult than it looked, at least for him, although he hadn't thought himself weak of arm.

Gray didn't seem to notice his discomfort, or much of anything else. He kept watch on the hills, as though expecting something awful to stream across them the moment he dropped his gaze.

Cully was more solicitous. "You'll hurt worse in the morning, but less every morning after, particularly if you stick with it." His horse seemed impatient with the speed of Niko's, and Cully had to keep giving little jerks on the reins to keep even with Niko. "Me, as well; it's been some years since I last forked a horse, and I'm cursedly clumsy."

It didn't show. It looked like Cully's hips were stitched to the saddle, just like with the other two.

That wasn't the only annoyance. This Pantelleria, or Bent el-Rhia, or you-know-where, wasn't a proper island. The rocks weren't even a normal rock color, but an almost pure black, both at the shoreline and where they jutted up from the earth here and there.

The shore had been honeycombed with caves, but not proper caves—many of them hissed and spouted steam and an awful smell, as though the island was rimmed by entrances to the hot Hell of the One True Church. Even past the shore, gaps in the earth still spouted an occasional gout of steam that Bear had said was "volcanic" when Niko had first screamed and shied away from one, as though that explained anything.

Another one, perhaps a hundred feet away, but hidden in the dark greenery, spouted steam and stink into the sky.

Niko still flinched, of course, but he didn't shy away.

He believed Cully—although how a priest of the One True Church would give credence to Hephaistos for anything— even under the false Roman name of Vulcan—was something that Niko didn't understand.

Still, he didn't want to discuss the matter. It was one thing for a priest to know about that sort of thing, but Niko wasn't supposed to even know about Hephaistos.

The island was too round and even, and the hills too low, as though they had grown old and too tired to thrust up toward the sky. There were no trees—and except where the black bones of the earth showed through, the island was covered by a carpet of greenery, molded into strange shapes that made them look as though they had been carved, to what purpose or intent Niko wouldn't have wanted to guess.

"Notice anything strange?" Cully asked.

"*Everything* here is strange."

Cully laughed. "True enough. The thing I've been thinking about is that we've been riding for several hours, straight up into the hills, more or less."

"Yes, Father?"

"The whole island is less than twenty miles around— it's just about five miles the long way, and half that across the waist. Ride straight across, and you should be over the top and down the other side in an hour or two, at most."

"But we've been riding much longer than that." He eyed the sun. They had anchored off the cove at the northeast end of the island just after daybreak, and the sun was now high in the sky at noon, more or less.

"That was, I believe, my point. I'll show you the charts, when we return to the port. The Montagne Grande is a mile from the Punta Karascia, but even allowing for the twists and turns in the road, we've ridden much farther than that, with more to go. Illusion? Or is the contained larger than the container? The pure of heart are supposed to be able to see through deception, even from the Father of Lies."

"So it's said," Niko said skeptically, although he wasn't sure whether he was more skeptical about the idea, or about Cully being pure of heart.

"No, not me—Bear," Cully said. "If ever there was such thing as the pure of heart, it would be Brother Bear. Yet if you ask him, he'll tell you he thinks we've been riding since dawn, as well. It's not the only thing that's strange here—have you noticed how you feel?"

"Feel? What do you mean?" The pain in his backside was intense, but other than that . . .

"The sense of misery and doom?"

"I don't feel a sense of misery and doom." Which was strange, come to think of it. Thoughts of Grandfather and his sisters had dominated his waking hours, and nightmares what little sleep he could manage. But . . .

"Yes. You have not happened to have eaten any lotus recently, have you?"

"Eh?"

"Never mind. There's something in the air here, and something else. The Wise control things here; they apparently don't like strong emotions about."

"Wise Ones? You mean wizards—"

The ground rumbled at the word, and another gout of steam shot skyward just a few oar lengths away.

"It's best to speak in . . . indirect terms hereabouts," Cully said. "Your father, perhaps, taught you not to refer to Tisiphone, Megaera, and Alecto by their names, or as the Furies? 'The Good and Kindly ones,' no?" Cully smiled. "Oh, please. Bear and Gray haven't been living in Pironesia for the past ten years, but I have, and I'm aware of what goes on when the, err, One True Church isn't thought to be watching, and who is to say that it's all just superstition?

"You've already decided what to sacrifice to Tisiphone, I suppose, and I can't see the harm that it'd do, although I know I'm supposed to. Saint Mani to the contrary, there is more than simple good and pure evil that struggles across the face of the world, more players than Him and the Foul One. Even the cursed Triunes have begun to recognize that their rejection of Manicheanism was correct, but for the wrong reasons—but save that for another day, when perhaps you know what an old man is rambling on about.

"For now," he said, pointing at the castle that stood at the crest of the hill ahead, "be careful in what you say or do. I think they'll be unlikely to offer the three of us food or drink, but you might be a different matter. Regardless of how thirsty or hungry you are," he said, "I'd advise against accepting it. Strongly."

"Poison?"

"I doubt that. It's possible, I suppose, though unlikely. It's certainly reasonable to trade with any of the villages along the shore for food and water, if you wish; there's no harm in that, and the port villages do a lot of trade, some of it between Crown and Dar. Pantelleria's got quite good cuisine, in fact. It's a function of having been conquered by everybody— the Sesioti, the Phoeniciasti, the True Romans, the Dar, and finally the Crown, just before the battles of the Age of Crisis, when the Wise Ones seized the central highlands. The food here—along the shore, that is—is very good. Sciakisciuka is one of my favorite dishes, even though it disagrees with me. If we stay ashore tonight, eat your fill, and enjoy." He shook his head. "But not here, not once you leave the coast, not until you return to the coast."

"Might I ask why?"

"Because I've never heard of anybody who accepted any food from the Wise ever having left." Cully smiled. "You may now say 'oh.' "

"Yes, Sir Cully," Niko said. "Oh."

The gates to the castle stood open.

Bear dismounted without waiting to see if he could force his horse to go through the gates and into the courtyard beyond. It had already been trying to shy away, and there was no point in trying to make the animal do something against its nature, not when there was an easier, gentler alternative.

He left the other three behind, and walked in through the open gates.

Bear had heard tales of the castle on the impossibly distant highlands of Pantelleria, but it was, at least at first look, much less interesting in reality than it had been in story. Life was often that way, he supposed.

He had expected something rather more exotic. The grounds, while well manicured, seemed strangely ordinary and utilitarian. The three-story main residence that stood in the center of the compound wouldn't have seemed much out of place in Pendragonshire. It had been built of huge carved stones, rimmed by carefully trimmed hedges that blocked his view of any entrance beside the main, arched one in front.

It all spoke more of careful maintenance than great age or great magic.

A low stone building clung to the east wall. The shutters had been pulled back, and the rows of narrow bunk beds, each with a variety of spears, swords, and armor made it clear that it was a barracks, although there was not a soldier, or anybody else, to be seen. The huge door on the taller building—the building was built of well-weathered wood, rather than stone—against the east wall would have proclaimed it to be a stable even if the wind hadn't brought the familiar and pleasant stink of fresh manure to his nostrils.

It all looked so ordinary, save for the absence of anybody in sight, although it certainly wasn't absent of sound.

The familiar clattering of metal on metal from beyond the residence told of soldiers at practice, as much as the distinctive metal-on-metal squeal of a pump, followed by clay shattering from behind the residence spoke of everyday dishes being washed—and some broken.

He quickened his pace and walked toward the sound. The hedges were layered; the gap in the outer hedge was several feet away from the gap in the inner one, and when he walked through into the small sheltered courtyard behind the residence, he was alone, the only evidence that there had been somebody there was the water-darkened ground beneath the very ordinary-looking cast-iron pump.

He knelt down and felt at the ground. Yes, it was damp, but there was no trace of fragments of any sort, clay or otherwise. But he had heard the sounds, and they had come from there, but—

"Good afternoon, David," sounded from behind him.

He spun about, quickly, his hand flying to the hilt of the Nameless by reflex, although the distant cold comfort was no real comfort at all, not here and now.

Be calm, David, the Nameless whispered. *If you can't be the stream, be the rock that the stream flows about, and not a leaf pushed this way and that at every whim of the flowing water.*

"Be easy, David," the stranger said. "There's no danger here. At least none for you—if you behave yourself, which I'm sure you will."

The stranger was a big, blocky man with a smiling face that looked familiar, although Bear couldn't have said where he had seen it before. His feet bare, he was wearing nothing more than trousers and a simple, blousy shirt that Bear would not have called peasant-style because of the whiteness and fineness of the cloth. The sleeves were rolled back to bulging biceps, which flexed as the stranger finished wiping his hands with a cloth made of similar material, then tossed it to one side and held his hands up, fingers spread, as though to show that he was carrying nothing else.

When Bear glanced down at the ground where the cloth had fallen, it was gone.

"In the name of—"

"*Please.* Don't say anything in the name of anybody, not here," the man said. "That would present both of us with some difficulties, you rather more than I. Let's just sit and talk, instead," he said gesturing to a stone bench that stood next to a round, wood-topped table. The surface of the old wood was deeply scored, the other brushed some chips from it; it had apparently been used as some sort of chopping board, and recently so, but there was no sign of a cleaver or knife in evidence.

"You have the advantage of me, sir," Bear said.

"True enough. Then again, what else would you expect, here? Still, you do need a name to call me by. Wolf will do. You're here about that live sword, eh?" Wolf sighed. "A bad business, that. There's power in necromancy, but—"

"Necromancy?"

Wolf shrugged. "Necromancy, death magic, call it what you will. At the very least, doing it even under the most ideal circumstances balances on the edge of the black arts, and it's a sharp edge indeed—but death-magic is always dangerous stuff. Powerful yes—as you should know better than I, worshipping it as you do."

"I?" Bear drew himself up straight.

"Oh, please. Take no offense, or if you do take offense, take it away from here. What would you call the origin of your curious religion, if not death-magic? God the Father sacrificing His Son to purge souls of their taint? He could safely involve Himself in it, but look what happened to Pilate, despite his marginal involvement." His eyes narrowed. "Oh, calm down. Wasn't it you who used to say that the truth is immune to blasphemy?"

His hand went to the Nameless—not to attack, but for the reassurance.

Words are just words, David, the Nameless whispered.

But he refused to let the familiar internal voice calm him. "It's not just me; Saint Jerome of Albans—"

"Then remove your hand from the hilt of that saintly sword of yours. Right now, if you please." Wolf's voice held no trace of heat or anger, and his expression was an emotionless mask. "This is not the place for your religious arguments, be they carried out with words, or with enchanted steel that I've little desire to see, and none whatsoever to feel. It's apparently not the place for you at all, alas; I had hoped otherwise." Wolf shook his head. "I think it would be best if you'd leave. Pity."

The gates to the castle stood open, freshly so—Gray could tell by the deep arc that the posts had scored into the hard-packed ground

Above his head, feet stomped in time along the ramparts, and torches set into the walls just outside the gates burned wanly in the bright daylight, fresh tar burbling and hissing, as though the torches had just been dipped and placed.

His horse refused to walk through the gate, as expected, and he hitched the nervous gelding to the square hitching post, giving the knots an extra turn and tug. He let his fingers rest on the wood for a moment—the pine was still sticky with resin, as though the wood had been freshly cut, although there were no trees of any sort, anywhere on the island.

He walked inside. He had only been on Pantelleria once before, and that had been close to twenty years before—that nonsense with the Barbaries—but was unsurprised to find things as he had last seen them: a central residence, its high, pointed arches covered with green vinery that should have held a thousand bird's nests, and which did, to the ear (the chirping was annoying, in a vague sort of way) but with no trace of beaks or wings to the eye.

Even the sky above held no sign of the ever-present gulls, although they had been in ample evidence near the shore. It was as though the castle was separate from the rest of the island, from the rest of the world, and he fought against the sense of calm that threatened to enwrap him.

The man Gray had been expecting sat on the steps leading up to the main building; he raised a slim hand in greeting as Gray approached.

He was a little bit above average in height, in the tunic and robes of the Order, but without any of the insignia— no silver piping along the cuffs, nor any sign of the Cross at all. While his boots were tightly laced, Order-style, with the loose trousers properly bloused, no medallions had been laced into the boots.

Beneath the open robe, his sash was bound tightly across his hips, but there was no sheath of any sort supported by it. The only thing that looked even vaguely like a weapon was a slim stick, perhaps two feet in length, that he held in his hands, just enough off-white that Gray couldn't decide if it was ash or bone.

His black hair, shot with gray at the temples, was freshly cut, as was his close-trimmed beard. Beneath dark, sunken eyes that didn't blink nearly enough, his prominent nose had no breaks or bends, and when he gave a brief smile, his teeth were white and even—somewhat too white and far too even.

"Hello, Joshua—Father Joshua, I guess I should say." His voice sounded familiar, as it had before, but Gray couldn't place where he had heard it. "Or should it be just 'Sir Joshua'?"

"You can still call me Gray."

"Gray it is, then." He patted at the stone next to him, inviting him to take a seat, which Gray did. "It's been some time since I've seen you."

Gray nodded. "Twenty years or more. We both looked much younger then."

"Well, yes, we did. But if I may still call you Gray, you can still call me Black."

"You have my permission."

Black's smile was thin and momentary. "Well, hand it over," he said, gesturing to the bundle under Gray's arm. "Please," he went on, when Gray hesitated. "Bad enough to have your Khan here—and I hope you'll oblige me by keeping your hand away from it?"

His palm itched for the Khan's steel, but . . .

"Yes, it could at the very least damage me, perhaps worse; it lives at the juncture of the godly and profane, the magical and the mundane, and is quite deadly in all three directions. It could of a certainty slice through my own defenses just as much as it could one of your pitiful wizards' protections. But you'd have to cut me with it first—"

Black was suddenly standing a dozen feet to the right of where he'd been.

"—and that would, I think, be difficult. I'd certainly try to make it so. There would be advantages to me to utterly prohibiting knights of your Order from setting foot on the island, but there are perhaps some potential advantages to permitting it, as well, as I hope you never have occasion to find out."

In the blink of an eye, Black was again sitting next to Gray. "Still, let's not have any unpleasantness, eh, Khan?" he said, addressing the sword directly. Black held out his hand. "As to the other sword you hold, well, hand it over, if you please. I would hardly want to keep such a foul thing here, even if you wanted me to. Which you should, I expect. Not that you will."

"Want to? Or leave it?"

"You'll do neither, I'm afraid. It would be the simplest way for you to handle things, but your kind has always made simple things complicated beyond my comprehension. It's worth trying, though—the simple thing to do, right now, is to hand the sword to me." Black's hand remained unmoving, palm flat and upraised. "Or you could simply walk away, with it tucked under your arm, raise sail for England, and let your Royal College examine it. Weeks to get there, and forever for them to make any sense of it. That's exactly what I'm talking about—a sadder group of men and women I could hardly imagine, learning more and more about less and less until they know utterly everything about absolutely nothing at all. Leave, or stay; go or hand it over; your choice, Gray. It's really that simple."

Gray handed Black the sword.

Black's long fingers barely touched the knots that held the blanket wrapped tightly around the sword, but the twine fell away.

"Ah. As I expected," Black said, as he unwrapped the sword. "If the likes of me started to take up death-magic, calling us the Wise would become foolish sarcasm instead of unintentional accuracy."

Black let the blankets fall away from the sword, and held it up in the bright sunlight, not even flinching when his fingers touched the steel. "Nicely done, for an awful thing to have done," he said. He examined the tang closely with a loupe that Gray hadn't seen him produce, much less set so deeply into his eye socket that it seemed to almost have replaced the eye. "No marks at all, save for the hammer. Can't think why such an artist wouldn't want to sign his work, unless, of course, he doesn't want everybody and his brother hunting him down. Or her, or them—there's no way I have of knowing. I could probably learn more by testing the edge against my arm, but I think I'll skip that; I'm fond of both of my arms."

Black touched his tongue to the tang. The loupe was gone, although Gray hadn't seen it go, any more than he had seen Black produce it. "Hmmm . . . it's tasted at least two souls, beyond the trapped one." He made a face. "Cully, for one, I suppose—no, Cully of a certainty; I'd not mistake that particular bitterness for anybody else's. Seared another and burned yet another worse than the others. Can't blame the man it seared—he didn't want to have anything to do with this, as who would, eh?"

Black set the sword down on the blanket beside him and smiled at Gray. "Nothing near the number that that Khan of yours has burned and damned, eh? But not bad for a baby."

"And that's all you can tell me?"

Black shook his head. "No. But that's all I *will* tell you—unless you'd care to join me in a drink and discuss it further? I could have a feast laid out by the time we walked into the great hall—your favorite dish is roast duck, I believe? Or would you prefer pottage-pig? Larks ingrayled?"

"I think not."

"You shouldn't think that you can avoid any contamination, Gray. You've breathed the air not just of Pantelleria, but of the . . . keep here. Of living knights of your Order, that puts you in a select crowd—a very select one if you still include those who are still bound to the live swords they've carried. You with the Khan, Bear with the Nameless, and John of Redhook—Big John, you call him?—with the Goatboy. It would connect you somewhat more to me, to here, were you to take more nourishment than what you can breathe in, but I think you'd find it interesting. And the duck, I can promise, would be the tastiest you've ever had."

"As I said, I think not."

"Well, have it your way, then. Off with you—don't come back with another one of these, not unless you're prepared to stay. And if you stay, you'll hardly need a live sword. Or be allowed to keep one."

"But—" Gray reached for the sword.

Black, still holding the sword, was again standing a dozen feet away. He made a shooing-away gesture with his free hand. "Off with you, Gray; as I told you, the sword won't remain here, for roughly the same reason that you might examine a viper, but not clutch it to your own bosom and think to make a household pet of it."

"Then—"

"Then nothing. Just go: discourses with the saintly are quite bad enough; talking to the damned is much more unpleasant, and every whit as pointless."

The gates to the castle stood open, although the interior was darkened, as though the blue sky above was filled with storm clouds.

Leaving his horse behind with the others, Cully walked into the gathering darkness, which only deepened with every step. By the time he was a dozen paces inside the gate, it was night. But a strange kind of night: the sky seemed clear and cloudless, but only one star shone, low over the walls, to the west. It was a silent night, as well; the crickets should have been out and chirping, but they weren't.

Lamps set into the entrance arch of the residence cast a wan light across the marble-floored courtyard, and each step echoed in the silence.

"Hello?" he called out.

No answer.

That was strange. He had expected that it would be like the other two times that destiny or chance—or both—had brought him here: he would see only one person, and that person would look like it could have been Cully himself. Oh, a different Cully—more at ease with himself, less world-worn and weary, but Cully.

"Is anybody here?"

Again, no answer.

Perhaps the distant star had grown brighter, and as he stood there trying to decide if it had, or what to do if it had, it grew brighter still. Not bright with the warmth of the sun, but bright in a cold, white-blue sort of way that dazzled without warming.

It flared into an awful, actinic whiteness that forced his eyes shut for just a moment.

He opened them.

"Hello, Cully," She said, Her voice low and musical.

A thrill ran through him; he fell to his knees.

"My lady—"

"Call me a lady if you wish, but I'm not Her. Not in any real sense, unless we are all of a oneness, and in that sense, I'm everyone, Morgaine included. Useless if true."

The last time he had been here, the Wise had appeared as himself—smoother of skin, less haunted of eye, but Cully nonetheless.

"Yes," she said. "That was when you trusted yourself rather more, as Gray and Bear do themselves, each in his own way, despite their protestations—although for a moment I was tempted to manifest as Wolf to Gray, and Black to Bear. As for you, these days your own opinion of Cully of Cully's Woode is not quite so lofty, is it? I do tend to appear as a trusted one; there are reasons for it."

"But—"

"Oh, I don't think appearing as your Lord would be a good idea, at all. He might take offense, and not just because He might think me to be mocking Him. I think it's wiser to simply manifest as Her, as I don't have need to worry if She does, not at this remove. Still, do give Her my greetings, when next you see Her, if you do."

She stood in front of him, the right side of her face and body barely illuminated by the light of the star, the left side cast into utter black shadow. Her hair, black as the raven, cupped the side of her face as it fell about her. Beneath the hair, her skin was pale as fine Han porcelain, so thin and translucent that he could see the traceries of blue veins beneath the slim arm that extended toward him.

"Then why?"

"Take my hand, as you would Hers, and I'll tell you all you wish to know," she said, smiling. "Love me as you've loved Her, with your heart even more than your loins, and all will be revealed."

A red apple stood balanced on her outstretched palm. "Just one bite—it will be good for you, Cully. I don't promise you the knowledge of all things, after all. And I'm hardly a serpent." She smiled. Her teeth were impossibly even, impossibly white, the white of sun-bleached bone;

the nipple that peeked through the black sea of raven hair was not the reddish pink of real flesh; it was a dark, deeper red, the awful red of fresh blood from the heart.

"I think not," he said.

"Of course not," she said. "If you'd turn away from Her, even loving and trusting Her as you do, you'd turn away from a simulacrum of Her, no matter how persuasive it can be, although I can be *very* persuasive, Cully, just as I can be many other things." She leaned close to him, her breath cold on his cheek. She smelled of roses and pepper. "Ah, to be young again, eh? Even if only for a moment," she said.

Her hand cupped his groin; her lips, red as her nipple, were just inches from his. Her tongue darted out for just a moment, its ordinary pinkness touching the frightening redness of her lips, then retreated, the lips quirking into a thin smile. "Although it appears that you are young again, if only for a moment, eh?" She drew away from him, and bit into the apple. "The stiffness my appearance has brought to your member is free, Cully. Knowledge," she said, talking around a mouthful, "always comes with a price. Wisdom is more expensive. Would you care to see a price list?"

He tried to breathe shallowly; her scent had his head spinning. "Lady, I . . . if I were to surrender to knowledge, or to wisdom—"

"It would be to Her, and not to me." She nodded. "Well, it was worth asking. You can't blame a girl for trying, can you?" She sighed. "Just when you think things are settling down, they get complicated, eh?"

"I had thought that myself," Cully said.

"You thought you would spend your last years on a hill

overlooking the sea, watching over sheep?" She laughed. "How foolish of you. Life doesn't admit of such simple ends, even if there wasn't danger about. As there is. Something that has slept long appears to be wakening. Is it some ancient power? Or just foolish lust and insensate greed in the hearts of modern men? Good questions, are they not?"

"I'm more interested in the answers," he said.

"Oh, good—very good, Cully!" she almost squealed. "You want to know the provenance of this live sword," she said, "so that you can go and destroy whoever it is that has created such a cursed thing."

"Yes."

"Just as well you've come here, then. She wouldn't allow one of these into Her presence. Not if She had any sense left. Which, perhaps She doesn't—the Great Ones do get tired, and while Merlin has been off having his little nap, She's been faithfully trying to protect Her nephew's family, even in Her weakened state, when She has little to offer beyond cautious guidance, and has to pay quite a price for dispensing that. Wisdom costs even more to give than to receive, and She's turned out to be quite willing to pay the price. I wouldn't have thought it of Her, but people do surprise me, from time to time, and there's much of the human in Her.

"You, on the other hand, don't surprise me much— your tired protestations to the contrary, you're far too much a Knight of the Order. 'Order,' that is the word— you prop up the order, the regulation, the status quo, the way of *is*, rather than could-be."

"Enough. Just tell me what it is that I have to do. Where I have to go."

She sniffed. "Why, nothing and nowhere, of course. Knowledge and wisdom come only with sacrifice—you could ask your Lord, or the One-Eyed, if you doubt me—but it doesn't have to be your sacrifice. Give me the boy. I have a use for him, and I can assure you it's not one he would mind, except at first, perhaps."

"He's not mine to give, and—"

"And you wouldn't even if he was, would you? You and Gray are cut from the same strange cloth, Cully. Either of you would sacrifice your own soul without hesitation, even if it's for nothing—as you have, and as it is. But if you could bring on the End of Days, with Heaven beyond, by torturing a small child to death—just one small child, a sickly one, one that was likely to die momentarily anyway—what would you do?

"Say that I make you that offer, right here and now, what would you say to it?"

Cully took a step back and reached to his side for Jenn, but, of course, she wasn't there. She hadn't been at his side for ten years, and he hadn't gone an hour without missing her, even more than he missed Her.

"She's lost to you forever, Cully. You can't count on her to answer your questions for you."

No, he didn't have Jenn. All he had was a walking stick. No; that wasn't all. He had the stick, and he had two feet and two hands, and by God's blood he had teeth.

That would be enough to end it, one way or the other.

He had long ago given up the illusion that he was more than any other man—not more in holiness, not more in wisdom, and less in loyalty and devotion than others—but he was, despite his wishes, Sir Cully of Cully's Woode, and he knew what was required of him.

"I'd do my best to take the life of the devil who made me such an offer, for that is a devil's offer," he said, taking the stick in his hands and settling his feet against the gravel. "No matter what form it took, even Hers. Particularly if it was Hers."

"You think so?" her smile mocked him. "You think that you could fight me, here, without Jenn in your hands? With just a simple stick?"

"Absolutely." He forced his shoulders to relax, and his feet to find stability and support on the ground. "I'd kill you, or I'd die trying."

"Ah. Then it's best for you that I haven't made you such an offer," she said. "I'll just send you on your way with somebody simpler and therefore far more sensible."

"Niko!" Grandfather's voice called out. "Niko—come here, boy."

No, it couldn't be—but it *was*.

Niko broke into a run, and almost fell over. It was one thing to ride a horse wearing these boots, but walking in them was strange, particularly on such a flat and unmoving surface. It was different than with the sandals that left his ankles alone.

Grandfather had been sitting on the flat stones of the entrance to the huge building, but he rose at Niko's approach and stood waiting, his arms open.

He folded Niko tightly in them, and hugged him to his bare chest.

"Niko, Niko, Niko," he said, his breath warm in Niko's ear. "I have something for you."

Chapter 5: Playing With Fire

———◆◆◆———

He who lives by the Rule will be hoist by the Rule.
                                                    —Gray

The night was cool.

Which, Gray decided, was a decidedly different thing than either the food or the conversation. "I don't like it any more than you do," he said to Cully, forcing himself to keep his voice level.

"I frankly doubt that." Cully shook his head, and then took another careful spoonful of the awful fish stew that he had specially ordered. "Then again, I'm sure that you don't like this sciakisciuka as much as I do, so things all balance out." He grinned.

"Father, don't try to change the subject." Gray set his elbows on the table, tented his hands over his plate, and leaned forward. "I'm over my head here, and I like that even less than this inedible . . . stuff.

"But I do know how to handle it: we set sail for England in the morning, and turn the boy over to the College—let them take the sword away from him. The sword is property of the Crown—do you think the Council will let it stay in the hands of some barefoot Pironesian boy?"

"He isn't barefoot; we bought him boots," Cully said. "Dressing him up isn't a problem. He's large for his age— just about your size, Gray, and I don't doubt that your tunics, leggings, and robes could fit him."

Gray snorted. "I don't think that dressing him up like an Order Knight would persuade the Abbot General to let him retain a live sword."

Cully shrugged. "No, of course it wouldn't. Not even if it's the wise thing to do. The Order is jealous of its prerogatives even more than the College is."

"Could we save your criticisms of the Order and the Council for another occasion?"

"No," Cully said. "Not if they're relevant, Joshua, as they appear to me to be. I don't think we should count on having time to consult with others before doing anything useful, and I'm not expecting Ralph to do the right thing, in any case. Much better to settle things in Napoli, if you're unwilling to handle them."

"It's not a matter of consulting," Gray said, trying to control his anger at the suggestion. "It's a matter of authority—and of getting the right authorities involved. The Duke of Napoli isn't the right authority, with all respect to Thomas Pendragon."

Gray understood why Cully would have wanted to get

the closest royal authority involved, and the fact that the third Duke of Napoli was one of His Majesty's uncles—just as the Duke of New England was—made the idea attractive, at least emotionally.

But Pendragon or not, anything involving the swords was a Crown matter, not a ducal one. Yes, Crown dukes necessarily had great authority in their own person and office, and the further they were from Londinium, the more so in practice, if not necessarily in theory. It was one thing for the Duke of York to send a messenger or courtier—or himself—to Pendragon Castle, and only a little more time-consuming for the dukes of, say, Northmarch or Normandie to do so. By the time one got as far away from the capital as Napoli was, it was impractical to wait for an answer to any pressing question. While English and French dukes were known to appear on their own behalf in Parliament, it was just this side of unknown for southern ones to do so; they were, in practice, always represented by their Court barons.

As for the colonies, William Pendragon, the second Duke of New England, was in practice rather more an independent prince than anything else, and it wasn't unusual that years would pass without him returning to Londinium to pay homage to his nephew and king, and there was always talk that, eventually, his nickname as the Prince of Whales would, eventually, become something more officially true, as well, although probably not under that name.

But there was an ocean in between Londinium and New Portsmouth, not just a couple of weeks.

"Perhaps we should consult the Fleet admiral, on Malta?" Bear asked. "It's not far."

"Better than sending off to England, and that's a fact," Cully said.

Gray shrugged. "What do you think Admiral DuPuy would do? Strip the Fleet to go chasing after this? We only lose a day or so by heading over to there, but—"

"No." Cully shook his head. "Probably not, if he's given an alternative. Cautious man, the admiral, which is as it should be."

"It's not just an alternative—it's the right one, and it's my decision. We go home."

Bear calmly conveyed another mouthful of the horrid local fish stew to his mouth, and chewed slowly and thoroughly, then washed it down with another glass of the inky wine. "I think that heading home would be unwise, Gray," he said. "Consider the time it would take. Three weeks just to get there, unless the winds, sea and tide all cooperate, all of the time."

"And as much time to get back," Cully said. "More, if the Council is as slow as they've been known to be, unless we can take the matter directly to His Majesty." Cully took a careful sip of wine from his glass. "Which is hardly the only problem with it." He gestured toward the bottle of wine. "Take a drink and relax for a while. We can't do anything tonight besides eat, drink and talk, and I intend to have my fill of all three."

Gray poured himself another glass, but imitated Cully by only taking a small sip. He needed to keep his head about him, and it would have been easy to guzzle it down, glass by glass, until his head was all abuzz.

The ride back from the castle had given him a painfully sharp appetite and a horrendous thirst, but Gray had not only refrained from drinking from their waterbags or the parchment-wrapped provisions in their saddlebags as they rode away, but had insisted that the others follow his example and throw the food and water away. It had been out of their sight, after all. He wasn't worried about poison, but it would have been a matter of just a few moments for somebody or something to pour a thimbleful of water from a Montagne Grande spring into any of their waterbags.

Would that mean that whoever drank from such would never leave? Gray didn't know, and didn't care to test the matter, not when the option had been simply a few hours of thirst, no matter how burning the thirst, as indeed it had been.

Quarts of water for drinking and gallons of water for washing had relieved some of the sense of having been turned into a piece of knightly jerky, and even the one glass of wine that was all that he had allowed himself had his brain buzzing.

He sat back in his chair, and tried to relax.

It should have been easy. It was a pleasant night out on the plaza.

The breeze was cool, but not cold, and ever so light and gentle; the waves *lap-lap-lapp*ed on the shore in time with the slow beat of his heart. Their suite of rooms at the inn was large and airy, and the small balcony off them jutted out over the water, giving the sensation that they were alone with the breeze and the night and the sea.

Barely visible beyond the waters of the cove, the *Wellesley* bobbed up and down on the gentle swells. Those of the crew who had been given shore leave had been gently encouraged to choose an inn down the coast almost half a mile away, and while the raucous cries and singing carried, they were far enough away to be an amusement instead of an annoyance.

All of which was just as well. A fat barkentine flying what Gray was sure was the sword-and-star pennant of the Dar—although which emirate flag flew below it he had no idea—lay at anchor a long bowshot beyond the *Wellesley*. Gray wasn't sure where the saracens were staying, other than that it wasn't in the village of Porto Pantelleria, and he wasn't eager to find out, although he would have guessed they had landed their launches no closer than Suaki or Sataria, what with the *Wellesley* anchored at the entrance to the harbor.

While the Wise rarely ventured down out of the hills or became exercised over goings-on on the shoreline at all, there was always the danger that anything perceived as misbehavior would change Pantelleria from a neutral state to an aligned one, and it was in the interest of both the Dar and the Crown not to bring the Wise in on the other side.

Would something as small as a fight in a shoreside tavern do that? Gray didn't have the slightest idea, and neither did Lieutenant Johansen, master of the *Wellesley*, who had restricted liberty to men he thought senior enough to obey his restriction to the village proper, upon threat of being treated as deserters. Gray would have kept them all aboard, and had briefly considered instructing the captain to do so, but had decided against it. Getting good service out of the Navy wasn't just a matter of giving orders, after all.

Neither was it with Cully, unfortunately, but regardless of whether or not Cully liked it, Gray was in charge.

"We'll have to get the boy and the sword home," Gray finally said.

"Niko's home isn't England," Cully said.

"Three weeks, perhaps," Gray went on, trying to ignore the distraction, "if we travel by sea. At that, we could stop at Malta and commandeer a smaller, faster ship. The *Wellesley's* reasonably fleet of foot, but it's hardly the fastest thing afloat. Or we could take the land route."

"You don't save much by taking the land route. Two, three days to Villenueve," Cully said. "Then another ten days, two weeks overland to Normandie and Calais. Perhaps a little less if you want to kill some horses and do without an old man who simply can't ride from dawn to dusk, but not much. Much more time when we detour around Borbonaisse, and we would." He took a careful bite, and smiled. "Capers. I love capers, and the pickled ones are but a pale relic of the fresh."

Gray waved away the attempted distraction. "Why would I want to detour around Borbonaisse?"

"You might not; I would. Monsieur le duc du Borbonaisse perhaps doesn't have my portrait hanging from every lamppost in the province these days, but I'm sure he would be happy to have me hanging from just one."

"*These* days?"

Cully shrugged. "I was involved in a . . . situation there after I left the Order, and I'm still wanted, I'm quite sure."

Gray really wanted to know what Cully was talking about, but he knew Cully too well—if Gray let him digress, he'd be listening to Cully's tales until morning, and no doubt that was Cully's intention. "If I tell you to go overland, you'll go, Brother Cully."

"Not anywhere where the fleur-de-lys flies under the bend sinister. Suicide is sinful, and it's not one of those sins I care to take up, not simply to save you some time if you're already wasting it by the bucketload. You may think I'm a knight of the Order, and my person sacrosanct—but without any way of proving it, not I'm confident that the authorities in Borbonaisse would readily agree." Cully tentatively dipped a hunk of fresh bread in the stew, then shrugged and spooned a huge spoonful of the fiery stuff on the bread, and stuck the whole thing in his mouth, an almost beatific expression on his face as he chewed. "I'll suffer for this before morning, but it's worth it, I do declare." His face darkened. "And it washes the taste of some other things from my mouth, if not quite my mind."

"I—"

"Excuse me," Bear said. "The Edicts say that when Knights of the Order meet on a matter of importance, the junior speaks first, do they not?"

Gray frowned. "Yes, of course they do. But what does—"

"As I understand it," Cully said, casually interrupting, "the idea of the junior speaking first arises from the fear that the junior will defer to the senior. When it comes to argument, if not obedience, Bear, I've never known you much for deferring."

"That may be so." Bear nodded. "I speak as seems wise to me. As I was taught to do—by you, among others. You'd violate the Edicts, Father Cully?"

Cully snorted. "It's not up to me. Talk to Gray."

"Very well." Bear nodded, and turned to Gray. "I had barely begun speaking when you interrupted me, much less finished." He looked Gray directly in the eyes. "Is this a matter of importance?"

"Of course it is, and—"

"And I take it you don't care to relieve me of my vows, Gray?"

What was Bear going on for? "I don't have any such desire. Or authority."

Cully shook his head. "You can speak better to your desires than any other man alive, but that's not the case, about the authority," he said, peremptorily tapping a rough-bitten fingernail on the table. "You were sent on this mission by the Abbot General, and travel with his authority—his authority both as Archbishop of Canterbury, *and* as Abbot General. That wouldn't supersede the Archbishop's-as-Archbishop authority in Sicilia—*primus inter pares*, and all, despite what some say about the Archbishop of Canterbury being the Anglican pope—not on ecclesiastical matters, but we're not in Sicilia at the moment."

Gray frowned. "That's just a technicality. Pantelleria's barely forty miles from Sicilia, and Sicilia is the nearest Crown possession—"

"From such *technicalities* does your authority arise." Cully tapped a finger against his own chest. "You had the authority to call me back into service because of the *technicality* of me having been relieved of my vows rather than cast out of the Order, and the *technicality* of your claim that I was essential to your mission. You have the authority not only to hear confessions and order penance but to permit Bear and me to do so because we are *technically* on mission, and our confessions and penance and absolution are *technically* just as binding as if they were given by the local priest, under the authority of the local bishop. Since there is no bishop—archbishop or bishop ordinary—whose diocese includes Pantelleria, *technically* speaking, you have the power of ordination while you are here, which necessarily includes the power to dismiss an ordination as improvidently granted." He smiled. "I don't mind at all if you release me, or Brother David."

"You're telling me that I should release Bear from the Order?"

"I don't have the authority to tell you what you have to do in the exercise of your office, Vicar. Yes, Vicar—your authority, here and now, is just the same as if you were the Abbot General himself, both in an ecclesiastical and temporal sense. You've used that temporal authority to pry the *Wellesley* from a reluctant admiral, and you've used your ecclesiastical authority to force me back into service contrary to my will, and if you're not going to listen to Sir David as required by the Edicts, you're obligated to relieve him of his vows. I thought you were the one who insisted that knights live up to their obligations, or was I wrong?"

"Cully—"

"You could just listen to him, instead."

Gray had been enjoying the fresh bread, although not the horribly spicy stew that came with it, but he found himself without appetite. In frustration, he heaved the chunk of bread high into the air, and wasn't at all surprised to see a gull snatch it out of the air as it reached the top of its arch. "Very well. Go ahead, Bear."

"You didn't apologize, Gray," Cully said.

Gray's hand had tightened on his wineglass enough that he forced himself to loosen his grip, for fear that he would snap it. "I stand corrected—you have my apologies, Bear. Please proceed."

"Thank you." Bear set his own wineglass down. "I think that it makes more sense to follow what clues we have where they lead, rather than just return to England and let the Council start over again."

"Which necessarily means leaving the boy in possession of the live sword."

Bear shrugged. "I don't see an alternative. It's bonded to him, every bit as much as the Nameless is bonded to me, and the Khan to you."

Or more so. Gray didn't understand the mechanics of it, but bonding a sword to a human's essence was by no means a trivial bit of wizardry, despite how easy and simple Black had made it sound. "Taking up a live sword," he said, "is difficult, yes, but no more difficult than putting one down." He gave a long look at Cully.

"Depends on the situation, Joshua," Cully said.

"There are other alternatives," Gray said. "Not that I like any of them."

A bond between live sword and its bearer could be broken by a wizard, just as it was created—or more simply, if brutally, by the death of the bearer, although Gray had no intention of running the boy through for the minimal crime of having been taken in by the Wise, or having fallen in with Cully.

"You shouldn't. If you're seriously proposing to kill the boy to break the bond between him and the sword, I'd be surprised." He smiled. "But since you're not, we don't have to see if I can manage to defeat you and the Khan with a walking stick, eh?"

Gray ignored the implied threat. He wasn't going to kill the boy just to make things easier, after all. Not unless it was absolutely necessary.

Cully turned to Bear. "Are you quite finished?"

"Yes, Father." Bear ducked his head.

"You're sure?"

What was Cully giving Bear such difficulty for? His quarrel was with Gray, not Bear. Bear was on his side, after all, and—

"Then that would make it my turn, no?" Cully asked.

Bear nodded, and after a moment, Gray joined him. Gray was, as strange as it felt, senior to Cully—not in service, but in authority.

"Very well," Gray said. "Speak your mind and then— since you've suddenly decided that I've the authority to make decisions, then I'll speak my mind, and then I'll make my decision, and you, Sir Cully, shall abide by it. All according to the rules."

"Fair enough." Cully smiled, and raised his voice. "Niko? *Niko.*"

The boy walked through the open doors and onto the patio, standing awkwardly in what was a naval utility uniform save for the broad sash about his waist. The sword, still wrapped and tied in a blanket, looked awkward in his sash next to the Navy-issue blade, although not quite as awkward as the boy himself appeared.

"I told you to speak your mind, Cully—"

"Shhh. It's my turn. Permit me." He turned to Niko. "You do realize that it wasn't your grandfather who you met up there," he said, pointing his chin toward the heart of the island.

Niko nodded slowly. "I guess so. But . . ."

"But what?"

"But it *felt* like Grandfather. Not just the way he looked, but . . ." He shrugged. "But the way he helped."

"And you think that him giving you this sword was a *help*?" The nerve of the boy.

"Shush, Gray. You're scaring him. Go ahead, Niko."

"Grandfather said it would help me find the ones who were responsible for his murder."

"In just those words?"

"Yes, sir. In just those words."

Gray drummed his fingers against the surface of the table, desisting only when Cully put his hand over Gray's.

"He didn't say the ones who killed him?" Cully asked. "He said 'the ones responsible'?"

"Yes, sir. I mean, no, sir—he said what I said he said."

"Did he happen to say how?"

"I tried to ask, but he just smiled, the way he always did, and said, 'Niko, you must trust me.' "

Gray snorted, and Cully smiled.

"Whenever somebody says I must trust him, that's my signal to put one hand over my pouch, another over my testicles, and another on the hilt of my sword," Cully said, smiling. "And never mind that I don't have three hands, and don't have or want a sword. Still . . ." He waved Niko to a seat. "Sit, boy—this concerns you, and you might as well listen to it."

"Yes, sir."

Gray didn't like where this was going. "You're suggesting that we let him keep it, and try to use it, somehow, to find the people who killed his family."

"Not precisely," Cully said. "But that's part of it, certainly." Cully's jaw tightened just for a moment. "What I think you really ought to do is relieve me of the call into service, and let Niko and me go about our business. You and David can trot back to England and lay it all in the laps of your betters, if you are so sure that you're incapable of handling matters. As for me, I'm minded to look into this, and—"

"As for *you*, Sir Cully, you're just as much a Knight of the Order as I am, and—"

"No. Not quite." He shook his head. "I'm betwixt and between, Gray. You've pressed me into service, but all that means is that my old oath compels me to obey you while you need me—"

"To the extent that you're compelled by an oath, which doesn't seem to be the case, at least not when you think it's best to do otherwise."

"A fair accusation, indeed." Cully laughed. "Well, that's not likely to change; I'm rather too set in my ways. But—"

"But you think that you'll weasel out of this because of your *status*?"

"One can only hope. I'll certainly try. You've pressed me into service because you claimed you needed me to help you test Niko's sword." Gray started to object at that characterization, but Cully plowed on: "Very well; I've complied, and I've followed you this far—but you hardly need me to keep you company on a trip to England, do you?"

"No, I guess not."

"Then I take it I'm released? I may do as I please, go where and as I please? Without you claiming that I've violated my oath?"

"Well, yes, I guess you may."

Cully was right. Gray had no need for him simply as a companion, and while most of the Knights of the Order were otherwise occupied or on mission, if he really needed more than Bear, the Abbot could surely assign one or more. Keeping four knights with live swords to serve as His Majesty's personal bodyguard was traditional and wise, but not obligatory, and there was ample precedent of replacing one or even all with Order Knights who carried only mundane steel, although the most recent precedent that Gray was aware of had come close to being disastrous, as Cully knew better than anybody else.

The Abbot General would hate doing that. Gray didn't much like the idea himself.

Cully turned to Bear. "Do we know where all the Red and Whites are?"

Gray tried not to smile. Cully had said "we," after all.

"Well . . ." Bear shrugged. "More or less. Eric and Lady Ellen are trying to handle some problems in New England—"

Cully snorted. "The Abbot still lets the two of them work together?"

"Shut up," Gray explained.

"—Walter and the Beast left on a peace mission to the Dar just a week before we left—"

"A waste of time," Cully said.

"Please?"

"—Big John was hunting Kali-worshippers in the Kush, last anybody heard from him; the Saracen is still recovering in Coventry, from that mess in Bosnia."

"He's still carrying Jerome?"

"Yes." Bear nodded. "For how much longer, I don't know. And then there's Guy of Orkney—"

"—who is proof beyond any doubt that innocence and idiocy are not incompatible."

"If I may go on? Or should we just leave it at that?"

Cully let air wheeze out through his lips. "Let's try it this way: who might be available?"

Gray thought about it for a moment. "There are eighty-three full Knights of the Order on the active list—eighty-four including yourself. Add another fifty or so brothers in teaching assignments at the abbey—perhaps a third of them young or undamaged enough to be of any use. They're scattered about, of course, but there's certainly three dozen or more in England."

"But none of them Red or White?"

"We're spread thin, as usual. Everybody else is on mission somewhere—although I guess it's possible that Guy is back, but I doubt it. In terms of who you can count on being in Londinium, it's just His Own—and the Abbot General himself."

"Who carries Jenn." Cully said softly. Too softly.

"There's three dozen or so on the reserve list, like poor Becket," Bear said. "None of them Red or White, of course."

Of course not. The live swords were too few to be left in the hands of somebody who wasn't able to use one.

"Your family is still watching over him?" Cully asked. "Very noble." The words could have been mocking, perhaps. It was hard to tell.

"Noblesse oblige doesn't enter into it," Bear said, his smiling warming in the night. "Truly, he's no bother; he and Father sit up telling old war stories most nights that Parliament isn't in session." Bear's smile widened. "Mother insists that her confessor have her tend to him as a penance, and bathes him herself, with her own hands—and with some help, granted."

"I want to be sure that I understand this—you two were the only Red and White available?"

Gray nodded. "There was some resistance to sending both of us." He shrugged. "The other choice was, of course, to second one or more of His Own."

Cully grunted. "A terrific idea—assuming that every possible heir was clapped in the Tower as a precaution." Cully was just blowing smoke, of course—'every possible heir,' after all, included all of the noble families.

Gray shook his head. "We talked about it—His Own, that is. Prince Eric's the junior middie on the *Tusk*, and Prince John's just started at Eton. Both have Order knights in attendance, of course. It would be difficult—not impossible, but difficult—to assassinate them both at the same time, and more so to kill both them and His Majesty and even after that . . ."

"After that, it would depend on the House of Lords," Cully said. "Which it does anyway, if the King were to die, given Eric's age; he'd need a Regent, and the idea of leaving that up to Parliamentary politics has no appeal at all to me, any more than it would to Ralph."

It bothered Gray to hear the Abbot General referred to so casually, but he didn't complain. At least Cully hadn't first-named the King.

"I don't like the idea of leaving His Majesty unprotected," Cully went on. "He doesn't like to mingle the way his father did, but he's always been far too eager to be seen in public."

Mingle. That was a nice way to put the late King's habits.

Bear nodded. "I've heard tales of the last time that the King was left naked."

"Just be glad they're only tales to you, Bear," Gray said, not at all pleasantly.

"I am, Gray," Bear said, gently. "I hope I would have served as well as all of you did, but I'd not wish to be put to such a test."

Niko was looking puzzled—not that Gray blamed him—but there didn't seem to be any point in going into detail for the boy's benefit.

So Cully, of course, did just that. " 'Naked' is just a figure of speech, Niko; the King doesn't prance about without trousers.

"It happened about thirty years ago. Kings tend to rely too much on Knights of the Order as problem-solvers, and His late Majesty was no different—for what he thought was good enough reason, he stripped himself of his personal guard of Red and Whites. His younger brother, John, the Duke of York, took the opportunity to try to assassinate both his elder brother—the King—and his son, the Prince, who was a baby at the time—"

"God save the King," Bear intoned; Gray ducked his head and echoed him, and gave Niko a long look until he repeated it. The boy was polite enough, but utterly ignorant of ordinary manners.

"Yes, God save the King," Cully said. "But it didn't quite work out that way."

Gray smiled. "Oh, I don't know, Cully. God works His will through stranger vessels."

It would have succeeded, if a young Order Knight hadn't seen through the plan and taken it upon himself to solve the problem in a particularly ruthless manner, with nothing more than his own mundane swords, a classful of novices who had only been at Balmoral for presentation and oath, and one lone, elderly Knight of the Table Round, who had, for some reason, decided to trust a knight of the rival order, rather than the Duke that he had known all of his life.

Saving the King's and the Crown Prince's lives had done

much for that young knight's status, as well as that of the surviving novices, although it had used up most of the novices and the knight of the rival order in the process, in about the same way that sending lambs through the door of a slaughterhouse used up the lambs.

The names of the dead novices had been added post-humously to the List, as was only proper. And while Sir Bedivere of Lincoln had been buried by the knights of his own order, as also was proper, every novice boy at Alton since had made the pilgrimage to Bedivere's grave to lay flowers, and to kneel down to say a prayer for the soul of that Knight of the Table Round.

To the end of his days, Gray would remember Cully standing in the doorway over Sir Bedivere's fallen body, Bedivere's sword naked in his hands, barely able to stand on the blood-slickened stones, barely moving from side to side as he blocked each spear thrust, ducked the cross-bow bolts that hissed through the gaps between the combatants, while Lady Mary, ignoring her own wounds, huddled in the far corner, shielding the baby prince with her own body as much as her borrowed armor, and Gray and Alexander had each grabbed one of the King's arms, holding him up against the wall to the side of the door, ignoring his shouted demands that he be given a sword and allowed to relieve Cully in the doorway.

Say what you would about the late King, he was no coward.

Not while I breathe, Cully had murmured, over and over again. Gray and Alexander had ignored the king's increasingly loud orders and obeyed Cully.

Gray raised a glass. "To lost companions."

"Lost companions," Cully echoed.

Gray stood. "So be it," he said. "By the power vested in me, as the Abbot General's Vicar, I hereby restore you to your full status as Knight of the Order of Crown, Shield, and Dragon, Sir Cully of Cully's Woode." He took his mundane sword from his belt and set it on the table. "Now take up your sword and stop this nonsense."

"You plan to go about with one sword?"

"You can give it back to me when you get a pair of Navy swords from the *Wellesley*—and stop trying to distract me."

"As you wish." Cully pulled the scabbard to him, and drew a few inches of the blade. "Nicely sharpened," he said, sucking blood from his thumb. "Now, if we're done . . . ?"

"I asked you to stop trying to change the subject. As the Abbot General's vicar, I direct you to return to the home abbey of the Order, with me."

Cully nodded. "As you command, Sir Joshua." His lips were white. "I'll want that in writing—particularly the restoration of my status." His lip curled in an uncharacteristic sneer. "So there's no dispute when I'm presented to the Abbot General? I'd rather not be clapped into irons for impersonating, well, Sir Cully of Cully's Woode." The sneer changed into a grin. "Although, in truth, I can probably do that better than any other man alive, eh?"

Gray forced himself not to answer angrily. Did Cully really think that Gray wouldn't admit what he had done? "Very well. Would the morning be acceptable, or—"

"You've restored me now, and you've ordered me now; I think that it all ought to be done now. Unless, of course, Sir Vicar, you order otherwise?" Cully's smile was mocking.

"As you wish." Gray picked up the bell on the table

and rang it, forcing himself not to shake the bell as hard as he wanted to shake Cully.

In moments, one of the servitors appeared.

"Yes, Your Excellency?"

"I need several sheets of parchment—not just paper—and pen and ink."

"Yes, Your Excellency."

"And some blotting powder, if you please?"

In a few minutes it was done. Cully tipped more blotting powder on the parchment Gray had given him, although Gray hadn't used a light hand with it himself.

"Dry enough?"

"Well, let's see." He blew away the powder, then carefully folded the parchment twice across, unfolded it, nodded, then refolded it and put it in his pouch. "It will serve, I think. Another drink, perhaps?" he asked, already pouring three glasses of wine.

"Very well."

Again, Cully raised his glass. "To fallen comrades," he said, drinking.

"To fallen comrades." Gray drained the glass angrily, then resumed his seat.

Sunlight was streaming down on his face, and Bear was shaking him.

Gray's head pounded in bright red agony with every heartbeat, and by the way Bear's forehead creased in pain with every shake he gave Gray, Bear wasn't much better off than Gray was.

"He's gone," Bear said. "He took the cutter, and the boy, and the sword—and apparently rummaged through your chest; I think some of your clothes are gone, as well.

He had Niko's skiff towed, but put the cutter's crew in it an hour or so out of port, and sent them back."

"Of course." It was important to keep his temper, despite the temptation. His hand found its way to the Khan's hilt.

May our enemies know great pain before they die.

Gray was knowing enough great pain at the moment, and, angry as he was, he wouldn't kill Cully over this. Probably.

"There's a note, I suppose," he said. Cully would leave a note.

Bear nodded, then grimaced in pain as though he regretted the movement. "Yes. He sent back to the captain—his runner woke me just a few moments ago." He held up a piece of paper. "You should read this."

Gray took the note from Bear's hands, but his eyes couldn't focus. He closed them and shook his head.

"He drugged the wine," Bear said.

"I've already figured that out." And he had drunk more of it than Bear had. "Can you read this? His cursed drug still has my eyes, damn it."

"I already have. He's off to find the source of the swords, with the boy, starting back in Pironisia, and—"

"And? There's more?"

"Well, yes." Bear hesitated.

"Out with it, please. Don't make me drag it out of you."

Bear spread his hands, helplessly. "It seems he's knighted the boy."

Niko had had things easier.

Sailing the cutter was really a job for at least four, preferably six, and it was more than a little difficult to do it with just two, particularly as the wind picked up—from astern, of course. The cutter was beautifully balanced, with just a trace of weather helm; much safer than lee helm, and Niko assumed that was deliberate, and under most circumstances, it would have made it relatively easy.

So, of course, the perversity of the sea being what it was, the wind was out of the east, and they had to sail almost exactly due west, before the wind, always watching for any sign of the wind changing, ready to turn into the wind and haul in the sheets.

There should have been one man constantly at the helm, at least while the wind was at their back, and another two or three for the sheets, at least.

Instead there was Niko, and Cully, and while Cully was probably stronger and certainly much nimbler than most men his age, he barely had sea legs at all, and Niko felt that if he didn't keep a constant eye on the old man, he'd be over the side before Niko could blink, and probably have long drowned before Niko could circle back for him.

Niko didn't grumble about it much, not even to himself. That was the way of the sea—it never seemed to manage to arrange anything for a fisherman's convenience. You had to settle for what you could get—when it didn't interfere with his life or his profit, the sacrifices to Poseidon were well worth it.

"Well, we could have taken your skiff, instead of putting the sailors in it and sending them back to Pantelleria," Cully said, as he worked at untangling the mainsheet from the capstan, while Niko kept the forward length taut around a bitt. "But that would have had other problems—there," he said, easing it off just a little. "Got it."

"Are you sure?"

"No. But try it anyway."

"Haul smartly, as soon as you get any slack."

"You've told me that five times already, Niko."

So now it's six, he thought, but didn't say. In some ways, Cully reminded Niko of Father and Grandfather, and was about as likely to tolerate insolence as they were. Had been.

Niko took a strain on the sheet, and released it from the bitt with a practiced flip, and, just as he'd expected, the sheet got away from him, although not from Cully. The mast rang like a drum as the boom swung out on its newfound freedom, but not far—Cully had hauled in on the sheet just as Niko had released it, and after a frightening moment, the cutter settled down again.

Niko didn't like it. Granted, the mast was keel-stepped—he had checked that for himself, although he hadn't expected any less from a Navy boat—and as far as he could tell, it was solidly so, but . . .

Niko released the wheel and pointed the cutter a few more degrees away from the wind, just in case, then pegged the wheel down again. Sailing with a steady wind at his back was one thing on the skiff, where he could either haul in the boom or just let it swing free if—when— the wind changed, but the cutter didn't just have more sails than the skiff, it carried far more sail, and the strength of the thicker mast hadn't grown proportionately, and Niko's own strength hadn't grown at all.

Cully just smiled, and said something about how the next leg would be easier.

Niko hoped so.

The sheets quickly wetted from the spray, and stayed wet, and fouled all of the time, particularly the mainsheet, which seemed to take any attempt to surge it as an invitation to tie itself into knots. What was just a matter of a taking a turn or two around a bitt on the skiff required several turns around a capstan, trying to simultaneously balance and put a brake on forces that could easily have dragged both Niko and the old knight over the side, and probably would have, if Niko hadn't made a decision that, even when the wind was light, jibing was out of the question, no matter how smoothly and easily the sailors had done it.

Coming about, particularly with the wind astern, was more time-consuming, but it was far safer, and the brisk stern wind certainly gave the craft more than enough speed to make it not only possible, but as easy as such a thing could be.

"You considered having us take the skiff, and sending them back in the cutter?" he asked.

"Not really. The cutter's faster than your little skiff, by rather a lot, carrying as much sail as it does. Wouldn't want to take it through heavy seas, but as long as the weather holds fair and the wind's not too heavy, it's faster than the *Wellesley*, which is the point. I want Gray chasing us, not catching us." Cully took another turn around a bitt, then tied the sheet in place around a brace with a knot that Niko didn't recognize, and didn't much like.

It must have showed in his face. "Oh, go ahead—fix it, Sir Niko," Cully said. "You're the captain of this; I'm just your crew."

"First a knight, and now a knight *and* captain," Niko said, retying the sheet properly. "I'm coming up in the world."

Cully laughed. "Well, don't get used to being a captain.

We'll take on a full crew back in Pironesia. You can expect some deference, but don't expect too much."

"A crew? For where? And what are we going to do in Pironesia, of all places?"

"Oh," Cully said. "We're talking about two different things—when I say Pironesia, I mean the whole group of islands, including the outer ones. You mean the colonial capital city on one island, the one for which His Majesty's Possession of Pironesia was named. We're not going to that one, at least not for now."

"Then where are we going?"

Cully looked at the compass, again. "At the moment, just a little north of west, which is what I want. Navigation's an arcane art, and it's one that I don't have, and you don't, either. We've no sextant, nor rutters, much less the art to use them well—so it's best to keep things simple. I know there's some sleight involved even with the compass—it doesn't quite point true north, although it's been too long since I studied such things for me to remember what to do about that, or even if it matters, at this latitude.

"If we're too far north, we can follow the shore south; even just a little too far south, and we could slip between Kithira and Kissamos, and not find any land this side of Seeproosh, or worse. Not that there'd be much worse for the two of us, even if the water did hold out that long."

"I didn't mean where are we going at the moment. What I meant was where are we *going*?"

"You're going to have to tell me that, eventually," Cully said. "For now, though, any one of the Pironesian islands in the outer cluster will be fine—any one of your neighbors—just like I said in the note I sent with the skiff. The Abdullahs' islands, probably. Are they good sailors?"

Niko shrugged. "There's good sailors among them."

"But you don't like them."

"They're neighbors. They *were* neighbors."

"Yes. I'm assuming that the sword came from somewhere to the east of you, so we're headed in the right direction. I hope. What I'm trying to buy is enough time to get some direction from you—and from it." He gestured at the hatch. "And before we make landfall, I'd best find some time to fit some grips to the sword, for that matter. I'm fairly good at that sort of thing—I can't promise you anything fancy, but I should be able to pull the grips from your Navy sword, fit the undersides to the live sword, and bind them in place without much difficulty, if I can find some gloves—I know there's a spool of brass wire aboard. And you'll need your hair cut, and a shave." He raised his right hand, miming gripping a knife but deliberately twitching it, as though he had the palsy. "I think that can wait until we're ashore, though; I assume you're attached to your nose, and wish it to remain attached to you. With that, and Gray's robes, you should look a proper knight."

"I've spent perhaps a dozen hours with a sword in my hands, Father Cully," Niko said. "I don't think you should count on me to be of much use."

"I'm counting you to look like a knight with a sword, and not like a boy carrying around something wrapped in a blanket, that's all. We've no time or materials to make a proper scabbard—but it will fit in one of the Navy scabbards, with a bit of wadding inside to hold it in place. Just be careful with it, and for Her sake, don't touch your hand to the steel. And no, I'm not expecting to have to fight, not at the moment."

Niko nodded. "Training." He felt awkward trying to take the positions that the marines had started teaching him, but there was something about it that appealed to him, even though it made him ache in unusual places, like the insides of his thighs. He was used to much harder work than taking up an awkward-feeling stance—it was strange that it was so draining.

"Training? Yes—but I'm trying, for my sins, to get you to be able to stand and move like a knight, nothing more. Turning you into a swordsman isn't something I can do in a few days, or even a few weeks."

"But—"

"Not with an ordinary sword, no." Cully smiled. "Not for another thousand hours of practice—if you're a fast learner. But using a live sword isn't really swordplay, not most of the time. You saw what Gray did to your island, and—"

"Yes, I saw that." Niko's jaw clenched.

"—and you saw what your sword did to your father. Live swords are . . . powerful, and the Khan is more so than most." He sighed. "Too powerful—it takes a certain something to use that power in combat with any kind of restraint, and it isn't accidental that Knights of the Order spend a dozen years in training before they can even be considered to bear one. Have you ever heard of a town called Linfield?"

"No."

"Are you sure? You've never heard of the Linfield Horror?"

"Yes, sir. I mean no, sir, I haven't heard of this Linafeld of yours."

"Linfield. But perhaps I shouldn't be surprised—there

isn't a Linfield, not anymore. Hasn't been for a little less than two hundred years. One knight of the Red Sword in one moment of uncontrolled, drunken anger—the idiotic feud with the Table—and land blackened for miles in all directions, deconsecrated for tens of miles in all directions, thousands of people dead. And worse."

"Worse?"

"Much worse. White swords are dangerous enough— you don't want to be in the path of the rage of a saint—but for most purposes, Red swords are worse, and the Sandoval is about as bad as it gets; the Sandoval is capable of doing far more evil than simple murder." He shook his head. "Darklings, deodands—the full range of the demonic. Churches changed, in a flash, into locii of dark horrors. Even ordinary things went black—you still hear, every year, about small children being carried off by death kites in Sussex. A wave of plague, carried throughout England and onto the Continent by things that had been rats. Locusts the size of robins, with a bite that paralyzed— and that's just part of it. It was bad. A little taste of the Zone, and it could have been worse."

"You think that my—that this sword can do that?"

"Unlikely. The Sandoval, like the Khan, is particularly powerful; I've got no reason to believe that your sword is anywhere near that dangerous. But it could be. Or more so, for all I know." He shook his head. "Although that would seem unlikely, all in all. We'll have some better idea once you actually take it in hand."

"But why—"

"Why all this?" Cully shrugged. "As the Jews say, *Ayn Brera*—I had no choice." He sighed. "Joshua was a good boy, and he's a good man—better than he thinks—but he's always taken the obedience part of 'service, honor, faith, and obedience' too seriously, just as David's too much a man of faith. Gray trusts in authority too much, whether it's the Abbot General, or His Majesty, or even such as me.

"That rigidity probably makes him a good candidate to carry something as awful as the Khan, but too much of anything is, well, too much of that thing.

"As for me, I think that this matter of the swords could be—*is*—too urgent to wait for Ralph to decide what to do, even if he'd decide the right thing, another matter on which I have little faith, and less influence.

"I would have preferred to lay it all on the lap of the Duke in Napoli. The Neapolitan navy is large enough, and good enough, and the Duke is independent-minded enough to handle things in his own court without worrying about being recalled to Londinium—but anything to do with the swords is a Crown matter, and that means Governor Halloran in Pironesia, and Admiral DuPuy in Malta, if action is going to be taken quickly. Halloran's not a problem—for Gray—and DuPuy will probably listen to Gray, given his letters of reference.

"I tried to talk Gray into getting Malta and the Fleet involved, but he wouldn't hear of it. So I'm forcing his hand. There's too much wrong going on . . . darklings this far south, the sword, the death of your family, and it all feels like matters are coming to a head, and—out with it, out with it."

"Sir?"

"You've got a question—out with it, boy. As I used to tell my students, there is no such thing as an impertinent question, just an impertinent boy, and I found I could beat the impertinence out of the boy just fine, thankee very much."

"You think that you can . . . handle this?"

Cully shook his head. "Unlikely. At best, I'm hoping to blaze a trail for Gray and Bear and the rest, and sound an alarm that DuPuy and Halloran and eventually Ralph can't afford to ignore."

That was the second time Cully had used the name; Niko hadn't recognized it before. "Ralph?"

"Sir Ralph Francis Wakefield, by the Grace of God and Order of His Majesty the King, not only the Archbishop of Canterbury, but the Abbot General of the Order of Crown, Shield, and Dragon, and for good reason and perhaps some ill, not one of my admirers.

"Right now, unless I know Gray far less well than I flatter myself, the *Wellesley* is making as quick time as possible toward Malta, intending to give chase once they put in there and pass the word—and, perhaps, if he's as sensible a boy as he used to be, take on what additional forces he can pry from the Admiral.

"Regardless . . . from Malta, a fast courier ship will be heading to England, and shortly, there will be the clopping of hooves on Londinium streets, and the sounds of a set of boots running up the stone cathedral steps and down the marble corridors." He chuckled at the thought. "I'd like to see Ralph's face when he opens the envelope, but if I could see his face, he'd see mine, and that would lose the virtue of it all—Ralph might decide that he doesn't have any better idea than I do as to how to find the origin of these new live swords, but he won't like the idea of me being off on my own, not with the authority that Gray was foolish enough to give me, and Ralph's not quite a fool; as tempted as I often am to think him one, he's a good man.

"He may not agree with me on the imminence of danger, but he surely will think that having me off on my own, getting involved in it—with you bearing a live sword—needs to be handled promptly, and I know he'll have to see the King about that.

"His Majesty will, I think, give me the benefit of the doubt as to how important this is, and whatever else can be said about Ralph, he knows how to obey an order from the King.

"A week or two at most, until frigates from Malta are in the eastern waters; figure six, perhaps seven weeks, and this part of the world should be crawling with Knights of the Order, ships of the line, and various and sundry other things and folk. Probably including His Own." He bit his lip. "If, of course, the purpose of the whole thing is to strip His Majesty of his best protection, I've just left the King undefended. I never was a very good chess player; still, that seems like an unlikely move, all in all."

Niko didn't understand most of what Cully had said. But—"Why knight me? Not that I'm complaining, sir—"

"Ah." Cully smiled. "Particularly since we're heading back toward your home, eh? Two hundred crowns of gold in a handsome strongbox, fine clothes on your body, and you're now Sir Niko Christofolous, at least for the time being, and not just Niko Christofolous, fisherboy.

"Seems little enough reward. But that's not why I did it. I have my reasons—several of them. For one, as a Knight, other knights are required to hear you out. It's important that that be in Cully's report—for your safety, among other reasons."

"They'd listen to me when they'd not listen to you?"

"They may not have that opportunity. Little loss." Cully shrugged. "I said I wasn't a good chess player, but not that I was an utterly incompetent one. If we have any luck at all, we'll have gotten closer to whatever is going on before they catch up with us; pawns like me tend not to survive contact in such circumstances." He nodded. "Which is only fair, after all. What isn't fair is that your chances are only a little better than mine."

"If that bothers me too much, we can turn the boat around?" he asked, not sure if he wanted to or not. There was something about Cully's intensity that was persuasive, even intoxicating.

"No. It wasn't right of me to get you into this without asking, but I don't always do what's right." His smile was crooked. "I don't even always do what's right on the rare occasions that I *know* what's right. As for this, I need the sword both for information and as bait, and that means that I need you, regardless of the danger I'm putting you in. The only way I can see that you can get out of this is to turn me in; you should have the chance soon enough."

"I wouldn't do that. These are the people that murdered my family that you're going after." It wasn't possible to forgive the gods and the sea, and a fisherman was no nobleman, who could hold a grudge for generations, but . . .

"Perhaps not. When one of the Wise tells you the truth, you can be sure that they've not told you the whole truth. I'm not at all sure what this sword will do in your hands, and finding that out, as soon as we've a safe place to do so, is our first order of business—for that and other reasons." He rose. "Enough talking. Let's take a more northerly tack for an hour or two so we're not running so before the wind—give us some time to eat, and I can fit some grips to the sword, if I can find a pair of gloves aboard this scow, and perhaps to work out."

"As you wish, sir."

"My wishes have nothing to do with it."

For just a moment, Cully's expression reminded Niko of Grandfather's, although he couldn't have said why.

Interlude 2: Serenity

◆◆◆

> Choose your enemies, before they choose you. Your friends will choose themselves.
>
> —Gray

The wind changed.

It brought the smell of hot pitch to Tucker's nostrils, making him shudder for just a moment.

Presumably at the first officer's command—although Captain Michael Tucker, RM, wasn't paying much attention to that, having other things on his mind—the helmsman slacked a few points away from the wind's new direction.

The last thing the *Serenity* needed to do right now was luff into the wind, not with nothing but the *Serry* blocking the open sea behind the pirate, and the two other ships coming up as fast as they could, which wasn't very. The *Serry* was the chaser because she was the fastest of the three, although the smallest, as well.

Behind and above Tucker's head, up on the quarter-deck, the captain called out some orders to the first officer, who bellowed them over the wind to the bosuns and mates rather than simply calling for the piping of All Topmen Aloft, and the bosuns and mates bellowed the commands at the topmen, and quick as you please—moving even before the piper had finished blowing the six notes of Topmen Aloft—the foretopmen were scrambling up the rigging like the rope-monkeys that they were, while, unsurprisingly, the mizzentopmen moved somewhat slower. It was call for more sail, presumably—getting the fastest speed under the circumstances was a matter of constantly reefing and unreefing; there was hardly time to fly additional sails, not with the pirates close at hand, although there were hardly more to fly, the *Serry*'s masts being loaded to the topgallants.

Tucker ignored what the topmen were doing as much as he could. After fifteen years in the marines, Tucker could have followed not only exactly what they were doing—which was easy—but make an educated guess as to why—something more difficult.

But he didn't bother. He had other things to think about, and, more important, other things *not* to think about, at the moment. The shouted commands and manic actions of the Navy crew—from the mangonel crews on the forecastle, to the hook crews off to the side of the main deck, to the port and starboard flinger crews, and never mind the constant yammering of the mizzentopmen and particularly the foretopmen—those were just noise to his ears, and the only way it would have distracted him was if it stopped, in much the same way as the rolling of the deck beneath his feet would have been disturbing only if it was absent.

He could have spent the time before battle second-guessing himself, and there always was the temptation as he looked over his section, crowded toward the middle of the forecastle mainly to be out of the way of the sailors on both sides of them. The marines were, at the moment, the bundles of bolts in the catapults: weapons, waiting to be used.

Soon. It would be soon.

Holtz had finished checking his squad, and was sitting on the deck with his back braced against Denton's, endlessly stropping the edge of a knife against the well-worn spot on the sleeve of his boarding-jacket. He seemed to be utterly immersed in the task, but to Tucker that just made him look as nervous as if Holtz had been, like Bartles, constantly looking back and forth, peering at everything like a rabbit trying to decide if it was safe to emerge from his hidey-hole.

Tucker didn't blame him for being nervous, for all the usual reasons, and more. He had promoted Holtz to corporal after Erikson's death, even though there were several privates who were senior, and even trusty old Fotheringay had disagreed, in the same blunt terms that had burned Tucker's ears when he was a new lieutenant and Fotheringay his batman—although, as always, in private. Fotheringay was now the company's sergeant, but he had never stopped looking after Tucker, and even slipped and called him "Lieutenant" every once in a while, when he was particularly aggrieved, as he had been this time.

But you had to go with your instincts and judgment in this bloody business, and while Tucker couldn't have exactly said why, he thought that Holtz was just a touch better for the spot than Fitzhugh or Kelly or Williamson, and that was that.

The time before contact was a time to relax. If Tucker couldn't really relax—and he couldn't, of course; the muscles in the back of his neck were so tight that it hurt to move—it was important that he be *seen* to relax. Nervousness was contagious, fear more so, and panic most of all—the commander of *Serenity*'s marines had no desire to infect his men with his own shortcomings.

Moving easily across the rolling deck, he walked over toward one of the mangonel firepots, noting with some relief that, at least this time, the idiots hadn't overfilled the bubbling vat, and that the heavy potmetal lids were lashed to stanchions nearby.

It'd be safe to borrow some fire; he reached for the pipe stuck into his belt, intending to light it with a straw— his first captain, back when he was a lieutenant, had always smoked before battle, and it had always looked reassuring—but he felt his fingers tremble, and stopped himself. Pity; he really wanted a smoke about now.

So he tamped the tobacco down, hard, with his thumb, and stowed his pipe in the pouch laced into the inside of his cuirass for just that purpose, then hooked his thumbs in his harness belt and continued his walk across the foredeck, pretending to be supervising the corporals as they checked the men's gear.

He didn't have to intervene; his marines knew what they were doing, and he affected not to see the way that

Nicol gave Wetterling a firm cuff across the back of the head, and then insisted on retying Wetterling's leather himself—accompanied by more than a few oaths and more cuffing—with the proper knots that could be released by a sudden jerk on the ball knots at the end of the thongs, at least half the time.

Armor was cheap. Working through the night with his knives and awls and dobbles, the Navy armorer could make a new cuirass in about a day's work. It took much longer than that to turn a landsman into a marine, although there were no landsmen among the marines on the *Serenity*—the marine commander of the chase ship got his pick among the volunteers, and the better food probably had as much to do with it as did better prize shares; it would be a bit much to expect marine privates to look beyond their next meal.

Unsurprisingly, fat Fotheringay waddled over to check Nicol's checking, and then went for'ard to where Holtz was waiting with his squad, carefully looking over Holtz's squad while pretending to chat with Holtz, going to far as to check the no-doubt shaving-sharp edge on Holtz's knife.

Tucker smiled. The edge of an oversharpened knife would break about as often as it would cut, and an oversharpened tip was even more delicate, but you could, if necessary, shove a snap-tipped knife into an enemy's face or chest, something Tucker knew from personal experience.

Nicol, of course, had been right—about half of the marines who went into the water would be able to release their armor and strip off their boarding clothes to make it to the rope ladders, but half was much better than none. For some reason, the fatter the man was, the better

chances he had of making it back to the surface—
Fotheringay had gone overboard three times that Tucker
knew of, and had bobbed up like a chubby cork each time.

Leather armor wouldn't even slow a crossbow bolt, but
it would turn a sword's edge reliably, which was the whole
purpose of it, after all. Of course, if one of the marines
went over the side—and while Tucker had heard of a
boarding where that didn't happen, he believed they were
just sea stories, as he'd never seen one—the combination
of the armor and the waterlogged padding attached to
the body-side of it would sink him just about as effectively as if it were plate armor, unless he managed to
release it, and Tucker preferred to avoid losing any more
men than necessary.

Wetterling was obviously of the opinion that he was
sufficiently strong that nobody and nothing could force
him over the side, but it wasn't his choice—it was Captain
Michael Tucker's, after all, and it was Corporal Flem
Nicol's job to see that Tucker's orders were followed to
the letter.

Nicol was much less good about enforcing Tucker's
orders against gambling, but since Tucker didn't officially
know about that, he didn't have to do anything about it
officially at all, and didn't bother doing more than telling
Fotheringay to keep a quiet eye on it, so it didn't get out
of hand.

Some hypocrisy was a necessary part of command. Men
who were about to go into battle tended not to think about
the long term, but their commander did, and having some
private owe a year's pay to another one—or, worse, to a
corporal—was bad for morale. Too easy to miss a half
step at the wrong moment, and never mind the possibility

of outright murder under cover of battle.

Tucker forced himself not to fidget with his own gear. It wouldn't be long now; the pirate ship was less than half a mile off the starboard bow, and the *Serenity* was closing fast, coming in from upwind.

A stern chase wouldn't have been to Rafferty or *Serenity*'s advantage, and Captain Rafferty had avoided it as carefully as he could, something that Tucker approved of, although the commander of the *Serenity*'s marines would no more have thought of offering Rafferty an unsolicited opinion on matters of seamanship than Tucker would have asked the captain's opinion on matters involving what do when—and it was when, he sincerely hoped, not if— *Serenity* closed with the pirate.

Which would be soon. The *Serry* had apparently been built with piracy in mind—but from the other side; it wasn't built for chasing down and taking other ships, not like the *Fairchild* and the *Buffalo*, the flagship, such as it was, of the pocket squadron. The *Serry* in fact was a prize ship that had been captured several years before in these same waters, or hereabouts.

Pirates had some of the same needs that those who pursued them had; the *Serry* was built along reasonably fleet lines, and faster than she looked, as though she was trying to live down her previous incarnation as a pirate ship.

He more felt than saw Finnerty walk up from behind to stand beside him. Finnerty had presumably finished his inspection of his own section on the raised poop deck and, as usual, had made his way forward to have a few final words with Tucker.

There would be no chance for any words once it all

started—Finnerty would have his section to handle, just as Tucker did his. Realistically, once it all started, they were no longer captain and his lieutenant, but two effectively equal commanders.

Like Tucker, Finnerty was in full gear: leather cuirass and greaves, leaving his arms bare save for his thick but supple leather boarding-shirt that had him sweating just as much as everybody else. A brace of knives was strapped to each hip; a scabbarded issue sword, twin to the curved saber naked in his hand, was bound diagonally down his broad back. His steel helmet was in his free hand rather than on his head—donning it would be the last thing before he made his mad dash down the boarding ladder.

"Captain," he said, not saluting. Naval traditions were different—and, in Tucker's considered opinion, more often stupid than not. Marines on a boarding mission all dressed the same, and salutes while in boarding gear were every bit as forbidden as they were compulsory under other circumstances. The pirate ship was too far off the bow for any of the pirates to be able to pick out individuals by sight, less to take an aimed crossbow shot from the murderer's perch or the deck, much less to hit when shooting from the one rolling deck or a perch on a mast . . . but the habit of ingraining good habits was itself such a habit that Tucker only thought about it to give his mind something to chew on less frightening than the thought of what a pirate's blade—or worse, a bucketful of pitch—could do to him, and compared to pitch, a bolt was something to laugh at.

Let them shoot at the Navy officers if they wanted high-ranking targets.

That said, stupid as he thought it was, if the *Serenity*'s

captain actually wanted to prance about the quarterdeck in his full undress blues, his cocked hat making him a prominent target, Tucker had no problem with that, and the bright yellow-and-red ribbon striped across his chest provided a fine enough target. The captain didn't owe Tucker any money; the first officer was a perfectly good sailor, and Tucker made it a point not to get too chummy with the Naval officers anyway.

Prize shares were divided among the living, after all; the sea swallowed the dead, and if the living hoisted a few glasses to their memory, that was all that could be asked. Tucker had enough memories of his own without having to add unnecessarily to them.

"Lieutenant," Tucker said. "I'd ask if you're ready," he said with a forced smile, "but I wouldn't want to insult you." Finnerty was not the brightest officer who had served under Tucker, but he wasn't bad—just overly eager, and too quick to take offense, even if sensible enough not to act on it, at least while shipboard. Then again, they wouldn't always be shipboard, and the proscription against dueling only applied when under sail or under orders, not back in Birmingham, as far away as home seemed at the moment.

"I'm ready, and so is my section," Finnerty said. "Just checked with the surgeons—tables are cleared, the water's hot, and the fires out." The surgery was aft, two decks down from the poop deck, and making sure that it was ready was Finnerty's responsibility, just as making sure that *everything* was ready was Tucker's.

"Checked with, or checked out?" he asked, keeping his voice casual.

"I saw to it in person, sir." Finnerty's blank expression

told Tucker that he didn't need to be told—a second time—that the way to see that something was done was to *see* that the thing was done.

"Good." Tucker didn't see fit to mention that Fotheringay had already been down to the surgery, and had reported to him just minutes before that that idiot of a chief surgeon hadn't yet doused the fires—then; Fotheringay had watched him do so with his own eyes. The fact that the chief surgeon carried a sublieutenant's rank was of no importance to Fotheringay any more than it was to Tucker—it was a Navy rank, after all.

Not that Tucker gave a tinker's damn about whether or not the thumb-fingered butchers burned themselves to ashes . . . after they had done what was needful for his marines.

The battle would be only a matter of minutes, but the screams of the wounded would go on for hours, or days. Tucker rubbed at the left side of his face, where a splash of burning pitch had barely missed his eyes off of Miskonos—or was it Teleria? It all ran together after a couple of years, and he had been at this for more than that.

He didn't give any last-minute orders to Finnerty; Finnerty knew his job, or at least the important part of it. Once the *Serry* came alongside of—more smashed into— the pirate, and the hook crew had sunk their irons, the ladders would go over, followed immediately by the marines.

Tucker would take the for'ard boarding party—for'ard in orientation to the *Serry;* locking nose to tail was hardly unknown, although unlikely for this encounter—while Finnerty would take the aft. First party to make it past the midpoint of the enemy ship and bury a knife in the mainmast would buy the beer when the *Serry* next made port, according to the tradition of the Fleet.

But that would have to wait.

For now, it was just a matter of waiting—waiting for the captain to maneuver close enough that the seamen on the mangonels could fire the pirate's sails while the crossbowmen and catapulters would pick off as many pirates as they could—damned few, usually—then waiting until the captain came abreast of the pirate long enough for the crew to fix the boarding irons, and then it would begin, at least it would begin for Tucker and the marines. If the pirate had been a bigger ship, they might well have had to simply hold off a desperate counterattack while the slower *Fairchild* closed, along with its larger complement of marines, but Tucker both thought that his company could handle a ship this size by itself, and had no particular desire to share the prize money with Colonel O'Neill and his men on the *Fairy*.

Bad enough to have to share far too much of it with Rafferty and his crew, for doing little more than bringing the marines to where they could do their own job.

Finnerty nodded, as though he was reading his commander's thoughts. "Figure maybe forty, sixty 'rats?"

"Shouldn't be much more. Could easily be half that." The pirate ship couldn't carry many more, not and keep enough hold space for supplies going out and booty coming back.

It all depended on what the pirates had been planning on hitting. This far east, the odds were it was fishing villages along the Kargizian coastline. Southwestern Turkee was, by and large, of little interest to the Balakaziri, being far more concerned, by and large, with seeing exactly what position they should take for convenient buggering by the Byzantines, who, even these days could have rolled over them but for the convenience of having Balakazistan as something between a state-as-catamite and a largely theoretical buffer against the Northern Caliphate. Nothing much to admire about the Balakaziri.

"Well, at least this lot hasn't hoisted the Scimitar and Star."

"There is that."

Absent unusual circumstances or orders to the contrary, a pirate crew was executed, man by man, on the spot. Crown and Dar generally left each others' ships alone, even in contested waters, and gave each others' naval squadrons a wide berth these days, stopping flagged ships only to make sure that they were what they said they were, and perhaps engage in a little unofficial trade between captains, navy or merchant.

Every once in a while, though, some idiot of a pirate captain or collective idiot of a pirate crew, particularly in waters close to the Dar, would reinvent the clever idea of raising the Scimitar and Star, sometimes with an emirate pennant below it.

Tucker hated that.

Them doing that meant that they would have to try to take some prisoners, to be turned over to the Dar in some trucal port, and while Tucker wasn't a squeamish man by any means—a life in the marines wasn't for those who couldn't take blood and screaming—he didn't like to think what the experienced torturers of the Commission for the Prevention of Vice and Promotion of Virtue would do to somebody who they believed had defiled the flag of the Dar al-Islam.

"Be interesting to see what cargo they have," Finnerty said. "Silks? Gold? Women?"

Tucker suppressed his own irritation. Granted, he himself had been daydreaming about what he could do with his prize share, but he wanted Finnerty to put his mind on the job that was shortly to be at hand.

Still . . .

A marine officer didn't make much money from his pay, and had few of the chances for graft that left many a Navy master well-off when he finally hit the beach for good, but prime duty like pirate patrol could leave Tucker enough to buy land rights to a small plantation in western Victoria when he retired, perhaps bringing Fotheringay and a few of the corporals along to manage the transportees. He wouldn't be the first marine officer to do that, and any men who could take on hardened Seeproosh pirates had little to worry about from some cowed transportees—or poxy, half-starving Chirokee or Kriks—after all.

He could end up as a land baron, in practice if not officially—the chances of a baron's crest were basically nil—and it was an attractive thought, at that.

He was jolted from his deliberate daydreaming by a shout of "Let *fire*!" followed by the distinctive *thumpwhoosh* of a for'ard mangonel cutting loose, that was immediately followed by the *thumpwhoosh* of the other one, and a yowl from some poor navvy who had gotten a small splash of pitch.

The wooden balls, heavily wrapped in flaming, pitch-soaked cloth, arced high through the air, but fell well short and to port of the pirate's broad beam, about as Tucker would have expected.

Somebody was overly eager.

But the mangonel-bunnies were fast in reloading, four landsmen working the twin windlasses with manic speed under the bosun's shouts urging them to even greater speed, while more experienced sailors stood by with other balls already pitched, and it was only a few seconds before another pair were arcing high through the air—

Only to bracket the pirate, splashing uselessly into the water.

"Clear, damn you, *clear*," the bosun on the bow catapult shouted, as some idiot of a landsman mangonel-bunny hadn't vacated the space between the two mangonels quickly enough for his taste, and for his shot, and he had to wait until the rise and fall of the bow suited his aim— aiming a catapult was far more art than science—until the moment was, so he thought, right, and he smashed his foot down, hard, on the release arm, sending the bundle of crude bolts whizzing on its way.

Most of the pattern arced well over the pirate—the bosun had either been rushed, or just plain unlucky— and some tore uselessly through the top of the mainsail, but a body falling from the crow's nest showed that at least one of the dozens of bolts had found flesh, pointless though it was to take out the pirate's lookout at this point.

Well, no harm done; the lookout would have to be taken out anyway.

The pirate turned toward the wind, trading off speed for angle away, but Rafferty had apparently been anticipating that, and the bow of the *Serenity* swung about, well past the wind. Tucker couldn't see the *Fairy* or the *Buff* from his vantage point, but he had no doubt that the *Fairchild* was moving to cut off that possibility, as well, although he hoped it wouldn't come to that, just as he was sure that Colonel O'Neill on the *Buff* and McPhee on the *Fairy* were hoping that the pirate would escape the *Serry* and fall to them.

Which seemed unlikely, but not impossible. Yes, the lateen-rigged felluca could sail closer to the wind than the square-rigged *Serry* could, of course, but unless the wind changed dramatically, pointing not quite into the wind was suicidal—that was why the *Fairchild* and the *Buffalo* waited downwind; it wasn't an accident that the smaller, faster *Serry* had sailed downwind past the pirate before coming about and turning back to close the trap around the pirate's unwashed neck.

The sublieutenant and middies officering the starboard mangonel crews had either anticipated that, or more likely had heard a warning that Tucker hadn't paid any attention to; as the ship came about, the starboard battery fired in unison, six flaming balls arcing high through the sky, and—

"Yes!"

Tucker didn't see where the others had gone, but one flaming ball caught the mainsail squarely, and wetted or not, the sail began to burn. The pirate started to heel over—perhaps one of the others had burned the helmsman?—and Rafferty responded immediately by turning to starboard to give the port mangonels a chance to fire, the *Serenity* maneuvering quickly and nimbly, as though the insensate wood of the ship smelled blood in the same way and with the same hearty appetite that her crew did, the same way that had Tucker's heart beating painfully hard in his chest as the *Serry* moved in for the kill.

Fotheringay walked up beside him, and gave the slightest of nods. He already had his helmet on, the shortened boarding pike that he preferred as a personal weapon clutched in one thick hand.

Broad as a lorry, the top of his helmeted head barely reaching Tucker's chin, Fotheringay was a preposterously ugly man. His thick nose had been broken enough times that it was now permanently flattened against his face, under his thick brows. Despite the earholes, his steel helmet hid where a Saracen had bitten off his left ear, back in that mess on the Barbary, and if his thick, battered lips had parted when he smiled—they didn't—they would have showed that he'd long since lost all of his forward teeth, leaving him with a lisp; Fotheringay couldn't even manage hardtack unless he soaked it in something—rum, usually, off-duty; and water on.

"Shouldn't be too long now, Cap'n," he said.

It's time for you to issue the ready order, he meant, and a fair enough comment, with the *Serry* coming up fast on the pirate ship. Nosed into the wind, it meant that Finnerty's section would be going in through the smoke at the stern, while Tucker's would be in clear air. There were advantages and disadvantages in both directions, but there was no point in woolgathering over them, when it was too late to change places with Finnerty, even if he wanted to.

"Mr. Finnerty, take your place." He didn't wait for Finnerty's aye, aye, and the sound of boots running across the deck before turning to Fotheringay.

"At the ready," he said, quietly.

"Make *ready*," Fotheringay bellowed, and to a man, the marines buckled their helmets in place, then squatted and gripped at the grab bars that had been made fast to the deck cleats, while the pirate grew ever closer. Tucker handed his saber to Fotheringay, and quickly buckled his own helmet under his chin before retrieving the weapon.

As always, Tucker feared for one horrible moment, that the *Serry* would crash, bow-first, into the side of the pirate, most likely sinking them both, despite the reinforcement of the *Serenity's* bow. A four-hundred-ton ship was small as Fleet vessels went, and the *Serry* was more nimble than most, but it couldn't be flipped about like a cutter or longboat.

"You, too, Cap'n," Fotheringay said, pulling on Tucker's arm until he knelt down next to the nearest deck cleat, fastening his own hands on the bar next to the sergeant's.

Slowly, too slowly, the ship started to turn as the pirate fellucca came up fast and faster, so close that Tucker could hear the crackling of its burning sails, and choked for a moment from the smoke. Something had caught fire—he hoped it was something on the pirate, rather than the *Serry*.

Then came the loud, sickening crunch that seemed to go on forever as the deck of the Serry bucked and reared as it tried to throw Tucker from his purchase.

Halyards sang and the mizzenmast gave a deep thrumm that was quickly overpowered by a scream, followed by a sodden thump as a body slammed into the deck just feet away from where Tucker and the sergeant crouched— one of the mizzentopmen had apparently lost his purchase; not Tucker's problem, and probably not the surgeon's, either, for that matter—and the sounds of the thin chains *clankety*clankety*clank*ing as they paid off of their well-greased spools in response to the port catapults firing off their gaffs.

"Heave now, *heave*," one of the bosuns shrilled unnecessarily, as the sailors on the chains were already doing just that. As usual, most of the gaffs hadn't found purchase, but three had, and sailors on other teams dropped their slack chains and raced across the deck to join those who were pulling and grunting and heaving the ships together, locking them into one unit.

"Boarding ladders," Tucker said.

"Boarding *ladders*," Fotheringay echoed, unnecessarily—each of the five-man teams had already retrieved its ladder the moment that the ship had stopped shuddering, and most of them not bothering with the quick-release knots when they already had a sword or knife in hand, some grunting as they moved the heavy iron ladders over to their deck cleats, quickly tying their ends in place.

The railing on both port and starboard had been removed for just this moment; the ladders smashed down onto the deck of the ship half a dozen feet below, smashing through railing and debris alike, one of them smashing down on a pirate, the spikes pinning him to the deck of his ship pointlessly, as the heavy weight had surely killed him anyway.

The more ladders the better, of course—give the pirates a narrow entry point to protect, and they could hold off the marines for minutes, perhaps longer.

Tucker tugged at the strap that held his helmet on his head; it held.

"Board," he said, quietly, the same way that the death sentence was usually passed.

"*Boarders, over the side!*" Fotheringay bellowed as he ran toward the nearest ladder. Holtz's squad was mostly over the side on the next ladder over before Fotheringay reached the closest one to him, his boarding pike held properly vertical, but switching to the horizontal the moment he reached the ladder; Tucker was just half a step behind him.

The rungs of the ladder were deliberately flat and wide, leaving only enough space between the boards for the easy insertion of a booted foot, and the flat soles of the marines' boarding boots had been designed to minimize the chance of any heel catch.

Some of the marines ran down the steep incline, more than a few falling forward as they did, but Fotheringay simply launched himself feet-first, sliding down onto the main deck of the pirate ship, with Tucker close behind him, feet widespread to get what purchase he could on the raised rails. The backplate of his boiled-leather armor smashed the padding beneath it hard against his back, not quite knocking the wind out of him, but he managed to gain his feet on the deck below, as the screams and shouts sounded from all around him.

A bare-chested pirate came out of nowhere to smash into Tucker's right side, but a blow from the butt of Fotheringay's pike stopped him for at least a moment, the slash from Tucker's heavy boarding saber opened him from shoulder to belly, and a kick from Tucker's heavy boot sent him sprawling away backward across the deck.

Tucker turned to square off with another one; the greasy bastard hesitated just a moment, and one of the marines—with the smoke Tucker couldn't tell who it was under the helmet, but it should have been one of Holtz's squad—economically planted a knife in the naked back with a cruel twist, then kicked him away, another of his knives already in his free hand. One hand for the ship and one for yourself was good advice, most of the time; a boarding wasn't most of the time.

The plan called for Holtz's squad to make their way as quickly as possible to the mainmast to cut the mainsail's halyards, both to drop the hoped-for burning sails on as many piratical heads as possible, but mainly because a boom swinging across the deck was likely to be more of a problem for marines whose helmets precluded any peripheral vision than for a gang of half-naked pirates.

But, as shouldn't have and didn't surprise Tucker, that hadn't happened yet, and while God may have looked out for saints and fools, He didn't seem to spend much time watching out for marines—the massive boom, propelled by a change of wind that filled its burning sheets, swept toward him, knocking pirates and marines about like skittles.

Tucker threw himself flat on the deck, but not quite quickly enough—the bottom of the boom clipped the top of his helmet, leaving his head and ears ringing, turning the world loud and bright, and then gray and distant, although for how long he was never quite sure.

He became aware that strong hands were gripping the collar of his cuirass, dragging him across the deck, and he lashed out with his empty hands—where had his knife and sword gone?—his fist impacting on hard leather.

"*Easy*, Cap'n," Fotheringay shouted, helping him to his feet. He slipped the hilt of Tucker's sword into his hand, while Tucker retrieved another one of his daggers from his hip. "You're not bleeding—you hurt?"

"No." Tucker shook his head. Doing that made him wince, and made the sparks dance behind his eyes again, but the sergeant wasn't asking if he was uncomfortable, but wounded.

Not this time, thankfully.

It was all ending almost as suddenly as it had, finally, begun. There was a bizarre symmetry to a ship-to-ship battle, where hours or days of pursuit and preparation would resolve themselves in but a few bloody minutes, leaving hours and days of clean-up after.

But it wasn't quite done, not yet. Holtz, his helmet gone, was at the mainmast, his saber already red with blood as he methodically walked among the bodies, spearing each economically while he moved to the next. You could never be sure that what appeared to be a dead man was, and—

One man screamed and tried to rise, but one of Holtz's squad—Tucker couldn't tell who it was because he still had his helmet on—kicked him in the head, hard, then held him down with a heavy boot until he stopped twitching, while Holtz kept thrusting into him, over and over, groaning with a passion that seemed almost sexual, or was perhaps more than almost so.

The sail was still smouldering in spots, but a couple of the marines had already taken buckets to it.

As usual, it had all been just a matter of a few moments. Training, preparation, the chase, and boarding—all of it had resolved itself into bodies silently bleeding on a deck now awash in red, and Tucker had missed most of it just by being knocked down for a few seconds.

A dozen enterprising sailors—or, at least, ones under an aggressive bosun's mate—had already made it down the ladders, and were busy detaching the boarding irons from whatever they had managed to sink themselves into, whether it was deck, mast, or pirate.

The only remaining fighting going on was where a single pirate had backed himself up and into the bow, holding off three marines, none of whom was eager to be the last man wounded or killed in the assault.

It was only a matter of time, and—

A crossbow bolt seemed to spring out of the pirate's bare chest. He screamed, a horrible, high-pitched woman-like scream, and dropped his wide-bladed scimitar to clutch at his chest, and one of the marines just lowered his helmet and butted him into the railing and over, rewarded by a distant splash.

Shouts and cries coming up through the hatch made it clear that there was still some fighting going on belowdecks. Tucker resheathed his knife to claw at the buckle of his helmet, shoving up and dropping the preposterously heavy thing to the deck; he stalked toward the hatchway, Fotheringay rushing up to join him, not quite barring his way with the butt of his pike.

"You in some sort of rush, Cap'n?" the old sergeant said. He had removed his helmet, too. His scraggly hair was plastered against his scalp with sweat, and the bloody wads of cloth jammed into his huge nostrils announced that he had, somehow, broken his nose yet again.

"See to the wounded," Tucker said, by way of answer. That was an order he should already have given, and—

"Done." Fotheringay's toothless smile was reassuring; he pointed toward the stern with the butt of the spear. "Lost five overboard from our section—don't know about the lieutenant's. Navy's already on it; boats are in the water. Another four down—that shitter at the bow was fast and lucky; he got Nicol through the throat." He shook his head and pointed toward where a limp form in marine leather had collapsed over a rack, then spat in the direction of the hatch.

"All of our people accounted for, I think; Lieutenant Finnerty's below, with most of his section; went down the aft hatch, slick as you please. You wouldn't want to rush down the ladder there and frighten one of Lieutenant Finnerty's babies, sir. Give 'em a few minutes to sort things out—I think that's the way of it."

It made sense, and, besides, he was hurting, and very, very tired.

"Very well," he said. He sat down heavily on a box and set his sword down beside him.

What he really wanted was a change of clothes, and a bath—he'd pissed himself again, unsurprisingly. The clothes would be easy to come by back on the *Serenity*, but anything other than a bucket bath would, of course, have to wait for port.

His fingers, seemingly of their own volition, had retrieved his pipe from its hidden pouch, and he was pleased to see that his fall hadn't snapped the stem. He stuck the stem in his mouth, finding the bitterness strangely comforting, and started looking about for the pirate's smudge pot.

Fotheringay, as he should have expected, had already anticipated him—the sergeant produced a tar-ended lighting stick, reached over behind Tucker, and cupped his free hand around the flame and bowl of the pipe.

The rich Victorian tobacco filled his lungs, and seemed to ease the pounding in his head.

The sounds from below had died out, as presumably had the pirates.

He was tempted to get to his feet and head down the hatch, but he could wait a few minutes without shaming himself.

Besides, some of Finnety's marines would, certainly, take a few small souvenirs—as would Tucker's, when they went below—and that was fine, as long as they didn't get too greedy. A few coins, here and there, were no problem, and unlikely to draw attention. He would, as usual, leave it to Fotheringay to make sure that it didn't go much beyond that, and to be sure that if it did, matters were adjusted before Tucker had to take any notice.

His job, in essence, was over for the moment. A captain in the marines didn't draw high pay, unless you calculated it by the few minutes—hours, at most—in his career that he actually was in the way of sharp steel and pointed wood, and then it was a princely sum indeed, despite how quickly and easily the money managed to spend itself.

The metal boarding ladders and deck irons that had welded the ships together had already been drawn up the *Serry's* side as a precautionary matter, and replaced with ordinary cable that could be severed by a few seamen with axes at a quick command, not that that was likely to be necessary. The pirate ship was in no apparent danger of sinking, although Tucker would not have been at all surprised if the *Serry's* deck hoist would shortly lower the spare pump to clear the bilge.

The sensible thing for a trapped pirate to do would be to smash the seacocks open, after all. Just as pirates preyed on coastdwellers, to one extent or another, the pirate patrol squadrons of the Navy preyed upon the pirates, and while you could never be sure what riches, if any, would be found in a pirate ship, a fast ship was itself a prize, and this would be the first time in a year and a half that Tucker had earned the boarding officer's shares.

The last blow against him that the pirate crew could have made was sinking the ship. Tucker certainly would have, if their situation had been reversed.

But Tucker didn't really expect a filthy, murdering pirate to take the long view of such things, although the thought amused him, and from his viewpoint, seated on a wooden box amid a scene of carnage, there was damnall to amuse him.

The thought of climbing up the ladder to the *Serry* had no appeal at the moment, even though he had no doubt that Finnerty could handle things here, for now. It was his job to remain aboard for the time being, and that was sufficient reason—although the cursed exhaustion that always followed a fight was in itself reason enough, as well.

Shouts and orders from the rail of the *Serry* drew his attention—the hoist had been deployed to lift the wounded marines aboard, as they shortly would any promising cargo, which would have to be carefully inventoried by the *Serry*'s purser, under the supervision of the first lieutenant.

Tucker could let the bastard hacks of surgeons do what little they could for the wounded—and hope to hell that there were none of the all-too-common belly wounds that would kill a man slowly, painfully, over days, nine times out of ten.

There was no rush.

He would have to turn the ship over to Captain Rafferty, of course, as law and tradition demanded, for the captain or more likely the commodore to assign a prize crew to bring it into port under the watch of the *Fairchild*, while the *Buff* and *Serry* continued to try their luck.

The fire had rendered pirate's mainsail useless, of course, but the jib had just been dropped when the halyards had been cut, and was probably more or less intact. A few seamen working a few hours could refly the jib and probably improvise some sort of mainsail from the *Buffalo*'s immense stores, even if the pirates didn't have a spare mainsail aboard. Turning the felluca into a proper sloop could wait for Malta, and the less work it needed, the larger the prize shares.

For the time being, though, the ship was Tucker's, and nobody else's. As always, he would take the chance to nose around the lower deck of the prize, just out of curiosity. No souvenirs for the commander beyond a trinket or two that would fit in his pouch—Hennessy, who served as his batsman when he wasn't seconding Nicol, snooped through his things, after all, and even sailors didn't gossip the way marines did when there wasn't anything better to do.

Feet thundered from the ladder below, and Richards emerged, his hands empty, apparently having left his sword and helmet below, once the fighting was over. That was something that Tucker would want to deal with later— a stiff word to Finnerty would suffice.

Richards took up a stiff brace.

"Lieutenant Finnerty's compliments, sir, and he said that you—he asks that you join him below at your convenience," Richards said.

He didn't salute, of course, even though the rule was pointless at the moment. He probably couldn't have—his right hand hung limp, bound up with a bloody strip of cloth, a twin to the one tied tightly on his left thigh, but his curiass was intact, which was all to the good, and likely would need only a good binding of his wounds and a light leeching.

"For'ard? Or to the stern?" Tucker asked, already rising. He was reaching for his sword when Fotheringay slipped it into his hand; his fingers closed reflexively around the familiar grips. It wasn't one of those wonderfully cursed swords that a well-born Navy officer might carry, but it had, once again, done a fair enough job, as Tucker himself had, come to think of it.

"He's at the stern, sir," Richards said. "We've some prisoners."

"Ours?" Why would that idiot Finnerty take prisoners? Tucker had just had that discussion with him, and—

"Theirs, sir. And there's something else, too, he said."

Tucker nodded, and turned to Fotheringay. "See that Richards gets to the surgeons," he said, walking away. Pour half a bottle of rum down the poor sod's throat, and the other half into the wound before the hacks sewed it up proper and then leeched him, and more than likely the arm could be saved—and the sooner the better, while Tucker was as far away from Richards's screams as he could be. Yet another reason not to hurry himself back to the *Serry.*

"*Holtz,*" Fotheringay shouted, "yes, you, unless there's another Holtz wearing corporal's stripes. Get this man up to the surgeons, and quickly now." He hadn't fallen more than a step behind Tucker as he barked commands at Holtz, and deftly made his way over the bodies and debris to beat Tucker to the hatchway, giving one of his lipped smiles as he nodded to the captain, then preceded him down.

Tucker had to chuckle. Well, he hadn't explicitly ordered Fotheringay to escort Richards back to the *Serenity*, after all, and truth to tell, he thought, as he carefully descended down the rickety ladder, Tucker liked having the old sergeant with him.

He stood still and puffed on his pipe for a few moments, hoping to adjust his eyes to the relative darkness belowdecks.

There were no lanterns lit. Sunlight filtering through gaps in the planking of the deck above striped the deck, showing the usual after-fight abattoir, one band falling across a pair of unblinking dead eyes so brightly that it was a moment before Tucker could make out that it was a naked pirate, and not one of his marines. The eyes always looked the same.

He took a step forward—

Ow. Again, sparks jumped behind his eyes as pain shot through his aching head. "God's *teeth!*"

He hadn't seen the lantern hanging from the hook above, and the godforesaken thing had managed to impact directly on the already swelling bump on his head, just above the hairline.

"Begging your pardon, sir," Fotheringay said, making his way around Tucker. He clomped a few steps up the ladder—"*McGarry*—is there some *other* McGarry? Do any of your bloody lot even know your own cursed *names?*—yes, *you*, McGarry—get me a torch down here. No, a *torch*, not a lantern—they got bloody *lanterns* down here, you motherless son of a motherless idiot, but—just get me a bloody torch, and be quick about it."

Fotheringay hadn't quite finished his tirade when the torch was passed down to him. He quickly lit the lantern, then extinguished the torch in a pool of offal on the deck, and led Tucker down the companionway, idly poking at each and every one of the bodies with the tip of his pike before he passed.

Past the compartment below the main deck, the companionway leading toward the stern was narrow, and the deck had been set high, presumably to allow more cargo space below; Tucker had to duck under each thick beam, although the shorter Fotheringay managed to clear them without any difficulty.

Except for the bodies, the companionway was neater than most, which didn't bode well. A well-laden pirate would have its companionways filled with booty of various sorts, what with the holds already full, and the wisdom of keeping the topside deck as clear as possible.

Pity. He had half hoped that the pirate was coming back from raids, not heading out from wherever its port was. It was best, taking the overall view of things, to kill a pirate before he did any damage, but the shares were always higher when they caught a Seeproosh pirate heavily laden with booty.

Seeproosl was more of a general term than a specific location; a large number of the Seeproosh pirates had their home ports in the arc of land from Kurtulus to Iskenderun, protected as much as the island-dwellers were by the alliance between Seeproosh and the Eastern emirates, as well as the ongoing chaos in the Turkish south.

Doorless compartments lay on each side of the companionway, and Fotheringay stopped at each one to stick the lantern in, whether out of curiosity or caution Tucker wasn't sure, and didn't object to, since he shared both.

Nothing unusual, and while the ship would require an intensive cleaning before meeting even slack Navy standards, it wouldn't apparently require much more. It was all fairly ordinary: each bulkhead supported racks of bunks, each barely large enough for a man to slip in and out of, with barely enough room for a blanket underneath him; a few rough wooden tables, apparently solidly fixed to the deck, rather than chock-wedged into place.

One compartment was half filled with hogsheads. Tucker was curious if they were empty or full—and what they were filled with, if the latter was the case—but that could wait for later, or simply be skipped altogether. Still, it would be interesting to see if this particular pirate was utterly free of wine or rum, as some were, giving rise to suspicions that at least some of what were putatively Seeproosh pirate crews were in fact Musselmen under the supervision of one of their sharp-eyed priests, who would tolerate any sort of mistreatment of Nasrani captives or smoking of kheef, but would cut a man's hands or balls off for having a glass of wine or a mug of beer.

One door stood closed, and Fotheringay reached for the handle, but Tucker just grunted a no, and he moved along. Finnerty's men had already cleared the lower deck, and while Tucker was curious as to what was behind a door that Finnerty or his men had thought worth closing, he wasn't curious enough to make Finnerty wait.

Pickering, one of Finnerty's corporals, was waiting with simulated patience at the aft, just above the open trapdoor that led down into the hold.

"This way, sir," he said, preceding them.

The hatch directly above was still closed—it would have

made things easier on everybody if the paired hatches had been opened, but the dripping of some dark fluid that Tucker was sure was blood explained why nobody had gotten around to it. The marines did the killing, but let the Navy handle the bodies afterward. Marines wallowed in enough blood as it was when they had to.

Let the sailors clean up; it gave them something useful to do for their quarter-shares.

He looked down. Quiet whimpering sounds trickled up through the dark hole, and Fotheringay stepped in front of him and stood there, his stubby legs widespread, blocking Tucker's path.

"Lieutenant?" he called down.

"Sergeant?" Finnerty called up. "I believe that I asked for the captain." He sounded irritated, but nothing more.

Fotheringay nodded—"He's right here, Lieutenant"—then stepped out of Tucker's way.

Tucker repressed a smile as he climbed down the ladder.

Too cautious by half, the old sergeant was, when it came to his old lieutenant's safety, but there was no point in trying to change the old sergeant's mind on such things, and, truth to tell, Tucker found it more charming than annoying, as useless as it was at the moment.

He hoped it had passed Finnerty's attention that Fotheringay never called him "sir," but always addressed him by his rank. Be kind of interesting to see how the two of them got on if Tucker was killed, but, then again, if Tucker was killed, he'd hardly be able to see it.

The hold was, surprisingly, compartmented; a broad bulkhead, running side-to-side, stood about halfway down the length of the ship, blocked off the rear, and distant clicking and clucking—clucking?—

Finnerty followed his glance, and nodded. "Rigged for slave-taking, in quantity, I think," he said. "Half full of livestock, at the moment—cages of chickens, and a couple of goats. Fair number of trade knives in the inventory—only a couple of barrels of rum, and those sealed."

"*Maska'paia?*" Tucker asked.

"Probably." He jerked his chin toward the door to his left. "What's in here is what's more interesting, to me—but watch yourself; they bite."

They?

"Well, at least one of them does; I don't suggest you test the others, sir." Finnerty knocked on the door. "Coming in," he said, taking the lantern from Pickering. He opened the door slowly, and Tucker followed him in.

In the dim light of the lantern, dull eyes widened in something that looked more like resignation than fear. Four young women, wearing nothing more than dirt and bruises, were chained to the far wall by the wrists. The blankets that served as their beds had been nailed to the deck, although one of the women had managed to tear part of it loose and had it arranged in her lap, in some sort of futile attempt at modesty, Tucker supposed.

Tucker started to take a step forward, but Finnerty held up a hand. "I'd take it slow, sir. Pickering tried to see to them, but the one on the left bit him, when he got too close. Still got some fight in them, surprisingly."

Fotheringay grunted. "Pirates supplied themselves with all the comforts of home. Wouldn't want to have to wait to dip their wicks until they hit the coast, eh?" He stepped in front of the two officers, and tried a few phrases in Arabic, Hellenic, Turkish, and a couple of other languages that Tucker couldn't quite place.

One of the women—girls, really—shook her head, but the others just stared blankly, as though they knew what was going to happen next.

Not that they were right. The marines had been at sea for only a couple of weeks, and it would take a lot longer for such filthy wretches to look good to even a sailor.

But it was more than that. There also was, as strange as the notion sometimes seemed, a matter of honor involved. Filthy wretches the women might be, but they had just been rescued by His Majesty's marines, and were not to be summarily mounted like the women of a sacked city—even if they had been the well-groomed beauties that they no doubt would become in the sea stories that the men would tell.

"Turkish, I think," Fotheringay said, squatting in front of the nearest one, who backed herself up even more tightly against the bulkhead.

"*Merhaba*," he said. "*Adim* Sergeant Fotheringay *bey. Adinoz nedir? Su?*" He mimed drinking.

She shook her head, then nodded.

"*Su*," she said quietly. "*Lazczia*."

"*Lazczia?*" His toothless smile was forced, as he shook his head. "No savvy *Lasczia. Ekmek? Su?*"

"*Ismim Lazczia*," she said, chains clanking as she touched a fist against her own chest. "*Istiyorum su, bey. Istiyorum ekmek.*"

"Pickering—get some water," Tucker said. He didn't know much Turkish, but he could manage *su.* "*Ekmek?*"

"Bread, sir," Fotheringay said. " 'Lazczia' is her name— she hasn't introduced the others. Pickering, get them some tack, too—I don't think the ladies have exactly been overfed, of late."

"Aye, aye, sergeant." Pickering mounted the ladder.

"Wait." Tucker held up a hand. "And get the armorer from the *Serry*—tell him to bring some tools—we'll need to get them out of the chains." The wrenches used to fasten the chains in place were, no doubt, somewhere aboard the ship, but finding them would likely take more time. This way, it would be only a reliable few minutes to get them out.

"Aye, aye, sir."

Finnerty's face quirked into a questioning smile.

"Well, we'll have to turn them loose," Tucker said.

"Soon enough, certainly," Finnerty said, agreeing. "But for me, I'd just as soon not get bit for my troubles. Absent your orders to the contrary, I think feeding them first to gentle them down a bit is in order." His mouth quirked into a smile. "But I didn't send for you to admire a four-some of Turkish lovelies," he said. "What do you make of these?"

These were four long wooden boxes, each about the size of a coffin, lined up on the deck on the opposite side of the compartment where the women were chained. It wasn't just raw pine, but some darkish wood—mahogany, perhaps—oiled and polished to a high sheen.

"If I had to guess as to where the valuables are," Finnerty said, "I'd guess they'd be in these. No need for such a fancy box to keep trade knives or beads in. Something interesting, more'n likely—perhaps some coins or even jewels a pirate might want to take out and play with after . . . refreshing himself?"

Tucker was curious, and he wasn't sure that he would

have waited for his commander before opening the boxes.

Then again, it would probably have been wise for him to have waited until he had a commissioned witness. Or, perhaps, called for a commissioned witness *after* opening a box of valuables and removing a few trifles for himself, which he more than half suspected was the case. Finnerty seemed just a little too pleased with himself.

Well, if a bit of petty theft was the worst thing that Tucker had to worry about with Finnerty, he'd be more than glad of the bargain.

The box lids had been pegged down, rather than being either left loose, or nailed down, which was curious indeed.

If Finnerty had already opened them, he wasn't about to reveal the hidden catch to Tucker.

"Is there a pry—"

"Got one here, sir." Fotheringay had found a rusty pry bar somewhere; he set it down on top of the box, then worked the end of a trade knife under the lid of the box, and carefully levered it up and down to create enough room to slip the tip of the bar underneath.

The box resisted; Fotheringay grunted, and pressed down harder.

"Doesn't seem want to give way, sir," he said.

Tucker joined him on the bar, and pushed down hard, putting all of the weight of his body behind it. For a moment, he wasn't sure if box lid wouldn't just shatter beneath the strain, but then the peg nearest the bar's tip broke loose with a loud *chunk*, and the others broke away as well, popping the lid right off and over onto the deck.

The women screamed.

Silently, a vague form in dark robes rose up, a curved

sword in its hands, and floated across the deck toward Finnerty, while the other three box lids shattered, and three more vague shapes, all in dark robes, each with a sword held in a vague, ghostly hand, rose into the air, the hems of their robes barely brushing the deck.

For just a moment, Tucker denied the evidence of his eyes. Darklings.

Finnerty was faster than either Fotheringay or Tucker; he shoved Tucker out of the way even before Fotheringay could—

"God save the King!" he shouted, as he snatched a dagger in either hand and launched himself at the nearest of the darklings.

Good enough for last words.

The darkling seemed to gain size and substance as it fed upon the sodden earth that half filled the box—the casket—and it didn't bother with its sword as it enfolded Finnerty in a grasp that seemed almost tender or even loving, muffling Finnerty's screams in its ghostly breast.

Tucker wanted to run, he wanted to flee more than he had ever wanted anything, but he found himself turning his back on Finnerty's dying screams to grab Fotheringay by the collar of his cuirass and more throw than shove him through the door, ignoring the way that the sergeant's mouth was working. Tucker couldn't hear him, anyway; the pounding of his heart, and the rush of blood in his ears drowned out everything except the screams of the women chained in the hold, and Finnerty's dying screams.

He slammed the door shut, and dropped the bar.

"Call abandon ship and break open the seacocks," he shouted, although Fotheringay should have, would have, known to do that without being ordered. He would know enough to dash any lanterns he could find to the deck, as well.

"Wedge this hatch shut, but move it, man, move it."

It was only a matter of moments until the darklings would overcome Tucker as they had Finnerty, and only seconds later that they would be swarming out the door and into the rest of the pirate ship, and from there up the side of the *Serenity*, killing as they went.

It might not stop there—could darklings sail the *Serry* or one of her boats? Were they intelligent and substantial enough to load their own cursed soil into a ship's boat?

It didn't matter if they weren't given the chance, and there was no point in waiting.

He dashed the lantern against the far bulkhead, on the off chance that the fire would slow the darklings down, at least for a few moments. It would stop here, with fire from the shattered lantern, and water flooding the damned pirate ship.

The women screamed even louder.

Fotheringay was still pounding on the door. "Dammit, Lieutenant, Lieutenant—open the door, Lieutenant, damn your eyes."

"Obey your orders, Sergeant," Tucker said, backing himself against the door.

He had dropped his pipe when he drew his own daggers, and almost smiled at the thought that if he stepped on it, he would break the stem. That didn't matter now.

Still, it would have been nice to have a last taste of tobacco and nicer to have a last drink of rum, he thought, as he turned to face them.

He considered for a moment the idea of launching himself at them, then decided that he would hold the door until they overcame him, all the better to give Fotheringay a few more seconds to do his duty, as the old sergeant surely would; and he thought about how it was a pity that he wouldn't be able to report that Finnerty's last words had been a credit to the Royal Marines, but knew that Fotheringay could, and would report, and would make up some for Tucker to have said; and he thought that perhaps his official last words would be every bit as good as Finnerty's. Maybe Fotheringay would think of something even better. Or maybe not.

And then there was no time for such thoughts, as all four of the darklings were upon him, and there was no room for thought in Alvin Tucker's mind save for the fervent prayer that death would be the end of pain.

Chapter 6: Affirmation

Life is properly a matter of balance, so Cully used to teach—in word, if not always in action. Balance is, I've thought, always much easier to find when things are quiet.
—Gray

Halloran tried to look on the bright side of things: he didn't miss Surrey, at least not at the moment. He *did* miss the Governor's palace in Pironesia and his chair by the fire, and even his desk piled high with papers, a pile that was surely growing by the minute—with Clarendon alternating between being too hesitant on routine matters and too aggressive on others, and would end up being more of a mess than if the man just left things alone.

But he missed sleep, mostly, and—strange though it was anywhere in Pironesia—he missed warmth.

The cabin was cold, and dank; he pulled his feet up into his nightshirt, buried himself more deeply in his comforter, and tried to go back to sleep.

He was irritated with himself for missing Pironesia, of all places. It was absurd.

Or maybe not totally absurd, at least not under the circumstances. The lieutenant—he preferred to be called captain, as most masters did, and Halloran avoided the issue by addressing him by name and rank—in command of the *Conveyance* had given his cabin over to Halloran with only the minimum of the good grace that protocol demanded, but exchanging the comfortable splendor of the governor's palace for a room that Halloran would have thought miserly for a kennel was hardly an improvement, and the constant rocking in the surf would have made sleep damnably near impossible anyway, without the constant ringing of bells and the stomping of feet on the deck over his head. He had the suspicion that MacKenzie didn't tolerate such comings and goings when *he* was trying to sleep, and was taking revenge for the governor's unwelcome presence in a petty way, but it was the sort of thing that one simply had to endure, as it would seem even more petty to take notice of it.

What were those damnable knights up to? Halloran knew his own limitations, which hardly included him being any sort of man of action, but he also knew his responsibilities, and the combination of the news and demands for information brought by the sailors from the *Wellesley* and the absence of the Order Knights appearing in person to brief him had drawn him out of the port, with barely a half-dozen secretaries and attendants.

Murder? Piracy? Swords?

It was enough to make a man turn to strong drink.

Not that it took much to turn the Navy to strong drink. Dinner at Lieutenant MacKenzie's table was far more drinking bout than dinner, and the sometimes-reliable Miconou reported that it was similar in the petty officers' quarters next to the captain's overly generously labeled stateroom—where Halloran's staff was billeted, more for Halloran's convenience than any other reason—although the usual fare there was more cheap New England rum from the ship's stores and much less properly casked French wine from the captain's private ones.

He was just drifting off to sleep again when there was a knock on the door.

"Yes?"

"Captain's compliments, and he prays you join him on the quarterdeck at your convenience," sounded through the door. Halloran couldn't tell which one of the middies it was, although he had made it a point to learn all of their names. Only one of the middies was a young nobleman—the *Conveyance* was hardly the sort of prestigious assignment that a noble would try to procure for his son—but today's midshipman might be tomorrow's admiral, after all.

"Thank you; I'll be there directly. Miconou? *Miconou?*" Where was he?

He sighed. As he should have expected, his valet was not waiting directly outside his door; Miconou would have announced the middie if he had been where he was supposed to be.

Well, it wasn't the first time that Halloran had dressed himself in recent years, and at least Miconou had laid out clean clothes on the lieutenant's desk before retiring, as well as leaving a fresh thundermug.

It was only a few minutes later that Halloran was climbing up the steps to the quarterdeck, ignoring the seamen scrambling out of his way.

"Good morning, Governor," MacKenzie said.

Halloran had had a look at his file, and it was in accord with what Halloran had subsequently observed: the thick-waisted MacKenzie was a Scotsman who had seemingly spent years to remove the last burrs of his Scots accent from his voice, ending up sounding like a poor imitation of an upper-class West Ender, under the clipped speech of the Navy that predominated. He was constantly grooming his short, unkempt Scottish beard; a Scottish heritage was of no particular benefit in the Navy, and it was vaguely surprising that MacKenzie had actually risen to a command, even a minor one, as he was from an Edinburgh merchant family—a second son, of course—with some minor wealth but no perceptible influence or noble connection.

Absent some unlikely heroic misadventure, MacKenzie's only hope for further advancement would have to come from influence and interest, and one would have thought that the man would have gone out of his way to ingratiate himself with Halloran, who had such influence and could generate at least some of the interest, but he was apparently too stupid to see the obvious advantage.

Miconou hurried up the stairs to join Halloran, his hair uncombed, tucking his shirt into his trousers. Halloran gave him a quick glare, but didn't say anything; a gentleman didn't upbraid a servant in front of others, after all. He would have words with Miconou later, in private. Short words, mostly of one syllable each.

"Good morning, Lieutenant MacKenzie," Halloran said. "Some news of note?"

The lieutenant nodded. "A cutter flying the Crown beached on the windward side of the island just after dawn," he said. "There appear to have been two Order Knights aboard. They're apparently asking some questions in the north-side village, and are busy hiring on a crew."

"They haven't had the courtesy to call upon me—upon you?"

"No. Curious that they'd pull in on the windward side of the island—it's much more rocky, and heavily shoaled." MacKenzie took a thoughtful pull on his rough-carved pipe. "I'd want a local sailing master if I was to try it under sail willingly, even with something as shallow-drafted as a cutter, particularly in any wind at all." He smiled around the well-bitten stem. "I'd suspect that they're trying to avoid the *Conveyance*, were I the suspicious sort."

If they were trying to avoid the *Conveyance*, which Halloran doubted, they could do that much more easily and securely by bypassing the Abdullahs' islands entirely. Still . . .

"I have a longboat ready to be lowered; I can send for them, if you'd like," MacKenzie said.

Sending for a pair of Order Knights as though they were servants had an evil appeal to Halloran, but it was impolitic, and he rejected it out of hand. "No, I'll go to them." He turned to Miconou. "I should wear something a touch less informal, I expect."

"Yes, sir; I'll lay out your brown morning-coat directly. Messieurs Bowman and Langahan to attend you? And myself?"

"Yes; I think so." Halloran nodded.

"Yes, sir." Miconou scurried off.

MacKenzie nodded. "I thought you might say that, Governor. I've asked Mr. Henderson to have two natives waiting on the shore as guides. Henderson, two of the middies, and four of the marines will accompany you, if that's acceptable."

"You're not suggesting I might need military protection. Here? With the *Conveyance* lying offshore, and a half dozen frigates in these waters?"

"Begging the governor's pardon, but we've had three very suspicious murders in these islands—"

"I know. That's why we're here." And why Halloran had recalled more than a dozen beached Navy officers, all of them with intelligence portfolios, or at least Crown Intelligence cyphers. He resented having to pay them out of his gubernatorial purse, but that couldn't be helped. Murder of a local was, of course, presumptively a local affair, and piracy more than presumptively a naval one, but Halloran had no intention of having this fall through the cracks simply because there had been no reports of pirates in Pironesian water, particularly with these Order knights nosing about. He had no conviction that he would discover anything of interest, but he wanted to be able to report that he had looked into it personally. This wasn't the usual thing of one drunken peasant knifing another, and, equally important, it wouldn't sound to the Administration as though it was.

"Yes, Governor—and until that's disposed of, I think it best that your personal safety be seen to."

"Mr. MacKenzie—"

"I'm afraid that I really must insist, Governor."

It was a delicate point of law. The master of a ship was, in law, the master of all aboard the ship; the deference shown to Halloran was from political necessity and tradition, not a legal requirement.

Then again, once Halloran set a booted toe on dry land—particularly dry land that was part of His Majesty's Possession of Pironesia—he was no longer under MacKenzie's authority at all.

But governing was not, Halloran had long ago decided, merely an application of law and regulation; and while one's authority would rust from disuse, Halloran hadn't let his own lapse and found no need to use it now, despite the definite temptation.

Still, even though Pironesia was hardly the Kush, where a sensible man wouldn't venture out into the countryside without a company of cavalry in attendance, you never really knew what locals would do, and it was unwise to trust them any more than necessary.

Besides, in his experience local headmen were always more cooperative when they had to keep glancing over Halloran's shoulder at a few marines. Marines did have their uses, after all.

"Very well, Mr. MacKenzie, although I doubt we'll have any difficulty finding these knights, and while I'll confess I'm perhaps a touch less fond of the Order of the Crown, Shield, and Dragon than I ought to be, I can't imagine that I'd be in any danger from two knights."

MacKenzie started to say something, then stopped himself.

"No, I know you weren't suggesting that, Mr. MacKenzie." Halloran smiled. Delicacy in political judgment was not restricted to members of the civilian administration, either, of course.

MacKenzie turned to the middie waiting patiently at the foot of the ladder. "Mr. Midshipman Turnbull—my compliments to Mr. Henderson, and please inform him that the Governor will be ready to go ashore—" he raised an eyebrow in a question; Halloran nodded "—as soon as the launch can be readied."

"Aye, aye, sir."

Niko had resolved to obey Cully's instructions to look knightly, and to keep his mouth shut as much as possible.

The second was easier; at least, he knew how to do *that*. He wasn't sure what it meant to look knightly—other than seeming to alternate between being self-confident and self-questioning, to judge by Cully, Gray, and Bear.

It seemed to at least have something to do with sitting up straight, and Niko knew how to do that, too.

Drinking coffee was another matter. He knew he was supposed to be honored to be offered a heavy mug of the thick, disgusting stuff, and doubly so that Samir insisted on serving him, as he had Cully, with his own hands, but he'd much rather have been honored with a simple mug of fresh water to wash the taste from his mouth.

Niko sipped slowly at the warm brew, hoping that he could manage to drink enough for courtesy's sake without actually emptying the mug and being offered more before Cully had finished his business with Samir Abdullah. It tasted awful, and it was all he could do not to make a face with every sip.

"What we require," Cully said, "is information, four or five good sailors familiar with small craft who don't mind being paid in Crown copper, and provisions. That's for tomorrow; for today, all we need is some cleared space, and privacy."

"My home is yours, of course," Samir said, his expansive wave indicating that he meant the whole island, and not just his admittedly impressive house.

"It would be better if there's nobody else around— safer, as well. Sir Niko says that that small island just to the north and west is yours, but unoccupied?"

"Yes," Samir Abdullah said. "Of course; consider it yours, please."

"Thank you." Cully sat back in his chair, idly adjusting his robes around him. He seemed comfortable as he sat back in the huge chair, sipping at his coffee as though he did it every day.

The Abdullahs were far wealthier than most in the islands, and the home of the patriarch of the clan, built of stone, was no ordinary house—not only had it been floored and walled in some dark wood, and polished to a high gloss, but the the shutters had been opened to reveal actual glass windows, so pure and clear that they had barely a bubble. Niko didn't like to think how much those had cost. He had heard that they made such glass in far-off countries, although he didn't know where.

The room was floored in contrasting panels of highly polished dark wood that Niko thought might even be real Injan teak, and all of the furniture stood on woven carpets whose provenance Niko couldn't begin to guess at.

It wasn't just the wood and the glass. The stones that made up the outer walls of the house hadn't been merely mudded to keep the wind out, but mortared, and the sharply slanted roof was covered in slate rather than thatch, as though the Abdullahs were bragging that neither wind nor rain would ever enter without permission.

The room reeked of wealth in other ways. A sideboard

held a silver tray covered with plates of food, and the walls were covered with shelves holding riches, prominently among them crucifixes, as though to reassure visitors that the Abdullah clan had not gone back to its Musselman ways. It was a strange notion—an entire room dedicated to the receiving of visitors!—but Niko had heard Milos Abdullah bragging, more than once, that as much business was done in the visiting-room of his grandfather's home as was done in many counting houses in major port cities, and judging from the look if it, perhaps that wasn't just Milos's boastfulness.

They were alone, at least in theory, although Niko was certain that there were still ears listening carefully beyond the beaded curtains, and not just because Samir Abdullah had only raised his voice ever so slightly when he had called for the refill of the elegantly inscribed silver samovar of coffee that sat on the sideboard next to the matching tray. Cully seemed to have an insatiable appetite for the horrible stuff.

But it was strangely quiet—the only sound that came through the open windows was the whispering of the breeze, and the distant, familiar crash of waves on stone.

Samir Abdullah reached out a withered hand and poured more coffee for Cully, then set the samovar back down and folded his hands in his lap.

The last time Niko had seen him, Samir had been down at the pier in an ordinary kirtle, his skin darkened from the sun just as much as anybody else's as he stood supervising the transfer of fish from the smokehouses to the waiting ship, watching everything and saying little, leaving the bellowing of orders to his sons.

Now, he sat back in his chair, brushing down the front

of his fine, white-linen robes. His white hair and beard had been freshly combed, and were vaguely damp, as though at some signal he had bathed and changed while Cully and Niko were being conducted across the island to where his house overlooked the sea, as, of course, was entirely possible.

Samir Abdullah nodded. "What I have is yours, of course, Sir Cully," he said, carefully looking at Cully, and not at Niko. "Defkonos is what the island is called, as Niko has told you, I'm certain—"

"Sir Niko," Cully said.

"My apologies, Sir Cully—and Sir Niko." Old Samir didn't seem terribly apologetic, but he ducked his head nonetheless, for just a moment. "Sir Niko it is. As to Defkonos, nobody has lived there for a generation, not since we bought the *Marienios*; you'll have all the privacy you need for your rituals, whatever they might be. As to crew, I can certainly find sufficient numbers of my grandsons who would be pleased to sail your craft where and as you please, although none of them have much of any head for trade." He frowned. "My sons are not much better, alas—if it weren't for the enduring bounty of the sea, I'm sure we would starve, for their failure to be able to get a fair price for anything. I'd think that they think we weren't in business at all, if I wasn't here to constantly remind them otherwise."

Cully smiled. "I certainly don't mind negotiating their wages with you," he said. "I noticed a fine barkentine anchored off your pier. Would that be available for hire?"

"At your command, of course." Samir smiled. "The *Marienios* is rigged for fishing, of course, and it might be difficult—" a brief flash of yellow teeth indicated that he meant *expensive* "—to reconfigure it to suit your needs. Perhaps I could be more helpful if I knew what your needs are?"

"I'm not entirely sure at the moment what my needs are, except that they're likely to involve travel," Cully said. "Certain to, in fact. As to where, that's something that Niko and I are going to go to—Defkonos, you said?— Defkonos to try to discover."

"Ah." Samir barely raised an eyebrow, as though asking for an explanation. His smile froze itself in place when none was forthcoming. "You will stay for the noon meal, of course—my daughters rarely have guests from outside of the islands, and we do pride ourselves on our hospitality, although rarely do we have an opportunity to display it, and I can't ever recall having the opportunity to display it for such honored guests."

"I'm greatful for the offer, of course," Cully said, setting down his coffee mug and starting to rise. "But I think it's best we be on our way."

"Supper then? My ancestors would rise from their graves and throttle me if they thought I was discourteous to a pair of knights."

"I'm greatful for the invitation, but at the moment I can only say perhaps. Perhaps we'll know more by dark. Sir Niko? Let's be on our way."

Niko set his mug down and rose, cursing himself for his clumsiness when he almost dropped the sword on the floor.

He snatched at it, and the sword rattled in the ill-fitting sheath; he clapped his hand over the hilt, the metal cold against his palm, and—

✧   ✧   ✧

Pain.

Fear.

Darkness, and fire, and a huge sweat-slickened face leaning over her, its thick mouth moving, making complex sounds just like the One Who Smelled Like Food did. She couldn't move, but it wasn't like when One Who Smelled Like Food had held her wrapped tightly to her chest; that was warm and comforting—this was frightening.

And her hands hurt. She had already wet and soiled herself on the cold stone but that wasn't out of fear, and she felt more wetness slither down her leg and this one didn't care about that, not like the One Who Smelled Like Food did. It didn't care.

Where was the One Who Smelled Like Food? Why had she abandoned her?

Cries mixed with her screams.

The face made more sounds, but not the cooing sounds that the One Who Smelled Like Food did—these were harsh and distant, somehow. It held something shiny and glistening in its huge misshapen hand, and—

Niko. A voice called to him from far away. Niko. Nikonikonikoniko*dammit*nikowouldyouwake*up*niko would you—

" . . . would you *please* wake up, Niko."

A face loomed over him, but it wasn't that huge, sweaty, greasy face; it was Cully, and Niko became aware that Cully's hand was shaking him with careful gentleness.

"Easy, boy," he said. Niko couldn't see to the side as Cully turned and spoke to somebody outside of Niko's line of vision. "Help me lift him him, and gently, gently."

Strong hands slipped beneath him and lifted him first to a sitting position, and then easily to his feet.

"No—don't set him on his feet. Back into the chair—and watch the sword."

The world went gray again as they placed him back in the chair, and when he could see or think again, somebody had tucked a blanket all around him, and tied a short length of rope around it. He struggled to get his hands free, and was only vaguely relieved that it was easy—

"Easy, boy." Cully was kneeling in front of him. "We've not tied you down." Deft fingers removed the loose knot, and Cully placed the palm of his hand against Niko's chest to steady him, and keep him from falling forward. "Don't try to move for a few moments—Samir? Do you have any of that arak handy?"

"Yes, of course, it's right here," Samir Abdullah said. Niko tried to turn his own head so that he could see the old man, but quickly found that it was too much effort.

He wasn't in pain anymore. The agony of the cut down his chest was gone—

Wait.

A cut down his chest? He could remember the bright, strangely curved knife, he could still almost feel the red agony as it sliced down his preposterously smooth chest toward his bulging belly—

But his chest wasn't smooth, and his stomach was fisherman-flat, not bulging.

Or was it?

Panicky, clumsy hands scrabbled at the front of his tunic, yanking it up. He let his head loll forward and was only mildly surprised to see that it was his own nail-bitten fingers that were doing it.

And it was still *his* chest, with the thin mat of hair, and the flat belly below it. He found himself strangely seized of the urge to make sure that his manstick was still where it ought to be, and wasn't sure why.

"Easy, boy," Cully said, pulling his tunic down and easily pushing Niko's nerveless hands to one side. "Sit back. Relax. You're not hurt, at least not on the outside." He rubbed a finger against a spot above Niko's eyebrow. "You banged your head when you fell—just a mark, though; no swelling. How do you feel?"

It was too much effort to answer, and besides, when he tried to talk, the only thing that came out of his mouth was drool that ran down his face and into his scant beard.

He didn't know what he felt, other than tired. It was as though he was a visitor in his own inhospitable body, looking out through his own eyes as though they were impossibly clear glass. The scars along his left index finger from the times he had slipped while sharpening knives and hooks were the same pattern of ragged white lines that they had always been, but it was as though he was looking at them for the first time.

Distant fingers forced something between his mouth, and he drank the stinging cold liquid to avoid choking, then did choke and cough most of it out in a distant spasm that burned his throat and nostrils.

His tunnel of vision slowly expanded, revealing Samir Abdullah and an ugly, thickset woman he didn't recognize at all, even though he had known Yassramiryam Abdullah, Samir's wife, all his life, as she was as famous in the islands for the excellence of her smoked cuttlefish sausages as she was for the sharp tongue that kept her vast brood of grandchildren and great-grandchilden under tight control—

Wait.

He *knew* Yassramiryam, and not just her name. There was a huge mole to the right of her flattened nose—Samir, so legend had it, had had some trouble with her in their early years of marriage—that was almost a twin to a similar one on the left hand that was hidden in her formal robes.

Her lips parted in a gap-toothed smile that was strangely ingratiating, and when she reached out with the clay bottle to refill the thumb-sized bronze arak-cup that Cully held out, he could see the mole. He didn't understand why she deliberately touched her fingers to her lips, and then again to Cully's hand before recorking the bottle, but by the time that Cully brought the cup back to bring it to Niko's lips, enough strength and feeling had returned to Niko's that he was able to cup his hands around it himself.

"Bad, eh?" Cully more said than asked, then nodded in self-agreement.

A fourteen-year-old boy would have agreed vigorously if he'd been honest, but whining wasn't part of a fisherman's life, as Father and Grandfather used to say, and behaving properly around others had been more important to them than honesty. "I've been hurt worse," he said.

Cully grinned. "That's a knightly thing to say." He gave Niko an affectionate punch on his shoulder, then started to say something, but stopped himself. "If you can stand, we should be on our way." There was an undercurrent of urgency in his voice, something Niko understood.

"No doubt you'll wish to pay your respects to the Governor," Samir Abdullah said, nodding. "I'll have my grandson conduct you to—"

"The governor will have the opportunity to pay his respects to us when it's convenient—for *us*," Cully said, his face grim. He stared at old Samir for a long moment until the old man looked away.

"Of course, Excellency, of course. Your pardon for misspeaking; I simply wanted to ease your course. No offense was intended—"

"None taken," Cully said, the snap in his voice not particularly convincing. "Not personally, that is," he said, his voice softening, "but it's a matter of the Order and its prerogatives. I am a sworn Knight of the Order of Crown, Shield, and Dragon, and I'm subject to His Majesty, and under the orders of the Abbot General and the Council—I'm not subject to any local authorities. I'm sure that Governor Halloran wouldn't disagree, and I wouldn't want you to think otherwise."

"No, no, of course not."

He gave a smile that Niko thought was entirely calculated. "I'll see the governor, but—as you've just seen—the matter of this particular sword is much more pressing, and Sir Niko and I had better attend to it directly."

"As you wish, of course, Excellency." Samir nodded. "My grandsons await you at the landing; they'll guide you over to Defkonos, and return here to await your signal, if that's acceptable. And then, perhaps, we can discuss what your needs are?"

And, of course, discuss what Cully would pay for them. Samir had recovered quickly from Cully's reproach, despite how much it seemed to have scared him.

"Of course. Let us be on our way, Sir Niko."

Getting to his feet was only a little more difficult than hauling a fully laden skiff ashore would have been, and for a moment Niko thought that his trembling knees would betray him, but they didn't, not quite.

Gripping the scabbard until his knuckles were white, Niko stuck the sword through his belt and preceded the old knight out into the harsh sunshine.

The Governor and his party met them on the steep trail that twisted up from the cluster of houses below toward where Samir Abdullah's modest home stood alone on the highest point of the island.

Cully cursed, but he kept his cursing to himself, and directed it at himself more than Halloran.

He probably should have simply sailed on past the islands when he had seen the sails and the pennants, but he had decided—probably foolishly—that the worst thing he could do would be seen to be running too soon, particularly since he didn't know where he ought to be running to.

The boy was a decent hand with sails and rigging—better than Cully, certainly—but their chance of escaping a crack Navy crew was nil. A Navy cutter could fly more than enough sail to capsize it in any kind of wind at all—cutters were built for speed, and with speed there were risks—and setting and adjusting the sails for maximum speed under constantly changing winds and sea was something for the constant attention of expert sailing hands, not a fisherboy and a shepherd, or even a couple of knights, real or faux. An Order Knight's training made him a master of a few crafts and a journeyman at others; novices were pressed into service on training voyages more to keep them busy and broaden their education than with any expectation that it would turn them into even ordinary seamen.

Cully's plan, such as it was, did call for the authorities to be alerted and set on his trail—but by Gray, and Gray would choose his words carefully, once the initial anger had faded, or probably before. Gray would be furious, of course, but he would see the danger, if not the solution, in much the same way that Cully had, and he would go along with Cully's solution when presented with no other choice, and Bear and the Nameless would act as a moderating influence on Gray's hot temper, and that of the Khan.

There was time to calm down. Gray would have sailed for Malta first, before chasing after Cully, and that added at least another few days in which to work.

The important thing, Cully had decided, at least in the short run, was to find out what the sword knew.

If it knew anything. He hoped it did. Jenn could have guided Cully to the village where she had died; Bear and the Nameless would have had no trouble in finding the spot where the Nameless's bo tree had stood; Cully had been in the very square where Emil Sandoval had been hanged. But the Goatboy didn't have the slightest idea where he had died of the black fever, and it was hardly the only live sword that couldn't remember.

Maybe this one could.

If, the word of the Wise to the contrary, it wouldn't simply burn the boy's soul the moment he took it in hand. The only time to trust the Wise was when you had no choice, and if—

If, if, if—you could put a thousand ifs in one hand, and a piece of reality in the other, and the ifs would always weigh less.

He had given serious thought to trying to find some

unoccupied island between Pallenteria and the coast, but he didn't know those waters—he cursed himself for having enjoyed the hermitlike nature of tending his flock up in the hills, often spending weeks on end without hearing the grating sound of a human voice—and he hadn't thought it wise to spend the few hours that he could count on Bear and Gray remaining unconscious pouring over the *Wellesley's* captain's charts and references. It would have been just as bad to put in somewhere unknown to Niko or to him, somewhere that might well have a suspicious local factor in residence.

It was best to make a virtue of necessity once more, as it so often was: he quickened his step, putting his hand behind his back for a moment to make a patting motion to Niko to slow down. "Governor!" He forced a smile— not too much of one—and broke into an easy lope and ran down the path to meet them.

Halloran was accompanied by a surprisingly small party: a young but well-turned-out officer with sublieutenant's braid on his sleeve, a couple of middies, four marines, a couple of clerks, and a swarthy, local-looking man who Cully remembered from the mansion as being one of the governor's servants—Miconou, that was the name.

"Sir Cully," Halloran said, nodding. "I was informed of your arrival here."

"As I was of yours," he said. "We planned on visiting you as soon as we'd completed more pressing matters."

Cully had no objection to lying, except when the lie could easily be discovered, so he decided to stay with the truth, at least as much as possible.

"Hmmm . . . I've always thought that there's always

ample time for manners," Halloran said, not quite with a sniff.

"I agree, and manners quite properly call for introductions," Cully said, turning to the sublieutenant. He bowed slightly, but properly, his left arm folded across his middle, his right hand steadying the sword stuck through his sash.

"Sir Cully of Cully's Woode," he said, surprised at how good the phrase felt on his lips, "Knight of the Order of Crown, Shield, and Dragon." His eyes on the sublieutenant's, he more felt than saw Halloran stirring to one side, and he pulled the folded piece of parchment out of his pouch. "My papers, sir."

The sublieutenant didn't unfold the parchment or even glance down at it; he drew himself up straight, his shoulders back.

"Sublieutenant Thomas Henderson," he said. "At your service, Sir Cully." He gave a slight bow.

Henderson was a compact man in his forties, clean-shaven despite his pocked face—most Navy officers who had survived the pox covered their scars with a beard, at least when at sea—and something of the lilt of the highlands in his voice, despite the lowlander name.

"May I present the midshipmen, Sir Cully?" he asked.

"Of course."

By the time Henderson had finished introducing the middies, Niko had caught up with them, and Halloran was only not fidgeting, Cully decided, because it was unseemly for such an important man to fidget. He eyed the folded parchment still in Henderson's hand, and at a gesture of permission from Cully, Henderson handed it over to the Governor, who opened it with unseemly haste.

Cully let him be. It would be unwise to seem to be in as much of a rush as he in fact was, and, besides, the taller of the two midshipmen seemed familiar. There was something about the sharp nose and dark, sunken eyes.

"Have we met before, Mr. Turnbull?" No, they couldn't have. The boy was perhaps fifteen or sixteen; Cully hadn't been back in England for ten years.

"No, sir." The boy shook his head. "I know I'd remember—I've never even seen a Knight of the Order before."

The other midshipman, Waldegrave, smiled indulgently, if perhaps patronizingly—Waldegrave, as the son of the Earl of Burnamthorpe, had no doubt been presented at Court, with His Own in attendance, watching the crowd with flat looks that hid a constant professional suspicion—but his expression sobered at a microscopic headshake and mouth twitch from the sublieutenant.

"Perhaps you're thinking of my uncle Simon?" Turnbull asked. "I'm told I favor him."

Cully shook his head. "Simon Turnbull? I don't recall the name."

"He's my mum's brother, sir. Simon Sebastian," Turnbull said tentatively, hesitantly, as though expecting somebody to correct him, "he was at Alton—"

"Yes. Started in twenty-three." Cully nodded. "Left in his third year. Yes, I do remember him. A good lad, as I recall; if you take after him, you'll do your family proud," he said, with just a slight emphasis on *your* for Waldegrave's benefit, and was rewarded by a smile from Henderson as the boy's face brightened.

Barely one in four dozen of the boys who started out

in first form ended up as Order Knights. Some were found wanting, and asked to leave. In some cases, they were moved to other seminaries with a less demanding physical regimen; others, with different failings, went to the military academies, or to Eton.

Many left of their own request, as had, no doubt, been their families' plan from the start. A year or two at Alton wasn't a blot on a young man's record, and in fact conferred a certain cachet, embodied in the ring given all those who completed first form, to be surrendered only upon taking the Oath; there were many such rings on hands throughout both the Navy and Army, and in Parliament.

Cully had suspected that was part of the reason that Baron Shanley had sent sent young David to Alton, and wouldn't have been at all surprised to learn that the Baron hadn't expected the boy to stubborn his way through.

Not that Cully had ever had any doubt about Bear, any more than he had about Sister Mary or Gray, although they both had been special cases.

There were some knights, like old Sir Alfred, who claimed that they could glance at the class of firsters and tell who would or wouldn't make it to the swearing-in, although Cully never had that knack. A few, certainly—he had seen something in the little ragamuffin named Grayling, and in Mary and Alexander and Bear and perhaps a dozen others, but he had been wrong about as many as he had been right on. He remembered Simon Sebastian, an intense little boy who threw himself into his studies with the same furious concentration that he put into his workouts on the parade ground. If Cully had had to bet, then, he would have put down quite a lot of coin that Sebastian would have ended up kneeling before His Majesty, to arise a Knight of the Order, but he would have lost. Just was well; gambling was a sin, after all.

"Yes, sir, He's spoken of you—often, sir. He's in the New England fleet," the boy said, with some obvious pride. "First officer on the *Reprise*, out of New Portsmouth. I'm sure he'd send his regards, if he'd known . . ."

"Of course, of course." Cully smiled. "When you write to him, send him mine, if you would—and tell him that I still remember his dreadful essay on the Age of Crisis."

The biblical injunction was against bearing false witness against others; Cully had never thought it applied to a gentle lie. Cully didn't actually remember the essay, but he did remember that Sebastian had been in his first-form history class, and the subject of the Age was irresistible to the sort of young boys who still hadn't had all the romance of the Order beaten and worked out of them, and young Simon Sebastian had definitely been one of those.

"I'll do that, sir." The boy smiled.

Halloran wasn't quite bursting at the seams. "Your companion, Sir Cully is . . . ?"

"Ah. My pardon. Governor Lord Sir Albert Halloran, Knight of the Guard, may I present Sir Niko Christofolous, Knight of the Order of the Crown, Shield, and Dragon? Sir Niko—Governor Halloran, Sublieutenant Henderson, Midshipmen Turnbull and Waldegrave."

Niko bowed, correctly, but no more. The boy was teachable.

"Christofolous?" Halloran raised an eyebrow. "That's a Pironesian name."

In a knight's robes, his hair properly combed back if not expertly cut, and the cheeks above his scraggly beard given a good shaving, Niko didn't look like a barefoot Pironesian fisherboy anymore, and his dark complexion wasn't unusual, but Cully would have thought that the Governor could have recognized a Pironesian at first sight.

"Indeed, it is, and quite properly so," Cully said, "as Sir Niko is Pironesian. If you wish to discuss the details of how and why he was made a knight, Lord Albert, I'll be more than willing to oblige, although I think that this is hardly the best place; it's a delicate matter that should, I would think, call for some privacy."

He wasn't sure whether he was finding it irritating or comforting that formal manners were coming back to him; he had long since gotten used to speaking plainly, when he spoke at all, and the Pironesian merchants he dealt with spoke only a little more than the sheep.

"But not at the moment, unless you insist—Sir Niko and I have to be off across the channel to Defkonos for some private Order matters. Might I call upon you this evening? Or had you intended on weighing anchor before then?"

"This evening will serve well enough, Sir Cully."

Cully nodded. "Samir Abdullah has invited Sir Niko and myself to join him for dinner—I'm certain that he'll press you with an invitation when you call on him." A safe bet, that. A much less clever man than Abdullah would hardly fail to miss an opportunity to play host to even a much less important dignitary than the governor. "Perhaps, then, we can take a few private moments for me to brief you?"

Halloran clearly wanted to talk now, but there was no obvious way to protest, so he simply nodded. "That will serve quite well."

"Come, Sir Niko," Cully said.

Interlude 3:
A Sad End for a Formerly
Honest Sailor

There is much that can be learned from etymology, which is why, I'm sure, that novices still have to start Latin in the first form, even though it's not been used for liturgy since Mordred the Great broke with Rome.

Back when he was teaching history at Alton, Cully used to start the novices' class with a quick lesson in Sanskrit, scratching symbols on the chalkboard. I think the purpose of it was to show the ideograph for "cow," and then "want," so that he could get to showing that, at least in Sanskrit, the word "war" means "wanting more cows," more or less.

I'm not entirely sure that the Khan is correct that the Monglian word for "music" comes from the phrase "the sounds one's enemies make when dying in great pain."

After all, if a man has committed mass murder, he just might lie.

—Gray

It was, he often thought, a sad end for a man who had once been an honest sailor.

DuPuy shook his head. He puffed hard on his morning pipe, although it gave him little satisfaction.

Admiral Sir Simon Tremaine DuPuy—not, by God, Admiral *Lord* Sir Simon Tremaine DuPuy; he had turned down a baron's crest yet again—stood at the crossroads of his world, taking his morning pipe and coffee out on the balcony overlooking the port, as he did, fair weather or foul.

He preferred foul; it tended to match his mood these days, these months, these years.

Perversely, a nice Levanter was holding steady from due east, under a sky that held not even a hint of a threat of rain, and the air was so clear that he fancied a younger man could have made out the coast of Sicily, even though it was well over the razor-sharp horizon.

He sipped and puffed some more, enjoying the quiet, as much as he could.

The early morning, just as the dawn was breaking, was his quiet time, his time to himself. On the lower floors of the building, the endless administrative work that supported the Malta Fleet—such as it was—was just beginning for the day. Clerks—some of them with officer's commissions, yes, but just clerks nonetheless—churned through their little portions of the endless sea of paper that floated the Fleet. The Fleet couldn't have gotten by without them—or without someone in DuPuy's combined office and living-rooms. After all, DuPuy was more of a clerk than anything else, these awful, clear, cheery days.

DuPuy didn't like to think on that any more than he had to, and he had to spend most of his day with the unending demands of the faceless busybodies who would, more than soon enough, be nibbling the rest of his day like a pack of rats gnawing on all that remained of a formerly meaty bone.

Rats, jackals, vermin all—he sometimes thought that every one of them had his hand out.

DuPuy did not. Ever. You had to make compromises in this life, and compromise he did, but he got his six crowns seven every payday, and while as a younger man he had augmented his pay by gaming, he had not once taken a bent penny in graft.

He would lie and cheat and steal, yes—and worse, much worse—but not to fill his own purse. Once you started down that road, you never knew where it would take you, and Simon Tremaine DuPuy had never had to find out, because he had never taken a step down that road.

He looked over at the drydock, and nodded as approvingly as he could. McCaulkin, at least, could reliably be counted on to get good value for what he spent from the purse, taking only the traditional five-percent kickback, and with a new load of good black oak just in, McCaulkin would soon be far more busy supervising the work in the drydocks than he would in counting his graft.

Work had proceeded on the three-master in the drydock almost directly below him at only a maddeningly slow pace, rather than an unacceptably slow one, but it was largely done, finally, and only a matter of a day or two until the ship would slide down the ways.

It could do that now—the hull had long since been

readied, and the masts solidly stepped, rudder affixed, hardware set in place—even the anchor had been catted. While there was endless carpentry still to be done, nothing essential remained except the rigging—the running rigging, of course; not the standing rigging, which had been completed in proper order, just after the stepping of the masts.

Sleepy-eyed mates—DuPuy couldn't see them well enough, but any man would be sleepy this early in the morning; DuPuy certainly was—were already at work, bossing the equally sleepy-eyed artificers who were, even now, up in the rigging on their ladders.

Old superstitions to the contrary, it was better to set the running while the ship was in drydock, when ordinary ladders could be employed for the use of McCaulkin's lot, rather than the ship's own rope-monkeys working at preposterous heights. A master could and usually would alter the running rigging later, of course, and McCaulkin had made that point repeatedly, despite DuPuy's invariable refusals.

Dammit, good as he was, McCaulkin didn't really understand that the purpose of the whole thing wasn't merely to get the ship out of drydock and off McCaulkin's plate, but to put it into service, and doing the work in drydock like this meant putting the ship back into service more quickly, rather than having it bob uselessly in the harbor for weeks until it could be properly sailed, and the running could be set above while the last bit of essential carpentry belowdecks was completed.

There had been more work to do than had been advertised, of course. Much more. DuPuy had suspected that there was a catch when Humphreys had agreed to the transfer of the ship from the Atlantic to the Med, and was sure that he was right when Digsworth hadn't tried to shortstop it at Gibraltar.

As he had known from just a quick perusal of the belly of the beast, the wily Mumbai thieves who had rebuilt the *Lord Fauncher* in ought-six had cut every corner they thought they could, and then some—substituting bleached black oak for good white oak for the ship's knees had just been the start, and hardly the end. DuPuy had not been at all surprised to find that all but the most accessible bolts were deviled, and only a little more when the notoriously stingy McCaulkin agreed with him that they would pretty much have to rebuild the ship from the keel up, recovering what they could.

And, to be fair—DuPuy prided himself on his fairness—they had recovered far more than he had initially expected that they would.

The former crew, now beached, was another matter. It would have been nice if he had been able to make a bonfire of them, as he had of the rotted wood that had been stripped off the *Lord Fauncher*—or, at the very least, hanged a few of the worst offenders, just to make an example of them.

But you couldn't hang an officer or man just because you knew he was incompetent. You had to at least find some hint of a crime, after all.

Hard to do when all the evidence was a thousand miles or more away. The officers' files, unsurprisingly, had still been "delayed in transmission"—a delay that was pushing a year now—but a quick inquiry had told him that every man, from the master down to the cabin boys, had been freshly assigned. Humphreys was, as could be expected, using the opportunity to rid himself of every bumbling nitwit of an officer and buggering thief of a sailor that he could. A few of the former had made decent clerks, surprisingly—but most had been set on half-pay, spending their nights in the seaside taverns drinking endless mugs of cheap beer, and their days sleeping off their latest drunks, while those crewmen who hadn't completed their impressment were pressed into service as dockmen.

But it would be done, soon, and the ship would join the Malta Fleet, such as it was.

Below, two dozen ships lay idly at anchor just outside the shallow harbor, although the moorages to the east were far busier than those to the west with supply boats coming and going with almost manic speed.

As well they should! DuPuy had thought he had made it clear to that idiot Bullworth that he expected Red squadron to sail on the tide, by which he had meant the noon tide, of course. Little chance of that—the squadron would be lucky to sail on the midnight.

The *Cowperstown*—he hated the name almost as much as he hated the last-century, five-deck design—had a damnably deep draft, and DuPuy had much less faith in Bullworth's first lieutenant's abilities as a sailing master than Bullworth did, or at least affected to.

It was just as well, all in all. DuPuy couldn't quite chit Bullworth for not quite having obeyed an order that DuPuy hadn't quite given, but he could demonstrate his unhappiness in another way, that would turn out to be convenient for reasons having nothing to do with Bullworth.

DuPuy had done his duty, and that was all that could be asked. For now. If DuPuy was lucky, the *Cowperstown* would run itself aground on the sandy bottom beyond the dredged channel to and through the breakwater, doing more damage to Bullworth's career than to the ship, and DuPuy could have Bullworth hauled before a board of inquiry in Northhampton, brevet Randolph to command of the squadron, and work to make the assignment permanent.

But, no; that wouldn't happen. Bullworth was a careful sailor, which is why he was waiting for the tide; he wouldn't run aground, and Randolph wouldn't be brevetted—even though he deserved it.

DuPuy smiled. Randolph, master of the *Redemption*, would have taken DuPuy's command to sail on the tide as meaning to sail on the previous midnight; were Randolph the commodore, there would not be two ragged squadrons crowding the blue waters off of Kawra right now.

He wouldn't say he liked Randolph—quite the contrary—but he did admire him. It most certainly wasn't a matter of Randolph being the son of the Earl of Moray—and the next earl, more sooner than later, what with the present earl's age and the news just having reached Malta of Randolph's older brother having broken his neck falling off a horse in some hunting accident. Hunting boars from horseback? Absurd.

DuPuy cut no slack at all for nobility or royalty, not when they wore a Navy uniform; he never had.

His Majesty himself, as a middie, had served under him on the old *Indomitable*, and Sublieutenant DuPuy had nearly come to blows when both of the boy's two Order knight attendants had objected to DuPuy having the young prince turned over the wardroom table for having fallen asleep on watch.

But DuPuy had done what was necessary, and His Majesty had taken every stroke without so much as a groan, and that had been that, as far as DuPuy was concerned from the moment that he had instructed Mr. Midshipman Pendragon to raise his trousers and return to duty, which, of course, he had done.

DuPuy's opinion that that had ended the matter had not been universally shared. The first hadn't much cared for DuPuy's disciplining His Majesty—affairs of the middies and the junior sublieutenant had been beneath the open notice of the captain, of course—and DuPuy had found himself summarily reassigned to supervising the training of the enlisted landsmen. DuPuy had been sure that he had sacrificed his chances of any promotion on the altar of duty until his name appeared on the next list, supposedly for his service in the Battle of the Samothraki Straits, although neither DuPuy nor any other sober man thought that that had anything to do with it.

It was by order of the King himself, undoubtedly at the urging of the then-Prince, the same urging that certainly had beached the *Indomitable*'s first officer, and retired the ship's captain.

DuPuy wasn't sure if the King was having a joke, every time he had been presented, when His Majesty invariably found occasion to rub a royal hand against his equally royal buttocks—but DuPuy had no apologies to make, public or private, and always kept a boot-face on such occasions.

He liked the King's attitude, and—not that he would admit it to anybody—he admired Randolph's, as well, as strange as it was for a grandson of a man hanged as a Republican to admit, even to himself, fondness for a nobleman's performance.

The *Redemption* was as taut a ship as there was in the Fleet, and never missed a tick—but to hear Randolph talk about it, all the credit was due to others. If you made a general compliment, you'd hear from Randolph that his first, Braithwaite, was due all the credit that couldn't be apportioned to the second, and that Randolph hadn't seen a better bunch of middies in years. If you made a comment about how the *Redemption* flew a nice set of sails, you'd hear about how Sticky Washhall and Sneaky Weems were the best damned sailmakers in the Navy, and not just the Fleet; that the least of Bosun's Mate Nivens's mizzentopmen would make a foretopman's bonus on most other ships; that the landsmen were coming along handsomely, and that Randolph took last week's flogging as a reflection on himself, as a decent commander shouldn't have to have a man put under the lash more than three or four times a year. If you chuckled about what damage the for'ard catapults had done to the floating target off the *Reddy*'s bow, the response would be that it was Flinger Fitzgerald who didn't believe in letting his hands loll about in port, and that Randolph had had to concede that Quarters Marino's theory about how Castelmareseian carrots improved eyesight ought to be given more general distribution—as should the carrots.

Much better than Bullworth's endless whinging about how the quality of seamen had slipped in recent years, and while-I'm-not-complaining-about-my-officers-Admiral—the phrase was one word to that idiot Bullworth—everybody knew that the up-and-coming ones put in for the Atlantic, not the Med.

Idiot.

The world was filled with idiots and compromises.

When the battle flags went up for real—and they would—they would go up in the Med first and foremost, where the Crown faced the Dar al-Islam most directly, and not in the Atlantic, where the Crown supply lines stretched from Londinium to the New England colonies but the Dar was even more overextended, not just from Darmosh Kowayes across the ocean to Rabat, but from Rabat to the heart of the Dar.

Cut the connection of the limbs to the heart, that was the way of it; the heart of the Dar al-Islam wasn't on the African coast, or even in the Caliphate capitals, but in the cities of the Egyptian delta that churned out soldiers the way a baker did biscuits. Cut the sea lanes of the Med, and land troops in Sfax and al-Tarabala, and it would be all over within a few years.

But there weren't enough troops in the Med to do that. An invasion of north Africa couldn't be done with ten times the forces DuPuy had at his command.

The Crown could just wait, of course. Let the Dar build up in Africa, and let them plot and scheme with the Empire, and soon, maybe only in five or ten years, the Dar would move north while the Empire moved south, cutting the Med in half. The late King had been a fool not to finish with the Empire when he'd had the chance. In its present shrunken state, granted, the anything-but-holy and no-longer-Roman Empire was but a fragment and a wraith of its former self, and not the threat, by itself, that the Dar Al Islam was, but it wasn't dead and gone, after all.

DuPuy let his hand rest on the wheel; it comforted him.

By design, his balcony resembled the bridge of the old

Sufficient as much as a landlocked balcony could, and he had pretended not to notice how the overly dramatic Bugeja winced at the ordered removal of the ancient marble to be replaced by the oak railing. What was left of the *Sufficient*'s wheel was mounted on the decking that had been laid on the stone, the hub that it now spun upon impotently although the hub was greased after every rain, just as the ancient brass smoking lamp from his long-lost love's quarterdeck smouldered from a hook on the outside wall.

It all reminded him of the one place in the world that he belonged; it was lost to him forever, but by God he could mourn it properly this morning as he did every morning, as he waited for the two men in the world he hated the most.

They would both be early, of course; he had invited one and ordered the other to join him at seven bells, but he had, as was his habit, risen early, for none of the reasons of duty that had never let him sleep through the night about the *Sufficient*.

That had been different.

He smiled. The captain's midwatch-to-mornwatch visits to the quarterdeck had been widely admired and copied throughout the Fleet; a generation of lieutenants given their first command had since taken to rising at the change of mid-to-morning, and probably no more really understood why they did that than they did their adopted thin, effete trace of the butter-thick Marseilles accent that Mr. Midshipman DuPuy had never been quite able to rid himself of, Lieutenant DuPuy had stopped trying to, and Captain and Admiral DuPuy had found himself more and more falling into, as though he was regressing with age.

Which he was, in more ways than one—now, he rose early because he couldn't sleep through the night, and tried to fool himself that it was the softness of his feather bed.

What had been a blot on the horizon had clearly become a ship, and he bet himself a half crown that he would be able to identify it before the shorewatcher did.

"My glass, Scratch," he said, not looking behind him for his secretary.

Instead of handing him the glass, Scratch knocked gingerly on the wood of the balcony's arch.

"Both of them are here, Admiral," he said. "At the same time," he added, the only reproach in the content of the words, not in the tone. "I've had Bugsted lay out your clothes," he said, resignedly.

"I'm fine as I am—you may have him put them away."

"Yes, Admiral." Scratch didn't quite sigh.

It was, of course, every bit as much a violation of regulations for the admiral to wear utilities on ordinary duty ashore as it would be for a bone-buttoned middie to, but one of the few nice things about this damned shore office was that there was nobody on Malta who was in a position to correct him directly, although his secretary tried to, of course, and as long as he wasn't too blatant about it, DuPuy let it pass.

He was, by necessity, frugal. There were definite disadvantages to being an honest man, and not supplementing his pay with even the ordinary graft was not the worst of them, given what the cost of uniforms still did to his personal budget, despite him spending his days in cheap utilities.

He didn't sleep well at night, but it wasn't from his

conscience bothering him—just his bowels and bladder.

"Show them in," he said.

"To the study?"

"Out here will serve," he said. "Bring a couple of mugs—mugs, mind you, not that cursed china that breaks at a cross look—and coffee for the both of them. And another cup for me, too." He'd rather offer the two of them poison—but coffee, brewed thick and rich with a pinch of salt added to the cup, would have to do. "And bring me my glass, dammit."

Scratch held out the tarnished old brass cylinder that had, of course, already been in his hand; the only apology DuPuy offered was a grunt as he accepted it and put it to his good eye, the left one.

Dammit, his good eye was going, too. Black flecks swum about his field of vision like a swarm of lazy flies, another of the indignities of age. He had no hope of making out any signal flags—much less pennants—until it drew much closer, but he had been hoping to get a feel for the sails. You could tell much about a master by the way he set his sails, as any schoolboy knew, although it went far beyond the elementary matter of Frenchmen and Spaniards typically flying two jibs when one was sufficient for an English master who knew how to use topgallants and stuns'ls.

All he could tell about this ship was that it was a two-master; its provenance or identity was beyond his ability to guess, at least for the moment, and he'd be unlikely to be able to spend any time on it for the next hour or so—he didn't need to consult a seer to figure that another half crown into the Widows and Orphans box was in his immediate future, as ill has he could afford it.

It shouldn't be a Crown ship.

DuPuy was more than vaguely familiar with Fleet schedules, and those of the fleet of merchantmen that serviced the Fleet. Neither of the two ragged squadrons at sea to the east were due in for some time, and the next slopman was either the *Refuge* or the *Spirits*, but the *Refuge* had been dispatched to Marseilles in large part as a message to the ever-greedy Bolognese merchants that the Fleet had other options; the *Reffy* would be coming in from the northeast, not the west. The *Spirits* had sailed west-norwest to Thessalonika, granted, and should be back any day, but it was a fat barkentine, and DuPuy's eyes weren't so bad or his mind so dull that he couldn't tell the difference between two and three masts, although he couldn't guess whether it was a schooner, brig, brigantine, ketch, or yawl, or even one of those strange two-masted fellucas you'd only find in the mild waters of the eastern Med.

Oh, well. He held out the glass, but Scratch wasn't there, of course, so he went back into the office to find the case. He had a much finer glass, presented to him along with his fancy-but-useless admiral's sword, in admonition that he would, henceforth, be watching things rather than actually doing things, but he had never once so much as put the gilded piece of frippery to his bad eye.

"Good morning, sir," Randolph said, stopping his limping pace to come to attention.

"*Ah-salam oo-allay-koom*," Abdul ibn Mussa al-Bakilani said. "A good morning to you, Admiral."

"G'morning, Lieutenant, and greetings, sir," DuPuy said.

Scratch arrived with the coffee, and both men, of course, accepted it. Al-Bakilani would have downed flaming piss if protocol demanded it, and he seemed to actually like the admiral's coffee, although that only meant that he thought it appropriate to seem to like the admiral's coffee.

Both of the men he hated most in the world were dressed as they should be—Lieutenant Lord Sir Alphonse Randolph in the impeccably tailored first-class blues that, certainly by no accident, showed off his broad shoulders and almost womanishly trim waist. He stood painfully straight, and not just because of the high starched collar of the white blouse beneath the jacket and waistcoat; Randolph was that sort.

His medals—the officer's uniform of the day on Malta specified medals, not just ribbons—had somehow been secured to each other and the short, waist-length jacket, and didn't click together to echo his boot heels as he drew himself up to an even stiffer brace. While it was traditional that a family crest was displayed on the right breast, Randolph's was on the left, beneath the medals that obscured everything except the second motto: *Fari Que Sentiat*. Save for a thin bristle of mustache below the sharp Moray nose, his face was shore-shorn, emphasizing the thick scar just below his cheekbone.

Technically, despite the medals, he was out of uniform. The sword at his waist was one of those overly curved Seeproosh-style sabers, not a proper officer's dress sword—as though to brag how he had obtained it, along with the limp. DuPuy probably wouldn't have corrected him, even if they weren't alone, and even if DuPuy wasn't in utilities himself. A bit of quiet braggadocio was a good thing in a master and commander, after all.

The Arab was arrayed in the long flowing robes of his people, only the high quality of the fine-woven linen and the silver stitching at the hems distinguishing him from any lesser man, although there was some significance to the tiny golden pendant secured by a preposterously thin gold chain around his neck, just as there was some scheme to the pattern of that rope-thing that would have secured his headscarf in place. DuPuy had never bothered to learn about such things, and the headscarf and rope-thing—called something like "argyle," if DuPuy remembered correctly—had been tucked into al-Bakilani's sash in a way that perversely reminded him of the way that Randolph had his handkerchief tucked into his sleeve.

A handsome enough man, for an Arab, if only because his smooth, dark face was free of pockmarks; the devil protected his own, after all.

Al-Bakilani had no weapon in evidence, although he did have a reputation as a warrior; the Caliphate's emissaries depending on other things than their prowess with weapons to protect themselves on Crown territory, and his unusual willingness to meet with DuPuy without the usual entourage that al-Bakilani's predecessor, a much less clever man, had always brought with him to any discussion. Al-Bakilani had gracefully dispensed with that, shortly after his arrival. Perhaps he thought that DuPuy, who strongly preferred simply getting business done and over with, would be more flexible—although that hope was in vain, of course. Or maybe it was that he thought he was probing for some sign that DuPuy might be corruptible.

Which, in a sense, he was, of course. But not by the likes of al-Bakilani.

Hanging a Western Emirates ambassador was something that DuPuy would have gladly ordered—the thought of al-Bakilani jerking and pissing and shitting himself on the end of a rope was an utterly loverly image—but there were good reasons, and, more important, there were standing orders that such persons were sacrosanct, after all, just as the delegates from the Crown to the Caliphate were.

DuPuy hoped that his opposite number in Sfax was every bit as aggrieved with his guest as DuPuy was with his. But life was rarely so just.

"I—"

"Admiral—"

Both men immediately shut up, al-Bakilani making an expansive gesture for Randolph to proceed, which Randolph returned with a stiff smile and a perfectly correct bow.

"I beg your pardon, sir," Randolph said, "most humbly."

"No, please; my fault entirely," the Arab said, turning to DuPuy. "It appears I've arrived shamefully early for my appointment with His Excellency." It was the closest that he would come to criticizing DuPuy for having committed the solecism of having the two of them arrive together.

"No, it's not your fault," DuPuy said. "I intended to make an introduction. Hope I didn't embarrass either of you—Shaykh Abdul ibn Mussa al-Bakilani al-Medina Hajji, may I present Lieutenant Lord Sir Alphonse Randolph? Randolph, Shaykh al-Bakilani. Should have done this a week ago, but I'd expected that—oh, never mind."

He hadn't expected anything, but it always made sense to give al-Bakilani something to think about. DuPuy had quite deliberately generated an impression of deviousness by the simple expedient of being as straightforward as he could, and while the smooth smile never dropped from al-Bakilani's face, DuPuy could tell that he expected something subtle and clever from him, which DuPuy did his best to provide.

"I am, of course, honored to meet the lieutenant," al-Bakilani said. "My condolences on your recent loss; I hope you wouldn't be offended if I were to say a brief prayer for your late brother?"

"Not at all," Randolph said, his own boot-face firmly in place.

"Seems strange to pray for a Nasranite, isn't it?" DuPuy asked, just to see how al-Bakilani would handle it.

"Not at all." Al-Bakilani ducked his head as he murmured a short phrase in Arabic, then raised his head. "Roughly: 'whether it be of the True Believers, or those who are Jews or Christians or Sabaeans, whosoever believe in God and the last day and act aright, they have their reward at their Lord's hand.' So may it be for Francis Mordred Randolph, son of Michael Francis Randolph, Earl of Moray, may Allah show him mercy."

Al-Bakilani gave DuPuy a thin smile. Since word of the elder Randolph's death had only just reached Malta two days before, al-Bakilani was more giving DuPuy to know that his sources within the Fleet were in place than he was, once again, showing off his apparently encyclopedic knowledge of British noble families.

Which meant, of course, that either al-Bakilani had no such sources in the Fleet itself—something DuPuy knew was not the case—and wanted DuPuy to send Weatheral to chase around looking for his nonexistent spies, or that al-Bakilani was playing a double-bluff game of some sort, as he was.

Well, DuPuy would be glad to be rid of al-Bakilani. What business they had was long since finished. Sad days when you had to reveal at least part of your schedules and timetables to an enemy to minimize unwanted encounters at sea. What he should have been doing— what he wanted to do—was to issue a general order that any ship flying the Star and Crescent was to be taken, and to have enough ships and marines to do that, and sack every city along the northern arc of the Dar, from al-Gaheer to Bayrut, something that would take rather a lot more than a puny six undermanned squadrons more suited to pirate patrol than real warfare.

There was no point in letting his mind churn that over and over again, but while DuPuy controlled his words and actions, he never had been able to get a rein on his thoughts, and was too old to start trying.

He cleared his throat. "The reason I arranged for the two of you to meet—should have done it before, Shaykh; my apologies, again—will be evident in a moment, I expect. Mr. Randolph, is the *Redemption* ready for sea?"

"Yes, sir." He said it with no qualification, and it hadn't escaped DuPuy's notice that the manic supply boat activity in the rest of the squadron's berthings didn't include *Redemption*. No need to rush about like a headless chicken if you'd already made yourself ready.

"And your first officer—a Mister . . . Braithwaite, I believe?"

"Yes, sir. Lieutenant David Braithwaite, sir."

"Would you say he's ready for his own command?"

"Absolutely, sir."

"As I thought." He looked past Randolph's shoulder to Scratch, and gave a quick nod. Scratch, as was usual, overly theatrical, patted at his breast pocket, and departed the room with atypical haste. "I'm giving him the *Reddy*; you're the new master of the *Lord Fauncher*. Throckmorton's already issued the orders; you should have them in hand within the hour."

"Yes, sir." No expression, although he was sure that Randolph resented it. DuPuy certainly would have.

He turned to the Arab. "The lieutenant and the *Lord Fauncher* will be your host on the trip to Sfax; you're due there on the thirteenth, as I recall."

"His Excellency recalls correctly, of course," al-Bakilani said, not rising to the bait. "And may I congratulate the lieutenant on his new command?"

"Thank you," Randolph said. "I'm very much looking forward to it."

DuPuy watched his face closely; if there was any indication that this was the first that Randolph was hearing of it, DuPuy couldn't see it. Good. Throckmorton was the only officer he had told, although he was sure that Throckmorton's secretary, like Scratch, knew as well. Throckmorton wasn't DuPuy's idea of what a port captain ought to be, but at least he could keep his mouth closed.

"Now, Excellency, if you'll excuse us?"

"Of course, Admiral," al-Bakilani said, smiling gently. "I'm sure that you and the lieutenant have much to discuss about his new command, and I believe that your captain Postlethwaite is expecting me?"

DuPuy waited until the door had closed behind the Arab until he spoke. Randolph was still holding himself in a stiff brace; silent insolence of a sort, but not the sort that DuPuy cared about.

"Sit, Lieutenant, sit," he said, then changed his mind and shook his head. "Better—let's finish our coffee out on the balcony," he said, as always careful not to call it 'the quarterdeck' out loud. A beached sailor was a silly thing in and of itself; no need to be laughed at behind his back, any more than he already was—although there were, of course, worse things than being thought to be an utterly useless old man: being an utterly useless old man first among them.

"Yes, sir." Randolph followed him outside. DuPuy found that his own pipe had gone out, and gestured an invitation to Randolph to light his own, which Randolph took as the command that indeed it was.

"Well, go ahead, speak your mind," DuPuy said. He raised his glass to look at the distant ship. A two-master of a certainty, understandably if a bit aggressively flying a full complement of sails in the light air, but he couldn't tell anything more than that, not without his glass.

"Aye, aye, sir," Randolph said, eying the ship as he puffed on his pipe. "If you don't mind me asking, is there something about the *Wellesley* that I should know?"

"*Wellesley*? You don't mean the *Lord Fauncher*?"

"I mean the ship coming in from the nor'west, sir." Randolph didn't quite shrug. "I'd think it the Welly, sir, unless there's another master who flies both unreefed royals and topgallants without bothering with stuns'ls, sir—that's one of Johansen's quirks. Doesn't much care for stuns'ls, for some reason." He took a thoughtful pull on his pipe. "Good man, though. Probably be able to run a shakedown on the *Lord Fauncher* as well as anybody else."

"Is that a complaint, Lord Randolph?"

There was a flash of expression before Randolph resumed his boot-face. "Lord Randolph isn't at issue here, Admiral," he said. "Lieutenant Randolph, sir, has no complaint to make whatsoever." His lips might have tightened, just a touch. Perhaps not.

"You're wondering why I'm reassigning you."

"Well, yes, sir, I am."

"Speak your mind, Mr. Randolph," he said, gesturing at the motto on his breast. "*Fari Que Sentiat* means 'say what you think,' no? Something about a trip to Sfax beneath you? You have some objection to my orders, Mr. Randolph?"

"No, sir." Randolph told the lie without blinking. "If I'm to be transferred, I'd have thought I'd be ordered to report to Assignments, rather than to the Admiral. But I'll wager I can have the *Lord Fauncher* flying the Blue Peter as quickly and as well as most others, and better and faster than some."

"She slides down the ways tomorrow. You've got five days before you set sail for Sfax." DuPuy expected an objection, in posture if not in words, but didn't get one. It was an absurdly short time to ready a ship even for the most tentative of shakedowns, but not quite an impossibly short one, given the state of the *Lord Fauncher's* repairs, and her hold, something that Randolph apparently was aware of. "You're not asking me about her condition, I notice. You've been following the repairs?"

"No, sir. I've been busy seeing after the *Redemption*.

The *Lord Fauncher* hasn't been a matter of my concern until this moment, and I think that one look about her is worth a thousand questions—I assume that Captain McCaulkin will find the time to receive me?"

"A safe assumption." DuPuy pointed his pipestem toward the drydock. "You can proceed there directly from here."

"Aye, aye, sir. Do I report to Assignments to find out about my crew, or do you wish to give me the bad news on that yourself? Sir."

More insolence, but DuPuy just smiled. "You can have your pick from the beach crew; see Shea, and then Throckmorton. He'll have them report to you by the end of the day, even if he has to have them dragged by the heels from every tavern and bordello across the island—as he more than likely will, with some of that lot."

"Yes, sir." If Randolph resented having to pick among the beach crew, as he surely should have, that didn't show in his face.

"Unless there's some officers or men from the *Redemption* you feel you need more than Braithwaite does?"

Braithwaite was probably a bit junior to be given the *Reddy*, but it would be interesting to see if he was as good a man as Randolph claimed—as he probably was; DuPuy had followed Braithwaite's career rather more carefully than he cared to let on at the moment.

"No, sir. Not with the *Reddy* about to sail on the tide—noon or midnight. I'll take my dogrobber, and leave it at that, Admiral."

Loyalty was a good thing. No doubt that Randolph would have preferred to have every crewman from the Reddy transferred—something that DuPuy had not quite openly offered, and a request that he would have denied, if it had been made—but, of course, Randolph wouldn't ask for any such thing.

DuPuy cocked his head to one side. "You haven't asked me why, Mr. Randolph."

"No, sir, I haven't."

"Carry on, Mr. Randolph."

"Aye, aye, sir."

And then he was alone again, with his pipe and the cold dregs of his morning coffee.

You couldn't persuade people with words, DuPuy had long since decided. If you couldn't order them, you had to let them see for themselves.

Randolph had taken the *Redemption* as the first command available, even though that had meant transfer from the far larger and more prestigious Atlantic Fleet to the hinter-waters of Malta, and had spent most of his year with the Malta Fleet chasing pirates. Give him a view, up close, of Sfax, and he'd at least begin to see—to see for himself, dammit—a fraction of the real forces arrayed against the Crown here.

DuPuy tried to do that with all his young officers, making sure that each ship, in turn, was seconded for a mission to a Dar port.

He was trying to take the long view; ten, twenty years from now—if there was to be a Crown in ten or twenty years—the Admiralty would have at least a leavening of senior captains and admirals who had seen the enemy for themselves, up-close.

That was important. Spending time around the likes of al-Bakilani was important, as well—let them know that the enemy could be charming, and soft-spoken, and even kindly, and they would be less willing to accept assurances that the Dar now believed that trade, rather than conquest, was the way to expand the Dar al-Islam.

But it was even more important to have that knowledge, that skepticism, and the passion created and represented by that knowledge and that skepticism in Parliament, and now he would have more of it, in the person of the Earl of Moray, sooner or later.

Preferably sooner, although he would have to think long and hard about trying to arrange that without doing something too obvious, or repetitious.

He made a *tsk*ing sound to himself. Weatherall had spies along the northern coast of Africa, although they were an untrustworthy lot, just as he was certain that al-Bakilani and the Dar had spies in Malta, even beyond the ever-reliable Scratch.

Pity. DuPuy had never had a better secretary, and Scratch had been—his treason aside—unwaveringly honest, never even taking a drink from the bottle of harsh issue rum that DuPuy kept in his desk. DuPuy could tell watered rum at a taste, and the level had never gone below his light scratch marks.

Oh, well.

He walked in to his office and unlocked his top drawer, pulled out the bottle, and poured himself a quick tot, habitually marking the bottle's level with the sharp edge of his ring, and then recorking it before downing the glass in one neat gulp.

With the bottle removed from the drawer, his private correspondence file was on top, and the hair he had placed between the second and third pages almost where he had left it. Scratch was almost as careful as DuPuy himself.

The latest letter from Francis Randolph, clumps of wax still attached, was at the very top of the pile. It was only reasonable, after all, that DuPuy would take a few moments to reread his correspondence with Francis Randolph upon being informed of Randolph's untimely demise.

The handwriting was excellent, if he did say so himself; it was just a matter of taking one's time, and never, ever using anything but his deliberately crude scratchings to sign his own correspondence.

> . . . *and you may have my assurances, my dear Admiral duPuy, that even absent our lengthy correspondence, I would have and indeed have fully adopted your view of the prevailing situation in the Mediterranean Sea, and will prevail upon both the earl and any others who will listen to my voice about the necessity of reinforcing the Malta Fleet, to the obvious necessities that we have discussed. I urge you to continue to take the long view on such matters, as this won't be solved in a fortnight or a month or a year, but it will be addressed, and what influence I have or will have is entirely in service of this necessity.*

Probably a touch too arch, but . . . it would serve. Forging Randolph's personal seal would have been difficult, but that hadn't been necessary—DuPuy had used his own seal, and a bar of privately bought wax rather than Navy issue, and then removed almost all of the wax, leaving just enough behind to show that it had been sealed, no more. The paper had been a problem, but a few minutes with a bar and razor had turned a sheet of good broadside into something that a noble might well have used for private correspondence.

Good enough; it would serve.

It *had* served; he had written this letter more than a year ago, the moment that he had been informed of the younger Randolph's transfer to the Malta Fleet, and it had sealed the doom of Francis Randolph, unless the hunting accident was just that, which DuPuy didn't believe for a moment.

Randolph the elder, like his father, was notoriously apolitical, and was widely reported to have been more interested in boar hunting than anything else. Brave of him, certainly, but even more useless of him, and while DuPuy admired bravery, it should be in aid of something worthwhile. If you were going to spend your life, there were better and far more worthy causes than chasing a pig through a forest, armed with nothing more than a spear.

Well, the letter had done its duty, and now it was time to be rid of it, along with a few of the others, as well; they would just go into the fireplace—although he would want to be sure that Scratch was away from the offices before that, and would, of course, stir the ashes after the burning.

Pity he couldn't simply lay the matter on the Intelligence desk, but he had no faith in that idiot Weatherall, who had been bequeathed upon DuPuy by his predecessor.

Now would be a fine time for the burning, if Scratch was off on some errand. Which he wouldn't be, of course, until DuPuy dispatched him, so sending him off would be the next item of business for this depressingly bright and cheery day.

"Scratch?" He barely raised his voice before his secretary was through the door.

"Yes, Admiral?"

"I'd better speak to Assignments—would you ask Shea to see me as soon as possible? Tell him to bring the list of ensigns and junior lieutenants on the beach crew—I want some recommendations for the *Lord Fauncher.*"

The last thing he really wanted were recommendations, of course; he had no intention of tying Randolph's hands any more than he already had, but he did want to make it implicitly clear to both Shea and Throckmorton that he would be most unhappy if the best available beached officers and jacks weren't easily available to Randolph.

Best of a slaggardly lot, granted, but that was the way of it . . .

"Yes, sir," Scratch said. "I was coming in to see you, Admiral—I'm sorry to bother you, I just got back from downstairs; the captain summoned me. There are two Order Knights waiting downstairs, on a matter that's clearly of importance."

His pipestem snapped in his hands. Order Knights? A matter of importance—that they had talked to *Scratch* about? The only reason that Scratch was still alive was that there were no Fleet secrets in the backwaters of Malta except those that DuPuy was busy manufacturing. The truth was simple, alas.

"It had better be important," he said, snarling loudly to cover his anger—at himself; his fury at Scratch had long since burned itself down to banked coals.

"I can assure you that it is—they confided in me, albeit briefly."

"Very well. Show them in. And stand by your desk, man—if it is something important, I'll want you close at hand."

It would most likely be. The Order, for all its faults, did not raise a bunch of panicky flibbertigibbets, after all.

And write your will, you bloody traitor, he thought at Scratch's retreating back *If this is indeed something important, and not just a couple of self-important knights, you'll not see another sunrise.*

It would be easy, and he had long since decided how to do it, when the time came, as it perhaps finally had.

Murder was best done in the dark and quiet. Tonight would do.

After DuPuy had gone to bed, he would arise, as though he had trouble sleeping, and walk down the hall to summon Scratch from his own bed for some late-night correspondence, bring him back to the office, and ask him to fetch his pipe from the mantelpiece.

Hmmm . . . it would be a kind of justice to take his saracen trophy battleaxe down from the mantelpiece, but Scratch might notice that it was missing. A simple baulk of wood from the wood bin wasn't as elegant, but it would serve just as well. He didn't need to kill him with a quick blow to the head, it would be enough just to stun Scratch— although DuPuy wouldn't *mind* if it actually killed him, of course—and then it would be just a matter of splashing Scratch with some rum and then pitching him over the rail, following him with the smoking lamp from the balcony.

And then back to bed, to be awakened at all the

commotion, or even in the morning, if nobody noticed. An empty bottle beside his own bed, and a few splashes on his sheets, would explain his having missed all the excitement.

Not that it would be all that much excitement. Nobody would suspect a thing. A thieving admiral's secretary would have merely been at the admiral's bottle, and have gone out to the balcony to get himself a smoke without having to fear the smell waking the admiral; the drunken Scratch would have lost his balance, fallen over the rail, and shattered on the stones far below.

Nobody would think otherwise—except, perhaps, al-Bakilani, and what would he say?

Nothing, of course. But he would know, and while DuPuy would have had it otherwise were it possible, he took quiet pleasure from the necessity of that, just as he did in the sealed envelope that was in Throckmorton's safe, to be opened only upon DuPuy's death, in which he expressed a belief that al-Bakilani had decided to have him assassinated—and referred to conversations with Scratch, who would now never find himself hauled in front of Intelligence to be questioned on the letter, alas—and the small vial of poison secreted beneath his bed that would end his days when he was recalled.

In life, he would do his duty, even if his duty called for lying and deception; so would it be in death, he hoped.

But not too soon.

He still had more to do, and if Simon DuPuy couldn't serve his King from the quarterdeck of a warship, he would serve him as best he could from his luxurious prison.

There was service in that, and that it would never be known made it no less a service; and there was loyalty, as well, even though it would not be appreciated even if it was known; and if there was no honor to be had, well, you couldn't have everything.

Strange for a man who had thought of himself one of honor to have descended into such depravity, but needs must, when the devil drives, eh, old fellow?

He smiled to himself. It would be a beautiful thing, in its own way, to end his days with a blow to the Dar that he could never deliver alive, and if it wasn't as much of a blow as he would have wished for, it was all he could do, and a man couldn't ask for more than that.

But not tonight. Tonight was the time for Scratch to shuffle off this mortal coil; DuPuy's turn would come soon enough.

Still . . .

It was, he often thought, a sad end for a man who once, long ago—too long ago—had been an honest sailor.

Chapter 7: Swordplay

Years ago, when Bear and Alexander and I were off chasing down what I sincerely hope and pray was the very last of the Linfield deodands, we followed a twisting trail too far into the depths of Bedegraine, probably no more than a mile from where our attendants had pitched camp, but far enough away that they didn't answer to Alexander's horn.

So, of course, we made camp for the night. Not the easiest thing to do without so much as a pot or blanket between us, and no food save for the jerky and waybread we had in our pouches. Gathering dead wood for the fire was difficult in the gathering dark, with only an occasional trickle of moon shining through the huge trees, but starting the fire was even more so, even though Bear had used his mundane sword as deftly as you could imagine to shave some birch scrapings into tinder.

A real woodsman would probably have been able to rub two sticks together and produce a roaring fire, a trick

I've never mastered, and which neither Bear nor Alexander had, and for some reason the small stone that I found couldn't strike a spark off of my mundane sword, nor either of Alexander's, nor Bear's, although we tried, figuring that the scratches on the spines of our blades could be polished out more easily than we could get through a cold night in the Bedegraine Forest without fire.

All we ended up with, though, were scratched swords.

I was looking forward to a cold night shivering in my robes beneath the trees with my usual equanimity—not much—when Bear, just a huge hulking shape in the dark, quietly asked the other two of us to step away, and drew the Nameless.

I had been expecting something dramatic—and had been about to curse Bear for using the Nameless's power for such a mundane task, if indeed he could—and I found myself more outraged than relieved when he knelt in front of the tinder pile, the stone in his hand.

Sparks flickered along the length of the blade, sending the tinder smoking, and quicker than it takes to tell, at least as I remember it, we were sitting before a roaring fire, while Bear, his leather gauntlets still in place, was polishing the Nameless before returning it to its sheath, while Alexander and I just sat, mouths open, while the Khan, at my side, muttered outraged threats at the sacrilege and disrespect—using a White Sword as a sparking iron? How dare he!

Bear just smiled, his face shiny in the firelight. "The Nameless said to remind you that he, like Our Lord, washed beggars' feet. Should we need to dig a latrine-hole, he says he'd be happy to be of service in that, too."

I'll likely never understand the Nameless. I'm sure I'll never understand Bear.

—Gray

The afternoon sun gave off light and heat, but, strangely, no warmth. Maybe it was the knight's robes that Niko wore, over the tunic and leggings, and them over the undergarments. It was still strange, if no longer entirely uncomfortable, to have so much cloth between his skin and the sun.

Niko sat cross-legged on the cold stone, the sword lying naked on the blanket in front of him, next to its scabbard and the heavy leather gauntlets.

He smoothed down the front of his robes, then snatched the hand away—it was trembling and sweaty.

The best thing to do, perhaps, would be to strip it all off and fold it carefully—if the single scrap of cloth for his kirtle was expensive, it was hard to imagine what these clothes would have cost—and let the sun warm him, if it would. If it could.

His fingers trembled; he fastened them together in his lap, which didn't help much, and seemed to more transfer the trembling to his chattering teeth than anything else.

"What am I supposed to do?" he asked, more to delay the inevitable than because he had any real doubt. He would grasp the hilt of the sword, and feel the pain and fear again.

"For now, just try to calm yourself," Cully said. "We have enough time. Let's not rush matters without need."

He sat, also cross-legged, on the other side of the blanket. Like Niko, he was dressed in the garments of the Order, and like Niko, he was freshly shorn, and then freshly bathed. His smile was as reassuring as a smile could be, which wasn't much. "I know that's easier said than done, but try. Or don't try—think about something unimportant. What do you think the Abdullahs will serve for dinner? Something good, I'd expect."

"Yes."

Niko wasn't hungry at the moment, but he didn't have to think very hard as to what the centerpiece of the feast would be, nor did he have to guess that Cully was trying to distract him. The wind brought the smell of roasting meat across the water—perhaps overly seasoned with fresh wild onion, as there had been no time to properly hang and then brine it—and it had reached Cully's nose as surely as it had Niko's.

Entertaining guests of such an elevated station was something that any sensible fisherman would wisely turn his hand to, and the Abdullahs were more capable of doing that than most.

"Very well. Now try to clear your mind—yes, I know you can't force yourself to think about nothing. Nobody can. But think of something simple and calming—a pool of water is the classic choice."

A pool of water?

It sounded like a silly thing to think about, but he would try.

A small pool of seawater, perhaps, cupped in a depression in the rocks at the shoreline, left behind by the falling tide. Sometimes the tide left a jellyfish in such, and it was a simple matter to scoop them out with a wicker basket, and carry them high to the ridge above to dry. Mara would crunch the leathery bits between her teeth, and laugh—

Mara. Gentle, clever Mara. And Lina. And Grandfather—all of them now rotting in the cold ground at the bottom of a pit, as though they were shit to be covered over with dirt, not even given the dignity of being returned to the sea from which all had sprung, and to which all would return, to be received by Poseidon at his court, far beneath the waves.

Were they in the cold arms of Hades? Or had Zeus taken them as His own?

He tried to swallow, but couldn't.

"Shhh . . . easy, boy, easy. Just take a deep breath, and let it out slowly. Slowly, now—you're not stoking your lungs for a dive beneath the waters. Slowly."

Niko did. It seemed to help, strangely enough, although only a little.

The sword still lay there, the pain and fear waiting for him.

"Better," Cully said. "Are you calm yet?"

"Yes, sir."

"If you're going to lie to me, boy, do a better job of it. Again: are you calm?"

He hesitated, then answered honestly. No point in lying. "No." How could he be calm at a time like this? His hand went to the front of his chest.

"Can you hear your heart beat?" Cully asked.

"No, of course not." A silly question, but . . .

"Hmm . . . well, we'll do it the first-form way, then: cup your hand, your left hand, against your ear."

"Sir Cully—"

"Just do it, boy. Listen carefully to it, and it will slow down. It'll take a few moments, but just be patient."

Niko did, and found that he could hear the *lub-dub-lub-dub* of his heart, and, even more strangely, that it seemed to slow, that it *was* slowing, as he listened and willed it to.

Niko found his mind turning to trivialities. It turned

out that the distinctive knights' haircut was simply a matter of fastening three fingers, tight against the scalp, in a clump of hair, and cutting off what remained, then repeating until all the hair on the head was of the same length. Cully had showed him how to do it while he was cutting Niko's hair, and then had Niko serve him in turn.

Trimming the beard had been much of the same thing, save that you scissored the beard hair between two fingers. The only difficult part of the preparation had been the shaving of the upper cheeks, which Cully accomplished for both of them with a strange-looking straight knife from a kit in his rucksack.

Even more strange: Niko hadn't been scared, even when Cully had had to put the straight knife against Niko's well-soaped throat.

Lub-dub. Lub-dub.

"Better." Cully's smile seemed sincere, and of a surety, it reminded Niko of Grandfather's. "Now, when you're ready—no rush, no rush at all—reach out and let your hand rest on the sword."

"Not grab it by the hilt?"

"Don't grab it at all. Reach out and touch it, gently, as though you were trying to calm a frightened dog."

Again Cully was talking about things that Niko didn't understand. Why would anybody want to calm a dog? The dogs that lived around Pironesia were just like giant rats, all in all, and about as useful. When you saw a dog, you looked for a stone to chase it away with; you didn't pat it, as you would a frightened child.

He could try to think of it as frightened child, though. That might do, and it was easier than arguing with Cully. Maybe if he thought of it as Mara—not the bloody hunk of meat left dead on the beach, but little Mara, as tiny as she had been, smiling up at him as she sat in his lap, giggling even as she wet herself, splashing him with warmth that echoed with laughter in the hut at his curses.

He smiled. It had washed off. And he had set her in Mother's arms before rushing out to wash himself.

So, Mara it would be. Perhaps that would do.

He reached out his hand to pat the cold steel, and—

She awoke to fear, and to pain. She immediately started to scream again, and—

There is no pain; be still, little one.

She didn't understand. It wasn't the One Who Smelled Like Food, but its thoughts were almost as gentle—although it was as every bit as frightened as she was.

More, I think.

It smelled like the other one that had touched her, the one that had recoiled in her fear and pain, amplified by its own fear and pain, and then had gone away, leaving her once again alone in the endless dark.

And it wasn't alone—another one was with it! And this one had a knife, too—a big knife, and—

Shhh. It's just Cully.

What was a Cully?

It didn't answer.

And what are you? And where is the One Who Smells Like Food?

I don't know, little one. I don't know much of anything. I'm just Niko the fisherman.

Its answers just led to more questions, and she didn't much like that. What was a Niko, or a fisherman? And where was the One Who Smells Like Food?

It didn't answer that, but she could feel it smiling in reassurance, although she wasn't reassured about anything. The way to reassure her was to *feed* her, to hold her to the warm flesh of the One Who Smells Like Food, to let her suck and suck at the sweet warmth, while the One Who Smells Like Food made those strange lilting sounds, and acted out the words with her hands:

> Dandinidandini dastana
> Danalargirmis bostana
> Kovbostanci danayl
> Yemisinlahanyl
> Eh-e nini, eh-e nini,
> Eh-e nini, nini,
> Nininini nini
> Eh-e, eh-e nini eh!
> Eh-e, eh-e nini eh!
> Eh-e, ninni, ninni, ninni,
> Eh-e, ninni, ninni, eh!
> *Eh-e, ninni.*

Sleep, my little Nadide-precious, my tiny Tezer-treasure, the One would say.

I don't understand.

It didn't understand anything important, but it was friendly—not like that huge one, with the knife, the one that hurt, and—

Shh. That one's not here. It's just me and Cully, and we mean you no harm, truly.

Maybe this Niko and this Cully would feed her? But she didn't feel hungry, strangely enough. She didn't feel much of anything at all. Just scared.

I'm scared, too, but there's nothing to fear, not here and now. Shh.

"*Enough*, Niko. Let go—and gently. That's enough for the moment."

She heard the words, although she couldn't tell where they were coming from, and they didn't make any sense. Ee-nuff? What was an ee-nuff, and why was an enuff important enough to yell about? Was this Cully another mean and cruel—

No. Cully isn't that. He wants to . . . to help you, to help the both of us.

It was strange that she understood that this Cully wanted Niko to let go of her—

Let go of her? No. Don't, please don't.

Shh. Not yet. In a moment. But I'll be—I'll be back, and you'll be with me.

That was nice. She wasn't alone, not really. She didn't mind resting in the cool darkness, where there was no time, no feeling, nothing. It would have been like death, she supposed, but she didn't have any idea what death was, although the idea of this death-thing frightened and angered Niko, and brought forth visions of another big one—of several of them, lying on cold sands, unmoving, although two of the big ones were small, and she didn't understand that, either.

Don't be frightened, Niko. I'm with you. But where is the One Who Smells Like Food?

I don't know, little one.

I'm not "little one." The One Who Smells Like Food called me Nadide-precious, Tezer-treasure.

You want me to call you Nadide, or all of that?

Just make those sounds that the One does. Or bring

her here? I think I'm hungry, but I don't feel hungry.

Shh.

Please? Make the sounds?

If you insist.

It started singing, but it didn't have a very good voice, and most of the sounds came out different. She had no trouble understanding them, but there were thoughts under the surface that didn't make any sense—what was a "trading language," or a "Hellenic?"

It didn't matter, though; this Niko was singing, in words that she had never heard, but which somehow made sense to her, just as if they'd been the right ones:

Into the garden the calves did stray.
Gardener quickly turn them away.
They'll eat the cabbages without delay,

—it began, with the same cooing sounds after.

Not as good, of course, but its intentions were comforting, and she would have put her thickfinger in her mouth and sucked on it if she could have.

Strange. Her thickfinger didn't seem to be anywhere around. Where was it? Was it with the One Who Smells Like Food?

She drifted off peacefully into the welcoming, warm darkness, thinking of the One.

Cully wasn't happy. Angry, even. He adjusted his robes about him, and gestured at Niko to do the same.

Niko felt stupid.

He wasn't sure what he was supposed to have learned, but—whatever it was—the only thing he was utterly sure of was that he hadn't learned it, other than it was a baby.

"A baby?"

Cully nodded. "A baby. That was the lullabye its—"

"Her."

"—her mother used to sing?"

"Yes."

"Hmph. It doesn't sound familiar to me. Do you recognize it? Your mother didn't happen to sing it to you?"

Niko shook his head. "No. Not that I remember. Not with, with my sisters, either."

"Well, it's Hellenic, not English, and that broad, lazy accent of yours is typical of the eastern islands. More clipped around Athenai, and some swallowed sounds in Thessalonika." He nodded, as though to himself. "She came from somewhere in the islands. That should be good, but it isn't."

"I don't understand."

"Because I don't quite believe it." Cully shook his head as he dug through his knapsack, producing a bottle. He uncorked it and took a long drink, then gave it a long look before shaking his head once again, then absentmindedly recorking it and putting it away without offering Niko a drink.

"Why don't I quite believe it? The timing of this all suggests a presence, but not an immediate presence. Let's say that the Abdullahs were the source of these swords, that it's right here." He rapped his staff on the rock.

"You don't really believe—"

"No, I don't." Cully shook his head. "We'd know of missing children in the islands, for one thing. Their own? I can't believe that. Samir Abdullah impresses me as having great control over his family, yes, but enough to take a baby from its—from her mother's breast and kill it? And where would he come by a priest and a wizard, at the same time?

"But forget all that, for just a moment—if it was them, if it was any of your neighbors, the right time to set upon you and your family was immediately—before the sword was brought to Pironesia, if possible. Not leave any bodies behind, no evidence at all, nothing that a man could hold on to. You, your sisters, and your grandfather would just disappear.

"But that isn't what happened. Word got out, and it took some time for word to reach, well, Them, whoever They are, whatever they are.

"That's easily enough done. Your Abdullahs are traders, as well as fishermen, and it's hard to imagine that their shore stories, of late, haven't featured the cursed sword that killed Niko the Elder, and the same for any of the other traders that stop in these islands, and for islanders traveling to Pironesia themselves.

"And I would bet copper to gold that Andros of the *Kalends* had many a good, public laugh about how he swindled your family out of the reward—and if he didn't, his sailors surely did, probably accompanied by complaints that their shares were insufficient, if he shared with them at all.

"Gossip travels precisely as fast as the fastest ship, yes, and a cursed sword killing a fisherman is, among other things, a good story, and They certainly took action as soon as They knew, but, still, it took two months for word to get to England and for Cully and Bear to arrive in Pironesia, and the darklings and whoever or whatever carried them weren't much ahead or behind that.

"Enough time, certainly, for word to reach Sfax or Tunis—or Baghdad, for that matter—and to dispatch killers by sea, and even for the killers to arrive here, in some sort of trader guise.

"But darklings? Give the devil his due—the Caliph is as black a villain as there has been since Arthur the Tyrant if not Judas Iscariot, and his courtiers strive to excel in murder as much as conquest, but the Dar has no more trade in the Dark than the Crown does, nor does the Empire." He stood silently for a moment. "Not that that would stop somebody dedicated enough, certainly. But traversing the Zone isn't something to be done lightly, and it certainly can't be done quickly, not from here of a certainty. So, Dar or no Dar, the darklings were waiting in Pironesia before we got there, and that's unlikely to be the only place."

"So, what do you do?"

"*We*. You should be asking, 'what do *we* do?' "

"Sir Cully, I don't know anything useful, and the only thing I can use this sword for is singing lullabies or knocking myself out, and—"

"Correct. You don't know anything useful. Neither do I, at the moment."

"So what do you—what do we do?"

"Shush. Let me think, and by God, another drink would help." He extracted the bottle from his rucksack again, and took another drink, this time holding the bottle out to Niko.

Niko accepted it and took a tentative taste, forcing himself neither to make a face nor spit out the horrible burning liquid.

"Not to your liking?"

"Well, not really."

"It may grow on you."

Cully sat silently for a moment, until a thin smile flickered across his face. "But news travels fast, and interesting news travels faster, and its speed is neither sped nor slowed by the truth of it." He cocked his head at Niko. "I don't take you to be a very good liar, so your task, by and large, will be to keep your mouth shut and look confident."

Niko swallowed heavily, but found his hand reaching to Nadide's hilt for reassurance, and he only stopped himself at the last moment.

"Good boy." Cully smiled. "Unless you feel like swimming back to the Abdullahs, it's probably time to signal for your friend Milos to come and pick us up." He pulled a small leather pouch out of his bag, and tossed it to Niko. "I'll gather more wood—you can start the fire," he said, walking quickly away before Niko could point out that there were ample driftwood scraps on the shoreline, and that they would have to climb down anyway.

Oh, well.

Besides, it was best to deal with the problem at hand, which was starting a fire without getting his fine knightly clothes dirty.

That was simply enough solved, he thought, as he began to undress. He knew how to undress, and he could fold and lay them on a blanket, and he knew how to start a fire. The rest would have to wait.

The food was good, and there was more than enough of it, which didn't surprise Niko.

He had been curious as to exactly who would be at

supper at Samir's, and how they would be served. He had, upon occasion, guested on the Abdullah's main island, of course, but he had always stayed in one of the unmarried-men's huts along the windward side of the island. That was far enough away from the cluster of houses and build-ings that the young Abdullah men could either have some privacy or, more likely, avoid the constant yowling of the babies. The food for their evening meal had always been brought down the trail by Abdullah girls, properly escorted by at least one of the older men, to avoid the impropriety of Niko being left alone with them.

This was, well, different.

The greeting room of Samir Abdullah's house had been cleared of all its furniture, and a huge table had been mounted and covered with what the Governor had smil-ingly praised as as fine a linen cloth as he had seen since leaving England.

There was some sleight to the seating—apparently one simply didn't grab the nearest spot on a bench—and the Governor had been ceremoniously shown to one of the three real chairs next to one end of the table—the "head" they called it, where Samir sat—while Cully and then Niko had been seated across from the Governor, Niko on the end of the bench next to Petros Abdullah, and then Henderson, with the two mid-ship-men past him, each with an Abdullah seated between them.

Niko wasn't sure about what the actual functions were of the men the Governor had brought along with him, but judging by their clothes, they were every bit as impor-tant as the Governor himself, which probably meant something, as did the conversation that flowed around the table. Mid-ship-man Winston seemingly paid rapt attention to Ari Abdullah's discourse on setting deep-sea nets in heavy wind, plying him with questions whenever he paused to take a breath or a drink—not that Ari Thumbfingers paused terribly often. While Niko had noticed that the wine at the "foot" of the table came from an earthenware jug while that at the "head" came from mottled-glass bottles, he doubted that wine was a common beverage for even the wealthy Abdullahs.

As for him, he could easily count on his fingers and toes the number of times he had been given a taste of wine, and except for two times it had been the horrible pine-tasting stuff used in the One True Church rituals to symbolize, the priests always carefully explained, the blood of the One True Church's god, although it didn't taste anything like blood, as Niko had sucked on enough of his own cuts to know. Blood tasted like the sea.

Niko tried to pay attention to the conversation and put in a question or comment every now and then, mainly because Cully didn't give a private triple-tap on Niko's boot as long as he was doing that, and triple-tapped if he went too long between talking.

They had only three signals: one tap meant "yes" or "go on"; two was "no," or "disagree with me," and three was "talk more." That was more than enough for Niko.

And, in truth, he did find the conversation interesting. He thought he might learn something about the handling of a ship larger than a skiff, and that might be of interest in the coming days.

He didn't think it would be of any use, of course, but he had found the constant shoutings and orders of the captain and first officer on the *Wellesley* to be incomprehensible, and while he had seen the sailors almost constantly climbing up into the rigging to make adjustments to the sails every time the wind changed, even a little, he had not had any real idea as to why, although he could speculate about some of it. It had been all he could do to learn the sails' names. Apparently, sailing a tall ship required that each sail have a name, and would refuse to cooperate if the top sail on the mizzenmast was called just that, rather than the "topgallant" or the "mizzen royale."

Henderson smiled at him, over the rim of his glass. "Interesting stuff, Sir Niko, eh?" he asked.

"Yes, it is, Lieutenant. I don't know much about the handling of big ships."

"Be that as it may, you and Sir Cully seemed to handle that cutter right smartly, if you don't mind my saying so. Fairly tricky with only two hands aboard."

A knight was probably supposed to sound self-confident without bragging, but Niko wasn't sure how to pull that off, so he just nodded. "We did well enough, I suppose. Most of it, though, was just avoiding being too aggressive, and watching the wind." He shrugged. "I learned not to try to get the last bit of speed out of a boat the first time I capsized our skiff, Lieutenant."

Henderson nodded, and conveyed another bite of lamb to his mouth with his eating prong, as though he had been using such a thing for all his life, as he probably had, come to think of it. Even stranger, he didn't take any apparent offense at Niko calling him by his rank.

Cully had cautioned him that he was to call the officers and mid-ship-men by their rank and never, ever call any of them "Sir" or "Excellency."

If Niko was irritated with one of them—that was what

Cully had actually said: "If *you* are irritated with one of *them*"—he was to express that without cursing, but by frowning and saying just what he would have said anyway, and just in the way he would have said it, but to call the man by his last name.

He hadn't done that. He was still perplexed by the notion that he would have to be told not to curse the officers and mid-ship-men; Cully apparently didn't think much of Niko's instincts for survival.

"Made good time," Henderson said, "from . . . where was it you set sail out of again?"

Niko hadn't said, but it wasn't a secret, as far as he knew. Still—

Cully's foot tapped three times on his. "Pantelleria," Niko said immediately, and all eyes near him widened. "They—we had a matter that needed to be seen to on the Montagne Grande."

That, too, was surely no secret, but the newfound pressure of Cully's boot on top of Niko's told him that he had said something he shouldn't have, even though he had been most specific that Niko was to find a way to work the word into the conversation if Cully didn't beat him to it. It was all Niko could do not to turn and ask what, but that surely would have been the wrong thing to do.

"Sir Niko," Cully said, turning to him, as all the other conversation stopped, "I'd very much rather you not discuss the events on you-know-where outside of the Order." His foot tapped twice against Niko's, the signal for "no," or "disagree with me."

Well, Niko couldn't claim to understand what Cully was up to, but at least he could count to two. The signal was two taps, he was sure it was, just as the three taps had told him to talk more. But apparently he wasn't supposed to have said what he'd said, and he hesitated for a moment, and Cully's boot came down on his again, harder, and again it was twice.

"With respect," Niko said—surely it wouldn't do any harm to admit respect, would it?—"I disagree, Sir Cully."

He wasn't sure why he was supposed to disagree, and was trying to decide what he should say next when Cully drew himself up straight, started to speak, and then stopped himself and held up his hands in mock surrender.

"Ah, you're quite right, Sir Niko; my apologies to you—to all of you—for my outburst." Cully tilted back his wineglass, then set it down on the table. "There's more than a few matters going on that aren't for general distribution, but the bare bones of what went on there isn't a secret." He chuckled. "Not that it can remain much of a secret, what with a live sword in that sash about your waist, eh?"

Governor Halloran looked like he'd bitten into a bad turtle egg. "I think, perhaps, we should not bore our hosts with such matters?"

"Bore?" Cully snorted. "*Bore?* The live swords are many things, Governor, but one of the things they're not now and never have been is boring, sir."

There was just a trace of slur to his words, although Niko didn't think it was from the drink; Cully was just acting.

"Nor," Cully went on, "I'm sure, would anybody find boring the facts and the reasons behind the necessity of knighting a Pironesian fisherboy and giving him a live sword, eh?—although, yes, you and I had best discuss that privately, later, and not . . . inflict that knowledge on anybody else, at least for some time to come." His face was a grim mask. "Enough of this is going to come out sooner than later, although I'd very much appreciate it if as little talk as possible were to reach the *Conveyance*'s wardroom, gentlemen."

"Yes, yes." Henderson ducked his head quickly. "Of course, Sir Cully," he said, looking at the mid-ship-men for a moment before turning back to the knight. "May I have your leave to discuss this with Captain MacKenzie?"

"Well, yes, of course," Cully said, then took another sip of wine. "Just don't go telling rail stories to the crew, eh?" He turned to Samir Abdullah. "Say what you wish to your family, and do ask them to be reasonably discreet . . . but don't worry about it too much—I'm not inflicting Crown secrets on you and your family, Samir."

Abdullah smiled genially over the rim of his wineglass. "We are, of course, loyal to the Crown, but it's good to know that when—and you did say when, Sir Cully; I made a particular note of that—this all becomes common knowledge, my family and I won't be blamed for that."

"Of course not." He waved the idea away. "The best way to keep a secret is not to share it with anybody, and particularly not where it might reach a bunch of chatting seamen—enlisted seamen, I mean, Mr. Henderson; no reflection on your officers and middies. But some things can't be kept secret, without hanging everybody who knows, and maybe not even then." He drained his glass of wine, and when he set it down on the table, Samir himself refilled it with a remarkably steady hand.

"As to what you asked me this morning, Samir, I think that it would be best if your barkentine sets sail at first light—or even before, if your son who commands it . . . would you remind me of his name?"

"Salim. My fourth son," he said, gesturing at Salim, who was sitting next to one of the Governor's assistants.

"If you and Captain Salim think that he can manage the shoals offshore before the sun's fully up."

It probably was difficult to seem offended and ingratiating at the same time, but somehow Samir Abdullah's expression managed it. "He's a clumsy boy, with no head for trade, but I do think he can be counted on not to stave in the hull on familiar rocks. The question of the crew comes to mind, as . . . hesitant as I am to discuss business affairs at table."

Cully laughed. "Well, as for me, I'm a confirmed commoner, and when it comes to discussing business, I've always thought that there's no time like the present," he said, "although at present my head is buzzing with this most excellent wine that you've provided, and talk of numbers is more likely to make my head swim off my shoulders than offend anybody."

"Perhaps I can help with that." Governor Halloran seemed relieved that the talk had turned to less dangerous matters. "I'm sure that Mister Langahan can work out a fair hire-price. If that would be acceptable, Sir Cully? Mister Abdullah?"

Abdullah just nodded, while Cully positively beamed.

"Acceptable?" Cully asked, his voice increasingly loud. "It's bloody generous of you, Governor, and so much so that I'll not even question whether or not your Mr. Langahan is willing, but jump upon the offer like a wolf on a three-legged sheep—and no offense intended by the comparison, Mr. Langahan, no offense intended at all, sir."

"None taken, Sir Cully." Langahan smiled genially. "It would, of course, be my privilege to be of any assistance I could provide."

"Ah, good. Well, then, to finalize this ugly talk of business, Samir, we'll just need the barest sailing crew, and they may leave their nets safely ashore here—I doubt we'll be doing much fishing, all in all. We'll take on more crew in Pironesia—I'm not going to take any more of your grandsons away from you than I need to, as I can't say how long we'll need the barkentine, mind you, but—"

"But the hiring-price will, of course, be by the week—or month?—and I see no problem, Mr. Abdullah," Langahan said. "Provisions, Sir Cully?"

"We'll provision in Pironesia; have to stop there anyway, and my suspicion is that the marines will be happier living on smoked mutton and beef than even the finest of dried fish, all in all—not to mention rum and beer. I don't like it when marines are unhappy—they tend to pout."

Henderson smiled, and Halloran merely nodded at the mention of marines, and old Samir's face was impassive, but Langahan leaned forward. "Marines?"

"You know," Cully said, his voice now definitely slurred, "those fellows in the blue uniforms? I'll definitely need a good company, and—oh, excuse me, Mr. Langahan, I'm an old man, and I've dined far too well tonight for a man of my age. God takes pity, so it's said, on drunkards and fools, and I fully qualify on both accounts, the latter in particular at the moment." He clapped a hand to Niko's shoulder. "Thankfully, another of our Order is behaving properly. Not that I'm surprised, mind you. The Order's always been lucky when it comes to our oddities—and no offense is intended, Sir Niko, but your knighthood is every bit as much an oddity as Lady Ellen's is or Sister Mary's was, may her soul rest in peace—and more so than the Saracen's." He stopped himself. His face was ashen white, and he looked like he was about to cry. "*Damn* me, I once swore I'd never speak Mary's name without remembering her properly, and here I am too old and too drunk, and . . ."

He held up a hand as he fought for control of himself, and the English all looked away, while the Abdullahs, understandably, stared.

"By your leave, sir." Mid-ship-man Turnbull, who had been silently watching, pushed back from the bench and stood himself straight. "I'm the senior midshipman, Sir Cully; it's my privilege, I believe."

"Indeed it is," Cully said, wiping at his eyes. "Please. If you would, if you know . . ."

"My privilege, sir," he repeated. The only criticism of Cully's drunken state that Niko could see was in the repetition, and in the way Turnbull held himself. He found himself more than a little jealous of Turnbull's self-confidence; Turnbull was, after all, no more than a year older than Niko, and still beardless—a boy, who held himself, at least for the moment, like a man.

"I'll need but a moment. Gentlemen, charge your glasses, if you please," Turnbull said, holding out his own. The Navy officers and the Governor were immediately on their feet, the Abdullahs only a little slower, and Niko the slowest of all.

Turnbull waited patiently until all the glasses were filled, then raised his own.

"Gentlemen, I give you Lady Mary Catherine de Camp et du Maurier," he said, pronouncing the name with a curious lilt to his voice, "late of the Abbey of St.

Almesbury; sealed Knight of the Order of Crown, Shield, and Dragon. Lady Mary, who protected the infant crown-prince-that-was and king-to-be from the traitors' knives and swords with her own body, having no more armor to offer His Majesty than her own back; Lady Mary, who bore her scars and her pain—and the cursed Sandoval—with courage and grace and unfailing courtesy to all for years after, until her last day; Lady Mary, most foully murdered by the cursed false knight Alexander Smith, while she slept in her bed.

"I don't ask that she rest in peace, gentlemen, because I know that she does. I know that God Himself rose to greet her upon her arrival at the Pearly Gates, and I say that any God who would not gather Lady Mary to His Bosom is no God I'd care to worship.

"*Lady Mary.*" He raised his glass and drained it.

"Lady Mary."

"Lady Mary."

Niko had expected Cully to stop leaning on him the moment that they rounded the bend, but Cully surprised him.

"Easy, boy," he said. "Let me rest for a moment." Using his stick to steady himself, he lowered himself to an awkward crouch, teetered, and would have fallen if Niko hadn't rushed to grab hold of his shoulders.

"Shit, boy, I'm getting too old for this." His voice was still slurred, although there was no need to keep up the pretense. "Think that it worked?"

"Worked, Sir Cully?" Niko didn't understand.

"Worked. It's a simple English word. Worked, as in, did they believe that I know far more than I'm saying, that I've figured out what the source of these swords is, and that all that's needed is to kill those responsible. Shit, boy, shit I hope it did. Gossip travels fast, but gossip about an old man making up stories won't do any good at all.

"Drank like a man who knows something awful—and that I do, that I am—but nothing useful, dammit all, nothing useful, nothing to do except paint a bright target on both of our backs and see whose arrows sprout out of it."

The drinking hadn't been some sort of ruse? "You're really drunk, Sir Cully?"

"If you know some way to down more than two bottles of wine without getting drunk, boy, you be sure to let me know. In the morning, in the morning. Now help me up."

Interlude 4: The Saracen

Envy is a sin, and we all are sinners.

I try to avoid sin, but I fail, time and time again. Lust I can usually conquer—always in deed, if not in the occasional momentary thought, as I've not had a woman since I shaved my head as a novice, and the occasional dreams of the flesh that haunt my nights are just demons to be cast out by awakening.

Greed has rarely tempted me; I think that's a gift of my birth and upbringing. I save my wrath for the appropriate. As critical as I can be of myself—and I do try—I don't think of myself as slothful.

But envy, ah, envy. I am filled to bursting with envy.

I envy my brother Michael his birth order; I envy Father his easy laugh. I envy the Abbot General his wisdom and authority, and I envy Gray his devotion—carrying Red is far more of a burden than White, as the Nameless has never other than lightened my load.

The thing that Gray most envies about me, I think, is

my home—what he thinks of as my home, although he's wrong. Fallsworth is a wonderful place, granted, and it's been my family's home for many, many years. I think I know every tree in the woods that's bigger around than a man's arm, and while Mother complains about the castle being drafty no matter how often the stones are mudded, it's always seemed warm and homey to me.

But just homey, not home. When Father dies, it will be Michael's home, not mine, and while I'm sure I'll be welcome when I visit, I will be visiting then, just as I do now.

My home, like Gray's, is the Order of Crown, Shield, and Dragon, and it always is with me, and while it comforts me, it doesn't merely comfort me . . .

In that, I fail again: pride, too, is a sin.

I am a sinner who cannot and will not repent of that.

—Bear

He had even started dreaming in English.

That was a good thing, he guessed. Probably.

Whistling in time with his quick pace, Stavros made his way through the twisting streets, down toward the docks, his teabag over his shoulder.

It was a long walk down from the hills to the docks, but he didn't mind, not at the moment. Even from the cluster of sunoikia up in the hills, he could see that there were new ships in port, and that meant work, which meant money—and other things, as well, and it was high time he got back to sea, if only to avoid the long daily walk, although he certainly had better reasons than that.

Sunoikia closer to the water were more convenient, and of better quality than the miserably stuffy room at the edge of town that he shared when ashore, but the ones at the fringe of the city were far cheaper, and he wouldn't have left his few miserable possessions unguarded even in the better ones, not when they would fit in his teabag, and when he could reliably assume that everybody in any of the sunoikia was a thief.

Like everybody else, Stavros used his seabag as a pillow, and was not unusual in making a point to empty and repack it in view of the others, to make sure everybody in the sunoikia understood the scantness of his possessions. Necessary, given how both Hellenes and their English masters tolerated thievery in practice, if not in law.

He would have smiled to himself if he ever much smiled.

Sunoikia, indeed. He was thinking in Hellenic, as usual, which he supposed was a good thing, one way or the other. He talked in his sleep from time to time, Elikina said, but always in English, which she thought strange—although it was unremarkable, under the circumstances.

He certainly thought in one or the other most of the time, and that was, certainly, all for the best. He didn't even think of the ZZZZZ as the ZZZZZ, or as *hay'at al-amr bilma'ruf wa al-nahi 'an al-munkar* or even as al-Bilma, but, rather, as "the Committee" when he did, and he tried not to think of it at all, and sometimes he even succeeded.

He thought about himself all the time, but as Stavros Kechiroski—known as "Stavros Andropolounikos" dockside because of his origin; Andropolouniki were not common this far south—and he never even thought of himself as Nissim al-Furat anymore, and, truth to tell, days and even weeks went by without him thinking of Nissim's home.

Once a month, at least when he was in the satrapal capital, he would find some time, privacy, pen, and paper—the privacy was the hardest to come by; time the easiest—and write down everything he had seen that even might be of interest, using the simple substitution code where Hellenic letters substituted for Pharsi ones. Pharsi, of course, not Arabic; even though it was highly unlikely that Royal Navy Intelligence ever would come across any of his writings, much less break the code, it could happen, and the added misdirection might be useful. Let them think that the near-mythical Hassasanites had been reborn, if they would. The Committee traced its lineage from much more reputable origins, even though it was said that there had been an assassin or two involved in the early days, and in the long run would do—it probably had done—far more damage to the Dar al-Harb than a bunch of screaming killers waving swords possibly could.

If he was to be seen writing, or even his writing was seen, what of that? Many a common sailor knew his letters, after all—the Hellenes more so than the English, for some reason—and he wouldn't be the only sailor ever to dream of striking for a purser-clerk's cushy billet and higher pay.

He always folded his reports carefully, then completely wrapped the folded paper in clay. The clay would be deposited in the same spot under an upthrust root of an old oak tree a mile out on the northern road out of the city. He had a woman in the village just beyond the vineyards—more of a whore, really; he was sure that Elikina took on other men when he was away, as she could hardly get by on the few coppers he gave her, despite her smiling protestations to the contrary—which would easily account for his travels, should anybody ever stop and ask him.

Not that anybody ever did, although dropping off his

reports was always the most frightening part of what he did; it always felt like curious eyes were watching him from the dark, and it took all his self-control not to look around. If somebody was there, the last thing he ought to be doing was engaging in some furtive looks.

Stavros had no idea who picked up his reports, or when, but whoever it was of necessity knew where he left his reports, and if his unseen brother—surely it would be only one?—fell into Crown hands, and could be made to talk, it would be a simple matter to lie in wait for Stavros. He had heard of an occasional spy of the Dar al-Islam being captured, although had never heard of one being captured alive.

A fist-sized clump of clay wouldn't draw attention by itself even if discovered, and was unlikely to be discovered by accident—particularly since Stavros always made sure to empty his bowels there on any trip, in or out of the city, whether or not he was leaving a message—but the weakness of it all came from the necessity.

The Committee was like one of the wonderful grinding machines that the Hellenes used to make their tasty, wonderful pork sausage—Hellenes loved their filthy swine, and of course, being a Hellene, so did Stavros—in went all sorts of scraps, and out came something useful, he hoped, although it would be a long time, he suspected, before he would know if he had, indeed, ever been of any use.

The only thing he knew for certain was that he had not been recalled, and that he was to continue, and continue he would. He had been pledged to the Committee for a full ten years, not counting his two years of training, and then—

Well, it was best not to think about then. It would only make his present life that much less endurable, and it was certainly a good enough life for the likes of Stavros Kechiroski, eh?

Stavros made his way through the twisting streets in the pre-dawn light, whistling a British sailor's tune, as though it would ward away the Press, were there gangs about this early, which there sometimes were, although usually not.

The tune wouldn't, not by itself; the sealed certificate sewed into the lining of his teabag, however, would and, at least these days, enough of the local sailors had such certificates that the Press rarely bothered any sailor who didn't run from them.

There would be no point in stealing it, although you couldn't count on a thief to be sensible, as it wouldn't do anybody else any good. It described him, as all such certificates did: the mole on his left wrist and the pattern of scars on his back were drawn in ink on the certificate, and while there were more than a few other men of his height, with black hair and short fingers, the scars and mole were distinctive.

There was another thing about him that would have been distinctive. Boys in Tikritiza had by tradition been held off from being circumcised until they joined the Arm at fifteen, and while that was not unique, it was unusual, and Nissim had long since suspected that Shaykh Tzidiki's fatwa on the subject had more to do with the Shaykh's involvement in the Committee than they had with anything else, as holy and learned a man as the Shaykh was.

Instead of participating in the Fitna feast and marching off to join the Arm, Nissim had been sent away to learn other skills, and his foreskin was to be left intact until his work was completed.

Another three years and he would, finally, achieve at least that level of fitnah—of fitness, *fitness*—and could think of himself as a true man, and not, even in the back of his mind, as an uncircumcised pig of a Hellene.

He patted at the spot on his bag where his certificate was concealed. While his training had included counterfeiting, his release certificate was entirely genuine; he had begun his real service to the Committee by being impressed, dragged off the streets by a press gang less than a mile from these very docks.

It had, of course, been unpleasant, particularly at first. The bosun's mate in whose charge the new landsmen aboard the *Holofernes* had been placed had taken a particular liking to him, unfortunately.

Not that it was all bad. Sullivan's influence had largely kept him out of the rigging and on the deck crew, which had been just fine with him, and provided him with more than enough gossip that eventually, when they were given leave on Malta—impressed landsmen, no matter how apparently docile, were never given leave where they might find some place to flee until they earned their buttons—went into his reports.

But he had kept his head down—in more ways than one, alas; the mate's appetites were insatiable—and obeyed orders, and accepted every bit of abuse and indignity with neither exceptionally much nor suspiciously little protest, and had received his discharge three months to the day before word had reached Pironesia that impressments were now to be three years instead of two.

But that was in the past, and this was a beautiful day,

and there were several new ships in the harbor, and likely a job to be had. What with the activity of the Press of late, masters were paying good wages for experienced seamen, and Stavros' dockside reputation was good enough that he would more than likely not have to produce his record book, much less his discharge papers, before signing on.

Rigger, topman, carpenter, deckhand, cook—he had done it all in the Navy and since, and he knew the waters around at least two dozen ports of call well enough to be a welcome hand at the tiller or wheel in the rocky waters around Malta, or near the sandbars that grounded many a merchantman off Fletesque at low tide to wait until either men in hard-rowing launches, or, more usually, the high tide, pulled them free.

He always preferred a Malta run, of course, as that was one of the three places he knew to look for signs. He had seen the chalked three wavy lines that meant "find instructions" in more ports than he could count, although they weren't intended for him anywhere except Malta, and here, on the corner of—

Really. The three wavy lines *were* chalked on the the side of old Nicolou's place. They hadn't been there yesterday; he always made a point of passing by the corner of Dog and Pony at least once a day whenever he was in the city.

He didn't miss a step or a note, of course, although he could feel his pulse quicken, and it was only because he was walking in time to the tune that he didn't have to force himself to maintain the same pace. He hadn't seen that sign in Pironesia in more than a year.

It meant something—one of three things. The best possibility, of course, was that he had been recalled, and the worst that his unseen proctor had been caught and made to talk. If it was the former, it would just be a matter of digging down deep into the soil where he had, when he had first arrived in Pironesia, buried the sealed clay jar containing his merchant's clothes, papers, and money, then walking up the coast far enough that nobody would recognize him as Stavros Andropolounikos, and taking passage to some trucal port where he could find a True Believer trader bound for Sfax, or Algiers, or any port along the coast.

If it was the second, he was likely a dead man, although he would take what pains he could, and hope that the brother had deliberately left out a few details as to how the message would be left—which would be a recall, of sorts, although not the one that he wanted.

And the third . . . well, that would be the most interesting.

He needed to do it as quickly as possible, but there was no reason to seem to be hurrying, and every reason not to. The British were not always as clumsy as he had been taught that they were, but there was some justice in that appraisal, and if he saw a squad of soldiers watching the tavern, he could and would just walk on, and wait until later.

But there were none such at old Ari's, and the common room was crowded with sailors, some getting an early start on their daily drinking, but most of them with their packed sea bags under one foot or clutched between their knees as they sat at their benches, bolting down the last decent meal that was likely to slip down their throats for some time to come. There were good things to be said about shipboard life, if not many, but the quality of the food was not high among them.

Over in the far corner, four were busy in a game of one-thumb, and the small stack of quarterpence in front of Marko the tailor showed that Marko, once again, had found himself some easy prey. Marko met his glance for a moment, then returned to his game, and Stavros let his gaze swing by, not having any particular reason or desire to ruin things for Marko. The others— Pireausians, from the look of them—would learn soon enough, although Stavros didn't understand why a perfectly good cooper would waste his time cheating for pennies in port when there was always work for a man of his skills, any more than he did why a cooper had a tailor's nickname.

Ari himself spotted Stavros, and scurried over, wiping his filthy hands on his not-much-less filthy apron. "Stavros!" he said, greeting him with a quick smile. "Shipping out?"

"I don't know," he said. "I thought I'd get something to eat before I checked down at the docks." He patted at his belly. "I think I can feel my backbone—bread and onions, and some wine, perhaps?"

Ari's broad smile became less real around the edges. "Oh? No berth yet?"

Stavros knew what that meant, and he produced a copper coin, and flipped it to the innkeeper.

The smile changed back. "Some sausage, as well?" The copper still lay on his fat palm, and he was apparently rethinking his concern about Stavros's ability to pay. "I'm sure you'll find a berth—you could sign a chit?"

"I think I'd better see if I can find a berth before I celebrate—as fond as I am of your wonderful sausages."

"As you wish, then," Ari said as he closed his hand around the coin.

A departing sailor always had good credit, at least until the ship left port—Ari's son made it a point to greet incoming merchantmen, a bagful of debt-chits in his hand, to be sure that Fat Ari's was paid off before any debtor sailors were. A sailor sometimes—often—didn't have two quarterpence to clink together, but as long as he had a berth, he had enough credit at Ari's for a good meal, and probably enough more for a quick turn with one of the whores in the back rooms.

Stavros took a seat on one of the benches, as the smell of freshly baked bread wafted in through the open door, followed a moment later by Ari with a head-sized loaf of bread and a bunch of onions on a clay plate, and a tall mug of presumably watered wine clutched in his big fist.

The walk had turned Stavros's normal good appetite into something urgent and painful; he gulped down his food and washed it down with the wine as though he hadn't eaten for a week, rather than just a little less than a day. There was nothing special about the bread, not really, but the one thing you could count on about freshly baked shore-bread was that you'd never take a bite and see half a weevil-worm wiggling back at you, although he had had to eat weevilled bread, and worse, in his time.

Conversation flowed around him, about as usual. It was possible to learn a lot in a waterfront inn; some of it was of use to a sailor, and perhaps to others, as well. The *O'Reilly* had taken on half a dozen new hands, and the *Spirikos* even more, and there were sailors on the pumps night and day, most likely because of shipworm, of which the *Spirikos* was sorely afflicted, and which would only get worse, as Aristides was either too pressed to fulfill some long-standing contracts, or too cheap—or, most likely, both—to spend a month or more on the beach at Athenai for even a patchwork refit, and the worms would likely get to the keel before he did give in and spend the time and money, and he would expect his carpenter to work miracles indefinitely in the interim.

Three Guild ships were in port, as well, and they were all taking on hands for a trip out to Darmosh Kowayes, a place that Stavros Andropolounikos had no particular interest in going, and Nissim al-Furat even less.

"You ever sail on a Guild ship, Stavros?" Fat Egidio more lisped than asked, as his mouth was full with at least his third fist-sized loaf of bread, to which he quickly added a swallow of wine. His mouth split in a grin that dribbled some of the glop into his thick black beard. Egidio—known as Egidio Aristides, as he claimed, at least when sufficiently drunk, to be the bastard of a Thessalonikan grandee, although which grandee his supposed father was did have a tendency to change, depending on just how drunk he was—was another ex-impressee, whose time of service had overlapped Stavros's, although they'd never served together on the same ship. "I understand life on a Guild ship can be . . . very interesting."

Stavros allowed himself to show some anger. "Well, I'm told that it is, and that you'd better know than I would how *interesting* it all can be, from how Bosun Flaherty used to say about how you had the prettiest mouth he'd ever had the pleasure of."

There probably was a Bosun Flaherty somewhere in the Navy, but Stavros didn't know one, and he couldn't, offhand, remember any of the names of the officers and bosuns and mates aboard either of the two ships that Egidio had been on, although he had at the time, of course, included what names and other information he'd had in his reports.

Egidio's face darkened, and he drew himself up straight, not quite rising from the bench. "I—"

"Oh, sit down, Aristides," another of the sailors said. "Or go outside—if the two of you knock over my wine fighting, you can each find out how interesting it is to have a foot up your back passage—and I don't have to take the time to tear my toenails ragged before I do, as I already did that last night." His tone was light, but he was a big man, and there was a serious undercurrent, and Stavros raised his hands, fingers spread, in surrender, smiling broadly.

"Ah," Stavros said, "I'm not looking for a fight—just a ship, and—" he let a pained expression come over his face, "—and my bread and onions are going through me like grain through a duck." He rose and scooped up his teabag, and quickly made his way through the back door and down the steps, across the stones, then up the steps to the pergula, the laughter trailing off behind him.

It was a four-holer, closed on all four sides but open to the sky, probably to help the odors escape on the wind—but from the smell, the slop barrels beneath hadn't been emptied in too long. More important, the chalk marks were in the right place on the door, and it was, at the moment, unoccupied, leaving him free from the necessity of grunting and loitering on the seat until he could have a moment of privacy.

Not that he needed much time. The second floorboard from the wall was disgustingly damp, but loose, and the fresh clay holding the folded sheet of paper was quickly in his hand.

He listened for the sound of footsteps, and hearing none, opened it.

Most of the symbols he could read at a glance, but it took a moment for him to puzzle out the words that had been spelled phonetically. Ah: "Marienios," and "hiring."

The Marienios *is hiring*, it said. *There are two knights aboard. Sign on. Important.*

There was still no sound of footsteps, so he quickly urinated on the paper and then folded the soggy mess in roughly the same way that it had been, mashed the clay around it, and put it back where it had been, then seated himself on the bench.

Interesting, and as interesting for what the note didn't say as what it did, although the symbol for "important" was very unusual, as though it was necessary to emphasize to somebody with Nissim's harsh training that a specific instruction was to be obeyed.

But it didn't say for him to report. Was that because his brother would trust him to report, as always? Or was it because, just possibly, he wouldn't need to, that he would be found, that his unseen brother would finally identify himself to Stavros?

That would be wonderful. He couldn't be left out in the Dar al-Harb with such knowledge. If that was to happen, he would either have to be recalled—or killed, of course, and if that was the will of the Committee, he would go to his grave with the same smile on his face that he would otherwise take to his hidden cache.

But enough of that. For now, the question was how to get hired on aboard the *Marienios*. That shouldn't be difficult. Stavros kept a careful eye on the coming and goings of ships in the port, which was perfectly natural for a sailor without a permanent berth, so he didn't even have to think about affecting ignorance.

The *Marienios* hadn't been in port the night before, so it must be freshly arrived, and that meant that it had been at most a scant few hours since his unseen brother had seen it, decided for himself that it would be useful for Stavros to be on it, then left both the note and the chalk mark, alerting Stavros.

Very interesting. The *Marienios* belonged to the Abdullah family, and while Stavros had had no reason to suspect that they were other than the heretic dogs that they affected to be, it wasn't impossible—

No, it was. A clan that large couldn't keep such a secret, not for even one generation, and certainly not for many.

Still, he thought, as he hefted his teabag to his shoulder, he wasn't alone, anymore. His elder brother was near, and watching.

Although it did feel otherwise most of the time, it gave him a warm feeling to know that he was not alone.

Stavros whistled as he headed down toward the docks, where the *Marienios* waited for him.

Chapter 8: Return to Pironesia

> There's reward—and as much joy as I'm capable of—
> in doing that which I do well. Every once in a while,
> though, it's useful for me to be reminded that I'm not
> nearly as good at any of it as I would wish, and some-
> times even believe.
>
> —Gray

There was a wizard at the bow.

Not that he looked particularly like a wizard, Gray thought. Sigerson was tall and slender—even skinny—but utterly healthy looking. Most wizards, at least most that Gray had met, looked like they were about to collapse at any moment, some from consumption and some from, well, overconsumption.

Not Eric Sigerson. Clear of skin, clean-shaven and almost dainty in appearance, his hair was slicked back, neatly combed into place, and remained so, despite the wind. He wore a distinctly unwizardlike but apparently genuine smile that seemed to be an almost permanent fixture on his long face.

His clothes were almost entirely conventional and, except for the boots—none of it looked, well, wizardly. While he had his formal robes aboard—Sigerson's taciturn manservant had commandeered the tailor's quarters to iron them—this morning he was dressed in a blindingly white blousy cotton shirt under his white linen jacket and matching waistcoat, and the ends of his trousers were neatly bloused into a pair of thick-soled boots that looked to be more suitable for the woods than anything else.

Expensive, Gray thought, although he had little experience with the cost of clothes; the Order provided for him. But the buttons on Sigerson's jacket and waistcoat appeared to be ivory, and not just bone, and the shoulders didn't bunch up as Sigerson moved, which spoke of good—and therefore expensive—tailoring.

Save for the massive silver ring on the index finger of his right hand and the slim ivory wand that, at least when aboard ship, was always looped about his neck on a thin and delicate-looking silver chain, it would have been easy to think of him as some wealthy Londinium merchant with noble pretensions, and Gray tried to think of him that way; it made it all the easier to dislike him.

"And a good morning to you, Sir Joshua," Sigerson called out, although Gray hadn't greeted him at all.

"Good morning, Mr. Sigerson," Gray said. "Did you rest well?"

Sigerson smiled, his knees automatically giving and recovering as the bow bounced up and down. "Not one whit, in fact—I spent most of the night heaving up what little I ate last night. Crawling about belowdecks doesn't agree with me." He seemed positively cheerful about it, which was strange, as was his apparent comfort at the bow.

Then again, there wasn't much about Sigerson that wasn't strange, at least from Gray's point of view. Even his ordinariness was discomfiting.

"Your morning coffee, Mr. Sigerson?" Midshipman Reifer already had a steaming mug in his hand, and Sigerson climbed down from the bow to the foredeck to accept it.

"Thank you, Mr. Reifer," he said, accepting the mug but not immediately drinking it.

The boy beamed as he walked away, not seeming to notice Gray.

Sigerson waited until the midshipman had disappeared down the forward hatch, took a sniff of it, made a face, and flung the contents overboard, noting with manifest irritation that the wind had splattered his sleeve with a few stray drops.

"Never did acquire a taste for the stuff," he said, "but I'd rather waste it than hurt the boy's feelings—he seems to have rather taken a shine to me, eh?"

"Yes. I believe most of the crew has, in fact." Which was understandable.

"Understandable," Sigerson said, echoing Gray's thoughts so closely that Gray looked twice to see that Sigerson's hands were nowhere near his wand, "under the circumstances, I suspect."

Sigerson had spent much of the previous two days in the lower hold with his bag, supplies—and manservant, who apparently functioned as his assistant, as well as his valet.

"Not that the *Wellesley* has what I'd call a bad case of shipworm," he said, "but the best case is none at all, and I think that I've made a good start on that." He cast a glance over his shoulder. "Be willing to take a turn in the *Winfrew* and *Cooperman*, particularly if we're going to be in port for some time. Best done in drydock, of course, but . . ." He shrugged. "Messier and less effective this way, but the mess cleans off." He frowned as he considered the fingernails of his free hand. "Eventually."

"I don't know how long we'll be there," Gray said. "Not long, I'm hoping. Depends on what the news is, I suppose."

"Yes, it would at that."

Off in the distance, a point or so off the port bow, the ancient lighthouse that marked the entrance to the port of Pironesia stood watching, as it had for centuries, and beyond that, Gray could make out two sets of sails, although little more than that.

He looked astern. Both of the two miserable sloops that were all that DuPuy had let him have had fallen far behind. He could barely see the pennants atop the *Winfrew*'s mainmast, and the other ship, was, he devoutly hoped, simply too far behind that, rather than lying at the bottom of the sea. He forced himself not to shake his head in disgust. The old admiral was as stubborn as a Lancaster mule, and had spent hours—literally hours, hours that Gray didn't have to spare—over maps, showing what he knew of the deployment of Dar warships, and emphasizing the miserably few ships that the Malta Fleet had to hold them at bay.

It was true, Gray was sure, but it was also unimportant in the larger scheme of things, and he was every bit as unsurprised as he was furious at DuPuy's refusal to see it that way. Gray had enough authority to get DuPuy to hear him out, but not to make him listen. The same orders that had had Halloran in Pironesia jumping at Gray's command had been met with little more than an upraised eyebrow by the Malta Admiral.

And this time, there was no jitney trip across town with the King at the other end of it to threaten with. Even if he had been able to make that threat, Gray had the definite impression that he would have had to follow through, and that it would have taken the King himself to pry a decent squadron from the Admiral.

The Abbot General would, of course, lodge a protest with the Admiralty, but if DuPuy gave a tinker's dam about that, it didn't show—he seemed to almost relish the idea.

Gray had had to accept what he could—a wretched two ships, crewed mainly by landsmen and beached officers, and a detachment of marines so few that calling them a company was a sad joke.

And then there was the wizard, who wasn't, strictly speaking, under the Admiral's orders, which was why he had come along. DuPuy had watched with cold eyes as Sigerson's man had loaded his trunks into the jollyboat for the trip to the *Wellesley*'s mooring.

Not that the Admiral had been openly combative, or even utterly uncooperative—the courier ship to Gibraltar had been dispatched a day early for the asking, even though DuPuy knew that it carried Gray's protest to the Abbot General, as well as his other letters.

There was another way to handle it. I had the definite

impression that Throckmorton would have been more sensible. Rolling the Admiral's head across the table would likely have persuaded him. I had one of my men do that at a peace conference with the Tien'shen, once.

And how well did that work out for you? Did they make peace?

It worked out perfectly well; I conquered Tien'shen, didn't I?

"If you let me know what you're thinking, Sir Joshua, I might be able to be of help."

Gray shook his head. "I wasn't thinking about much," he said, not caring to share the Khan's thoughts with anybody, Sigerson in particular. "Just enjoying the morning, such as it is."

He never slept well on a ship, and there had been too many shipboard nights of late. Far too many; a minor thing to resent Cully for.

Bear, on the other hand, was still snoring below, his broad face in his usual sleeping smile. It didn't bother Gray that Bear would bear up under discomfort with more equanimity than Gray could manage—but to find the rocking of a ship to be an aid to sleep was almost an insult.

Sigerson nodded. "If you don't mind a personal comment, Sir Joshua . . . ?"

The Khan seemed to brighten at his side. *I don't mind him making a personal comment, if I can kill him for it.*

Shh.

"Not at all, of course."

"You don't seem to be much for enjoying things," he said. "Me, I've spent most of my time in Malta crawling through the bellies of more ships than I care to count, in pursuit of the repellent but crafty shipworm, and there's nothing at all pleasant about that, I can assure you. Deucedly filthy work—necessary work, of course, but, nonetheless disgusting for all of that . . ." He shook his head and looked down at his sleeve again. "A moment, if you please?"

He reached into his short jacket with his free hand, and pulled a pinch of some powder out of somewhere and quickly rubbed it against his sleeve, thoroughly smearing the coffee stain into a larger, dirtier one. He unlooped his wand from around his neck, careful not to muss his hair and, muttering something under his breath, lightly tapped the wand against the stain, then blew on his sleeve.

The stain vanished, as though it had never been there.

"There," he said, smiling as looped his wand's chain back of his head with a practiced flip, then tucked the wand away into his jacket. "That's better—as I was saying, it seems to me to be sensible to enjoy what one can, when one can, even if it's something as trivial as having one's favorite jacket clean, eh? You should enjoy yourself more, perhaps?"

"You have some suggestion, maybe? My sleeve is perfectly clean."

"Well . . . since you ask, I fancy myself a decent singlestick player, and I'd expect that a Knight of the Order of the Crown, Shield, and Dragon would be a better one—could I persuade you into going a few rounds with me before we get into port?" He gestured toward the open space on the main deck that Gray and Bear did their daily practices on. "There seems to be ample room, and I can have Bigglesworth chalk the lines while we dress?" He had an affectation of sometimes making a simple declarative sentence a question, and used it just often enough that each time it was an annoying surprise rather than a reliable irritation.

"You have your pads aboard?"

"Of course," Sigerson said. "And my sticks, and my slippers, and a spare set of slippers and sticks, if you don't have such handy."

His smile was insulting, somehow, although Gray couldn't quite put his finger on how. He wished he could. Surely Gray couldn't dislike the man for no reason?

Do it. I'd like to see you beat him until he pisses blood.

Well, there was something in the young wizard's manner that just cried for a beating, and Gray had, like all Order novices, mastered the sticks before being given even his first practice sword.

Gray wouldn't hurt him too badly. The padding minimized damage, but couldn't prevent it, and Gray would have to be careful not to finesse past the padding at the juncture of gauntlet and tunic, as he had made a habit of back in his youth, when irritated, as he could easily break Sigerson's wrist without half trying.

But it would do him good to hurt somebody, at least a little, and if that meant he had been carrying the Khan too long, well, he had, in fact, been carrying the Khan too long.

"I'll see if I remember how." Gray smiled.

"It will, I'm sure, come back to you." Sigerson smiled back. "Probably more quickly than I'll care for, but what of that, eh? So, have we a match?"

"Well, as you say, it's a fine morning, and let's enjoy it, shall we?"

"After you, Sir Joshua."

The cut over Gray's right eye had closed up nicely, and his left wrist had stopped throbbing by the time he was ready to climb down the ladder and into the jollyboat for the trip into the dock.

Too many of the sailors were grinning, although none of them met his eyes.

Kill one or two, then. That will establish that you're not to be taken lightly.

Gray ignored the Khan. Truth was, Sigerson was simply better with a pair of sticks than Gray was, and being a poor loser wouldn't make that fact any better, but worse.

Still, he was seriously considering inviting Sigerson to join him and Bear in their daily workouts. Under those less restrictive sparring rules, he could return the injuries with what Sigerson would be likely to decide was usurious interest.

Did he want to do that because he had to maintain his status with the Navy men, or because he resented being beaten by a skinny, ascetic wizard?

"Sir Joshua?" Captain Johansen called out from the quarterdeck, where he stood, alone, sipping a cup of coffee and leaning against the rail. "Might I have a moment?"

Oh, what was it now?

You know what it is.

"Any orders in particular, Sir Joshua?" Johansen asked, straightening as Gray mounted the steps. "Other than my keeping the crew aboard?"

That again.

Gray shrugged. "I didn't tell you to keep the whole crew aboard," he said slowly, patiently. "I said that just an anchor watch won't do—I don't know when we'll be leaving, or for where. I want you to be prepared to raise sail the moment the jollyboat puts me back on that ladder. Same for the other two ships," he said, with a jerk of the thumb skyward to where a commodore's pennant floated from the mainmast, as he couldn't point toward the *Winfrew* or the *Cooperman*, neither of which had rounded the lighthouse yet.

DuPuy hadn't been agreeable about much, but he had gone along with the necessity of the brevet promotion, since the lieutenant in command of the *Winfrew* was senior to Johansen, even though half his career had been spent on the beach, and probably deservedly so.

"In the Navy, Sir Joshua, we say 'aye, aye,' when given an order, and then we carry it out, whether or not it makes much sense."

"Which you don't think this does."

"No, sir; I don't. I can't see how, say, a two-hour recall is likely to make much of a difference, one way or the other, on the other end—wherever the other end is. And while the crew of the *Wellesley*, sir, can raise sail and get the old girl moving as fast as any ship in the Navy, I wouldn't want to claim that for . . . other ships, necessarily." His eyes hardened. "I'll do what I'm ordered, sir, so will every officer and man aboard—but I don't much like denying my men anything they've earned, not without necessity, and they've earned a good drunk, and—and other recreations that can't be afforded aboard."

Well, you could always haul a boatload of whores for the men from shore, Gray thought, but didn't say. It was just his irritation. No, Johansen couldn't do any such thing, even more than he couldn't increase the rum ration for the men on the ship. Bad for discipline, and a master who started to let discipline slack would find it hard to take up the slack later.

They were being watched, of course, by every officer and man on deck, although Johansen kept his voice low, as did Gray.

Gray sighed. Part of it wanted to punish every man and officer for seeing him humiliated by Sigerson, and while it would have been easy to blame such pettiness on the Khan, it was entirely his own, and it disgusted him. That didn't mean that it had to rule him, one way or the other.

You think too much, Gray. You can hardly empty your bowels without meditating over whether it's the morally correct thing to do.

He yanked his hand from the Khan, then put it back. No; he would handle this as he wished that he would have had the decency to do by instinct, the way Bear would have.

"You could have them back on board in two hours?" he asked. "Have your mates chase them down wherever they've gone to ground, all over the entire port?"

Gray expected Johansen to admit the absurdity of it, but the captain just smiled and nodded.

"Yes, more or less." Johansen took a puff on his pipe, then went on: "Not that it's difficult. Port section is first up. Finch has a preferred dive just off the docks, and he and Bartlesby tend to hang together ashore, anyway. I'll just have them stay there—even with Finch's, err, stamina, he won't be able to work his way through all the whores for a couple of days. It's just a matter of ordering the leave crew that they're to be within a whistle of that place. Fifteen minutes after I get your signal, sir, there'd be mates blowing pipes all around there, and we'd not lose more than a man or two, if that. Captain Henslow's got a good sergeant—he can do the same sort of thing with the marines. If we're here for a few days, it's just a matter of rotating the mates and corporals on, err, whore duty."

"And the other ships? When they stagger in?"

"I'll tell their masters to restrict leave to Dog Street, half a section at a time. Can't swear I'd get the same compliance that I can promise for the Wellies, but we'll get most of them, and either of them could sail with a section and a half if they had to."

"And if they're late?"

"Adjustments can be made." Any lapse would give Johansen an obvious excuse to put one of his lieutenants on board as commander, something he was probably aching to do. "But you give me two hours warning, sir, and I'll have your squadron anchors up, and heading out the harbor with sails flying from mainmast royales down to the spanker. You have my word on that."

There it was—Johansen had made it a matter of his word. Gray should just have refused to let the captain engage him in conversation at all, but . . .

"Very well, Commodore. Make it so."

Johansen's eyes twinkled, just a little. "Aye, aye, sir. Where are you staying in the city?"

Gray shrugged. He didn't much care where he slept. "Probably at the Governor's palace, in the guest quarters."

"I'll have a sailor on duty at the gate, around the clock. One word from you, and you'll have no cause to regret the two hours. Thank you for hearing me out." He gestured with his pipe toward the ladder. "I'll not delay you any longer. Best of luck ashore, sir."

"Thank you, Commodore," Gray said, not meaning it for a moment, as he headed for the ladder.

Had Gray been first down, he would have held on to the ladder so that the boat wouldn't rock when Bear got in, but Bear just sat primly on the bench next to Sigerson, trusting to the sailors to keep it all steady, and surely enough they did.

"Going ashore, Mr. Sigerson?"

"Thought I might, if you don't have any objection," Sigerson said. "A good meal on solid land would suit me well. And perhaps, I thought, you might find me of some use, one way or another." He patted at his bag. "And if not, well, I don't know much about whistles and signals and suchlike, but Bigglesworth does—eh, Biggles?"

Sigerson's man had just sat still, not speaking. He didn't talk much. "Yes, sir," he said. "I finished with my twenty some years ago, but I think I can remember Recall All Hands. If you want to stay with the *Wellesley*, I'll have you aboard well before she lifts anchor, Mr. Sigerson, and no worries on that score."

He was speaking to Sigerson, but the message was for Gray, and Gray nodded.

"So be it, then. I'll be glad of the company." Gray forced a smile. "Although I don't think we'll have occasion for another lesson in the sticks, not right away."

He had lost, and was sore, but he wouldn't be a sore loser, and he carefully took no notice of what appeared to be a hint of a ghost of a smile on Bigglesworth's face.

The Khan was strangely quiet at his side; Gray guessed that his loss had embarrassed the old warrior. The Khan had only lost once, after all, at anything.

The boat pulled away from the *Wellesley*'s broad side, accompanied by comments from Finch about the slaggardliness of the shorebound oarsmen, whose strokes seemed to Gray to be deep and well-coordinated enough, and it was only a few minutes later that they were climbing up to the solid wood of the dock.

Bear seemed to be wobbly on his feet, as did Sigerson and Finch, something Gray didn't understand. Returning to land was such a natural thing that he didn't have to try to balance himself against the no-longer-rolling motion of the wood beneath his boots, thankfully.

"Governor's palace, I think," he said, hefting his bag to his shoulder. Probably the best place to look for some word of Cully. Cully, of course, would be off somewhere, counting on Gray to follow—and, of course, he would have to do just that—if only to retrieve the boy's live sword, and the boy, Niko, for that matter. He might be hard to find, but it wouldn't be difficult for Gray to set himself on his trail.

Gray hoped that Cully at least had left a trail of breadcrumbs behind him. Bodies would be more likely, under the circumstances, he thought, and for a moment had to glance down to be sure that he hadn't fastened his hand on the Khan.

"Excuse me for interrupting," Sigerson said, "but I think we've already found what you're seeking."

Two knights stood at the far end of the dock, waiting patiently.

Well, two knights of a sort—it was Cully and that Niko boy, hardly a real knight.

That said, he didn't have a bad look about him: he stood easily on the rough wood, if a bit stiffly, the hilts of two scabbarded swords stuck through his sash within easy reach of his hands, and at their approach, his right hand dropped to the hilt of the uppermost of the two swords in a gesture that Gray well recognized, and found himself duplicating, even though the last thing he wanted at the moment was to hear from the Khan, and he snatched his hand away.

The clothes that Cully had stolen from Gray fit the boy well enough, in fact. The only question in Gray's mind was whether he would be sensible and just have them washed and rewashed when this was all over, or burn them.

I would bet on the burning, myself.

Cully gave a knowing smile. "Sir Joshua," he said, as they clasped hands. "Good of you to join us, finally. We've been waiting. You know Sir Niko, I believe, but I've not met your companion."

So that was the way Cully wanted to play it?

Very well; Gray could go along, for the moment. Airing a dispute with a brother knight wasn't something he would want to do out in the open, for that matter, even if—particularly if that knight was Cully.

Bear didn't hesitate; he stepped forward. "Sir Cully," he said, enfolding Cully's hands in his larger ones, "it's good to see you. I was . . . concerned." He released Cully's hands and bowed toward the boy. "Sir Niko."

"Sir David." Niko returned the bow properly, then accepted Bear's hand-clasp as though he had done it a thousand times before.

Dammit, he carried himself well, looking much more knight than fisherboy.

Sigerson stepped forward. "Eric Sigerson," he said, offering a hand instead of bowing. "Fellow of the College."

"Cully of Cully's Woode, of the Order."

"The Order of Crown, Shield, and Dragon, I take it?" Sigerson arched an eyebrow.

"Yes, of course. And when you say the College, you mean His Majesty's College of Wizardry, I take it?"

"Indeed." Sigerson smiled. "And while I'd love to chat with you further, unless I'm missing something—always a possibility—I would think that the four of you have some catching up to do. Would it suit you if I meet you at the Governor's palace in a few hours?"

Gray nodded, but Cully shook his head.

"No," Cully said. "I think it would be best if you accompanied us there now. There have been a few developments."

He gave Gray a long look as though to say that it wouldn't hurt to trust him, just for a while.

You can always kill him later.

It wouldn't come to that.

We'll see.

The old sergeant seemed to find it difficult to relax into his chair; he seemed to have himself at a permanent posture of attention.

He probably sleeps that way, the Khan murmured.

Shh.

"You're sure it was darklings?" Gray asked.

"No, sir. I'm not sure of anything, except what I said. Never shaw a darkling before."

And I hope to never see one again, Fotheringay didn't have to add.

Bear looked up. Bear, with Niko at his side, was bent over Langahan's desk, with maps and charts spread out, going over the report from Rafferty of the *Serenity*, probably for the twentieth time. Gray hadn't been able to draw anything useful out of it, or from the charts, but maybe Bear would, and at least it kept the boy out of Gray's way, for the time being.

"Brought their own soil?" Bear asked.

"Well, whoever dispatched them did," Gray said.

"No." Sigerson shook his head. "That's a common superstition—confusion with the vampire myth, I think. The unholy don't need the soil of their burial place. I doubt that darklings are ever actually buried, in any case, and certainly not in a conventional way. Anything cursed will do to maintain their strength."

"Cursed how?" Niko asked, clearly regretting the question after a quick, irritated look from Cully shut him up.

Sigerson's fingers twitched in his lap. "Any of a number of ways—sprinkling the blood of somebody murdered unshriven is the classic way to deconsecrate soil, but it's not difficult. The Hezmoni used to rape Christian women with bottles of sacramental wine, then drink the wine and piss it out. It's not like there's actual magic involved—just a defilement of holiness. You could probably just burn a cross and do it well enough, if you were of a mind to." He shook his head. "Not something I much like thinking or talking about, not under such pleasant circumstances, eh?" He gestured at their surroundings. "Much better than what was available shipboard."

Cully had commandeered Langahan's office, the one just across the inlaid marble hall from Halloran's, and while, he said, Langahan occasionally popped in to retrieve something from his own files, he didn't make a habit of it.

What Gray really wanted to do was get Cully alone—

in private—but Cully had carefully avoided that, although why, Gray didn't know. It wasn't as though he was afraid of the sharpness of Gray's tongue.

That would have to wait, Cully had said.

No, we'll do it now, Gray had wanted to say, but he kept his tongue under control.

"Took half of the company down with them," Fotheringay said. "Can't say how much of it was these darklings, or the fire, or the sea—we held them off as long as we could, so the *Serry* could break away, and then every man, marine and sailor, went over the side just as fast as we could."

Cully nodded. "Understandable."

"Understandable?" Fotheringay's lips tightened. "To flaming hell with your 'understandable,' sir." There would have been something comical about his lisp, under other circumstances. "It was me orders, sir. Lieutenant—Captain Tucker gave me them orders, just before he slammed the door in my face. Open the seacocks, push her away and abandon ship, he said, so we did."

Bear started to say something, but desisted at a gesture from Gray. The bandages on the sergeant's right hand were fresh, granted, but he had been badly burned all along the right arm, and his face seemed flushed.

"A trace of the fever, I think," Sigerson said. "Are you feeling well, Sergeant?"

"I'll do, sir."

"I'd rather have an honest answer, all in all."

"Yes, sir. I been leeched from crotch to throat, sir, and it don't seem to help much. Seems to make it worse, all in all. But I'll do, sir."

Was it the burns, or the encounter with the darklings?

They hadn't quite touched the sergeant, he had said. Of a certainty they hadn't gotten their hands on him, but . . .

"You saw no sign of swords?"

"Saw plenty of swords, and most of them felt like they were pointed right at me and my captain," Fotheringay said. "But nothing cursed, far as I could tell. The company might have had some more difficulty taking the pirate if there'd been that sort of thing aboard."

Some difficulty? Does he really think that a bunch of marines could stand up to the likes of me?

Of course not, any more than they could have beaten the darklings. But they would have tried.

"Sergeant—"

"If I may, Sir Joshua?" Sigerson leaned forward. "The sergeant has told us at least most of what he knows, I think, and it's probably better that he get some rest before any further interview."

"I can manage. Sir."

"Yes, I'm sure you can," Bear said, after a quick look toward Gray, and Gray's answering nod, "but you can probably manage better with some rest. Burns are nasty things. If I have any more questions about Captain Rafferty's account, I'll come see you later."

Gray kept silent. On the field of battle, a deck of a ship, or in a governor's aide's office, they divided the work so automatically that it only occasionally occurred to Gray that that was just what they were doing. Bear's gentle manner could probably get the sergeant to talk more throughly and certainly less reservedly than Gray could. People tended to relax in Bear's presence in a way that they never seemed to be able to in Gray's, although Gray certainly tried hard enough to force them to relax, when the situation required it.

"Yes, sir." The sergeant struggled to his feet. "But can I see the report, sir?"

"You haven't been shown it yet?"

"No, sir. Not my place. Mr. Rafferty—the *Serry's* captain, came down to the galley and talked to me, but he didn't show me nothing."

"Do you think he misrepresented something, Sergeant?"

There it was. If Gray had asked just that question, in just that way, Fotheringay would have drawn himself up to a stiff brace, focused his eyes on a distant nothing, and grunted a quick "*no, sir,*" but with the same words from Bear, he just shrugged, even though the movement clearly caused him pain.

"No, sir," he said. "I got no complaints about Mr. Rafferty. But I was a little out of my head when he come down to talk to me—got bunged up a little, along with the burn. I just want to be sure that he got—that I got Captain Tucker's last words right. My cap'n died a hero, sir, doing his duty—wouldn't be right if an old sergeant's mumblings made the record wrong."

Gray would have just told him to go away, but Bear nodded, and leafed through the pages. "Ah. Captain Rafferty says his last words were 'For King and country,' just like Lieutenant Finnerty's."

"Shit. Then I got it wrong. Can you—can you do something about it, sir?"

"We can't tamper with a Navy report," Bear said. "That's just a copy that one of the clerks made. But I can ask the Governor to submit a supplement, if you'd like."

"I'm sure Governor Halloran will be happy to comply," Cully said. "What did the captain say?"

"You tell him," the sergeant said, breathing heavily, "you tell him that after Captain Tucker told me to see to the seacocks, and stepped between those things and them women, he shouted, 'Not while I breathe.' "

The sergeant's jaw was clenched so tightly that it was a minor miracle he could speak at all. " 'Not while I breathe,' he said. You tell them that, sir. You tell them all that."

"As you wish, Sergeant." Cully's voice sounded too calm, too mild.

He drew himself up to attention, gave a stiff nod in Cully's direction, and marched out of the office and into the hall, the regular *slap-slap-slap* of his boots quickly becoming uneven and ragged.

Bear started to rise, but desisted at a motion from Gray. The sergeant didn't need any help, or, if he did, the stiff-necked prig could damn well ask for it himself.

"Sentimental man, the sergeant," Cully said, lightly.

"You don't—"

"Of course not. Only a pompous fool would say something like that." Cully grinned. He rose and walked to the desk and tapped a forefinger against the report. "This Tucker doesn't seem to have been a pompous fool. Sergeant Fotheringay's just trying to motivate us a little more."

"Well, he's motivated his way aboard one of the ships, when we leave," Gray said. He wasn't at all happy with the marines aboard the two slopships DuPuy had given them. Whatever you could say about this Fotheringay, he had a proper military manner, and it might be infectious. Then again, so might any fever he had. Something to think about.

But when they were leaving was a more important subject than whether or not they added one damaged marine sergeant to the company. He turned to Cully. "As to when we leave, and for where, that's something that—"

"It's something that I'd just as soon keep between you and me, at least for the moment. With all due respect to Mr. Sigerson, this is an Order matter. And, for all I know, there may be be other reasons for some discretion," he said, tapping a finger against his ear, "and I know for a fact I could use some fresh air, and maybe a simple meal."

"Eminently sensible, I'd say." Sigerson didn't seem to take offense. "If you don't mind, I'm going to take a look at that report, and at the maps. It's not utterly impossible I'll come up with some useful insight."

"Very well." Gray nodded. He rose, adjusting his swords in his sash. "Let's walk down toward the plaza. Bear? Niko, you should probably stay with Mr. Sigerson, or, better just turn in for the night—"

"Sir Niko should definitely come with us." Cully said. "It is, as you say, an Order matter."

Gray drew in a deep breath of the cool night air, then let it out slowly. It was supposed to relax him, although it wasn't doing much good at the moment.

Night had snuck into the city, exposed in its daily stealth by the half-moon that had fully risen, casting everything below in silver and gray.

Beneath the sputtering of lamps, shops along the Street of Sails had long since been closed and barred, and the only things that remained of the market day along the docks were a few scraps of discarded vegetables here and the odd pile of donkey turds there, waiting to be swept into the sewers and dumped into the harbor by the next rain.

Off in the distance, where the hills rose, blackness upon darkness, a distant wolf howled, whether in triumph or frustration Gray didn't know, and didn't much care.

The Street of Sails was set high enough in the city that Gray could look over the low buildings and see the ships lying at anchor in the harbor. Two others were berthed near the *Wellesley*; the stragglers had, finally, made it in, and he had no doubt that firm orders had been given to keep them readied for a quick departure, although he had less confidence than Johansen did that a quick departure would actually happen.

Although to where? If Cully knew, he wasn't saying.

Maybe it would be best to simply take up residence in Pironesia for the weeks it would be before relief would arrive from England. A Knight of the Order, of course, was expected to handle many things by himself, and Gray had no cause to fault himself for his willingness to take matters into his own hands—although he didn't fault himself for not overreaching, the way Cully always did.

But what to do? A live sword, and threats of others about; darklings in the Mediterranean, being conveyed by pirates and God-knows-who-else?

That was more important than Cully having over-reached himself, yes, but Gray didn't know what to do about that. Either.

The Plaza of the Order was quiet, save for the quiet sussuration of the fountain. Gray half expected more darklings to move out of the shadows at them, and the Khan, at his waist, almost vibrated with eagerness, but . . .

But nothing. The evening wind caught the spray from

the fountain and turned it into a light misting that, annoyingly, more refreshed than chilled Gray. It should have made him uncomfortable.

Cully threw a hip over the lip of the fountain and folded his arms across his chest.

"Well, that's about as I should have expected. Nothing." His voice was pitched low. "Too obvious, I expect."

"Obvious?"

"Well, yes. Niko and I have made it a point to stop and pray here the last three nights, before the fountain. I'd have dragged along a chain and anchored myself here like a goat, but I thought that would be, well, a little much. If they're out there, whatever they are, they're patient and cautious, I hope."

"You *hope*?"

Cully gave Gray a look that made him feel like a clumsy first-former again, and Gray didn't know why that didn't bother him as much as it should have.

"Well, the other explanation is that they're gone—along with any clue or hint as to what they are, where this sword came from, and what this is all about. We're short of leads—we don't have any of those pirates to question, and I doubt that we would be able to make darklings talk, even if we had any captive, which we don't.

"Niko and I have been . . . chatting with merchant captains, and going over berthing reports; nothing of any use that I can see. There's a couple ships that regularly call out in the islands that are just enough off-schedule to be of some interest—including that Captain Andros's *Kalends*—but if he stopped off in the outer islands on his regular circuit, he might well have decided that Pironesia is a trifle too hot for his tastes, at least for the time being, for reasons having more to do with his little swindling being exposed than anything else.

"All we have is darklings where there shouldn't be; a fragment of a song, a song that could come from anywhere; a hint of a curved knife—and God knows that curved knives aren't unusual—and a sword that has nothing exceptional about it, save for the soul trapped inside." He spread his hands. "Am I missing something?"

"Yes," Gray said. "A plan to do something about it. Something useful."

"My first notion was to already be out chasing after the source of the sword—of the swords." He frowned. "You were supposed to be chasing after me, bringing along a heavily manned squadron, and not just the *Welly* and two ships that ought to be in drydock."

"I wasn't supposed to catch you in Pironesia?"

"Catch me? I've had the *Marienios* tied up at the dock, waiting for you as confidently as I knew how to wait. I'd rather be off on the trail, but I don't have a trail, dammit."

"And now I've arrived, and—"

"What I can do, I've already done," Cully said. "I've given Ralph a swift kick in the ass, which should get things moving, although I'm sure that he doesn't know any more than do you or I about what the threat is, or where it comes from. Word of pirates carrying darklings about the Med should get Admiral DuPuy some more ships, perhaps . . ."

"Just as likely to get the Gibraltar fleet to inspect things more closely in the Straits," Bear said.

"A lot of good that would do." Gray shook his head. "What are they going to do? Open every box? Wade through every ballast-hold?"

"Regardless, all of that will take some time." Cully rapped his stick against the stones. "But they're here—at least some of them. I can feel it."

"And how reliable is your intuition, Father?" Bear asked, as gently as such a question could be asked.

"It was reliable when I knew that you and Gray would end up kneeling before His Majesty to rise as knights, just as it was unreliable about Alexander, and many other things. But I think the darklings—the ones that attacked us—is more evidence than mere intuition." He turned to Niko. "You don't seem to be saying much, Sir Niko."

"I . . . I don't really have anything to say, Sir Cully," he said.

He still sounded hesitant, and tentative, but at least he had stopped cringing every time anybody so much as looked at him. That probably had something to do with his grip on the hilt of his sword—the live sword, of course, although Gray couldn't tell by looking.

"Well, does your sword have anything to say?" Bear asked. "Anything at all?"

"No." Niko shook his head. "She just wants me to sing to her. I don't think she understands much of this, much of anything."

"Sing?" Gray's forehead wrinkled. Why would a sword want him to sing?

"*Sing,*" Cully said, firmly. "Lullabyes. The sword is a baby."

Bear scowled, an unusual expression on his face. "A baby. You said that the sword wasn't old, but I thought that you meant it was newly created."

"I did." Cully shook his head. "At least, I think I did." He shrugged. "I'm not sure what exactly I meant, or how much of it was me, and how much the sword—and if you're expecting me to apologize for not taking it in hand, you'll have a long wait. Niko, how long does she think that her soul has been locked into that sword?"

Niko gripped the sword even more tightly. "She doesn't know, and she doesn't like me asking about that. It reminds her of the Big—of the man with the knife. She . . . she doesn't seem to think much about time. She knows that she should be hungry, but she isn't . . . and that's about all, I think."

"Can you describe him?" Gray asked. "The man with the knife?"

Cully held up a hand. "I've already asked him that, and he's—"

"And he can damn well answer the question again, Sir Cully." Maybe there was something that Cully had missed. That was at least possible, wasn't it?

Cully's nod was cold. "That may well be," he said, as though answering Gray's thought rather than responding to what he had said. "Try asking her again, Niko."

Gray nodded to himself. At least the boy was well disciplined, if utterly untrained. Niko clearly wanted to protest, but he just settled himself more firmly on the lip of the fountain, and, again, clenched his hand over the hilt of the sword.

"Large . . . sweaty, and the knife, shiny, shiny, shiny, shiny," the boy went on, his eyes tightly closed, his voice high pitched and thick, and trailed off into whimpering, and pleas to bring the baby her mother or something equally pointless.

Cully wasn't watching Niko; he had his eyes on the edge of the plaza, as did Bear. Gray started to turn, but desisted at a quick, be-still movement from Cully's hand.

Did that mean that they saw something? That—

Cully shook his head. No. They didn't see anything. They were just staying alert, as they should be.

Of course there wouldn't be something. It would be nice if a bunch of the conspirators were to march themselves into the plaza, right about now, but it wouldn't happen. Life didn't work that way—that would be too bloody useful, much more so than listening to a Pironesian boy's mumblings.

" . . . and where is the One Who Smells Like Food? She should be here; she loves me . . ." The words trailed off into a series of whimpers, and cries, that sounded for all the world like a baby's. It was just as well they were alone; shameful for somebody presenting himself as a Knight of the Order of Crown, Shield, and Dragon to be crying like a baby at all, much less in public.

It's a baby, Gray, the Khan whispered to him. *And it cries like a baby; that's all. Don't blame the boy, and don't blame the baby. Babies cry.*

Gray wasn't at all sure that he liked being lectured on patience and tolerance by the Khan.

Then show some without my reminder, the Khan said. *I've heard many a young baby cry. Send for the women to see to it if you're not man enough to endure it yourself.*

"Shh . . ." Niko whispered, in his own voice. "Shh . . . yes, yes, Nadide, I'll sing you the lullabye, again, just like she used to . . .

> Into the garden the calves did stray.
> Gardener quickly turn them away.
> They'll eat the cabbages without delay,

> Eh-e nini, eh-e nini,
> Eh-e nini, nini,
> Nini nini nini
> Eh-e, eh-e nini eh!
> Eh-e, eh-e nini eh!
> Eh-e, ninni, ninni, ninni,
> *Eh-e, ninni, ninni, eh!*

"*Eh-e, ninni*," it went, and continued on, ever more softly, as the boy's body swayed in time, ever slower, the nonsense syllables of lullabye growing every quieter, until Gray could barely hear him.

Cully rose from his seat and walked carefully, quietly, over to Gray. "Does that sound familiar to you?" he whispered.

"No," Gray said, lowering his voice at Cully's glare, and switched to a whisper. "I don't know much about lullabyes." Gray's childhood hadn't been filled with that sort of thing.

Other than the nonsense syllables, the boy was singing in Hellenic, of course, but there wasn't anything unusual about the accent, or much of anything different from the way that Niko usually spoke.

"Mmph. Doesn't sound familiar to anybody else, either, far as I can tell. Had Niko do it on board the *Marienios*, the other night, and none of the crew said it sounded familiar." He grinned. "I just smiled and looked secretive."

"So what happened?"

"Well, Salim Abdullah trotted out a lullabye that the women of his clan sing to their babies, and more of the Abdullahs joined in—nice voices, that lot—and some of the new-hired sailors did the same, and we had a nice little sing-along on the dock. A very pleasant time, all in all, but I don't see as it accomplished much."

His smile was more than a little irritating, and Gray was about to say something to that effect when Cully gave him a look. "Yes, this is very serious; certainly, it's important, but if I've taught you anything, I hope I've taught you to enjoy the moment, when you can." He patted Gray's arm. "You were always too serious a boy, and you've not shed that as a man. Tending to your duty doesn't need to mean that you walk through every step of your life with a gravedigger's expression on your face, Joshua." Cully cocked his head to one side. "Lots of curiosities about the sword, though. Paste a curious expression on your face, and we can talk about them."

"Well, if you insist, I'll—"

At a sound behind him, Gray spun around, the Khan in his hand, only realizing that he had drawn it at the clatter of the Khan's scabbard on the stones.

Yes.

The world changed about him.

It always did, in much the same way, but each time more intense, sharper, brighter, darker, than it had been the time before, as the two of them came alive once more.

Yes, alive. He was more fully alive than he ever had been, as Gray or Khan.

It was one thing to rest his hand on the Khan's steel, and another to remove it from its scabbard, and hold the slim blade, as familiar to him as his own hands, raised high above his head, ready to slice not just through flesh and bone, not only to part boiled leather and welded steel with an effort that was no effort at all but the purest of joy, but to cleave through life and not-life.

His skin tingled and stung, as though he had been set upon by a million angry but impotent wasps whose stingers somehow hurt without hurting; as always, he felt like he was growing, becoming taller, larger, something more than merely human. The distant aches of his wrist and head didn't quite vanish. If anything they became more intense, but they were utterly unimportant and irrelevant.

The strangest part was his sight. After, he always described it even to himself as though it felt like he was an observer behind his own eyes, and again, he knew that that was wrong, just as he always forgot about it, somehow, between the times that he held the Khan in the dark—Gray-as-Gray always thought of the night as dark and colorless.

But, again, he was reminded that he was wrong—there had been the subtle, inky blue-black of the sky, and the moon had been the blue of steel heated in the hottest forge. The fish-oil lamps dimly flickering on their poles had held just the barest of flames, yes, but while they had been but a dim echo of the rich orange and red of the sun, they had shared their color generously, even lovingly with the night.

Had . . .

That was all gone.

Now, just as it would have been in the brightest of daylight, the world was painted only in black and white, with no shades of gray to divide the two, no true color at all save for the fiery orange and red of the Khan that he held out and over his head.

The sky overhead had become a solid black, marked

with pinpricks of oppressive whiteness that should have blinded him, but didn't, any more than the simple round whiteness of the moon did, or the sun would have.

Cully's face, eyes wide and mouth open, was like a moving sketch, his features bright white drawn against a background of the blackest of charcoal.

And, as always, the world slowed down, capturing the moment like a fly frozen into a block of slowly melting ice. He could hear the agonizingly slow beat of his heart speed up, he could even feel it try to beat faster than mere flesh possibly could—but still, it pulsed so slowly, too slowly, and he gasped for the breath that could fill his burning lungs but never quite satisfy them.

The worst or best of it—he was never quite sure, at such times which, although he would later have no doubt—was the Khan. The Khan was no more just speaking to him—it was him, and he was the Khan.

He was the one-who-had-been-two, who had ridden his pony down from the grassy steppes that the effete, weak Westerners called Nova Monglia, taking first the Xi Xia, and then the Qin, and then the Na-Chung. The world thought that he would stop there, on the shores of the Nipponese sea, or, if not strike across the sea for Nippon, defying the holy wind that had drowned the others who had tried to do the same. Caution and cowardice wouldn't stop him—of course he would head east.

So he had turned west, across the rocky desert, far colder and inhospitable than the mild, sandy ones of the weak south, sewing destruction and reaping the harvest of it, knowing that nothing could stop him until he reached the sea to the west, just as he had to the east.

Yes, he had been a conqueror, and there was nothing

greater than that. But he had been more than that—not
greater, of course—but more. He had been a father, who
had loved his sons—and, in a lesser way, as was only
proper, his daughters—although undoubtedly he had sired
a legion of bastards on his slow, inexorable march toward
the true western sea, over the Khwarizm, barely slowed
by the pitiful Uzbi and all the others, as with each mile of
land he took, his strength grew, and it was no shame or
hindrance that it grew just a little, with every day's ride,
with every village and every plot of tilled soil where his
whim became law, and his word became real.

It had been wonderful.

No, it *was* wonderful, and it was always with him, not
just as a vague generality, but with all the little details:
the way that his favorite pony would whicker and shy in
the morning, as though from eagerness to be on with
today's ride; the comfortable feel of the well-worn saddle
beneath his ass; the fear in the eyes of the women and
the taste of their trembling lips, the sounds of their groans
as he mounted them; and how he could look before and
behind him, at the ponies and horses and wagons and
campfires, and never see the end of them, as though he
was a boat floating always in the center of the sea of conquest, as though it was his very manhood that grew with
every *clop-clop-clop*, stiffening beneath him from sea to
its final destination in the far sea.

No, that hadn't happened.

He had been infuriated by his defeat and capture on
the shores of the Black Sea. He had always been able to
divide his enemies, and play them off against each other,
not for a moment pausing in his inexorable, unstoppable
advance.

Until this one time, this one defeat, this one and final humiliation—or so he thought.

Then there had been another: to be strapped to that upright post, while a bearded wizard and one of their hideous priests murmured spells—it was wrong that he should, that he could end like that, in the hands of his enemies. Being ripped apart by horses, or his skin flayed off by sharp knives, or even dropped from a height to be stopped by a rope around his neck—he had expected that, but not *this*.

And, of course, he hadn't ended like that, or ended at all. He had simply traded his failing flesh for shiny, enduring steel, and the sharing of the flesh of the score of others who had held that steel in his time pleased him even more than the taste of the blood and souls that he drank.

And of all of them, of all who had joined themselves with him, Gray was most the kindred soul—deny it as he would, when he would.

He wouldn't now. Not when they were now one, not when the blood-turned-to-fire coursed too slowly but still powerfully through their shared veins, carrying with it a power that grew with every year, every use, and could shatter now walls and perhaps, one day, make the heavens themselves fall, to scatter before his feet, where they belonged.

The Gray-Khan towered above Gray's companions, although he couldn't say quite how, as he could look them in their black-and-white faces, rather than on them from a height, as though he were seated on the back of his horse and they were but the men of a dozen races who had spent their entire lives waiting to die beneath his sword, as was only proper.

But they were nothing beside him. A flick of the wrist would send Cully tumbling through the air, shattering him against the fountain, and Niko would take less than that.

The only danger was Shanley—him and that idiotic White one, still sleeping in his scabbard, who didn't understand what power was, what it was for, who—

"Gray, no," Cully said, his mouth and voice working so slowly it was an effort to make out his words, and only the trace of him that was still Gray was willing to make the effort. "It was nothing. No danger. Look—"

Cully tried to grab the Gray Khan's free hand, and while it would have been easy to avoid the old man's honey-slow motion, the Khan let him grip it, then used that grip to toss Cully aside, barely capable of admiring the way that the old man was able to turn the throw into a tumble and roll that carried him halfway across the plaza.

He was in no danger from this Cully, not now, not with Cully armed with nothing but ordinary steel, trapped in slowtime—it was best to save his strength for that meddling Nameless, although had no doubt that he had strength enough. Save Cully for later.

For now, there was Shanley.

And still there was time, for the lumbering fool who carried the bumbling saint stood anchored in time, like all the rest.

The Gray-Khan turned to face the retreating backs of the man and women fleeing the plaza, running in such leaden panic that they had left their donkey behind, the woman barely taking the moment it took to pull the squealing infant from the animal's back.

It should have run, too, but it stood as though anchored, braying loudly as it voided itself and—

Then the three of them faced him, moving more quickly than they should have been able to in slowtime, but not as fast as the Gray-Khan.

Shanley slowly, too slowly, was drawing the Nameless from its sheath. It would have been easy to blast him to ashes before he finished the draw, but—

Yes, he had better do that. Without Bear, the Nameless was no threat at all.

"No." The boy stood before him, that absurd little girl-sword in his hands. Clumsy stance, with the legs spread too far apart, as though he was anchoring himself in place, refusing to consider the possibility that he would have to retreat.

Of course he wouldn't retreat. He and she would die right then and there. Her soul glowed through the metal, yes, but it was a dull, dim glow, the orange-red of an autumn leaf, nothing that pierced the white and black like a needle through an eyeball; it was a soul that had known nothing of life beyond the taste of the sweet milk it had sucked from its mother's breasts—nothing like the white fire of the Nameless, or the beautiful, blazing, burning red and orange of his own.

Kill the boy, kill the Nameless, and then Cully, and—

No.

Yes, yes, it was yes, now was the time. Start with them, and work his way outward, through the city, through—

No. Let go, Khan. There's nothing here.

Nothing? How could there be nothing? There were stone statues—they were something. There were three men, bearing weapons—that was something. There was a city filled with people, and there was the countryside beyond, and the ships, and there were stars in the sky that needed to be—

No. We're damned, you and me, and that's as it should be. But we'll not worsen it. Not now. Not ever, I hope. But not now.

Yes; there must come a time; on that they were in accord. Let that time be now.

Yes.

But somehow, for just a moment, the Gray-Khan hesitated. Not even for a quickened but too-slow heartbeat, perhaps, but long enough.

"No!" Gray shouted, and he flung the sword away from him as though it had burned his hand.

And then he was just Gray again, standing in the darkness whose warm colors had returned, with the Khan lying lifeless, for the moment, on the hard stones before him.

His heart pounded fast and hard in his chest, and his lungs burned as he tried to get enough air, but couldn't. His knees threatened to buckle beneath him.

No; he locked them into place. *No.*

Nothing but his own will would ever bring him to his knees again.

They were smiling at him. Cully didn't seem to notice the trickle of blood that ran down through his thinning hair and onto his cheek.

Bear reached out a hand. "Gray—"

"Be still, Bear," Cully said, catching Bear's sleeve. "He's back, but . . ."

Nothing but his own will would ever bring him to his

knees, he swore. He had sworn that before, and he would again.

So it was by his own will that Joshua Grayling knelt, the cobblestones cold and hard beneath his knees, and bowed his head, clasping his trembling hands together before him.

"Forgive me, Father, for I have sinned," Gray said. "I almost—I would have killed you, Father, all of you. I would have. I almost . . ."

He wept and wept, his chest heaving, his body shaking. He wept as though he was a child who had been beaten too much, and could stand no more.

Bear shook his head and sighed.

Gray was sleeping, finally, the Khan, now scabbarded, lying on the bed beside him, its hilt scant inches from Gray's right hand.

Gray was shivering in his sleep, although it wasn't cold in the room, so Bear pulled the blankets up around Gray's neck, moving as slowly and gently as he could, so as not to wake him.

Bear considered, for a moment, removing the Khan, despite how improper that would be. You simply didn't ever so much as lay a finger on another knight's weapons or armor without permission—and a Red Sword? That wasn't just hideously impolite, but dangerous.

But if Gray touched it in his sleep . . .

That would be bad. Bear didn't have to take it from the room; the guards outside would see. He could just lay it on the floor beside the bed.

No. That would be wrong, and it would tell Gray that Bear didn't trust him.

He straightened himself and walked to the door, closing it gently behind him, then turned to the two marines who had been set on guard, at Cully's insistence. "If he wakes, send for me—don't go in. Don't let anybody in."

"Aye, aye, sir," the senior private said. "And if he wants to go out?"

It was only because he was so shocked that he didn't slap the man across his face. "Then come to a stiff brace, Private, and you hold the door for him while you ask if there's anything you can do to be of assistance," he said, regretting the anger. It was just ignorance, not disrespect.

But he couldn't help adding, "Suicide is a mortal sin, Private. If you were so foolish as to lay an unwanted hand on Sir Joshua, Red Sword or no Red Sword, you'd not have time to repent of it."

The younger one, who couldn't have been all that much older than Niko, looked as though he was going to say something, but desisted at a quick glance from the older. It wouldn't do any harm to bide a moment longer, and for a fact, Bear was not eager to go back down the hall to the others, reconvened in Langahan's office over a bottle of wine—and a pipe for Sigerson.

And, besides, while he had not been as harsh with the private as he had been tempted, he had been harsh, and while it had been only necessary and proper, Bear nevertheless regretted it.

"Go ahead," he said, gently. "It's always best to ask questions, I think, even if you may not get a good answer."

"No, sir, I just . . ."

"You just don't know your place, Platt," the other private said. "I'm sorry, sir."

Bear smiled. "Not knowing one's place seems to be a

common enough ailment, Private, but it's rarely a fatal one, at least around me. Go ahead, Platt—out with it, please."

"Well, sir, I was just wondering—word around the docks is that Sir Joshua actually drew his sword tonight. The live one, sir."

"The rumors are true. There was a minor disturbance in the Plaza of Heroes. Sir Joshua . . . responded, but it wasn't necessary for him to actually use the Khan."

That was true enough, but it was only part of the story. It left out how Gray had had no real reason to draw the Khan in the first place—some farmers, heading home late from a market day, were hardly any sort of threat that called for the display of naked mundane steel, much less so much more than that.

And it left out how Bear and the Nameless had been prepared to at least try to do what was necessary, and Bear's uncertainty that they would have been able to stop Gray, even though he thought that duty would have moved him to try to do what was necessary.

No, it was only part. But the part would have to do, at least for now. There was something in Bear that rejected the notion that a knight should seem to be above it all: untouchable, even inhuman. For his own part, Bear tried to strike a balance between the necessity of maintaining the dignity and the authority of the Order with his own sense that all were equally sinners before God and in some sense, therefore equal, despite the natural differences of race and class, though he was never sure that he struck quite the right balance.

But Gray was different; the cross he bore through life was heavier. Gray thought that he was required to embody the Order in himself, openly and always, and a sign of weakness before outsiders would not just embarrass him—although it would—but it would make Gray feel that he had failed in his duty.

Bear would have had him otherwise in many ways.

Still, he would not share the image, burned into his brain, of Gray kneeling in the plaza, begging and pleading for forgiveness for another's sins. Bear hoped that that was mainly because doing so would have embarrassed Gray, rather than the Order, but it was certainly much of both.

It was hard going through life thinking that you were damned, and perhaps Gray was. That was in God's hands, where it would have to stay. There was only a little that Bear could do about the matter, but . . .

Later. Gray was not the only knight who could do his duty, and right now, Bear's duty called for him to join the others. "Good night, Privates," he said, and walked down the hall.

All eyes were on him as he entered the room: Cully, Sigerson, and the boy. The night had been warm, but perhaps the stones of the residence held more cold than was usual; Bear found himself squatting in front of the fireplace, rubbing his hands together in the heat.

"I did that, too." Cully nodded, and seemed to relax. "Seems to be more of a chill in the air than, well, the chill in the air."

Bear had to nod.

"Well, he's sleeping peacefully," Cully said.

"Yes."

"Oh, go ahead, Sir Niko; don't fidget about. Just come out and ask me why I know that Gray's sleeping peacefully." Cully grinned.

"I . . ." Again, the boy's hand fell to the hilt of the sword that lay across his lap, in a reflex that Bear had seen—and done—far more times than he cared to count. "Very well, Sir Cully—how do you know?"

"Mr. Sigerson?" Cully raised an eyebrow. "You don't seem curious—are you uninterested?"

Sigerson leaned back in his chair and puffed on his pipe. "I'm interested, certainly enough, but I think it's obvious—Sir David's expression suggests that he's not overly concerned, and more than that: he's here, in fact, joining us rather than summoning you."

"I'd hardly leave him if I was needed," Bear said.

"Well, yes—I believe, in fact, that was my point." Sigerson leaned back in his chair, his feet still propped up on the low table, careless of what minor damage his slippers were doing to it. He was in a robe, yes—but not wizard's robes, just an utterly conventional striped cotton night-robe over his sleeping shirt, the only unusual thing about it the half-dozen pockets scattered, seemingly randomly, across the breast and skirt. He drew a small metal tool from one of the pockets, and manipulated the contents of his pipe, a homey gesture that reminded Bear of how Father used to do much the same thing, as the family would sit in front of the roaring hearth on a cold night.

"I wish I'd been there to see it," Sigerson said. "Heard much about what happens when a knight takes a live sword in hand, but, of course, I've never seen it."

Bear found himself irritated, but Cully just smiled. "Well, you may have the opportunity to learn better of such eagerness. I do hope you survive it."

"As of course, do I." Sigerson stretched and yawned. "And with that hope, I think I'll bid you all a good night;

I expect that tomorrow will be a busy day, and I'm curious to see just how."

"Good night, Mr. Sigerson," Cully said, and waited silently until the door had closed behind him.

He touched a finger gingerly to his forehead, then gave Bear a questioning look. "Is it just that I'm slowing down with old age, or is Gray even faster than I remember him being?"

"He's faster." Bear lowered himself into a chair. "Much faster, I think, Father." He shook his head. "Not quite as much so as Big John with the Goatboy in hand, perhaps, but close to it. More than the Nameless and me, of a certainty—the Nameless doesn't seem to do that at all, at least not for me."

"Didn't do it for Sir Edward, either." Cully shrugged. "I'd say it had something to do with the Khan's redness— just like it is with the Sandoval's—but then there's the matter of Big John and the Goatboy, although I can't think of any other Whites that confer that attribute. Jenn certainly doesn't. Didn't."

Niko spoke up—without asking permission, even with a look. "Does that mean you couldn't have . . . stopped him?"

Unfortunate that he had shown such impudence at the same time he was showing self-confidence. "That is *not* a proper question. Gray is—"

"—human, and therefore imperfect, and he's carrying the Khan, David," Cully said. "That's an entirely proper question to be asked, privately, among Knights of the Order. I'd like to hear your answer—and *his*, for that matter. You may take a moment to think it over, if you like. It's perhaps not unimportant."

Bear had already taken the Nameless's hilt in hand, of course, and that had immediately extinguished his anger at Niko. He was, after all, just a boy, and it was better for as humble and reserved a boy as Niko was to come out of his shell than to cower in it, peering out like a frightened turtle.

It's a matter of balance, the Nameless whispered, amused, *and moderation. Moderation is a virtue, when it is taken in moderation.*

"I don't know, Niko," Bear said. "It's said that the White drives out the Dark, and that's true in general, in the long run. All the Nameless knows is what will be, will be, and I'm certainly no wiser than he is."

"But with that speed—"

"Speed isn't everything. The Nameless and I don't have the Khan's speed, or his fury, but . . . the Nameless is not just a decent man imprisoned in a sword; he's something more.

"Who would win? I don't know. 'The race is not always won by the swiftest, the battle not always by the strongest; prosperity does not always belong to those who are the wisest, wealth does not always belong to those who are the most discerning, nor does success always come to those with the most knowledge, for time and chance may overcome them all.' "

Niko looked puzzled.

"You don't recognize Ecclesiastes?"

"My—my grandfather read to us from the One—from the Bible, but I don't remember that part."

Bear gave Cully as stern a look as he could manage. "You said you were training him."

"Yes, I said so, and I am—and I've had to set my

priorities. For right now, him learning to walk and talk
and carry himself like a knight is more important than
anything else. I've had scant enough time for that, and no
time at all for Bible study, Bear, and—"

"Father, if you'll excuse me, there is always time for
such."

"Fine," Cully said, with more than usual heat. "You
tell me—should we engage in a little planning, right now,
or spend the shank of the evening delving into the mysteries of Ecclesiates? I wouldn't have any objection to
some of the latter, if we'd decided on the former. Which
we would have—if Gray hadn't interrupted our discussion with his little fit."

Bear started to object, but Cully silenced him with a
quick, chopping motion in the air.

"Yes, it was a fit—there was no need for it, and Gray
above all should know that you *never* draw a live sword
without need. That boy—he's always been that way, keeping himself under control for days, weeks, months on end,
and then he lets it drop, for just a moment. Bad enough
for any man, worse for a knight, and much worse for a
Knight of the Red Sword." Cully shook his head. "He
never should have been given a Red Sword, David—he's
not nearly as strong as everybody thinks he is, and I've
known him longer and better than any man alive, you
included."

"You've not known him a day of his life for the past ten
years, until very recently, Father," Bear said, wondering
to himself why was saying any such thing. Just because
something was true doesn't mean that it needed to be
said here and now, or ever.

Cully was on his feet. "Yes, yes, I've abandoned you

all," he whispered, visibly straining with the effort of keeping his voice low. "I'm just a miserable old man, undeserving of any of the honors ever placed upon my head or belted about my waist."

"Father—"

"But I'm *right* about this, Bear, and you know I am, and while I've always loved you for your loyalty, boy, as much as for your gentleness, there is a time and a place for everything, and . . ." He threw up his hands. "And this is hardly the time or the place for an old man to be preaching to you or ranting at you, even if you'd listen."

This was, after all, Father Cully; Bear didn't need the Nameless's help to answer him gently.

"Always, Father," he said, "always I will hear you out, just as I'll always want your blessing. You're quite right, though, this is not the time or the place for such discussions, and I humbly beg your pardon for suggesting otherwise. You have some ideas?"

"Since you asked, yes." Cully regained control of himself seemingly without effort. Had his outburst been a show, a lesson? "Take a look at this chart," he said, beckoning Bear over to the desk. "Niko's island is here," he said, indicating a spot on the map, "and, if I read Mr. Rafferty's report right, they first spotted the pirate right about here, almost due east. Yes, and if you drew the line straight, it would lead through Seeproosh, and to al-Qabilyah, and probably beyond."

"You think the source is Seeproosh? And they simply load these swords in ships and ship them east?"

"No, of course not—and keep your voice down. Not that I'm saying it couldn't be Seeproosh, mind you, although why they'd come all the way to Pironesia to grab a baby girl when they could raid for such much closer is something that doesn't make much sense. No. I am saying, though, that it certainly appears that the origin is somewhere to the east, and that while we know we don't know where that is, They—whoever They are—might suspect otherwise. They might worry about what we know, what we suspect. What I'm suggesting is that we set out, to the east, as soon as possible, making it clear to everybody in the port that we have a definite plan, a definite destination, and intend to proceed somewhat indirectly toward it, for our own reasons." His mouth quirked. "Although, of course, we need to make it clear without making it clear, if you catch my meaning."

"And then hope somebody tries to stop us." Bear shook his head. It didn't seem likely, but—

But possible. It was possible. The one thing you could be sure of about anybody involved in such a filthy business was that they would live in fear of being discovered. Perhaps they could be panicked into doing something overt, something—

And, besides, Bear had no better idea.

"And what do you need from me?"

"A few hours ago, I'd have said I need you to talk to Gray, and try to persuade him. He'll listen to you." Cully grinned. "And, just maybe, he'd listen to that damned Khan, who would never sit still for a moment, not when there was a chance of murder and mayhem." He shrugged. "As for now, I need for you to decide."

"Father—"

"It's not much of a plan, but perhaps by the time the others show up, we'll have discovered something of use? Possibly?

"Or would you rather we just sit in these admittedly comfortable surroundings and wait? We could spend the time in Bible study, which I know would please you. Go ahead, take your time and think on it, but don't take too long. If we delay in port much longer than overnight, just long enough for you to resupply your ships and give a quick leave to your crews, there's no point in doing anything but just sitting here."

That was true enough. If Cully had been waiting for them, with some destination in mind, why would he wait any longer than that?

"Gray should decide that," he finally said.

"Gray is all-in; what he needs now is rest. And besides," Cully added before Bear could decide whether or not to point it out, "he might not be so flexible, but if you've signaled for recall, and ordered this ragtag fleet of ours to sail at first light, he may not like it, but he won't try to stop it. The trick with Joshua is to present him with a *fait accompli*—that's 'a thing accomplished,' Niko—let him complain about it, then force him to make it work." Cully nodded, as though he was trying to persuade himself.

"Is that why you put guards on his door?"

Cully gave him a disgusted look. "I put guards on his door because it seems to me to be safe to assume that whoever is behind all this has noted that I was waiting in Pironesia for him, and sure enough, he's well worth waiting for, as he demonstrated tonight.

"Word has gone out in the city about the Khan being brandished tonight, and will soon be echoing across the countryside. Not altogether a bad thing, although it could easily have turned out worse than merely badly. No," he said, forestalling Bear's question, "I don't have any reason to distrust anybody in the Governor's mansion, not in particular. But I don't have any reason to trust each and every one of them, either." He gestured at the food remaining on the tray. "Which is why, when he wakes, he eats from that—and if you see me peering into corners and think me mad, you may be right, but it's not without reason that I've been driven so." Cully folded his hands over his chest. "So, Sir David, decide: stay? Do we go, on your say-so? Do you wake Gray, or wait until he wakes himself?"

"We go," Bear said immediately, thinking how unlike himself it was to take matters into his own hands, when Gray was just down the hall. "We'll sail at first light. Get what sleep you can, the both of you." He rose. "I'd best go notify the sailor at the gate; I'm sure Captain Johansen will be glad of six hours notice instead of his promised two."

Cully stretched broadly. "That sounds sensible. I'll be glad of some sleep myself," he said, rubbing at his eyes. He looked around. "I think I saw a bottle somewhere—a drink would go down well. Bear?"

"Thank you, no," he said. "I recall what happened the last time I accepted a drink from you, Father."

Cully grinned. "Well, it did help you sleep. Would you take my word that this bottle contains only Mr. Langahan's presumably excellent whiskey?"

"I would, of course, but I think I'll take a short walk instead. That will probably help me sleep more than whiskey would."

That was true, but it was incomplete. There was something he should do, and no need to discuss it even with Cully.

But Cully just nodded, and Bear gathered up his swords and left the room.

He walked down the hall—past the marines who were still stiffly on duty—and walked down the broad, curving steps to the front arch, and then down the walk to the gate, gravel crunching beneath his boots.

Unsurprisingly, Johansen had been as good as his word—a sailor, his red-and-gold brassard proclaiming that he was on alone-duty ashore, and not to be bothered by the Watch, was waiting for him, standing rigidly at attention just beyond the gate. He had, no doubt, been leaning against the bole of one of the two ancient oaks that stood like a pair of ancient watchmen just beyond the gate, but Bear wouldn't have corrected him. He was there; that was enough.

"Sir David?"

"We sail at first light," he said. "Please have the commodore inform the other two ships, and Mr. Abdullah on the *Marienios*, as well. It's a matter of some urgency."

"Aye, aye, sir. Sail at first light; Captain to pass the word to both *Winfrew* and *Cooperman*, and to Abdullah on the *Marienios*. On my way, sir."

The sailor broke into a run that quickly carried him down the street and out of Bear's sight, only the echoes of his footsteps left behind.

He should, of course, have gotten some sleep himself. And he would try, of course, although there wasn't much point; he could sleep better with the rocking of the ship cradling him like a baby, and once they were on their way, he'd get as much sleep as he could, while he could.

But there was another matter to attend to, first. It had

been too long, and he'd not had a private moment in an appropriate place.

Bear quickened his steps as he walked down the street, turned down another one, a steeper street that led down toward the shore.

The city was quiet at night, although it didn't have the feel of a Londinium street, where decent people shuttered their windows and barred their doors, where only those with the most urgent of reasons came out at night at all, rushing through the darkness from lamppost to lamppost, as though the wan overhead glow could somehow protect them.

Here, it just felt quiet. Oh, if he listened carefully, the sounds of raucous laughter and drunken singing carried across the water, but he didn't listen carefully, as that made him feel strangely lonely, and that was an unaccustomed and uncomfortable emotion, so he quickened his pace.

At a seven-note blast on a distant whistle, Bear allowed himself a smile; Captain Johansen appeared to be a man of his word in this, as well.

Whistles were piping Recall All Hands dockside before Bear found what he had been looking for, although it didn't take long, and he hadn't expected it to.

But he did want to finish quickly. Not for the sake of sleep. If he took too long, questions might be asked that he would not wish to answer honestly, and therefore wouldn't answer at all.

He hadn't been here before, but he had marked the location in his mind. Just a few short weeks ago, when they had sailed into the port, Bear and had taken note of the red-slate-topped cupola, adorned with nothing more than a simple stone cross.

The church had been built by the Romans, he decided, and whatever else you could say of the Romans, they built well, and while from the look of it the chapterhouse had been added sometime later, the builders had the good sense or good taste—or both—to duplicate the style as best they could.

Not nearly as ornate as what he had grown up with, granted. Bear always thought that the intricate windows of glass, metal and stone that flowered into a rainbow of colors in the sun were somehow a call to prayer and contemplation themselves, just as the vaulted ceilings high above were a reminder of the presence of Heaven.

But this was much plainer, and there was virtue in that, too; that it was different didn't make it wrong. There was something very pleasant about the way that the two smooth columns of the entry, adorned only at floor and ceiling, gracefully supported a triple archway, and as he climbed the few steps he noted with approval that they had been freshly swept.

Both of the massive oaken doors stood open, as though the very presence of the stone cross beyond them could and would frighten away thieves. As might be so—the earthquake, twenty years ago, that had shaken most of the city to the ground had spared the church. It was possible that thieves would be deterred, as well, although Bear would have been more reassured by somebody watching; it was impious, he had always thought, to depend on God to do what man should do for himself.

Bear walked inside, and, as always, felt both peace and dread descend upon him, as was proper. While God was everywhere, it was right and proper that one should be reminded of both His love and His sternness when one entered His house.

No candles were burning on the altar, although lanterns set into the walls of the nave cast a flickering light; the nave was not allowed to go dark.

Feeling a little like a thief himself, he walked past the altar into the apse. Perhaps he could find what he was looking for by himself, although there should be some—

"Excuse me?" The fluid Hellenic voice held a trace of fear, and Bear forced himself to turn slowly for fear of adding to the fright.

It was just the priest—or one of them, probably the most junior, given the hour—and he doubted that the vicar or prelate would have appreciated one of their juniors taking up his crook of office more as a weapon than anything else.

But the priest lowered the stick, his eyes wide. "Who—are you? Are you really—"

"I'm sorry to disturb your sleep, Father . . . ?"

"Brother." The Pironesian visibly relaxed. The sight of an Order Knight's distinctive garments sometimes had that effect, although often it was the opposite one. "Brother Michael. I'm of the Anglian brotherhood; we wear the same caftan as the priests, and—"

"I'm David Shanley, Brother Michael, and I'm more than vaguely familiar with the rule of the Anglians. I'm sorry to have woken you, and sorrier to have alarmed you."

Whether he was impressed by being in the presence of a Knight of the Order, or just relieved that the man who had entered the church in the middle of the night was not a thief, Brother Michael's smile was warming, nonetheless.

Bear dug into his pouch for a coin, and pulled it out. "I need a candle, please, Brother." He placed the coin in the monk's palm, and Brother Michael's fingers closed around it immediately.

"Yes, Father David, of course—I'll bring you our largest; it's back in the—"

"No, please. Whatever this would normally buy."

The monk looked down into his hand, and his eyes widened. "But that's a silver crown—I don't think we have anything big enough—"

"Anything. Please. A candle. Just a candle." It was hard to talk. "Any candle."

"Yes, Father, of course, of course."

With the unreliable, occasional Pironesian economy of motion, a foot-long candle, thick around as a strong man's arm, was quickly produced, and brought to the altar, where wax drippings told of hundreds and thousands that had been placed before, testimony to wishes, if not always to piety.

"Will this do? I know we have some larger, but they're in the curate's office, I think. I could get the key—there's a huge one, took three days to pour—"

"This one is splendid," Bear said.

The candle was quickly set into the votary altar, and even more quickly the monk produced a taper, lit it from one of the lanterns, and presented it to him.

"Thank you, Brother Michael."

He didn't have to ask for privacy; the monk quickly disappeared behind the altar before the taper had burned much at all. Bear lit the candle, blew out the taper, and knelt before the altar.

He didn't bow his head right away. The Nameless was

unusually silent, and that bothered him. He usually said something at these times. Nothing inappropriate, not really, except in the sense that the Nameless's gentle humor usually had a trace of self-mockery in it.

No comment? he asked. Nothing about how I've often said that God does not need to be nagged?

I don't know, David. I've never claimed to know much or little about the divine.

You've mocked me before.

Oh, never. I've mocked myself, certainly, and perhaps some others, from time to time. I don't recall that I've mocked you, and I've certainly heard of worse pretentiousness than yours. I've heard tell that there are stories told of a supposedly holy man who swore that he would not enter heaven until all humanity could go before him, the Nameless said.

I'm not that holy.

Or that pretentious? Bear didn't answer, and the Nameless went on, *Well, they are just stories. I wouldn't believe them, myself, were I you.*

I believe them, about that man.

And I would do nothing to try to shake your faith, David. I've little hunger for the futile. But your candle is burning, and the night gets no younger, eh?

True enough.

David Shanley bowed his head, and once again, as he had so many times before, more begged than prayed that God spare the soul of Joshua Grayling, if He could, in His infinite mercy, see fit to do so.

And if not . . .

If not . . . there was an alternative.

And it was far more Bear's demand than his prayer

that, if God would not spare Gray, He would send Sir David Shanley, sworn and sealed Knight, Brother, and Priest of the Order of Crown, Shield, and Dragon, to burn alongside his brother in Hell.

Somebody had to watch out for Gray, after all.

Interlude 5: The Saracen

I once used the old expression "you don't use a sledge-hammer to kill a housefly" to the Khan. Of course, then I had to explain why one would want to kill a housefly, and while the Khan didn't seem to understand that, he said that he thought that if it was so very important to do so, a sledgehammer was a perfectly appropriate tool for the task.

Most don't think the Khan has a sense of humor.

I am one of those most.

—Gray

The English were strange.

Everybody knew that, of course, but these knights were strange even for the English; on that Stavros Andropolounikos and Nissim al-Furat could easily if privately agree.

The gossip among the hired-ons aboard the *Marienios* had it that the knights had spurned the luxurious captain's quarters aboard the *Wellesley* for what was available on the *Marienios*. Stavros wasn't sure he believed that; English commanders had great power aboard their own vessels, even when there was nobility aboard, and perhaps the captain had simply told them to travel aboard the *Marienios*, rather than having them underfoot on the Navy vessels.

Which, of course, would have meant that Salim Abdullah should have been expelled from of his captain's quarters at the stern, and probably Matir Abdullah from his, as well.

Instead, the four knights had taken up residence in a compartment in the now-empty forward cargo hold, having had a couple of the marines stringing up sleeping hammocks rather than asking the ship's carpenter and mate to build them proper beds—something that the carpenter and mate could have done both easily and quickly.

That neglect didn't bother the carpenter, a diminutive Thessalonikan named Spiros, who would certainly have cooperated, but would probably have considered such a thing beneath him and simply assigned the task to the carpenter's mate.

It most certainly didn't bother the carpenter's mate, the mate being Stavros, and the mate having more than enough work to do as it was.

Nissim al-Furat felt differently. Nissim would have very much liked to have had the opportunity forced on him to spend some time with the knights. The English were an indiscreet race, and some interesting things might drop from their lips. And, had he been put to work in their quarters, it wasn't impossible that he could find a few private moments to go through their things—although that would have to be carefully done, if it were to be done at all.

But, alas, the Fates and the knights had made things otherwise.

Still, on a boat the size of the *Marienios*, you couldn't get far away from anybody, although it felt like you could, when you had a deck between you, so he had expected that he would have some time to observe them.

But most of their time seemingly was spent on deck, while almost all of Stavros's was below, under about the most disgusting conditions possible.

Maintaining a ship was a constant race between repair and decay, and the Abdullahs, merchants all, were getting every hour of work for every copper they—or, more likely, their English employers—paid out. The aft hold looked and very much smelled like it had not been cleaned out in years, and the two-layered decking had to be replaced; there was only so much that wood could do.

The tearing-out had only taken a day, with all hands that could be pressed into service—all of the hired-on ones, save for the cook and his mate—and both Spiros and Stavros had been surprised to discover that the rot hadn't actually gotten to the knees.

That would have made things easier, he supposed, as there would be little point in replacing the deck over the rot.

Samir Abdullah, after a careful inspection—accompanied by both Sir Cully, and the young Pironesian knight, who apparently had never seen the actual insides of ship before—had pronounced the knees fit, and the real work begun, with Spiros up in the fresh air the most of the time, working with plane, froe, saw, and chisel, and Stavros spending his days up to his knees in the stinking bilge water, setting the diagonals and joists for the underdeck, and only then moving on to fitting the underdeck, plank by plank.

The only time that Spiros deigned to join him, it seemed, was to check the underside of the underdeck. When he got tired of working, Spiros would have Stavros stop his work to improvise a cofferdam of unset planks and waxed sailcloth, then have Stavros take a pail of fresh seawater and pour it over the partially completed deck while Spiros went into the bilge with a lantern, only emerging to point out spots where the underdeck leaked—usually at the joints, of course—and peremptorily ordering Stavros to recaulk those spots.

And then, usually, while Stavros was working, Spiros would just stand and talk.

His great theory, which he explained in far more detail and at a greater volume than Stavros cared to hear about, was that a proper deck shouldn't rely on the pressure of the planks against the hull to help the caulking maintain its seal, but on the anchoring of the deck planks to the joists.

That theory would have sounded more reasonable, all in all, if it hadn't resulted in Stavros spending endless hours on his knees with caulking iron in hand, swinging the oak caulking hammer to drive the heated mixture of pitch and horsehair and God-knew-what-else into every gap—

—and then having to redo the whole cursed thing every time that a plank would tear loose.

To hear that idiot Spiros tell it, it was only Stavros's particularly clumsy pounding that could tear a plank loose, and as tempted as he was to invite the carpenter to switch places and demonstrate, Stavros kept his head down and stayed at work, saving his complaining for when he took his evening meal up on the poop deck. It would have seemed strange if he hadn't eaten with the others or voiced any complaint, after all.

The work left little time for anything else save for smearing fat over his blisters, and by the end of the day, his ears were ringing incessantly from the steady *thwock-thwock-thwock* of his caulking mallet against the iron.

But as night fell, he finally climbed up the ladder, through the hatch, and onto the deck, relishing the taste of the fresh air, which was about the only thing he was capable of enjoying the taste of, at the moment. Another day in the hold, the reek of the tar fighting with the stench of long-dead fish, had left him no appetite at all.

Not at first—but a quick bath on the cutoff barrel mounted on the poop deck, followed by a change into his clean kirtle, thoroughly refreshed him, and he tore into his evening meal along with all the other hired-ons. Say what you would about the Abdullahs—and he heard plenty, little of it complimentary—they did feed you.

Shkelqim frowned over his bowl. "I think that Milos washed his kirtle in the soup tonight." Safer, all in all, to blame the Abdullah in charge of the cook and cook's mate, rather than Arno, who was sitting just a few feet away.

"I don't much care what I eat, long as there's enough of it," Stavros said. Shqiperese were always complaining, as they were a whiny race by nature, and since Stavros hadn't objected the last five times that Shkelqim had whined about the food, it was his turn, more or less.

"Andropolouniki,"Shkelqim said, with a derisive sniff, "don't care what they eat, or futter, eh?"

"I don't think there's anything wrong with the food," Arno said. "But if it's not to your taste, I can have a word with Milos Abdullah, and perhaps you'll be happier living off tack and water?"

As if he'd heard his name mentioned, Milos Abdullah walked up, spoon but not bowl in hand, and dipped it in the kettle, then tasted it. He nodded, as though to himself, then thought about it for a moment and, ignoring Arno's openly hostile glare, pulled some powder or other out of his many-pouched apron, stirred the pot, and tasted again, seemingly unbothered by being assigned to do a woman's work. Or had he volunteered? He was a pretty enough boy, at that—or, at least, he would have been if he hadn't insisted on trying to grow a beard that insisted on being thin and stringy, rather than manly.

With one of the owners present, the conversation lagged. Complaining was the staple of rear-deck talk, as usual, and also as usual, objection was much less often taken to complaints when the target of them was absent.

Stavros just ate and drank, and let his body sag back against the rail's upright, and watched.

He had a private bet with himself that Sir Niko would find an excuse to join Milos Abdullah on the deck, and it wasn't long before he won.

They didn't much like each other, that was certain, although Stavros didn't know what the source of the enmity was, and he would very much have liked to, if only because he didn't know much about these Order Knights, other than the legends and stories, most of which he didn't believe.

But they were important personages, certainly, and the fact that there were four of them aboard was probably important, and so obviously so that it would have been much more risky to pretend a lack of interest than it was to show one.

"Good evening, Milos," Niko said.

"And a good evening to you, Sir Niko." If Milos Abdullah's tone and posture were just a touch too formal, Niko didn't take apparent notice or manifest offense. The two boys didn't like each other very much, and while Stavros didn't know if that was significant, it was interesting—like the Hellenes said, all is sausage that comes to the butcher's back door.

The story was that on the short trip from the Abdullah's island to the city, Milos had first-named the young knight, and had been quietly taken below to be beaten by two of his uncles. Stavros wasn't sure whether or not he believed that, but for a fact there were fading bruises on Milos's broad back.

Not that such were uncommon; Stavros himself had several fresh injuries from when his first attempt at setting the diagonals had collapsed on him. Life was, Stavros often thought, little more than a series of cuts and bruises interrupted by a few moments of ease and joy, only to be punctuated, finally, with death.

Hmmm . . . now, that was interesting—Niko didn't present the bowl in his hands to Milos to fill; he just dippered some stew into it himself, then tasted it.

"Does it suit you, Sir Niko?" Milos asked.

"It's fine, Milos." The smile could have been intended

to be friendly or insulting. "But it's not for me. One of the knights—one of the *other* knights seems to like yours and Arno's cooking. Even more than I do. So I thought I'd get him some more; I'd thought perhaps it had too little pepper in it, but it seems very good, and I'm sure that Sir Joshua will find it to his taste, as well."

"I'm honored."

Ah. So the junior of the knights was acting as food-taster for the others? That spoke of some suspicion, or perhaps simply a habitual caution.

Probably the latter; if they thought there was somebody aboard who would look to poison four knights of the Order, they would not be aboard, after all.

Stavros certainly would have tried to poison them, if he'd had any such orders. His training included the preparation and use of poisons, and while he knew of nothing aboard that would be particularly useful, he certainly could find something ashore, when they landed in Rodhos. No monkshood, of course—he had never seen monkshood other than in illustration—as Pironesia was too far south, but stavesacre or hellebore wouldn't be difficult to come by, although the trick would be in the administration, even more than in the acquisition.

His orders, of course, had given him no such instructions, but it was something to think on. He might just take a walk outside of the city when they made landfall in Rodhos, and see what he could find. If anybody was going to search through his sea bag, they had already had ample opportunity, and a sealed bottle or packet could be concealed in the bilge against possible need.

Better to be prepared than to be found wanting.

The young knight had walked away, and Milos

Abdullah, unsurprisingly, didn't offer to ladle Stavros more soup, so he helped himself, and returned to where he had been sitting.

Hmmm . . . it did taste better with more pepper, at that.

Chapter 9: Rodhos

The nice thing about service in His Own is how simple it is. The rules are plain, and straightforward, and irrelevant of all the machinations that go on around the Court itself, and in Parliament, and anywhere else.

The real problem with it is that once you've done a tour with His Own, others—even those on the Council, who should know better—think that means you should be able to handle less important matters than protecting His Majesty.

They're wrong in their major assumption—as His Majesty himself has said, on more than one occasion.

—Gray

The inn became very quiet.

It had been anything but quiet before they walked inside. The noise trailed into silence when they did.

The chatter trailed off as though all had gone suddenly mute, and the musicians in the far corner ground to a clumsy halt, the tamboura player giving a few tentative pats to on the drumhead, while the gaida gave out a wheezing sound that sounded halfway between a whine and the passing of wind.

Cully gave Niko a reassuring smile, but then just let his own gaze sweep across the low-ceilinged room, resting for a moment on one man, and then another and yet another, all of whom avoided his gaze. Niko didn't blame him; he didn't much like meeting Cully's eyes, not at the moment.

The Crossroads of the World didn't seem to cater to any particular nationality, unlike the two other taverns they had already visited that night. The Hellenes-Only—that was what the sign said, in Hellenic and in the awkward letters of the trading language, as well as several other kinds of writing that Niko couldn't begin to guess at—unsurprisingly, had been filled with Hellenes only; the Laughing Turk had, equally unsurprisingly, been host to Antalyans, Izmiri, and Balakaziri.

At least, that's what Cully said. Niko couldn't have told the difference between any of the three nationalities, but he had no problem taking Cully's word that *he* could. Cully seemed to know everything. He had even been right about this horse-riding thing. By the time they had left the Cyclades, Niko had probably spent the better part of a week on the backs of several hired horses, and it didn't make him sore anymore. Much.

He still didn't like it, mind, although it was preferable to walking into yet another room filled with strange-looking strangers. Then again, most things were.

As usual, Niko couldn't begin to guess at the nationalities of most of the men, but the long, flowing robes of a half dozen in the corner spoke of their Musselmen origin, as did their unusually long beards. He was sure that Cully could have told him which country they were from, but had no way to guess, any more than he could guess what they had been doing with the immensely fat, completely bald man with the strange, slanted-looking eyes—how did he see?—and the sallow complexion.

What they were doing wasn't necessarily disreputable, but one of the Musselmen put his hand on another's arm, and then all heads at the table bent toward each other, engaging in some whispered discussion just as soon as the music started up again, which it did only after the skinny man in the strange-looking overlarge trousers clapped his hands and gestured urgently at them.

The proprietor scurried over, wiping his hands on a none-too-clean piece of cloth, a weak smile pasted on his face. "Good evening to you, Excellencies," he said. "And welcome, welcome to the Crossroads of the World—"

"Your name," Cully said, flatly. If his usually expressive face held any trace of emotion, Niko couldn't make it out.

"Zeferino, Excellency." If anything, the smile became wider and weaker.

"My name is Cully. I'm addressed as 'Sir Cully,' not 'Excellency.' This is Sir Niko."

"Of course, Sir Cully. I beg your pardon."

"It's granted. 'Zeferino,' you say? Do you mean to tell me that you are the only Zeferino on this whole island? Have you no other name?"

"No, Sir Cully—I mean yes, Sir Cully. I was christened

Zeferino Marianious by the One True Church, and am known all across the island as Zeferino Erasmus, due to my easy and gentle disposition."

"Wine," Cully said. "Three cups. A table."

"Yes, of course, Excellency—I mean, 'Sir Cully,' of course."

Niko felt embarrassed for the way the man almost groveled before the knights, as he shooed three men away from one table and ushered them to it. It took a moment for Niko to recall that he himself had used almost the same words in almost the same tone when he had first met Gray and Cully and Bear, and that made him feel more embarrassed, although he wasn't quite sure who for.

Then again, Cully had said almost the same words to Niko that he had said to Zeferino. It wasn't the words that were different; it was the way he said them, and perhaps Bear's presence then and absence now, as well.

It felt like all eyes were on the two of them, although as Niko looked around, none seemed willing to settle on his, with the exception of the strikingly beautiful woman who had, again, started puffing away at her gaida. Her eyes seemed to lock on his, and made him even more uncomfortable than he already was. There was something about the combination of raven-black hair and the sea-blue of her eyes that made his stomach turn over, even though he avoided staring at the wisp of cloth that bound her ample breasts, somehow more drawing his eye to them than they would had they simply been hanging free.

The tambouri player next to her gave her a glare and picked up the beat, although he quickly let his gaze slide by Niko's, for some reason or other.

Zeferino returned with a clay bottle and three glasses—

blown glass, not just the clay mugs that everybody else was drinking out of. "May I pour for both of you, or—"

"Pour for three." Cully dropped a copper coin on the table. "Sit."

Zeferino sat, and Cully's boot came down twice on Niko's.

Niko tugged gently on Cully's sleeve. "Sir Cully, with respect, I think the word 'please' is missing from your vocabulary this evening," he said, frowning, as Zeferino seated himself.

Cully started to protest, then nodded. "Yes, yes, as you wish, Sir Niko," Cully said. "Please sit, Zeferino Erasmus—but you're already sitting. Then, please, remain seated, please." He gave an irritated look at Niko. "To your health, Zeferino Erasmus, please." He pushed the glass that had been in front of Niko over to Zeferino, and gestured at him to drink.

"My pleasure, of course, Excellency—Sir Cully, that is." The innkeeper downed the wine with one quick swallow and no sign of hesitation. "Is there anything else I can be of help with?"

"We're looking for the town's mayor."

"Mayor? We have no mayor in Lindos, Sir Cully."

"The town bailiff, then. Surely there's a bailiff."

"Again, my apologies—but no, not at the moment." He held himself still, as though he expected some outburst, then went on. "Old Andros was the bailiff, but died last year, and his Excellency the Governor has yet to appoint another. We're an open port, Sir Cully—we've little need of such, all in all. Rodhos is the crossroads of the world, Excellency, and Lindos the crossroads of Rodhos, and my establishment the crossroads of Lindos."

"Yes, I noticed the roads."

"If you need a mayor, Sir Cully I know you'll find one in Rodhos—the city, that is—and I believe he has several bailiffs, as well. We don't have—we manage to get by without such, hereabouts. It's a quiet town, for all that it's the crossroads of the world."

"Which is why those Sebiani?" Gray jerked his thumb toward four very large men sitting over in the far corner. "To help with the quiet?"

"Oh, they're old friends of mine, and large as they are, it's worthwhile letting them hang about, as they tend to help settle the small sorts of disputes that one has, from time to time." Zeferino gave a small shrug. "You know; if you mix men of difference races, and drinks of different preferences—even if it's just the thick coffee that's all that the True Be—that's all that the cursed Musselmen drink, and, well, every now and then—"

"Send for one."

"A Musselman—? As you wish, of course—"

"No. One of your Sebiani."

"Why, of course, Excellency. Filikos—that's what I call him, Excellency; I doubt anybody not bred to it could pronounce what he claims to be his name—Filikos, over here, please."

One of the men rose and walked over, slowly.

"Sit," Cully said. Filikos sat.

Niko turned to Zeferino. "Thank you for your help, Zeferino—we'll not keep you any longer."

Cully waited until Zeferino had walked a few steps away, then turned back, seen Cully's eyes on his, and had chosen to disappear into the back room.

The music was apparently too quiet for Cully's

preference, he caught the eye of the tamboura player, made a bring-it-up gesture with his hands, and both the speed and volume picked up.

Niko didn't recognize the tune, although heads throughout the room were swaying and feet tapping to the rhythm, and some of the Hellenes were singing in such low voices that he couldn't make out the words.

Obedient to his instructions, Niko tried to avoid looking around the room, but out of the corner of his eye he could tell that several of the tables had been emptied, the men at them apparently having decided to seek a less stressful place for their evening's recreation. He didn't blame them; Cully, with his present mask, frightened him, too, and he knew—or at least thought that he knew—that it was just an act.

Cully had let Filikos sit long enough. "We're looking for some information," he said, quietly.

"I don't know much," Filikos said. He had a deep, gravelly voice, and his thick beard didn't quite cover an old scar on his throat. "I do know that I haven't had a taste of the good wine in longer'n I care to think about, though. Zeferino doesn't believe in pampering us."

Cully nodded, and filled the glass that Zeferino had used; Filikos sipped at it, and smiled. It wasn't a very pleasant smile, between the absent teeth and the battered lips. One ear was mostly missing, as were, also mostly, two fingers of the right hand, and a deep cut over his left eye hadn't quite healed. It didn't take long experience as a knight to conclude that Zeferino's "occasional disputes" more than occasionally required somebody beating on somebody else, and that while he might have been good at it, he was just as capable of being injured in a fight as anybody else might be.

"You might think on telling me what exactly it is that you're looking for, you know?"

"I've thought about that. I've also thought that if I did, the moment after we left, Zeferino and everybody else with a pair of ears might hear about it, as well."

"That's possible, I guess." Filikos sipped more wine, and shrugged. "You'll never know unless you try."

"If I did tell you something, it would be a very bad idea if it got back to me that you'd bandied it about."

"Yes, it probably would," Filikos said, gesturing at Cully's swords. "I don't think I could take on a man who's actually drawn a sword." He grinned. "Then again, when we have problems in here, me and the rest don't wait until the swords or knives actually come out."

"You think you could take on a Knight of the Order, even a weaponless one?" Cully seemed very interested.

"Oh, I'd probably have some trouble with the boy; he carries himself well enough. Nothing I couldn't handle, mind you, but I'd be more worried about your marines or the bailiff over in the city coming looking for me after than I would about the likes of you." He touched a blunt finger to his forehead. "All respect intended, surely."

"Surely." Cully nodded. "And if you were promised that there'd be no marines, no bailiff looking for you, no sword drawn? On the word of a Knight of the Order."

"Then I wouldn't worry at all," Filikos said.

"Anytime, then. Anytime at all, if you'd rather fight than talk."

"I don't mind either. I just don't know what you're looking for, and you're not telling me." His fist lay on the table, the thumb pointing in the general direction of the

Musselmen. "We don't get a lot of Syrians in Lindos—they tend to do their business in the city, and then leave. If I had to guess, I'd guess that they and the Balak are working out some deal for slaves from Kizmir."

"And doing it here to keep Seeproosh out of it?" Cully nodded. "It's possible, I guess."

"Well, when Zeferino buys the barrels of his sorry excuse for wine, he goes upland to Dimilia and buys it there, rather at the port. Probably not the only man ever to skip around a go-between." He eyed Cully levelly. "I wouldn't want you to think I'm afraid of you, though, just because I pointed them out. I wouldn't want people to think I'm afraid of anybody, or I'd have to prove that there's reason for me not to be more often."

"I wouldn't want you to think that any Knight of the Order of Crown, Shield, and Dragon is someone for a swaggering Hellenic turd to take lightly," Cully said, then sipped at his wine.

"Hmmm . . ." Filikos shrugged. "I've got a suggestion, if you're of a mind for one. How about you and I each decide that we're each the most dangerous man in the room—in all of Rodhos, and just leave it at that?"

"If you prefer." Cully rose, slowly, and Niko did the same. "I think we're done here."

He didn't say any more until they were outside.

"Well, that was probably useless," Cully said, sighing. "Let's see if the good sergeant has had any better luck."

Niko was impressed with how well Cully had handled himself. For a moment, he had almost believed that the old man could have fought that huge man, and won.

He had likely persuaded Filikos that there was a chance, at least, although perhaps Filikos had been more worried about Niko? Probably not, but it was a nice thought, although Niko didn't know anything about fighting, with a sword or bare hands, that he hadn't learned over the past weeks from Cully, and not much of it at that.

Down at the foot of the street, the marines had half a dozen men sitting on the hard ground under the oil lamp. Niko only recognized a couple of them from the Crossroads of the World, but he hadn't been trying to memorize faces, after all.

"Swept 'em up nice, Sir Cully," Fotheringay called out. "That lot we caught coming over the back fence—these others tried to make it down the street."

Fotheringay and Mr. Sigerson had each taken one man aside, and each was listening patiently to his own man's quiet but urgent protestations. For some reason that Niko couldn't imagine, Sigerson was taking down notes for himself, while his manservant, Bigglesworth, was doing the same for Fotheringay.

Fotheringay gave Cully a quizzical look, and Cully made a shooing-away motion with his hands.

"On your way, then," Fotheringay said, gruffly, and the man gave a quick look at Cully and Niko, as though he was deciding whether to say anything, then clearly thought better of it, and took off down the street, walking at first, then breaking into a run, the *slap-slap-slap* of his sandals diminishing as he vanished into the dark.

Fotheringay started to beckon to another of the men, but gestured at the marines to keep him in place, and walked over to Cully, drawing himself up to attention.

"Nothing of interest, sir," he said, quietly. "Wouldn't be surprised if that last one was a deserter, but I wouldn't be surprised if he wasn't. If you ask me, it'd make sense to tattoo landsmen, just like they do indents before they haul them over to New England."

"More sense, if anything—but I don't recall His Majesty ever asking me about that, and we're not looking for deserters."

"I know that, sir, God's truth I do—it's what we *are* looking for I don't know."

"Well, two ways to look at it, sergeant. One way is that we're looking for something that's not right. 'The wicked flee when no man pursueth: but the righteous are bold as a lion.' If you find one that seems, well, more not-right than he should be, hang on to him. Otherwise, just let him go, along with the righteous."

"Damn few righteous, in this life." For whatever reason, the sergeant had . . . loosened up around Cully, although not the other knights.

Then again, so had Niko.

"True enough. But if you were somehow involved in whatever this is—whatever's behind the swords and the darklings—and you saw the likes of the two of us show up in town, what would you do?"

"I'd sit tight, sir, I would."

"Yes, you would. But you know that we know damnall—and I'm hoping that somebody hereabouts doesn't. 'Course, that means we've put every deserter, smuggler, and outlaw on the run, except maybe for a few smart ones, with a level enough head to stay put." His mouth quirked into a smile. "Rather have stayed with the *Wellesley*, Sergeant?"

The *Wellesley* had been left out at sea, close enough to cut off any escape to the east from the main port at the eastern point of the island, at least, and far enough away that it would be invisible from the shoreline, and would have to trust the two sailors stationed at the harbor lighthouse to signal that there was a ship trying to sneak out at night.

The entry to the harbor was heavily shoaled. Niko wouldn't have wanted to sail it at all with anything of a deeper draft than the skiff, and even the locals didn't come in or out at night—not without dire need.

"Yes, sir, when you beat the bushes, whatever's in them is going to fly out, even if it's not what you're looking for. And you might just frighten what's in the next bush, too, sir."

"True enough. Let's be on our way, Niko—Private Weatherall must be getting tired of the horses' company by now, and if Sir Joshua and Sir David have joined him, he'll be even happier to see the last of their company for a while. Gray tends to make people uncomfortable, as you may have noticed." He turned back to Fotheringay. "Just be sure you don't get bit by whatever jumps out of the bush."

"Yes, sir." Fotheringay came to attention, then relaxed. "You do the same, sir."

"Well," Cully asked, "who has spotted the spy?"

Niko looked up, startled. Bear's forehead wrinkled, and Gray just scowled.

A spy?

Niko looked behind him. Below, beneath the silver of moon, the road twisted down to the dim lights of Lindos, and while he was no more comfortable on the back of the hired pony than he had been on Pantelleria, at least they seemed to be less than an hour's ride from Lindos, as nearly as Niko could guess, which seemed reasonable, as they had definitely ridden for less than an hour.

He didn't have to guess where they were—Cully had said that this hill was called the Agios Stefanos, the Mountain of the Smith, as though that should have meant something to him, as well as Gray and Bear. It hadn't, but they had gone along with as little protest as Niko had.

To what purpose, he couldn't guess.

It was far too slow a pace to have been of any use in chasing any of the men who had been questioned, although it did give the three knights a chance to talk.

Gray and Bear had reported a similar haul of scared men to be questioned and released on the other side of town, and the silence of bosuns' whistles spoke loudly of a lack of anything important found by those that they had left behind.

The road grew ever steeper, and Niko had trouble holding on, despite the promised sure-footedness of the horses, and the ease with which the three knights stayed in their saddles, without any apparent effort.

"Well, of course there are spies here," Gray said. "I think it's damnably foolish to make every landing on the island a free port, without so much as a squadron stationed here, and no government to speak of, but I don't recall the Governor asking me, or you, if he should change that."

" 'Rodhos is the crossroads of the world,' eh?" Cully smiled.

"Damn near *everywhere* is the crossroads of the world," Gray said. "If you ask the locals." He sighed. "But they've got a point here—I counted two Guild ships, half a dozen

Western and Eastern Caliphate feluccas in the harbor, and I wouldn't be at all surprised if that sleek bark flying the Izmiri pennant is really from Seeproosh."

"The Izmiri are far more victims than traders, these days; I'd be surprised if it wasn't." Cully shook his head. "But no, I wasn't talking about a spy here—but on the *Marienios*. Or the Navy ships, possibly."

Gray just scowled, and Bear seemed puzzled.

"Niko?" Cully asked. "You?"

Niko shrugged. "I don't . . . I don't have any idea, Sir Cully. What makes you think there's a spy on board, and for whom?"

"Them, whoever they are. If I was them—whoever they are—and I knew that we were headed their way, I'd certainly try to put one of my own people aboard. My guess would be it's one of the hired-on seamen. Which one, I couldn't say. I doubt that he'd be whispering to himself in dark corners of the ship, as convenient as that would be. But I think he's there—I certainly hope so."

"Which is why you insisted that the Abdullahs rent you the ship with just a skeleton of a crew?" Bear nodded. "I should have wondered about that."

"It seemed reasonable. All is fish that comes to the net, or whatever the Hellenes say. I haven't noticed anybody showing any . . . unusual curiosity over exactly where we're going, have you, Niko?"

Niko wrestled with trying to keep his feet in the stirrups while he thought about it for a moment. "Everybody seems to be curious about where we're going next."

"But that's not unusual, under the circumstances. I haven't noticed any of the sailors trying to engage you in conversation about it. Have you?"

He shook his head. They were all treating him distantly, the way that strangers should—although it had even spread to the Abdullahs. Milos's resentment was almost palpable—not that Niko had complained, or taken advantage of it. When this was all over, he would have to go back to the islands, after all, and while he would go back a rich man, he would not wish go back to become a man whose neighbors took a view that he thought himself better than they were. "I don't know," he said. "I'm not fond of Milos, true—"

"The girl?" Gray asked.

"Kela," Bear said. "She seemed . . . very pleasant. Quite pretty."

"Do I detect a note of lust, O saintly one?" Gray asked, but there was a smile in his voice.

"I'm not saintly, Gray, though I do try. And it's hardly sinful lust to note that a girl is pretty." He sobered. "It's best not to speak of it, all things considered. Do you think there's some spy for this Them aboard?"

Gray fiddled with the hilt of the Khan, and shook his head. "The Khan doesn't think so. He thinks that's too subtle for a bunch of Westerners."

Cully laughed. "Well, thank him for me."

"Thank him yourself," Gray said.

"Oh, what is it, Joshua? If I've offended you yet again, tell me how, and I'll consider apologizing."

Niko could more feel than see Gray scowl in the dark, but he didn't say anything. Other than the quiet whisper of the wind through the brush, the only sound was the shuffling of the horses' hooves and grunts—these ponies seemed to grunt a lot, for some reason or other.

"Perhaps, Father Cully," Bear finally said, "you could

tell us where we're going now?"

"I wanted to keep you alert," Cully said. "I was rather hoping that we'd scared up something that would try to put a stop to us." He pointed to the right. "Twenty years ago, there was a foot trail over that way, and somebody with enough motivation could have gotten ahead of us along it." He shook his head. "But even these ancient ears would have heard something."

"In the future, if you wish me to remain alert, Father, could I ask that you just ask me?" Bear said, gently. "I've been listening, mind you, but I've not heard anything."

"I have." Cully pointed a thumb to their right. "Something moved in the brush back there a few yards. Something small—perhaps a rabbit."

"If you wanted bait for some trap, you might as well have dragged a goat along behind us," Gray said, interrupting himself to swear at his pony when it stumbled.

"I don't have a goat handy, Gray, and, somehow or other, I don't think it would be the right bait in any case. On the other hand, four knights—"

"Hold up, please. I'm going to walk this poor excuse for a horse—"

"Very gentle of you."

"—rather than breaking my legs underneath it when it falls on top of me," Gray finished.

"We're almost there," Cully said, and pulled his pony to a halt. "I think, and—yes; there's the path."

They tied the horses' leads to brush by the side of the road, and followed Cully up the steep path that led over a heavily grown saddle.

Niko let go an involuntary gasp. The ruins seemed to glow from an inner light, or perhaps it was just the moonlight.

Whatever it was—whatever it had been—had been settled into the top of the hill, the huge stones moved from who-knew-where, who-knew-how.

"Welcome to the Acropolis of Lindos," Cully said. He pointed toward where what looked like it had been a series of perhaps twenty curved, massive steps rimmed the side of the hill. But they weren't the sorts of steps a person could have used; they were far too large, and too wide.

He caught himself moving to make the sign of the Trident, and stopped himself, but Cully caught the move and just grinned. "No, Niko, there's no need to cross yourself—although they do look like steps that one of the, err, one of the local false gods would have used, eh? It's nothing quite that grand, although it was grand enough, I'm sure. See that flat space below? That was, I think, the stage, and those were the seats of the theater, I believe, where plays were performed for the pleasure of the gods—and the local populace, perhaps, as well, who sat there."

"False gods," Bear said, his hand dropping from the Nameless, as though it had rejected the hand.

"Well, that would depend on your opinion, David," Cully said. "The locals didn't think so, and perhaps some still don't. I've heard tell that there's occasional homage paid to the old gods all over the islands, here and there."

Bear turned to him. "Niko? Could that be true?"

Niko didn't know what to say. Well, that wasn't true.

Niko-the-fisherboy knew what to say: *Of course not*, perhaps. Or *I've never heard of such a thing, Excellency— we all worship the One God at the One True Church throughout the islands*.

But—but the three of them, Bear and Cully in particular, had treated him well, better than one of his station in life had any right to expect.

He owed them at least some honesty, and he ought to pay it. A strange feeling for a fisherboy to have, although maybe he wasn't just a fisherman, not anymore.

But here? Here where, so Cully said, the gods had actually been worshiped? That idea chilled him thoroughly, and he had to clamp his jaws together to keep his teeth from chattering, despite what had been the only pleasant coolness of the night air.

"Niko."

His hand fell to Nadide's hilt, and it warmed him.

Niko? Niko, I'm scared.

Me, too, Little One.

Sing to me?

"Niko, I asked you—"

"Easy, Gray. Just give him a moment."

Later, he thought. I—I. Shhh. Just go back to sleep.

I'm scared, Niko.

Shh.

It had been wrong to wake her; his fear was infectious. He put his free hand to his ear, as Cully had taught him, and listened to the slowing beat of his heart until he could breathe slowly again, and in his mind he sang her the lullabye.

Slowly, at first with protest, Nadide drifted off into her own warm darkness, thinking of her thickfinger and, as always, her mother.

He let his hand drop.

All three of them were looking at him, and he felt his own fear return. "I'm . . . I'm sorry—I let my hand rest wrong, and I had to—"

"Easy, boy." Gray, for once, sounded amused. "We've

all done that." He actually chuckled. "Well, at least I'm
willing to bet that Nadide didn't try to persuade you that
killing all three of us was the right thing to do."

"No," he said. "She didn't." But the distraction had
given him a moment to gather his thoughts. Cully knew
about the worship of the Old Ones, and Niko didn't like
the idea of lying in front of Cully almost as much as he
didn't like the idea of Cully knowing that he was lying.

It just didn't seem right.

"As to what you asked me—"

"Please, Niko, hold for a moment," Cully said, shaking
his head. "Sir David, I think you owe Sir Niko an apology.
If Niko had seen such a performance on his island, he
would have mentioned it, and surely would have if they'd
made sacrifices to the local gods."

"Father, I—"

"You implied that Sir Niko is some sort of heretic, is
what you did. At the very least, you implied that he'd tolerate heresy, pagan rites, and the like. If that's not an
unknightly way to treat a brother of the Order, David, it
certainly ought to be."

Gray scowled, but Bear nodded. "You are, of course,
entirely correct, Father." He turned to Niko, and bowed
stiffly. "Sir and brother," he said, "I have given offense,
and must apologize."

"Now wait one bloody moment." Gray took a step forward. "Bear—"

Bear straightened and faced him. "Yes, Gray, I must."
He held up a hand. "As for you, sir and brother Joshua, I
must ask you to hold your peace."

"He's only a knight because—"

"He's a knight, by God, because I made him one," Cully

said, "with the authority you forced on me."

"The authority you tricked me out of."

"But it's real nonetheless, and his knighthood is, at this moment, every bit as real as is yours and mine," Bear said, gently, then raised a hand to forestall Gray's objection. "Yes, that can be changed, and perhaps shall be changed, by order of the Abbot General and Council, or perhaps His Majesty himself. Perhaps, at some point, it should. But, right here and now, he is Sir Niko Christofolous, Knight and Brother of the Order, and I did neither the Order nor myself any honor by implying that he would behave so."

Their eyes locked.

Niko started to say something—what, he didn't know—but Cully gripped his arm with unusual strength, and shook his head. "No," Cully whispered. "Let them be."

"Yes, let us be." Gray looked away and sighed. "Ah, very well, Bear. You win, as usual. Have it your way," he said, and turned to Niko. "And you may have my apologies, too, Sir Niko," he said. "If you'll accept them."

"Of course he will," Cully said. "Now, as I was saying before I was so rudely interrupted, Gray, the plays were a city thing, although every bit as much a worship of their ancient false gods as sacrifices were." He beckoned to them. "But follow me."

He led them down the path, past the steps of the gods—the seats of the theater, down a dip in the path and then up to the top of a low ridge.

"Now, here, here's something more interesting," he said, leading them single-file through a natural path through the thick scrub. "Those blocks over there, I think are what's left of the columns that used to support the temple."

"A temple to these false gods?"

"Oh, don't sound so indignant, Bear—the Inquisition did the dirty work, a hundred or more years ago. Happened all over the islands—the local populace, under the watchful eyes of the priests, tore down all the altars to the local false gods, just like they did to the Musselman mosques, when they didn't just remake them as churches, like in Pironesia."

"That—church was—"

"Yes, of course. And it was properly purified, properly consecrated, although why you'd be bothered by such things escapes me. Hmmm . . . none of you would happen to have a lantern in your kit, by any chance? I thought not," he said, digging in his pouch.

In a few minutes, he had fashioned a torch from a rag and stick, and doused the rag in some oil from a bottle from his kit. For some reason, Gray insisted on lighting it with the flint and steel from his own pouch.

The torch burned with a loud crackling, casting dark and ever-moving shadows from the stones. "This may take a while, and more than one—Bear? Would you mind improvising a few more?"

"Not at all."

While Bear sat down on one of the benches with his sticks and rags, Cully led Niko and Gray past the stunted uprights of what had been columns toward the altar.

Cully held the torch over the smooth, even surface of the altar. Niko didn't know what to expect, but he found himself relieved when the surface gleamed back, spotless and unstained. There were no markings of any sort on it. It was just a rectangular slab of marble, vaguely convex. There were chips along the edges of the surface, and the sides had been left rough and unpolished.

But it was just a piece of stone, just an ordinary altar, like the one that was—that had been atop Niko's island. The locals, here, certainly worshiped the old gods, just as Niko's family did—had. But they had been careful, too, and that was more than just as well.

Gray's shoulders seemed to ease, too, and he let out a loud sigh. "You were beginning to frighten me, Sir Cully. I'd half-expected that the altar would be stained with blood, or that we'd find some child's body open to the sky."

"Don't be more of a fool than you have to, Gray."

"I'll endeavor to try," Gray said. "But it's difficult at times."

"Try harder." Cully held the torch's flame near the smooth stone surface, and leaned over as though he was looking for something, although Niko couldn't have said what. "The Hellenes no more engaged in human sacrifice than the Hebrews did—the story of Abraham and Isaac aside. And if you want to condemn human sacrifice, then consult the Khan, and ask him how he died—"

"That was different."

"It always is," Cully said. "Everything's always different." He rose and shook his head, then walked over to one of the stone benches rimming the cleared area around the altar, and rubbed his hand along it, then stood, one hand on a hip. "Now, that is interesting—the bench is dusty, as it should be. But the altar itself is clean, as though it's been recently washed—scrubbed clean, perhaps?"

"Perhaps." Gray sounded grim again, all trace of the light tone in his voice vanished into the dark. "What do we do now?"

"Well, we look. It's worth bringing back a party of marines in the daylight, but . . ." he said, as he walked off, the torch still in hand, " . . . my guess is that the refuse pit would be nearby."

"Refuse pit?"

"Certainly. No matter what you do with a sacrifice, there'll be . . . spare parts left over. If they burn the sacrifices, there'll be charred bones, and if they don't think that the old gods actually want to eat the meat, they have to dispose of it some way, so let us look."

Niko relaxed; he knew what they would find, if the rituals here were anything like they had been at home: nothing.

Zeus and Demeter, so he had been taught, had no use for most of the meat—beyond the heart, the seat of the soul of a goat, or a bull—any more than the Good and Kindly Ones did.

Poseidon himself wanted only blood and viscera— nothing of even the fattest of fat tunnyfish, nothing save the acknowledgment that the bounty of the sea was his to grant or withhold, an admission that any fisherman would be a fool to deny.

There would be nothing to find, so it was best to get to finding that nothing, and be done with it.

Bear had finished the torches, and handed them out. Niko, like the other two, touched his to Cully's lit one, and started to search the ground, although he didn't know what he was supposed to be looking for. The local people surely wouldn't leave the viscera here, any more than Grandfather had. Hides were always useful, and separating them from the meat could be done later—and bone was useful for hundreds of different things.

"Well, look here," Gray said, as he planted his torch in the ground. "Loose soil—I think there's some sort of pit here."

Cully smiled. "Ah—sharp eyes. I was hoping so." He knelt, digging in the soft dirt with his bare hands. "Niko, would you mind helping me?"

There was no way to object, although Niko wished that there was, so he knelt.

An insect whizzed by Niko's ear, making it itch. He reached up to scratch at it, and his hand came away wet— with blood?

Something large and dark came out of the night and struck him, knocking him over, and he started to struggle as well as he could, but strong hands battered his own away, and he found himself pressed hard into the ground, stones sharp against his back.

"Easy, Niko," Bear's voice whispered in his ear. "Stay down."

Cully and Gray were already gone, off somewhere in the dark, having disappeared without a word.

Bear didn't wait for Niko's response before he too was gone in the dark, leaving Niko cowering behind the altar, awfully and terribly alone.

He had been, Gray decided, a fool. A blind, clumsy fool who had lost his focus, just for a moment, too eager to see what was in front of him to pay attention to what was going on all around him, too distracted over his anger at the humiliation of Bear in having to apologize to that— to Sir Niko to focus on the moment.

Enough of *that*.

At the sound of the bowstring, he had flung his torch

high into the night, in the general direction of where he had heard the twang, and launched himself in a flat dive in the other direction, onto the loose gravel surrounding the pagan altar, rolling as he did, so that his shoulders would take most of the damage, and got his scabbards in hand then rolled some more, half pulling, half crawling until he was just over the crest of the mound, the heavy scrub clawing at face, trying for his closed eyes.

Seeing could wait—it was important to get off into the dark, and if at all possible to steal a few moments to lose the cursed torchlight that persisted behind his eyes.

The Khan was silent; Gray wouldn't need his advice at the moment, and, besides, he didn't have a free hand.

He took a moment to rest, yes, but mainly to listen. The boy was whimpering quietly in the direction Gray had come from, but Bear and Cully had moved off quickly and quietly enough that he didn't know where they were, just that they had been moving away from him, the three of them reflexively spreading out into the night to wreak their own damage separately.

Gray dimly remembered feeling a tug of some sort, on his left side, and when he reached down he felt a hole torn in his robes—but the flesh underneath was unhurt.

It had been close, and that was bad enough, but . . .

The first thing was to check on the others, and then deal with the attackers. It couldn't be many of them— even a distracted fool like Gray wouldn't have been able to ignore more than a few. He grinned for just a moment. He was angrier at himself than at the men who had just tried to kill him. That was reasonable, perhaps, but it was strange that it seemed so reasonable.

His mouth was dry as dust, and it took him several

tries licking his lips before he could give off a single low whistle. No need to add any tongue-clicks—he had a dozen bruises and cuts on his back, and a deep scrape along his left arm, but he was, at the moment, unwounded.

Two whistles a dozen or so yards to to his right told of Cully having continued in the same direction he had taken off, and of having reached the other side of the mound, and it was a long moment before Bear's own low triple whistle sounded, followed by a scrabbling through the brush to Gray's left. Moving quietly had never been one of Bear's strengths.

Gray wanted, as badly as he wanted anything, to draw the Khan—to shatter these murderous idolaters into flaming little pieces was an image so enticing that his mouth belatedly watered.

And—no.

One didn't draw the Khan out of anger, but of necessity, with a mind purged of the fury and emotion that could so easily go further than where calm, iron control should let it. He had been, he knew, wrong, horribly wrong to draw the Khan in Pironesia, and that his nerves had been as taught as a crossbow's string had been no excuse then.

If he did it now, he would do so out of cold necessity, which could be, which *would* be more than bad enough.

Neither Cully nor Bear had said anything, beyond whistling their condition, but low voices cursing to the north and east told of idolators who weren't well trained at all, although they certainly had come upon the knights quietly enough; Gray had to give them that. Idiots—if they had just had the sense and self-control to fire in a volley, they would have nailed all three—all four of them.

The temptation was to take them lightly because of

that, and Gray had to restrain himself, but not too long—the others would be waiting for him to take the lead.

He slung the Khan diagonally over his shoulder, and tied it in place with the strings from his robes. He could still reach over his shoulder and draw it, if need be, but it would stay out of the way in the interim.

His scabbarded mundane sword in his left hand, he whistled for Bear and Cully to hold in place—implicitly meaning "in a safe place, if possible."

Gray already had a target. One of their thrown torches had lit a patch of brush on fire, and one of the attackers had started trying to put it out, his crossbow held to the side, while he stooped to throw dirt and sand on the blaze.

A stupid thing to do, yes, but the world was full of stupidity, and Gray never minded taking full advantage of it, particularly since he had contributed more than his share to the pool.

Drawing his mundane sword, Gray rose to a crouch and ran at the man, allowing a deep-throated shout to push its way out of his throat.

The idiot turned, his broad face greasy with sweat in the firelight, bringing his crossbow up, but Gray kicked it to one side with a booted foot, the bolt discharging harmlessly into dirt. Gray took the moment to bring his saber around, slashing down across the Hellene's face as Gray barely broke stride in his run past into the darkness beyond the ragged circle of torchlight.

The man's scream was warming in the dark, but Gray didn't stop to enjoy it as he continued to run. Something had moved in the bushes beyond him, to the left, and he broke in that direction, his sword held out to one side, ready to slash.

Slash, rather than thrust, was the way of it—injure if not kill the man in front of you, then on to another, until they were all down, and could be finished off at leisure.

A dark shape rose from the bushes slowly, far too slowly, something cradled in its arms. Gray slashed again, this time kicking the man's legs out from under him, unwillingly giving him a precious half-second to make his peace with God before Gray cut his throat.

It was all distant, but sharp, the way it usually was, as though he wasn't involved; Gray felt like he was outside himself, like a puppeteer at a children's show, pulling the strings and watching Gray-as-toy-puppet wreaking death and destruction on other puppets, and if the screams and grunts and particularly the smells should have made him feel otherwise, they didn't.

"How many?" he called out. "I've got two down."

He should have whistled—it was much more difficult, particularly for an untrained man, to make out the exact direction of a whistle, even if he understood it to be a signal, and none of the enemy would know what the signal meant—but Gray wanted to draw them toward him, to him.

A quick series of five-then-three notes to his right told of Bear having counted five, and having added another one to Gray's count of the downed, but the querying three-note theme after that said that Bear wasn't entirely sure about the number, not that Gray would have or should have relied on his count as anything but a minimum, anyway.

The man who had been foolish enough to try to put out the fire was still screaming as he knelt on the ground, his face in his hands, and Gray listened hard, trying to sort out the sounds in the brush and along the gravel.

There.

There were the sounds of running feet—at least two pairs of them, perhaps three—down the path that led past the amphitheater. Two or more of the idolaters had had enough—unless the boy had taken off, and was among them.

There were distant sounds of a scuffle from that direction, three truncated cries of agony, and a few moments later, the All-Clear whistle from Cully.

Well, there would be ample time to worry about the boy later. Cully, soft-hearted Cully, wouldn't have killed the boy for fleeing, any more than Bear would have. Gray—Gray wasn't sure what he would have done, and it didn't matter at the moment. What was more important was the obvious question: had Cully miscounted? Had Gray? Was one of the attackers waiting, silently, out in the dark? If one or more of them had been smart and self-controlled enough to go to ground—

"I think we can do without lighting more torches," Bear said, his voice coming from behind and to Gray's right, "but that's all of them, I believe."

Probably.

Cully wouldn't have whistled All-Clear if he hadn't been sure, Gray decided, and he got to his feet slowly.

The man Gray had wounded was still screaming, which was just fine with Gray. If he could scream, he could talk, and from the sounds of it, Cully had been somewhat rushed with the two he had taken down, and this one was the only survivor.

Bear brushed himself off as he walked toward toward the altar where the boy had been hiding. "You can come out now, Niko, everything is fine," he said, and started to say something more, but his voice caught in his throat.

No.

Niko rose from behind the moonlit stone altar, Nadide held high over his head, glowing with a deep crimson fire that dazzled the mind far more than it did the eyes.

It was the screaming that had done it, finally.

He had heard the whistles, and at least at first the movement of bodies through the dark, although Gray and Bear and Cully moved so quickly and quietly that Niko lost track of them almost immediately.

Something slapped against the other side of the altar, and for some reason he reached up and felt at his ear.

It was only then that it started hurting; his hand came away all wet and even stickier, and it felt like his ear was going to come off in his hands. He clapped his hand over the ear, his other arm around his belly, trying to keep the cries inside. If he made any noise, Gray would probably kill him outright, if these others didn't.

It hurt so much.

He was supposed to be able to ignore pain; a fisherman's life wasn't one for some weakling who would cry out at every little cut and bruise that life had to offer. But his heart was pounding so loud and hard in his chest that he was sure that everyone around him could hear the *boom-boom-boom* of it, and he found himself unable to move from where he lay, curled up on the ground against the rough, cold stone, cradling Nadide's sheath in his arms, as though that could somehow protect him, and he could somehow protect her.

And then the screaming started, loud, echoing from

hill to hill, and even more in his head, until he found his tearing eyes jammed shut, and both of his hands on his ears, trying to keep the sound out.

But he couldn't. He didn't know who it was, but whoever it was was hurting badly, more than the agony in Niko's right ear, as bad as that was. It was probably as much as Lena and Mara had screamed when—

His hand fell to Nadide's hilt.

He's hurting, like that horrible one hurt me.

I know, but—

Make him stop hurting, Niko. Please.

I can't—

Yes, you can, you can, we can, I can, you can . . .

The sword slid smoothly and silently from the sheath. He was never sure whether he had drawn Nadide, or she had drawn him. There wasn't a him or her anymore, not really, but something else, something that was not merely a combination of a scared fisherboy and a soul locked in metal, but something more, something simpler.

His own aches became distant, even more distant than Nadide's ancient fear of the horrible man with the more-horrible knife.

That should have frightened him, and it should have frightened her, but it didn't frighten them, as they could not feel fright, any more than they could feel pain.

Were they beyond any pain, past any reason to fear? They didn't know; the one person that was Niko-Nadide didn't know, but somehow it didn't matter at all.

Ruddy light coursed through their shared muscles and veins, and their tendons sang like the plucked wires of the lavta that Nadide's mother used to play, before the Ugly Ones took them all away, before—

But that didn't matter. Not here and now.

What did matter was the man screaming in pain before them, writhing on the ground as he held his face in his hands, sucking in air in great, liquid gasps, only to release it in screams that reminded them of their own.

It was a wrongness. Nobody should hurt like that. Worse: nobody should fear in a way that they could smell with their joined soul far more than with Niko's nostrils that flared and contracted in time with his distant, ragged gasping.

Gray rose to block them, his own lifeless sword naked in his hands, and Bear, gentle, loving Bear, was running toward them, his arms and fingers spread wide, his head moving slowly, laboriously from side to side as his mouth moved—but he was moving slowly, so slowly, that it would have been hard to pay attention long enough to make out his words, and far too much trouble to try. They were just words, after all.

Bear wouldn't want the man to hurt, and neither did they. Gray was built of harsher stuff, yes, but his relentlessness couldn't rule them, not here and now, not with the screaming man's mind no longer hot with anger nor boiling with hate, but filled to overflowing with the fear and the pain from the blazing, agonizing darkness that had taken his eyes, and now threatened to take his all.

It had to stop, but even though he was moving with exquisite slowness, Gray had managed to plant himself, legs spread wide, between them and the hurt man, and that was a wrongness in and of itself. Gray shouldn't try to stop them. Nobody should. And Gray was the one who had hurt the screaming man.

Part of him wanted to burn Gray where he stood, but

he wasn't an evil man, not really, despite the harshness of his manner and his core—just a scared one, and that was not only understandable, and forgivable, but necessary. Everybody was scared, just as everyone was scarred; life etched wounds into every soul in a myriad of ways, day by day.

Gray's soul lay open before them, battered and scarred, razor-sharp at the edges and dangerous to the touch, but not wrong, just . . . misshapen. For her to burn that soul was entirely possible, of course—the heat from her fire burned more than hot enough, high over his head—but that would have been a wrongness in itself.

So he lowered her point, and he lowered his shoulder, and ran at Gray, swinging her out to one side to avoid Gray's body, so that the point of his shoulder rather than the point of the sword caught Gray in the pit of his stomach, knocking the slim man to one side, out of the way, barely slowing Niko and Nadide at all.

Behind them, Bear was still saying something, and for just a moment, Niko turned, and looked up.

The brightness of the stars dazzled him, but the silver of moon had somehow dimmed. He had never before noticed that the stars were not just white lights in the sky, but had a richness of color and tone; fiery reds, cool blues, and somehow cooler oranges spread across the sky.

But they didn't let the glorious wonder of the dome of sky slow them down, any more than they had permitted the leaden movements of Gray, or those of Bear to do so.

They stood over the hurting, screaming man, cowering with his face in his hands.

The part of them that was Niko lowered the part of them that was Nadide, and they touched him with fire and ice, with warmth from the cold of his fear just as much as with coolness from the heat of pain, and most of all with a dark and loving peace, and in the brief moments before his soul flickered into a dark fog that rose to join with its brothers in the sky, they knew that they had done right, and it was with a sense of overwhelming peace and joy that they themselves drifted off into a blanket of warmth that covered them from all the pain and fear and coldness of the world.

"Shit," Cully said.

Bear looked up from where he was attending to Cully. That exclamation wasn't very much like Cully at all, but Bear bent back to his work, rather than saying anything. It was probably just the hurt, and loss of blood. Bear didn't think he had hurt Cully, at least not any more than was necessary.

"I could wake him," Gray said, looking down at the boy's prostrate form, sprawled out on the ground beyond the still-smouldering ashes.

Niko still held the Red Sword, but the glow had faded to the dullest of reds, barely discernible in the moonlight; it wouldn't have been visible in daytime, he decided, although he didn't know what to make of that. Every live sword was different, just as every person was.

"Don't," Cully said.

"I could just poke him with my scabbard," Gray said, "or a stick. It might wake him up, and he might let go." His voice was too loud, as though he hoped that it might wake Niko.

"Yes," Cully said, "it might. And it might startle the both of them, and I don't want to know what happens then, not with his—their—speed." He gestured with his free hand toward the smoking remains of where the man Gray had injured lay. "Let him be, *please*."

Niko was alive, no question of that, and in no apparent danger, although even in the moonlight, Bear could still see the slow ooze of blood from the cut on his ear. But it was slow, and slowing, and Niko's chest rose and fell slowly and regularly. If he wasn't lying so straight and still, Bear would have thought him only asleep.

Niko wasn't the worst hurt of the three of them; Cully was. Gray had only taken a few cuts and scrapes, and Bear had only come off a little worse, where a headlong slide along the sharp stones had flayed his forearm and right leg, but Cully had taken a bolt through the fleshy part of his left arm.

Hand pressure had stopped the blood from flowing, and Bear had torn strips of cloth from Cully's tunic to bind the wound closed; Cully's sash had been improvised into a sling. That should hold until it could be properly washed and rebandaged.

"Wiggle your fingers, please," Bear said.

"If I can't wiggle my fingers, what do you propose to do about it?"

It was a reasonable objection, granted; poor old Sir Thomas had lost most of the use of both of his arms from wounds, and little of it had ever come back, despite the attention of the best surgeons.

But it was best to know. "Please," he said.

Cully shook his head and muttered something Bear didn't want to make out under his breath, but he obliged, and surely enough the fingers moved, although Cully winced with each twitch. "Are you satisfied?"

"Yes, Father. I'm sorry, but—"

"Oh, be still, Bear, and stop apologizing at every turn. I'm just an old man, with an injury that hurts more than such a thing would have even a dozen years ago, and that among other things puts me in less than the best of moods; nothing to worry about, and certainly nothing that's your fault." He looked over to where the boy lay. "I don't think you should touch him, Gray, not with the sword still in his hand," he said. "You saw how fast he moved—and more than saw it, eh?"

"Yes, I did see it." Gray took a step toward the boy, then stopped himself before Bear or Cully could say anything. "Idiots."

"Who?"

"Us. Them. Us, for getting so involved in what we were looking at that we didn't see them coming up from, from wherever they came from. Them, for whichever one of them panicked, and let fly too early. Some discipline, and they would have had us all for the taking."

Bear nodded. Gray was, of course, correct, and while he didn't quite say so, Bear knew that he was blaming himself more than anybody else.

"Gray," Cully asked, "how does the three of us being idiots make touching the boy any wiser? Just leave him be; he'll wake soon enough, I hope."

"I'll go see to the horses," Gray said. "Don't light any more torches." The only reason Bear wouldn't have described his movement as stomping away is that Gray moved smoothly and quietly, as usual.

The aftermath of a battle, even as small a one as this had been, was always much the same: crumpled bodies lying on the cold ground in whatever pose death had left them.

None of them had yet drawn flies, but come sunrise, they would, of course.

"Gray," Cully called out, "I'm going to light a torch—I want to take a look at that pit."

There was no answer. He cocked his head to one side. *"Quitacet consentire videtur*, no?"

Bear knew that Latin, and he nodded, regretfully. Gray wouldn't like it.

"And it's *auto de to sigan homologountos esti sou*, in Hellenic," Cully went on, and 'silence gives consent' in any language, eh?"

"I don't know why you're asking me, Father—you're going to do it anyway."

"Well, that's true enough." Cully grimaced as he moved. "But I do have a very good reason for asking you: I want you to light the torch, and do the digging." He patted, gently, at his slung arm. "My part will be to just stand over you and try to look wise, eh?" He gestured over to where Niko lay. "We can keep an eye on him while we do it."

Well, Gray hadn't actually forbidden it—he must have heard Cully, after all, and hadn't said anything—and they were, all three of them, knights, and while even Gray had stopped haranguing him about his habit of leaping to Cully's every command as though he was still a shaved-headed novice, it was a reasonable thing to do.

What had these idolaters been trying to conceal? Did Cully know more than he was saying?

Well, there was one way to find out.

Bear pulled his battered old fire-making kit from his pouch and fumbled around on the ground for one of the torches that they had made before. Wet dirt from the ground had stuck itself to the oiled cloth, and it spat and hissed as he struck flint to steel, but it did catch, and he planted it in the ground next to to the pit, surprised at how vulnerable and naked his back felt.

For a moment he regretted that all of their armor was aboard the *Wellesley*, and faulted himself for that regret. A crossbow bolt could pierce armor, after all, just as King William had long ago proved at Crecy, and while the craft of armor-making had gotten better over the years, so had bow-making.

"What's bothering you?" Cully asked. "Other than the obvious, I mean."

"Oh, I'm just being foolish, Father—I was thinking that if we had armor, I'd not be feeling so naked at the moment. No point in worrying about that now."

"And what's so foolish about that?" Cully asked. "I haven't looked for one of their crossbows, not yet; I think the one over by the . . . ashes was burned by Niko and Nadide, and I don't feel like thrashing around the bushes in the dark. We can do that when it's light. I doubt that they're windlass-driven; they reloaded and fired too quickly for that. Perhaps they used a belt claw; more likely, they finger-nocked the bolts. Men certainly grow strong enough hereabouts, but I doubt that their hand-drawn bows will put a quarrel through good Sheffield plate, although it probably would through leather.

"Still, all in all, even at my age, under most circumstances I'd rather rely on being able to move around than being slowed in heavy, hot armor—and hello, there. Hand me that."

That was, of course, the end of a bone, exposed by Bear's digging. Bear locked his fingers around it, and pulled. At first it resisted, but he pulled harder, and with a tearing sound, it came loose.

A few rotted bits of flesh and tendon still clung to it as he pulled it from the dirt; he brushed as much as he could off with his sleeve.

"Damn—ow!" Cully held up his good hand. "Never mind—I just moved my arm. All the excitement, and then the disappointment."

Cully took the bone in his unwounded hand. "It's a leg bone—from a sheep. I've certainly seen enough of those." Cully flipped it end-over-end into the night, and shook his head. "Well, keep digging—there may be something more interesting there, but I doubt it. My guess is that we've just discovered just what it appears to be: a coven of worshipers of Apollo, or maybe Demeter or Zeus; nothing more."

"You thought it might be more than that?"

"I hoped, at least, it was more than that. It would have been deucedly convenient if we'd found the source of these new swords here on Rodhos, and I thought that our stirring things up in Lindos would have flushed that game. And it occurred to me that since there seems to be . . . a very horrible kind of sacrifice involved, it might well take place here.

"If it was here. Which, alas, it appears not to be." He sighed. "Life is, alas, rarely arranged for the convenience of the likes of you and me, Brother Bear. Still: dig. Perhaps we'll come up with something more interesting, although I doubt it."

Bear dug.

✧   ✧   ✧

Niko came awake slowly, the dawn sun prying his eyes open.

He tried to go back to sleep, but the ground was hard beneath him. It was good to rest, to sleep, to wrap himself in a dark warm and dreamless dream, where there was no pain, no fear—nothing except him and Nadide, sleeping under the watchful gaze of Grandfather, and Father, and Mother, and Mara and Lina, just as much as under the gentle rocking and singing of the One Who Smelled Like—of Nadide's mother.

It was with a sense of loss that he let himself swim back up to the light, to find himself lying on—on a blanket?

He reached for Nadide, and—

"Easy, boy." Cully's lined face was leaning over him. "She's just to your right—and safely in her sheath, although I'd ask that you hold off from making contact with her until your head clears." He tapped his leather gloves against Niko's chest. "Are you able to get up by yourself?" He raised his head. "Bear? Gray? He's awake."

Cully grunted as he straightened. He had been injured, somehow or other; his bare right arm, wrapped with a bloody cloth, was strapped against his side, and his robes had been tied in a strange-looking way that tucked them under his injured arm, leaving it mostly exposed.

Niko stood, and for a moment the world swum about him, and he thought he would fall over, but the dizziness passed, and he retrieved Nadide in her scabbard, as well as the Navy sword that had been laid beside her.

He kept his hand from her hilt as he adjusted his clothing and put the swords away. Cully was right; that would be for later.

He very much didn't want to think about the night, and he certainly couldn't talk about it, not now. Particularly not with Nadide.

They were no longer alone. A group—no, a *squad* of very tired-looking marines was busy digging up the waste pit, under the supervision of an even more tired-looking Sergeant Fotheringay. While they couldn't have been at it terribly long—how long had Niko been sleeping?—the pile of dirt had grown large enough to hide the altar beyond it.

The pinch-faced wizard, Sigerson, walked from around the dirt pile, his manservant beside him. His gray robes were stained.

"Well?" Cully asked.

"Well, no." Sigerson shook his head. "Well, if there's any magic involved, it's beyond me," he said, directing his words to Cully, rather than Niko.

"Holiness? Or its opposite?"

Sigerson shrugged. "I'm color-blind to that, I blush to admit; most wizards admit they are, and the others, I think, lie." He produced a small bone from somewhere. "If there's some necromancy involved in these bones—these goat bones or those sheep bones—it's too subtle for the likes of me, and I flatter myself to be a subtle enough man." He tossed the bone to one side. "Still, it was worth looking into it."

"I'm so glad you approve," Gray said from behind him.

Niko started—he hadn't seen Gray walk up.

"It would be a shame to have gone to all this trouble," Gray went on, "if you thought it wasn't worthwhile."

Sigerson's lips made a thin line. "Apparently, I've given offense, and for that, of course, I apologize, Sir Joshua," he said.

He turned to Cully. "If there's nothing further you need from me, I'm of a mind to return to Lindos, and see about bathing myself—at the moment, I smell, I think, rather too much like a dead goat, and I'll confess it's not my preference in a gentleman's cologne."

Cully's face was pale, almost colorless, and the dark circles under his eyes spoke of exhaustion almost as much as did the unusual stoop of his shoulders. "A good idea, Mr. Sigerson," he said, quietly, "a bath, that is—I could use one myself. And thank you for your help."

"You're welcome, of course." He gave Niko a brief smile and Gray the slightest of nods before walking off, his manservant's eyes sweeping across all three of them as though they weren't there.

Cully shook his head, wincing at the movement. "Now that you're done antagonizing the wizard, Joshua, what do you think we ought to be about next?"

"I don't know why you're asking." Gray eyed him levelly. "I think that's obvious. We've got the bodies—*most* of the bodies of the men who attacked us. They can't be the only idolaters around here—we need to find out what village they came from, and—"

"And what? And burn the village from post to thatch? And kill everyone who might be an idolater, any child whose father or mother might be? Perhaps they came from Lindos itself, or several villages—do you want to set every house on the east coast of the island on fire from post to thatch?" Cully asked. "I don't see how that would be a good idea, or even possible—have you even seen any thatched roofs in the islands? They've plenty of slate, and wood, and—"

"Cully. *Stop*."

"No." Cully shook his head. "No, I think it's you who should stop—you and that cursed Khan. Please, please, stop and think, Joshua. What we have here is just a bunch of local idolaters, that's all. It's not that important."

"Idolaters who tried to murder three knights of the Order? That's not important?"

"*Four* knights of the Order, Sir Joshua, and all who tried to kill us are dead; you have no need to worry about some savage bragging that he managed to bag a Knight of the Order. If you want to hang the bodies by the ankles from tree branches, with signs around their necks, you go right ahead; there's trees and branches aplenty.

"But if you do, do it quickly, man, and be *done* with it. As to the worship of the old gods, there's much of that all through the islands, and if His Majesty determines to start a Crown and Church inquisition to wipe it out, that's for him to decide, and not for you to start, no matter how much your bloodlust is upon you now and always, Joshua."

"Father, I—"

"You're angry, and you're tired, and you're letting your weariness and that damned Khan rule your thinking, is what you're doing. And perhaps you're a little embarrassed, having been knocked off your feet by a boy less than half your age, with no training worth speaking of, and—"

"That was just the sword," Niko said, before he realized that he was interrupting Cully. "I mean, it was me and the sword. I'm not blaming Nadide, Sir Cully, Sir Gray, really I'm not, and I'll take whatever punishment is due to me without complaint, but I couldn't have, I wouldn't have . . ." He let his voice trail off.

He wouldn't have what? He wouldn't have been able

to knock Gray down without that? Of course not; he had seen the three of them move through the night, fast as fish in water, and as surefooted as wild goats.

He wouldn't have killed the man?

It hit him then. His knees shook, and threatened to buckle beneath him; it was all he could do to keep to his feet.

They had killed the screaming man, he and Nadide.

He had killed a man.

"What are you crying for, boy?" Gray asked, his voice utterly scornful. "I've had worse than your pitiful few scratches. Perhaps, since Sir Cully is avoiding doing the necessary, we should take time for a little sparring to show you how—"

"Oh, be still, Gray," Cully said. "Just because you and the Khan kill more willingly than I'll step on ants doesn't mean that it's that way for everybody—that's what's bothering him."

Gray took a long breath, and let it out. "True enough," he said. "I'm a red-handed killer carrying a Red Sword, and nothing more than that, nothing at all—but I'm hardly the only one in the world, and perhaps, Father Cully, you could let me beat myself for it without your help?"

"And the idolaters in this part of Rodhos are hardly the only ones in Pironesia, or in the Med, or in the world, for that matter, eh?"

"But they're here, and we're here."

Cully didn't say anything. He just gave Gray a long look, his head cocked to one side.

After a moment, Gray sighed, and nodded. "Yes, Father, I know: only an idiot would be chasing after a bunch of local idolaters when there's far more important matters to be handled, eh?"

"Well, yes," Cully said.

"And while I'll confess myself a fool in more ways than one, Father Cully, I'm not so much of a fool that I'll delay us any further; as usual, you may have things your own way." He bowed, and turned to Niko. "Sir Niko."

Gray walked toward where the marine sergeant was supervising the digging. "Fotheringay—get those bodies into the trees. By the ankles."

"Aye, aye, sir."

"And then load them up—we're done here."

He walked off.

"Well, he's close to the edge," Cully said, as he shook his head. "But in most ways, he's got a good heart, that boy, I think."

Niko didn't say anything.

"I wouldn't mind seeing you actually *move* your lazy ass, Lowrey," Fotheringay shouted. "Once we finish here, we've a nice little march to Rody-city, you know, and I can arrange to make it the most god-awful miserable day marching that you've ever spent since your mother squatted behind the plow she was pulling to push you out."

Cully smiled, and nodded. "Fotheringay, too, I think." He patted Niko's arm. "You think I have a strange notion of what constitutes a good heart, don't you?"

Niko shrugged. "It's not my place to say."

"Perhaps not. Then again, I think you've got one, too. And with that, Sir Niko, let's be going—we've got a long day ahead."

Interlude 6: Promises

It is the business of every officer in HM Navy to keep in mind that HM Navy is *not* a business. It is a calling, every bit as much as holy orders are, if not more so, and to Hell with anybody who considers the comparison impious.

—Admiral Sir Simon Tremaine DuPuy

It was tempting, but . . .

Strangling Owlsley would probably not make matters any better, DuPuy decided, although there was that strong temptation, and Owlsley's skinny neck really did cry out for a pair of strong hands to wring it. No, words would have to do—and they'd have to be carefully chosen words.

DuPuy waited until Throckmorton had closed the door behind him before saying anything. Owlsley hadn't risen to get the door for Throckmorton, either, although that was a more minor problem.

"The purpose of having you maintain my schedule," he said, slowly, as though he was explaining things to an idiot, which seemed to be more than reasonable under the circumstances, "is to make sure that my time is left free for important things."

"Yes, Admiral," Owlsley said, ducking his head. "Of course. Admiral."

Then why did you tell Throckmorton that he could have an hour when McCaulkin sent a note that said he needed to see me? he didn't ask.

Perhaps it was too much to expect, at this point. And more than perhaps he should have taken up Throckmorton's or Shea's offer—or any of the half-dozen other such offers—to have their own secretary replace his, after Scratch's . . . unfortunate accident. He had probably been overly concerned about some residue of loyalty to their former captains. But given the way that both Throckmorton and Shea treated their own secretaries, that was probably an unreasonable concern.

Something to learn from, he decided.

DuPuy knew of other officers who didn't believe in second-guessing themselves, but while he wasn't immune from folly, at least he was immune from that particular folly: if he didn't acknowledge errors, at least to himself, how the blasted hell would he ever learn to avoid them in the future?

The truth was, he missed Scratch. Not his treason— but his efficiency. He wondered how much of that efficiency had come from Scratch's resolve to keep his position, so that he would be able to sell the Navy's secrets to his Dar paymasters, and—

Damn him. Damn him to the blackest of black hells for having forced DuPuy's hand too soon. But Owlsley—DuPuy couldn't think of him as Scratch—had been left waiting and sweating long enough.

"Well," he said, slowly, carefully, as though he was speaking to an idiot—as indeed he was, apparently, "let's start from first principles, shall we? Captain McCaulkin and his men take ships that don't float, or don't float well enough, and he and they fix that. Do you follow me? Captain Throckmorton shuffles around the least likely batch of beached officers, landsmen, and pox-ridden bunch of alleged bosuns and mates that one can imagine—some of whom are expected to sail aboard those ships. When Throckmorton has a routine appointment and McCaulkin sends a note that he says he'd like to speak to me as soon as is convenient, which do you think is most needing of my attention? Well, speak up, man."

Owlsley cleared his throat. "Sorry, Admiral, I—"

"I don't give a sodding Spanish sou for your sorriness—I asked you a question, Owlsley."

"Yes, sir. Captain McCaulkin's more important."

DuPuy shook his head. "No. Every officer and every man in His Majesty's service is equally important. A ship can sail without a master better than it can without topmen and riggers. But Captain McCaulkin's need, in this case, is more important than Throckmorton's. Understood?"

He didn't wait for an answer, but stalked out of the office, shaking his head, mostly at himself. It wasn't an emergency—the excitable McCaulkin would not have sent a messenger with an ambiguous note in a real emergency—but whatever McCaulkin had in mind was likely more important than giving a mild chewing-out to Owlsley.

The only justification that he could offer himself was that, all in all, it was important to the efficiency of the Fleet that he have a capable secretary.

The damn fool.

While the road to the dockyard was not as straight as it should have been—he had to skirt around the bursary, rather than having every man-jack in it leaping to attention—it took him only a few minutes, and gave him time to calm himself. It was best to be seen as a man of short temper—you got better service when your subordinates feared failing you as much as they relished not only obedience, but success—but that was not aided by actually being a man of short temper, after all.

Oh, well. He couldn't do a damned thing about his temperament, but he could, by God, control his temper, no matter how the trying made his stomach boil, and his fists clench themselves.

The bulk of the *Surprise*—God, he hated that name—loomed over the shack that McCaulkin used as his office, and at DuPuy's approach, the rating catching a quick smoke outside the office ducked quickly inside.

Good. McCaulkin had been informed that the Admiral was present, and would join in a moment.

The *Surprise*, unless DuPuy missed his guess, was in somewhat better shape than he had feared. Not that he could tell the condition of the keep or the knees from here, but the few gaps in the planking on the hull spoke of McCaulkin having decided against having to do the sort of lengthy and expensive reconstruction that had been all too common of late.

Worth seeing for himself, at that.

High above his head, a long gangplank ran from the scaffolding that cradled the hulk onto the poop deck, and while it looked rickety from here, it was stable enough for a pair of men to be coaxing a heavily loaded wheelbarrow across it. Good enough for DuPuy.

He silently cursed every step up the scaffolding, notseeing the men who scampered up and down it, although part of him secretly hoped that one would stop his work and salute him, giving him a chance to tear the poor sod a new asshole. Any man who didn't have both of his hands full with work, relieving him of the necessity of saluting, had damned well better find some work, and quickly, as far as DuPuy was concerned.

By the time he reached the top he was half out of breath, and paused for a moment.

A pair of artificers, each carrying a pair of muslin bags depending from a yoke, actually waited to let DuPuy proceed. He would have liked to have a stiff word with them, but he didn't want them to believe that he actually needed the rest, dammit, so he stomped across the plank and lowered himself onto the deck of the *Surprise*, making his way quickly past the waist toward the quarterdeck.

You could tell a lot about the progress of a ship from a distance, but to get any real feel for it, there was no good substitute for seeing for yourself. True for most things in life, and one of the manifold and various frustrations of DuPuy being beached in practice, if not in theory.

For some reason or other, the steps up to the quarterdeck were much easier to take than those up the scaffolding had been. Probably just that there were fewer of them; that was most likely it.

There were hints that things were going more quickly than he would have expected—the quarterdeck's decking was fresh, which meant, of course, that the work beneath it had been done. He hadn't looked to see if the rudder had been unchocked, but knowing McCaulkin, the fact that the wheel had been remounted and not tied down indicated that it indeed had—and probably connected to the whipstaff, although that was obscured from here—so he walked over and took it in his hands.

Even in drydock, where he couldn't fool himself even a little that he was really at the wheel of a sailing ship, it felt good to have the spokes in his hand, although he didn't try to turn it. That would have been silly, just playing at being a steersman, much as he was playing at having a ship beneath him once again.

What he should have been doing was sending one of the men to tell McCaulkin that he was here, and—

"Admiral."

DuPuy snatched his hands from the wheel, and turned in irritation.

Heavy boots thundered on the deck as McCaulkin ran up, almost daintily stepping over the cordage and other detritus littering the deck. DuPuy had tried to ignore that—it was perfectly legitimate, he supposed, to leave equipment lying all over the deck in drydock, but it reminded him even more than the lack of motion beneath his feet that the ship was, after all, in drydock.

"Good to see you this morning, sir. Thank you for coming over so quickly."

"Hmph."

Captain Rodney McCaulkin was a stubby, fiftyish man,

barrel-chested and thick-fingered, and gray: his close-cropped hair—what there was of it—the deeply sunken eyes, and even his skin had an unhealthy-looking gray pallor that seemed utterly invulnerable to alleviation by the sun, although McCaulkin certainly spent enough time out of doors.

As was usual in the morning, his freshly shaved face was spattered with freshly clotting cuts—DuPuy thought that a man with such unsteady hands should have grown a beard—and, as was also usual, be it morning, noon, or night, McCaulkin's utilities were a mess.

Not that that bothered DuPuy. If anything, the notion of the captain of Malta's Repair Depot demonstrating by example that he wasn't afraid to get his hands and uniform dirty was, DuPuy had always thought, a good thing, although McCaulkin tended to take it further than DuPuy would have recommended, all in all.

But he was a tireless worker—even at this early hour, the underarms of his utilities were already darkened with sweat, despite the mildness of the day, and his fingernails were utterly filthy.

He ran those filthy fingernails through his too-long hair. Perhaps he thought it was a salute?

"Well, Captain, I'm sure you've brought me over for some reason—what is the bad news? The keel going? Knees turn out to be balsa wood? Masts stepped with glue?"

McCaulkin smiled. "No, not bad news, Admiral—surprising news, though. Given her logs, I was expecting that we'd be dealing with deviled bolts again—one of the reasons I wanted her out of the water, so that I could get at the keel from the underside."

"And . . . ?"

McCaulkin shook his head. "Nothing of the sort, sir. I pulled a couple—dirty work, but I wanted to see for myself. Good copper—and thicker by a good quarter-inch than standard. Somebody in Mumbai seems to have actually done his job, for once."

That was suspicious, in and of itself. "And you're quite sure."

If anything, the already broad smile widened. "I knew you'd be skeptical, Admiral—I was myself. But one look's worth a thousand words, if I do say so—care to take a look? I've got a couple of the bolts down in the master's cabin—been using it as an office aboard the ship."

That wasn't unusual; McCaulkin seemed to spend most of his waking hours aboard whatever ship was in the drydock. He had probably slept aboard. Probably in that set of utilities, from the look of them.

McCaulkin could have, of course, simply sent a report over to DuPuy—along with a bolt, perhaps—instead of sending for him, but DuPuy didn't complain; it was good to get out of that damned fur-lined prison for a while, at that. Putting off getting back was a luxury, and a spot of self-indulgence, but it was one he could afford for a few minutes, perhaps.

It might even help him keep himself from strangling Owlsley.

"Lead the way, Captain."

"Aye, aye, Admiral."

As DuPuy remembered it, there was a hatch at the stern end of the quarterdeck that led directly down to the captain's cabin, just as there had been on the old *Sufficient*. Back then, DuPuy had logged standing orders that the officer of the deck was to stomp three times on the hatch if, <u>for any reason</u>—he had underlined the phrase twice—there was any reason to believe that it would be better for the captain to come on deck.

DuPuy wondered if the *Surprise*'s log would show similar orders. Worth looking at, as long as they were going to the captain's quarters—to what would be the captain's quarters; the *Surprise* had no master at the moment.

For that matter, DuPuy was curious to see if he could squeeze his bulk through the narrow hatch. Nothing like land duty, with food that was far too good and far too readily available to make a man fat.

But the after part of the deck was still cordoned off, and McCaulkin led him down the ladder, to the open deck, then through a path among the piles of rope whose destiny was to become lanyards of the shrouds and back-stays to the open door of the captain's cabin.

"I think you'll find this interesting, Admiral," McCaulkin said, then started in manifestly affected surprise. "Lieutenant—I hadn't realized that you were still here."

Lieutenant Lord Sir Alphonse Randolph, who had been sitting at the master's desk, leaped to his feet. "My apologies, sir; I found myself caught up in the logs," he said. "Admiral."

DuPuy gave him a cold nod. "Good morning, Mr. Randolph."

"Morning, sir."

DuPuy eyed him carefully. He would tolerate McCaulkin's sloppiness of dress, for good reason, but if Randolph had one tarnish on a jacket button . . .

But, no. Randolph's first-class uniform was impeccable,

as usual. No lack of starch, and it looked as though he'd had his dog robber take a chamois and rouge to his buttons, as well as his medals; his collar points were sharp enough to make DuPuy think that they might almost be able to slice his throat open for him. A well turned-out officer, by the look of him—the only thing that DuPuy had to complain about the bastard was that he was *here*, dammit.

As to why, that was clear. Randolph wanted to talk to him, and rather than going through channels and asking for an appointment, he and McCaulkin had arranged this little charade. Perhaps Randolph was fool enough to think that a back-channel chat could get him off the *Lord Fauncher*? Well, it could, at that—but not in the way that Randolph was, perhaps, thinking, and not at the moment.

DuPuy briefly considered dismissing Randolph; let him apply for an appointment like anybody else.

But Randolph had piqued DuPuy's curiousity—what was he up to?

More to the point of the moment: what was in it for McCaulkin? That was something that DuPuy could save for later—if money had exchanged hands, DuPuy would make it his purpose to give McCaulkin reason to regret it.

"I didn't know you were visiting the Captain, Mr. Randolph," he said, coldly. "I would have thought that, perhaps, the *Lord Fauncher* is keeping you busy enough that you'd not have time for social calls."

"Err, Admiral, it wasn't a social call—Mr. Randolph had some issues with the way I set the flying rigging, and wished to discuss them."

"Hmm. And you've settled those matters?"

"I think I've handled his questions, yes, Admiral."

Whatever you could say bad about Randolph, he wasn't stupid enough to be unprepared—if DuPuy asked what the issues were, he and McCaulkin would, no doubt, have been able to lecture him for hours, hours that he didn't have. "Well, let's see this non-deviled bolt, eh?"

"Yes, of course." There were three of them on the captain's desk—each more than a foot long, two inches around, and apparently of thick copper. Two had been sawed or cut in half, and DuPuy reached for the nearest.

"That was one off of the *Lord Fauncher*, Admiral."

"Before the repairs were completed," Randolph added, as though DuPuy was some sort of idiot who couldn't have figured that out.

DuPuy nodded as he examined the bolt. It was well-enough done—somebody fairly clever had sheathed what appeared to be decent oak in copper, all the way around, rather than just at the heads.

"On the other hand," McCaulkin said, grunting overly dramatically as he picked up another sawn bolt, "this is one that I pulled out of the *Surprise*."

Now, that was another matter entirely. It was as heavy as it should be, and copper through and through. DuPuy pretended to give it a close examination, although he didn't know quite what to pretend he was closely examining—it was just solid copper, after all. Ah: "You've assayed it, of course."

"Of course. As I was telling you, Admiral, it's good news, and I've pulled half a dozen more—all of them good and solid. We could take the ship apart, of course, but I'd wager my pension that if we haven't found any deviled ones yet, we're not going to. I figure I can have her back in the water in perhaps a month, six weeks at the most. Faster, even, if Captain Throckmorton might find me some more hands who can tell a froe from a hammer."

That again. DuPuy didn't say anything for a moment. Then, "Well, then, make it so—I'll have a word with Throckmorton, although I think he'll think that your ability to get this ship back in service so quickly suggests that you've already ample hands, eh?"

"My thinking, as well," McCaulkin said. "Which is why—"

"You'd rather the word come down from me that that's not the case, to preempt the problem?"

Hmm . . . that didn't sound at all like McCaulkin's sort of thinking. He was a direct sort, and he and Throckmorton had been bumping heads for years.

DuPuy looked at Randolph, whose face was studiously neutral. There were, it appeared, other ways for the young earl-to-be to pay off McCaulkin than simply putting coins in his hands.

"Yes, sir," McCaulkin said, shifting his feet back and forth, like a schoolboy. "Thank you, Admiral, and . . ."

"And you'd best be getting back to it, eh?" DuPuy nodded.

He waited until McCaulkin had left, and silently stared at Randolph.

"Well, Randolph," he finally said, "as long as we're both here, I guess I could ask you how the shakedown went, although I assume you've filed a report."

"Last night, sir, just after we dropped anchor." Randolph nodded. "Yes, sir. It went better than could be expected—crew's shaping up nicely, and more quickly than I would have guessed, all in all."

Randolph wasn't a whiner; you had to give him that.

"And further work needed?"

"A hundred minor things, Admiral, or more. But nothing that can't be handled—more quickly if I can borrow a few carpenters and riggers from Captain McCaulkin, but we can manage aboard, if need be. If it wasn't that I didn't think that the flinger crews weren't quite up to it—as of yet—I'd say the *Lord Fauncher* was ready to be returned to full duty."

"And you thought it was more important to tell me all that than to be training them?"

"All in all, yes, sir. Mr. McHenry can run the drills just as quickly as I can, and at the moment, he's doing just that. I'd say they're fairly river-trained about now—give me another few weeks, and I can certify them ready enough for full service."

That was interesting. "I would have thought that it would have taken months to get that batch of useless mouths and clumsy hands to that point. What's your secret, Mr. Randolph?"

"No secret, sir—just work, rewards, and punishments." His mouth tightened. "Had to go to the lash more than I'd like to—rather more—but my orders were to make the *Lord Fauncher* ready to be posted to the squadron as soon as possible, and I took some liberties in that."

Well, DuPuy would have to see that for himself. Still, as far as he was concerned, Randolph could flay half the men to their backbones if that would add another ship to Fleet quickly. And Randolph hadn't hanged anybody, as of yet; he would have mentioned that.

"Any other . . . liberties, Mr. Randolph?"

"Yes, sir." Randolph seemed to hesitate for a moment.

"Out with it, out with it."

"It's in my report, sir, and it's going to come to your attention soon enough, but I put in on Pantelleria on the way back from Sfax, to give the top men in each section some overnight leave."

So there it was. Standing orders were to avoid Pantelleria, for obvious reasons. But the orders were "avoid" and not "avoid at all costs." It wasn't unusual or forbidden for a ship to put in offshore to refill its water barrels, and while DuPuy didn't want any boarding or searching to take place in the waters immediately offshore, immediately was a flexible term, after all—Gold Squadron had nailed a pirate under false colors just a few months before, just east of the island.

It didn't surprise DuPuy that Randolph would take responsibility for violating his orders. It was the violation itself that was curious.

"Leave, Mr. Randolph?" DuPuy arched an eyebrow. "You thought that giving a few sailors leave was worth violating standing orders?"

Randolph drew himself up to a position of attention. "If the Admiral decides that I have violated any orders, I'll take any consequences, sir. My interpretation—"

"Interpretation, Mr. Randolph? Orders are to be obeyed, and not merely 'interpreted.' "

"Yes, sir." Randolph didn't seem apologetic, which was just as well, perhaps.

"I'd like to see orders that could be 'interpreted' so." DuPuy didn't know what he would do if Randolph had bribed Shea to permit leave. Tossing every corrupt officer off of DuPuy's balcony would likely draw attention—and create a large pile of bodies.

"Aye, aye, sir." Randolph reached into his breast pocket and produced a folded sheet of paper, then handed it over.

To Lieutenant Lord Sir Alphonse Randolph, *Lord Fauncher*, Port Valletta, HM Possession of Malta:

You are hereby required and directed forthwith to, upon your determination that His Majesty's Sloop *Lord Fauncher* is in all ways victualled to Four Weeks of all Requirements for her Established Complement and in all ways ready for Sea, if not for restoration to Full Service, to hoist such Flag and Flags as are proper and necessary, and then without loss of time to sail His Majesty's said Sloop under your command to Sfax, that City in Tunisia, to safely convey His Excellency, Shaykh Abdul ibn Mussa al-Bakilani al-Medina Hajji, Emmisary of the Caliph of Tunis, to that City, showing him all Courtesies, Respect, and Consideration due to his Inviolate Person, and those of his Attendants.

You are not to permit any of your Company to go ashore at Sfax save under the direst of Emergencies.

Upon your completion of the successful conveyance of Said Persons, you are to continue to sail the HM Sloop no less than one Day Adverse Sailing from any Coast and no farther than Five Days Adverse Sailing from HM Port of Valletta, for all purposes required in the Evaluation of HM Sloop's readiness to be returned to Full Service, and the Training of the Ship's Complement in said endeavor, to which end you are to take All Measures keep your men together to their Duty and cause them to be diligently employed in putting out her Weapons,

Stores, and Provisions, and to keep yourself diligently employed in preparing both Ship and Crew for Service.

The Lord Fauncher not being in Full Service, you are to refrain from Battle with other ships of any kind, save under circumstances of being Attacked, or should you be signaled by one of HM ships for rescue and succor.

When either the Ship or Crew are in all ways ready for Service, or Three Weeks from this date have elapsed, or you have determined that further Making of Readiness must necessarily be performed at Port Valletta, you are without loss of time to repair to Port Valletta, provision & victual for another Four Weeks sailing, but remain there till further order, giving us a Full Account of your proceedings.

Given under Our hands this 5th Leeds the 1625th Year of Our Lord

By Order of Admiral Sir Simon Tremaine DuPuy

Morton Shea, Captain

Well, that could be interpreted as Randolph had chosen to, although it was perhaps a stretch. There was some sense in it—DuPuy had been known to say, publicly and often, that rum and other rewards were every bit as important in maintaining good order and effectiveness as as a good master-at-arms who knew how to use a lash, and Pantelleria had been the only port within Randolph's orders, save for those in Tunisia, or on Malta itself, and returning to Malta would have not permitted much of any liberty, given the way that Throckmorton had written Randolph's orders.

"Hmmm . . . what trouble did they get in there?" It couldn't be terribly bad, or DuPuy would have heard about it already.

Randolph shook his head. "None, sir. None whatsoever—I took some precautions." His brow furrowed. "But the waters seemed awfully full of ships—it's in my report."

"Ships, Mr. Randolph? There are many kinds of ships, Lieutenant—" DuPuy stopped himself. "Hmm . . . perhaps you'd better tell me about it."

"I'll be most willing to tell the Admiral about it, of course, but I do have a suggestion, if the Admiral doesn't mind one."

"I'll always listen to suggestions, Mr. Randolph, particularly for an officer who has gone to as much trouble and taken as much risk to his career as you seem to have in order to bring this to my attention." He had hoped Randolph would at least blanch a little at that, but he didn't. "Your suggestion would be, Lieutenant?"

"I know the Fleet is undermanned, sir, but there's a lot more ships around Pantelleria than I think should be normal—Guild, unflagged, merchantmen from Crown and Dar, and half a dozen other flags."

"And you didn't think to have your men ask around as to—" DuPuy stopped himself.

Of course, Randolph had thought of doing just that, but it was damnably inconsistent with keeping a close leash on them. He probably had them confined to one tavern or bordello, with his master-at-arms and a few marines to make sure that they stayed there. Turning even a snap-to crew into a bunch of spies on the instant would have been too much to task any man.

Enough of that, and more than enough of letting Randolph tease DuPuy's curiosity without coming out and making his case, whatever it was: "Well, what is your advice, Mr. Randolph?"

Randolph didn't answer right away.

"Well?"

"I don't know, sir. I'd advise sending a squadron closer to Pantelleria than has been the practice of late. Or perhaps a port call by a ship with a carefully chosen crew—some of Captain Shea's lot, perhaps?" He didn't quite shrug. "I'd take the *Lord Fauncher* back myself, if I had the orders, but I'm not sure that I have enough of the . . . right sort of crew to look into things."

"How quickly do you think you get could get there?"

"If the wind holds, perhaps twenty, twenty-four hours."

That sounded more than a little suspicious—Pantelleria was closer to a hundred miles away than farther from it, and while the Levanter was still blowing . . .

Randolph wasn't bragging of being able to set a record, by any means, but it was an ambitious boast, particularly for a new crew.

"I'd like to see that," DuPuy said, nodding.

"I'm at your orders, Admiral. We can raise anchor within the hour."

So Randolph had anticipated him, eh? Fair enough. "Make it two hours—I'll have to make some additional preparations if I'm to leave Malta, even if only for a few days. I trust you have a bunk and a seat at your table for an old man, and perhaps a few more for some of his staff?" Some of Shea's people were not utterly incompetent, and putting a junior lieutenant or two in a jack-tar's shirt and trousers would be easy enough.

He had finally managed to get a reaction out of Randolph, and was only a little surprised that it wasn't more than, "Yes, sir." Randolph drew himself up to attention, again. "By your leave, sir? I'd best be back to the ship, and quickly."

"One your way, then, Mr. Randolph."

Randolph's feet didn't start pounding on the deck until he was several feet from the door.

DuPuy didn't have time to waste, either. Two hours? Owlsley had damned well better be able to pack his things in short order; no worries on that score. Shea had better have a few good men ready to be hauled off on short notice—and if they didn't have the right clothing for their disguises, the *Lord Fauncher*'s sailmaker could quickly alter some dirty, used issue clothing, or DuPuy would know the reason why. Shea wasn't—had better not be—a problem.

Throckmorton, on the other hand, would need a short and pointed lecture on the difference between being left in charge and left in command, and—no; to blazes with Throckmorton, and Shea.

He stepped outside the captain's cabin, and beckoned to the nearest of the sailors working on deck.

"Tell Captain McCaulkin I'll see him in my office, on the double. Move it, man, move it."

It would do Throckmorton and Shea's souls good to have to jump when McCaulkin barked, even if only for a few days, and DuPuy had no doubt that there would be plenty of barking done; McCaulkin was that sort, and while he would have enjoyed Throckmorton's expression at having to stand to attention before a man with dirty fingernails, the reality would probably not be nearly as amusing as the mental image, and if he had been there, Throckmorton would have been standing at attention in front of DuPuy, instead, after all.

He should be hurrying, but it was best that he not be seen to hurry, so he took a moment to light his pipe, and let the rich smoke fill his lungs and nostrils, trying to slow the pounding of his heart.

Of course, it was totally irresponsible, looked at any reasonable way, and Shea and Throckmorton and a dozen other senior officers would be certain to make certain that reports of DuPuy's irresponsibility reached the Admiralty, one way or another. They might even beat DuPuy's own report, which might be written on his return, but wouldn't be dispatched before the next courier ship left for Gibby, and home.

Not that that mattered. The trip would give DuPuy some time to feel out Randolph—he was far more interested in what the future Earl of Moray thought of what he had seen in Sfax than in some temporary excess of activity on the wizard-controlled island of Pantelleria. The age of the Wise Ones had ended with the Age of Crisis, no matter what those pompous knights of the Order seemed to think. Pantelleria was just a local irritation and problem; nothing more.

Even if this bit of irresponsibility lost DuPuy his last command—and it well might—enlisting Randolph in his quiet, informal conspiracy to keep the main threat firmly in mind in Londinium and elsewhere would be of more value to the Crown than whatever service DuPuy had left as a land-locked sailor.

And if Randolph hadn't taken the point? DuPuy was not, by any means, a terribly persuasive man—what if he couldn't get through to Randolph? Or worse—what if Randolph had been taken in by that too-smooth al-Bakilani? What if he were to become part of the Accomodationists?

DuPuy didn't think that was likely, but that could be handled, too. Nights at sea were dark, and a man could go over the side without drawing notice, if he were careful in the doing of it.

Earl or no earl, a man who had lost an Admiral on a calm Mediterranean night—even a poor landlocked excuse for an Admiral—would find himself discredited in and out of Parliament. And given their personal history, with DuPuy having relieved him of as desirable a posting as could be had out of Malta, and given a beached crew, it would be thought, and it would be widely whispered, that perhaps it had not just been carelessness.

Hmm . . . perhaps DuPuy had time to leave behind a memorandum? He and Randolph had had a long discussion about the threat of the Dar, and Randolph had disagreed, then invited the Admiral on board to discuss it further?

No; he could do that shipboard, and hope that Owlsley wouldn't use the memorandum to wipe himself.

It was best to hurry. There wasn't much time, after all. He really should have given Randolph more time than a scant two hours. Still, it was justified in that the sooner he was off, the sooner he would see for himself these strange and supposedly significant gatherings of ships on and off Pantelleria.

Yes, that was it.

And that this would give him a deck rolling beneath

his feet for three days, that couldn't have affected his decision, in any way.

It wouldn't be his deck, after all. It would be Randolph's ship and Randolph's deck and while, of course, Randolph would offer DuPuy his cabin, Randolph would still be the master of the *Lord Fauncher*, not DuPuy, and DuPuy would have to watch himself constantly so as not to forget it, as Randolph would no doubt be more than happy to remind him, all the more pointedly for it being done with exquisite courtesy.

Simon DuPuy made his way across the waist, toward the plank that led over to the scaffolding. It was all he could do not to let his feet break into a run across the plank from the all-too-stable deck of the drydocked ship to the normal and proper stability of the scaffolding.

Dammit, it would be good to be a sailor again, and if he wasn't to be an entirely honest one, well, Simon DuPuy could live with that, just as long as was necessary.

And not a minute longer.

Chapter 10: Lullabye

I have never quite understood the unusual compassion that Cully has always had for children—although I was the beneficiary of it—any more than Bear's wistful nostalgia for his childhood.

I envy the latter, of course, given my own, but that's another matter.

—Gray

The wizard was drunk.

There was really no question about that, Bear decided, as he stood at the foot of the dock, watching Sigerson sitting on the far end of the dock under the stars, his legs over the side, a bottle his only company.

Bear crossed his arms over his chest and stood silently for a moment. At least arguably, he should just leave Sigerson alone, and he tried not to be impulsive. Gray was more than impulsive enough for the two of them, and Cully . . . well, it was hard to tell about Cully.

Still, although it was hard to be sure by what little light there was, Sigerson's seat appeared to be less than steady, and as he tilted the bottle back it appeared, for at least a moment, as though he might lose what balance he had and tumble into the water. Since it was closer to low tide than farther from it, he would more likely smash himself to death on the rocks rather than drown. The usually omnipresent Bigglesworth was nowhere to be seen, which was surprising, and more than a little irritating. Perhaps Bear should go find Bigglesworth, and have him see to his master.

No. There was no point in Bear trying to fool himself— he was not going to walk away, so he might as well get to it.

Bear walked down the pier quietly, so as not to startle the wizard. It would be a cruel irony indeed if Bear's attempt to see to Sigerson's welfare, spiritual and temporal, managed to kill the man, after all.

Halfway across the harbor, three ships of their ragged convoy lay anchored at neighboring berths, a short distance from any of the others. For whatever reason, the *Cooperman* and the *Winfrew* had been berthed to either side of the *Marienios*, and he couldn't decide if it looked more like they were standing guard or preventing escape, although perhaps it was a little of both—Gray, like Cully, was perfectly capable of doing one thing for two reasons, or more.

From here, Bear couldn't see where the marines had been stationed on watch, but he had been impressed even more by Sergeant Fotheringay than he had by Captain

Madsen, the titular commander of the marine detachment, and he was confident that everybody was where he was supposed to be.

One of the interesting things about Cully, Bear decided, was his luck in the people who found themselves bound to him by choice or fate—or, usually, both.

He wasn't sure what the cause of it was, and assuredly it wasn't a completely reliable talent. But he had plucked Gray and Alfred from Londinium back streets, and Sister Mary from her convent, and they were hardly the only examples. Bear flattered himself that Cully had seen something special in David Shanley, as well, and he had certainly tried to live up to it. Fotheringay seemed to fit the mold, as well.

And, of course, there was Niko. Facing off against Gray, at the plaza—that had taken courage, more than one would expect from an untrained boy, even of a noble family, much less some Pironesian fisherboy.

Sigerson, though . . . well, Gray and Bear had acquired him, not Cully. Perhaps that was it.

He sat down on the wood beside the wizard, letting his legs dangle over the side, just as Sigerson did.

Sigerson started, and Bear thrust out an arm to block a possible fall, then let it drop when Sigerson seemed to steady himself.

"Sorry, Sir David; I didn't see you walk up."

"So I could see. I don't see your man." Where was he? Letting his master out and about while this drunk—Bear had thought better of Bigglesworth, who seemed to be both competent, and devoted.

"Nor will you—Biggles and I have an understanding: when I'm in my cups, he makes himself scarce. In return,

I don't dismiss him for bothering me when I've been drinking. Seems to me to be a reasonable arrangement, and Biggles doesn't seem to complain. There's a . . . certain efficiency in doing it here—when it makes me sick, I can simply relieve myself over the side. As it shall, and as I shall. I doubt you'll find that entertaining, Sir David."

Drunkenness wasn't precisely a sin in and of itself, not really, but . . .

"Is there some problem I can be of help with?"

Sigerson didn't answer at first. Bear decided to wait him out.

He had been intending to take the launch over to the *Marienios*. Gray and Cully, both of whom seemed to sleep better on land, were ensconced in a dockside inn—with a squad of marines in attendance, just in case. Bear, for some reason he couldn't have explained, slept better aboard—and, besides, Niko had gone over to the ship shortly after they had returned to the city, and he had had a hard night, and been mostly silent during the long ride back from Lindos to the port city.

Understandable, really. There was no sin in killing, not in battle, and the battle had not been over when Niko and his sword had slain the last of their attackers, and been more of a *coup de grâce* than anything else.

But it hadn't always felt that way to Bear, and it probably wouldn't feel that way to the boy. Bear had seen it before—in himself, both longer ago and more recently than he cared to think about.

And it's easier to see to others' consciences than your own, perhaps? the Nameless said.

That was true enough, certainly.

"For somebody trying to pry a confession out of me,

you're awfully quiet, Sir David," Sigerson said. He took another long pull from his bottle. "I do have a problem, though."

"Yes? Something I might be able to help with?" Bear brightened. This might be easier than he had feared.

"It's a fairly delicate matter."

"Go ahead, please." It wasn't the words of the ritual of confession that were important, but the substance. Bear had, of course, learned the words almost before he could walk, and had both heard and given more confessions than he could count, but there was no magic in the particular words, any more than in the location.

A valid confession could be made in English or Hellenic or French or Arabic or Tien-Shien; Bear had heard confessions in a church, during a walk in the woods, or even when kneeling in the muck over a dying man in a Southampton backstreet alleyway, hoping that the man would be able to gasp out his last sins before he died.

Sigerson knew that Bear was a priest, after all. A full and knowing confession to a properly ordained priest, followed by an act of contrition—and if Sigerson didn't think it was a confession, well, that could easily be changed.

The one thing that bothered him was his own status— there was a bishop in the city of Rodhos, although Gray said they didn't have time for a courtesy call. Back home, a seaside diocese extended to the high-tide marks, but were the rules different here?

It was something to ask Cully about; he would know. And, in any case, it would still count, and if Bear exceeded his authority, that was a matter for Bear to make his amends to the bishop for; it would not affect Sigerson's soul.

Sigerson nodded. "Well, I was gently raised, believe it or not, and taught manners, but here I am with no proper glasses, and I'm trying to decide whether it's a worse crime against courtesy to offer you a drink from a bottle that's spent most of the last hour between my lips, or not offer one at all."

Bear tried not to sigh. "And that's all that bothers you, Mr. Sigerson?"

"It's a serious enough problem, at the moment," Sigerson said.

Bear held out his hand for the bottle. "A drink would go down well, at that, since you appear to be offering."

"Ah." Sigerson handed over the bottle. "Would that all problems were so easily solved, eh?"

Bear took a cautious sip, and forced himself not to make a face. While he certainly enjoyed an occasional glass of wine—wine had always been available when sitting table at home—the raw bite of rum never particularly agreed with him.

He handed the bottle back to Sigerson, and they sat silently for a moment.

"See that little island there?" Sigerson asked. "The one just next to the lighthouse?"

It was hard to see anything clearly out in the dark, but Bear could make it out, if only barely. Just a dark mass, huddled against the sea, dwarfed by the way that the lighthouse jutted up. If there was a building of any sort on it, it was unlighted.

"Is there something in particular there?"

Sigerson shook his head. "No, not now. But there was before . . ."

"And before?"

"Hmph. Does the name Chares of Lindos mean anything to you?"

Bear shook his head. "No, I'm afraid not. Might I ask what the—"

"I didn't think it would. He's been dead for more than a thousand years, and he wasn't terribly important, in the larger sense, when he was alive. That little, unremarkable island is where the Colossus of Rhodes stood, a hundred feet tall—Chares of Lindos built it." Sigerson took another drink, and wiped his mouth with the back of his hand. "It would have been something to see, eh?"

"I don't see the—"

"—the point, Sir David? Think on it—the Hellenes built a statue to honor their god Apollo. More than a dozen years in the building, it stood watching over the harbor, a bronze statue, a hundred feet tall, gleaming in the sunlight atop a marble pedestal of perhaps another fifty feet. Passing ships could have seen it for perhaps twenty, fifty, a hundred miles."

He took another drink. "And now the many-times-great-grandchildren of those same men who built that are reduced to strapping a goat to a slab of marble and cutting its guts out to, to, wave them around and bellow under the noon sun, all the while fearing foreigners—us—hanging them if they're caught." He shook his head and took yet another drink—did the man want to drink himself to death? "There's something more than a little sad about that, isn't there?"

This wasn't the sort of confession that Bear had had in mind, and it bothered him for more reason than that. Blasphemy, idolatry, apostasy, heresy—all of those were wrong, but there was also something wrong with the picture that Sigerson had painted.

"Oh, please," Sigerson went on, "I'm not pointing fingers at others that I won't point at myself. Look at me—a full Fellow of the Royal College, the very institution founded by Merlin himself, in the days of the Tyrant—a time when Avalon could be hidden and unhidden, before Excalibur and the Sword of Constantine shattered on each other, before the end of the Age chased almost all of the Old Ones away and crippled the rest.

"There was a time—not in living memory, granted, but a time nonetheless—when a Pendragonshire nobleman had to think carefully about taking a walk out his back door of an evening, for if he walked too fast, too long, too far, he might find himself face to face with the Queen of Air and Darkness, herself—and, yes, I know that you've met her, and I know that all who do say she's but a ghost of what she once was.

"As we all are, I think. The poor, sodding, goat-killing Hellenes; the pretentious, supposedly all-conquering Musselmen—all of them, and all of us.

"I say 'us,' as I've no pretensions of being anything better. I spend my days crawling through the foul-smelling bellies of ships trying to come up with better ways of killing shipworm, that's what I do, when I'm not trying to figure out ways to ensorcel a scroll so that only the intended recipient can read it, or place an even more effective curse on an officer's sword, or—" He shook his head. "Me, I kill worms, and perform a few parlor tricks, and keep myself focused on that—because if I don't, I'll start thinking about the black arts, and while there's power aplenty there, I'd much rather be a useless little man than a great and evil one, Sir David." He shook his head. "Yes, I know that it's said that if you so much as dip your toe in the blackness, it'll swallow you up before you think that you're as much as up to your ankle, and I know of enough cases to think that's true, but I flatter myself that I could, that I could . . ." He sighed. "And it's best not to think too long on that, eh?" He turned to look Bear in the eye. "Will you hear my confession, Father?"

"I thought I was already doing that." Bear took the bottle from him and took another drink.

The rum wasn't really all that bad, and, besides, the Nameless always preached moderation in everything— even in temperance, as Saint Timothy had. New England rum wasn't exactly "a little wine for thy stomach's sake and thine often infirmities," but it would serve.

"Oh, really?" Sigerson sounded skeptical.

"Why, yes. At least, I had hoped to. Both for the sake of your soul and because I've found that confession is, well, good for the heart, as well."

Sigerson nodded. "Well, then, let me confess a mortal sin: envy. And another: lust." Sigerson took the bottle back and had another, longer drink. "I envy you and your brothers, Sir David. What you do matters, doesn't it?"

"I would hope so." He nodded. "Some things more than others, perhaps, but . . . I would hope so, for all of it."

"And this, this . . . quest we're on matters." He shook his head. "There's something out there, something hungry, something awful, and I should be utterly excited, delighted to be part of it, and part of me is. No, it's more than part. But part of me is more than a little scared, and it's not just scared of what we'll find when we find it, if we ever do—although I do swear that has me frightened, Father; I don't claim to be a brave man—but of what I'll do after that." He shook his head. "I saw what was left of that man, when the boy was through with him. My senses are perhaps too well attuned—there was something more horrible about it than about the other bodies that the four of you scattered around, like a bunch of tenpins."

"And you envy that?"

"Not that, no. Not even the ability of doing that—but the sense that you'll be at the heart of what matters, all four of you, and I'll just be on the periphery, that when we're all done with this, you'll go on to something else important, while I know I'll just go back to my studies, and my spells and potions, learning more and more about less and less until I have the complete knowledge about and utter control over absolutely nothing at all." He shook his head. "And I do confess that I lust over the doing of important work." He tilted his head to one side. "And now that I've confessed, what shall be my penance?"

"Not so quickly, please," Bear said. "There's other sins than the awful seven, and they manifest themselves in many ways. Perhaps, it would be best to be more formal?"

"Formal? Sitting on a dock, drinking out of a bottle? That doesn't seem to argue for much formality."

"I don't see any harm—do you?"

"Well, no."

"Then please, proceed."

"Father, forgive me, for I have sinned . . ." Sigerson started, and went on, haltingly. It had apparently been some time since the wizard's last formal confession, or perhaps it was just the drink—he stumbled over the words several times, and Bear had to gently remind him.

But, finally, Bear nodded.

"And my penance, Father?" Sigerson asked. He seemed indecently anxious to do a penance. That wasn't uncommon, though, in Bear's experience, although he often thought that it missed the point. One could never balance wrong with penance, after all.

"I almost never give heavy penances. That's always seemed to me to be . . . presumptuous." Bear shrugged. "A single rosary should do, I think—but in the morning, when you're sober. And perhaps, you should abstain from strong drink for a day—no, make it two days, two *full* days, and let's have no perhaps about it, and you're to have no wine, even watered, as a substitute. And—"

"And?" Sigerson sounded almost eager.

"Accompany me to see to Niko, now. Maybe you can do something for him that I can't. Do you accept your penance?"

"Well, of course I do, and—"

"And do you truly repent of your envy, and your lust, and your other sins?"

"More than you can know."

"Well, there we have it." He rose stood over Sigerson.

The words needed to be said, and while simply the saying of them, under these conditions, were what were needed for Sigerson's soul, for the sake of his own soul Bear, as always, concentrated on the words, and on their meaning. It was important to understand what he was saying, as he said it:

"May God who loves humankind, in His mercy, grant you forgiveness for all your sins, both those which you have confessed as well as those that you have forgotten.

"I absolve you of all the sins that you have committed

in thought, in word and in deed; it is my privilege to absolve you, and I do so in the name of the Father, and of the Son and of the Holy Spirit."

He offered Sigerson his hand, and the wizard gripped it with surprising strength. Bear drew him to his feet, and let him totter ahead down the pier, toward shore.

Well, he had heard the confession, and, as was true all too often when he did, he had learned more than he had really wanted to, and probably less than he should have.

As so often is the case, Bear.

Hmph. He hadn't intended to rest his hand on the Nameless's hilt again, but—

There are fewer accidents in this world than you might think.

"Perhaps."

Bear took a final drink from the bottle of rum, then threw it over the side.

Niko sat by himself in the not-quite-darkness of their cabin.

Well, not quite by himself. The oil lamp hanging from the wall was some company, and every now and then he could hear footsteps moving on the deck overhead, and occasionally quiet voices talking about something, although he couldn't make out what.

Nadide was by his side, of course, lying on the box next to the one he was sitting on, the one he was using as a work table, rather than a seat.

The hammocks were fine for sleeping, once he had figured out how to get in one without spilling himself on the deck, although he still hadn't quite mastered getting out without regularly doing just that.

Their rocking was comforting, for some reason he couldn't quite figure out. But they were, really, only useful for sleeping—he couldn't curl up in a hammock the way he used to at home, on his spot on the floor, and work.

And he couldn't sleep. He had tried, but the rocking wasn't comforting tonight, and he had given up on it, despite how dry his eyeballs felt, how his backside still ached from the saddle, how he found himself uncontrollably yawning.

So he had gotten down from the hammock—spilling himself on the deck in the process, again; he was glad nobody had been there to see it—and taken out his swords.

Best to keep his hands busy. He should have checked Nadide—he hadn't been the one who had sheathed her, after all.

But he couldn't quite bring himself to touch her hilt, even gloved, and he had temporized by taking out the leather pouch that the *Wellesley*'s Navy armorer had given him—along with the strange lecture, punctuated with it's-not-my-place-to-tell-you-what-to-do-sir, and if-you-don't-mind-me-pointing-out-sir, the gist of which was that the Navy sword should be regularly cleaned and oiled, but only sharpened when needed, and preferably not by Niko.

It still felt strange to have so much time on his hands, even at night, even when he should be asleep.

He should be sitting on the floor of the hut, with the damp netting splashed out across the floor, working with bone needle and string to mend rips and reinforce loosening knots, while Mara and Lina stitched and sewed, and Grandfather worked with his still-strong fingers, building new crab traps to replace ones that had washed out to sea, perhaps even while reading out loud. Grandfather could do both.

It was late, and a fisherman's day was long. Perhaps Niko would just be sleeping, woken only occasionally by the low, slow breathing of his sisters as they lay curled up in their blankets, or by Grandfather's horrible, rattling snoring that always seemed to threaten to shake their house apart.

But they—

No. Best not to think about that. They were gone, and he was—

No.

He was better off just concentrating on polishing this sword. There wasn't anything else he could do, nothing useful. Maybe that was the trouble here—he just didn't have enough to do. Too much time to think, and if he concentrated on working, perhaps he wouldn't think so much.

The sword—the Navy sword—lay across his lap. Gray in particular spoke disparagingly of Navy issue, but Niko couldn't see anything wrong with it. It was certainly sharp enough—he tested it against the hair of his arm, again; and once again, when he leaned his head close as he carefully slid the blade along his skin, he could hear the quiet *pop-pop-pop* as the hairs snapped off.

The sword seemed like a terrible waste of steel, though—you could easily make a dozen fisherman's knives from just one of these, and the *Wellesley*'s armory had, literally, dozens of spares, beyond the swords that the marines and the Navy officers themselves had been given—no, *issued*. The English were terribly rich.

He held the lamp closer. Yes, there was a small rust spot along the edge, despite Niko having thought he'd been careful with it. He certainly had always been careful with Father's knife, after the one time that Father had found a spot not much larger than this on it, and beaten him.

Understandably.

Well, he could probably just polish it out. He pulled the strange leathery cloth out of the pouch—no, Bosun's Mate Thatchery had called it a "kit," and called the cloth a "shammy," and Niko should try to do so, too. He wrapped his index finger in the shammy and rubbed at the rust spot until the metal beneath gleamed brightly.

That wasn't bad, not bad at all; he gave the rest of the sword a quick polishing, then oiled it, and rubbed the oil mostly off with the oil rag from the kit.

Truth to tell, the sword did fit his hand comfortably. He got to his feet, ducking under an overhead timber, and took a position near the bulkhead. He moved into the stance that he had been practicing, under Cully's tutelage: the sword gripped in his right hand, the scabbard in his left, with his feet about a shoulder's width apart, slightly diagonal to the bulkhead, the sword held firmly in his hand, elbow bent, point low-but-not-down-dammit-Niko, the scabbard held in his left hand. At least that was coming naturally to him—understandable, given all the hours he had stood that way.

You didn't step forward to lunge, Cully explained— you just straightened your arm, raised your foot, and leaned forward, and let gravity do the work. It seemed awfully simple—and the knights and marines made it look easy—until you tried to actually do it, but Cully said that after he'd done it only a few tens of thousands of times, it would start to feel natural, and Niko wasn't even a good part of the way there, any more than he was with any of the strange rituals that the knights practiced.

It really didn't make any sense for him to bother with doing this, but it was something to do, something more useful than sitting in a box and feeling sorry for himself, as silly as that was.

There were others to feel sorry for, like the man he and Nadide had killed. The peasants were just protecting their own, after all. That was something that anybody could understand, anybody should be able to understand, and—

No.

Sword fighting, so Cully had explained, was the simplest of things. There were only eight moves, after all, and if a dung-footed Sherwood peasant could learn them, and he could, then so could a fish-scented Pironesian boy. It was just a matter of practice, practice, practice and then varying and combining the moves, something that would only take a few years of constant study to learn the rudiments of.

Cully had grinned. Not that that was all, he had said, or even the most of a novice's education. Theology, history, poetry; fluency in at least three languages beyond the trading-language—beyond English—and then there was smithing, armorcraft, horsemanship, court manners, and the strangely varying customs from Londinium east and west to everywhere that the Crown pennant flew; woodsmanship—Cully thought those arts had been shamefully neglected in recent years—as well as at least the rudiments of sailing and navigation. And then there were mathematics and clerkship, and a dozen other subjects. A Knight of the Order was of necessity a journeyman of many trades and the master of several.

The rest of it was far beyond his abilities, but if he was going to impersonate a knight for the time being, Niko thought he could learn to hold a sword and lunge, and he was certain he could do that much more easily than he could try to reconcile the subtle—the utterly incomprehensible—differences between Bear's view of the way that the One True Church should be obeyed and Gray's, or Cully's.

He lunged and recovered again, and again, and kept at it.

The muscles of his right thigh began to ache, but anybody who had been a fisherman had to learn to ignore pain—and probably everybody else did, as well. Life was hard, and work was hard, and if you concentrated on it, if you didn't let your mind wander, if you paid attention, it could all be managed, whether you were hauling buckets of fish up a narrow path to the ridge, or—

"*Very* nice, Sir Niko."

He almost dropped the sword.

Bear, with Mr. Sigerson with him, had somehow come into the compartment while Niko had been busy practicing; he hadn't heard the door open.

Feeling more than a little foolish, Niko set the Navy sword down on the box, next to Nadide's scabbard, while Bear hung his lantern on a peg on the wall on the other side of the door from where Niko's hung.

"I'd suggest a little less of the leg extension, though," Bear said, "you've got to be able to retreat as quickly as you lunge forward." Bear set both of his swords down on the box beside Niko's. "May I?" he asked, gesturing.

It took Niko a moment to realize that Bear was asking if he could pick up Niko's Navy sword. Why he would be asking—oh. Cully had explained to him that a sword was considered a special sort of personal possession, like a kirtle, and that others—even others of much greater status—weren't supposed to touch it without asking permission.

"Yes, yes, of course, Sir David."

Bear picked it up, and gave it a practice shake. "A solid enough weapon, certainly. Grips are a little small for my hand, but they seem to suit you well enough." He turned to Sigerson. "What do you think? Did he have too much extension in the lunge?"

"I think," Sigerson said slowly, his voice blurry around the edges, "that I'd not want to argue with a Knight of the Order on such matters, even if I thought he was wrong, even if he didn't have a sword in his hands."

Bear seemed to lose some of his usual friendliness as he pointedly lowered the point of the sword.

"I think, perhaps, there's a reason for you to speak your mind, just as I know you're not truly afraid that I'd so much as think of running you through for disagreeing with me, Mr. Sigerson."

"True enough; my apologies, Sir David." Sigerson shook his head. "I don't disagree—I thought it was far too much leg extension, myself, although I'm much more of a singlestick player than a swordsman, I'll freely con—admit."

"Then see if you can procure some sticks, if you please, and join me and Sir Niko on deck."

Sigerson looked like he was going to say something, but he just nodded.

"Of course, Sir David." He closed the door slowly behind him.

Bear looked Niko up and down. "Well, then, young sir knight—one thing you've got to learn is that when you have a question, there's a proper time and place to ask it, and seeing as there's nobody but the two of us in the room at the moment, there could hardly be a more proper time and place."

Niko didn't know what to say. Which was strange, given that it was Bear. But Bear was waiting for him to say something, so he had to.

"I don't know. I . . ." He swallowed heavily. "I'm sorry. I just couldn't sleep, and—"

"No, there's no need to apologize for that, Niko. You have good instincts." Bear nodded. "A wise man once spent some time sitting beneath a tree, thinking. He didn't do it because he thought that sitting beneath a tree was the best thing in the world to do, but because he knew how to do that, and he didn't know how to do anything more useful at the moment.

"And if the moment grew longer, as moments have a way of doing, that was entirely suitable, and proper."

He looked over at the boxes where Niko had spread out his sword-cleaning pouch—kit, kit, it was a kit—then held Niko's sword close to the lantern on the wall, carefully examining the blade.

"Good enough, certainly. And while I'd not think that cleaning and polishing a sword would look to an outsider as the same thing as more usual contemplation, it might serve you well enough." His eyes grew vague and distant. "We have to find our own ways about many things in this world. You're bothered by the man you killed, and there's nothing wrong with that—such things shouldn't be taken lightly, even when they're necessary."

"You—you and Sir Cully and Sir Joshua didn't hesitate."

Bear shook his head, matter-of-factly. "No," he said, simply, no trace of sadness or apology in his voice or manner. "You can put it down to years of training, if you'd like, or to the various stains on all of our souls, if you insist, but when things . . . snap into place like that, you do what you have to, and sort out how you feel about it later on, if at all."

"Like Gray did in the plaza in Pironesia?"

He regretted the words the moment that they were out of his mouth, but Bear just nodded.

"Yes," he said, sadly, "precisely like that. Although I think the difference between doing so when it's necessary and not is rather important—and so does Gray." He looked at Niko's sword, still in his hands, as though it were something foreign and perhaps foul. "I think, perhaps, I'm not in the mood for practice at the moment," he said, setting the sword down next to its sheath. "But some exercise would be good for you, as well as me—get your swords, and let's take the boat to shore, and walk for a while; we can sleep when the ship leaves in the morning, perhaps?"

It was really more of a command than a question, so the only thing that Niko could say was, "Of course, Sir David."

Something had changed in Niko, perhaps.

Either that, or the world seemed to have both grown and shrunk at the same time, although the idea of that seemed even more strange.

The easiest thing to do was walk, so he walked, and tried not to think any more than he had to.

The city of Rodhos jutted out into the sea, and the rough path along the coast to the west traced the shoreline, sometimes climbing up to the low plateau, often dipping to within but a few feet of the high-tide marks. It reminded Niko of such paths that circled his home island—it looked so much more a natural path than a road, although years of plodding feet had beaten it into some semblance of stability.

They walked quietly above the rocky shore to the east, quickly leaving the city far behind them.

Niko had thought of Pironesia—the city—as almost impossibly huge and sprawling. Rodhos was, perhaps, only half the size, or even smaller, but it felt tiny. He wondered if that was because of the flatness of the land. It wasn't nearly as hilly as seemed natural, as though some thing or some one had worn it down.

He said something to that effect to Bear and Sigerson, but they both just chuckled, and exchanged funny looks, and Sigerson muttered something about what flat land was really like, and Bear urged him to take the lead as they reached a steep grade, and walked up the rocky path above and along the shoreline.

For some reason, the two others seemed to have some trouble with the steepness of it, and Sigerson in particular was breathing heavily. Niko didn't see what the problem was; it was nothing like the daily climbing up and down at home had been, and the path, whatever its origin, was wide enough in most places that two could have walked abreast without fear of falling.

The night was alive with sounds, although the east wind

tended to carry those from around the port away, and out to sea. The noise of the port behind them—did sailors ever stop drinking and singing?—soon had faded, and the squawking of the ever-present gulls, which seemed to sleep quietly even less often than sailors—quickly predominated, sometimes almost in rhythm with the regular beat of the waves against the shore below.

The wind from the east picked up. Below, it seemed to flatten rather than magnify the waves, turning the star-spattered sea all glossy and shiny, rippled like the scales of a beached tunnyfish.

The path branched off in several places, presumably leading to houses and olive groves, Bear said. The land was too rocky to grow much up here—Niko knew that from his family's experience—but olives apparently didn't require much.

They approached a small group of houses close enough to the edge to see—too few to call it a village, Bear said.

Niko didn't want to ask what the minimum number of houses was that constituted a village, as the two of them would probably just have laughed at him again, and he was finding that he didn't much like being laughed at.

No, that wasn't really true—he had never much liked being laughed at, but it wouldn't have occurred to him, at least until recently, to have resented such a thing, even silently, when his betters did it. That probably had something to do with the strongbox now aboard the *Wellesley*, and the leather pouch still on its thong tied to his waist beneath his robes. A rich man could afford to take offense, after all; rich men could afford all sorts of such luxuries.

The path forked as it had before, one steep incline

leading up to the ridge, the main branch continuing along. Niko stopped when Bear touched him on the shoulder.

"Let's wait for a moment," Bear said, quietly.

"Of course, Sir David," he said.

For some reason, Sigerson was falling far behind again, and his steps didn't seem terribly steady—perhaps he wasn't used to walking?

Still, there wasn't far to go, and the way would get easier soon. If Niko's sense of direction was as good on land as it was on the sea, all they had to do was continue on for a while, and they should soon reach the Lindos-Rodhos road, and be able to return to the city on flatter land that would, presumably, not have Sigerson audibly wheezing.

"We'll give him a moment to catch his breath, and then walk on—visitors probably don't come calling in the middle of the night hereabouts." Bear's voice was low, barely above a whisper, although a normal speaking voice wouldn't have carried very far above the steady wind that had their robes flapping.

Niko nodded. He had never, of course, on his family's island, heard somebody outside at night—but it would have terrified him, too. Maybe, though, people on the larger islands thought differently about such things?

Still, while drawing attention from the houses was probably unwise—and most certainly unkind—it couldn't hurt to look, not from here, could it?

What kind of people lived here? Not rich ones, certainly—the houses were much more the sort of thing Bear would have called a shack than anything finer, and there was no sign of the smoke-houses or drying nets that would have indicated that the people were fisherfolk. Niko couldn't hear any chickens, although he wouldn't have been surprised if the smaller of the shacks was a coop. Chickens slept, too.

There was no sign of olive groves, although Niko couldn't see very far in the dark, although he could make out a few small plots where something had been planted, although he couldn't have said what.

The only windows on this side had been shuttered against the wind, but two of them on the nearest of the shacks, even at this late hour, leaked light, striping the surrounding rocks in flickering crimson and yellow.

A distant sound came: a low, woman's voice, quietly singing.

"Shhh . . ." Bear whispered—although Niko certainly thought he was standing quietly enough. What did Bear want him to do? Stop the wind from flapping his sleeves? Sigerson's wheezing from down the path was louder than that. "It sounds like somebody is up late with a baby."

It had been years since Niko had heard Mother singing to Mara late at night. Maybe that was what sounded so familiar. Did all mothers, everywhere, sing to their children?

Still, there was something about the voice that sounded more than familiar, and strangely so. He took a few tentative steps up the narrow path, walking silently. If Bear objected to it, he could say something.

It was *very* familiar.

"Wait," Sigerson whispered, loudly, from behind him. Niko turned; he and Bear were just dark outlines against the star-spattered sea.

"Just a moment, please." It wasn't just that the tune was familiar—the skin on the back of Niko's neck tightened, painfully so. It was the *words*. He couldn't quite make them out, but . . .

He found himself climbing quickly, one hand gripping the brush to the side of the path, his other clapped to Nadide's hilt, ignoring the increasingly loud whispers that turned to cries from behind him.

Niko, it's the One Who—no. But it sounds like her; it does. Niko—

"*Dandini dandini dastana,*" the woman's voice was singing.

> "*Danalar girmis bostana
> Kov bostanci danayl . . .
> Yemisin lahanyl . . .*"

"Niko, stop." Bear made a tentative grab at the hem of his robes, but Niko shook it off, and ran toward the sound.

> "*Dandini dandini dastana*
> Danalar girmis bostana
> Kov bostanci danayl
> Yemisin lahanyl . . .*"

He scrambling clumsily over the broken ground, but struggled to keep his feet beneath him.

"Niko, come back. Niko . . ."

He ran.

> "*Eh-e nini, eh-e nini,*
> Eh-e nini, nini,
> Nini nini nini
> *Eh-e, eh-e nini eh!*
> Eh-e, eh-e nini eh!
> Eh-e, ninni, ninni, ninni,

Eh-e, ninni, ninni, eh!
Eh-e, ninni . . ."

He pounded on the door. "Please," he said. "Please."
Please.

Turkish. Bear nodded.

It had been *Turkish*, not Hellenic—the boy had, of
course, sung the words in his own language, and with his
own broad accent. He hadn't even thought of them in
Turkish, any more than Bear thought in Hindi when talking to the Nameless, or Gray in Xingcha when conversing
with the Khan. Nadide had understood enough of the
words, and communicated that understanding to Niko.
Of course Niko had sung the lullabye in Hellenic by preference, English by second choice, and always with the
same Pironesian accent.

Bear nodded, and raised his hands, fingers spread, trying to reassure the seven wide-eyed people who watched
his every move, as though expecting him to do something
horrible to them at any moment.

He had deliberately seated himself on the hard dirt
floor, so as not to tower above them, but that didn't seem
to be making much of a difference. Not that he blamed
them.

"Please, Ercam," he said. "I know this is all very frightening, but . . ."

"Yes, Excellency," Ercam said. "We're just . . . surprised
to have visitors in the middle of the night, but . . . honored,
of course." His Hellenic accent was thick with Turkish
overtones, which was approximately as unsurprising as
that he was lying about how honored he felt.

The father of the family was Ercam; the boys, in descending order of age, were Melik, Nedim, and Orcan. The mother, baby Zahara held too-tightly in her arms, was Safeena, and the elder daughter, who appeared to be Niko's age, was Yasmine.

Despite—or perhaps because of—their understandable fear, Ercam was trying to act as though he were a host with guests, rather than a man whose rented shack had just been invaded. The girl, Yasmine, huddled in her blankets in the far corner of the shack, and made it a point to avoid any of their eyes, something that angered Bear, although he didn't express that.

What did they fear two knights and an English wizard were going to do? Rape the girl and her mother in front of their family, or drag them out into the night?

That was probably it, and it was understandable; they had gone through horror enough, he decided. Having their village raided by men from Izbir, the men slaughtered, the women and babies carried off up into the hills. Ercam had spoken of how he had fought off the attackers, but the scornful looks from his sons made it clear that that was a lie—they had run and hidden, Bear suspected.

Not that Bear blamed them for that. They had been fortunate to get away.

They had been more than lucky to make their way to Rodhos—and were silent on the subject as to how they had managed to work their passage even across the few miles that separated Guhlice from Rodhos, although Bear had his suspicions on that score, and made a point not to look closely from the baby to her supposed father.

And while working the groves for a Rodhos farmer was the sort of living that barely brought them enough to eat, that was better than what had happened to the rest of their village.

Sigerson stood leaning against the doorjamb. The walk had, as Bear had hoped, driven at least much of the rum from his head, but the pallor of his skin and his unsteadiness suggested that he would have an extra penance to pay, particularly in the morning. But if Bear hadn't known about his drinking, he would probably have taken the scowl on Sigerson's face as threatening, and didn't blame the family for doing so.

Niko, who had also seated himself on the floor, edged closer to where Safeena sat up against the rough-hewn wall. She pushed herself back against it, holding the baby so tightly that it—she—woke and began to cry. Safeena reached into her shift, as though to give the baby to suck, but stopped, and contented herself with gently shaking the baby clutched in her arms.

"Shhh . . ." Niko said. "You're in no danger from the three of us."

"I've heard that before," Melik said, starting to rise, then stopping himself. "That's what the men said, when they took my mother and my sister—"

His father grabbed him by his shoulder, and hissed something at him in Turkish, probably telling him to shut up.

"I'm sorry, Excellency," Ercam said to Niko. "I'll punish my son as you see fit; there's no need to dirty your own hands with him. If you wish to watch me beat him, I—"

"*No.*" Niko uttered the word harshly.

Ercam blanched at that, and more so when Niko rose.

"There will be no hurting of anybody here, not tonight,

not in the presence of two Knights of the Order of Crown, Shield, and Dragon."

His hand fell to his sword, but he made no effort to draw it. "It's . . . avenging the hurting of innocents that brings us here, and not to hurt more, I swear—on my grandfather's and sisters' souls." His chin trembled. "We need to talk to you, and that's all." He turned to Bear. "Cully will need to see them, as soon as possible. Gray, too."

Bear nodded, and tried to keep the surprise off of his face. This . . . aggressiveness was very much not what he had come to expect from Niko, and he wasn't sure what the source of it was. He found himself thinking of a butterfly emerging from its cocoon—a particularly fierce butterfly, at least at the moment, granted.

"As you wish, Sir Niko," he said, trying as hard as he could to keep any trace of irony from his voice.

He must have succeeded; Niko simply nodded. "We should all be off, I think, darkness or not. All of us."

"But, Excellency, we have work here, and—"

"Shh." Niko held up one hand and dipped another into his robes. It took him a moment to bring out a coin—a gold crown. He held it on the flat of his palm for a long moment, as though he was studying the buttery metal for some insight, then smiled and shrugged and squatted down—in front of Safeena, not her husband.

"I believe this will more than compensate your family for whatever work you'll lose," he said, quietly. He smiled. "I'm sure that you will want to put it somewhere safe."

She eyed the coin greedily, but with the baby cradled in her arms, she didn't have a free hand. Ercam took half a step toward her, but stopped at Bear's quick headshake.

The boy was handling this as well as anybody could—let him handle it without interference.

"May I?" Niko said, gently, holding out both of his hands for the baby.

Whether it was the gold or his manner that had worked the magic—or, most likely, both—she didn't resist as he gently removed the baby from her arms, and she instead quickly crawled across the floor to give the coin to Ercam, then turned back, obviously to reclaim the baby.

She was too late. Niko—no, by God, Sir Niko Christofolous was already sitting tailor-fashion on the bare dirt floor, the baby cradled gently in his arms, rocking back and forth and singing so softly that Bear would have had trouble making out the lullabye if he hadn't heard it before.

> "*Eh-e nini, eh-e nini,*
> Eh-e nini, nini,
> Nini nini nini
> Eh-e, eh-e nini eh!
> Eh-e, eh-e nini eh!
> Eh-e, ninni, ninni, ninni,
> Eh-e, ninni, ninni, eh!
> *Eh-e, ninni . . .*"

The baby quickly was back asleep, and while the family kept giving frightened looks in the direction of Bear and Sigerson—when they didn't simply try to look away—even the girl Yasmine watched Niko with quiet, trusting eyes.

"*Eh-e nini, eh-e nini,*" he sang.

"Eh-e nini, nini,
Nini nini nini
Eh-e, eh-e nini eh!
Eh-e, eh-e nini eh!
Eh-e, ninni, ninni, ninni,
Eh-e, ninni, ninni, eh!
Eh-e, ninni . . ."

Chapter 11: Crusade

Faith is, often I think, overrated.

Faith in people is guaranteed to disappoint, sooner or later; people are fallible, me more so than most. Faith in things is necessary, as anybody who has ever stepped down onto the top rung of a ladder can say—but it's dangerous, anybody who has seen a man fall from a ladder where the rung has broken beneath his feet to shatter himself on the stones far below can attest. Faith in magic is as reliable as magic is.

And faith in the Holy?

I wish I knew.

—Gray

Gray was hungry.

Not for food—he had eaten but a few hours ago, and

never much cared what he ate, as long as it filled his belly—but for . . . something.

Revenge?

Possibly. Blood, certainly. And most particularly, to be rid of that annoying boy, who carried himself as though he were a knight.

The coast grew before him, as the *Marienios* led the *Wellesley* toward it. Rocky and inhospitable, the only question was how soon the Johansen on the *Wellesley* would drop anchor. Close enough, he hoped, for the onager and catapult crews to cover a retreat, if one was necessary. Then again, staving in the hull or running the ship aground would make the ships even more useless than ones too far off would be.

Well, that was not the only question—the other question was how long it would take for those two slow slaggards of excuses for ships that DuPuy had foisted on them to catch up.

He would have rather been on the *Wellesley*, of course. By now, he was sure that Lieutenant Gordon Cooper would have the marines ready to go ashore, and presumably his counterparts on the *Winfrew* and *Cooperman* were doing the same—certainly true on the *Cooperman*. While Gray didn't think much of the marine lieutenant on that sad excuse for a ship, he had been impressed with Fotheringay. It wouldn't have bothered Gray for a moment if Lieutenant de Ros happened to break his neck going down the ladder, leaving Fotheringay fully in charge.

I'm wondering if that would occur to Fotheringay, the Khan said.

Stranger things had happened. A good sergeant wouldn't much care, other than in a personal sort of way, whether or not he liked his officers, but incompetence was another matter entirely, and this all was going to be difficult enough as it was. You couldn't mount an invasion with two hundred men—but a raid was another matter, even if the only purpose of the raid was to establish a temporary beachhead, to make sure that the knights had a way to get back to the ships.

Interesting that de Ros had sent Fotheringay ahead in the *Cooperman*'s launch to discuss the details with Gray, and while it was probably more than time for Fotheringay to be getting back to the *Cooperman*, it probably made as much sense for him to be taking his ease on the poop deck of the *Marienios*, puffing away at his pipe—easier and probably safer to drop the launch, and let Fotheringay signal the *Cooperman* where to drop anchor, just in case its idiot master couldn't read the *Wellesley*'s signal flags in the darkness.

Of course, it was entirely possible that Fotheringay's time would have been better spent supervising the final preparations of de Ros's marines, and even more possible that de Ros didn't want any more criticism—most likely implicit criticism, but Gray wouldn't have been surprised if Fotheringay spoke above his station—from the sergeant who had been forced upon him as to how sorry a state that was.

He shook his head. If it went wrong, it would be his problem, but there was nothing that Gray could do about it—leave it to the marines.

Be interesting to see what they would find. The Turks that Bear had found—granted, with the boy Niko's help—were from a village not too far from the coast, and they reported as least the direction that the captors had taken the people of their village.

Had Nadide been one of their villagers? Hard to say. Niko seemed to be sure of it, but the boy seemed utterly sure of everything of late, after all, and that didn't mean much, other than that he was overreaching himself, something that seemed to amuse Bear, for some reason.

"Nervous, Joshua?" Cully had joined him at the bow. Thankfully, he had left the boy below; Gray didn't have any particular desire to talk to him.

"Of course not." Gray shook his head. "You think we'll find what we're looking for here?"

"Possibly." He shrugged. "The only reason that I think perhaps not is that nobody's tried to stop us, so far."

Gray snorted, and gestured toward the shoreline. "Plenty of places to do that between here and Bear's friend's village, or what's left of it." Marching their company of marines up into the back country might have been a wiser choice, but Gray had vetoed that idea—you couldn't do that without drawing a lot of attention, and while leaving them on the beach to be prepared to cover a retreat had its own risks, he liked the idea of being able to get in and out, as quickly as possible.

See what they could see, talk to who they could talk to—and if they could find out where the villagers had been taken, that might, just might, lead them to whoever it was who was creating the new live swords.

Possibly. And if not here, then somewhere else.

"Hmmmm . . ." Cully hitched at his—two swords?

He caught Gray's glance, and smiled. "Always good to have a spare sword around, just in case." His face sobered. "And a spare knight or would-be knight, or two, as well, come to think of it."

And who shall be the spare, expendable knight, this

time? Gray didn't ask. As irritating as he often found Cully, he knew what the answer to that was: Cully himself.

You could fault Cully for a lot of things, but not that. It wasn't just a matter of a lack of cowardice—it was something much more cold-blooded.

"Very well," Cully said. "We've got marines to set up to cover our retreat, if retreat is necessary. We've got enough provisions for a couple of days, at least, save for water—and we can find water. We've Ercam as a guide, and his elder son as a spare guide, just in case."

"If we have them, where are they?"

"Below, spending a few moments with their family; they can be last up. I've had some words with Salim about them, by the way."

"You thought the Abdullahs would . . . interfere with the women?"

"No, not really—but I'm not sure about some of the hired-ons, and I wanted Salim to understand that the family is his responsibility. Probably should have put them aboard the *Wellesley*—but it's a bit late for that, now.

"As I was saying, before you started complaining, we've got Sigerson, to at least smell out the wizard—if we find him—and his manservant, who seems a capable sort, all in all, and probably the best substitute for a burro we've available. And the rest of the gear." He pointed down, as though toward their quarters, where Bear was presumably finishing packing up what they would carry with them. "Money for bribes, and the usual things one needs to live off the land."

"And your point would be?"

"That's easy." Cully's mouth quirked into a frown. "What am I missing?"

Were they teacher and student again, or was Cully just talking to pass the time? "Horses, for one," Gray said.

Cully nodded. "Certainly. I'd love to have some silent horses, ones that could be reliably counted on to be swum ashore—might make faster progress that way. I think going on foot makes sense." He grinned. "Should we turn around and go back and see if they've been breeding these silent, swimming horses back on Rodhos?"

Despite himself, Gray returned the smile. "If you think we could find some? Do let's."

"Why, Joshua, you've learned how to smile. You should try the expression out more often—I think it's hurting your face."

"I'm not sure where that came from, either." His hand fell to the hilt of the Khan.

I'm sure. The prospect of killing always made me smile, back when I had a mouth to smile with.

No, it wasn't that.

Cully stamped his foot three times on the deck, then looked up at Gray's look of surprise. "Well, I thought it was about time that the others joined us, and it's faster than sending for them."

It was, at that.

It was only a few minutes later that the rest of the party was on deck with them. That they all had rucksacks on their backs didn't make them look all the same, of course; they were each different.

Bear, of course, was as even of voice and manner as usual, and if that wasn't in its own way so reassuring, Gray would have been irritated. Both of the Turks were obviously scared—Gray wouldn't have been surprised if they quickly abandoned the knights as soon as they hit the beach.

Or maybe not. Their family was aboard. Hostages? That depended on your way of looking at things. Gray wouldn't hurt the children or the wives for the sins of the father and brother, but they didn't have to know that. They were being more than well enough paid for the risks they were taking, although they should have been willing to take any sort of risks as a matter of honor.

Then again, honor wasn't something you could count on, most of the time.

Sigerson had his usual amused expression pasted to his face, and his manservant his usual lack of any expression at all.

The boy, well, he looked scared, but he was a boy, after all, and you could hardly blame him for that, and he certainly had ample reason to be. This wasn't probably a good time to remind him that somebody who wielded a Red Sword was more than likely hellbound, after all, despite the temptation.

Yes, yes, of course you could repent. But Gray, for one, couldn't sincerely repent of his joining of his soul with the cursed Khan. It was the way that he could best serve the Crown, after all, and while there were men who would put their own interests ahead of their duty, Gray devoutly hoped that none of them were of the Order of Crown, Shield, and Dragon.

Cully? You could never tell about Cully, but . . .

And . . . wait.

At first, Gray thought it was a seagull dropping down out of the sky.

But it wasn't. It was a bird, though, larger than a seagull. A crow? No—a raven. A raven, at sea?

It swooped down out of the sky and landed on the deck

just a few feet in front of him, and in a blink, it was Black.

"Black?"

"Yes." He swallowed, hard.

Not the same as Gray had seen him before. He still wore his presumptuous imitation of a knight's robes, but the robes were bloody, tattered, and torn.

Which wasn't the worst of it. His right arm was covered with blood, and hung limply at his side, and his face was battered. His left hand was pressed tightly against his middle, as though trying to hold his guts in.

Probably the worst of it was his expression. The eyes were wide, the jaw trembling, and for some reason the whole effect was to remind Gray of a frightened, beaten little boy that he had known long ago, a boy standing before an Order knight, on the verge of collapsing in terror.

"Help me, Gray," he said. "Please."

Bear had shouldered his rucksack, and bounced up and down a few times, rewarded by a smile from Niko, who just stood watching, trying hard not to seem as amused as he obviously was.

Bear just grinned. "I'm much more concerned with making sure that the straps fit tightly and properly on my shoulders than I am in not looking foolish in front of you, young sir knight."

The boy spread his hands. "No offense—oh, very well: it did look strange."

He shrugged into his own rucksack, and accepted Bear's help in adjusting the straps. A fisherboy, of necessity, was used to long hours and hard work, perhaps even more so than a peasant, as difficult as that was to imagine.

But a more-than-one day march across country, a rucksack on his back, was a different thing entirely, and it was good that Niko's newfound confidence—at least, that's what it appeared to be—hadn't degenerated into an unwillingness to listen. Bear would have corrected him on the issue, as a matter of duty—but he was just as happy not to.

"Now," Bear said, "you try it."

"Jumping up and down?"

"Please."

He did. The straps were a little loose for Bear's tastes—more than what was required to make it possible to discard the rucksack quickly—but after some work on the straps, and more bouncing up and down by Niko, they met with Bear's approval.

Niko started at a triple thumping from the deck above. "It's just Cully, getting impatient."

Niko frowned. "I think I'm supposed to say something more."

"Eh?"

He shook his head. "Just a—"

"—code that Cully worked out with you? One for 'yes,' two for 'no,' three for 'more'?" Bear grinned. "Ah, yes—it's been a long time since I learned novice usages. Very well, Sir Niko—what is the more that you should say now?"

"That we should get going, perhaps?"

Bear grinned. "That will do. You'd better go get Ercam and Melik."

"Yes, Sir David."

His own pack shouldered, Bear gathered up his swords and followed Niko into the passageway, then climbed up the ladder to the deck while Niko continued on toward where the refugees were billeted in a stern compartment.

Cully and Gray were waiting for them, and Sigerson, his valet, and Niko, the two Turks in tow, were only a few moments behind.

"Shouldn't be long now," Cully said. The *Wellesley* was already down just one sail on each of the masts, and those had been heavily reefed. Bear couldn't see well enough from here to know if the topmen were all aloft, but their Abdullah counterparts here were, and he expected that they were.

The Abdullahs and the rest of the crew seemed to be making a point to keep the bow deck clear. Even the lookout, that Milos boy that Niko apparently had some grievance with, perched high in the foremast, kept his gaze fixed firmly on the water and land before them, although Samir Abdullah, taking the wheel himself, had apparently gone to some trouble to follow the *Wellesley's* course in.

The bird spread its wings widely, beating them madly against the air as it struggled to make it to the deck, and not splash into the water.

It succeeded, and with a final flurry of wings, landed, hard on the deck, skittering forward a few feet until it—

—changed.

For a moment, Bear didn't recognize the man.

He was still large and blocky, vaguely peasant-looking in the face and shoulders, particularly. But all of the elegance was gone—his shirt hung on him in bloody tatters; a cut on his right cheek had gone to the bone, and the blood oozing from a dozen wounds spoke of far more serious damage.

If any of it could be believed.

Wolf took a staggering step forward, and fell to his knees; he would have fallen face-first on the deck if he hadn't stopped himself by putting out an arm.

Wolf looked up at Bear. All of the serenity and confidence that Bear had seen in his face was gone, washed away in blood and agony.

There was nothing in that face save pain and despair.

"Help me, Bear," Wolf said. "Please."

The Wise, battered and bloody, knelt before Cully in supplication. He, she—it didn't look like Her, not this time. Nor had it manifested itself in some sort of idealized form of Cully himself.

It had, for whatever reason, chosen Sir Bedivere, precisely as Cully had seen him the last time, so many years ago: the fletching of an arrow just barely projecting from his chest, what was left of his left arm from the elbow down hanging by a tendon and a scrap of skin, his usually preposterously well-combed beard all askew and drenched in his own blood and vomit. And, as it had been at Bedivere's death, the coat of arms on his tabard was intact, the only part of his clothing or armor that had been untouched in his battle with the traitors.

The eyes, though, they were not the same. They had been, and always would be, sharp in Cully's memory, a fierceness and joy in Bedivere's eyes, a ghost of which had persisted even when those eyes had gone all dull and lifeless. Bedivere had gone to his death knowing that he had died in service of his Order, and his King, and he had laid himself down with joy as much as with pain.

These eyes had none of that joy, though all of the pain.

If anything, they reminded him of a deer he had once brought down in his long-lost Woode, and he found his hand going to his belt for the dagger that he would have used to give an animal the blow of grace.

But, of course, the dagger wasn't there. Nor, of course, was Bedivere.

"Help me, Cully," the image of Bedivere said, its voice a horrible, liquid rasp. "Please."

It was Grandfather, again, of course. Or, more accurately, it looked like Grandfather—but not the healthy, vibrant man that Niko would always remember, but something more like the murdered body that he had seen on the shore at home, back when he had a home.

It had fooled Niko before—but it wouldn't this time, not again. Niko didn't like to be fooled.

"Help me, Niko," the lying image said. "Please."

Chapter 12: Pantelleria

When I was serving with His Own, shortly after one minor incident at Balmoral where I acquitted myself apparently adequately, I was sent to sit in on what I was told was a fascinating theological argument between a couple of scholars at the Old College. He said that it was intended to be a reward, but perhaps HM was just having a joke at my expense. I'm told that he has a subtle sense of humor, but not having any such myself, I'd hardly be the person to judge.

The subject, as I recall, was something long and involved about the nature of Unintended Evil Consequences of Morally Proper Acts vs. Unintended Good Consequences of Morally Wrong Ones. They started with Judas Iscariot and Pontius Pilate, and how the betrayal of the first and at least the moral indifference of the second led to Our Lord dying for all of our sins, and went on from there.

By the time they got to the required pieties about the

Tyrant murdering all those babies—although missing the
baby Mordred—and forcing Mordred the Great, both for
moral and practical reasons, down the path that led him
to have to take the throne, all I'd learned is that good
things sometimes flow from evil intent, and vice versa.

I think I already knew that.

—Gray

It did look strange.

It *still*, apparently, looked strange. DuPuy hadn't
thought that Randolph was lying, but . . . it was different
to see it for himself. There were just too many ships. And
too many kinds of ships, dammit.

As soon as he lowered his glass, Admiral Sir Simon
Tremaine DuPuy found himself, once again, pacing back
and forth across the quarterdeck, so he stopped. Out of
the corner of his eye he caught the steersman grinning at
the first, and the first grinning back, so he just stared at
the two of them, and they quickly found themselves utterly
engaged in their work, as did the rest of the crew.

Unsurprisingly, every time that DuPuy was on deck,
there wasn't an officer or man aboard standing at ease—
save for Randolph himself, whose own quarterdeck style
seemed to involve as little activity and motion on his own
part as was humanly possible. Still, it probably wasn't a
coincidence that Randolph's preferred posture—leaning
against the quarterdeck rail, smoking his pipe—kept all
of topside under his immediate observation.

Which was better than what DuPuy had witnessed their
first day out—Randolph had stripped off his jacket and
boots and climbed up the foremast's rigging, like some
sort of ropemonkey—a damnably common sort of thing

to do. Perhaps when you were gently born, you felt you could get away with that sort of thing, although who would want to was something DuPuy couldn't fathom, and there were more important matters at hand, at least at the moment.

Randolph had reported a little more than a dozen ships crowding the Porto Pantelleria harbor—fifteen, DuPuy remembered—but there were easily twice that many here, just off Khamma and more headed in.

It was the combination of the number and the variety that was so strange.

He shook his head, and put the glass back to his good eye. Granted, Pantelleria was but a day's sail from Tunis, just as it was from Agrigento, and not an uncommon place for some trade between Tunisian and Sicilian merchants to take place, despite the lack of anything resembling decent-sized warehouses, or docking capable of taking a ship. As to what got traded there, well, that was among the things that DuPuy didn't know, and didn't much want to know.

Not his business.

The orders for Navy ships to avoid the island were, well, naval orders, not local ones, and the Earl of Sicilia had not, as far as DuPuy knew—and he would have known—prohibited it, nor had his sovereign Duke, so there was no surprise in seeing two ships with the Trinakria on the mast, fluttering beneath both the rampant stallion of the Duke of Napoli and, of course, the Crown and Dragon.

Nor was DuPuy surprised to find the Star and Scimitar on several of the fellucas' masts, with various Caliphate and satrapal pennants below them.

And then there were Guild ships, their masts bare of any flag save for the preposterously plain red-over-white that the League and Guild had flown since time immemorial, and, of course, all of them flew several of the dozens of pennants that announced what they had to trade as well as what they claimed to be seeking in trade.

And not just Guild—that low-slung four-master had Izmiri lines, and the fat bark was clearly Sebiani.

Something was going on. It was probably nothing terribly important, granted, but . . .

Randolph emerged from his cabin at his usual leisurely pace, asked a quick is-everything-as-it-should-be of the first, and barely waited for Caldwell's quick nod before walking over to where DuPuy was standing.

"Afternoon, Admiral," he said.

"Captain."

Randolph turned to the quarterdeck runner, but DuPuy preempted him by passing his glass over. Randolph put it to his eye, lowering it quickly enough to irritate DuPuy. Damn his eyes.

"A bit thicker than it was before," Randolph said. He put the glass back to his eye. "But about the same, all in all, and—hmm." He shook his head. "We're not the only ones to have seen something of interest—that's al-Bakilani's personal pennant on the nor'most fellucca."

DuPuy almost asked if he was sure, but stopped himself. Randolph had flown the pennant—well below any of the other pennants—while conveying al-Bakilani to Sfax.

"A clever man, al-Bakilani," Randolph went on. "I wonder what he's doing here."

And, of course, it didn't do Randolph's credibility any

harm to point out to DuPuy that the same thing he had observed had also been noticed by al-Bakilani and his people, and presumably drawn him here.

If, of course, al-Bakilani himself wasn't the cause of all of this activity.

Well, DuPuy had seen it for himself, and the sensible thing to do was probably just to turn the *Lord Fauncher* around after dropping off a longboat with the three of Shea's people that he had. Granted, that might as well announce that they were from Naval Intelligence—but the late, unlamented Scratch had certainly already passed along that word to al-Bakilani.

"Dangerous man, al-Bakilani," Randolph went on, giving DuPuy a sideways glance.

The feeling-Randolph-out part of this all, at least, was an apparent success—Randolph had gone to some trouble to make it clear to DuPuy that he had been impressed with the number and quality of the ships in the harbor at Sfax, and had, last night after a remarkably and atypically sober dinner, put his officers and middies through an interesting sandtable on a hypothetical landing and sack of Sfax.

Not a bad plan, at that—Randolph's scheme involved mustering ships and southern troops at Siracusa, bringing the Napolitans over the Messina Straits, with the Gibby Fleet making a diversionary attack at Tunis, splitting off to join the Med Fleet for the landings. A tricky thing, yes, and it would have to be set up carefully enough, but it could be done, at least in theory, if enough troops could be shifted south to reinforce it all.

Although it would have to be well timed; necessary to land in Morocco at the same time, to seal up the sea routes out of the Med, something that Randolph hadn't fully thought through.

Maybe. If it worked, it would cut off the Western Dar from the East, effectively isolating the heart of it from its rich Darmosh Kowayes colonies, particularly if the new trebuchets at Tarifa were as accurate as they were claimed to be and as numerous as they ought to be.

Gibraltar was the neck—grab them by the neck and then cut their throat at Sfax and eventually Tunis, and then turn privateers loose in the Atlantic, and it would be only a matter of time before the Darmosh Kowayes colonies would fall to the Duke of New England.

Of course, the Dar wouldn't be standing idly by while that happened, and Randolph was making the typical junior officer assumption that everything would go as planned. And—

"Admiral?"

DuPuy shook his head. "Just an old man woolgathering, Mr. Randolph."

Well, if they were going to go ashore, the obvious thing to do was to send Shea's men into Khamma—with a company of marines at least pretending to look like they were on shore leave. The *Lord Fauncher* wasn't going to be fighting its way away from Pantelleria, after all, at least not successfully.

As to what DuPuy himself was going to do, well, that was obvious, too.

"You think your first can handle an anchor watch, Mr. Randolph?"

Randolph hesitated for a moment, then: "I think a button-boned middie can handle an anchor watch, Admiral—if nothing exciting happens." He pointed his chin toward the ships anchored offshore. "But if, say, two of those Dar feluccas were to move toward us and try to board, I don't have any confidence that *I* could raise anchor, fly the sails, and get the ship moving away quickly enough to prevent them from locking on and boarding." He looked DuPuy in the eye. "And I've a fairly high opinion of my own abilities—at least so I've been told."

It would have been difficult to brace the man for that sort of uppitiness on his own quarterdeck, sore as the temptation was, and it was typical of Randolph to take responsibility for the problem himself—he hadn't even suggested that such a thing would be a problem because of his shipload of idiots and rejects. There was some truth to that, too. Still, a crack crew—topmen taking their ease aloft, with most sails flying but reefed to the point where they wouldn't strain the anchor chain—could get a ship moving awfully quickly, if need be, even absent the possibility of cutting the anchor chain.

The other choice, of course, was to have the *Lord Fauncher* simply circle the island. But that had its own problems—it would, of a certainty draw attention to the ship, and it would mean that the shore party would have to wait for its return before being able to reboard.

And never mind that that sort of thing would challenge the first well beyond DuPuy's confidence in his abilities—Hempstead would probably manage to run the *Lord Fauncher* aground, as he had, repeatedly, when he had been the master of the *Silkie*, which was what had gotten him beached—unless, of course, he gave the shoaled waters around the island a wide enough berth that DuPuy might as well have sent him back to Malta.

Randolph could, DuPuy decided, handle either, despite

his apparent desultory command style. DuPuy could take the shore party himself, and not bring Randolph along, which had been his intention until Randolph had seen al-Bakilani's pennant.

Perhaps he should just stick with that—but he very much wanted to see how Randolph reacted in the Arab's presence.

Well, decisions didn't get any better by standing on deck. "Let's go ashore, and see what our old friend al-Bakilani is up to, shall we?"

"Of course, sir." He turned toward the first. "Mr. Caldwell—prepare the longboat for the Admiral and myself. You have the deck."

"Aye, aye, sir."

DuPuy frowned. Randolph's face hadn't so much as twitched at DuPuy's characterization of al-Bakilani, and Randolph had been less than responsive to DuPuy's attempts to feel him out. For some reason, most officers found it difficult to bare their souls to Simon DuPuy.

"Some concern, Admiral?"

"Well, we can hardly call on him in our utilities, can we?"

"No, sir, I think it would be impolite," Randolph said. "Shall we?"

They headed below to change. DuPuy couldn't get the frown off his face. The danger didn't bother him—but he'd have to put on the damnably expensive first-class uniform, unless that idiot Owlsley hadn't packed it.

That possibility brought a smile to his face.

Unfortunately, by the time that DuPuy made it down to his—to Randolph's cabin, Owlsley already had all of it laid out on the bunk, and was busily engaged in polishing the ivory-hilted dress sword and matching dagger, and it was all DuPuy could do to say "Well done"—which he did—rather than "Why did you have to pick *this* bloody occasion to be suddenly competent and efficient?"

It wasn't a difficult matter to find out where al-Bakilani was staying. Even if their inquiries in Agma hadn't immediately born fruit—and they had—with his ship anchored offshore that village, the most likely place for him was the Bagno della Acqua, and, sure enough, his personal pennant flew from a stanchion off the largest and grandest of the small homes just off the edge of the Bagno della Acqua, what the locals called the "shore."

To the extent that it had shores. The famous "bath of water" looked to DuPuy more like an oversized pool of steaming mud than anything else, although a preposterous profundity of people, apparently from the various dammusi circling the mud puddle, had descended down the black, rocky slope to sit in it, and the wind across the mud puddle brought a distinct smell of sulfur to DuPuy's nose. Judging from what he could see, every passing merchantman's officers and perhaps paying passengers took the opportunity of pulling into Pantelleria to sit in mud no different, save for the stench, than could have been found on any road in Suffolk after a good rain.

They had left the marines and the so-called Intelligence men behind in the village. While DuPuy didn't much care about manners when it came to the enemy, showing up at al-Bakilani's rented doorstep at all was enough of a challenge without making it worse by committing the further solecism of arriving in force, albeit even in small force.

The home—they were still called "dammusi," DuPuy recollected—was rather small by what DuPuy thought would be the Arab's standards. Wisps of smoke rising from behind it, only to be immediately shattered on the wind, suggested that whatever kitchens it had were outside, hidden behind the bulk of the dammusa.

An arch led to the patio at the front of it, protecting the massive front door from the wind. The windows at the front were dark, but unshuttered, making it clear that the dwelling was built of remarkably thick stones of the black local rock, although from what DuPuy could see across the mud puddle about the backsides of other dammusi, didn't make them look like they'd be terribly resistant to an attack from that direction, and the low, waist-height wall was just a decoration, although it probably helped protect the gardens well enough from wind-driven sand, which was probably its only intent.

The roof, like all of the rest, was domed, rather than flat—that was probably about the wind, as well.

There was no gate—the low wall simply opened on the flat stone walkway up to the door.

"Begging your pardon, Admiral," Randolph said, "but do you propose to simply knock on his door?"

DuPuy nodded. "Yes, and leave my card with his servant, of course," he said, producing a card from the breast pocket of his first-class uniform. He had no pen to write with, of course—he could hardly carry around pen and inkwell in his first-class uniform, and he had deliberately left Owlsley, with all of his kit, aboard the *Lord Fauncher*—but DuPuy's name on the paper should be message enough.

Let al-Bakilani come looking for him.

He ran a finger under his collar. Damned uncomfortable thing—the heavily starched white collar always scratched his neck, and one of the few fears that Simon DuPuy had was of falling down and damaging the bloody expensive uniform beyond the ability of easy repair, guaranteeing hours of time wasted in fitting and more money that he cared to think about in the replacement.

He would be willing to bet heavily that he would quickly hear from al-Bakilani—whatever al-Bakilani was up to, he would want to know to what extent that the Crown in general and DuPuy in particular were on to him, and not wish to wait for a report from Scratch, even if he hadn't heard about DuPuy's secretary's unfortunate accident.

There were no servants or anybody else outside the low stone fence around the dammusa—DuPuy had expected that there would be at least some sort of guard on duty, to whom he could present his card. Their absence probably meant that, pennant aside, al-Bakilani was not there at the moment.

Well, there was no point in standing out here and waiting. He marched up the walkway, his card in hand. There was no proper knocker on the door.

"No knocker—and I'm not about to pound on it with my fist."

Randolph, wisely, didn't say anything.

"Probably just slide it under the door, I think," DuPuy said.

Since there was nobody there to properly receive it, or him, and while leaving it pinned to the door with his dress-belt dagger had a certain appeal, it probably wasn't the right thing to do—and, besides, he'd need to replace the dagger.

He handed the card to Randolph—let him do the stooping—and just as Randolph bent to do so, the door wheezed open, and al-Bakilani himself was standing there, an easy smile on his face.

"Your Excellency," he said. "As it happens, I was just speaking of you."

"A coincidence, I suppose?"

"Oh, not at all, for any number of reasons." Al-Bakilani's smile, if anything, broadened.

He looked no different than the last time DuPuy had seen him—what DuPuy had hoped was the last time he would ever see al-Bakilani, although instead of the the long flowing robes, he wore only a single linen garment that, irritatingly, reminded DuPuy of a mockery of priest's cassock, down to the Musselman rosary that depended from the left side of his waist. At least he was armed, in a way—there was a dagger of sorts on his other hip. DuPuy found that vaguely reassuring, for reasons he couldn't quite have explained.

Al-Bakilani bowed deeply. "Would you be so kind as to grace my home?"

Randolph at his side, DuPuy followed al-Bakilani into the hall, and into the large central room, only idly wondering if al-Bakilani could turn about before DuPuy plunged his dagger into al-Bakilani's broad back.

A door led off down a hallway that was brightly lit by the afternoon sun, the only exit other than the ones that they had walked in, and sounds coming through the door told some activity beyond them, although DuPuy couldn't have said what it might be.

Two Arabs had been reclining on their strange-looking couches, and both of them sat up at DuPuy's entrance, one of them in an ordinary, desultory sort of fashion, although the other leaped to his feet and took a step forward, as though to move between DuPuy and Randolph and the other.

Al-Bakilani made a patting motion with both of his hands, and murmured something in Arabic, and the man assumed a position that looked to DuPuy more like parade rest than anything else.

His eyes seemed to fasten on DuPuy's as he accepted al-Bakilani's command with a nod, then crossed his hands over his chest.

There was something strange about him, particularly around the eyes. Perhaps it was just that his sun-bronzed skin was a few shades lighter than the others', or that his beard seemed a little, well, bushier.

The strangest thing about him was the sword tucked through the sash at his waist. It wasn't the curved Musselman scimitar, but a straight blade, plainly wood-gripped with no sign of decoration, in a simple wooden sheath.

Al-Bakilani ignored him, but addressed the other man, who nodded, and rose, slowly.

He was an immense, fat man, but from the way he moved to his feet it was clear that there were muscles, as well as fat, beneath his simple shift. He was taller than al-Bakilani—himself not a short man—although he stood half a head shorter than the swordsman. His thick fingers were heavily laden with jeweled rings, and a small silver chain, looped several times around his forehead, held his oiled hair in place.

His eyes were neither warm nor hostile, although he seemed not to blink at all.

"Admiral Sir Simon Tremaine DuPuy, Lieutenant Lord Sir Alphonse Randolph, may I have the honor to present Abu Abdullah Mohammed ibn al-Sharif al-Idrisi?"

It was all DuPuy could do not to sputter. If al-Bakilani wasn't lying through his too-white teeth, this was . . . preposterous. Al-Idrisi was the Sharif of Tunisia, the equivalent—to the extent that the filthy Musselmen could have an equivalent—to a Crown Duke, and of a certainty the most important and powerful man in the Dar al-Islam this side of the Nile, and, at least arguably, this side of Mecca.

What was *he* doing *here*? And why had DuPuy been admitted to his presence? And where were his guards? His army? He would be no more likely to venture out of Tunis into contested waters without soldiers aplenty in attendance than the Duke of Napoli would—less so, perhaps, if there was something less likely than the inconceivable.

Randolph was quicker on his feet. "Honored, Your Excellency," he said, bowing deeply.

Well, there was nothing for it but to go along, at least for the moment.

"Honored," DuPuy said.

Al-Idrisi smiled, and turned toward al-Bakilani. "I think, perhaps, my friend," he said, "that I see a trace of doubt in the noble Admiral's face."

If anything, his English was more puzzling—first, that he spoke it at all, and more-so, that he seemed to have no accent, save perhaps a touch of Brigstow? And why would the two Arabs be talking in English to each other? Surely it couldn't be to reassure DuPuy.

There was not a damn thing about this that was in any way reassuring.

Al-Bakilani nodded. "I can hardly blame him, Excellency," he said. "I think some explanations are not only in order, but in all of our interests."

"And inevitable, at that," al-Idrisi said. "And they can be given here just as easily as I'd intended you to convey them to his Excellency on Malta—and perhaps even more persuasively?"

Al-Bakilani bowed. "Your wisdom does not surprise me." He glanced at the window. "We have enough time—sundown is hours away, as of yet." He clapped his hands together, the sound of running feet in the small courtyard behind the house were immediately followed by a short, dark man, manifestly a servant—he wore only blousy white pantaloons, and was naked from the waist up—appearing in the open doorway.

"We have guests, Efik—and the hospitality of the al-Bakilani family suffers every moment they are kept thirsty and hungry."

"I'm not—" DuPuy started.

"We are, of course, honored," Randolph put in, interrupting. His timing had best not have been deliberate, even if the effect had been to prevent DuPuy from being impolite.

"It's my hope that you will be more than honored, but delighted—Efik has been my personal cook and attendant for . . . would you remind me, Efik? In English, please; I know you speak it."

"Yes, Excellency. I've had the honor of serving you in one capacity or another for the past twelve years, and as your cook since old Salim died, three years ago." He was a compact little man, his hairless chest splattered with the scars of old burn marks, although his back was unmarked. "I hadn't expected you to have guests quite so soon, but I can assure you I'll manage—and, if not," he said, gesturing toward the open door, "I can send for assistance."

Al-Bakilani gave DuPuy a smile. Of course al-Idrisi would bring along his personal entourage, which probably was somewhere nearby—perhaps in some of the other dammusi along the shoreline. It was entirely possible that the men sitting in the mud of the Bagno della Acqua were lookouts for soldiers stationed inside, and certain that the Sharif of Tunisia would not be depending on merely one man for protection—nor would he believe that DuPuy would be so gullible as to believe that.

"Very well, Efik. Please impress our guests—but quickly, quickly."

"Of course, Excellency." Efik gave only an economical bow before hurrying off.

The supposed Sharif gestured both of them to nearby couches, and there being no graceful way around it, DuPuy sat. Randolph actually reclined on his, only straightening after a quick glare from DuPuy. No matter what the local custom was, one of His Majesty's officers didn't sprawl on a couch like a whore about to be mounted, by God.

The other Arab remained standing, eying both DuPuy and Randolph with a look of something that had as much of evaluation as hatred in it, as though he was deciding how to kill them, not when.

DuPuy looked him right back in the eye. There were things in this world that frightened Simon DuPuy, yes, but death wasn't one of them.

Al-Bakilani started to talk, but stopped when Efik, at

the head of a team of four more servants bustled in, carrying well-laden trays, and it took a few minutes to make sure that everybody—save for the big man on his feet—was served.

DuPuy ate—it was obviously required—but didn't taste anything. He was more interested in making sure that he didn't drip anything on his uniform—and vastly more so in watching al-Bakilani, al-Idrisi, and particularly the man who had not been introduced—than he was in whatever the various porridges were that he was supposed to sop up with the flat Arab bread.

The man was obviously a soldier of some sort, although his robes were fine enough for a Dar noble. He ignored the servants, and even al-Bakilani and al-Idrisi, but just stood, not quite motionless, and continued to watch DuPuy and Randolph, as though he expected them to leap up and attack the supposed al-Idrisi at any moment. DuPuy looked around while trying not to look as though he was—where were the rest of this al-Idrisi's guards?

Al-Bakilani muttered something in Arabic to al-Idrisi, who nodded.

"Of course," he said, "but please, if you would, let us try to keep the conversation in a language our guests can follow."

"My apologies, of course." He turned to DuPuy. "I beg your pardon; I find it . . . uncomfortable to quote the Prophet to a fellow True Believer other than in Arabic. It was one of the hadiths, and it seems to apply. 'If you stay with some people and they entertain you as they should for a guest, accept their hospitality, but if they don't do as they should, take the right of the guest from them.'

"Englishmen are, so I understand, fond of their pipes.

I'm of the opinion that such things are . . . discouraged for True Believers, but both His Excellency the Sharif and I are more of the opinion that the Prophet, peace be upon him, considered the obligations of hosts rather more important than such preferences, and, truth to tell, I've never found the smell of tobacco unpleasant—if you'd honor me by lighting your pipes, I'd take that as a sign that we were fulfilling our obligations."

Getting their pipes out and packed was but a matter of a few moments, and the ever-efficient Efik quickly provided them with lit tapers, and—truth to tell—DuPuy found the smoke comforting, and the supposed al-Idrisi's attempts to hide his clear discomfort with the smell even more so. DuPuy didn't have the slightest idea whether al-Bakilani relished or detested the smoke, but at least he could read al-Idrisi's face.

Or was he intended to think that he could?

Al-Bakilani sipped at his coffee. "Where to start? Ah. Do let's start with what must be most puzzling to you—His Excellency the Sharif's presence here?"

"That would be the second thing, I suspect." The supposed al-Idrisi shook his head. "My identity, perhaps?" He gave DuPuy an infuriating smile. "Were I the Admiral, I'd likely be skeptical on that point. One would expect somebody who Allah has honored with my status to travel with an army to protect him, even so short a distance from Tunis."

Some response seemed called for, so DuPuy nodded. "I had been thinking of that. They're concealed in the nearby dammusi, I suppose."

If anything, that caused al-Idrisi's already broad smile to broaden even further. "Actually, no. I traveled aboard my friend's ship, with but a few men, and they're stationed along the roads where they can give alarm, rather than protect my person. As for that, another introduction is in order, I believe." His flipperlike hand gestured toward the other Arab. "Admiral Sir Simon Tremaine DuPuy, Lieutenant Lord Sir Alphonse Randolph, may I present Abdul ibn Mahmoud?"

DuPuy didn't quite shrug. Al-Idrisi cocked his head to one side. "Abdul is a . . ." He looked to al-Bakilani.

"Convert, Excellency."

"Convert, that's the word. He was born Alexander Smith, I believe, and known at one time as Sir Alexander Smith, Knight of the Order of the Crown, Shield, and Dragon."

Randolph was on his feet immediately, his pipe clattering on the tiles.

"Sit down, Mr. Randolph," DuPuy said. The Arab's—no, this Alexander's hand was resting on the hilt of his sword, and if this was who al-Idrisi said it was, then Randolph would have no chance at all. And probably none anyway, even if al-Idrisi was lying, or not al-Idrisi at all—al-Bakilani had obviously considered the possibilities, and al-Bakilani was not a fool.

"Sir, I—"

"Sit *down*, by God." There was nothing more that Simon DuPuy would have liked to do than have seen that traitor's, that murderer's blood spill across the floor, and his own and Randolph's life would be a pitifully small price to pay for that.

But that wasn't going to happen here and now.

Randolph wasn't moving, and his hand was clapped to the hilt of that curved Seeproosh saber, but at least he hadn't drawn it yet.

"Please, Lieutenant, do as you wish," the murderer said. "The Sandoval is always ready, and hungry—and I'm none too fond of highborn English dogs—"

"*Cease.*" Al-Idrisi had gotten to his feet faster than a man with that bulk should have been able to, and squared off against Smith. Al-Idrisi started to say something in Arabic, then stopped himself, and went on in English: "You've lived long enough among us to know of the obligations of a host to guests."

From al-Idrisi's tone, DuPuy had expected more reaction than "Yes, Excellency."

DuPuy wasn't watching his expression; his eyes were on Randolph, who hadn't moved. "Lieutenant . . ."

"Aye, aye, sir," Randolph said, his boot-face once again firmly in place, if you didn't quite notice the way that his jaw clenched. "Sir, I—"

"Sit, boy," he said, gently.

"Aye, aye, sir." Randolph sat. "Permission to speak, sir."

"Save it for later." It was more important to find out what this was all about. Were they prisoners?

DuPuy didn't like the way al-Bakilani shook his head. "No, Admiral, you're not prisoners. You're guests, free to leave when and as you please. But I do think you'll want to hear His Excellency out," he said. "It's in your interest as much as ours, I believe."

Those were fine words, but they would be all the better for the testing.

"On your feet, Mr. Randolph," he said. "Return to your ship. Raise anchor, and be prepared to take flight at any approach—do so in any case before dark. No orders to the contrary from me are to be entertained unless delivered in person—and if there's as much as one man in the boat along with me, or a place where one could possibly be hidden, you are to assume I'm a prisoner, acting under duress, and act accordingly."

"Aye, aye, sir." Randolph tugged at the edge of his jacket, and looked down, momentarily, at his pipe on the floor, then visibly decided not to bend down in the presence of an enemy to pick it up.

He turned and marched toward the door, then stopped. "Admiral, I will send a man—a volunteer—back here to report that I've safely arrived on the *Lord Fauncher*. I'd recommend that you assume I've been assassinated by a cowardly murderer should that man not arrive within the hour, and take any protestations about your being a guest as worth what I believe they *are* worth."

DuPuy nodded. Randolph was thinking—better than DuPuy was, in fact. "Very well."

Randolph turned to this . . . Smith. "And I'll disobey my orders to the extent of saying this, and take what discipline the Admiral deems appropriate without complaint. You—"

"Lieutenant—"

"No, sir; not 'Lieutenant'." Randolph's lips were white. "I'm speaking as Lord Sir Alphonse Randolph, Admiral. If you want my commission for doing so, Admiral, you may have it, with my thanks." He didn't wait for an answer, but turned back to Smith. "I've had the honor of laying flowers at the grave of Lady Mary, Mr. Smith—in the company of both the Earl of Moray, and of His Majesty. I thought then, Mr. Smith, long and hard about the sort of . . . person who would cut her throat while she slept, and I swore to myself that were I ever to find myself in the . . . company of that piece of filth, one of us would not survive.

"I never thought that likely, mind you, but here I am, and here you are. I've no doubt that stolen Red Sword of yours could easily take my life, and perhaps you could even best me fairly, in a duel—not that your kind would face a man with steel in his hand.

"But Admiral DuPuy says no. Admiral DuPuy says I must violate my oath, here and now.

"Very well. I'll violate that oath, obedient to my orders, and not because I've also sworn to obey my lawful superiors. I am, at the moment, a lieutenant in His Majesty's service, and while I'd gladly, eagerly lay down my life and my oath for a chance at yours, I happen to believe that Admiral DuPuy is as wise a man as ever has worn a uniform, and he apparently believes that you ought to be allowed live to for the moment.

"So I'll do that—this one time. But not again. And if I live through this day, I will make it my purpose to see that there will be another occasion.

"I'll think long and hard about you every day until I lay your head at the foot of her grave, Mr. Smith, and then I'll not think about you ever again."

He spun on the ball of his foot and marched from the room.

"Very prettily spoken," Smith said, loudly enough for the words to carry. "I'll not lose any sleep, though."

Realistically, there was no reason why he should. It wasn't as though Alexander Smith wasn't already a wanted man, and while DuPuy thought and certainly hoped that His Majesty had agents all throughout the Dar al-Islam, if it had been easy or even practical for Smith to be assassinated, it would already have been done by now. There had to be some sensible men in Londinium, after all.

And this?

What was Randolph going to do, even assuming that Smith would stay in Tunis—an unlikely possibility; he had clearly been seconded from the Caliph for just this occasion. Did Randolph think he could take passage on an unflagged merchantman to Tunis, and then march up to the gates of al-Idrisi's palace and throw down a glove? Randolph had been speaking from the heart, not the head.

But DuPuy shook his head anyway. "If I were you, Mr. Smith, I would think—"

"My name is Abdul ibn Mahmoud. And I'm not interested in what you think, DuPuy."

"But I am," al-Bakilani put in. "There are other matters that are perhaps more important at the moment, but . . ." He frowned. "And while the Admiral's presence has . . . complicated things, and perhaps hurried along matters that could better have waited until His Excellency sent me to Malta, as we had been planning, there's more than enough time, I believe, to hear him out."

DuPuy resumed his seat, and deliberately took a moment to puff on his pipe. Surprisingly, it hadn't gone out. He bent over and picked up Randolph's pipe from where it had fallen on the floor, wondering if he was going to be able to return it to the lieutenant.

"What I was going to say, Mr. Smith," DuPuy said raising his head to look Smith in the eye, "is that if I thought that Alphonse Randolph was after my head, that head would not rest easily on my pillow. You've not taken the measure of the man—I have."

Smith started to say something, but desisted at a microscopic headshake from al-Idrisi. If this . . . charade was a matter of trying to persuade DuPuy of the identities of two imposters, it was working, although to what end DuPuy couldn't imagine.

And yes, of course, DuPuy's warning had been all bluff and bluster, but if that bluff and bluster caused al-Bakilani and al-Idrisi to take DuPuy less seriously, there might be benefit in that. Then again, al-Bakilani might decide that DuPuy was just trying to get him to think that—was there ever a wheel that didn't have another wheel rolling around inside it?

But, that aside, there had been a benefit from Randolph's speech—for Randolph. A man with that sort of appropriately directed hatred in him would make a fine Earl of Moray, from DuPuy's point of view—and the sooner the better. Have to figure out a way to pin a medal or two on his chest.

Hmmm . . . and while he wouldn't give Randolph a hint of it, there was now nothing Randolph could say or do that would cause DuPuy to want to ruin his reputation— quite the contrary. That threat had passed Randolph by without him ever having known of it.

The next Earl of Moray would, if Simon DuPuy had anything to say about it, leave the Navy with as respectable a record as he could manage. Command of a squadron was an obvious step. The only question was how to manage it—and that would be arranged, even if it required DuPuy to go over Bullworth's account books himself, pen and ink in hand. DuPuy's honor was as expendable as Bullworth's career, after all.

But he could save that thinking for the trip back to Malta—if, indeed, he would be allowed to leave.

And, if not . . . many eyes had seen the flags fluttering from the mast of the *Lord Fauncher*, and were it to disappear, with all hands, in waters this close to the Dar, some of the right conclusions would likely be drawn. Wars had started over less. It was likely that al-Idrisi and al-Bakilani would permit Randolph to make it back to the *Lord Fauncher*, and the *Lord Fauncher* to Malta, with or without DuPuy on board. They obviously wanted to persuade him of something, after all, and DuPuy would not be persuaded of anything were Randolph's messenger not to arrive, and if the *Lord Fauncher* were not to make it back to Malta upon his return, DuPuy would know who to blame.

And if al-Bakilani and al-Idrisi intended to kidnap DuPuy? That would be a silly thing to do, granted—of what use was an old, beached sailor?

But, if so, he could handle that. You struck at your enemy with the tools at your disposal, as effectively as you could. The dress dagger on DuPuy's belt was near enough to his hand, and sharp enough to shave with. DuPuy had never been able to stomach a weapon that wasn't a weapon.

Of course, with Smith standing there, DuPuy, even twenty years younger and three stone lighter, would not be able to reach al-Bakilani or al-Idrisi, and it would be futile to try.

If there was a chance that the outrage over the murder of a British Admiral focused attention and intention properly—and there was, at least a chance—DuPuy would laugh as he cut his own throat. But there would be time for that, later, if need be. For now, he could hear al-Bakilani out.

"Now," he said to al-Bakilani, "what was it you were going to be sent to Malta to tell me?"

"You'll permit me, my friend?" al-Idrisi asked. "Admiral?"

"Of course, Excellency."

DuPuy nodded, and took another puff on his pipe. "Please."

There had been rumors about these swords for some time, al-Idrisi explained.

Then again, there were *always* rumors. Rumors were a fact of life, on matters of faith. Thus had it always been: the Hidden Mahdi was about to surface in Tikritiza, shattering the legitimacy of the Umayyad dynasty; the Jews were momentarily to break out of Judea, carrying the Ark of the Covenant before them; or the Maasa'pi were revolting—not unusual, particularly, although their rebellions were quickly put down, as neither their warriors nor their promised shaman never seemed to be as immune to swords or arrows as the legends promised—or Avalon had reappeared, the Holy Grail found, the shards of the Sword of Constantine restored and reforged, and the remnants of the Holy Roman Empire would once again become invincible as they swept east and west and south.

Could such things happen? Well, of course they could—but a practical man would no more worry about them than about anything else that he could do nothing about. When it came to all matters, it would be as Allah willed, as it was from the beginning.

And, of course, rumors didn't merely circulate about the sacred and the profane.

Admiral DuPuy would, of course, forgive al-Idrisi if he didn't go into any detail about family squabbles in the Dar Al Islam, although he was sure that the noble Admiral was aware of tension between the various Sharifs in Darmosh Kowayes and the Caliph—blessed be his name—just as al-Idrisi was more than passingly familiar with similar tensions between the Duke of New England and His Majesty the King, and it was a safe prediction that, sooner than later, the New England colonies would choose to break away from the Crown, and that might be a rather different thing for the British Crown than it would mean to Mecca, should some Sharif in the Darmosh decide to stop paying his appropriate tribute.

In the long run, though, it didn't much matter. The triumph of Islam had been ordained by Allah himself, and it being eventual rather than immediate was of no particular importance to Abu Abdullah Mohammed ibn al-Sharif al-Idrisi than it was to the Caliph himself. Patience—proper patience—was a virtue, and the uneasy truce between the Dar and the Crown and Empire could easily go for years to the benefit of the Dar al-Islam, and probably to both Crown and Empire, as well.

Yes, there were tensions, and the tensions might result in an occasional battle that would send True Believers to paradise and infidels to hell, and that was as it should be. Swords—both real and metaphorical—got rusty with disuse.

And speaking of swords, al-Idrisi wished to convey his compliments to His Majesty on the . . . utility of these wonderful live swords. It would probably not be best to go into details—he didn't wish to bore the Admiral with such matters—but the former Sir Alexander Smith had been a terribly effective servant of the Caliph, in many matters.

And that was where the rumors that the Sharif wished

to bring to the Admiral's attention had started.

New live swords? That whole notion had disturbing echoes of the Sword of Constantine. In truth, Constantine's armies had been almost as effective in spreading the previous revelation as those of the Dar al-Islam had been of the final one—well, at least as long as the sword had been unbroken.

There was something . . . impious about relying on such artifacts, though, handy as they were. Al-Idrisi could speak from personal experience that Abdul ibn Mahmoud had been of great service to the Caliphate, in various matters that would, no doubt, be too boring to dwell on. Not essential, of course, any more than they had been for the Crown. But it was decidedly convenient to be able to solve a problem by sending one man.

Rumors of more live swords? Those would, of course, be very useful, and entirely valuable—the honors and, to be blunt, the gold paid to Abdul ibn Mahmoud had been a wise investment.

There had been . . . contacts. The Admiral would understand, of course, that al-Idrisi would not wish to go into the details of exactly how and where, but messages had been conveyed, and exchanged.

With whom? That was an interesting question. Al-Idrisi could hazard a general sort of guess—as the Admiral would be able to, perhaps, shortly—but the messages in both directions had been sent and received in ways that concealed the identity of the original sender, or senders.

There were, so it was said, a dozen such swords—produced over many years, at some serious difficulty—that would be available. And, were certain guarantees given about the future of certain areas in and around the

Mediterranean, after the inevitable victory of the forces of the Dar al-Islam, those might be provided.

The guarantees would, of course, have to be unambiguous. And the sender would be interested in discussing the nature of those guarantees.

It was, of course, preposterous. Yes, the swords were of great value—but enough to give over *countries* for? That was the part that bothered al-Idrisi the most, actually—as any merchant in the souk could tell you, the only thing more suspicious than an absurdly high asking price was an absurdly low one. Attacking the Crown? Yes, of course, eventually—the Dar al-Islam was destined to expand. But now, when Crown armies stood firmly astride almost all of Europe, and it would be years, perhaps centuries, before the forces of the Dar al-Islam were sufficient in number that moving north again would not be a manifest attempt to flout the Prophet's instructions about patience.

After all, was it not written that "Therefore bear up patiently as did the apostles endowed with constancy bear up with patience and do not seek to hasten for them their doom. On the day that they shall see what they are promised they shall be as if they had not tarried save an hour of the day." And "Whoever takes Allah and His prophet and those who believe for a guardian, then surely the party of Allah are they that shall be triumphant." And so it would be, of course, and perhaps al-Idrisi might be honored to live to see it.

But not now.

Twelve live swords wouldn't make that possible, even if each of them was a mirror of the Sandoval. Oh, certainly, a squad of Red Knights of Allah could do terrible damage if inserted anywhere into Crown territory, particularly if they were as powerful as the Sandoval or the Khan—much less so for lesser ones. But the swords rendered their bearers powerful, not invulnerable, and while it might, at least in theory, take a large army to kill such a squad, the Crown had large armies, just as the Caliphate did.

And if he was wrong? If these swords, born by True Believers, could lay waste to the Crown? Surely, the amount of damage that His Majesty's Red and White Knights could do in the Dar al-Islam would be a horrible thing to witness as well, and the English were known for their tastes for revenge, as the honorable lieutenant had been kind enough to demonstrate.

The Empire, even if they could be trusted, was hardly a terribly useful ally, and of a surety, they would turn against the Faithful to aid their . . . coreligionists, after all.

Ridiculous.

So what was it all about? Well, it wasn't going to be about launching a . . . precipitous war between the Dar al-Islam and the Crown, that was a certainty, and while the Caliph would, of course, be more than happy to pay a preposterously generous fee for the delivery of these twelve—or was it now eleven?—live swords—and such would, al-Idrisi hoped, be in Tunis within a day or two, and the gold on its way to their former owners, al-Idrisi intended to deliver into the Crown's hands the person of whoever it was who was due to arrive at this very dammusa at sunset.

"An interesting story, Excellency," DuPuy said. His pipe had gone out, and it was more irritating than reassuring that it was only a few moments after he puffed uselessly on it that Efik was in front of him, with another lit taper.

"But it is the sort, I supposed, that would go all the better with proof?"

"There is that." Red Swords in the Dar? There was something indecent about the idea, more so even than that traitor, Smith.

Yes, if the numbers were right, it wasn't as frightening as it sounded. The live swords had been created to use against the Dark, during the Age, and were one of the main reasons that northern Europe hadn't been overrun, and the Zone contained. Yes, for the past centuries the King had used the Knights as his personal bodyguards, emissaries, and problem-solvers, and it was only a slight exaggeration to say "one rebellion, one Order Knight"— and when it came to dealing with magical . . . problems, they had no equal.

Then why did it bother him so much? And what could he do about it?

"Well, the proof will be available shortly," al-Bakilani said. "If this . . . emissary is able to answer the questions that his master knows will be asked, he'll know other things of interest, no doubt."

He would, of course, if he could be taken alive, and if he could be made to talk, and—

Al-Bakilani smiled. "Yes. One often has many reasons for doing the same thing, and Abdul ibn Mahmoud has other uses. I'm sorry to say that had you tried to use your dagger to take your own life, he would have interfered with you." He raised his palms. "You may cut your throat should you wish, my friend, and I think that your King and the Crown would be poorer for the loss, but you'll not do so when it could be blamed on His Excellency, or me."

DuPuy tried to ignore that, although al-Bakilani's cleverness was as grating as usual, if not more so. "And you think that he can make this . . . emissary talk?"

Al-Idrisi snorted. "Him? Abdul ibn Mahmoud specializes in other matters." He waved his hand toward the back door. "The next-over-but-one dammusa contains several . . . ZZZZ?" He looked over at al-Bakilani.

"Experts, I think, Excellency. Experts."

Al-Idrisi nodded. "Yes, experts. We have several *experts* in such matters from the *hay'at al-amr bilma'ruf wa al-nahi 'an al-munkar* waiting, and they're quite good at what they do."

Al-Bakilani smiled. "But do let's not go into the details. I understand that they are, by and large, somewhat unpleasant." He spread his hands. "Now, it's just a matter of waiting until dark." He gestured toward the arched doorway that led to the back of the dammusa. "Would you care to try the famous Bagno della Acqua in the interim? I had the pleasure myself of it this morning; it's very relaxing."

"Well, assuming I'm not a prisoner, despite your protestations, I think I'll take a stroll," he said, rising. "although I'll be sure to be back before sundown, if you don't think that my appearance will frighten this emissary away." Not that one other man would make a difference—whoever this was had probably already figured out how to handle the problem of his capture by the duplicitous Arabs, even if he hadn't counted on the speed and skills of Smith, as was possible.

Not that DuPuy blamed them for the duplicity, not

here and now. They were, for the moment, rivals rather than enemies, strange as that felt.

"As you wish." Al-Idrisi gestured permission.

Al-Bakilani rose, nodding. "Of course, I hope you wouldn't think it wise to land the marines off the *Lord Launcher* and attempt to interfere with matters here. That would be . . . unfortunate, and unproductive." His smile dropped for just a moment. "It's one thing to not wish to start a war over such things, but it would be quite another to permit one ship of the third class to bear them away, and do I have to point out that we would be able to easily thwart such an attempt?"

"Very well, I—"

There was a distant *boom*.

The ground shook beneath his feet, rattling the dishes on the low tables. DuPuy tried to maintain his balance, but he was a fat old man, after all, and he crashed down, hard, on the tile floor, smashing all of his body weight down on the dress sword on his left hip.

But it was just pain, and Simon DuPuy was no stranger to pain; he struggled to his feet, not sure if the ground was still trembling, or if it was DuPuy himself.

Al-Idrisi had still been stretched out on his couch, but had tumbled to the floor, and al-Bakilani, like DuPuy, had been unable to keep to his feet.

Of the four men in the room, only Smith had kept his balance, and by the time DuPuy looked up, he was already at al-Idrisi's side, making no effort to help the Sharif up from the floor, but having positioned himself to block any approach through the door. Say what you would about the traitor, he was fast on his feet, and fast with his mind.

Al-Idrisi muttered something in Arabic, and al-Bakilani

shook his head and answered in the same language. He gave a quick glance at DuPuy, then turned back to al-Idrisi. "Perhaps I had best go look," al-Bakilani said. The bastard had, somehow or other, both acquired and drawn a sword and dagger. "Likely just an earthquake—"

One of the servants ran in, chattering in Arabic, his eyes widening at the naked weapons in al-Bakilani's hands.

"No, not an earthquake, apparently," al-Bakilani said. He sounded too calm, and if DuPuy hadn't seen the sweat on al-Bakilani's brow, he might have almost believed it. "Faryad thinks that the top of the mountain is exploding. Admiral?"

Well, if the volcano was going off, the thing to do was to get the hell out of there—but it was miles off, and it was likely that they had either ample time or no time at all to make it to the shore and the ships.

And, besides, DuPuy was more than a little curious.

He followed al-Bakilani out the back door.

Off in the distance—it looked like only a couple of miles, but distances were bloody hard to calculate on land—the top of the Montagne Grande was lit up, certainly enough, as though it was on fire, a curious red fire without a trace of yellow in it, and without the smoke and ash that one would expect from a volcano. DuPuy had never seen a volcano himself, but he had always made a habit to read anything by explorers that he could, and had read more than a few descriptions—most of those from native stories that a sober man would not take as gospel, of course—and seen some illustrations.

A volcano wasn't just curiously red flame flickering across a mountaintop, but the earth itself belching out rock and steam and . . .

And this wasn't it.

Damn his eyes, and damn him for not having brought his glass—there seemed to be other colors mixing with the red.

From behind him, al-Idrisi spoke. "I'm . . . not pleased." He turned to al-Bakilani. "Do you have the slightest idea what is going on?"

Al-Bakilani shook his head. "I'm sorry, but no, I—"

"Excuse me." Smith was still standing so as to protect al-Idrisi, but his boot-face had dropped; he actually looked scared. "Those are Red Swords—I can feel it." The Sandoval wasn't naked in his hand, but he had his hand clapped to the hilt. "I'd suggest that we get Your Excellency out of here, as quickly as possible—whatever my former brothers are up to is not intended for his benefit. Now, if you please."

"Excuse me," Efik said, again surprising DuPuy, who hadn't seen him come up from behind, either. "I think it would be best if you all stayed—it would be to your benefit. And it does not involve those cursed Knights of the Crown, Shield, and Dragon, either." He gestured toward DuPuy. "But you might as well kill him now. You'll be killing the English aplenty shortly, I'm quite sure."

There was something strange about his speech, beyond the lack of any hint of tone of servility in it.

DuPuy had never seen shock or surprise in al-Bakilani's face until moments before, but al-Bakilani had quickly regained his composure then, and he did now.

"Efik, you must not address—"

"Please." Despite his mumbling, Efik was smiling as broadly as DuPuy had ever seen a man smile. "I've waited and worked, in my own way, for this day for half my life.

And while I'd not say a word if it would do you any good—any of you—it might, perhaps, make things easier for you if you let me speak for a moment." He gestured up toward the mountain.

"Some years ago a man, a wizard, developed or rediscovered a way to put souls into swords, just like the Great Wizards did in the Age of Crisis. No, he wasn't a Great Wizard himself, just a very dedicated one, and no, he wasn't able to do so with great souls, be they great for purity or evil; that art is lost.

"Just with babies, and then only some of the time. A baby's soul, he discovered—and yes, he discovered it by as awful a means as you can imagine—is not attached to this world as strongly as an adult's.

"And, of course, as he wasn't a Great Wizard, and the sacrifice of innocents is as black an art as there is, he knew full well that he'd die in the making of the first sword.

"So he took his time, and he raised and trained sons, and gathered others about him, and told none of them any more than they needed to know, and not too many years ago he began to make the swords. The doing of it killed him, of course—the black arts are not easy on those who practice them, and while there's no wrong in binding somebody like Sandoval to steel to expatiate his sin, or in permitting a dying pure one to remain bound in steel rather than receiving his or her reward, he was, after all, killing babies, as did his sons.

"Rather a lot of them." He looked over at DuPuy. "If I recall correctly, and I do, your own Mordred the Great revolted against his father because his father sought to slay children for his own purposes.

"Ah—we were back to the swords. Yes, they're of value,

but they in themselves wouldn't be of enough value for what he wanted for his people, and as to who his people are, well, his grandsons will tell you that soon enough."

"But you said—"

"Oh, yes," Efik went on, "he and his sons and his grandsons will have only those eleven live swords—it should be twelve, but . . ." He shrugged. "Well, just let it be said that what was done was explained at the wrong time to the wrong person, and leave it at that." He laughed, he actually laughed. "I've no complaint—I'd expected it to take more years for this all to come to fruition. Things seem to have been hurried along.

"There's one other thing he discovered, something that you, Admiral DuPuy, a good believing Christian man, should have no trouble in accepting: what passes for the soul of the Wise, or the Great, or the Godly is even more powerful than a sinner like Sandoval or a saint like Gautama." He stretched out his hand toward the mountain. "And even if you could run like the wind up there, Abdul ibn Mahmoud, by the time that you would get there it will be all over. The Wise won't be able to stand against eleven live swords, even of the dimmest red, and the grandson of that beloved old man will come down from the Montagne Grande bearing *it* in his hands." He shrugged. "A little past nightfall, perhaps, but close enough."

"You won't live to see it," Smith said.

"Ah. Entirely correct." Efik bit down hard, and there was a crunching sound. He buckled at the knees, and sprawled out on the stones.

Al-Idrisi barked out a quick order to Smith, who began to run, tossing the scabbard of his sword aside as he did.

DuPuy would have watched as the light flared and Smith blurred away, but he was more interested in the way that Efik, manifestly dead on the ground, was still smiling.

"Well, Excellency, that was bloody brilliant of you," he said, letting the sarcasm drip from his voice. One man with a Red Sword against eleven? And never mind what the sword with the soul of the Wise imprisoned it would be like to face—if there were any doubt in Efik's mind that it would not be all over before Alexander ever reached the Montagne Grande, he would not have spoken.

Still, a man who had waited and plotted and schemed and worked toward an end for half his lifetime would want to see the faces of his enemies when it all came to fruition. DuPuy, of all people, could understand that.

Al-Bakilani nodded. "Well, yes. He just removed His Excellency's main protection, didn't he?"

Al-Idrisi bowed his head. "It will all be as Allah wills," he said. "In the meantime, is there anything we can do but wait?"

Wait for what? Wait for whoever was to come down from the Montagne Grande bearing a sword that would make the Sandoval look like a paring knife by comparison?

With that in hand, it was obvious what al-Idrisi would do, would have to do: make whatever promises he could, and with this, this thing in his possession, the man bearing it would be more than able to force adherence to any promises that would be made.

The only thing for DuPuy to do was to put off the promises being made, and that required—

—but al-Bakilani was, damn his eyes, thinking faster

than he was, and had his sword out, and just inches away from DuPuy's throat.

"I'm sorry, Admiral, but I think that you'll serve your King better as my prisoner for the moment than you would dead on the ground." He actually managed to sound sincere, the bastard. "If you'd slowly unbuckle your sword belt, and let it fall to the ground, I'll see that it's returned to you when this is all over."

He sighed. "Which, I'm afraid, won't be very long now at all."

Chapter 13: Crusade II

The three pillars of the world are faith, wisdom, and justice. Is it any wonder that the world shakes on its foundations? Faith is so often misplaced and, perhaps as often, not-placed when it should be; wisdom is only clear in retrospect, if then; and justice . . .

Father, forgive not this sinner, for he doesn't deserve it.

You gave Your only begotten Son for the salvation of those who would accept it, and regardless of how much I wish that I could and have, I am reminded that I reject His Sacrifice every time I lay my hand on the damned Khan.

I haven't, and can't, repent of having taken such an evil thing to hand, to mix my soul with his, as I did so and do so believing it necessary to serve my King, my Order, and my brothers, and have seen the necessity many times over.

You are, You have said, a jealous God. Punish me as

You see fit for loving them more than You, as I do; may my eternal screams be sweet music in Your Ears.

Absent the repentance that I can't give, there'd be no justice in forgiving me, and the world already shakes enough on its foundations as it is; I do not ask that You shake it even a little more for such as Joshua Grayling.

I don't ask that. But I do beg this of You: in Your infinite Mercy, please grant me the knowledge that I have, indeed, served my King, my Order, and my brothers.

When the Fallen One laughs at me for having thrown away Heaven for nothing, I beg the comfort of the knowing, as well as the faith, that he is, in this as in so much else, the Father of Lies.

—Gray

There was much in life that Stavros Kechiroski didn't understand, but one of the things he did was keeping silent, and trying to avoid being noticed, while taking notice. If you just kept your mouth shut and your eyes open, you could learn a lot, and if you'd mastered the art of opening your mouth only occasionally and carefully— while making sure that it didn't *look* like you were being careful—you could learn even more.

And he had been very interested in watching these knights and the marines prepare to go ashore, even though that had meant rising earlier than any of the other hired-ons, save for the cook and his mate. The—well, other people, no need to think about precisely who they were—*other people* probably knew as much about their techniques as they needed to, but Stavros found it interesting, and his presence could easily be explained, were it necessary, as the product of him being unable to sleep.

The marine sergeant, Fotheringay, had had a quick

discussion with the two the knights at the bow, then had gotten out of their way, and joined Stavros—in location, if not in any social sort of way—at the stern. Stavros didn't blame him—while Nissim al-Furat would have very much liked to have eavesdropped on any conversation between Cully and Gray, Stavros Kechiroski was the sort of man who would give such men a wide berth, if possible. They made him nervous.

Still, it was an easy morning, so far. Spiros was still asleep below, and given the prodigious amount of work that he and Stavros had already accomplished—and, more likely, the Abdullahs' preoccupation with more immediate matters—Stavros was left alone to dawdle over his morning porridge and tack.

Whether Fotheringay had already eaten aboard the *Cooperman*, or wasn't interested in such ordinary fare, he didn't so much as glance at the kettle, but set his gear down on the deck in front of a stanchion of the aft rail, then sat down on the deck itself, his legs over his gear, more likely to prevent any concern about it falling overboard than out of fear of theft, folded his arms over his massive chest, and leaned his head back against the rail, letting his eyes sag shut.

All told, it should be an interesting day. Too bad that there was no obvious need for a carpenter's mate on the shore party. When they returned—if they returned—no doubt Stavros would find out much of what had gone on, but there really was no substitute for seeing for oneself, after all. It would have been more than a little suspicious for him to have asked to join the marines, and more so to join the knights and their companions who were to go inland, but . . .

Well, there was nothing to be done about it. They were apparently going to use the Turks as porters, as well as guides. Still, if he saw one of them talking to the Abdullahs, it might be because they had decided that they'd need some extra porters, and being caught trying to sneak below would have a good chance at earning Stavros the job. Something to keep alert for.

Milos Abdullah came on deck, giving a quick stir to the porridge before he slipped the steel cover over the cooker. Breakfast was apparently over. When Spiros came up, he could eat either cold porridge and tack, or go hungry until the evening meal—something that only bothered Stavros because it would likely do nothing to improve the carpenter's temper.

The rest of the shore party gradually joined Cully and Gray. There were the two Turks, as Stavros had anticipated, and the wizard with his manservant, and—

What?

Stavros had been watching the activity toward the stern; not the sky; he didn't notice the huge raven until moments before it dropped onto the deck.

A raven? Here?

Fotheringay leaped to his feet. "What the bloody *hell*?"

Milos Abdullah took a step forward, but stopped himself. None of the other Abdullahs moved, save for Salim, the captain, who raised his hands, fingers spread wide, making push-back motions, as though anybody would approach.

Sigerson started to take a step forward, but his man gripped him by the arm and pulled him back. Understandable, and sensible—but the strange thing was the knights—they didn't do anything.

They just stood there, motionless.

"Help me, please," Black said.

Gray took a step toward him, but Black held up a hand.

"No—you can't do any good that way. Not here." Black's outstretched hand was covered with blood and cuts, and as he held it out, more appeared; Black only winced a little, and looked down at it with a remarkably detached sort of interest when the tips of the two outer fingers disappeared, as though sheared off, then formed the hand into a fist that dripped with blood.

Gray wasn't interested in Black's opinion—the first thing to do was to get him some help; Gray reached out to grab him by the collar and drag him away—but his hand went right through the collar, and Black, who was still kneeling on the deck before him.

"No." Black shook his head. "You've got to come with me—I can . . ." He swallowed once, hard. "I can open a way for you, you and that damned sword of yours, and perhaps, perhaps bring others along as well, but I—" He shuddered as a gash opened up along his forehead. "It has to be done now. Please."

"Me? Only me?"

"You, David, Niko, John of Redhook, of your Order; I can't reach many others, and they wouldn't do any good, in any case. I cry out to a few of my own kind, or near enough to my own kind—but She is too weak, and I think too frightened. Coyote will think on it until too late, wondering if I'm joking with him, and be happy that the joke appears to be on me; the One-Eyed's sleep will not be broken for this, any more than that of the rishis. Holowaka's wings are too weak, Huitaca is too drunk;

Julana and Njirana are still in the Dream Time; the Litae offer to bind my wounds, but wouldn't do more than that even if they could." As Black spoke, more wounds blossomed all over him, as though he was being cut by swords every bit as invisible as his own form was intangible here.

"What did Bear say? Big John?"

Black laughed, although that sent him into a spasm of coughing; bloody phlegm issuing from his mouth as he did, drops and globs that disappeared as they hit the unmarked wood of the deck. "John of Redhook asks the same about Bear, as Bear does about you." Black wiped his mouth on the back of his sleeve, smearing blood on his face. "Can't any of you decide for yourself?"

They were close to the source of the swords; Gray could feel it. This was probably just some diversion—a wizard who could make a live sword, after all, should be capable of creating an illusion.

What harm, though, could an illusion do?

He turned to ask Bear, but . . .

He was alone on the deck. The heavily reefed sails still fluttered on the *Marienios*'s masts. Back at the stern, the wheel was still moving, both back and forth, as though turned by invisible hands.

But there was nobody there.

"No, you'll have to decide for yourself. I . . . can't."

Gray shook his head. "My duty is not to you, Black."

"Duty, no—but can you have, for once, just a little faith? Can't you accept that by saving me, you might just save yourself?"

"You've chosen to present yourself, at least to me, much like me, Black. Perhaps your soul is as . . . wrong as mine.

I'd not be distracted from my duty to save my own life—
I won't for yours."

"Then—"

"Then: no."

"Help me, Bear," Wolf said. "Please."

Bear tried to scoop him up in his arms, but his arms
went right through.

"No, no—that won't work." Wolf's voice seemed to hold
almost as much frustration as pain. "Come with me; help
me. I swear on all that's holy that it will be worth your
while, for yourself, for your Order."

Bear sighed. "I've heard many an oath sworn in my
time," he said. "That's not the way to manipulate me."

Yes, Bear took oaths seriously, and was hardly the only
one who did, in or out of the Order—but all that you
could know when someone promised something was that
those were the words he could speak.

"I'm not—" Wolf's words were strangled in his throat
by a scream as half of his right ear disappeared; he clapped
what was left of his right hand to it. "I'm not trying to
manipulate you, Bear—I'm begging for your help."

He started to look around—where was Gray? Where
were all the others? It was just like it had been at the
castle on Pantelleria—and it was all he could do, here
and now, to think about the others.

"Why do you all do that?" Wolf let out a groan. "You're
all the same, you are. No, no, you're not, but—please.
I . . . if you wait much longer, Bear, you may as well not
help at all. I don't know what they're going to do with
me—I don't even know who they are, but . . . Gray *won't*.
He doesn't trust me, and—"

"Trust is earned; trust is given; trust is not taken by demand, nor is it created by begging."

It was not Bear's to judge if the Wise had been justified in holding himself separate from the rest of the world. And, in truth, it had done less of that than some others, and despite the Wise's appearance when Bear had been on Pantelleria, it could have been that he was, like She was, too old and tired to do more.

"Can you not spare some for me?" Wolf pleaded. "I can promise you much, and—"

"No." Bear shook his head. "You've nothing to promise me at all. I serve my Lord, my King, and my brothers. I've no room left in me to serve you, Wolf."

"Cully—"

Cully shook his head. "You choose foolishly when you appeared as Her, and perhaps even more foolishly to mimic Bedivere."

The false Bedivere sprouted another arrow, right next to the first; the fingers of his one working hand pulled weakly, impotently, futilely at it.

It was, of course, the eyes that bothered Cully.

"What do you want of me?" Cully asked. "How can you even reach out to me, here?"

"I think you know." The false Bedivere shook his head. "Most would say that that wizard broke your bond to Jenn, and there's surely some truth to that. But it's still there, remnants of it are, traces that nothing short of death can break—just as your bond to Her is, and to the others. Deny it if you will, but it's what has made it possible for me to beg you." The Wise shook his head sadly. "But Gray and Bear have said no, and you'll be no different. Not that you'd be enough, a man with just an ordinary sword."

Cully nodded. "That is, indeed what I am, an ordinary man, with no claim to virtue or nobility beyond other men—less than many." He let his shoulders relax. "But not enough? What does that matter to the likes of me?"

Niko wouldn't be fooled, not by this lying image that proclaimed itself to be Grandfather. It had fooled Niko before—but it wouldn't this time, not again. Niko didn't like to be fooled.

"Help me, Niko," the lying image said. "Please. I . . . make no promises, no guarantees, no offers. I tell you, in truth, that if you come to my aid, whatever you seek ashore will likely long be fled by the time you could return. I don't tell you if it's there, or not, and not just because you'd not believe me, but because I don't know. I don't think that you and your one sword could defeat all of them—there's far more of them than of you."

He spoke calmly, as though he were Grandfather, discussing how to set the nets on a flat sea. He went on: "It could be that the ones who killed your family are not even ashore, and that if you help me now, you'll never avenge them, even if you live out the day."

"Then what are you asking?"

Grandfather—no, the lying image of Grandfather—swallowed once, hard.

"I ask the help of Sir Niko Christofolous, Knight of the Order of Crown, Shield, and Dragon, the Order that lives by 'service, honor, faith, and obedience; justice tempered only by mercy; mercy tempered only by justice.' I ask for rescue, for aid—I ask for mercy, Sir Niko."

Niko clasped his hand to Nadide's hilt, and felt her warm presence.

I don't trust this one, Niko.

Nor do I, Nadide-precious. It lied to me before, and it's probably lying now, about many things. But I do trust that it's in pain, in desperation—like my sisters were in their last moments, like you were. It begs for mercy, Nadide.

Service, honor, faith, and obedience. Justice tempered only by mercy; mercy tempered only by justice.

He could almost feel her smile. *Then there's no question, is there?*

Not for you and me, little one. Not here, and not now.

Niko drew Nadide, her redness flaring in his mind, the scabbard held properly in his left hand, just as he had been taught.

Not taught enough, of course—but he, at least, knew how to hold himself.

"Then let it be so," he said, quietly.

At those words, the sea went all dark before him, dark as the blackest of night, and a single, huge swell rose up before the bow of the ship.

Sir Niko Christofolous ran for the bow, ignoring Cully's cry of "Niko, no!" from behind him as he leaped to the rail. Nadide was warm in his hand, and his mind, and his soul; he wasn't alone.

And, then without pause or hesitation, he jumped into the darkness.

Interlude 7: The Saracen

My beloved brothers: I try to avoid thinking about who I was, most of the time.

Being—well, let me not say who I am being, shall I? Writings can fall into wrong hands, and codes can be broken. Being the one who you have asked me to be is rather a full-time preoccupation, and leaves little time for thinking about being the one who I was.

When my service is done, though, I would very much like to become that man again, if it be your will.

And, if it not, I am not only a slave of Allah, and a servant of the Prophet (peace be upon him), but of yours, as well, and know that you will do that which is right.

—Nissim al-Furat

"What the bloody hell?" Fotheringay said.

None of the knights were moving. Not at all—they just

stood stock-still like living statues for a long moment, as though frozen in time before the perched, equally motionless raven.

For just a heartbeat—a long, eternal heartbeat.

And then, with no warning, the raven was gone. Stavros was just turning to Fotheringay to say something, he wasn't sure quite what, when darkness swept down across the sea, covering the land in an impenetrable blanket; a single huge wall of water, blacker than dark, black as black could be, rose up before the bow of the ship, towering so far above the top of the foremast as to dwarf the *Marienios*.

There were shouts and screams, and it took Stavros but a moment to realize that some of them were his own—but the black wave just hung there, not crashing down on the deck and smashing the ship to flinders, as it should have.

The boy, Niko, drew his sword, and ran for the rail. Cully moved to intercept him, shouting something that Stavros couldn't make out over the rush of blood in his own ears, but the boy didn't stop; he leaped to the rail, and off into the darkness, vanishing without a splash, without anything to mark his passage.

The black wave began to shrink, to recede.

Cully shook his head, and turned to Gray and Bear. "Stay—I can't let him go alone."

"No," Gray said. "We have our own—"

There was no preliminary, no warning. One moment, Gray was standing between Cully and the for'ard railing, the two of them still dwarfed by the black wall of water, and the next Gray had fallen to his knees, bleeding from his nose, clutching at his crotch.

"Take care of him, Bear," Cully said, not looking back.

"Don't follow. Be sensible. I've always loved you for your good sense."

"Father Cully—*no*."

But he was already gone, vanished into the black wall, just as the boy had.

Gray struggled to get to his feet, but fell back to the deck. "Bear, help me." His words came out in a croaking shout, horrible to hear. "I'm not . . ." He gasped for breath. "I'm not going to—I can't let him die without me at his side, any more than I could—throw me through, please, Bear, please. Please don't make me beg—no, no, I don't mind begging, Bear, just do it." He forced himself up to his knees. "Please, Bear. There's no time, there's no time at all."

Moving far more gracefully than a man his size had any business doing, Bear scooped up Gray, and threw him over his shoulder. "As you wish, Gray."

"No, Bear, not *you*. No, please."

"Don't be silly, Gray," he said, as with the weakly struggling Gray on his shoulder, he struggled up to a precarious perch on the bow rail, and leaped into the darkness.

Fotheringay had not just been standing there—he had donned his backpack, belted on his sword and dagger, and retrieved his curiously short boarding pike.

He gave a quick glance at the rapidly diminishing wall of water.

"Who's with me?" he shouted. His brow was furrowed—Fotheringay didn't understand what was going on any more than anybody else did. The only thing he knew was that the knights had leaped into the dark wall.

To what purpose? Stavros didn't believe for a moment

that the marine sergeant knew any better than Stavros did, but . . .

Stavros had thought the wizard had stood motionless while it all went on, but he had obviously been mistaken— Sigerson had somehow managed to get into his robes. The hems fluttered in the wind, and the tip of the wand clutched with surprising delicacy in his long fingers sparkled against the receding darkness of the wall of water behind him.

"If it will be done, Sergeant, it had best be done quickly," he said.

And then, just like the others: the wizard, his manservant, and the sergeant vanished into the shrinking blackness.

Well, it was obvious what Stavros Kechiroski would do under such circumstances: he'd simply sigh with relief as the wall of water continued to recede rather than smashing the ship, and be as puzzled and frightened and confused as anybody else.

Nissim al-Furat, on the other hand, was of the opinion that whatever was going on on the other side of that diminishing wall of water was probably of greater importance to the Dar al-Islam in general, and the *hay'atal-amr bilma'ruf wa al-nahi 'an al-munkar* in particular, than whatever Nissim would be able to discover from whatever expedition—if there was to be one, now—on the shore here.

Of course, the problem would be in reporting whatever that something of interest was, should he live through this. Why would Stavros Kechiroski do such a thing?

Well, he'd just have to think up a good story, later.

If there was a later.

Chapter 14: Redemption

I am not a good man; I know that, I accept that, and perhaps it could be said that I indulge myself in it. So be it.

But while I'm not a good man, the Khan and I are good at one thing, and that one thing does have its uses.

And as to that, too, I say: so be it.

—Gray

The corridor stretched ahead.

Niko found it hard to breathe; his heart, in the slow red time, beat too slowly in his chest, and the song in his muscles and tendons was a thing that spoke of both agony and pleasure and he wasn't sure which predominated, only that if he let it go, he would only be partly alive until he felt it again.

But still, the corridor stretched silently ahead—no

break, no sound, no threat. Nothing. Where was he? It was hard to focus his eyes—it seemed to keep changing. Not in any useful way—the floor beneath his feet turned from a solid expanse of curlicued black-and-white marble to tiles of some rough green stone, and then to a slick white expanse, as he looked.

It was the screams from the end of the corridor that drew him. He ran down it, Nadide held high over his head. The world was in slowtime, and as he tried to brake himself at the sudden bend in the corridor, his booted feet *chitter-chitter-chitter*ed on the interstices between the floorboards, and he slid, slamming hard into the rough stones of the wall, barely able to keep his feet.

And then the other was there, running up the broad stone steps, a sword reddened both from its inner glow and the blood that ran down its length held over his head.

He could feel Nadide's fear and anger reach out from her length, manifesting itself in a gout of too-slowly-flickering flame that—

—that dispersed itself without touching the other man, like a bucket of water vanishing into steam upon the hottest of fires.

And still the man came. He wasn't trapped in slowtime, like the rest of the world; his bare, hairy chest, glistening with sweat, heaved in and out, as though he, like Niko, couldn't fill his lungs with air quickly, thoroughly enough.

Niko had to run—but where? His back was to the wall, and the swordsman was at least as fast as he was, if not faster; it would be a simple matter to cut off any escape.

So there would be no escape.

Niko took up the stance he had been taught: Nadide's grip firm in his right hand, the scabbard still clutched in his left, his feet a shoulder's width apart, slightly diagonal to the onrushing swordsman. Elbow bent, point low-but-not-down-dammit-Niko, and as the man swung at him, he straightened his arm, raised his right foot, and lunged forward.

His vision blurred as the other sword whizzed past his head, its red glow blinding him momentarily, filling his eyes with tears that only squeezing his eyelids shut could dispel.

He had failed, he was certain. His lunge had met no resistance, and there was no time for—

No.

A smouldering pile lay at his feet on the smooth gray tiles, shards of metal, some of it still glowing red poking up through the ashes. But the red wasn't the red of Nadide—it was the red of steel, heated in a hot fire.

"Nnniiiikooooo—"

He spun at the too-slow voice from behind him, swinging Nadide about as he did, barely able to stop himself, and her, inches away from the blade cutting through Cully's neck.

It was hard to think, and—

Let me sleep, please, Niko. I need to rest.

In the part of his mind that was Nadide-and-Niko, she was crying. Not in fear—he had drawn her fear into himself, and it didn't slow him—but in exhaustion, and from something more, something he couldn't put a name to.

Please.

He slipped Nadide back into her sheath, and let his hand sag away from her hilt, and the world spun back into normality. Aches that had been distant and unimportant became real and immediate; the drumming of his heart was echoed by the slow counterpoint of his gasps.

His knees started to buckle; if Cully hadn't caught him, he would have fallen; he sagged into the old man's free arm.

"Easy, boy," Cully said, as he slipped an arm around Niko's waist, bearing him up. "It's just me." His sword was drawn, but down and at his side, and he had lost his scabbard somewhere. For some reason, Cully was smiling, although what there was to smile about escaped Niko entirely.

Cully looked down at the smoking mass at his feet, and frowned. "Well, there's one down."

"Sir Cully," he said, still gasping, "I—"

"Shh. We handle this now, as best we can. We feel about it later. One down, which leaves . . ." He shrugged. " . . . others."

"One what?"

Cully shrugged. "One enemy—one enemy with what was a live sword." He frowned at that, and shook his head. "Well, what are you waiting for?"

He set out down the corridor at a fast trot, one that would have done credit to a much younger man, although Niko, in fasttime, would have been able to pass him easily. He stopped, and turned. "Are you coming?"

"Yes, Father Cully."

The courtyard could have been anywhere, Nissim decided. He could have been anywhere—anywhere he hadn't been before. He would have remembered this place, not because it was so horribly grand or unusual, but just because that was his way.

The stone residence that stood at its center was large,

certainly, by both Pironesian and Tikritizan standards, but not huge, although the cornices and square archways made it seem more English than anything he was used to.

There were sounds beyond the building—strange sounds, like the wind, although Nissim couldn't feel any breeze at all, what with the keep's walls all around him.

But a barracks, seemingly empty, stood against the keep's walls to his right. He would investigate—anybody would, of course—but neither Stavros Kechiroski nor Nissim al-Furat would want to do so empty-handed. Maybe there was a weapon in there.

He set off at a trot.

"Halt there," came from behind him. He turned to see Fotheringay running toward him, his boarding pike held up and across his chest. "You're that carpenter, from the *Marienios*?"

"Yes, Excellency—"

"Fotheringay—you can call me 'Sergeant.' " There should have been a smile to go along with the words, but there wasn't. "You fell through, or did those Abdullahs throw you through?"

Best to stick with the truth, at least until he could think up a good lie. "I came through the wave myself, Sergeant."

Fotheringay snorted. "And why would you want to do a fool thing like that, half naked and unarmed?"

Stavros ignored the question. "There's what looks like a barracks over there—I was hoping to find some sort of spear, or perhaps a bow." That came naturally, as did, "I used to hunt wild goats, as a boy."

Fotheringay grunted. "Take a strange bow, and no time to practice with it, and even if you were a wicked-good bowman as a boy, you'd be useless as tits on a boar-hog.

Let's see if we can find you a spear." He frowned down at his waist, then shrugged, and drew his sword, tossing it hilt-first to Nissim. "Hold on to this in the meantime— not that it'll do you a lot of good."

They set out at a fast trot toward the barracks. The sounds of the wind—could it be wind?—and cries from beyond the hedgerow seemed to beckon to Fotheringay, and he waved Stavros toward the barracks, as he himself dashed off toward the hedgerow. "Better get something you can use, and if you can find some spares, maybe I can use them."

Stavros hefted the sword. Yes, of course—naturally, both Stavros Kechiroski and Nissim al-Furat would want to get involved in somebody else's fight.

In—how did the English put it?—a swine's eye.

The barracks was empty of people, but there were what appeared to be freshly made bunks for eighty or more men, and bundles of spears stacked in the far corner. And a rack of bows, too, strings hanging limply from one end— and quivers, already filled with arrows, on the shelves beside it.

He tossed the borrowed sword onto one of the bunks and retrieved a spear, then went to the door, standing just inside the shadows, to watch, then thought better of it, and went for a bow and strung it, grunting with the effort, before he retrieved a quiver, and then a spear, for his own defense.

He had said that he was going to go for a bow, and it would be best to be found with one, when this was all over.

Whatever it was.

❖   ❖   ❖

Gray tumbled to the dirt, banging his head against the hard-packed ground so violently that lights danced behind his eyes.

Or were all the lights behind his eyes? Crimson flashes had seemed to pierce the air and the sky as much as his mind, and when he forced his eyes open, he caught the sun setting full in the eyes, dazzling him into bright blindness.

As he fought to his feet, he could more feel than see Bear beside him, as was only right and proper. But it wasn't Bear that he needed, now. No—that was wrong. Gray needed Bear—but Gray needed to be not-Gray.

His hands fastened on the familiar steel.

Yes.

And then the Khan was in his hand.

The world changed about him.

It was all much simpler, much purer now—purer in a way that only the Gray-Khan could have appreciated.

His vision cleared, resolving itself into the black and white that was the only proper way for a man—or something more than a man—to see, and the actinic whiteness of the sun no more blinded him than did the coal blackness of the sky.

His own body was somehow more distant and immediate; the blood still dripping from the nose where Cully had struck him but an annoying wetness.

The pain was there, but it was just the pain of a human man, and he was something far more than that. He was not just a witness standing behind his own eyes, although he knew he would remember it that way; and he knew, as he always did, that his memory, once again, would lie, that it was just Gray trying to deny that he and the Khan had become one thing, one soul.

There were others here. Even in quicktime, he could barely make them out in the dark, black shapes upon blackness, but the flames of the swords shot back and forth across the courtyard, as though they were pursuing something, a pack of wolves chasing a rabbit through the black night that was relieved not even a little by the harsh whiteness of the sun.

Yes, the world was, once again, as it always should be: black and white, and always, always red, with no gray to it, and no Gray in it.

"Help me, Gray," came from the blackness. It was Black's voice, but where? And, more important, where was Cully? Was he already dead?

It didn't matter. It was Gray who loved Cully, Gray who took the man who had pulled that sniveling little boy from the waterfronts and given him a life—the Gray-Khan was above such matters.

What mattered was the power, the glory of it, the way that the redness of the Khan cut through the darkness, the way that it filled his veins and muscles and brain, making the world all simple and sensible once more.

Because it was, finally, sensible.

Things were always too complicated for Gray. For the Khan, they had been simple—the world was divided into four parts: himself; those who walked or rode beneath his banner; the conquered; the dead. The Khan had reveled in that simplicity, and now, the world was more straightforward and not even four-times-complex, but two: there was the Gray-Khan; and there was everything and everybody else; he would crush them, and then the world would be even simpler, and more beautiful:

Just black, just white, and no red save his own.

There were enemies here, and if they wouldn't have been the Khan's enemies and perhaps shouldn't have been Gray's, the Gray-Khan had nothing in this world, here and now, but himself and adversaries.

Behind him, he felt the Nameless flare into white reality, and it was all he could do to not turn to deal with him first, despite the temptation. These flickers of red were not the threat that the Nameless's whiteness was, yes, but the Nameless was weak, weakened by mercy, crippled by compassion, neutered by detachment.

Not the Gray-Khan.

One of the flickering flames dashing in and out of the blackness dashed within his reach, and he stretched out his own fire to encompass it, relishing, bathing in the smell and taste of its burning and shattering, the silent screams of agony that echoed through the pure darkness to end in dark silence.

That was one, and he quickly dispatched another, and—

Agony flared in his side—not the distant pain of the Gray-body, but real pain, pain that touched the body and soul of the Gray-Khan—and he turned to face the source.

Had he been so mistaken?

Had the Nameless finally come to his senses?

No—it was another of the flickering little reds. They were small, but they were clever, and they worked in packs, like the dogs that they were. While he had been dispatching one, another had snuck up into the blackness behind him, and he could feel the strength drain from his Gray-body.

He drew strength from his total self, and spun about, sending this one into blackness with a dispatch and a fury that almost surprised himself.

No. There was no surprise. There was just darkness, and the reds hiding in it, and the white incandescence of the Nameless couldn't dispel it. Like a pack of wolves, they would nip at him, satisfying themselves with bite after bite until they brought him down.

No. That would not be.

It could not be allowed to be. It—

It always reminded Bear of the wine.

There was something almost indecent about how good it felt to join himself with the Nameless. And, of course, something more.

But it always reminded Bear of the wine.

Father had always insisted that decent wine was the right thing for Communion—it was wrong, Father had always said, for the Blood of the Lamb to be some insipid squeezings, barely aged enough to be called wine; it should be at least a decent vintage, properly casked and aged in good wood, whose taste would remind all who partook of the sacrament that God's power could turn a humble grape into something with at least a hint of wonder in it.

Mother would always laugh at Father's arrogance and presumption—if the sacrament itself wasn't wonder enough, then even the finest of bottle-aged Burgundian cabernet would hardly be sufficient, would it? She was under the impression that the baronial purse would not last long if he were to take that route, but if he insisted, perhaps—

Dammit, if he was going to provide the wine for the Fallsworth church—and he was obligated to support the church, in case she had forgotten—he could damn well decide to give the faithful a taste of decent wine, couldn't he?

And so it would go. Mother and Father loved their arguments, and never worried about the effect that they might have had on young ears listening in.

Intrigued by all the talk, David and Matthew and Michael—David had been the instigator, even though he was the youngest of the three—had snuck out at night and taken the winding path to the winery and into the cellar, late at night, and swallowed mug after mug from one of the barrels that had been set aside for the church.

All been discovered in the morning, brought before Father, and quite properly and thoroughly thrashed for it, of course.

But there had been a moment, just a moment, in between, as he recalled, his fourth and fifth mug, that a sense of peace had descended on him—before the passing-out that night, and the shaking-awake, and vomiting, and the the hangover, and the thrashing of the next day—a moment.

Or maybe a Moment.

He couldn't have described it to anybody else. It was a moment not just of peace and relaxation, and perhaps the illusion of clarity, but of connection—connection with his drunken brothers in a way that David, the odd duck of the family, had never really had, before or since; connection with serenity, with peace, with the uncovered dirt of the cellar floor, with the trees that had provided the wood for the barrel he leaned against, with . . . with everything.

Drawing the Nameless was like that. Always.

He was One—not just with the Nameless, not just with the rough bark of the tree beneath which the Nameless had sat—but with everything.

It wasn't intoxicating, just as that moment with the wine hadn't been intoxicating; it was clarifying.

The blurred shapes dashing across the courtyard in pursuit of their quarry didn't slow in their mad pace, but became sharp and clear. One of the men, the Red Sword glowing above his head in the dim light of the dawn, had a quirk in his thick eyebrow, as though it had grown over an old scar; another's mouth was wide in fear that should have had him trembling, but didn't. None of the stones of the gravel-strewn courtyard was just a stone, but each had its own shape, its own identity, different from all the others.

And then there was Gray and the Khan. He didn't pity either of them—it was only right that they be precisely as they were, the two of them, and the two-as-one, and though he would have cut them down, without anger or hatred, if that had been proper, it wasn't . . . it wasn't clear now.

The only thing that didn't gain clarity was the blur of the Wise—or maybe it was otherwise? Maybe the Wise really was of an indeterminate shape, never quite coalescing into something sharp-edged and substantial?

It was all so sharp and real that it was all he could do not to dive into the individuality, the uniqueness of each stone, of each blade of grass that had worked its way through the gravel, reaching for the sun.

But, of course, that was not was required. The world was the stream, and he was not the rock to be washed over by it; he was a drop in the stream himself, glistening more than some and less than others, and he was never more aware of it as he lowered the Nameless to brush away the other glistening drop that had attacked Gray, sending it spattering into a million drifting motes without anger, without hatred, with only the sense that it was right that this drop be dispersed, right here and right now; and then another, and another.

And it was only right and only proper, he thought, when another drop splattered into him, sending the Nameless dropping from his nerveless fingers, and making him one with the stream, no longer having any need to be a distinct drop himself.

It was a pity, all in all, he thought, that he would never know how it all ended.

And the pity was part of the perfection of it.

Cully grabbed Niko before he could make it out the doorway into the courtyard.

"No," he said. "Wait. It's beyond the likes of me, and even of you, right now."

"But—wait. Give them a chance—they should be able to, perhaps."

He shook his head. "No. There's too many."

"Then we—"

"No. Wait."

Blurred forms moved quickly, too quickly across the gravel, sending stones flying into the air. Niko thought that he saw some of them pursuing some other blurred shape, but he wasn't sure.

Gray and Bear stood, back to back, in the center of it, almost unmoving, but as one of the blurs approached Gray, he seemed to do nothing more than perhaps twitch—

—and a broken body tumbled through the air, to lie still, on the gravel, shards of metal raining down with a horrible clicking that seemed never to end.

Gray's smile was awful to see. He seemed to lower the Khan slowly, yet its tip cut back and forth through the air so quickly that it seemed to vibrate, and—

—he fell, clutching at the stump that was all that remained of his right hand, while the Khan clattered to the ground.

And then Bear fell, and Cully turned to Niko, ignoring the two knights lying bleeding, dead or dying on the ground. It was hard to read his expression—but was there, perhaps, a trace of a smile? How could that be? How could he smile as the tears ran down his cheeks and into his beard?

Niko didn't understand, and he wanted to ask, but the words choked in his throat.

And, besides, there wasn't time.

Cully looked down at the scabbard held in his left hand, and threw it to one side, then tossed the sword after it. They clattered on the hard stones as he drew his stick from his sash, and touched the end of it to his head, as though in a salute.

"I'll go first, and try to distract them as well as I can—while they're killing me, you'll have your chance. Don't draw Nadide until you have that chance—they'll see her fire as easily as you see theirs." He clasped his free hand to Niko's shoulder, once, the way Grandfather used to. "Make the most of it, Sir Niko."

"Yes, Father," Niko said. "As you will."

Cully walked quickly out into the courtyard, though each footstep anchored him to the earth before he went on to the next. Balance was the way of it, as he had long ago learned, and longer ago taught.

Three of the flashing reds were left, blurring around the courtyard in pursuit of the Wise, the speed of their passage whipping dirt and gravel into the air. Too fast, too strong for the likes of him, and once again, he had let his children throw themselves against against forces too many, too strong for them, and once again, most of them lay, dead or dying, on the ground.

He had murdered more of them.

Gray and the Khan could have brought down the whole keep around them in a hellish inferno, killing them all, but that would not have protected the Wise.

Was that why Gray had not done the needful?

No, of course not—he would have sacrificed the Wise, and himself, but even under the influence of the Khan, it would not occur to Gray to bring Bear and Cully down with him, not if there was another way, another chance, another possibility, and there had always been an arrogance in the boy of sorts, about his own abilities if nothing else, one that had not been tempered by his years carrying that Khan. Gray had thought that he could win, that they could.

A chance? For winning? None. Niko would try, of course.

The boy had a good sword, good instincts, and a good heart, but Cully had thrown boys with good swords, good instincts, good hearts and better training into the meat grinder before—and not just when he and Bedivere had done so directly against York's men.

Cully had also done it indirectly, distantly, but not one whit less responsibly back when he was teaching at Alton, every time he had signed the approval for a first-former to graduate to second-form; every time that he stood, his silence mute consent, as sealed fourth-formers knelt before His Majesty to arise as knights of the Order.

He had done the same to Gray when he had let Ralph give him the Khan, opposing it only with his threat to appeal to His Majesty—as he had done; His Majesty had heard him out, and refused him—and to Her—She had, too, refused him—and finally his threat to leave the Order, a threat that Ralph had taken as the opportunity that it indeed had been.

Words and pleas and threats had not been enough. Cully should have cut Ralph down when the decision was made, and not relied on his failing abilities to persuade, not counting his value to His Majesty and to Her.

If they were not to be persuaded, they would not be bullied with his threats.

Was it cowardice that had stayed his hand, or obedience? He wished he knew.

The one thing he knew was that he didn't deserve to die with the sword of a knight of the Order in his hands, and that was something that he could control.

Mordred the Great had been right: Arthur the Tyrant had murdered all those babies, and he had not been fit to rule. Yes, certainly the Great had other reasons for taking the Crown, but a decent man could have selfish reasons for doing the morally requisite, couldn't he?

And how many babies had Cully already murdered? How many of his own, as much his children—*more so* than if they had merely sprung from his seed?

And how many more to come?

One, certainly. But let that be the end of it.

There was at least the chance that Cully could make it to Gray's and Bear's sides, and make his last stand there, and give a good account of himself.

Let the ones who cut him down remember their own fallen comrades and know that knights' lives might be taken, but not easily or cheaply. No, it would not end here. The Order had feuded with the Table for centuries, and whoever was behind this would forever have to look over their shoulders, worrying that the last thing they saw would be the face of Big John, or Walter, the Beast, Lady Ellen, or even that idiotic Guy of Orkney.

Let them fear; let them die. Let the world know.

But since it would end for Cully here, let it end as a knight. For a moment, just one last moment, let him be Sir Cully of Cully's Woode, sealed Knight of the Order of Crown, Shield, and Dragon.

"Over *here*," he shouted, as he raised his stick over his head. "You won't be able to kill the Wise until you've killed the last of us. It isn't over," he said. And then he smiled. "Not while I breathe."

One of the blurs detached itself from the pack and streaked toward him, and Cully dropped back, his stick held out to one side, an extension not just of his arm and his body, but himself.

One blow. Give him just one blow.

It was time, Niko decided. He had waited long enough. He felt almost, well, rested, at least by comparison with but a few minutes before—he felt like could actually breathe again, and while he didn't have to listen to hear his heart thumping in his chest, it didn't pound painfully anymore.

It was time. His hands fell to Nadide's hilt.

Will it hurt, Niko?

I don't think so, little one. Not for long, in any case.

I miss her, Niko. Will I be with her?

I wish I could tell you yes, but I can't lie to you, Nadide. I just don't know about such things. Perhaps. I hope so.

Then what do you know?

That these are the ones, or part of the ones, that hurt the One Who Smells Like Food, and my sisters—and Father and Grandfather.

Will we hurt them?

We will try.

I'm scared, Niko.

That's . . . as it should be, I expect.

He drew her, and she flared from a close presence to an intimate one. Oh, yes, he thrilled to the way that the fiery redness pulsed throughout his body with every too-slow heartbeat, the deep thrummm of his bones that echoed through every tendon.

But it was much more. It was . . . *right*.

Perhaps it should have bothered him that each time it became more comfortable, more intimate—Cully had said there were dangers in the drawing of a live sword from such things—but it didn't feel that way.

It felt like being whole.

He leaped from the steps and ran across the ground in as low a crouch as he could, hoping that the man bearing down on Cully would not feel their flame; he couldn't see them, not with his back to them.

And, perhaps, neither of the other two would notice? That was the part of them that was Nadide; Niko didn't believe it for a moment.

He was going to be too late; Cully's attacker was every bit as much in the quicktime as they were, and his treacherous heart refused to pound any more quickly, his traitor body refused to move any faster, and—

They cut down through the swordsman's back, the soul-and-steel cleaving more than just flesh and blood and bone. The fiery end of both of them should have bothered them, but perhaps it was just that babies were selfish, or that Niko was enraged, or perhaps it was something else.

But he was—*they* were moving so quickly that it was impossible to stop, and they slammed into Cully, bowling him over, and knocking him—them to the ground, as well. He tried to protect Cully as they fell, but the action slammed both their bodies' weights down on the hand holding the sword, and his fingers opened as they rolled across the hard stones.

And then he was just-Niko again, struggling to free himself from Cully, so that he could get Nadide back in hand. The old man was trying to help, he was sure, but his struggles were more interfering than helping. In desperation, Niko kicked away from the old man, his finger clawing at the gravel as though that could bring him the scant few inches he needed, knowing as he did that they were two and he was one, and that he would not—

And then the twin streaks stopped, and resolved themselves into two men, shards of metal that had been swords falling from their nerveless fingers, who writhed and screamed as their skin crackled and popped like meat cooked on the flat rock of the fireplace, and then more fell in on themselves than fell to the ground.

A man stood panting in front of him, his face streaked with dirt and sweat.

He was dressed in an Arab merchant's flowing robes,

although the robes were filthy with dust and twigs, and tattered, as though he had just crawled through some thicket that had somehow torn his clothes but left his skin intact; if he had a wound on him, Niko couldn't see it.

But the scabbarded sword that he held in his left hand hand was straight, the hilt plain, plain as Nadide, plain as—

A knight. It was another knight.

The knight snickered as he kicked Nadide away from Niko's outstretched hand, sending her halfway across the courtyard.

"You may . . . as well stop smiling, boy. I'm no . . . friend of yours," he said, still gasping for breath.

Cully had started to rise, but despite his obvious exhaustion the man immediately gave him a quick kick in the head, and Cully fell flat on the ground, motionless.

The man then moved toward where Gray and Bear lay bleeding, carefully not getting any closer than necessary to them before kicking the Khan and the Nameless away from them, as well.

He wasn't moving quickly, but he was obviously as bone-tired as Niko was, and he started to sway, his knees trembling, but he managed to right himself. "Haven't had the sword in hand for that long in a long time," he said, as though talking to himself. "And I'd not care to take it in hand again, not at the moment. Dangerous, eh?" There was nothing friendly in his smile.

Niko forced himself to his knees, readying himself to lunge at Nadide, but the man stepped between him and the sword. "Easy, boy. I . . . I don't want to have to serve you right now, not with the Sandoval, but I will if you rush me. Go easier on all of you if I do it with ordinary steel, I expect, and it'll surely go easier on me." He smiled down at Cully's prostrate form. "And don't think I'll come within range of you, Father Cully, not without the Sandoval in hand—I'm dog-tired, for a fact, and feel weak as a newborn, but I'm not stupid."

Sandoval? That meant—

"Yes, yes, I'm the one they used to call Alexander, although they surely call me something else now. And you, Father Cully, you may lie there if you'd like, or rise no further than your knees. Any more, and tired or not, I'll let the Sandoval eat you."

Cully lay on the ground, his legs sprawled over Niko's, unmoving.

"I can see you breathing, Cully." Alexander cocked his head to one sided. "And that bastard Gray is still breathing, too. Have to fix him after I fix you." He glanced quickly around the courtyard. "Hmm . . . didn't any of these fools have a mundane sword on them? Apparently not." He shrugged. "Then again, neither do I. Special circumstances, he? Well, Bear's will have to do. Good old Brother Bear, always happy to be of service."

He carefully walked around, keeping Bear's body in between himself and Gray's prostrate form, then stopped for a moment, his brow furrowed. "No, that's a bit too close, eh?" he asked, answering himself by stooping and seizing hold of Bear's right boot.

Bear had been a big man in life, and death hadn't changed that; the stranger—Alexander grunted and groaned as he dragged the body just a few feet away, never taking his eyes off where Cully and Niko lay, always seeming to watch Gray as well.

He'd have to make a try. Perhaps this Alexander would

set the Sandoval down on the ground when he turned Bear over. Nadide was far away, too far away, but he had to try, and Niko could feel his own strength returning with each breath.

He stared Alexander right in the eye. Maybe if the traitor was watching his eyes he wouldn't see Niko make the slight movements necessary to set his hands and feet into the ground for his lunge.

Cully was still motionless next to him, facedown on the ground, his left leg sprawled over Niko's.

It twitched twice.

Twice. Two for "no." Two for "disagree with me." Two for "not yet."

Two for "Cully was still with him."

He forced himself not to smile as Cully's foot twitched again, three times. Three times for "talk more."

Niko could do that.

"Why?" he choked out.

"Why what? Why is Bear so damned heavy? That's what I'm wondering," he said. "Why did the noble fool fall covering his scabbard? Why, when I dragged him, didn't the damn thing work itself a little loose, so I could get hold of it? I'm wondering that, too." He managed to get his free hand and a foot under Bear, and rolled him over. "Ah, now, that's better."

That was it. With all of the live swords out of reach, Alexander would slip the sheathed Sandoval into his sash, and then Niko would make his move.

That's what Cully was thinking.

He forced himself not to look at Bear's dead face, at the way that his open eyes, already glazed over and covered with dirt, stared unblinkingly at the sun. No. You couldn't think about that at times like this, you couldn't dwell on Bear's gentleness and kindness, and—

Cully's foot twitched once. And then again and again.

Talk more? Talk about *what*?

"Mr. Alexander?"

The only reason that Alexander didn't look up was because he never had looked down. But at least Niko had stalled him, if only for a few moments. His fingers fumbled clumsily for the hilt of Bear's sword. "My name is Abdul ibn Mahmoud," he said, showing anger for the first time. "If you want to beg for your life, boy, you can at least beg me by my name, eh? Ah. There it is." His fingers had found the hilt.

For one moment, Niko hoped that, by some miracle, Bear had managed to sheath the Nameless, that what Smith had kicked away was just Bear's mundane sword, Smith would be laying his hands on a White Sword that would burn him at the touch.

But, no: the sword slid smoothly from its sheath.

And then a miracle happened.

It wasn't a big miracle, granted. Niko had been read to enough from the Bible to know that real, big miracles were things like the sun standing still, like water being turned to wine, the raising of the dead.

But a strand of grass, just about halfway between Niko and this man who wanted to be called Abdul ibn Mahmoud, but who was the murderer Alexander Smith, poked its tip up through the gravel, and grew quickly, becoming the length of a fingertip, and then a finger, and then a hand.

Smith saw it too, and his brow furrowed.

"What the—"

There was a shout from behind Niko, and Cully's foot twitched, once.

Yes, it meant.

Niko lunged forward, scrabbling on the gravel, trying to gain his feet while Fotheringay, his short pike held out chest-height in front of him, dashed out of the bushes, the sound issuing from his mouth something somewhere between a battle cry and a growl.

Niko was already at a dead run around Smith, toward where Nadide lay. There was a chance, if not much of one, that Smith wouldn't have time to both draw the sword, and then kill Fotheringay and Cully and then Niko before Niko got Nadide in hand, and even if he could, could he and Nadide possibly defeat Alexander and the Sandoval?

He had to try.

Smith had been startled for a moment, but not for long; he dropped Bear's mundane sword and reached toward the Sandoval—

—stopped by an arrow that seemed to sprout from his chest.

It staggered him for a moment, just long enough for Fotheringay to reach him. The old sergeant slammed the butt of his pike into Alexander's chest, knocking him back, then slashed out with the pike's point, cutting into his sword arm.

Alexander fell back, the sword falling from his arms, but as Fotheringay moved in for the kill, Alexander's fingers managed to grasp it, and the redness flared.

And then he was blurring *away*—leaving behind a trail

through the smashed hedges from which Fotheringay had emerged.

And Niko's fingers were reaching for Nadide.

"Wait, boy," Cully shouted. "Both of you. He's fled. Don't take the swords in hand—but keep them near."

Gray had somehow or other managed to crawl across the gravel, leaving behind a trail of blood, and while what was left of his right arm was thrust into the robes over his chest, his left hand was but inches from the Khan.

He sagged down to the ground, and stretched his hand out.

Niko didn't see where Sigerson's man Bigglesworth had come from, but he quickly ran up to Gray. "Easy there, sir," he said. "You been hurt, hurt bad. Best just to rest." He raised his head.

"Help me up."

"Sir, you—"

"Help him up, Biggles," Sigerson said, walking quickly toward them.

His voice was preposterously calm as he unfastened the belt that held his wizard's robes tight against his waist. He tossed it to Bigglesworth. "Bind up his arm—and hold his sword for him, keep it ready for him, but hold it by the scabbard; don't touch the metal with your flesh."

"You don't have to tell me that twice, sir," Bigglesworth said. "Matter of fact, and meaning no disrespect, Mr. Sigerson, you didn't have to tell me that once."

Cully gripped Niko's hand and helped him to his feet, then tore a scrap of cloth from his own robes and wrapped it about Nadide so that he could pick her up. "Easy, Niko," he said. "Stand easy."

"No," Gray said, more of a grunt than a word.

"Alexander's not stupid. He'll not come back . . . not injured, not to face two . . . two knights of the Red Sword."

Bear lay dead on the ground at his feet, but Gray didn't look down at the body.

He looked over at Niko, and he smiled, and his smile was an awful thing to behold.

Sigerson took charge; there was no objection.

Gray's arm was quickly bound, and the stump didn't seem to bleed much at all. Fotheringay quickly gathered up scabbards, and the Khan was, safely scabbarded, in Gray's hand where it belonged, freeing Bigglesworth to be to find something to cover Bear up with.

Niko, with Cully at his side, just stood on watch, as did Gray, his back to them, watching, ignoring the way that Bear just lay there, dead eyes staring up at the sky.

Niko didn't look away.

It wasn't that he forced himself to look at the body. He could look at it, or not. It didn't make any difference.

It was all very strange.

He should have been feeling . . . something. He should have been recalling Bear's kindness and gentleness, and the knowing that it was gone forever, that what had been a big, gentle man was now just a pile of dead flesh rotting in the sun should have made his heart ache—it should have made the stones weep.

But they didn't, and neither did Niko.

He didn't feel anything. It was just a body, and there were bodies, and pieces of them, aplenty scattered about the courtyard, and it didn't matter.

He kept his hand near Nadide's hilt, but didn't touch it. If he touched her, he would feel something. Cully and

Gray were as silent and motionless as he was, and Niko almost jumped out of his skin when Cully laid a hand on his shoulder and squeezed it gently.

But it just startled him. That was all. Maybe he could feel something later. Maybe not.

He ignored the chattering of Sigerson and Bigglesworth and Fotheringay—

No. That was unfair. It wasn't chattering—they were getting necessary things done, and if they were congratulating themselves, just a little, they more than deserved it.

Bigglesworth and Sigerson had intercepted Fotheringay in the hedges, and the three of them had waited for the right moment, before making their move— Sigerson coming up with the only distraction that he could improvise on the spot, and Fotheringay charging Smith, hoping that he would get through, while Bigglesworth had run around the far side, hoping to get around behind Alexander, and the fact that it hadn't worked out quite as well as they hoped, well . . . it could have been much worse.

Fotheringay dashed off toward the building that he said was a barracks in search of a blanket to cover Bear up with, and came back with both a blanket and the man that Niko recognized as the carpenter's mate, the one on the *Marienios*—Stavros Andropolounikos.

Of the lot of them, Andropolounikos was the only one unmarked and unbruised. He carried a short bow in one hand, had a quiver of arrows belted about his waist, and wore a crooked smile across his face.

Fotheringay silently covered Bear's body up, but when he turned away, he was almost jolly. "Damn me for a fool," he said. "But this man is by far the best bowman I've ever had the pleasure of knowing, and I've known some damn fine bowmen in my time, I do swear," he said. He looked like he was about to hug Andropolounikos. "What a bloody marvelous shot, you beautiful son of a—of a wonderful Hellenic woman, and I'll hold down any man who says otherwise while you bugger him, or carve on him, or do whatever the hell you want, eh?"

If Niko could have felt anything, he would have wanted to slap Fotheringay silly.

"Thank you, Sergeant. It was . . ." Andropolounikos shrugged. " . . . it was all I could do to help."

Fotheringay snorted. "*Damn* your modesty, man. That would have been an impressive shot if that'd been the bow you'd practiced with from the minute your mother squirted you out—I would have sworn that you'd have been just as likely to hit me as that traitor, if I'd had to bet."

Andropolounikos seemed to have trouble speaking. "I'm . . . pleased to have been of service," he finally said.

Cully finally spoke. "Perhaps . . . perhaps your arrow was guided from above. Miracles do happen," he said.

Andropolounikos just shrugged again.

Cully's hand rested on Niko's shoulder. "Can you spare me?"

"Eh?"

"I think it's safe now, for now," he said quietly. "Keep on watch, the two of you. Please. *Please*. I have to. Somebody has to—and Gray can't."

Please? Please what? Please watch?

It was easy to just stand and watch.

Cully walked over to the blanket covering what was

left of what had been Bear, knelt down, and made the Sign over Bear.

"Glory be to the Father, to the Son, and to the Holy Ghost," he said. "As it was in the beginning, is now, and ever. Amen." There was no emotion or intensity in the words; he just spoke them quietly, quickly, as though trying to get them over with. "Incline Your ear, O Lord, unto our prayers, wherein we humbly pray Thee to show Thy mercy upon the soul of Thy servant David, whom Thou hast commanded to pass out of this world, that Thou wouldst place him in the region of peace and light, and bid him be a partaker with Thy Saints, through Christ our Lord. Amen."

He knelt there, silently, for the longest time. And then he buried his face in his hands, his body shaking silently.

"My lambs," he finally said, his voice a low whisper, barely audible, "my poor, poor babies. I murder you all, don't I?"

Cully knelt there for a long time, weeping, while Gray stood watch over him, his face without a trace of expression.

Niko just stood. He knew how to do that.

Chapter 15: Recall

Not all knowledge, not even all holiness, is contained within Christendom. The Inquisition would have burned me for saying this, but for all my sins, I've never served that Church.

In truth, the Nameless himself was never a Christian; and it's worth remembering that even His Son was born a Jew.

When the Jews say their prayer for the dead, there is no mention of the dead. They talk of God, and of their people—and that's about all; there is no mention of the dead.

I think I understand that, now.

I wish I didn't.

—Gray

It had been a long morning, and a longer afternoon. The red fires on the Montagne Grande had died off well before noon, and while al-Bakilani had two of his servants out behind the dammusa keep their elegant glasses trained on the long trail that snaked down from the distant hilltop, all they reported was that they had seen nothing.

Nothing.

The only surprise was that Randolph's junior midshipman had actually arrived, and DuPuy had been permitted a quick whispered conversation in which Mr. Emmons reported that, in fact, Randolph had been returned to the *Lord Fauncher*, and was standing by, in accord with his orders.

The boy was scared, but he carried himself well enough, and when he thought that nobody was looking, his raised eyebrow asked the obvious question.

DuPuy just shook his head. Emmons had been thoroughly searched, of course, and after the soldiers had found the third hidden knife he had been taken into the other room to return in, of all things, a spare set of al-Bakilani's elegant robes over his blushes; his uniform, down to his boots, had been unceremoniously dumped in a pile in the corner.

Al-Idrisi had called for a chessboard, and amused himself in winning game after game with one of the dozen soldiers who had been summoned after Smith's departure. DuPuy tried to follow the game—it would be interesting to see just how clever the man was in letting the Sharif win—but it was hard to concentrate on such things, and DuPuy had never been much for chess, anyway.

DuPuy watched for an opening, of course—not on the chessboard, but in the main room of the dammusa.

Equally, of course, he didn't find one.

It was midafternoon when al-Bakilani, who had been trying to engage DuPuy in a pointless conversation about horse-breeding—a subject about which DuPuy knew little and cared less—sat up at a quick exclamation from one of the watchers out behind the dammusa.

"If you'll excuse me, Admiral," he said, rising with his usual catlike grace, his voice level and calm as always, "Adil appears to be somewhat excited."

He walked quickly out the back door, to return but a few moments later, nodding calmly as he tapped the glass against his wrist. He spoke quickly in Arabic to al-Idrisi—and DuPuy cursed himself once again for not having learned the language.

Al-Idrisi was not quite so self-controlled. He shook his head, and reached for the chessboard, as though to throw it, but stopped himself, shrugged, and laid his king over, then rose, and stalked into the other room, his guards backing away, their eyes never leaving DuPuy and Emmons.

"Admiral?" Al-Bakilani's face was unreadable. "If you'd accompany me outside," he said, holding out the glass. "I believe you'll find this of interest. You, too, Mr. Emmons, if the Admiral will permit it."

DuPuy wished he'd had the self-control not to rush out the door, but he knew himself all too well, and he didn't even try; he snatched the glass from al-Bakilani's hand and dashed out through the door.

At first he couldn't see anything of interest. The idiot mud-bathers were still bathing in the stinking mud, and beyond them, the top of the Montagne Grande was as quiet as it had been. But the road . . . there was something moving on the road down from the mountain.

He put the glass to his good eye, squinting pointlessly, as though that would dispel the dancing black motes, as of course it didn't.

And then it came into focus.

It was a curious procession. The first thing he was able to make out was what looked like an oxcart, being pulled by two men, one of them in what appeared to be—yes, by God, it was marine utilities. He couldn't see what was in the cart, but . . . it didn't matter. That wasn't what had frightened al-Bakilani and al-Idrisi: the procession was led by three men. They all were hobbling, and one appeared to have a bandaged arm.

But they were all in the distinctive robes of the Knights of the Order of Crown, Shield, and Dragon.

Simon DuPuy let the arm holding the glass fall to his side. "If you're going to kill me, al-Bakilani, go right ahead. I don't mind." He tapped the glass against al-Bakilani's chest. "Go right ahead. They might not even avenge me. They might never know I was even here."

"Oh, they'd know, Admiral." Al-Bakilani's smooth face was as calm and impassive as always, damn him. "I'm sure that Lord Randolph would mention it." He shook his head. "You're utterly safe from me, at the moment, I can assure you. Although I suspect that the converse isn't necessarily true, given my earlier behavior." He shrugged. "There are other options, of course."

"Options?"

Al-Bakilani nodded. "His Excellency the Sharif has asked me to serve as an emissary to the Court of His Majesty the King. His Excellency is of the opinion that I might soon have some information to share that would be of . . . mutual benefit?" He gestured toward the dammusa behind them. "The late, unlamented dog, Efik? Perhaps he left some trail that points toward his own masters, and, all in all, I think that the Crown and the Dar al-Islam have some mutual interest in sending hunters down that trail." His smile was as calm and maddening as usual. "It's my understanding that a ship—or more than one ship—will soon be dispatched to both Malta and Londinium with all the information that the Commission for the Prevention of Vice and Promotion of Virtue can provide on such matters, and they are quite . . . diligent at such interviews, and quite good at extracting information, and will be more than happy to share it—well, if not all of it, at least all of it that would be of more use to the Crown than to the Dar al-Islam."

"And that won't happen if I wring your neck?"

"Oh, no. It will happen nonetheless. The state of my neck, as fond as I am of it, doesn't affect such matters of our mutual interest, alas. But I would hope that my own good offices would make any information flow more quickly and effectively, all in all."

DuPuy shook his head. The gall of the man. Still . . . "We could just wait," he said. "I don't see your . . . Abdul ibn Mahmoud here, or there. Do you think that, that, dog of a Sharif's soldiers could stand up to the likes of Sir Joshua? And Sir Joshua," he added, gesturing with the glass, "is hardly alone."

Al-Bakilani shook his head. "I rather doubt it. Which is why His Excellency and his guards have already departed with what would normally be unseemly haste, while we've been standing here talking. You could, of course, give chase—but I think the knights are perhaps closer to an hour away from here than farther from it, and by that time, it's my expectation that, even if you choose to try to interfere, even with the aid of the estimable Midshipman Emmons, His Excellency's ship will have already set sail by the time they arrive."

"And I'm expected to load you and a bunch of your attendant spies on the *Lord Fauncher* to convey you to England?"

"Well, no." Al-Bakilani shook his head. "Much as I would like to have my own people in attendance, I'm not sure that everyone that His Excellency and I brought to Pantelleria is entirely trustworthy—and I trust that you'll find that they've all taken to their heels with His Excellency the Sharif. Should I be your guest, I'll have to trust to the Crown's graciousness, for the time being, while I wait for some . . . very carefully interviewed staff to arrive to serve me." His smile broadened. "If I'm your prisoner, well, prisoners rarely have much of a staff at all, at that. And if you choose to—how did you put it?—wring my neck, well, then, the issue of how I'm to be served won't be of any further interest to anyone at all, myself included." He spread his hands. "What happens next is up to you, Admiral. I'm sure you'll serve your King honorably and wisely, however you decide."

DuPuy wasn't a hesitating sort. "Lieutenant Emmons?"

"Err, Admiral, I'm a midshipman, sir."

Well, Emmons was right, but there was a deep and profound glee in DuPuy. He could make the boy wrong, and by God, he would! "And I'm a bloody Admiral, and if I say you're a lieutenant, you're a bloody lieutenant."

"Yes, sir."

"You're out of uniform. I'll forgive the midshipman's

braid on the uniform, but get the hell out of those robes and into that uniform—if the damned Arabs have left it intact. Put it on, and then conduct . . . our guest to meet the knights. Ask them to report to me at the port. I've got to stop the *Lord Fauncher* from leaving, and Randolph is expecting to see me, and me alone."

"Yes, sir." Emmons started to turn away.

"Wait, dammit. I'm not done, Lieutenant. Our . . . guest suffers from a spastic condition. He requests that you tie his hands—and tightly, mind you—behind his back, and that he be gagged, to avoid any unwanted sounds, and that he be conducted to the meeting at sword point. Should his condition cause him to to try to free himself, or make some sort of outcry before he's taken in hand by the knights, or should anybody try to interfere with you or him—and I particularly direct your attention to the fact that that Smith-character is devilishly fast, and that I've not seen his head—His Excellency and I both request that you stick that sword in him to avoid any embarrassment. From him it's a request; from me it's an order. You know how to obey an order, Lieutenant?"

"Yes, *sir*."

"You have any problem with that, Excellency?"

"None at all." Al-Bakilani shook his head. "I'm pleased of course, but not surprised that I'm to live. The Admiral, as I've long said and even longer thought, is a most wise and careful man. And may I congratulate Lieutenant Emmons on his promotion?"

"Shut up, Excellency," DuPuy said. "Move it, Emmons. And smartly."

"Yes, sir."

It all mostly decided itself: get the knights home, and

quickly, and don't spend a moment regretting losing the services, for the time being, of the most . . . promising captain to ever have served under Admiral Simon Tremaine DuPuy. Get al-Bakilani into the hands of His Majesty—without having it let out that he was ever in Crown hands. Or perhaps not—perhaps he had suffered an accident on Pantelleria?

DuPuy would have to have quick words with Randolph on that subject, but . . . no. Realistically, too many people would know that al-Bakilani had been taken aboard the *Lord Fauncher*, and DuPuy was sparing his life, and not just postponing an execution. No sense in fooling himself.

The only real decision DuPuy had to make was how to get himself back to Malta.

And that would, all in all, be easy—the *Lord Fauncher's* cutter would serve, and the blowing Levanter would make the trip fast.

Getting the knights and whatever information was in their hands and their heads back to England as quickly as possible was too important to be delayed for even two days by carrying a fat, old, useless man back to his furlined beach billet, after all. Randolph could live without the cutter on his trip to England.

Have to take a few men from Randolph's crew to man it, of course, and that would give DuPuy an opportunity to evaluate them himself.

And dammit, it would be good to have a tiller in his hands.

Chapter 16: The Voyage Home

"Service, honor, faith, obedience. Justice tempered only by mercy; mercy tempered only by justice."

Fine words, yes. For me, they are all lies. Save one.

One word to live by; one word to live for: *service*.

There is no justice; Bear's mute lips speak loudly as to that. Me, I am drained of mercy and impoverished of faith, and care not a whit about such fripperies as honor.

And obedience? Let's not be silly.

But there is still service, and I will still be of service. I swear it. I wish I could swear it on Bear's grave, but I'd not let any man pollute his resting place with the oaths of the damned.

But I will be of service.

Do not think well of me for that; it's no sacrifice.

I really don't have anything else left.

—Gray

There was brief talk of burying Bear at sea. He put an end to that.

Randolph made the short formal offer, although Gray could tell that he didn't expect Gray to accept, and Gray didn't, and Randolph just said, "Of course, Sir Joshua," and returned to his duties, and added not one word nor raised an eyebrow over sailors' superstitions about carrying corpses; he just nodded stiffly, and walked away.

Which was just as well, all in all.

Sigerson, Bigglesworth at his side, asked Gray for permission to preserve the body, and Gray had nodded. Bear's body had already started to stink, and even with favorable winds, tides, and seas it was four or five days good sailing to Gibraltar, and probably another ten past that to Londinium, and who knew how long after that it would take to bring the body home to Fallsworth?

Sigerson was closeted up in the rear hold overnight, and emerged, as sagging and tired-looking as Gray had ever seen a man. He nodded, and reported that it was done, and Gray said, "Thank you," and Sigerson said, "You are welcome, of course." They didn't say anything else; they didn't have anything else to say to each other.

They held a brief mass on the main deck the second night out. Orders were orders, and Randolph's were to repair to England at all possible speed, so the topmen remained aloft throughout, prepared to reef if the wind picked up, as the *Lord Fauncher* had every scrap of sail flying from the foremast topgallants to the spanker, all the way aft.

Gray had heard Randolph instructing the first, who had the deck, that there was to be no slacking in activity, and if the situation called for orders to be piped or shouted, that was to be done, no matter the state of the service, and when he had seen Gray watching him, he had stood silently until Gray had nodded.

Of course. Orders were orders. The work had to go on. Gray could hardly fault Randolph for that.

They all gathered there: Randolph, of course, resplendent in his dress blues; Gray, and Niko, and Cully, and Fotheringay, Sigerson, and Bigglesworth—and, of course, Andropolounikos, visibly uncomfortable in the shore clothes borrowed from one of the officers, and which the ship's tailor had altered for him; his index finger kept running around the inside of his collar.

The knights' gear was hundreds of miles away aboard the *Marienios*, but the ship's sailmaker had done a fine job of laundering and as decent a one as was possible of stitching up their clothing, and if they looked shabby, and they did, Bear wouldn't have minded, so Gray pretended not to, either.

Gray said the Mass for the Dead, with Cully having done the preparations. Gray didn't feel anything; he just spoke the words. There was no question of doing Bear's death baptism aboard the *Lord Fauncher*; that would be done at Fallsworth, of course, along with his burial.

And it was just as well that first-form novices at Alton had learned all the masses by rote, and tested on them every year, and that what was early learned is one's possession for life, for it had been a long time since Gray had celebrated mass, and he wouldn't have wanted to stumble over the words that swam on the page of the missal minor that Cully held for him.

And then it was over, and Cully had taken the tray and missal minor away, and he and Niko had done the rest of the cleaning up, leaving Gray alone at the stern rail.

He wasn't sure when or how, but Gray had somehow ended up with Bear's sword—his mundane sword, of course—stuck through his sash, along with his own two. Part of him wanted to just throw it over the side, although he didn't know why, and he would, of course, return the sword to Baron Shanley, along with the body.

Gray stood at the stern rail for a long time.

Strange thing: his fingers hurt. Not the fingers of his remaining hand—the ones that should have been where his right hand used to be. Not the stump—it hurt, yes, but not much, not more than he could stand; the red had burned it clean to the bone, just above the wrist, but when he held it up, it felt like he could wiggle his fingers, and once or twice he tried to touch his own cheek with the ghostly fingers, and, of course, didn't feel anything in his cheek, or with the lost hand.

But the absent fingers ached, constantly.

Strange. Although why it should be strange, he didn't know. It wasn't as though he didn't already understand how something missing could hurt more than a strong man could bear.

He just stood, watching the water, trying to ignore the whistles and shouts of the deck crew, and not for a moment laying his remaining hand on the Khan.

He was left alone for what seemed to be a short time, or maybe it was a long one, but he became aware that Cully was standing to one side of him, and Niko to the other.

They didn't say anything at first.

"The Nameless is locked in the captain's strongbox," Cully finally said. "Marines on watch, and Fotheringay watching the marines—the other marines."

"I don't think there's anything to worry about," Gray said.

"Neither does Fotheringay," Cully said.

Gray nodded. He didn't care much for, or about, the sergeant, but Fotheringay would do his duty as he saw it. Probably just wanted to keep busy, since he had no real work to do.

Al-Bakilani was locked in the first's cabin, and there were guards on his door, too. Whether he was to be a prisoner or an ambassador was probably an interesting question, but it was one that other heads than Randolph's would have to answer, and he would spend the trip below.

The three stood silently again.

Then Niko spoke. "What happens next?"

Gray shook his head. He didn't know. He didn't care.

"For the three of us, it'll be up to the Council, which means the Abbot General," Cully said. "I suspect you and I won't have any trouble being relieved of our vows, eh, Niko?" He smiled in the dark. "Life goes on, until it stops. We go on. Worst case? You've got two hundred crowns of gold in the strongbox aboard the *Marienios*, and—"

"I wasn't asking about the money."

"I didn't think you were." Cully shook his head. "But a man—knight or fisherman—has to eat. Speaking of which," he said, turning to Gray, "you're going to have to eat something, Joshua."

"Tomorrow."

Cully nodded. "Good enough. Your word is always good enough for me, Joshua."

"I wasn't aware I gave my word."

"I thought you were doing just that."

"If you insist."

"Then we're agreed—and the boy does have to eat, as well. In a figurative, as well as a literal sense. That'll need to be seen to."

Gray shrugged. "Easily enough handled. Take him—*I* will get Sir Robert to come with me and take him—"

"Which Sir Robert? Cooper or Linsen? Or some other Sir Robert entirely?"

"—I will ask Sir Robert *Linsen* to come with me and take him down to the City, and to whichever banking house Sir Robert uses. My word is good enough bond for Linsen, and his should be good enough bond, all in all—we'll get Sir Niko an advance on the money, enough to live on, while word's sent to the Governor's office to collect it— Langahan will probably end up handling that—and send a note back. Have to take a serious discount, given the distance, but we can leave it to Linsen to handle." He wasn't worried about the Abdullahs stealing the boys' money—the only people who had to worry about the Abdullahs stealing the boy's money were the Abdullahs— but there was, of course, the possibility that the *Marienios* wouldn't make it back home. Storms, pirates . . . and the Others, whoever they were.

The only question was how to handle the details. That was the sort of thing that he would have had Bear deal with.

His missing hand ached.

"How soon do you think we'll be there?" Cully asked. "Have to stop for water somewhere, if not other provisions. Gibraltar probably."

"No, not Gibby," Gray said, shaking his head. "Likely to make things too complicated—Digsworth would probably insist on being briefed, and that would delay things. Little love lost between Gibby and Malta; he might even decide that DuPuy overreached himself on having al-Bakilani clapped in irons, and I expect that Randolph will want to see that his own reports are the first to reach Londinium."

"It was ordinary rope, as I recall."

"You know what I mean. I don't think al-Bakilani would or will complain, mind you—I think he's as eager to get the Crown on the trail of these Others as His Majesty will be, and won't want to distract anybody's attention from that issue. And—" he stopped himself. "I see," he said, nodding. "You get me wrapped up in the details of the world, bind me to it more tightly . . ."

Cully patted him on the arm. "I think I'm supposed to say that I don't know what you're talking about." He gave a thin smile.

"Then again, you only do what you're supposed to, be it accident, or coincidence, Father."

"True enough." The smile vanished. "Do you think they'll make—let you keep the Khan?"

Gray stopped his hand an inch from the Khan's hilt. "Well, I could hardly serve on His Own with just one hand, now, could I?"

"I wasn't asking if you'd be allowed to serve on His Own. I was asking if you expect to be taken off the active list, or relieved of the Khan."

"I hadn't been thinking about that."

"Well, then, do so."

That wasn't quite true—he had been avoiding thinking about it. He couldn't even tie his bootlaces or knot his sash for himself. And he would never be able to hold his mundane sword in his lost right hand, the scabbarded Khan in his left, prepared to drop the mundane sword and draw the Khan as quick as a man could blink.

But there was precedent. While he had not served with His Own after the loss of his arm, Linsen had carried the Goatboy for years; it was age that had finally taken it away from him, not the disability. Then again, the Goatboy was White, and the Khan was Red, and while releasing holiness was not to be taken lightly, it generally fell more lightly on the world than unleashing evil always did, eh?

"I don't know," he said. "We'll see." It wasn't his choice, after all. He would argue against it, if anyone would listen to him.

Cully probably thought that Gray wouldn't notice how he tapped against Niko's arm, but he did. Talk more? About what?

Niko piped up obediently with: "Could I ask a question?"

"You already did." Cully smiled. "But, yes, you may ask another, although I don't know what you'd have to ask about right now."

Niko tried to seem puzzled. "It's not important, I guess, but—what are those pennants at the top of the mizzen mast? I don't remember seeing them before."

Gray looked up.

The foremast, of course, flew the black flag of the Crown, Shield, and Dragon; and below it, the red-and-gold pennant of the Royal Navy. No solid-colored pennants, there, which was just as well—there wasn't a solid color that was good news.

The mizzenmast flew four pennants, and only one of those was solid: the topmost was black-and-white striped, and below it a red-and-white checkered one, a solid red, and another black-and-white striped.

"Oh," Cully said, nodding. "I see what you mean. The black-and-white one means that the *Lord Fauncher* is on courier duty. The red-and-white is 'urgency' or 'emergency,' and the solid red is speed. Captain Randolph is announcing that we're on courier duty—reasonable under the circumstances—and repeating the flag under the other two is him asking for any fast courier ship to come alongside. I think that's why he's back down in his quarters, writing dispatches. The *Lord Fauncher* is fast enough, but she's no courier sloop—my guess is that the captain wants to get his dispatches to Londinium ahead of us, if possible. Not the worst of ideas, for any of us."

Gray shook his head. "I couldn't write."

"You could dictate. I can write."

"And you could just have said, 'Gray, I think it would make sense to get your report to the Abbot General ahead of the *Lord Fauncher*, if possible,' instead of putting Sir Niko through this charade."

"Yes, I guess I could have."

He sighed, and let his hand rest on the hilt of Bear's sword.

"Let's get to it, shall we?"

Chapter 17: Knighthood

———◆———

> The words I'm used to living by are "the fish are running, Niko," "pull harder, Niko," and "the day isn't getting any younger, Niko." I understand how to live by those.
>
> But these other words . . . it's all very strange to me. We'll see.
>
> —Niko

Niko just happened to be on deck, going through his daily workouts, when the cutter came for them.

He might have noticed the sail, but they had seen plenty of sails over the past days. The closer that they got to Portsmouth, the more they saw.

The captain, eying his charts and logs and the coastline, had said that morning that he expected to make Portsmouth just before dark, but it was only midafternoon, and Niko and Cully had gone into their usual routine, while Gray, as he did at all such times, just went below, not saying anything, while land grew closer, and the pace of tacking increased until it seemed like it was only minutes between the cries of "Prepare to come about."

Niko would have taken a broad reach north, and then tacked back. Then again, he didn't know these waters at all, and Captain Randolph certainly did. Probably sensible seamanship.

The wind had picked up, and Poseidon had apparently not wanted them to hurry into Portsmouth, as the wind seemed to be coming directly from the distant twin lighthouses marking the way into port.

This would probably be their last workout, all in all.

Niko didn't quite see the point, but . . . no, he had. He was, for the time being, Sir Niko Christofolous, and it was only right that he be as little a pale imitation of a real knight as he could be, and it gave him something to do.

And, truth to tell, there was something about the ritual of take-your-position, of lunge-and-recover, of high-guard-outside-dammit-Niko-outside and all the rest that was good for more than just working up a sweat, as though one would want to work up a sweat.

He hadn't really had anything else to do. Whatever else could be said about traveling aboard a ship you weren't involved in the sailing of, it was boring, and left too much time for thinking. There had been more than enough of that, lying in his bunk, trying to sleep, finally reaching out a finger to touch Nadide's steel, and silently singing the lullabye that put the both of them to sleep.

The truth, as Cully seemed to insist, when he talked about it—and he seemed to want to talk about it more and more, as the days had passed, although he never did so in front of Gray—was that what had happened had been a great victory. A live sword, with the soul—or what passed for it—of the Wise, raised against the Crown? They had stopped that, and the stopping of that was worth far more to the Crown than the life of one knight, even one like Bear.

He'd say that, as though to persuade himself, but his eyes would say *but, of course, there was none like Bear*.

And Niko would just say, "Yes, Sir Cully," and let his eyes speak for themselves, and had looked forward to their afternoon workouts much more than he did to further talk, about Bear or anything else.

"Cutter approaching," the lookout sang out, "signaling 'stand by.' Carrying the Admiralty flag."

The First, who had the deck, called out something to the bosun, and Topmen Aloft was immediately piped, followed by a seven-note theme that Niko hadn't heard before, not that it was hard to figure out what it meant when the sailors scrambled up the ropes and immediately began lowering the sails.

Cully tossed Niko a soft cloth. "Practice time is over—for today, at least," he said. "Wash up, as quickly as you can, mind, and get dressed. I expect that all of us will be taken aboard, and I don't want you to appear all dirty and sweaty in front of, well, whoever it is we're going to be hauled in front of. The Navy, I expect, although I wouldn't be surprised if we're in front of the Abbot General sooner than later."

"And you?"

Cully smoothed a hand down the front of his tunic. "I haven't been getting myself all sweaty, and I'm known to be a worthless old man. Now, if you'll get a move on, I'll see to Gray."

Niko hurried down to the cabin he and Cully shared, and gave himself a quick rinse in the water bucket, careless of the way he was splashing the deck. He was halfway into his trousers when there was a knock on the door.

"Yes?"

Fotheringay walked in, a bundle in his arms. "Well, Sir Niko, it took a bit of doing to get that lazy bastard to finish early, but it appears I won't actually have to shove my foot up his lazy ass quite as far as I thought I would—he finished for all three of you." He dumped the clothes on the bunk, and beckoned to Niko. "Come on, sir, shake a leg—you don't want to appear in front of the Admiral in mended clothes, do you?"

"Admiral?"

"Well, it's an Admiral's flag that's flying from the launch, and they haven't sent it for the likes of me—I wouldn't be at all surprised if there'll be a lot of folks wanting to hear what you have to say, all in all, and perhaps a few who want to hear from me, by and by. If you could move it a bit more quickly, sir, it'd be a favor. They're going to want to see you quickly, I'd wager."

"Not you?"

Fotheringay chuckled. "Me? Me, I'd best worry about not being hanged, for the moment." He didn't look worried, and Niko didn't have the vaguest idea of what he was talking about, but he kept talking as he insisted on helping Niko into the clothes that Niko was perfectly capable of putting on without any help. "Oh, it's nothing—but here I am, a marine sergeant assigned to the Blue Squadron, Malta Fleet, on a ship that's not part of the

Blue and not officially accepted back into service in the Fleet, for that matter, and never mind that Mr. Langahan had me seconded to service with the *Wellesley*, which is where I'm officially supposed to be, and while you and I know that Admiral DuPuy put me aboard the *Lord Fauncher*, Captain Randolph's been a bit, well, distracted to write me out a set of orders, and truth to tell—and I do like telling the truth, young sir; it keeps things simpler— I've not mentioned the matter to him, as I long ago learned that you get yourself more into trouble than out of it by bothering officers, and I'm not sure that somebody's not going to decide, at least for the moment, that I'm 'absent without orders,' although I doubt they'll even lock me up, much less actually get around to hanging me without checking, and . . . there you go." He nodded. "That looks proper enough, although I think maybe somebody needs to have words with Fogarty about his stitching, but that's not my place, and I do know my place, by and large, young sir."

He gave the hem of Niko's tunic a quick tug, then nodded approvingly as Niko slid both Nadide and his Navy sword into place. "Now, that's what a fit and proper young Knight of the Order looks like, I'll say." He snapped to attention, then dropped the position. "Do you mind?"

Niko didn't have the slightest idea what Fotheringay was asking, so he said, "No, I don't mind."

Fotheringay smiled as he stuck out a hand. "Don't know as we'll see each other soon, if again. It's been a privilege, Sir Niko."

"I'm . . . not really very much of a knight, Sergeant Fotheringay," he said, as he took the sergeant's hand.

"You tell that to the dead men, Sir Niko," Fotheringay

said. "You tell that to men who were going to raise Red
Swords and I don't like to think what else against the
Crown, young sir, the ones that the gulls are dining on
back on you-know-where. They won't object." He shook
his head. "But meaning no disrespect, sir, you don't need
to bother telling that to the likes of Nigel Fotheringay, as
he bloody well knows better."

"You did more than I did, Sergeant."

Fotheringay gave him a toothless smile. "I only did me
duty, sir," he said, "but it's kind of you to say so, most
kind, and—"

There was knock on the door. Fotheringay opened it,
then snapped back to attention.

It was Sutherland, the senior midshipman. "At your
ease, sergeant," he said, frowning. He turned to Niko,
and dropped the frown. "Captain's compliments, Sir Niko,
and he'd be much obliged if you'd report to him on the
quarterdeck with your gear. There's a launch coming aside,
ready to take you."

"I'll be right there, Mr. Sutherland. Thank you."

Sutherland turned to Fotheringay and handed him an
envelope. "And while he didn't send any compliments,
Sergeant, he sent me to tell you to get your kit together,
and smartly, and to haul yourself to the quarterdeck, and
do so *right* smartly—you're going, too, apparently. And
I'm to say, and I quote, 'Here's the orders you should have
asked me for days ago. Do you want to be hanged with a
medal around your neck?' "

Sutherland smiled.

The cutter tacked back and forth even more rapidly
than the *Lord Fauncher* had, and it was only a few minutes

before they passed between the lighthouses, and the oarsmen quickly lowered the sail to set about rowing, while Niko and the others just sat on the benches.

It was all of them, unsurprisingly: Sigerson and Bigglesworth; Fotheringay and Andropolounikos; and, of course, Cully and Gray. The Nameless had been removed from the strongbox and lay in a cloth bag across Gray's lap. Bear's body, like al-Bakilani, were still aboard the *Lord Fauncher*.

He looked behind him. The *Lord Fauncher* already had its sails back up, and was starting to move, although not nearly as quickly as the cutter had under sail . . .

. . . and then it was gone, hidden behind the spit of land at the entrance to the harbor.

It was a nastier and rockier harbor than Niko was used to, and there was something wrong with the air. He shivered.

"Easy, boy," Cully said, his voice low.

There was a reception committee of sorts on the pier: easily one hundred soldiers, all in strange-looking black uniform jackets, with preposterously tall feathers on their rounded hats.

"Marines?" Niko asked.

"No," Cully said. "Not marines—army. Portsmouth Guards—the earl's troops."

"No," Gray said, quietly, leaning forward, his good hand down, as though fiddling with his bootlaces. "It's the Porties' uniforms, but my eyes are good enough to recognize Atkinson at the head of it, and he's Marsh Guard." His voice was too low, too calm. "Not likely to be seconded to the Porties. And I'm none too impressed with the way the jackets fit—some of those supposed Porties are busting their buttons."

"Hmm . . ." Cully said. "I don't like that. What's a captain in the Marsh doing here?"

"I don't like it, either. Let's see what it means." His hand—his remaining hand—was half tucked into the front of his robes, probably by no coincidence bringing it near the hilt of the Khan. "I doubt it means much. Maybe I'm wrong; maybe Atkinson just has a cousin that favors him."

Was there a flicker of a smile on Gray's face? Niko wasn't sure.

"His family from around here?" Cully asked. His voice had gone all low and quiet, too. One hand rested with something that looked like affection on Gray's shoulder.

"I don't know," Gray said. He reached up to cover Cully's hand with his own, then let it drop. "I don't know him well. I don't know many people around Court all that well, and the Marshies were only in Londinium for half a year or so, back before they got sent to Kurcik. But I don't like it. We've got three live swords, and they're of . . . some value. If it all breaks—"

"If it breaks, it breaks on my signal," Cully said, sighing as he let his hand fall from Gray's shoulder. "Not the Khan's. And not yours."

Gray didn't answer for a moment, then he nodded. "Yes, Father. You'd better carry the Nameless, though. If it does all go to pieces, I'll need my hand free." There was something different in his voice that Niko couldn't quite place. Confidence? Comfort? He couldn't have said for sure.

Cully started to protest, but then just shrugged and took the bag from Gray. "I thought I was done with bearing one of these, even in a bag."

"Would you be still?"

"I hope I will." Cully nodded. "Niko, I go up the ladder first of the three of us—Gray last. Make sure you've got some clear space, and don't let anybody lay a hand on you. Nobody has the right to lay a hand on an Order Knight."

"And if they do?"

"Then it's all gone bad." He leaned forward and whispered something to Fotheringay, who just nodded, and bent momentarily to adjust his boots, then leaned back and stretched broadly, his hands clasped behind his head.

Fotheringay looked over at Niko for a moment, then gave him a flash of toothless grin and a nod. "It'll be fine, Sir Niko," he said, tilting his hand just for a moment so that Niko could see a flash of the knife he held in his hand, the grip reversed, blade flat against his arm, concealed by his sleeve, before he let his hand drop. "Just keep behind me, young sir. I'll buy you the time you need to get your sword out. You can't count on much in this world, but you can count on that, Sir Niko." He said it all matter-of-factly. "Kechiroski," he said, "you got that bow in your kit?" At Kechiroski's nod, Fotheringay shook his head. "Don't get it out; too much of a signal. If it all goes to shit, you break right and do the best that you can, as long as you can."

"Yes, Sergeant."

Sigerson started to turn, then stopped the motion at Cully's headshake.

"We've been sent for by Admiral Dempsey," Cully said, quietly, "and our escort should be marines, not army, and if it's army . . ."

"It should be the Porties, and not just look like them."

"You saw it, too."

Sigerson smiled. "It's not a question of seeing, Sir Cully, but of observing. And yes, I observed it, too."

"Ship oars," the coxswain called out, and oars were quickly brought aboard.

Niko looked at the sailors without trying to look like he was looking at them.

The coxswain in the bow of the cutter rose to catch hold of the dock ladder, then one by one, each sailor took his turn pulling the cutter along the ladder until it was amidships, and the two sailors on either side held the boat steady, so that they could all depart.

"Excuse me," Fotheringay said, perhaps a little too loudly, leaned past Bigglesworth and addressed Sigerson. "Got a touch of the mal—mind if I'm first up?"

"Not at all, Sergeant." If Sigerson's voice was a little too loud, too, his usual smile was still in place. "If you'll be sure to be quick enough about it that I don't need an umbrella?"

"No worries on that score, sir." He made his way across Bigglesworth and Sigerson, bumping into Bigglesworth as he did, then climbed up the ladder more quickly than a man of his age and bulk would be expected to.

Bigglesworth was next, and then Sigerson followed, and then Cully, and then Niko, with Andropolounikos behind him.

By the time Niko got to the top, the others were arranged in a rough semicircle, between him and the Guard captain, who Cully was talking to. Fotheringay gave him a momentary look, then took half a step to one side, putting himself between Niko and the nearest of the soldiers.

Cully looked the guard captain up and down. "You're

here to conduct us to the Admiralty, Captain . . ."

"Atkinson, sir. And no. My orders are to take you to the Earl's residence—his town house, Sir Cully, not his estate." He gestured toward the city. "About half a mile, sir; it won't be long."

"And the Admiral is meeting us there?"

"I don't know much about such things, sir. I'm just following the orders I was given."

"You are, eh, Atkinson?" Gray's hand was but inches away from the Khan. "And why would the earl or the Admiral put a Marshie in a Portie's uniform?"

Niko nodded. If they were going to have it out, they would have it out here and now. He could more feel than see Fotheringay tense up, as Gray took a step to one side, and—

"Wait *please*." Atkinson threw up his hands. "I didn't think you'd recognize me, Sir Joshua. You and I've barely exchanged a dozen words, if that. Easy, man, easy. No need for trouble—the earl's waiting for you, yes, but it's not just him. I've been seconded to the Household Guard, and His Majesty thought it would draw less attention if we came in Portie uniforms. We're all House Guard . . . I'm sure you know some of the . . . Simperson, yes, you— over here. On the double, damn it."

"*Sir*." A sergeant in an ill-fitting jacket marched over. "I don't know if Sir Joshua will recognize me, but—"

"Simperson." Gray nodded. "You made sergeant? Or is that just the uniform?"

"*Sir*. I made sergeant. I'm still with the House Guard, sir."

"So—"

"Yes, yes, yes," Atkinson said, "you're going to see the

King. He's come down from Londinium to see you, in fact. We're your escort, man, not your enemies. Now will you come with me, or do you intend to stand on this drafty dock while I go fetch His Majesty?"

There was a problem at the door to the great hall in what had been described as a "town house," but was actually a gated palace, not quite the size of the Governor's mansion in Pironesia. Niko had been puzzling over that as they walked in, but was distracted by the argument about his own status.

The others hadn't had any problem, or any issue.

The guards—these ones in the red tunics with the red piping of the House Guard—had thoroughly searched everybody else except for Gray and Cully.

It seemed that few people were allowed to come armed into the Presence, which was understandable. Certainly nobody else had complained at the search. Bigglesworth and Fotheringay had turned over their weapons— including the daggers that each of the two men still had concealed in their hands, the flat of the blade still against the arm—and Sigerson and Andropolounikos weren't carrying any.

Cully and Gray, of course, had been allowed to keep their swords with no protest—they were Order Knights, after all—but the guard frowned, and looked down at his list, and said that he knew of no Sir Niko Christofolous of the Order of Crown, Shield, and Dragon, and begging Sir Niko's pardon, it would probably be simpler if he turned over his swords like the others had.

Niko started to say something, but desisted at a peremptory motion from Gray.

"No," Gray said.

"Perhaps I could send for one of His Own?" the guard asked. "Meaning no offense, Sir Joshua, but—"

"*Do* that, then. Send for one of His Own. Send for whomever you care to," Gray said, his voice tight. "Now, please. You're keeping His Majesty waiting."

"Oh, send them in," a voice called from behind the door. "I'm quite sure that Sir Niko isn't a danger. To me, at least."

The doors opened.

His Majesty, Mordred V, seemed more amused than displeased, although the four Order knights who stood halfway across the great hall of the earl's home watched them all, even Cully and Gray, with no expression whatsoever, even as all of them knelt, Niko and Cully quite properly sweeping their swords back, Gray having trouble with it.

Niko hadn't known what to expect of the King, but this wasn't it. He was of more than average height, perhaps, but certainly not much more. His face didn't look much like it was on the pennies—the jaw wasn't quite as square, and the eyes seemed tired. And the hair, well, it was black, shot with just a little gray, and not copper-colored, and ever-so-slightly messy.

"Well, it seems that you've come close to causing even more commotion today, eh? Oh, get up, the lot of you," the king said, more flopping into than sitting in the chair next to the great hearth. He threw a leg over the arm of the chair, then clearly thought better of it and seated himself properly. There was a table at his elbow, holding a ragged pile of papers. He picked one up, glanced quickly at it, then set it back down.

"Let's start—just find yourself some seats, all of you." There were couches and chairs on the thick rug, and they all walked slowly over and found seats, under the gaze of the knights. To the right of the king's chair, a long table had been set, with fine glazed pottery holding pens, and half a dozen inkwells and several stacks of paper; six elegantly dressed men sat there, waiting patiently, watching Niko and all the others with expressions almost as neutral as the knights', but not nearly as implicitly hostile.

Of course, the fact that the secretaries didn't have swords within reach might have had something to do with that.

"This is important enough," the king said, "for me to have come down here, but it's not the only important thing going on right now—I've dragged a dozen ministers, half the Privy Council, and more secretaries than I care to think about with me, and there are other matters that I must attend to, even this night." He beckoned to one of the . . . scribes? Niko decided that they were scribes. "I'll want to call Shanley first," he said. "Then the Archbishop. Ask them to wait outside." The man nodded, rose, and quickly walked from the room.

The king gave Cully a smile. "Yes, yes, I'm going to make Ralph wait while I talk to you. He'll already have noticed that, as I intend; I don't want you to point it out to him, Cully. Understood?"

"I'll obey, Your Highness," Cully said, slowly. "I'm not sure I understand."

The king shook his head and raised a hand. "We can get to that in a moment. I want to take the easy parts first, and then we can go on to more difficult and unpleasant matters. And, truth to tell, the easy parts are among my pleasures. Speaking of which . . ." He looked over at Andropolounikos. "Stavros Kechiroski, better known as Stavros Andropolounikos, would you be so kind as to rise?"

Andropolounikos was already quickly on his feet before Niko realized that the King was speaking in Hellenic. Andropolounikos seemed surprised, too, and that seemed to amuse the King.

"I've read Lord Randolph's and Sir Joshua's reports—reread them, in fact, although I've been told I'm a quick study," he said, lapsing back into English. "Then again," he added, with a brief smile, "I'm told many nice things about myself, and I'm not sure I believe all of them. Not sure what to make of all the details—secondhand reports are bad enough—but I do believe that you made an incredible bowshot in Our service, and showed great courage.

"You, Stavros Andropolounikos, are the easiest one—you're to be knighted and pensioned. Knight of the Guard, I think, along with the OC; you'll be able to live decently in Londinium, better out in the country, and like a baron, if not nearly an earl, if you decide to return to Andropolounikos. Your choice. Every man should see Londinium before he dies, and you'll do that—but you might find yourself more comfortable at home. I know I do.

"I'm not in such a rush that we have to knight you now, on the run—you'll be properly and publicly knighted at the already-scheduled ceremony in Londinium on . . ." He paused momentarily.

"Four weeks from tomorrow, Your Majesty," the scribe on the left said, looking up, while the other two were writing quickly. "Eighth of Cornwall."

" . . . on the Eighth of Cornwall. You'll spend the time between now and then talking to the Intelligence people." He gave a quick shrug. "I suspect you don't know much that they'd find of interest, but the simplest way to find that out is for you to talk to them, at some length." He turned to one of the scribes. "And make sure that Sir Stavros is treated properly, please? The man's a hero, and he should be dressed appropriately at the ceremony. Royal Tailor; Privy Purse."

"Of course, Your Majesty." He didn't make a note; Niko suspected that he already had. The man made a gesture to one of the other scribes, who rose, and beckoned to Andropolounikos, who quickly followed him out of the room.

The king was silent until the two had left, and the door closed behind them. He turned to Fotheringay.

"You're a problem, Sergeant Fotheringay."

Fotheringay had already leaped to attention when the king had started to speak, but he didn't say anything.

"What I'd like to do is give you a knighthood and commission, but . . ." The king shook his head. "But I don't have any reason to believe that you'd make a good officer, not at your age, even with a knighthood to ward off problems of your station, and I can't knight you and send you back to the Fleet as a sergeant, for whatever poor lieutenant you're assigned to having to call you 'Sir Nigel.' " He smiled. "I've served aboard a ship or two, you know. So you get the Order of the Crown for now, and the knighthood comes when you retire. Unless you want to retire right now?"

"No, sir. I mean, 'No, Your Majesty.' "

"No, you meant 'no, sir,' but that's fine. The OC comes

with a pension, you know. You won't need to stay in service. You're eighteen months from your thirty, but that can be waived." He grinned. "I believe I have that authority."

Fotheringay almost shrugged. "It's what I know, Your Majesty."

"Ah. The tailor to his needles, the cobbler to his last, and the marine sergeant to his company. So be it. Report to the Admiralty—Assignments, of course, in . . . ?"

"Three weeks from today, Your Majesty," the scribe supplied. "Need to allow some time to get back from Fallsworth."

". . . three weeks from today. Until then, you're on duty with Intelligence—just as Sir Stavros, is, and just as I'm going to do with Bigglesworth in a minute, and Mr. Sigerson—and the rest of you, as well, over the next weeks. Answer questions thoroughly and honestly, and spend the rest of the time enjoying yourself." The king smiled. "Avoid getting the pox."

"Aye, aye, sir—Your Majesty."

He turned to Sigerson. "You can have Bigglesworth back, Sir Eric, when they're done with him. But he gets the same KHMG and OC that you do, and the same pension that Fotheringay and Kechiroski get. I'd offer you the pension, but I know about your family's affairs, and I'm feeling cheap at the moment. There'll be other work for you—Lord Belknap will be having some words with the College, and your name will be prominently mentioned."

Sigerson nodded. "Of course, Your Majesty."

"And now, if the three of you will excuse me, I think I have some matters to settle with my Order Knights." The king rested his elbow on the arm of his chair, and cupped his hand, and a servant quickly set a surprisingly plain pipe in it, while another produced a lit taper, and the king sat and puffed on his pipe while the other three were led from the room.

"And now, it gets to the hard part. You three." He gave Cully a look. "I know your history—you don't take orders well. My father used to speak of that, every now and then. I'm not sure whether it was in admiration or irritation. Probably both."

"I'm . . . sorry for any distress I've caused the Crown, sire."

"No, you're not. I don't really have time for any of this, but let's have it out, anyway. You and the Abbot General fought over Sir Joshua—Gray—being given the Khan. The Council backed him, which isn't surprising, since for all practical purposes, the Abbot is the Council. You went over his head to Father, and he refused to overrule the Abbot, and when you tried to go over Father's head to Her, She turned you down, too. Not that he was in the habit of hopping about at Her command, but . . . am I missing anything?"

"Rather a lot, Your Majesty," Cully said, evenly. "I think that—"

"That the Khan is too much a burden on Gray, that carrying it, even for less time than he has, is likely to break him." The king shook his head. "Do I have that about right?"

"Yes, Your Majesty. You have it precisely right, Sire."

The king frowned. "I spend men like they were coppers, Cully. I'm not the only one. I remember hearing tales of a man who threw a classful of novices at the late, unlamented Duke of York's troops to get a chance to save my father's life—and my own—and how many of them survived?"

"Two, Your Majesty," Cully said.

"Two." The King nodded. "Would you do it again?"

"I . . . I don't know. I know that it would be my duty, but . . ." He shook his head. "I don't know if I have it in me, not anymore. I've killed enough of my students, Sire. More than enough."

"Then it's just as well that I'm king and you're not, isn't it?" He thumped his hand on the arm of the chair. "It could be my late uncle Daniel sitting here, instead of me, and almost every English duke, most of the earls and probably half the barons eying their own chances, with the Empire and the Dar—and whatever else is going on— playing one off against another until they divided the Crown among them. Bad enough now with what's going on in New England, and worse with the intrigues on the Continent, and . . . well, we'll get to that." He shook his head. "That's not the sort of throne I'd wish on my son; he was an ass to wish it on his." He looked over at Gray. "I treat you as expendable as an archer treats an arrow. Nice if I can recover you and use you again—you're a fine arrow, Sir Joshua, and the combination of you and the Khan is damn near perfect—but I've got other arrows in my quiver. Do you have an objection?"

Gray shook his head. "No, Your Majesty. I . . . I am your servant, and I wish to be of service."

"Very well, then. We'll dispense with that, first off. My uncle William, the Duke of New England, has been responding to my repeated indirect suggestions that he really ought to attend the next Parliament with protestations as to how busy he is minding the affairs of the Duchy.

I don't like that. More to the point, I don't intend to tolerate that. I need to send someone to have words with him—pleasant words, but pleasant words spoken by a man carrying the Khan are better than pleasant words alone. Don't threaten to drag him across the Atlantic by the ear, but make it clear that We do wish to see him. You leave after the knighting ceremony—and, if you possibly can, would you manage to pry passage out of Admiral Dougherty without me having to hear about it again?"

"If possible, Your Majesty," Gray said, slowly, carefully. "That largely depends on the Admiral."

"Mmph. Not a lot of give in you, eh, Sir Joshua?" The king waved his pipestem. "Then again, if there was a lot of give, you'd be less useful of an arrow, eh? Well, never mind that; do what you must. As you will. I know that it's the tradition that Order Knights do for themselves, but you'll need attendants, given your hand. You could pay a sailor to dogrobber for you, of course, but, all in all, I think that I'd rather you be attended by a couple of promising novices from Alton that I've had my eye on. Talk to the Abbot General about that—but not tonight." He gave Niko a quick glance, then shook his head as though dismissing the idea.

"Yes, Your Majesty."

The king turned back to Cully. "And now to you, Sir Cully of Cully's Woode. You're as stubborn a man as I've known, and We are not ungrateful for your service—quite the contrary. But, if you read your Apollodorus, you'll find that after Heracles killed the Nemean lion, he was sent after the Hydra."

"And later, after the wild boar of Erymanthus, the Augean stables, Your Majesty."

The king laughed. "Well, this may stink as much, all in all, but I rather think it's more the Hydra than the stables I'm setting you on. We'll see. I'm . . . concerned about these reports of darklings in the Med, and this whole matter of the live swords, and it's not clear to me, for one, that it's all over." He shook his head. "That bothers me, and I'd have a lot more faith in Crown Intelligence handling it if they'd had some whiff of it happening until, well, it almost happened.

"Not good enough. So I'm appointing a commission. Going to be a tough job to handle it, given that there's going to have to be some cooperation with the Caliphate, and cooperation with the Dar isn't exactly a hallmark of Crown Intelligence, for obvious reasons." The king paused to puff on his pipe. "Whoever is running it is going to have to be able to listen to Intelligence, and to whatever information al-Bakilani forwards along, and tells me when he thinks they're missing something—and then, at the least, comes up with suggestions for how to handle it. Whatever *it* turns out to be."

"I don't think I'd be at all suitable to run it, Sire."

"*You?*" The king snorted. "I've done stupid things, but not that stupid. I'm grabbing Admiral DuPuy to head the commission—I don't know any other military man who's worked so well with the Dar—and I think he's wasted in the backwaters of Malta. Good man, DuPuy." For some reason, the king actually reached down behind himself and seemed to, well, rub his buttocks, before he went on. "No—what I need is somebody to run errands for the chairman of the commission, somebody who isn't afraid to argue with his superior, somebody who has demonstrated that he's willing to come to the king and argue with *him*, if he thinks it necessary. Somebody who can, if necessary, be sent into the lion's mouth, and while it'd be all the better if he can come back out again, that's not essential. Deputy commissioner? A baronet's crest? Both? Neither?" The king shrugged. "The task comes first— the titles later, if ever. It's your task."

"I take it I'm not being asked?"

The king snorted. "No, you're not. 'Service, honor, faith, obedience.' Does that sound even vaguely familiar? You managed to get yourself relieved of active service—even though you seemed to stay rather active over the last ten years; le Duc du Borbonaisse is probably not the only person to notice—but you also managed to swindle Gray, here, into returning you to full status." The king smiled. "So, Sir Cully of Cully's Woode, full status it is. We Pendragons have had a tendency to overuse Order Knights, but I can't think of a better use for you, and can easily think of many worse." He cocked his head to one side. "And I'll convey the . . . good news to the Abbot General—you'd probably gloat."

Cully shook his head. "No, Sire. I wouldn't gloat."

The king had been puffing on his pipe; his snort sent streams of smoke issuing from his nostrils. "See that you don't. You'll be seeing him in two weeks, and you're to be on your best behavior. As is he." He let out a deep sigh. "Which leads me to one sad but inevitable matter, before we solve the problem of you, Sir Niko." The king sat silently for a moment. "We—and I emphasize: *We*—bury Sir David Shanley at Fallsworth Church, two weeks from today. You'll all be in attendance, as will be the other comrades-in-arms who were with him when he died. Knights of the Order will carry his casket, and lay him to his rest; the Archbishop of Canterbury will celebrate the mass, and the King—that would be me—will be the first and the last to put a shovel-full of dirt into his grave."

The undercurrent of humor was gone from the king's voice, and there was no smile on his lips, or in his eyes. "Sir David was, by all accounts, a good and kindly knight, and he died in Our service, and not just in Our service—he was protecting his brothers."

His eyes bore in on Niko's. "Which, by an indirect route, leads me to you, Sir Niko." He frowned. "The sensible thing, perhaps, would be to simply go along with the Abbot General's . . . strong suggestion that your knighthood be revoked, as improvidently granted. That might be a more appealing suggestion if the Abbot General had bothered to take the time to meet with you, and make his own decision that you were not knightly material, rather than just dismissing it out of hand, simply because of who it was that knighted you." He shook his head. "I've met you, and you seem to carry yourself well, and you certainly acquitted yourself well. I'd be inclined to take my chances on you, at least to the extent of giving you a try." He puffed on his pipe, and shook his head. "But you're not trained—an Order Knight isn't just a man who walks around with a sword, be it mundane, or Red, or White. I'd give you a Guard knighthood and a Guard's sword without a second thought, but I don't know if you can be trained, much less up to the standards of the Order, and that presents a problem. Sir Cully, what would happen to him if I sent him to Alton?"

"With or without the Red Sword?"

The King shrugged. "Whichever you think would go easier on him."

"Neither would go easy on him, Your Majesty. He's already served as a Knight of the Order, and the sort of petty jealousy that you see in boys everywhere else isn't absent at Alton. Sent there by royal decree? They'd eat him alive."

Gray nodded.

"Well, speak up, Sir Joshua."

"Father Cully's right; it wouldn't work, Your Majesty. A bunch of fourth-formers having to call a first-former 'Sir Niko?' No. You'd have to dismiss his knighthood, and then—"

"And then he'd be a boy—a man, more than boy— having been sent to Alton after having been found wanting as a knight, and they'd run him right out."

"I can be stubborn, Your Majesty," Niko said, finding himself surprised that he had spoken at all.

Eyes widened at the secretaries' table, but the king just chuckled. "Well, we'll see about that, but not at Alton." He made a beckoning motion with his fingers; two of the servants opened the door, and a man hobbled in, supporting himself mostly on his cane.

Niko was on his feet almost as fast as Cully, and faster than Gray.

"Giscard, Baron Shanley," the king said. "I believe you know Sir Joshua and Sir Cully."

He looked nothing like Bear. Where Bear had been big and wide, the baron was slender, elegant. His father?

"Baron, this is Sir Niko Christofolous," the king said, gesturing at Niko. "He was a friend of your son, David."

"So I understand," the baron said. There was no hint of any emotion in his voice. His eyes tended to blink not quite enough. "I'm pleased to meet you, Sir Niko," he said.

Niko didn't need for Cully to tap him three times on the back. He knew he had to say something.

"I'm honored, Your Lordship. And I'm very sorry about Bear—about Sir David."

Shanley didn't blink. "His brothers of the Order always called him Bear," he said, nodding. His voice was preposterously calm and level. "You will please continue to do so." Shanley looked from Niko to Cully to Gray. "My son—he died honorably?"

"Your son," the king said, before even Cully could open his mouth, "died as honorably as any man ever has, a credit to his family, as well as his Order. You'll have an opportunity to hear the details later, if you must. And, of course, you must." The king paused for a moment. "I have sons, too," he said, quietly, then shook his head and turned back to the knights.

"The baron was in Londinium when word of his son arrived, and I had the sad duty to convey the news to him. He's not always my strongest advocate in Parliament, but, well, we do see eye to eye on most matters, and I've found his counsel of more than a little interest, on more than a few occasions.

"And we have another occasion.

"I've been discussing my . . . quandary with the baron, and he made an interesting suggestion. It seems that Sir Martin Becket is resident at Fallsworth, and the baron's of the opinion that, while Sir Martin is barely able to hobble out of bed, his mind is still sharp, as are his eye and tongue. You've much to learn, young knight, and while some of it can and will be learned sitting at a table with Sir Martin at your elbow, not all of it will be. He won't be able to spar with you, nor teach you how to ride a horse, not directly. But other teachers can be provided, if need be, and they will—with Sir Martin to supervise them." He turned to Cully. "You know Sir Martin. What are the chances he'd approve the boy if he wasn't satisfied with his learning?"

"None, sire." Cully didn't hesitate. "Becket's a hard man."

"You approve?" the king asked.

"It's not my place to approve or disapprove—"

"That's never stopped you before; don't let it stop you now. Do you approve, Sir Cully?"

"Yes, Sire. I do."

"Good. Gray?"

"I've only met him a couple of times." Gray shrugged. "Bear spoke well of him. I'd take Bear's word."

"As would I. As do I." The king nodded. "So, that's what we'll do. We'll see if—and how quickly—Sir Martin can turn you into a knight in reality, and not just in title. Even with all that personal attention, it will take at least two years, probably twice or three times that; shorter if he decides that you can't do it—and you'll find them long years, Sir Niko." He shook his head. "Although you may not find them unbroken years—I can think of several possibilities where you might be useful in the interim, on other matters, and I'd very much like to have you and your Red to hand if any of those possibilities turn real. A bowman needs all sorts of arrows."

Cully nodded.

"I'm so glad you continue to approve, Sir Cully," the king said, with no particular kindliness. "And now that we've settled the matter of Sir Niko, we can—"

"Excuse me."

The king raised an eyebrow, while eyes widened around the room.

"You've not asked Sir Niko, Your Majesty," Cully went on, quietly.

The king just snorted. "I'm not used to asking people, Sir Cully. But perhaps I should make an exception. I wouldn't want to have another unwilling knight of my Order." He turned to Niko. "Speak, Sir Niko. Do you wish to remain in the Order of Crown, Shield, and Dragon?"

Niko's tongue was thick and clumsy in his mouth.

"Go ahead," Cully said. "Speak your mind."

Gray nodded. "Yes, Sir Niko. It's your decision," he said, his face as hard and impassive as a mountain. "No one else's. Not mine, nor Father Cully's, nor even His Majesty's."

"Quite so." The king's words silenced the quiet gasps from his courtiers. The king nodded. "Your choice, Sir Niko?" he asked.

He didn't have the words. Not his own.

But there were others.

" 'Service, honor, faith, and obedience,' " he managed to choke out, feeling his voice become stronger and his words clearer as he spoke. " 'Justice tempered only by mercy; mercy tempered only by justice.' I . . . I can't say that I understand all that, Your Majesty. But I can swear that I'll do my best to live by it." His fingers were trembling; he forced himself not to fasten them on Nadide's hilt.

The king nodded. "And if you're-ever-so-slightly impertinent, I can live with that. Understandable," he said, giving Cully a pointed look, "considering the company you keep." The king sat back in his chair and puffed on his pipe in silence for a moment.

"You're excused," he finally said. "All of you. I've got to break the bad news to the Abbot General that I'm letting Sir Niko keep his knighthood and the sword, at least for now, and then there are other matters that need to be dealt with." He made a flicking motion with his fingers. "I'll see you in Fallsworth, in two weeks."

Baron Shanley's carriage was waiting, and while there was room for all four inside, it was crowded; it hadn't been designed to hold so many, apparently.

Shanley sat facing backward, next to Gray, with Cully and Niko facing them, and before he was even fully seated, he rapped three times with the head of his cane on the wall of the carriage, and it immediately started off, the sudden jerk almost causing him to lose his balance and fall into Niko's lap.

It was possible to see his expression in the light of the flickering lantern set into the carriage wall, but there wasn't much to see.

After a while, he spoke. "I know it's late, but it's a two-day trip to Fallsworth, and . . . and there's nothing for me here, not now. Would you very much mind if we rode through the night? The carriage is stocked, of course, and . . ." His voice trailed off, but into silence, not the sobbing that Niko felt inside.

"No," Cully said, "of course not."

Shanley swallowed once. "And can you tell me about David as we ride?"

It was, fittingly, Gray who spoke. "Yes," he said, quietly. "We shall tell you everything. You've every right to hear it, all of it."

"Yes," Cully said, "But let's start with what His Majesty said: 'He was a good and kindly knight.' "

"Yes," Gray said. "That is, always, where you have to start with Bear." His face might as well have been graven from unmoving stone, his voice was calm and level, and his hand was away from the hilt of the Khan. " 'He was a good and kindly knight,' " Gray repeated, so softly that Niko could barely hear him over the clatter of the carriage.

Niko just nodded, for his heart was in his throat, and he touched his hand to Nadide's hilt.

Niko? Is everything . . . all right?

As much so as it can be, little one. It appears that we're going to be together, at least for now—

Together? You were going to leave me?

Shhh. We're going to tell stories about Bear. Would you like to listen? Or would you rather go to sleep?

I'd rather you sing me the lullabye, but . . .

But what?

He was nice. I liked him.

Epilogue: Her

Only a hero or a fool enters the Arroy without need.
I'm not a hero. The only question is whether I go because
I have the need, or because I am a fool.

Both is most certainly a possibility.

—Cully

The path wasn't the same.

Cully had expected that; it was never the same. That's
one of the ways you could know that you had entered the
Arroy; there was no sharp, bright boundary between the
Arroy Forest and the massive Bedegraine Forest that
encompassed it.

He had left the horses and most of his gear at the village
of Bedegraine itself, at the eastern edge of the forest,
and proceeded on foot, with nothing more than his

rucksack, his two swords, and his walking stick.

Best not to enter the Arroy on horseback, all in all—more than one knight had found his horse chasing something or running from something and had learned the hard way that the Arroy's other name, the Forest of Adventure, was well-deserved, and that adventures tended to be much more pleasant in retrospect than they were to experience. Not that there was any guarantee of immunity by entering it on foot. It was just a little safer, perhaps, and the changes seemed to come a little slower.

The change was like a man aging.

Bedegraine had been, well, as ordinary as a forest could be, which wasn't very ordinary at all. The path had taken him past trees of all shapes and sizes; the ancient towering giants, their tops concealed by the leafy greenery, loomed over smaller ones, sometimes seeming almost parental. The undergrowth was thick in some places and thinner in others; the land rose and fell sometimes so gently that it could have been almost flat, and sometimes so steeply that he had to use his stick for fear of slipping and falling on the detritus that littered the paths. While the trails sometimes ran straight along a ridgeline or across an open glade, most often they twisted down through tree-lined gulleys and folds of land so much that he had to be sure to frequently turn around to catch an occasional glimpse of the sun through the leafy canopy to be sure that he was still heading west.

The woods were always alive with sound. Squirrels chittered in the trees, and occasionally the crashing of something larger moving away quickly, and there were always birds singing off in the distance, becoming silent at his approach. Once, a partridge leaped out of the brush and into the air, its wings thumpthumpthumping together as it panicked into the sky.

Not that there was anything to panic about; his bow had been left behind, and while he fancied that he still could have downed a fleeing bird if he'd been moving through the forest with an arrow nocked, he wasn't, after all, hunting.

Still, more than once, he caught himself falling into a woodsman's pace of step-step-step, then pause, then a few more irregular steps and another pause. Ancient habits died hard, and Cully had to force himself to keep a steady pace. If the regular beat of his footsteps carried through the air or the ground to frighten away a deer, that was fine with him.

It was, he thought, so much like aging that it was almost painful. One moment, you were a young man, full of health and energy and ideals, leaping out of bed in the morning having slept off whatever aches and pains the previous day had brought, and in the blink of an eye that young man had turned old and aching, cursed by a body that seemed to obey your will just a little less each day, each day that was framed by a night of the cursed sleep that brought no rest.

And so it was with the forest, as Bedegraine had given way to Arroy.

As it always had been before, it had all happened too gradually to notice as it was happening, but he had left the last of the young trees behind him a long time ago, and the twisting path was now walled by leafy giants that utterly blocked the sun, giving him not even an occasional bright spear of direct sunlight as respite from the cool dark greenness that was far more chilling than refreshing, despite what had been the warmth of the day. It was almost strangling in its darkness and stillness, where gnarled roots looped up from age-packed earth littered only by rotting leaves, with no undergrowth working its way from the soil up into the wan light.

There was no sound. No animals moving in the absent undergrowth, no whisper of wind or rustle of leaves, nothing save the sound of his own breathing, and the beating of his heart.

A single brown oak leaf fluttered down from high above his head to settle itself silently on the ground; he knelt to pick it up, and was only vaguely surprised that he could hear it crackle as he crushed it in his hand, then wiped his hands down the front of his tunic.

He took off his rucksack and took out the battered brass compass that he had acquired what felt like a lifetime ago aboard the *Wellesley's* cutter, and snapped the cover open, although he knew what he would see, and indeed the needle swung free, refusing to settle on a direction. He put the compass away, and slipped one strap of the rucksack over his shoulder, and continued down the path, forcing his pace to a walk, although he wanted to run— he just wasn't sure in which direction. No, that wasn't true—he wanted to run in both directions at once: to run to Her, and to flee from Her at the same time.

Cully smiled. He should be used to that by now, eh?

He walked on.

There was something always comforting about walking down a trail in the Arroy, knowing that when you reached a fork in the trail, it didn't make a difference which one you took. Life was rarely like that; most of the time, decisions mattered. But not here. Left, right; north, south; the well-trod path or the one so overgrown with brush and thorns that you would have to draw a sword to chop your way through—it didn't make a difference. It would bring him to Her.

Cully always took the easier path. It only made sense, after all, and it was a comfort to be able to do that in good conscience.

Not that even the easier paths were particularly easy; there had been a rain the night before, and the ground was still soft and muddy. Crisscrossed by tracks, as well, although not as many deer tracks as he would have expected.

The trail crested a hillock, then fell into a deep gully; at the bottom a stream twisted its way, the steep banks dead of any growth for easily a dozen feet on either side, save where mammoth ropes of roots from the leafy giants above emerged, looking strangely naked and vulnerable, despite their size.

As good a place as any, and it wasn't likely he'd find a better one. He sat down on an upthrust root and removed his boots, then the rest of his clothing, tying it into a neat bundle; he lashed the bundle and his swords to the rucksack, then carefully heaved the bundle, the scabbarded swords on top, across the stream to the opposite bank.

He stepped onto the sharp stones hidden beneath the icy water. The water went barely knee-deep as he waded across the stream, ignoring the cold as well as he could.

He crouched, shivering, over his rucksack and untied the straps again, removing two thin blankets. The first he spread out on the riverbank, just a step beyond the rushing waters, and set the other, still folded, on it, then removed his fresh clothes from his rucksack and spread them out on the blanket, as well, before untying his bundle of dirty clothes to remove his boots and set them aside on the ground next to the blanket.

From his rucksack he drew a packet of brown paper containing a small bar of soap and a mesh bag, into which he inserted his dirty clothes before tying the neck of the bag tightly, tugging hard against the string to make sure that it would hold.

Holding tightly to one end of the string, he tossed the bag into the water, then pulled it back to shore. He dumped the damp clothes into a pile, and then, one by one, removed each garment and rubbed the soap on it in turn before, thrusting it into the string bag, and retying the bag.

He tucked his bag of dirty clothes under his arm and walked back into the icy water.

Bathing in a stream was always cold, and always tricky; if he lost his grip on his clothing bag, it would be washed away before he could go after it. He solved the problem, as usual, by the simple expedient of kneeling on the bag, pinning it in place until he could be sure that he had the string properly anchored under a sufficiently heavy rock, then backing off downstream, to give him a chance to catch it if he had been wrong.

But the bag held, and he lowered himself all the way into the water to wet himself, then lathered himself down from hair to crotch to toes. Still soapy, he walked to the riverbank to rewrap the soap in the brown paper and toss it to the blanket before ducking once more into the stream to rinse himself off, and retrieve the clothing bag.

He emerged, naked and shivering, and dried himself as best he could with the spare blanket, then wrapped it about his waist while he hung his wet clothes on the upthrust roots to dry.

He had no brush in his rucksack; as usual, he hadn't thought of everything.

Oh, well—he finger-combed his hair into place and dressed as quickly as he could, taking extra pains to make sure that his boots were laced tightly, and his trousers bloused properly, then slipped his swords into place.

He continued down the path, with only the clothes on his body and the swords in his sash. He left everything else behind—particularly his stick. He could retrieve it on his way back. Cully would not hobble his way into Her presence.

The path twisted up the side of the hill, and then down, into a deep valley full of stones.

A long table that would have done justice to the finest home Cully had ever seen stood on the stones, with two places set at one end.

She stood at the head of the table, waiting. Her black hair should have glistened in the bright sunlight, but it there was no gloss to it, and it fell about her shoulders like a shadow. Her skin, too white and pale, should have been burning beneath the light of the noonday sun, but if it bothered her at all, there was no sign of it on her perfect face.

Her lips, red as fresh blood, parted in a smile, revealing the too-even, too-white teeth behind them.

She was in person, as She always was in his memory, inhumanly perfect.

"Hello, Cully," she said. Her voice was as it always had been, as it had to be: half an octave lower than he had expected, sweet as honey, bracing as a cold stream, and as always he didn't know what he wanted to do, although he wanted to do something almost more than he could stand.

So he just stood there.

"My Lady," he finally said. "It's been a long time."

"Yes, it has. Too long. It would have been a few minutes less long if you hadn't dawdled so," She said, with just a touch of petulance.

He shook his head. There was much he was sorry for, but he had no apology for that. "I couldn't appear before You in dirty, tattered clothes, could I?"

"Of course you could—if you thought what I needed was your strong arm and your sword."

He nodded, conceding the point. He would have, and not thought twice about it. "But that is not the case."

"No, not at the moment. I could summon some ravening beast from the Arroy, if you'd like. It could attack me, and you could slay it, and I'd be glad of the effort, if that would make you feel better about your uncombed hair."

"I don't see the need, not at the moment."

"Very well. Will you sit?" She gestured toward the chair next to Hers. "I've been waiting for you. I think you'll find the food to your liking."

"No." He shook his head again. "I don't think so. I'll willingly kneel before You, if You wish, but I don't think I can sit and break bread with You."

She nodded. "As I'd expected." She cleared Her throat. "How was the funeral?"

He didn't know what to say, so he didn't say anything.

" 'Art thou greatly wroth?' " She asked.

"Yes," he said. "Greatly wroth." He nodded. "Among other things."

She smiled sadly. "And the other things would be . . . ?"

She was suddenly before him, close enough to touch, if he dared. His right hand, as though of its own volition, reached out to cup Her cheek, but he held it back, less than an inch from that all-too-perfect skin. She started to take his hand in Hers, but stopped. "I can't touch you if you won't let Me, Cully."

"And I can't let You, Lady." He shook his head. "It's temptation enough to be here. More than enough." His jaw hurt, and he forced himself to unclench it. "But I had to."

"Yes, you did." She nodded. "All of the boys love Me; it's part of what I am, and what all of you are. Most of them let Me go, one way or another. But you, Cully . . . you can't let go of Me any more than I can release you, Cully. Of all of them—and there have been several, over the centuries—you've been . . . different. Special?"

"I'm . . . touched," he said, trying to sound sarcastic, and failing. He was being silly. Of course, She knew that. She knew everything there was to know about him. That was the way of it, and he couldn't have changed that if he wanted to.

"You love them more than you love Me?" She asked.

He shook his head. "It's more complicated than that." He shrugged. "Everything is always more complicated than everything else. It's one of life's great contradictions. You . . . You don't need me, Lady. My lambs do."

She looked at him. If she spoke the truth, that the way he served his lambs was ever and always by leading them to the slaughter, he didn't know what he would do. There was no sin in speaking the truth, and he certainly deserved to hear it, but he didn't think he could bear to hear it from Her lips.

"Oh, Cully, my Cully." She sighed. "And if your choice is them or Me?" she asked.

He could feel the warmth of her cheek, even though he didn't trust himself to touch it. "That decision has long since been made, My Lady," he said.

She tilted her head to one side, and he had to move his hand lest he touch her. "I was hoping that you would reconsider," She said.

"Reconsider?" He laughed. It sounded every bit as forced as it felt. "I reconsider every day. There was a time that I reconsidered every minute. Then every hour. Perhaps in another ten years, it'll be every month."

She smiled. "But you'll not change your mind?"

"Of course not."

"It wasn't a serious question. I know you too well."

"We have different loyalties, My Lady. Yours are to Your family—"

"And yours aren't? He's a good boy, this Mordred; he wears his crown with honor and dignity and wisdom—and more than a little courage. His sons will wear the crown even better, if they're permitted."

Sons? Not son? Was she speaking metaphorically, or was She seeing something about the princes? He would have asked, but she wouldn't have answered. "He's more than that, my Lady. I . . . admire my King. But . . ."

"But he, like Me, will stand by while your lambs go to the slaughterhouse."

"Worse. Much worse. He'll stand by while I send them there, in his service, and if it bothers him—I think it does, and I hope for his sake that it does—he won't so much as lay a cheap salve upon his conscience by letting it show."

"And you, Cully, must let it show; you'll wear your self-inflicted grief like a blood-stained medal pinned not merely to your tunic, but into the flesh of your chest. Does that make it better, or worse? You don't need to answer that."

"If I knew, I would."

"You're a stubborn man, Cully."

"Yes. And I will do what Cully must, as I am, willy-nilly, Sir Cully of Cully's Woode," he said. "It's not a choice, not for me. I'd thought that—but never mind what I'd thought. That matters as little as what I'd hoped."

"Yes."

"Would you have me otherwise, my Lady?"

"No." She shook her head, and then She sighed, and She nodded. "Very well; have it your way." She sniffed. "I'll send for the king, and ask him to relieve Gray of his Red Sword, if you wish." She held up a hand. "I'll make him listen, Cully. From his viewpoint, yes, Gray and the Khan are a fine arrow, but he does, as he's said, have others."

He closed his eyes. She was tempting him with the impossible. But even the impossible wasn't enough. "And you'll relieve Gray of his willingness to be damned for the carrying of it? You'll grant my—you'll grant the boy repentance and hope?"

If She could do that . . . no.

"Cully," She said, "you ask too much."

He opened his eyes. "Yes. I do. But it's no more than I must, Lady."

"I can't do that—it's not a matter of I-won't, but I-can't. But if I did grant that? If I *could* grant that? What more would you demand?"

"I don't know." He shrugged. "I don't know much, not anymore."

"Yes." She nodded. "So: we find ourselves still in opposite camps, with no room for compromise, and my vision of necessity pitted against your resolve, with neither breaking."

He didn't quite stop himself from sighing. "One thing we have in common, Lady, is that neither of us has ever been much for compromise." He let his calloused hand rest on Her perfect cheek, and the hand burned with a fire that was as much of pleasure as of pain. He had done harder things than let that hand drop down to his side, although he couldn't remember when.

But it didn't matter. He was, after all, despite what were his wishes, despite what had been his hopes, despite what should have been his prayers, himself. Just as She was the Queen of Air and Darkness, and neither wishes nor prayers could touch that, he was Sir Cully of Cully's Woode, sworn and sealed knight of the Order, and he would be what he must be, and do what he must do.

And he would feel what he must feel, as well.

"But, still, I remain, in my own way," he said, "Your faithful and loving servant, and whatever else I've been."

"Yes," She said. "You are that. Your lambs come first, which is, perhaps, not as it should be, or, possibly, as either of us would have it, but that is as it is, my Cully. And do I remain your Lady, Sir Cully?"

"Of course." He nodded. "Always, Morgaine." He cocked his head to one side. He smiled. "It couldn't be otherwise, could it?"

She smiled back, and arched an eyebrow. " 'Not while I breathe'?"

"Yes."

And then he turned and walked away, the stones hard beneath his boots.

The following is an excerpt from:

KNIGHT MOVES

by

Joel Rosenberg

available from Baen Books
December 2006
hardcover

Prologue
The Knights and the Night

At least his feet had started hurting again.

It could have been worse, Edward thought. Possibly. No: definitely. No matter how bad things were, they could always get worse. That was a simple fact of life, and he should be used to that by now, particularly on this cold, horrid night.

Pain was certainly safer than the numbness that had overtaken them the last time that Fat Harold had called for a break. Cold was dangerous; numbness was the beginning of the end.

It shouldn't be very far to go, he thought, although every step seemed to last forever, from the moment when he lifted a boot to when he set it down again, and the long, frightening moment after, until when he was confident enough that his forward foot could support him to dare lifting the one behind.

There was no such thing as steady footing on the frozen

trail; steady enough would have to serve, even though that kept their pace maddeningly slow, as rushing would be lethal.

It was, he thought, the night as much as the cold, although the cold was bad enough.

Edward didn't care for nights, generally. And particularly not for this one.

Didn't like cold, either.

The exposed tip of his nose had only stopped being numb and started being painful again when he had taken off a glove for a few moments, and he had warmed it with his hand, and then shoved his freezing hand back into what little warmth was left in the glove, and flexed his fingers, hard, until the pain returned as the blood began to flow there.

Pain was safe; numbness was the onset of frostbite.

The cold was going to get worse before it got better, with morning. He had hoped they would have reached the shack by now, but he had been hoping that for the past hour, or more. Stopping for the rest of the night was certainly possible, if a man didn't mind freezing to death.

There was a storm coming; far to the north, the clouds glowed with the dimming light of the moon, as they massed to overcome it. Darkness would triumph over the weak light, yes, but only until morning.

That was reassuring, he decided. Saint Albert of Leeds had written that only the impious would doubt that darkness would eventually fall to the light, and Edward de Vigny flattered himself that whatever his limitations and failings, he was not an impious man.

But piety didn't make him one whit warmer.

He picked his way carefully up the rocky path, trusting

to his balance more than the hobnails of his heavy boots, or to Fat Harold's ability to catch him if he fell backward. He had already fallen half a dozen times, but each time had managed to fall forward, which, he was sure, had bruised at least a couple of ribs, and left a cut over his left eye that had come damnably close to blinding him.

Better to fall forward than falling over backward, when his swords where strapped to his pack—even if he didn't tumble down the path, with Fat Harold watching helplessly.

Behind him, Fat Harold grunted. "Hope we can find the shelter before it hits," he said. "I'm not that fond of the cold, either, Butcher."

As Edward hadn't ever gotten used to, Fat Harold spoke too loudly, but his words wouldn't carry very far, not over the howling of he wind. And, besides, even if the distant wolves did hear it, they weren't very likely prey. Nor, for that matter, would even a pack of such find a pair of Order Knights to be soft prey, either.

Fat Harold kept complaining, and Edward would have ignored him, if he could.

But he couldn't. God, in his infinite mercy, had not given the ears lids in the way that he had protected the eyes, and Edward's hands were occupied, and unable to cover them.

Fat Harold went on, and on and on: it was too cold; it was too high an altitude; they should have waited in the village; there was more than a hundred miles left on this long patrol anyway, and while, yes, they might need to take a side trip, they could do it in the daylight.

Edward wished Harold would just keep quiet. For a knight of the Order, Fat Harold—more formally, Sir

Harold O'Reilly, like Edward, a knight of the Order of Crown, Shield, and Dragon—was far too much of a whiner.

He would have guessed that that was why Fat Harold had never been raised in estate to White or Red, but Sir Guy of Orkney—who, so Sir Guy apparently thought, was far too dignified to have a nickname—was a notorious whiner and complainer, something that Fat Harold was known to hold forth on at great length, on the rare occasions that Edward upbraided him, as though that was the key to such a raise in estate.

Edward thought it rather unlikely.

As to Edward, well, he would of course accept the honor if it was offered, but the live swords were rare and— at least until recently—thought to be utterly irreplaceable, and he would serve as best he could until and unless the Abbot and the Council decided that he was worthy.

His present status was hardly an indignity, after all, the present moment aside, which—as bloody uncomfortable as it was—was far more discomfort than indignity. He was, after all, a knight of the Order of Crown, Shield, and Dragon—and that was quite a rise in estate from that of the son of a butcher, eh?

Nothing to be ashamed about, and in fact, the sin of pride was a temptation.

He didn't doubt for a moment that he had earned fully his swords, but many men in this life failed to get what they earned, after all.

Even most Order Knights who made it to retirement, and the Reserve List, never went Red or White. If Edward was a jealous sort of man, it would have bothered him that when most Englishmen thought of Order Knights, they thought of the Reds and Whites, and often seemed to somehow assume that there was something lacking with the majority of Order Knights who were never entrusted—or burdened, depending on whom you listened to, among other things—with a live sword.

When was the last time you heard a ballad about an Order Knight who wasn't a Red or White? Well, yes, there were all the songs and stories and talkes of the Final Battle at Bedegraine, but that was in the old days, long before the Age of Crisis, long before the live swords.

Then again, some song about Sir Edward freezing his toes off in this godforsaken place probably wouldn't be all that interesting, anyway. He tried to imagine some ditty—"he froze, he froze, he froze, and then he froze"— but couldn't come up with anything but a light tune that didn't either warm him or fit the words.

But the oath wasn't "for glory," after all. It was: "Service, honor, faith, obedience. Justice tempered only by mercy; mercy tempered only by justice."

In the meantime, while the Reds and the Whites served on His Own, or sent—as Gray had been—to *have words* with important nobility or on missions almost as glamorous, the likes of the Butcher and Fat Harold got to make the rounds in what wasn't quite the most godforsaken territory over which the Crown held domain.

Quite.

But it was service, and obedience, and there was honor in that, and he would just have to have faith that he was being useful.

And he was, of course.

For one thing, it was a good thing for Crown subjects

to see an Order Knight every now and then, and remember that whatever duke or earl or baron or headman or margrave that they mostly thought of themselves as serving, they were in reality His Majesty's subjects, and that the arm of the Pendragon King was long, and that the fist at the end of that arm every bit as lethal as necessary.

And, besides, with the Zone so close, and with rumors of more darklings south of Aba-Paluoja, them walking the northern and eastern boundaries, and being sure to bless the ground, was important, and something that had to be done by a priest.

The country was rough enough that if the priest wasn't to be regularly expended, it had to be done by a priest who was also skilled with weapons, and all the better if the priest was an Order Knight, who would rarely find himself having to prove those skills to any sane man.

Darklings and other things from the Zone couldn't cross running water or hallowed ground—not without assistance, at least—and making sure that they never had a route to the south was as important to the Crown here as it was to the Empire, to the east.

Not enough rivers, and those too often frozen.

Yes, the blessings came from Him, but the unholy had their ways, too—defiling ground wasn't particularly difficult, if you didn't give a fig for your immortal soul.

It was a matter of intention—deconsecrating a church's sanctuary, so that it could, say, become a school, was a matter of proper intention every bit as much as the ritual, and would no more endanger your immortal soul than would building a school rather than a church on the same plot of land in the first place.

Defilement was another matter; the hezmoni used to

rape Christian women with wine bottles—after, of course, raping them in other ways—then drink the wine and piss on the ground, which had seemed to serve.

There were, of course, other, less dramatic ways to accomplish the same effect.

The wind picked up, and off in the distance, a lone wolf howled his complaint over the cold, a complaint that Edward was sure that Fat Harold would have shared aloud, if he could have figured out a way to do so while puffing his way along behind Edward.

Edward had gotten awfully tired of Fat Harold's complaining, but even without that—even without having to trudge up the side of the mountain—he wouldn't have cared for this night in any case.

He had never liked the cold. Sir Edward de Vigny, despite his name, was no northerner. In fact, he was from Pinet in the south of Borbonaisse, a small village whose minimal fame was far overshadowed by that of nearby M•rifons. And, like M•rifons, Pinet was only a mile or so off the warm waters of the Bassin de Thau.

The only thing he had in common with the northern, noble Hautmont family of the same name *was* the name, and that was of dubious origin, and the one winter he had spent near Hautmont had been far too cold for his taste, colder than English winters, although not nearly as wet and damp.

This was worse.

Spring, *pfah*.

He would have spit if he hadn't thought that the spittle would likely freeze and shatter on the rocks.

What passed as a pitiful excuse for a spring night near Hostikka was no spring at all, and not just because it was more than six hundred miles to the north and east of the warm waters and gentle winds of the Mediterranean. Blame it on the cold waters of the sea to south, or the one to the west, or, if you liked, you could blame it on the Zone.

But blame on whatever cause, there was one thing certain: it was just too damned cold.

At least the fur leggings and long bearskin coat he wore over his Order robes kept the worst of it out, although whenever the wind picked up, the sleeves of the coat seemed to act like funnels for the wind, and would have chilled him to the bone if his pack's straps hadn't been so tight about his shoulders, preventing it from piercing him quite to the core.

For the moment. He didn't worry about his extremities, as long as they hurt—but his core was awfully cold as it was, and his testicles were trying to retreat up into his body.

He allowed himself a quick look behind, past where Fat Harold was huffing and puffing.

Half a mile below and miles further than that back, the lights in the village burned invitingly, promising warmth and food, and warmth. Their reception had been more than acceptable, which was just as well, for all concerned, despite some apparent nervousness about the presence of two Order knights, and constant glances at the their swords, with the obvious unvoiced question never quite asked, and never answered at all.

The talk of the town was, of course, as it was all across the region, that the Blue Skolt Same were very late in their spring migration through, and should have been through sometime in York—a month which the locals irritating still called "Huhtikuu," although they spoke English well enough, albeit a formal, Church English—and here it was Marsey, already, or "Toukokuu," as they had it.

In spring, the locals would be trading with the Skolts for the leather and bone goods that the Skolts made during the winter; in the fall, it would be fattened reindeer. A good pair of Skolt Same boots were highly prized, and some thought that there was perhaps a little magic in their construction, rather than just careful sewing of the reindeer hide.

But there was no sign of the Skolt Same.

In a more civilized country, the local barons or earls would have already sent out search parties, but the Duke of Suomaland could barely be bothered to send taxmen out in the fall of the year, and he kept his subordinate earls—really minor court barons, in all but titles—close to him in Helsinki, as though afraid of revolt, although it passed human understanding as to why anybody would want to seize control of this misbegotten frozen wasteland.

So, unsurprisingly, the task fell to Order Knights. It was part of what their patrol was, more or less.

Most likely, the Blue Skolts had simply taken an alternate route to the south. Yes, they lived near enough Zone as it was, but . . .

Well, they'd see.

"I still think we should have waited until morning," Fat Harold wheezed.

Yes, they could have waited until morning, and instead of climbing in the dark to the old shack at the top of the ridge, they would have been climbing in the light— through the storm—and reached the shack after dark.

At least, this way, they might have a chance for a distant view from the top in the morning, maybe even before the storm broke.

It shouldn't be much longer, and—

Ah.

He had been told by the village headman that it would be impossible to miss the cabin, and for once, a local had spoken truthfully, if only by accident.

The twisted pine that marked the crest of the hill really did look like the letter zed, even against the dark sky, and shelter was now just minutes away.

Whatever you could say ill about Fat Harold—and there was much that you could—he was a fast hand with a fire kit, and even if the headman had lied about the shack being faithfully restocked with wood in what passed for summer hereabouts, the hillside was littered with trees that had literally exploded during the worst of winter, and Fat Harold could make a good fire out of even frozen, wet wood, if necessary using a splash of the lamp oil to get it started.

And then there was the flask of good Scots whiskey in Edward's pack, wrapped with every bit as much care as the lantern, and for much the same reason. Once they had a fire going, it would warm him inside as much, or more than the fire would his outside.

He forced himself not to quicken his pace. It was always best to approach such things slowly, and not just because it would be a sad irony if, just as he was about to reach his goal, he tumbled back down the mountainside. It was, after all, not impossible that the shack would be occupied.

Not that a sane man would consider wintering up here,

but Sir Edward had found hermits in crazier places, if not much crazier.

And there was always a chance that a bear had decided to make the shack his den for the winter, and that the bear would have sense enough to sleep through what the locals lightheartedly thought of as spring.

But, no. In the harsh moonlight, the drifted snow in front of the cabin was unbroken and unmarked, and both the door and the roof appeared to be intact. If there was anybody inside, they had been inside since the last snowfall, and with the lack of fire, that would mean Edward and Fat Harold would find either vacancy and shelter, or frozen bodies . . . and shelter, too.

One thing you could say for building by laying stone upon stone is that it didn't rot—not that much of anything would rot in this horrid climate, not when it could just freeze solid instead.

The door, of course, was frozen shut, but it only took a couple of kicks for Fat Harold to break the ice loose, and knock it down—thankfully, without breaking the wood, which would have meant that they'd have had to fix the door in the morning.

"Turn around for a moment," Fat Harold said. For such a normally sluggardly man, he was preposterously quick in getting the lantern out of Edward's pack, and he knelt in the lee of the side of the hut with his fire kit, lighting it. Fat Harold was not quite as clumsy as he looked; he managed to manipulate the fire kit even with his gloves on, something that Edward couldn't have done.

"Give me ten minutes, Butcher," he said, his fat face grinning in the light of the lantern, "just ten bloody minutes, and I'll have a good fire going that will warm you, from toe to head, until you complain of the heat, and—"

His breath caught in his throat, and dropped the lantern to the ground, careless of the way that it shattered, sending flaming oil scattering about.

Silently, without even a whisper where their robes dragged upon the snow and dirt, two dark shapes glided slowly out of the hut.

The priest had promised. He had *sworn* that he had said the appropriate blessings at not only the four corners of the village, but had renewed the blessings from one end of the county to the other, including making the pilgrimage up here. Prayer could not kill such as these, but they couldn't cross water, or hallowed ground, not without help.

But they were here. Darklings, they were called. Were they really demons from Hell? Edward didn't know. What he knew about them was bad enough.

Here, so close to the Zone, they didn't even have weapons—they were themselves the weapon. Their touch would burn both body and soul, and while a live sword could kill them, there was little else in the world that could, not here. And certainly not the mundane swords that the two knights carried.

Fat Harold didn't even try to draw his swords from where they were strapped to his back; there was no time for that. Say what you would about him, Fat Harold was neither a fool nor a coward; they would be upon him before he could so much as turn and take a step.

He leaped at the darklings, his only words a shouted "Run, Butcher, for the love of God, *run*—" and his strangled screams were awful in the night.

It was Edward's only chance. An exorcism, this close

to the Zone, couldn't kill them—but it could repel them.

All he had to do was run down the trail, run away, while the darklings finished with Fat Harold, and try the exorcism.

He could, at the least, flee—it wouldn't be cowardice; this should be reported.

No.

He was, after all, a knight of the Order of Crown, Shield, and Dragon; an emissary of light, not dark. The light was supposed to triumph over the dark, but there were no guarantees in this world.

Save one: what he would do was in his own hands, and those were the hands of an Order Knight, who would not abandon his companion.

How it would turn out would be in the Hands of God. He drew his swords and tossed his scabbards aside. He would make the sign of the Cross with his swords . . . and they had other uses, as well.

"I exorcise thee, thou foul and unclean spirit, in the name of God the Father Almighty, and in the name—"

Edward de Vigney died, his exorcism turned to screams in his own throat.

He never did see the plain beyond, where the bones of the Blue Skolt and their reindeer herd lay, still frozen on the hard ground.

—end excerpt—

**from *Knight Moves*
available in hardcover,
December 2006**

The following is an excerpt from:

HELL'S GATE

BY

DAVID WEBER

& LINDA EVANS

Available from Baen Books

November 2006

hardcover

Chapter One

The tall noncom could have stepped straight out of a recruiting poster. His fair hair and height were a legacy from his North Shaloman ancestors, but he was far, far away—a universe away—from their steep cliffs and icy fjords. His jungle camo fatigues were starched and ironed to razor-sharp creases as he stood on the crude, muddy landing ground with his back to the looming hole of the portal. His immaculate uniform looked almost as bizarrely out of place against the backdrop of the hacked-out jungle clearing as the autumn-kissed red and gold of the forest giants beyond the portal, and he seemed impervious to the swamp-spawned insects zinging about his ears. He wore the shoulder patch of the Second Andaran Temporal Scouts, and the traces of gray at his temples went perfectly with the experience lines etched into his hard, bronzed face.

He gazed up into the painfully bright afternoon sky, blue-gray eyes slitted against the westering sun, with his helmet tucked into the crook of his left elbow and his right thumb hooked into the leather sling of the dragoon arbalest slung over his shoulder. He'd been standing there in the blistering heat for the better part of half an hour, yet he seemed unaware of it. In fact, he didn't even seem to be perspiring, although that had to be an illusion.

He also seemed prepared to stand there for the next week or so, if that was what it took. But then, finally, a black dot appeared against the cloudless blue, and his nostrils flared as he inhaled in satisfaction.

He watched the dot sweep steadily closer, losing altitude as it came, then lifted his helmet and settled it onto his head. He bent his neck, shielding his eyes with his left hand as the dragon back-winged in to a landing. Bits of debris flew on the sudden wind generated by the mighty beast's iridescent-scaled wings, and the noncom waited until the last twigs had pattered back to the ground before he lowered his hand and straightened once more.

The dragon's arrival was a sign of just how inaccessible this forward post actually was. In fact, it was just over seven hundred and twenty miles from the coastal base, in what would have been the swamps of the Kingdom of Farshal in northeastern Hilmar back home. Those were some pretty inhospitable miles, and the mud here was just as gluey as the genuine Hilmaran article, so aerial transport was the only real practical way in at the moment. The noncom himself had arrived back at the post via the regular transport dragon flight less than forty-eight hours earlier, and as he'd surveyed the muck below, he'd been struck by just how miserable it would have been to slog through it on foot. How anyone was going to properly exploit a portal in the middle of this godforsaken swamp was more than he could say, but he didn't doubt that the Union Trans-Temporal Transit Authority would find a way. The UTTTA had the best engineers in the universe—in *several* universes, for that matter—and plenty of experience with portals in terrain even less prepossessing than this.

Probably less prepossessing, anyway.

The dragon went obediently to its knees at the urging of its pilot, and a single passenger swung down the boarding harness strapped about the beast's shoulders. The newcomer was dark-haired, dark-eyed, and even taller than the noncom, although much younger, and each point of his collar bore the single silver shield of a commander of one hundred. Like the noncom, he wore the shoulder flash of the 2nd ATS, and the name "Olderhan, Jasak" was stenciled above his breast pocket. He said something to the dragon's pilot, then strode quickly across the mucky ground towards the waiting one-man welcoming committee.

"Sir!" The noncom snapped to attention and saluted sharply. "Welcome back to this shithole, *Sir!*" he barked.

"Why, thank you, Chief Sword Threbuch," the officer said amiably, tossing off a far more casual salute in response. Then he extended his right hand and gripped the older man's hand firmly. "I trust the Powers That Be have a suitable reason for dragging me back here, Otwal," he said dryly, and the noncom smiled.

"I wish they hadn't—dragged you back, that is, Sir— but I think you may forgive them in the end," he said. "I'm sort of surprised they managed to catch you, though.

I figured you'd be well on your way back to Garth Showma by now."

"So did I," Hundred Olderhan replied wryly. He shook his head. "Unfortunately, Hundred Thalmayr seems to've gotten himself delayed in transit somewhere along the way, and Magister Halathyn was quick enough off the mark to catch me before he got here. If the magister had only waited another couple of days for Thalmayr to get here to relieve me, I'd have been aboard ship and far enough out to sea to get away clean."

"Sorry about that, Sir." The chief sword grinned. "I hope you'll tell the Five Thousand I *tried* to get you home for your birthday."

"Oh, Father will forgive you, Otwal," Jasak assured him. "*Mother*, now . . ."

"Please, Sir!" The chief sword shivered dramatically. "I still remember what your lady mother had to say to me when I got the Five Thousand home late for their anniversary."

"According to Father, you did well to get him home at all," the hundred said, and the chief sword shrugged.

"The Five Thousand was too tough for any jaguar to eat, Sir. All I did was stop the bleeding."

"Most he could have expected out of you after he was stupid enough to step right on top of it." The chief sword gave the younger man a sharp look, and the hundred chuckled. "That's the way *Father* describes it, Otwal. I promise you I'm not being guilty of filial disrespect."

"As the Hundred says," the chief sword agreed.

"But since our lords and masters appear to have seen fit to make me miss my birthday, suppose you tell me exactly what we have here, Chief Sword." The hundred's voice was much crisper, his brown eyes intent, and the chief sword came back to a position midway between stand easy and parade rest.

"Sir, I'm afraid you'll need to ask Magister Halathyn for the details. All I know is that he says the potential tests on this portal's field strength indicate that there's at least one more in close proximity. A big one."

"How big?" Jasak asked, his eyes narrowing.

"I don't really know, Sir," Threbuch replied. "I don't think Magister Halathyn does yet, for that matter. But he was muttering something about a class eight."

Sir Jasak Olderhan's eyebrows rose, and he whistled silently. The largest trans-temporal portal so far charted was the Selkara Portal, and it was only a class seven. If Magister Halathyn had, indeed, detected a class *eight*, then this muddy, swampy hunk of jungle was about to become very valuable real estate.

"In that case, Chief Sword," he said mildly after a moment, "I suppose you'd better get me to Magister Halathyn."

Halathyn vos Dulainah was very erect, very dark-skinned, and very silver-haired, with a wiry build which was finally beginning to verge on frail. Jasak wasn't certain, but he strongly suspected that the old man was well past the age at which Authority regs mandated the retirement of the Gifted from active fieldwork. Not that anyone was likely to tell Magister Halathyn that. He'd been a law unto himself for decades and the UTTTA's crown jewel ever since he'd left the Mythal Falls Academy twenty years before, and he took an undisguised, almost childlike delight in telling his nominal superiors where they could stuff their regulations.

He hadn't told Jasak exactly why he was out here in the middle of this mud and bug-infested swamp, nor why Magister Gadrial Kelbryan, his second-in-command at the Garth Showma Institute, had followed him out here. He'd insisted with a bland-faced innocence which could not have been bettered by a twelve-year-old caught with his hand actually in the cookie jar, that he was "on vacation." He certainly had the clout within the UTTTA to commandeer transportation for his own amusement if that was what he really wanted, but Jasak suspected he was actually engaged in some sort of undisclosed research. Not that Magister Halathyn was going to admit it. He was too delighted by the opportunity to be mysterious to waste it.

He was also, as his complexion and the "vos" in front of his surname proclaimed, both a Mythalan and a member of the *shakira* caste. As a rule, Jasak Olderhan was less than fond of Mythalans . . . and considerably less fond than that of the *shakira*. But Magister Halathyn was the exception to that rule as he was to so many others.

The magister looked up as Chief Sword Threbuch followed Jasak into his tent, the heels of their boots loud on its raised wooden flooring. He tapped his stylus on the crystal display in front of him, freezing his notes and the calculations he'd been performing, and smiled at the hundred over the glassy sphere.

"And how is my second-favorite crude barbarian?" he inquired in genial Andaran.

"As unlettered and impatient as ever, Sir," Jasak replied, in Mythalan, with an answering smile. The old magister chuckled appreciatively and extended his hand for a welcoming shake. Then he cocked his canvas camp chair back at a comfortable, teetering angle and waved for Jasak to seat himself in the matching chair on the far side of his worktable.

"Seriously, Jasak," he said as the younger man obeyed the unspoken command, "I apologize for yanking you back here. I know how hard it was for you to get leave for your birthday in the first place, and I know your parents must have been looking forward to seeing you. But I thought you'd want to be here for this one. And, frankly, with all due respect to Hundred Thalmayr, I'm not sorry he was delayed. All things being equal, I'd prefer to have *you* in charge just a little longer."

Jasak stopped his grimace before it ever reached his expression, but it wasn't the easiest thing he'd ever done. Although he genuinely had been looking forward to spending his birthday at home in Garth Showma for the first time in over six years, he *hadn't* been looking forward to handing "his" company over to Hadrign Thalmayr, even temporarily. Partly because of his jealously possessive pride in Charlie Company, but also because Thalmayr—who was senior to him—had only transferred into the Scouts seventeen months ago. From his record, he was a perfectly competent infantry officer, but Jasak hadn't been impressed with the older man's mental flexibility the few times they'd met before Jasak himself had been forward-deployed. And it was pretty clear his previous line infantry experience had left him firmly imbued with the sort of by-the-book mentality the Temporal Scouts worked very hard to eradicate.

Which wasn't something he could discuss with a civilian, even one he respected as deeply as he did Magister Halathyn.

"The chief sword said something about a class eight," he said instead, his tone making the statement a question, and Magister Halathyn nodded soberly.

"Unless Gadrial and I are badly mistaken," he said, waving a hand at the letters and esoteric formulae glittering in the water-clear heart of his crystal, "it's *at least* a class eight. Actually, I suspect it may be even larger."

Jasak sat back in his chair, regarding the old man's lined face intently. Had it been anyone else, he would have been inclined to dismiss the preposterous claim as pure, rampant speculation. But Magister Halathyn wasn't given to speculation.

"If you're right about that, Sir," the hundred said after a moment, "this entire transit chain may just have become a lot more important to the Authority."

"It may," Magister Halathyn agreed. "Then again, it may not." He grimaced. "Whatever size this portal may be—" he tapped the crystal containing his notes "—*that* portal—" he pointed out through the open fly of his tent at the peculiar hole in the universe which loomed enormously beyond the muddy clearing's western perimeter "—is only a class three. That's going to bottleneck anything coming through from our putative class eight. Not to mention the fact that we're at the end of a ridiculously inconvenient chain at the moment."

"I suppose that depends in part on how far your new portal is from the other side of this one," Jasak pointed out. "The terrain between here and the coast may suck, but it's only seven hundred miles."

"Seven hundred and nineteen-point-three miles," Magister Halathyn corrected with a crooked smile.

"All right, Sir." Jasak accepted the correction with a

smile of his own. "That's still a ridiculously short haul compared to most of the portal connections I can think of. And if this new portal of yours is within relatively close proximity to our class three, we're talking about a twofer."

"That really is a remarkably uncouth way to describe a spatially congruent trans-temporal transfer zone," Halathyn said severely.

"I'm just a naturally uncouth sort of fellow, Sir," Jasak agreed cheerfully. "But however you slice it, it's still a two-for-one."

"Yes, it is," Halathyn acknowledged. "Assuming our calculations are sound, of course. In fact, if this new portal is as large as I think it is, and as closely associated with our portal here, I think it's entirely possible that we're looking at a cluster."

Despite all of the magister's many years of discipline, his eyes gleamed, and he couldn't quite keep the excitement out of his voice. Not that Jasak blamed him for that. A portal cluster . . . In the better part of two centuries of exploration, UTTTA's survey teams had located only one true cluster, the Zholhara Cluster. Doubletons were the rule—indeed, only sixteen triples had ever been found, which was a rate of less than one in ten. But a cluster like Zholhara was of literally incalculable value.

This far out—they were at the very end of the Lamia Chain, well over three months' travel from Arcana, even for someone who could claim transport dragon priority for the entire trip—even a cluster would take years to fully develop. Lamia, with over twenty portals, was already a huge prize. But if Magister Halathyn was correct, the entire transit chain was about to become even more valuable . . . and receive the highest development priority UTTTA could assign.

"Of course," Magister Halathyn continued in the tone of a man forcing himself to keep his enthusiasm in check, "we don't know where this supposed portal of mine connects. It could be the middle of the Great Ransaran Desert. Or an island in the middle of the Western Ocean, like Rycarh Outbound. Or the exact center of the polar ice cap."

"Or it could be a couple of thousand feet up in thin air, which would make for something of a nasty first step," Jasak agreed. "But I suppose we'd better go find it if we really want to know, shouldn't we?"

"My sentiments exactly," the magister agreed, and the hundred looked at the chief sword.

"How soon can we move out on the magister's heading, Chief Sword?"

"I'm afraid the Hundred would have to ask Fifty Garlath about that," Threbuch replied with absolutely no inflection, and this time Jasak did grimace. The tonelessness of the chief sword's voice shouted his opinion (among other things) of Commander of Fifty Shevan Garlath as an officer of the Union of Arcana. Unfortunately, Sir Jasak Olderhan's opinion exactly matched that of his company's senior noncommissioned officer.

"If the Hundred will recall," the chief sword continued even more tonelessly, "his last decision before his own departure was to authorize Third Platoon's R and R. That leaves Fifty Garlath as the SO here at the base camp."

Jasak winced internally as Threbuch tactfully (sort of) reminded him that leaving Garlath out here at the ass-end of nowhere had been his own idea. Which had seemed like a good one at the time, even if it had been a little petty of him. No, more than a little petty. Quite a bit more, if he wanted to be honest. Chief Sword Threbuch hadn't exactly protested at the time, but his expression had suggested his opinion of the decision. Not because he disagreed that Fifty Therman Ulthar and his men had earned their R&R, but because Shevan Garlath was arguably the most incompetent platoon commander in the entire brigade. Leaving him in charge of anything more complicated than a hot cider stand was not, in the chief sword's considered opinion, a Good Idea.

"We'd have to recall Fifty Ulthar's platoon from the coast, if you want to use him, Sir," the chief sword added, driving home the implied reprimand with exquisite tact.

Jasak was tempted to point out that Magister Halathyn had already dragged *him* back from the company's main CP at the coastal enclave, so there was really no reason *he* shouldn't recall Fifty Ulthar. Except, of course, that he couldn't. First, because doing so would require him to acknowledge to the man who'd been his father's first squad lance that he'd made a mistake. Both of them might *know* he had, but he was damned if he was going to *admit* it.

But second, and far more important, was the patronage system which permeated the Arcanan Army, because patronage was the only thing that kept Garlath in uniform. Not even that had been enough to get him promoted, but it was more than enough to ensure that his sponsors would ask pointed questions if Jasak went that far out of his way to invite another fifty to replace him on what promised to be quite possibly the most important portal exploration on record. If Magister Halathyn's estimates were remotely near correct, this was the sort of operation that got an officer noticed.

Which, in Jasak's opinion, was an even stronger argument in favor of handing it to a competent junior officer who didn't have any patrons . . . and whose probable promotion would actually have a beneficial effect on the Army. But—

"All right, Chief Sword," he sighed. "My respects to Fifty Garlath, and I want his platoon ready to move out at first light tomorrow."

The weather was much cooler on the other side of the base portal. Although it was only one hour earlier in the local day, it had been mid-afternoon—despite Jasak's best efforts—before Commander of Fifty Garlath's First Platoon had been ready to leave base camp and step through the immaterial interface between Hilmaran swamp and subarctic Andara in a single stride. The portal's outbound side was located smack on top of the Great Andaran Lakes, five thousand miles north of their departure portal, in what should have been the Kingdom of Lokan. In fact, it was on the narrow neck of land which separated Hammerfell Lake and White Mist Lake from Queen Kalthra's Lake. It might be only one hour east of the base camp, but the difference in latitude meant that single step had moved them from sweltering early summer heat into the crispness of autumn.

Jasak had been raised on his family's estates on New Arcana, less than eighty miles from the very spot at which they emerged, but New Arcana had been settled for the better part of two centuries. The bones of the Earth were the same, and the cool, leaf-painted air of a northern fall was a familiar and welcome relief from the base camp's smothering humidity, but the towering giants of the primordial forest verged on the overpowering even for him.

For Fifty Garlath, who had been raised on the endless grasslands of Yanko, the restricted sightlines and dense forest canopy were far worse than that. Hundred Olderhan, CO of Charlie Company, First Battalion, First Regiment, Second Andaran Temporal Scouts, couldn't very well take one of his platoon commanders to task in front of his subordinates for being an old woman, but Sir Jasak Olderhan felt an almost overpowering urge to kick Garlath in the ass.

He mastered the temptation sternly, but it wasn't easy, even for someone as disciplined as he was. Garlath was *supposed* to be a temporal scout, after all. That meant he was supposed to take the abrupt changes in climate trans-temporal travel imposed in stride. It also meant he was supposed to be confident in the face of the unknown, well versed in movement under all sorts of conditions and in all sorts of terrain. He was *not* supposed to be so obviously intimidated by endless square miles of trees.

Jasak turned away from his troopers to distract himself (and his mounting frustration) while Garlath tried to get his command squared away. He stood with his back to the brisk, northern autumn and gazed back through the portal at the humid swamp they had left behind. It was the sort of sight with which anyone who spent as much time wandering about between universes as the Second Andarans did became intimately familiar, but no one ever learned to take it for granted.

Magister Halathyn's tone had been dismissive when he described the portal as "only a class three." But while the classification was accurate, and there were undeniably much larger portals, even a "mere" class three was the better part of four miles across. A four-mile disk sliced out of the universe . . . and pasted onto another one.

It was far more than merely uncanny, and unless someone had seen it for himself, it was almost impossible to describe properly.

Jasak himself had only the most rudimentary understanding of current portal theory, but he found the portals themselves endlessly fascinating. A portal appeared to have only two dimensions—height, and width. No one had yet succeeded in measuring one's depth. As far as anyone could tell, it *had* no depth; its threshold was simply a line, visible to the eye but impossible to measure, where one universe stopped . . . and another one began.

Even more fascinating, it was as if each of the universes it connected were *inside* the other one. Standing on the eastern side of a portal in Universe A and looking west, one saw a section of Universe B stretching away from one. One might or might not be looking west in that universe, since portals' orientation in one universe had no discernible effect on their orientation in the other universe to which they connected. If one stepped through the portal into Universe B and looked back in the direction from which one had come, one saw exactly what one would have expected to see—the spot from which one had left Universe A. But, if one returned to Universe A and walked *around* the portal to its western aspect and looked *east*, one saw Universe B stretching away in a direction exactly 180 degrees reversed from what he'd seen from the portal's eastern side in Universe A. And if one then stepped through into Universe B, one found the portal once again at one's back . . . but this time looking west, not east, into Universe A.

The theoreticians referred to the effect as "counterintuitive." Most temporal scouts, like Jasak, referred to it as the "can't get there" effect, since it was impossible to move from one side to the other of a portal in the same universe without circling all the way around it. And, since that held true for any portal in any universe, no one could simply step through a portal one direction, then step back through it to emerge on its far side in the same universe. In order to reach the far side of the portal at the other end of the link, one had to walk all the way around *it*, as well.

Frankly, every time someone tried to explain the theory of how it all worked to Jasak, his brain hurt, but the engineers responsible for designing portal infrastructure took advantage of that effect on a routine basis. It always took some getting used to when one first saw it, of course. For example, it wasn't at all uncommon to see two lines of slider cars charging into a portal on exactly opposite headings—one from the east and the other from the west—at the exact same moment on what appeared to be exactly the same track. No matter how carefully it had all been explained before a man saw it for the first time with his own eyes, he *knew* those two sliders had to be colliding in the universe on the other side of that portal. But, of course, they weren't. Viewed from the side in that other universe, both sliders were exploding out of the same space simultaneously . . . but headed in exactly opposite directions.

From a military perspective, the . . . idiosyncrasies of trans-temporal travel could be more than a little maddening, although the Union of Arcana hadn't fought a true war in over two centuries.

At the moment, Jasak stood roughly at the center of the portal through which he had just stepped, looking back across it at the forward base camp and the swamp they'd left behind. The sunlight on the far side fell from a noticeably different angle, creating shadows whose shape and direction clashed weirdly with those of the cool, northern forest in which he stood. Swamp insects bumbled busily towards the immaterial threshold between worlds, then veered away as they hit the chill breeze blowing back across it.

This particular portal was relatively young. The theorists were still arguing about exactly how and why portals formed in the first place, but it had been obvious for better than a hundred and eighty years that new ones were constantly, if not exactly frequently, being formed. This one had formed long enough ago that the scores of gigantic trees which had been sliced in half vertically by its creation had become dead, well-dried hulks, but almost a dozen of them still stood, like gaunt, maimed chimneys. It wouldn't be long before the bitter northern winters toppled them, as well, yet the fact that it hadn't already happened suggested that they'd been dead for no more than a few years.

Which, Jasak told himself acidly, was not so very much longer than it appeared to be taking Fifty Garlath to get his platoon sorted out.

Eventually, however, even Garlath had his troopers shaken down into movement formation. Sort of. His single point man was too far from the main body, and he'd spread his flank scouts far too wide, but Jasak clamped his teeth firmly against a blistering reprimand . . . for now. He'd already intended to have a few words with Garlath about the totally unacceptable delay in getting started, but he'd decided he'd wait until they bivouacked and he could "counsel" his subordinate in private. With Charlie Company detached from the battalion as the only organized force at this end of the transit chain, it was particularly important not to undermine the chain of command by giving the troops cause to think that he considered their platoon CO an idiot.

Especially when he did.

So instead of ripping Garlath a new one at the fresh proof of his incompetence, he limited himself to one speaking glance at Chief Sword Threbuch, then followed along behind Garlath with Threbuch and Magister Kelbryan.

—end excerpt—

from *Hell's Gate*
available in hardcover,
November 2006, from Baen Books

THE FANTASY OF ERIC FLINT

THE PHILOSOPHICAL STRANGLER

When the world's best assassin gets too philosophical, the only thing to do is take up an even deadlier trade—heroing!

hc • 0-671-31986-8 • $24.00
pb • 0-7434-3541-9 • $7.99

FORWARD THE MAGE with Richard Roach

It's a dangerous, even foolhardy, thing to be in love with the sister of the world's greatest assassin.

hc • 0-7434-3524-9 • $24.00
pb • 0-7434-7146-6 • $7.99

PYRAMID SCHEME with Dave Freer

A huge alien pyramid has plopped itself in the middle of Chicago and is throwing people back into worlds of myth, impervious to all the U.S. Army has to throw at it. Unfortunately, the pyramid has captured mild-mannered professor Jerry Lukacs—the one man who just might have the will and know-how to be able to stop its schemes.

hc • 0-671-31839-X • $21.00
pb • 0-7434-3592-3 • $6.99

And don't miss **THE SHADOW OF THE LION** series of alternate fantasies, written with Mercedes Lackey & Dave Freer.

IF YOU LIKE...
YOU SHOULD TRY...

DAVID DRAKE
David Weber

DAVID WEBER
John Ringo

JOHN RINGO
Michael Z. Williamson
Tom Kratman

ANNE MCCAFFREY
Mercedes Lackey

MERCEDES LACKEY
Wen Spencer, Andre Norton
Andre Norton
James H. Schmitz

LARRY NIVEN
James P. Hogan
Travis S. Taylor

ROBERT A. HEINLEIN
Jerry Pournelle
Lois McMaster Bujold
Michael Z. Williamson

HEINLEIN'S "JUVENILES"
Rats, Bats & Vats series by Eric Flint & Dave Freer
Cosmic Tales I & II, ed. by T.K.F. Weisskopf

HORATIO HORNBLOWER OR PATRICK O'BRIAN
David Weber's Honor Harrington series
David Drake's RCN series

HARRY POTTER
Mercedes Lackey's Urban Fantasy series

THE LORD OF THE RINGS
Elizabeth Moon's *The Deed of Paksenarrion*

H.P. LOVECRAFT
Princess of Wands by John Ringo

GEORGETTE HEYER
Lois McMaster Bujold
Catherine Asaro

GREEK MYTHOLOGY
Bull God and *Thrice Bound* by Roberta Gellis
Pyramid Scheme by Eric Flint & Dave Freer
Forge of the Titans by Steve White
Blood of the Heroes by Steve White

NORSE MYTHOLOGY
Northworld Trilogy by David Drake
A Mankind Witch by Dave Freer

ARTHURIAN LEGEND
Steve White's "Legacy" series
For King and Country by Robert Asprin
& Linda Evans
The Dragon Lord by David Drake

SCA/HISTORICAL REENACTMENT
John Ringo's "After the Fall" series
Harald by David D. Friedman

SCIENCE FACT
Borderlands of Science by Charles Sheffield
Kicking the Sacred Cow by James P. Hogan

CATS
Larry Niven's Man-Kzin Wars series

PUNS
Rick Cook
Spider Robinson
Wm. Mark Simmons

VAMPIRES
Tomorrow Sucks ed. by Cox & Weisskopf
Fred Saberhagen's Vlad Tapes series
Nigel Bennett & P.N. Elrod
Wm. Mark Simmons